SAVAGE

Also by Keith C. Blackmore

Mountain Man
Mountain Man
Safari
Hellifax
Well Fed
Make Me King
Mindless
Skull Road
Mountain Man Prequel
Mountain Man 2nd Prequel: Them Early Days
The Hospital: A Mountain Man Story
Mountain Man Omnibus: Books 1–3

131 Days
131 Days
House of Pain
Spikes and Edges
About the Blood
To Thunderous Applause
131 Days Omnibus: Books 1–3

Breeds
Breeds
Breeds 2
Breeds 3
Breeds: The Complete Trilogy

Isosceles Moon
Isosceles Moon
Isosceles Moon 2

The He-Dog Chronicles
White Sands, Red Steel
Savage

The Bear That Fell from the Stars
Bones and Needles
Cauldron Gristle
Flight of the Cookie Dough Mansion
The Majestic 311
The Missing Boatman
Private Property
The Troll Hunter

SAVAGE

A HE-DOG ADVENTURE

KEITH C. BLACKMORE

Podium

All rights reserved. No part of this publication may be reproduced, stored in a retrieval system, or transmitted in any form or by any means electronic, mechanical, photocopying, recording, or otherwise without prior written permission from Podium Publishing.

This is a work of fiction. Names, characters, places, and incidents are either products of the author's imagination or used fictitiously. Any resemblance to actual events, locales, or persons, living, dead, or undead, is entirely coincidental.

Copyright © 2024 by Keith C. Blackmore

Cover design by Chris Rallis

ISBN: 978-1-0394-8919-6

Published in 2024 by Podium Publishing
www.podiumentertainment.com

Podium

SAVAGE

CHAPTER 1

Heat.
He hated the heat.

Hated every scalding lick of the sun.

Turquoise seawater foamed about He-Dog's ankles as he staggered out in the frothing surf. Every pulsing wave stopped him, threatened to swipe him off his unsteady legs and roll him onto the white sands at his back. The desert winds branded him from behind, however, keeping him upright, not that he appreciated the help. Its wheezing breath simmered at his back like an angry bellows, urging him to wade farther from shore.

When the water reached his knees, He-Dog stopped and sighed and set his feet.

A large swell rolled toward him.

Swaying, he bent over and let the wave break over him.

Seddon above, that was good, but not near the relief he needed. Worse, the salt sizzled and stung every blood-crusted bruise and cut carved into his sun-scorched hide. Grimacing, he straightened, braced himself, and peered out toward the horizon.

Spotless. Seamless.

A line as sharp as a blade's edge. Without blemish.

Feeling his many hurts, he slowly doused himself before stumbling out of the creamy water. After what seemed a lifetime of heat and sweat and sand, he swore he'd head north if the opportunity came along, up into the Ice Kingdoms. See what they were about. Anything to get away from the hot sun, winds, and sharp blowing dust of Big Rock.

Chop stood at the edge of the retreating surf. He had stripped to the waist, including his leather mask. His ghoulish face lifted to the sky, and when he moved, his scorched flesh and scars stretched to the point of ripping. Or at least it looked that way. He-Dog didn't dwell on it. He was an oddity himself, growing up with his breed blood. Though there was nothing outwardly different about him, some sensed his *offness*, which was perhaps best manifested in his physical attributes. But even his strength and stamina had limits and, as proven time and time again, he bled like anyone else.

He-Dog groaned, feeling the stickiness of the sea on his skin. He picked up his leather cuirass and slapped the sand from it. The armor's godlike physique had been split down the middle, ruined by the beastmen's armored Koja. Still, he couldn't bring himself to toss the piece away. It was just too damn pretty. Perhaps he could find someone to repair it. If he and Chop survived the killer desert, that was . . .

Beastmen, he fumed wearily. He was glad to be clear of the brutes. Wanted nothing more than to get free of the land they called Big Rock. Years ago, at the peak of its imperialistic appetite, the Zuthenian Empire had claimed Big Rock as theirs. They enslaved the beastmen tribes and used them to chip away at rich, bloated veins of copper and gold in the mountains. And chip away the beastmen did, until they'd had enough of their Zuthenian overloads whereupon they put aside their tribal differences and united. Using the very tools given to them to smash rock, the beastmen started smashing skulls instead.

Only now did the Zuthenian Empire realize their mistake.

With the fall of Foust, the beastmen wouldn't stop sacking cities and towns on Big Rock until every Zuthenian was slaughtered, devoured, and their bones tossed into sand, sea, or fire pit.

He-Dog knew of the Zuthenian king. Heard his name was Narijo or something of the like. Also heard he was an unfit stubborn sort. If that was the case, war would be coming to Big Rock, and on a much larger scale than the mayhem of Foust. If King Narijo was smart, he'd abandon all claims to the distant continent and let the beastmen have it. Be glad there was an ocean between Big Rock and the mainland. He'd be smarter still to have ships patrol the Zuthenian coast, to ensure the monsters didn't overcome their instinctive fear of the Big Water and attempt to cross it.

To continue their smashing.

Foust had fallen. He-Dog, Balless, and Chop had escorted the last two hundred or so survivors to the coast to escape the beastmen's bloody purge of the fabled city. Fleeing with that handful of souls had been part of the plan, but it didn't work out. He-Dog and his companions had made the decision to fight off the pursuing Koja, to give the last of Foust's survivors a chance to escape to the coast. Although victorious, He-Dog's brother, Balless, had died in that final confrontation, and his death pained He-Dog more than he would have dared to imagine. Not since Rige's death had he experienced such miserable agony. A deep ache had clutched his heart and refused to let go. To add further sting, He-Dog had somehow lost the gold he'd collected from the survivors for their protection. And to finish off this streak of unfit misfortune, he and Chop had reached the sea only to witness their survivors already aboard a ship, pulling out of the harbor, and disappearing into the depthless horizon.

Leaving both men stranded on a fat ribbon of beach, parched and frying under the sun.

With an army of beastmen somewhere behind them. An army very much looking forward to killing anyone who was *not* a beastman.

The situation wasn't favorable, and truth be known, He-Dog despised situations. Situations required *thinking*, and he wasn't one for thinking. His skills lay elsewhere.

Chop pulled his impassive black mask over his melted face, the stitches in the material uneven and many. He then gripped the twin pommels of his short swords hanging from his waist.

"Othil is that way," He-Dog said with as much enthusiasm as if he were looking upon a corpse.

The Nordish man nodded.

"Farther up the coast," He-Dog muttered, inspecting his cuts and bruises. He didn't remember receiving any of those licks, but they'd introduced themselves in the days that followed his battle with the remaining Koja. Every mark and gash throbbed and pulled and demanded attention.

He-Dog took that pain. That misery. That hate. And used it all for power.

Truth be known, the alternative—listening to Balless's ghost *wuffing* in his mind—hurt far more.

"Othil might be preparing for a siege," he said, not really knowing. "Or caught in a panic. Nine days from Othil to Foust. That's a straight walk."

He regarded the coastline for some time before shaking his head in doubt.

"We'll never make it," he muttered. "Probably perish from the sun first, but I can't think of anything else." He turned to Chop. "Unless you want to swim for the mainland? I think that's only four days. By ship."

Chop didn't reply.

Seddon above, He-Dog grumped, not impressed with the silence. Balless never thought for them either, but at least with Balless, he wholeheartedly supported whatever the plan was, even the bad ones.

"Othil it is, then," he muttered, deciding for them both. "Let's get moving. Before I start drinking this."

He nodded at the creamy surf.

Still sticky from the sea water, He-Dog pulled on his loose shirt, then his cuirass, leaving it hanging open. He yanked his dog skull blade free of the sand where he'd stabbed it. Chop suited up as well, managing to furnish his armor by himself. He knotted a set of bronze greaves and bracers last.

That drew a look from He-Dog. "You'll fry with them," he said, indicating the metal bits.

Chop ignored him.

The lack of conversation annoyed He-Dog, which was strange. When Balless was alive, he could barely get the big man to shut up. Chop couldn't really talk, and the silence was starting to feel like solitude. Before, when He-Dog did try talking with him, he'd usually had a few mugs of beer or mead or firewater in him first. The drink helped with the understanding.

At the moment, however, he had nothing of the sort.

The blue-green sea growled and hissed across the white sand, tempting He-Dog to just sit and watch the sun go down. He faced the bright waters, mesmerized by their motion. The smell of brine filled his nose, pleasing and cleansing of mind. Strangely enough, the scene appealed to him. Balless would have certainly enjoyed the sight.

Balless.

"Unfit," He-Dog muttered, tight-lipped and taking it all in. Sadness gripped his throat and threatened to rise further, so he began walking, sloshing along the shoreline, hoping to Seddon above to find some shade before his hide burst into flames.

Othil was a long way away, and it wasn't going to get any closer while he stared out over the water.

He didn't look to see if Chop followed.

CHAPTER 2

Hargan didn't know when things had first begun to go wrong. Perhaps earlier this evening, before the purpling sky turned black. Back when he still had most of his coin, a tight purse stuffed with silver and gold cutaros, rubbing and bouncing against his thigh like an eager honeypot. Now, however, that pleasant weight was gone, and all he had was the grind of wooden dice in his tightening fist. And a growing, quiet dread that he was about to lose everything.

Reflecting on the day, but really delaying the next toss as much as possible, he suspected he should've taken himself and his coin and found a honeypot instead.

Wealth was always a fleeting thing with the once-Sujin from Sunja, except he wasn't a Sujin anymore but a mercenary.

Memories of his homeland, then. It had been years since he'd left, and he didn't really miss it. Or the war with Nordun. A war that still raged, according to the sailors loading the merchant galleys tied up in Othil's harbor. Hargan remembered his share of campaigns against the Nordish maggots. Remembered smashing ranks of Jackals, knee-deep in the perished or soon-to-perish, in chilling downpours of rain and the punishing heat of the sun. Not that the fighting ever bothered him. Not at all. He enjoyed a hard fight. Relished it. Even appreciated a good old-fashioned slaughter.

Until the Field of Skulls.

That summoned cold memories of fear and an all too familiar burn of shame.

The entire first Klaw of the Sujin military had died that night, five thousand fighting men slaughtered, plus the hundreds of supporting professionals who leeched a living off the army. For one who was happiest in the thick of a fight—a *winning* fight—the Field of Skulls was Hargan's first taste of butchery on the *dying* side.

And, truth be known, he didn't enjoy it. At all.

Like a rapid poison, the Nords had somehow infiltrated the entire force during the night. No one really knew how they had managed it, but the Jackals made the most of their insertion, cutting up as many enemy soldiers as possible while they slept. When the alert finally came, chaos ensued. A confused carnage where it was damn near impossible to tell friend from foe. All semblance of an army dissolved in a cauldron of death and, as far as Hargan knew, only a handful escaped with their heads. To this day, Hargan believed he may have stabbed at least two of his own during the confusion. And when the blood really started to fly and the Nordish butchery reached its grisly pinnacle, he and his brother, Marrek, fled for the deepest parts of the forest.

In the shrieks and echoes of the haunting dawn that heralded a complete Nordish victory, later recorded as history, Hargan and Marrek ran.

The Field of Skulls broke Hargan.

Crippled him, really. In the head.

Dreams still haunted him. Miasmic, choking clouds that clutched and grabbed him when he slept. Nightmares where he and Marrek soaked and shivering, crept through undergrowth stinking of blood and shite during the night. A horrifying night, where the piercing screams of men and even a few women spiked the dark. Screams for mercy—sweet Seddon above have *mercy*—before being silenced by the meaty thud of an axe. All while the Jackals roamed the night, sniffing for any further scents.

In those nightmares, he and Marrek failed to escape, and were held down by faceless Nordish infantry before being stabbed or chopped into spraying pieces.

When Hargan woke, those images and sensations haunted him and left him cold.

He and Marrek had escaped, however. Neither brother could understand *how* they had managed that feat—and in their minds, they never made it out of the Field of Skulls. They'd *survived*. Anyone sensible could see the Nordish had the First Klaw right and proper that night. Had them by their kogs and bells even before their Sujin commanders knew it.

Make no mistake, both men knew how their peers would judge them for fleeing.

So they convinced themselves they'd had enough of the Jackals.

Told themselves Sunja was done, regardless of whether they ever returned home to make war against the Nordish anew. And since going back meant facing an executioner's axe just because they'd *survived* while others perished, well, it was an easy choice to make.

So they struck south, selling their bloody skills to whoever paid, putting the Field of Skulls far behind them.

Besides . . .

Everyone in the trade had a lapse of judgment. Sooner or later.

The brothers excelled in their new lives as wandering soldiers. It didn't matter where or what they fought as long as they were paid. Somewhere along the way, Hargan discovered he didn't rightly care who he killed, because killing was what he did best. Marrek was his equal, and dare he think it, perhaps even better. They made a formidable pair, plying warcraft in Mademia and Kree, initially working for criminal types before the prince convinced the two brothers to join his company for hire. The prince had a nose for conflict, and the coin to be earned from it.

The more sword arms they possessed, the bigger the battles, and the richer the plunder. Or so said the prince.

Lords above, he was right.

From then on, Hargan and Marrek worked the trade once more. Their new companions knew they were Sunjan. Knew they were once Sujins. Didn't care in the least. The world knew Sunja had lost its war, even if the country itself still refused to acknowledge it, bleeding out like a man stabbed through the guts but pressing a wad of cloth to the wound. Though Hargan wouldn't admit it to his brother, he swore he'd never go back. Not after that night of slaughter, where every breath had the potential to reveal his hiding place to the Jackals.

That memory bothered him more than he cared to admit.

Hargan discovered a way to free himself of that torment, however.

Through fighting.

The others noticed it. Talked about him. In time, Marrek saw it as well. Hargan took more risks than anyone on the battlefield. Terrible risks. The more danger involved, the more Hargan liked it. Wherever the fighting was thickest, was bloodiest, Hargan was there. Strove to be there. Every fight, every war, terrorizing the enemy with berserker energy.

Even more disturbing, however, was what he did with the *bodies* of the slain enemy.

Never going back, he would remind himself, thinking he meant Sunja, suspecting something else.

And earlier this day, Hargan had received a hefty purse of gold and silver cutaros, his share from the looting of an Ossaki pirate vessel. He enjoyed his coin as much as the next hellpup, and spent it either carousing or gambling. Usually gambling. Not that he was much good at it, but he enjoyed it all the same.

If he couldn't find bare fistfights to partake in, he'd wager coin on the dice, wherever he found a game. When fortune blew into his sails, it lifted him to dizzying heights. It also let him drop, however, for when he lost, he lost mightily, usually everything he'd earned from cutting people up.

This particular evening, a full gale had blown his way, lifting him high before dropping him neck-deep in a shite trough.

His choice of entertainment this evening had been Cloves, a Zuthenian dice game he wasn't familiar with.

That was his first mistake.

His opponents consisted of a group of sailors and brutish street men unknown to him—his second mistake.

As far as he could tell, Cloves didn't rely on any skill. Chance ruled. And if it didn't concern killing people, Hargan's fortune was considered to be the worst. In any case, the men he played with—who'd been quite friendly earlier in the evening—explained the game as being easy to learn. And it was. One merely had to toss the dice into the air and keep track of the number of points resulting from the toss, being mindful to keep clear of the cloven number of three or its deadly increments, else all coin wagered be lost. Winnings were quick to change hands.

Easy to understand. Easy to play.

And easy to enjoy as Hargan had been tossing and winning practically everything.

But then the friendliness got a little hard around the edges. The smiles became sneers. The jokes became jabs. All the while, Hargan's purse emptied. Far too quickly, really. Almost magically, even. That puzzled him. Poisoned him.

His hair was soaked in sweat, flattened to his skull where he patted it. He'd hoped the hard contact might wake him, to help him reason why things had gone into the pisspot so fast. The skies overhead had only just turned dark and he had already lost nearly every coin in his once fat purse. That missing weight left him none too pleased.

Seddon above, he was feeling exceptionally *unhappy* about it.

The hanging lamps barely lit the black flagstones and stout crossbeams of the back of the inn. Fish traps lay piled up against one wall, the netting rich with brine and fish bits only just starting to decompose. Shadows played across Mobos's face as the sailor smiled slyly, exposing the black nubs that were his remaining teeth. Dark-headed moles the size of fingertips dotted his face.

"Dying Seddon," the sailor cackled in a voice screamed hoarse. His breath reeked of sour ale and pickled fish. "If'n my fortunes change like a quick squat. Like a quick and satisfying squat. And timely enough, too, eh cutthroat?"

Although Hargan was kneeling on the other side of the game floor, a good three strides away from Mobos, he still caught too much of the man's foulness, smelling like a fishy pisspot in need of a scrubbing. The stink didn't drift but *leaped* across the flagstones, backing his head up on his shoulders.

Mobos's companions were smiling as well. Right and proper vicious they were, a pack of wharf rats that slapped their champion on the shoulders while talking fine praises. Mobos grinned hugely, salting Hargan's loss even more by clawing up his winnings and letting the coins spill through his fingers in glittering dribbles.

Then Hargan saw it.

Companions.

He had been too absorbed with his earlier streak to notice how the circle of gamers had fragmented into two camps.

Five men were on Mobos's side.

Hargan was alone.

"What'll it be now, ye hellion?" Mobos leered, daring him.

Hargan didn't like that smile. It was far too saucy. Too certain. Too . . . *knowing.*

"'Nother try?" the sailor pressed. "Or would ye rather slink away and see if'n ye can't scrounge up more coin?"

Hargan squeezed his last few cutaros. Squeezed them tight. It was still Mobos's toss. Seemed to him when Mobos had begun tossing, Hargan began losing.

The sailor's mouth dropped in feigned shock. "Believe he's actually *considerin'* it! Saimon's *balls!* They grow 'em *stupid* where ye come from, now don't they!"

The walls of the alley closed in tighter, and Hargan's vision narrowed to the clump of sea snakes opposing him. Laughter ripped through the lot of them, great gusts over quips not funny in the least, and Hargan had a sense of humor. One man appeared serious, however, perhaps sensing the mercenary's mind. Or seeing his stance.

The Sunjan didn't like being studied, either. Hargan stroked his tangled beard patiently, stretching out the time before making his decision.

More scalding laughter from the collection of rogues.

"He *is*!" Mobos squealed with rancid delight. "Saimon on a honeypot! Yer goin' to try again, ain'tcha? Haven't had enough, have ye? Fine with me. Just fine. I'll send ye away without a coin. Ye must like sleepin' in the streets, hm? With the drunks emptyin' their bulls overhead, hm? Where's the place ye say ye hailed from?"

"Sunja," supplied one of the gang.

"Aye that," Mobos growled. "I've heard about them toppers and their lack of sense. Ye surprise me, lad, truth be known. Didn't believe ye could talk the common tongue up there. Though I did hear some folks say ye spoke funny. Is that true? Do ye speak funny, boy? Lad? *Son?* Do ye? Speak some of that funny Sunjan talk for us, then. The way you speak with those unfit Sunjan asslickers ye called brothers. Go on, I'll even pay ye. With yer own coin, that is. Imagine I'll get it back soon enough, anyway."

Mobos cackled. His ratty companions joined him.

Hargan rubbed at a nose that had been broken perhaps twice over the years. His gray eyes became slits. "Your toss, Mobos."

The sailor's eyes widened in surprise. "Was that it?" He chuckled and tossed the Sunjan a coin. "Well, that *was* funny! Barely worth the coin but we had a bargain. Don't worry, I'll win it back."

And he winked.

Hargan placed his last few cutaros onto the flagstones one at a time.

"Stupid as rain over an ocean," Mobos declared sadly, shaking his head. He scooped up the dice and swished them around in his open hand, rattling them before Hargan's face as if invoking a spell. "Watch them now," the sailor said. "Watch them. I'll show ye some sorcery, Sunjan. Some black *wharf* sorcery, right here. Right in these alleys."

Mobos winked, and smiled, showing off teeth rotting inside his mouth.

He heaved the dice into the night.

The sailor watched them go up, but not Hargan. His gaze stopped at the other's ugly face. There was no need to watch, because Hargan knew, just *knew*, what the roll would be.

So he crushed Mobos's nose with one punch, laying him out flat.

The man beside the sailor looked down in time to have an elbow smashed into his face.

The rest of the pack splintered to the sides.

Things turned grim for Hargan then.

Gurry though they were, the gang had still survived the back streets of Othil. Knew how to fight in an alley.

They swarmed the Sunjan from the sides, grabbing his face and limbs, pushing him back into a wall. Four men pinned him there. Strong as he was, Hargan wasn't powerful enough to escape their combined clutches.

A recovered Mobos drifted into sight. The sailor's nose and mouth were a grisly smear of red. He grabbed Hargan's tunic with bloody hands, reared back, and punched his face. Twice. Granite hard shots that bounced Hargan's head off the wall. Still snarling, Mobos inspected the damage done before pulling back his fist for a third.

"Lords above, this is fun," Mobos said and struck, snapping a crooked ridge of knuckles into Hargan's face.

The once-Sujin's head rebounded again.

"That hurt?" Mobos puffed, his breath horrid.

As a reply, Hargan's leg snapped free of one captor's grip and flashed into the sailor's crotch. Mobos released a breathless squawk and clutched his man-bits. He hunched over and staggered back two steps, his face pinched and tortured, and dropped to his knees.

In the quiet surprise of the alley, a stricken Mobos crumpled to the flagstones.

"Not as bad as that," Hargan muttered.

That got the attention of the shite rats still holding him.

A fist rocked his head to the side. Someone punched his stomach, twice, two rapid blows that left the once-Sujin gasping. A set of arms secured his legs. Then the serious one from earlier stood before him. He clamped a hand around Hargan's throat while his other hand gripped a knife, wicked and worn down to a curve from years of use.

After being in the business for so long, Hargan could recognize the worrisome ones, and this particular maggot worried Hargan.

The sailor rapped the knife's pommel against Hargan's nose, breaking it in an explosion of black stars. Pain whipped and crackled to the back of his skull.

The Serious One didn't flinch, didn't speak. Instead, he studied Hargan's wincing discomfort and drew back the knife. This time, however, he angled the evil tip toward an eye.

"Let the little man go," someone commanded.

The authority in that voice fish-hooked everyone's attention.

Though it was dark beyond the glow of the lamps, no one had any difficulty seeing the monster standing at the alley's end.

Hargan was just below average height, thick as a barrel, and coiled with muscle.

Compared to his brother, however, he was a cub alongside a bear.

"I said Let. Him. Go." Marrek stood in the dark, eyeing each man before turning his full glare upon the Serious One.

Who still had a hold of Hargan's throat. He measured up the bald ogre stepping toward him into the lamp light.

As a warning, the Serious One smoothly placed that wicked blade to Hargan's hairy throat.

That stopped Marrek in his tracks.

"I'll cut him," the Serious One said in a dead tone. Hargan suspected the topper meant every word. Suspected he'd done it many times before without blinking.

Not that it bothered Hargan, not in his current state.

"Kill him, Marrek," he slurred in pain, his words warped with a nasal whine.

"Shaddup," his brother rumbled and then pointed at the Serious One. "Leave him, and we'll be on our way."

"He started this," one of the others blurted. "We're teaching him a lesson."

Silence. Then, "That so now?" Marrek asked.

"They were *cheating*, Marrek," Hargan grated.

The words hung in the air for long heartbeats, until Marrek moved closer, his height and size growing even more imposing at ten strides away.

"Saimon's hell we were," declared one of the wharf rats pinning Hargan's arms. "He was *losing* is what the problem was."

Grunts of agreement all 'round then.

"All right," Marrek said. "Let's just call truce and go our separate ways. You keep the coin."

"Marrek," Hargan squirmed.

"Shaddup. You lot never mind him. Keep the coin and we all go home, tonight. No need for any more blood."

The Serious One never wavered, his knife poised just below the bobbing nut of Hargan's throat. The Serious One considered the offer. Considered it for long moments. Both he and Marrek were reading each other quite well.

"We keep the coin?" the Serious One asked.

"Keep it. For your troubles."

Hargan's eyes rolled.

No one paid him any heed, however, and Marrek showed his palms in a gesture of *Well?*

The Serious One didn't waste any more time. He withdrew the knife, and Hargan had to admit he didn't mind that at all. Truth be known, he felt a great deal of relief—but only for a moment before he started fuming again. Over the conditions.

That was his coin. *His.*

"Done, then," the Serious One said, not taking his eyes off Marrek. "Let him go."

The other shite rats released Hargan, letting go of their holds but not their suspicions. They still sensed the man was not quite done.

For his part, Hargan straightened his tunic and wiped the blood flowing from his nose with a sloppy swab of his hand. He sniffed, exhaled, and scowled left and right before shattering a man's knee with one kick. Nearly took the head off the other with a vicious straight-arm punch.

The Serious One readied himself to rush Hargan but then remembered the ogre in the alley. He spun about in time to have both ears mashed by calloused palms.

Marrek stepped over the crumpled form and yelled at his brother. "You unfit bastard. You brainless *pisser*. Why can't you simply back *down* for once? Surprise me for once. This was over and *done*."

Hargan slammed the last sailor against a wall before brutalizing the man in a flurry of punches, where every strike sprayed fine oil. One final blow and the unconscious man slumped to the flagstones, chin down and legs splayed.

Everything got quiet again, except for the lamenting grunts and groans from the fallen.

"You finished?" Marrek asked, clearly not impressed.

Hargan kicked the last man he'd brutalized. Then another quick boot before backing off and nodding.

Marrek pointed a finger. "You're enjoying this too much."

"The asslickers cheated me."

"But did they? Truly? Or did you get all damn twisted with the thought and just started smashing?"

"They wanted a fight."

A stunned look flashed across Marrek's face. "*Six* men wanted a fight? You took on six, Hargan. With your fists. This is getting unfit, boy. Unfit. You're not some damned hellion, freshly escaped from Saimon's hell. Seems to me there was only *one* wanting a fight."

A sailor, the one holding his leg, moaned and rolled over.

Hargan kicked him in the head.

"*Damnation!*" Marrek grabbed his brother by the tunic, made fists in the material and slammed him against a wall. "You and I are going to talk. You're getting to *like* this too damn much."

"That's my business," Hargan shot back.

"No, Hargan. *Our* business isn't smashing heads into walls over a few words. You might think it is, but it's not. Never was. We're better than that, because we know the difference. We can think. But . . . you're *not* thinking anymore. Not one bit. I'm not even sure . . . I mean . . . Seddon above, I'm not sure you're . . . *you*, anymore."

Hargan squirmed and met his brother's flinty eyes, identical to his own. "Let me go, Marrek."

"Not until you've listened, so keep still. I've been watching you, and lately, seems you're not caring too much about what the fight is. Or the odds. Just as long as it's a *fight*. That seem right to you? Doesn't to me. That pirate scow we boarded. Those men you cut up. You *butchered* them, hellpups. I mean *butchered*. Then the ones who surrendered. Hargan—I *saw* you knife them and toss them over. You thought I didn't, but I did. What was that, Hargan? Four bound captives—*ransom* even—and you gave them the chop and tossed them to the sharks. What was that?"

"Shay gave the order."

"Oh-ho, I thought you'd say such gurry. But I asked Shay. Asked him and he said he gave *no* such order. I even asked Bartus—who was with Shay the whole time—and *he* said the prince never gave such an order. So where did you hear it? Tell me?"

"I said *he* gave the order."

"Except he *didn't*."

They grappled then for a few beats before Marrek rattled the smaller man against the wall, ending the exchange.

"You're no different," Hargan glared, holding onto his brother.

"Oh, I am. I'm different. I'm still a *soldier*. You don't see me rushing headlong into a fight as if my ass were on fire, breaking formation and endangering others on the line. I certainly don't cut up prisoners. But you? You're heading somewhere dark, Hargan. Someplace I don't understand and don't want to go. Seddon above, maybe you're already there. You're becoming . . . an *animal,* and I'm the unfortunate bastard straining with the chains."

Hargan started struggling again. "Then let me go, before—"

Marrek slammed his brother against the brick, jarring him, then yanked Hargan in close. The big man's glare softened, and his voice filled with horrified wonder. "What's the matter with you?"

They studied each other, attempting to read each other's thoughts.

"Let me go, Marrek."

"Or what?"

Hargan's features hardened. Marrek responded by tightening his grip, his knuckles crackling from the pressure.

"*Think*, Hargan," he warned. "You *think*. Before whatever you do next. *Think*. Before this leash becomes a noose."

They stared at each other, two hard men unwilling to back down, until the other did first. Hargan realized his brother had no intention of releasing him, so he squirmed even harder. Blood trickled from his smashed nose. He adjusted his grip, probing, searching for an escape.

Sadly, and perhaps even a touch worried, Marrek drew breath to speak when a streak of silver flashed across his throat, opening it to the bone. Blood as warm as soup spurted across Hargan's face.

And instead of holding onto his brother's wrists and expecting to fight him, Hargan suddenly held on because Marrek was *collapsing*, his throat gushing, *gargling*, from the killing slash. The big warrior fell over like a tree, a hand smacking the wall. One foot kicked out, knocking over a lantern. The glass broke and fiery light threw back the dark.

There, retreating a step from the spectacle was a recovered Mobos, clutching a bloodied knife.

"That's one," the sailor promised with a bloody grin. He crouched, poised with his knife directed right at Hargan and waggled his fingers at the man. "Right 'ere ye bastard. Ye unfit *scab*. I'll teach ye to scream some."

Hargan stared.

Marrek's neck was already a dying fountain.

Reality stretched in curious directions. Distant laughter rang out in the street's night, cutting and cruel. Mobos stood there, snarling a mouthful of rot and ready to kill again. The fire colored him, and he held onto that pitiful knife, waiting, inviting Hargan to make the first move.

Hargan's scowl became a murderous thing as the once-Sujin considered the sailor and the little blade he held.

As if realizing his knife might not be enough, Mobos's expression paled, and his weapon arm faltered.

Hargan lunged for the foul-smelling sailor.

A heartbeat later, the streets of the port city echoed with a man's shriek, before it was silenced by the sound of shattering wood.

And the roar of a monster.

CHAPTER 3

"I am Stephanak. *Captain* Stephanak of the *Blue Conquest*."

Lazy pipe smoke parted as the captain leaned over the table, his deep scorched voice drawing in his guests. On the alcove walls above his head hung sconces of iron molded in the shapes of dragons, their muzzles clamping down on burning candles. The light revealed a husky man dressed in tasteful, dark clothing. A thin beard covered his chin while his hair, threaded with silver, had been pulled back and tied in a knot. Wide set eyes, almost grandfatherly in the way they crinkled about the edges, studied his guests.

"Listen and share my wine, if only for a moment," the captain gestured at the cups and bottles upon the table. "And if you do not like what you hear . . . then . . . you are free to go."

The presence of wine guaranteed Prince Shay's attention, if only for the time it took to fill his first cup. But there was something about the older man that he liked almost right away. He placed it a moment later. The sailor's raspy charm reminded Shay of his father, back in Valencia. That was it.

Shay helped himself to the drink while Bartus, another Valencian, sat on his left. On the prince's right was Grage, an old hellpup fashioned from iron and scarred by lightning. An impressive beard hung off his chin, matched only by the wild strip of hair growing across his brow. Above that, however, his scalp was surprisingly barren.

They weren't the only lads Shay had brought along to this meeting. Jers Snaffer and Talso, hard-looking on any day, stood guard at the alcove's entrance, their attention split between the captain and the activity within the alehouse.

All five of them suffered through the heat of the day in their well-kept shirts of chainmail. Each carried an imposing assortment of blades.

Stephanak waited, watching, until the prince and his lads finished filling their cups. "I am *glad* that you came at such short notice," the captain said. "Not many would. Not so late at night. It speaks well of your character, good Prince. I must admit, I'm not used to being in the presence of royalty."

Shay smiled, showing strong teeth marred only by a missing right incisor. The expression brightened his weathered face. He was a large man. Powerful of limb. A dark beard crusted his chin, neatly trimmed like the rest of his hair. Shay kept his appearance clean, his clothing simple—odd for one with the title of "prince." It noticeably puzzled the old captain, just as it had many others.

"Well, just between us," Shay said, leaning in to share a secret, "I'm not really a prince. Not at all. My men call me that."

Stephanak's eyes narrowed.

"We call him 'Prince' for several reasons," Grage said, his voice solid like granite. "Generosity is one. And his understanding of a battlefield is nothing short of farseeing, like that of a king. Or a prince. That's two. And three . . . he has more honor in his topper alone than most royalty alive today."

"The lads actually wanted to call him 'King,'" Bartus quietly added from the other side.

"Couldn't have that," Shay said with a frown. "Didn't sound right. But 'Prince' I liked very much. As for the rest of what they say? Ask them again when I'm not present."

Stephanak's features darkened.

"Don't worry," Shay assured him before smiling. "I imagine most of it is true."

After a moment's thinking, the captain sighed and raised his cup. "Well met, Prince Shay."

They drank.

"I rather like Zuthenian hospitality," the prince remarked, studying the bottles as Bartus took the time to refill their cups.

"It is not much, I'm afraid," Stephanak said, "but one cannot discuss business without something to drink. To do otherwise would be uncivil. I like this particular wine. Not sharp at all. Unlike others of my age, I've grown fonder of the sweeter drinks."

Shay understood the sentiment. Though he knew Grage would later mock the captain for those words.

"And who are these men who praise your name?" Stephanak asked.

"Grage, you know from your first contact. Hails from the northern hole of Kold Keep, one of the Ice Kingdoms, which is why he's so . . . pleasant to behold. This is Bartus of Valencia. Both he and Grage are my appointed Koors. Guarding the entrance there and brooding like an ogre is Jers Snaffer. He's also from Kold Keep—followed Grage all the way down from what I understand. Talso, the other brute you see there, is Mademian. I'll have you know, Captain, that I have the highest regard for all my boys. Especially Snaffer and Grage. Frosty they might look, but as the Mademians say, 'Old steel carves the deepest.'"

Grage frowned and Shay knew he'd be sworn upon later. Snaffer, with his face covered in a thick beard, didn't appear to hear the prince.

"Welcome to my table." Stephanak raised his cup and they all tipped again. "Ah," the captain said, smacking lips. He studied his drink, then his guests. "Bartus, you say. He looks to be your age, Prince Shay."

"He is. Like a brother to me, actually. And the voice of reason before I commit to madness." Shay grasped his friend's shoulder.

"Excellent," the captain approved. "One must have dependable men about to rely on. To trust. I endeavor—can I say that?—I *endeavor* to do the same with my crew. Thus far, my caution has kept me away from the rocks." With that, the captain rapped the wooden table twice, banishing whatever foul influences lurked nearby.

"How long have you sailed?" Shay asked.

"Ah," Stephanak waved a hand, dismissing the question. "I don't keep track of the years. Time, you see, is a measure created by people and I . . . I do not accept it. Thus, I . . . am timeless. I have been on the water for as long as I can remember. And you? How long have you been in this far-flung city belonging to Zuthenia?"

"Almost a week," Shay answered. "We just finished some business to the east of here and decided it was time to leave Othil. If one believes the stories coming from the south, this place is in great danger."

"It is, it is," Stephanak agreed gravely. "And you should believe the stories. *I* believe the stories. The city of Foust has fallen. Ravaged. Every man butchered. Every woman and child devoured like sweet tarts. *Devoured.* Can you imagine? The beastmen were—*are* a problem that Zuthenia knew of, yet failed to properly deal with. Since this land is across a considerably large ocean, King Narijo's armies are every bit as distant as his throne. A shame. All of these," he gestured toward the other guests patronizing the alehouse, "are drinking what will be their last carefree mug of wine or beer for a very long time. Or short time. Foust's walls were *twice* as high as Othil's."

The captain let that sink in.

"You could stay and offer your services to the city's Kratoe," the old sailor suggested. "I'm sure he would hire you as he awaits reinforcements from the mainland."

"No," Shay smiled. "Sieges are not to my liking."

"No . . . I suppose not. Well, then. To issues of a more grand nature." The captain glanced about before leaning in close and whispering, "What do you know of the Sanjou?"

Shay shook his head. "Nothing."

"Ah, I see. Fortunate. For me." Stephanak cleared his throat. "You see, I'm preparing to sail to that place. In search of a lost fortune. I offer a partnership in this matter."

"Please continue."

"An even share of the prize. To be distributed into equal portions among our people. You and your soldiers—me and my crew. My task will be to safely bring you, aboard the *Blue Conquest,* to our destination, that being the Sanjou. Truth be known, I believe I have the easiest part of the undertaking. It is you who will have to endure the tangles of that hellish place."

"Careful with your honesty, Captain," Shay rumbled through a half smile. "You don't want to frighten us away."

Stephanak eyed him, his tone suddenly grim. "You were honest with me, Prince Shay, and I shall be equally honest with you. I won't take anyone unless they fully understand what they are agreeing to. It upsets my sleep, you see. And you are the first of my guests who have remained at my table *after* I mentioned the Sanjou. You really don't know anything about that place?"

"It's an island?" Shay guessed.

"You are correct," Stephanak brightened before his face clouded with trouble once more. "Roughly ten days' sail from Othil. Due south . . . southwest. It's an unfriendly wall of mountainous rock stabbing into the sky. A crown of the tallest cliffs you'll ever see. An unforgiving barrier that surrounds an interior lake, like a smashed bowl. Inside that broken thing, guts of jungle, green and foul and damn near impassable. A place haunted by headless ghosts and monsters of blackest legend. It is marked as . . . an island, but truth be known it's big enough to be a continent. Perhaps it is, as I have yet to sail all the way around its shores. Maybe that will be an undertaking for another day. Regardless, it is a place . . ." he waved pinched fingers, "*untouched* by civilization. A vast nest teeming with wildmen. Tribes of primitive people. Cannibals. Unfit hellions that joyfully hunt for the heads of voyagers like myself and who take them without hesitation. In Othil and Foust, people know of the Sanjou and"—the captain's smile flickered at Bartus— "are glad an ocean separates the two lands."

"But we're going there?" Shay asked.

"Aye that, we are. Yes. For a ransom of gemstones." He paused, allowing the words to sink in and imaginations to flourish.

"A ransom," Bartus said, squinting in thought. "A fortune you've never seen, I'll wager."

Stephanak winked at the man's doubt. "I have seen . . . a *sparkle*. Just a sparkle. But it's left me with the desire of wanting more. Two years ago, I was skirting the coastline of the Sanjou, for among its high cliffs there are places where sailors can climb up and enter the jungle. From there they can replenish their ship's stores with fruit, fresh water, and small game. One must do so quickly, and quietly, before rousing the wildmen there. This particular day, we found an adventurer floating in the sea, more dead than alive, stripped to his breeches and bobbing in the water like . . . like a piece of cork. A satchel was tied across his back. We fished him out, for I"—Stephanak pressed a hand against his chest—"am not a heartless man. So we fished him out. Landed him on the deck. And in a delirium, he offered payment for safe passage to the nearest port. Far be it from me to turn away a fare, so I accepted. Unfortunately, a murderous fever soon overcame him, possibly from an infected shoulder wound. An ugly gash swollen and turned to a rotten shade of red and yellow. He would perish from that wound before dawn, but not before telling his story to these ears."

The captain tweaked one lobe. "It scalded them forever, especially after I found what was in his satchel."

"Gemstones," Shay guessed.

"A *ransom* of stones," the captain insisted. "Greener than the eyes of a cat! *Emeralds*, my good prince, emeralds! Worth enough to outfit my ship for several voyages. Enough to endear my crew to me for life. And though I'm certain the poor dog had more before he took to water, the handful he did have were but pebbles groomed from a mountain."

"So there's more?" Shay asked, his interest growing.

"Much more. If a dead man's ravings prove true, there is so much more. A mountain streaked with green veins of stone. *Sparkling* green. Just waiting for someone to claw them free. The poor bastard even spoke of a waterfall where the constant flow had unearthed a . . . an emerald shelf that . . . that *blazed* through the water's depths . . . causing the very water to *glow*."

"But . . . it's in the Sanjou."

"It's in the Sanjou," Stephanak repeated in a defeated tone. "Where, I don't know. I only know where I fished that poor soul from the sea. So that would be the place you start your search. And for that alone, you need me. After I bring you there, you are tasked with searching for it, and, truth be known, those wilds are not a place for civilized men. Truth be known, my Prince, you are not the first group I've talked to about this. I've told the same story to four different leaders commanding packs of mercenaries. All of them, *all*, left the moment I mentioned that green, tangled hell. One cursed me for even mentioning the place. Think upon that. Many a treasure seeker has gone beyond those high cliffs and never returned. Think on that, as well. I did, for many a day, until I realized my best chance for an expedition was to contact, as you say, mercenaries with no ties to Zuthenia. Foreigners with no knowledge of the Sanjou. But even then . . ." he shrugged. "I must tell you all there is to know about that place. As I said, I wish to be honest."

"Well," Shay admitted. "I see."

Stephanak waited.

"Go on," the prince encouraged him.

A fog of pipe smoke drifted across the old sea master's features as he waited, perhaps believing an insult to be hurled at him. When there was none, he smiled in relief. Shay smiled back, as the captain's manner suggested everything he'd said was indeed true. The Sanjou was a place to avoid, despite hosting vast riches.

And yet, it was the kind of story that attracted Shay. The kind that made songs of people.

Clearing his throat, Stephanak smiled again and nodded. A moment later, he continued.

Shay leaned closer for the details.

CHAPTER 4

The pungent stink of expelled stomach soup, piss, and shite threatened to choke Shay and Bartus. That breath-stealing blend left them wincing and wishing for clean air. The jailor's expression remained indifferent—perhaps even bored—as he led the men deeper into the dungeon. The jailor was a big man who didn't appear to miss too many suppers. Truth be known, by the look of him, he probably had three or four suppers every time he ate. Breakfast was unquestionably a couple of supper-sized meals, as was lunch. The lad was hugely fat, waddling along on stumpy legs. His clothes were rough but clean, peeking out from underneath various slabs of tough leather strapped to his hide. Where skin peeked out, a sheen of what might've been sweat coated it, glistening in the light of a torch held in a massive fist. Despite his trade and environment, the jailor was a complete professional with the two mercenaries. Not only did he agree to take Shay and Bartus to see the recent additions, but he even took time to point out puddles best not to tread through.

"There," he said, the fat rolls of his throat deepening his voice. He stepped around a wet spot. "And that one there. That one as well. Well, well, well."

He held aloft the torch, its glow pushing back the foul darkness, causing rats to scurry away. Closed doors of wood and iron scrolled by, each cell barred at the top and bottom by stout timbers. Iron grates served as windows in some of those doors, offering a glimpse inside. Some cells were full, their occupants staring blindly ahead. One lad had his entire arm weaseled through the bars, swinging it back and forth like a cat's tail.

The jailor put the torch to the limb, and the owner, with a growl of pain, jerked it back into the dark.

The jailor regarded the two mercenaries. "Apologies," he rumbled, slightly embarrassed. "He knew he shouldn't be doing that."

Shay and Bartus exchanged looks.

They marched deeper into the depths, descending rough stone steps as the rats again scampered to escape the light. On the next level down were more cells, and more than a few faces lurking beyond the windows. The prince didn't recognize any of them. Hargan and Marrek had been missing for three days, prompting Shay to send his lads out to search for the two brothers. He presently had twenty-eight men under his command, all veterans of various campaigns, all more than capable.

But Marrek and Hargan were his best.

And Shay had no desire to go stomping about any jungle island without his most skilled, most valued men.

So he spoke with Stephanak, who graciously granted him time to search the city. The captain cautioned him to hurry. More people arrived at Othil's gates every passing day as word spread of the approaching beastman threat. Stephanak wished to set sail soon, well before any trouble came to the outer walls, as Othil appeared destined to fall victim to siege, much like Foust. Sieges were nasty, ugly things, drawn out and overdone. Shay had never been in one, mind you. Had better sense than to be caught in one. But he'd heard plenty of stories. He wasn't interested in being anywhere near Othil when the beastmen started beating their war drums and tearing down the outer walls.

It would be a bloody fight. A long fight, which would test the resolve of the inhabitants, as well as the stores of food and water within the city. Worse still . . . it would be a fight without pay.

All good reasons to be gone from this place as quickly as possible.

For three days, Shay's slayers had scoured the city, searching the local jails, the docks, the alehouses, and the taverns. Nothing. Hargan and Marrek were nowhere to be found.

Then Grage had suggested the city's prison, where he'd heard the worst of the worst usually went. Shay and Bartus decided to visit the place, with a purse full of coin, just in case.

The jailor stopped and waved a torch at a cell. The light revealed a prisoner, turning away from the unexpected attention and failing to hide the rat he was eating.

"Apologies," the jailor said. He sounded like he meant it. "The lads only eat once a day here."

Shay and Bartus exchanged looks again. "Was that it?" the prince asked.

"Oh, no," the jailor said, and continued on without another word.

The men followed.

With every step, the smell grew worse.

"Lords above," Bartus gasped and pinched his nose.

"What?" the jailor asked, stopping and turning around. When one was that big, turning around in a corridor was an event. "Something bother you?"

"You don't smell that?"

"Smell what?"

"The stink," Shay grimaced.

The jailor's eyes narrowed. "The what?"

"The shite," an offended Bartus said. "The shite. And everything else with it."

"It is foul," Shay added.

The jailor glanced from one to the other, the wheeze in his breathing troubling. "What? I don't smell anything."

"You're joking," Shay said after a moment of shock.

"About what? The smell, you say? Been jailing this place for nearly fourteen years. I don't smell anything. Not a single blessed thing. Fresh air to me. All fresh air. Well, as fresh as you'll get down here. We throw open the shutters once a week, rain or sun. Whether we need to or not."

That admission stunned the two mercenaries.

Recognizing the conversation was over, the jailor turned back—another large undertaking—and continued on his way. In short time, he stopped before one cell, scratched hard at an armpit, and slapped the door—the noise startling in the close quarters. He thrust the torch forward, revealing a figure beyond the bars.

"This one came in a few days ago," the jailor announced, hooking a thumb into a leather belt while stepping back. "He yours?"

Shay peered inside. A lump lay on the floor, facing the wall.

"Hargan?" he asked.

The figure stirred.

"Hang on, then." The jailor fiddled with a ring of keys, his tongue pinched into a gap in his teeth. Finding the right one, he unlocked the cell. He opened it and, with a reassuring nod, bade his guests to enter.

With a glance at Bartus to stay outside, Shay ventured in, realizing the floor of the cell was actually sand.

Hargan sat up and blinked against the torch's glare. Blood caked his nostrils and mouth and darkened the shirt he wore. His upper lip appeared twice its original size, as did parts of his smashed face. Bruises purpled his features and his hair hung in stringy clumps.

Shay sighed. At least he was alive.

"Lords almighty," Bartus whispered, trusting the jailor enough to step inside. Shay knew Bartus wasn't overly fond of the Sunjan, but he also recognized not many could give the little brute such an unfit thrashing.

"He's mine," Shay muttered with a nod. "We'll take him."

"Can't," the jailor informed him. "Not this one. Apologies. He killed seven men. Seven. One he tore apart with his bare hands. You can't have him. He'll be given the chop soon enough."

"Given the chop?" Shay asked.

"Executed?" Bartus blurted.

"Oh, aye that," the jailor said. "Bounce that skull right offa deck, we will. Even give it a kick or two. Guaranteed. In Othil, the kind of killin' he did is only punishable by death." The big man shrugged. "Only right. And generous, really. He'll leave this world easier than them souls he perished. Strange thing, though. Only took five of the street watch to bring him here. He didn't fight any of them. Tired out, we figured."

Shay straightened. Dark news indeed.

"He's a real killer, though," the jailor declared.

Hargan was. Shay *knew* he was. "Listen. He comes with us. I'll pay to get him out."

The jailor appeared cross. "This man broke Zuthenian *law*. He's as good as dead. *Dead*. You can't pay to get him out. What part of that do you not understand?"

"The part about Zuthenian law," Bartus muttered.

"Bartus," Shay cautioned and reached for the leather purse at his waist. "Hold out your hand," Shay instructed the jailor.

The big man did so.

Shay placed the purse in his palm. "That's all I have, and all I have is about twenty-one, twenty-two cutaros. Count it if you like."

The jailor blinked, his features glowing from the raised torch. The light wavered for an instant as he opened the purse and jabbed two hairy fingers inside.

"Hargan," Shay asked. "Hargan. Where's Marrek?"

Hargan didn't answer.

A grunt distracted the prince.

The jailor.

"What?" Shay asked.

"I don't know about this."

"You have all my coin right there," Shay pointed out.

"S'all you got?"

"That's it."

"S'not enough. How much he got?" The jailor indicated Bartus, who didn't appreciate the question.

"He doesn't have anything," Shay said.

"What? He's got a purse right there."

"That's bait for thieves," Bartus informed him.

"Bait?"

"Bait," the mercenary said, his warning scowl only a fraction of how murderous it could become.

"All right, then," the jailor muttered, back to being indifferent. "Not that I care, mind you. Just so happens, your lad's been good enough here. Not a problem at all. Makes me wonder, really. Anyway, take him. Go on. Just know . . . this is just a one-time arrangement. All right? You remember that. One time. Which is to say . . . if the street watch brings him or any of you back in here . . ."

"Price'll be doubled?" Bartus asked.

That stopped the jailor, who clearly didn't appreciate the remark. "Was that a jab? Because that sounded like a jab."

"Toss me one of them coins and I'll tell you."

The jailor glared at the mercenary. The mercenary glared back. Both held those looks for long heartbeats, before the jailor sniffed with the same indifference as before and turned to leave.

Bartus cleared his throat, pausing the larger man, whereupon the soldier snatched the torch away from him.

Muttering something about foreigners, the jailor ambled off into the gloom.

"Hargan, can you stand?" Shay asked once the jailor was on his way. "Hargan?"

"You've outdone yourself this time, you pig bastard crust of shite," Bartus added from behind.

Shay scowled. "No need for that right now."

"I'd say there's every need. He knows he's done wrong."

"You're not helping."

Bartus shook his head.

"Hargan," Shay tried again to no response, which worried him. "What do you think?" he asked Bartus.

"I think he killed someone."

"We *know* he killed someone."

"No, I mean he killed some*one*. Someone *important*. Best we leave now before that jailor remembers something. Or tells someone about this little payment who'll *remember for him*."

Shay mulled that thought. "Don't know what you did this time, Hargan old dog. Something bad, that's obvious enough. Part of me doesn't want to know what you did. I know one thing. Marrek will have your hide when he finds out."

"Or I'll tell him," Bartus said, earning another harsh look from Shay. "Oh, I will."

Hargan showed no indication of hearing anything.

"Perhaps he got smacked about the head," Bartus suggested, "and now he's unfit."

"You're not making this easier."

"I'm not about making matters easier. I'm about what's what."

"You're a pain in one's pisshole, is what you are."

"Look at him, Shay. The man's a cold junk. Nothing in there anymore. There wasn't much in there before, truth be known, but there's less now. My opinion? It's for the better. I think even Marrek suspected something was wrong with him."

"Well, I'm not leaving him here. We'll get him back to Gusper. Have him take a look at him. See if he can do anything. Who knows?" Shay lowered his voice. "Perhaps the jailor and his lads had a go at him. Seddon only knows how many people perish in here without anyone batting an eye."

"He did put down six men," Bartus supposed. "Would draw my attention. And boots. You hear that, Hargan? You black-hearted, brazen-ass packer. You're fortunate to have Shay watching over you. Saimon's crusty hole, I certainly wouldn't."

Hargan said nothing.

Bartus frowned. "Well, this isn't sporting at all. If he's not going to try, I'm not going to bother anymore."

The Sunjan remained fixated on the far wall.

That unflinching stare worried the prince. "Hargan?"

Nothing.

Shay hunkered down and studied the soldier's eyes. "Damnation."

"Unfit, isn't he?" Bartus asked.

"Shaddup. Hargan? You there?"

Dead eyes bore into Shay's, unnerving the prince even more. The face belonged to Hargan, but the man was nowhere to be seen in that husk. The fire in the hearth had somehow been extinguished. Doused by dirt or blood or something worse.

"Hargan," Shay persisted. "Listen now. Where's Marrek? He's missing as well. You know where he is?"

Hargan dipped his head. "I know," he eventually answered. "I know."

Bartus leaned forward, concern clouding his usually stoic face.

Then it all spilled out of Hargan in a dead gush. The Sunjan started talking of his gambling. Talked about what had happened a few nights back. Then he told them of Marrek's murder. Hearing it all robbed Shay and Bartus of speech and thought. Marrek had been a beast of a man. A brute who towered over companions and enemies. To think he was no longer among the living was ... damn near unthinkable.

Even *more* worrying was Hargan. It was understood that Hargan was the animal and Marrek his keeper. Shay himself sometimes relied on the big man to bring Hargan to heel when his orders fell upon unhearing ears. Now, with Marrek gone, unease about Hargan's safety clouded over any grief Shay had for Marrek.

The prince cleared his throat. "Come on then. We ... we have work to do."

"Work?" Hargan asked, as if pickled from a week's hard drinking.

"Work."

Hargan studied Shay's face. Then he looked at Bartus.

In time, he got to his feet.

CHAPTER 5

Three weeks.

    Much longer than He-Dog had thought.

Three weeks of marching along the coastline, feeding off crabs and handfuls of little fish more bone than meat, drinking from dusty wells and cavern trickles that were at times more mud than water. The journey had left He-Dog and Chop sunburned and parched and damn near delirious from the scutters.

Three weeks. During that time, they kept to the shade when they could, sickly and staggering and weak from repeated squats to empty what was left in their bowels. When the sun went down, they trudged across stretches of sand that quickly fatigued them. Several times they would stop, collapse, and rest, marveling at the moon and the surrounding starfield, as vast and sprawling as the desert. They followed the shore, the hissing surf accompanying them until the rosy dawn, when the sun drove them back into the shade. Shade had been a scant thing, ranging from boulders to sandy bluffs. When there was no shade, they hiked until they found it, the sun cooking them while mites and other things sampled their blood.

Three weeks of that.

After recovering at the infirmary in Foust, He-Dog had felt lean. Looked lean. Now, however, any fat he might've had, that *Chop* might've had—and they didn't have much to begin with—had melted away. The leather cuirass He-Dog wore hung off him like an open shirt, two sizes too large. His fingers strummed bones he never knew he had. Cords of muscle had become even more pronounced and dangerously sculpted.

Truth be known, they were right and proper starved.

A breath away from dying.

But they had survived. Were alive.

He-Dog's guts churned and twisted like hot snakes, and he knew it was from the few drops of well water that passed his lips, moisture licked from his palms that was probably more poison than water. He stopped, swayed, and pointed at the city. At this distance, it was more like a low fence studded with even pickets, glimpsed between a few sandy hills.

"There," he croaked. His dry and dusty tongue licked at scorched lips and tasted grit. "Othil. Seems . . . like years. Since . . . we last saw. The place."

With Balless, but he left that unsaid.

Borus was around too then, for that matter, but he was neither family nor friend. The one-eyed archer was simply a miserable saucy kog—though he had made amends with He-Dog in the end. After the wreckage of Foust, He-Dog wished Borus no misfortune.

Swaying and saying nothing, Chop regarded the far-off city. That was fine by He-Dog. He appreciated the mute mood of his remaining companion. In fact, he found himself paying less attention to Chop's grunts and incoherent gibberish, until he realized one day the Nordish swordsman had stopped talking entirely.

Not that he dwelled on it.

A seemingly endless march in unfit heat would do that to a person.

Long stretches of mutually shared silence dominated the days leading to Othil, unless Chop *really* had something important to point out. After the fight on that stony ridge, the man had walked for half a day wearing his mask. Then, at some point, he'd simply taken it off. He-Dog remembered glancing back and scowling at his companion's frightful face. All that mess had robbed the Nordish man of both looks and coherent speech. Not that he needed them, as Chop's talents lay elsewhere. He-Dog didn't think there was a finer swordsman about. *Including* himself.

Unlike Balless, who was only good for one thing. Even now, He-Dog didn't want to ruminate on what that was. He didn't want to remember . . . yet often did. His brain took every opportunity to remind him Balless was no longer with them.

"Othil," He-Dog repeated, barely getting it out, and even that was too much to say.

The port city was where they were first hired to travel to Foust. They'd been paid quite handsomely, in fact. They spent damn near all of it before leaving—because when one thinks one is headed for certain death, one will throw coin at just about anything.

Now, they had returned. Not in the state He-Dog would have liked, however. And nowhere as close as he wanted. It would take them half a day's walk to get there, especially in their condition. Maybe even a full day.

Chop walked by in a stricken shuffle, his arms hanging by his sides and his mask once more covering his face.

Sunbaked and hurting, He-Dog forced himself to follow his companion.

They left the coastline and eventually linked up with a wide road scuffed and flattened by thousands of travelers on their way to Othil. He-Dog didn't like the city. Didn't like any city, really, but he didn't have much choice in the matter. So, he followed Chop, keeping a few steps behind him.

"Hot," Balless said, suddenly beside him.

"Shaddup," He-Dog whispered, his sun-blasted lips barely moving.

"Only said it was hot."

That stopped He-Dog in his tracks, to face his brother, except he was no longer there. Just another memory. *Heat did that*, He-Dog knew. Twisted one's mind.

"Unfit," he muttered.

He followed Chop's shuffling form, who hadn't stopped at all.

In time, the low barrier surrounding the city grew until its solid rock facade towered above them. Spires stretched into the sky. Banners flew. Smoke rose, perhaps from chimneys sprouting out of alehouse kitchens, where all sorts of delicious things were cooking. And where beer could be had. That got them both walking a little faster, finding strength they didn't know they had. Other travelers soon dotted the road leading into the city, until the road was littered with crowds. The city gates appeared, and the closer He-Dog and Chop got, the better they could see what lay ahead. A thick knot of bodies mashed themselves through a thin opening, choking the city entrance, struggling to not only get themselves through but also their wagons, carts, and livestock.

A hundred strides out from the city walls, soldiers flung sand into the air, digging deep trenches and pits. Shovels flashed, scattering their load. More soldiers lined the city's battlements, faceless little figures bearing spears and bows.

Othil was a much busier place than He-Dog remembered.

A fight was coming.

A hot breeze blew past him, sprinkling his face with grit and carrying the smell of unwashed bodies and animal shite. That stink grew worse as He-Dog and Chop neared the rear of that long line of refugees fleeing the beastman threat. Zuthenians of all ages, shapes, and sizes glanced around anxiously, telling grim tales of Foust and its fate. Some of them led horses. Others led mules, goats, or cattle. Most carried sacks or containers of personal belongings. A child high up on a wagon ate what looked to be a fist-sized knob of bread covered with a thick and rosy jam, hooking He-Dog's attention and causing his mouth to water. Just a drop, a feeble drop, but even that surprised him. He didn't think he had a drop left in him.

The notion of asking any of these travelers for something to eat didn't enter his mind. They eyed both him and Chop with suspicion, not liking their looks at all. He-Dog didn't blame them.

Within the crowd, He-Dog realized he had been separated from Chop. He eventually found his companion a little way off, staring silently at a cart of caged chickens. The owners pulling the cart watched him with open distrust. He-Dog gripped the man's shoulder and that effort alone nearly dropped them both.

Someone jostled He-Dog hard then, hard enough to distract him, but he didn't have the will or strength to push back. Didn't have the strength to *glare*, even. The press and tide of desperate bodies edged them along. In short time, they entered Othil. That alone made He-Dog sag with relief. He considered stealing something, just to celebrate, but that risked a fight. Perhaps even death. Neither Rige nor Balless would have approved if he actually did steal something from the honest or the wretched, so he did nothing of the sort.

It was going to take every last bit of control, however, to keep his hands to himself, especially if they had to pass by food stalls.

"Docks," He-Dog croaked, guiding Chop free of the crowds and toward an alleyway. He remembered the way to the water, where there might be ships in port. Only the truly skittish ones would have already sailed. The rest would follow soon enough, however.

Shadow and light filled the alley as the two men limped along, appreciating the firm flagstones underfoot. A junction loomed ahead, where a building built of stone and wooden beams stood three levels high.

He-Dog considered one way over the other just as a hammer started pounding an anvil. The shrill banging made his skull ache.

"This way—no, wait." He rubbed his head. "This way."

Nothing from Chop. Not even a grunt. He-Dog frowned. At least Balless had offered a thought now and then. They weren't *intelligent* thoughts, but thoughts all the same.

Though facing a long and terrible siege, the city carried on with its day-to-day bustle, if at a more nervous pace. Threading their way along, all manner of smells accosted the two sun-scorched men, including that of roasting meat. He-Dog's stomach clenched for just a taste. He didn't pursue the matter—it was doubtful he could stop at just one bite, and he didn't want a confrontation. Still, there was food all around them. Just waiting. They had to get some. *Where* was a good question. The city had swelled to thrice its population and the people didn't bother with them.

Then He-Dog smelled it.

Water.

Carried along by the barest of breezes and sweeter than overripe fruit.

Dying Seddon above.

He-Dog followed his nose, redirecting Chop until they stopped at a public fountain. A stone maiden sat on a small dais at the center, tipping a jug. Dozens of people circled the place, talking or drinking their fill. Three old men saw He-Dog coming and got out of his way. The basin wall stopped just below his waist, so he fell to his knees and leaned over the water's surface. Smooth green stone inlaid the pool, only glimpsed before He-Dog drew two cupped hands' worth of clear water.

The very touch of it, warm from the sun, woke his entire well-cooked frame.

And it tasted glorious.

"*Gah,*" he exclaimed after the first few swallows, aware not to drink too much too fast, but needing much more. He settled for splashing some over his face, almost hearing a sizzle as it made contact.

Chop knelt next to him, his mask hitched up over his mouth. He drank handfuls, looking as if he was praying. Perhaps he was.

Only a few handfuls, but the water brought them back to life, at least a little bit.

The patrons sitting around the fountain moved back a ways, allowing the two men to drink their fill. Which they did, slowly, not wanting their guts to revolt.

After a time, they stood, their shrunken bellies stretched and sloshing.

"I know where we are," He-Dog remarked, his voice now well greased. "This way."

They shuffled away from the fountain, the crowd parting for them. Into another series of alleys, winding, twisting, until they walked along the side of a large, yellow stone building. He-Dog stopped at the corner and peeked out before proceeding, Chop trailing a few paces behind him.

A single enforcer stood guard at the alehouse's entrance. A tall individual, well suited to his profession, glaring at anyone passing by his employer's establishment. A mop of hair covered his head, clipped squarely two fingers above the eyes.

He-Dog and Chop approached the enforcer—who smelled them long before he saw them. The man held up a hand even before they got anywhere close to the entrance.

"No," he said quietly, shaking his head. "You'd empty the place with your stink. No."

Though the water had given some of his strength back, He-Dog still wasn't himself and was too tired to argue. So he decided to beg. "Look. We're very tired . . ."

"Don't care."

"And hungry."

"Still don't care."

"We've had a long, hard march. From Foust."

That got a hard, scrutinizing look. "You came from Foust?" the enforcer asked, looking doubtful.

He-Dog took a moment to reply. "Aye that."

"You marched?"

He-Dog nodded.

"Is it true what they say about the city? That it's fallen?"

He-Dog nodded again.

The enforcer tilted his head back, studying them down the length of his nose, or simply offended by the stink coming off them. "Unfit times," he rumbled, more to himself.

He-Dog didn't have the strength to talk any longer.

The enforcer regarded them both before finally conceding. "We have a stable behind the house," he said. "It'll cost the same as a room."

"How much is that?"

"Five cutaros."

"Will you take a sword?"

The enforcer thought about it. "Let's see it."

He-Dog turned to Chop, who stared back until he shook his head in dismay.

"Just one," a tired He-Dog said. "You've got the other. I've only got the one."

Chop absorbed that before relenting and unsheathed one of his two prized swords.

He-Dog took the weapon and showed it to the enforcer, who was impressed. "Good quality."

He-Dog nodded. It was. Taken straight from Foust's armory, in fact, but he decided not to say anything about that.

"All right, the stable's yours. It's empty right now, and there's a water barrel."

He reached for the sword.

"We want food as well," He-Dog said.

The enforcer frowned. "All right."

"Good food. Enough for tonight and tomorrow morning."

"You have to be out in the morning," the enforcer countered.

He-Dog handed over the weapon. "We will . . ."

When the enforcer visited the stable in the morning, the lads were already gone.

Long gone in fact.

Under an orange and purple sky, He-Dog and Chop made their way to the docks. Judging by the lack of activity in and around the city, the beastmen army had not yet arrived at Othil. That would change. Perhaps today. Maybe tomorrow. Maybe next week.

Didn't matter to He-Dog.

The beastmen would come for Othil. Which was reason enough to leave the city that very morning. If they could get onto a ship.

With a little more energy in their step, the pair caught the smell of salt water laced with the distinct tang of fish offal. Above the peaks and arches of the stone and brick buildings was the golden glare of a strengthening day. Foot traffic was more abundant here, which made He-Dog feel a little more anxious about getting out of the city. People walked all around them, overtaking them at times, or simply darting past. *People.* Some calm, some angry, and others with long drawn faces, possibly feeling the same unease that He-Dog felt. The closer they got to the docks, the busier and more crowded it became. He-Dog wasn't a sailor, but he'd crossed over the Big Water in ships to and from the Zuthenian mainland. He had no love for sea travel, but he had no desire to remain in Othil.

A short time later, the streets ended at the sprawling waterfront.

At least a dozen docks stretched out into the ocean. Thick ropes secured two- and three-mast vessels sporting high spars, square rigging, and lowered sails. High-prowed galleys and tall ships floated proudly at the ends of long piers made of stone and sand. Their sleek hulls creaked upon gentle swells while flags of scarlet, green, and yellow twitched in a scant breeze. Barrels and crates of all shapes and sizes waited to be carried off or loaded onboard, destined for unknown ports. Sacks of grain and other foodstuff lay in guarded piles and, between it all, an assortment of soldiers, sailors, and common folk bustled and fussed over everything, often stepping into each other's way and swearing mightily because of it.

In fact, commoners flooded the docks, swarming the main walkways and gathering about the ships. Zuthenian soldiers in full battle dress patrolled the scene, while steadfast knots of armored street watch glared at passersby. All were calm and collected, heedless of the approaching doom, or perhaps not yet grasping the scale of the beastman threat.

That would change once Two-Bite and his dogs arrived at the city's gates.

He-Dog and Chop threaded their way through the activity, toward the nearest galley with a single mast, which was off-loading sacks and livestock. Chickens fluttered in cages carried off ship by half-naked sailors. Some of the men working spied the approaching warriors and slowed their efforts.

"Ho there," He-Dog called to one man overseeing the off-loading of the ship. A stern-looking fellow, sporting a black moustache that drooped almost to his collarbones, who appeared none too pleased at being disturbed.

"We're looking for passage," He-Dog said, suddenly distracted by a pair of sailors on deck eating a breakfast of salted strips of meat with bread, *smelling* it even, some ten strides away. It smelled better than the small roasted lizards the enforcer had brought them the night before.

He-Dog focused on finishing his thought. "We'll work for it."

"Not here, you won't," said the stern man with the bush on his lip, regarding them with an expression of pure loathing.

"Do you need any fighting men?" He-Dog asked, figuring to clarify his offer. "Guards, perhaps?"

"Said there's no work. Move on." To further that thought, the stern man turned away, more interested in the activity behind him.

He-Dog didn't like the punce's attitude and was about to say so when something caught his eye. Namely, the four crossbow men standing on the ship's deck, eyeing him with loaded weapons.

Not needing the trouble, He-Dog turned away with a sigh, scratching at his nose. "Brazen toppers," he muttered to Chop, and spotted another ship. He went for it, leading the Nordish man along.

After a brief conversation with another brazen topper, they were again turned away.

Noon came and went as the pair moved from one dock to another. Some of the shipmates were gruff, while others were indifferent. Some of them blatantly told He-Dog to move on. No one needed extra hands. Especially not ones looking as ragged and done as He-Dog and Chop.

Until they reached a large galley with thin striped sails and enough rigging about her three masts to resemble a spider's monstrous webbing. The vessel's weathered sides lay heavy in the water, and a line of hard-looking lads trudged over her gangway carrying chests or pushing barrels toward her hold. A second group of men stood just to the side of the gangway, talking among themselves.

With only a night's real rest in him, and his belly no longer partially full, He-Dog scuffed toward the group standing on the dock.

"Who's the captain of this ship?" he grumped, interrupting the men's conversation, expecting the worst.

One man, on the late end of his twenties and perhaps two fingers shorter than He-Dog, turned and studied him. His companions quieted and turned as well, eyes narrowed at the disturbance. And for the first time, He-Dog noticed these weren't just men, but a seasoned pack of brutes ready to split heads upon an order. All wore cloth and leather vests that showed off powerful arms covered in scars or ink. All had the look of men not easily intimidated. Beards were long and full and resembled the thick scruff of bears. Scabbards filled with swords hung off broad belts. Daggers as well. One older war hound with an impressive head of wild gray hair glowered at He-Dog.

"What do you want?" one of them asked with equal bluntness.

"Bartus," the first man said. "Relax a moment. No need to bite just yet."

"There's no time for these shaggers," Bartus replied, glaring at He-Dog and Chop.

"Yes, well, you have to realize, though, they might *look* like shaggers. But they might be something more entirely," remarked the first man.

Smart lad, He-Dog thought, but he kept that to himself. The other pissers continued giving him unfit looks and he couldn't fathom why. Another mystery of civilization. One day they smiled at you, the next they were emptying the bull across your face without warning.

The one called Bartus didn't seem too happy, so He-Dog ignored him. "You the captain?" he asked the first man.

A smile exposed a missing incisor. "Of this ship? No. Not at all."

"I'll speak with the captain of the ship."

"What about?"

"I'll discuss that with him."

"Ah."

Another man, shorter, thick with muscle, and looking right and proper battered, trudged down the gangway. The man slowed to a stop when he laid eyes upon Chop. Angry eyes became slits. His mouth drew up in a tight line, screwing up a pale beard.

"Shay?" the short barrel of a warrior said, addressing the fellow with the missing incisor.

"What is it, Hargan? I'm conversing here."

"That," Hargan pointed at Chop. "Is a Nordish Jackal."

Under a sky that was becoming bluer by the moment, everyone, including He-Dog, turned to face the masked swordsman. A rooster cried out in the distance. Rigging creaked. Someone dropped something mid-deck.

"A Jackal?" Shay repeated, breaking the moment.

"Aye that. Look at the mask. Only Jackals wear them, you right, black-hearted *bastard*." Hargan aimed the insult at the Nordish man.

Chop gave no indication of hearing.

"Nordish," Bartus sighed with a shake of his head, as if the afternoon had just taken an unfit turn for the worse.

"Nordish," Shay repeated, sounding a touch more interested than before.

The brute called Hargan stopped not three paces away from He-Dog's companion. Looking ready to kill right there, Hargan stuck out one muscular shoulder and slapped it. Etched upon sun-browned flesh was a hooked talon. One dripping a single drop of ink.

He-Dog saw it and didn't know what to make of it.

Chop saw it, and his reaction was much different. He drew back a step, one hand feeling for the pommel of his remaining short sword.

"Aye that," Hargan sneered. "First Klaw. Served for years, until I got tired of butchering Nordish shite. I *was* thinking about heading back to Sunja, just so I could carve up the Jackals once more. Cut my name across a few."

Hargan stepped closer to Chop. "Maybe I'll start with you."

Another bout of tense silence. Someone coughed on the next dock over. Another started swearing over there as well, an inventive string of curses that failed to break the tension.

He-Dog cleared his throat. "Ah, seems your lad has a problem with mine," he said to Shay.

"Does seem that," Shay agreed and brightened. "How about a wager then?"

"A wager?"

"Aye that. On who bests the other in a fight?"

"They look half-dead, Shay," Bartus said of the two new men, not impressed.

"He doesn't have to fight," the prince nodded at Chop. "Only if he wants to."

He-Dog wanted it, recognizing the opportunity at hand. He-Dog wanted it badly. "All right," he agreed without looking at Chop.

"Excellent," Shay said, his face lighting up. "How much?"

He-Dog rubbed his chin. "Five cutaros."

"Done."

The quick agreement left He-Dog suspicious. "And . . . free passage on your ship. Away from this place."

"Away from this place?"

"If you're leaving," He-Dog clarified with a dour look.

Shay smiled. "Oh, we're leaving. In any case, done. You agree with all that, Hargan?"

"Whatever, Shay," the Sunjan remarked, glaring pure murder at the Nordish man.

Chop stared back without fear. He certainly was not backing down.

"Fists only," He-Dog said. "And not to the death. Agreed?"

"Agreed," Shay said. "Fists only, Hargan. And no killing. Agreed?"

"Fists, fingers, claws, boots," Hargan rasped, his mouth now an angry button. He stepped in close to Chop, so close that one intake of breath and their chests would touch. Though not tall, the Jackal stood almost four fingers above the once-Sujin. The Sunjan soldier was twice as thick with muscle, however.

"Not to the death, I said," He-Dog warned, feeling the need to say it a second time.

"Agreed. Hargan, no killing," Shay ordered.

Showing no indication that he heard, Hargan stared into the eyeholes of Chop's mask.

"Hargan!"

That distracted the Sunjan. "What?"

"Not to the death. Understood?"

Hargan didn't respond.

"Answer him, you brazen asslicker," a scowling Bartus warned. "Else you get my fist upside your head. And you know I don't need a reason."

"Agreed," Hargan rumbled before focusing on his opponent once more. "I'll plug your hole with that mask."

That cocked the Nordish man's head.

"The captain won't want a fistfight on his part of the wharf, Shay," Bartus muttered, knowing it made little difference.

"We can ask," Shay said brightly and faced the galley. "Captain Stephanak! What say you to an early afternoon fistfight? Eh? Some entertainment for the lads?"

A portly man dressed in resplendent blue and sea-green appeared at the rail. He quickly located the men at odds, his face breaking into a smile. "Let them at it, Prince Shay! One of your lads fighting?"

Prince Shay? He-Dog sized up the topper once more, taken back by the man's rather ordinary choice of clothing.

"One of them is," Shay answered. "That half-naked brick right there is mine. The other is Nordish. A true Jackal, they're called. Or some of them, anyway. Unfortunately, and herein lies the problem, Hargan is *Sunjan*, and served with the Su-*jins*. A rather . . . fearsome group of Sunjan infantry. And the Nord is, well, a Nord. Both countries are currently at war with each other."

"I know about that war," Stephanak called back and gestured at the two men. "They'll tear each other apart. Truth be known, I'm surprised they haven't done so already."

"Been agreed upon already. This isn't to the death, captain."

"Interesting if it stays that way. Be a shame to spill blood on the docks. Perhaps a bad sign for our journey."

"I guarantee you no one will die here this day," Shay said, sending a warning look straight at Hargan.

"Carry on then," Stephanak yelled and gripped the railing, bracing himself for the match.

"Clear a space," Shay ordered, and the sailors did just that, moving crates and sacks to create a small arena upon the wharf.

While the men prepared, He-Dog inserted himself between his Nordish companion and the vicious Sunjan, breaking the stare with one of his own.

Hargan didn't lift his head, but rather eyed the taller man, fixing him with a killer gaze.

"Step away, Hargan," Shay called out.

Knowing hard looks never killed anyone, He-Dog turned his back on the Sunjan and guided Chop to the opposite side of the formed circle.

"I'll take that," he said, indicating the swordsman's remaining blade. "Good thing we didn't trade away the second sword, eh?"

Unimpressed, the masked man undid his belt and handed the weapon over.

He-Dog leaned in close. "Don't kill him," he cautioned. "Bruise, bloody, or knock him out. All are fine but . . . don't . . . kill him. Understood? Not if you want a pleasant trip aboard that ship."

For a moment Chop didn't respond, and He-Dog wondered if the man was still angry about having to give up one of his blades the previous day. Then the black mask slowly nodded. Relief coursed through He-Dog, quickly dulled by a feeling of nervousness. They'd only had a night and a meal to recover from their three-week ordeal of reaching Othil. A fistfight would be exhausting for anyone, but for Chop it might be too much too soon. Not even He-Dog felt up to such a punishing task, realizing the long journey to Othil had physically drained him dry.

He wished Balless was about.

Hargan, who stood at his end of the circle, threw his meaty arms back and forth and looked ready to rip out a throat or two. He snarled and stomped a foot twice. Then he shook his head behind raised fists before snapping out a combination of punches so numerous that He-Dog quickly lost count.

Lords above.

"Looks eager," He-Dog observed, trying to sound calm while Chop stripped to the waist. The Nordish man glanced at him, took a longer look at Hargan, then glanced once again at He-Dog.

"You ready for this?" He-Dog asked.

The answer was less than encouraging. Chop's shoulders slumped, and he realized the Nordish man was every bit as exhausted as he was. A sudden chill lanced through He-Dog, as he took greater stock of his remaining companion.

"Are you certain?" he asked, a note of undisguised urgency in his voice.

Chop nodded wearily.

"I'd fight him, but . . . he's clearly taken a liking to you."

The Nordish man cocked his head, agreeing with the thought.

Across the way, Prince Shay spoke to Hargan in low tones—tones which the diminutive hellpup seemed not to hear. The prince paused, poked two fingers into the man's thick chest, and received a scowl and a nod. None too pleased, Shay straightened and addressed He-Dog and Chop.

"We're ready," he said and got clear of the makeshift battle circle.

He-Dog held up a hand to show he'd heard. He then offered his fist to Chop, who pressed his own against it, knuckles to bare knuckles. Unlike any other time, there wasn't much resistance. That worried He-Dog even more. With what he hoped was an encouraging slap on the shoulder, he got clear of the fight circle and wedged himself in between a pair of barrels.

"All eyes on the fighters, now," Shay shouted, receiving a cheer from the gathered sailors. Men had stopped their work on the ship and lined the railing, watching with eager faces. The prince's own small group of fighters appeared eager but less vocal.

He-Dog figured he'd be cheering too if he was only watching.

"Watch," Shay warned, holding a finger aloft. "It might all be over in a blink." He sized up one man and then the other. "On my word, you begin." The prince drew breath and again glanced at both fighters. "*Begin!*"

Another cheer from the watching sailors as Hargan tensed into a crouch.

Then he charged.

The Sunjan thundered across the circle, screaming as he crossed the midway point.

The abrupt charge surprised Chop and that, coupled with his still weakened condition, slowed his reaction time. He ducked under the first swing of a meaty arm, but Hargan's fingers clawed his shoulder, hard enough to draw blood. That dreadful hook whipped the Nordish man around so that he faced Hargan's back, where he rebounded and punched the Sunjan's ribs three times. Short, hard blows that blurred into the warrior's side.

The Sunjan backhanded with a rock-sized fist, clipping Chop's forehead and staggering him.

The connection impressed the onlookers, drawing a pained chorus of "*Ohhhhh*" from them.

He-Dog only frowned, however.

The Nordish man withdrew, arms lifting to guard.

Hargan rushed in, pulled his fist back—*way* back—the windup terrifying to behold, and punched. He sent that catapult shot of a fist whistling at the masked man's head.

Chop ducked under the boulder of meat and bone and pushed his foe off-balance as he went.

The two men reset at opposing ends of the circle, while the audience leaned in closer, very much entertained by the show.

The once-Sujin charged across the space once more. He punched for the liver, the chin, and the stomach, each blow punctuated with an expulsive grunt of air.

Chop evaded everything, coming dangerously close to a group of warriors who scattered out of harm's way.

Undaunted and perhaps even furious, Hargan stomped forward and lunged, firing a fist straight from his shoulder.

Chop ducked and countered with a hard set of knuckles to the gut.

The blow enraged the Sunjan, who lashed out as his foe sought to distance himself. That arching fist cracked Chop's head, driving him against a stack of barrels, where he staggered once more.

Hargan pounced, wrapping both arms around the taller man's waist and lifting him from the wharf.

Chop hammered at the once-Sujin's head, short jabs straight to the side of his foe's face—before he was slammed into the barrels. Wood and bones rattled as the masked man fell to the wharf. The rest of the audience *Ohhhh*ed once more at the brutal landing, a beat before the cheering commenced again.

The sight of Chop sprawled across stone and sand rotted He-Dog's hopes about the whole contest.

Breathing hard but far from done, Hargan backed up for everyone to better see.

With agonizing grace, Chop rolled onto his hands and knees and stayed that way for long moments. Blood ran down his back where the barrel's metal raked scarred skin. That silenced the onlookers, and a few men clutched their foreheads at the sight.

Fists balled and ready, Hargan crept forward, not waiting any longer.

Sensing the other's approach, Chop looked up to check on his foe.

The once-Sujin's fist struck like a blacksmith's hammer, cracking the masked head aside and uprooting everything attached below. Chop crumpled to the wharf, his hands quivering for a moment, and became still.

Much to He-Dog's undisguised dread.

"Fight's done!" he announced, waving his hands and catching Shay's happy attention.

But Hargan didn't hear. Or didn't want to.

The blocky Sunjan took two steps and kicked the fallen man. The sharp slap of boot leather to midsection rang out and caused more than a few onlookers to cringe.

Chop flipped onto his stomach, clutching at the tender spot.

"Fight's *done*!" He-Dog shouted at Shay and pointed at Hargan's back.

"Fight's done, Hargan," Shay yelled in agreement, smile gone now, recognizing the danger.

Hargan ignored them both. He jumped on the fallen man. He cocked that war hammer of a fist, lining up the jaw of the unmoving man trapped beneath him.

Not that the fist would fall.

Unwilling to let the Sunjan brutalize his remaining companion, He-Dog tackled the warrior in a clap of flesh. Both men rolled off the senseless Chop. They crashed against a wall of sacks, one of which broke open with a puff of dust.

"Fight's *done*—" but hands flew up into He-Dog's face, fingers went into his mouth, stretching out a cheek. Hargan twisted and mashed him into the grain sacks, and both men broke apart.

He-Dog scrambled to his feet. He spun, his frame coated in grain dust, to face a standing Hargan. Madness filled his eyes.

And that unfit bastard flew at him.

Only to be stopped dead in his tracks by a stunning volley of long jabs and follow-up punches that rocked the smaller man's head left to right and back again. He-Dog whipped hard knuckles into that bearded face, marking cheek and breaking skin. He hammered a jaw, an eye, and a forehead, the final strike snapping Hargan's head back in a spurt of scarlet, the skin splitting wide.

He-Dog broke off, aware of the sudden *heaviness* in his limbs. "Fight's *done*," he panted.

But Hargan didn't hear.

In fact, Hargan straightened, spat blood, and rattled his shaggy head, spattering the wharf. He smiled red and started stalking, leering at his new foe from behind upraised fists with bloodied knuckles.

He-Dog kept his hands up, realizing the whole arena had gone very quiet.

He also noticed Shay wasn't saying a damn word.

And that no one attempted to stop the Sunjan.

"Fight's done," Hargan scoffed. "Fight's *far* from—"

He-Dog jabbed, straight from his shoulder, turning his body into it for a few extra fingers of distance, and getting it. The blow mashed Hargan's nose square, warping his words into a garbled note of pain. His eyes squeezed shut and He-Dog waded in, intending to finish before his strength left him completely. He pitched punches into the smaller man's face, knocking that head left and right, sending blood and sweat flying and driving him backward. He buckled Hargan with a fist to the gut. Slammed home an uppercut that straightened the Sunjan's spine and backed him up several steps more. He-Dog followed and unleashed more punches to that battered face, spraying blood. Then another straight punch that clipped the whole head and twisted it sharp to the right. Yet another punch, thrown with a gasp of effort, cracked off the smaller man's hairy jaw.

Hargan did not fall, however.

Hargan did not even stagger.

Instead, the Sunjan threw his arms wide. "*Harder!*" he roared and pounded his own chest before offering up his chin.

He-Dog knew then that he had a problem.

So with whatever he had left, as much as his arms were fatigued, he still did as he was told.

Three punches crashed into the Sunjan's face, each thrown for maximum damage, drawing upon whatever strength He-Dog had left. Thing was, he didn't *have* much left. If he were fresh, he figured he would have ended this thing with the first punch.

That's what he told himself, anyway.

When he finished the barrage, he was gasping, sweating, his shoulders heaving and arms burning.

Across from him Hargan's beaten and battered features—with one eye swollen to a purple slit—twisted into a smile.

At that frightening display, desperation bloomed in He-Dog's chest.

The Sunjan would not go down.

Over the man's shoulders, Shay's smiling face hovered.

He-Dog decided to end it.

He swung for an eye but the punch was stopped—*easily*. The once-Sujin shrugged off two more strikes, each one slower than the last. Another punch was blocked. Then another. He-Dog grunted, teetering on exhaustion, and backed away.

Whereupon Hargan stepped in, his face as dark as thunderheads looking to drown the world.

He-Dog flailed a fist, which was swatted aside, and suddenly he had nothing left. Sweat streamed down his face and found his eyes. His stomach twisted. He sucked down air in mighty gulps and struggled to keep his aching arms at guard.

Still unmoving on the wharf lay Chop, and He-Dog had just enough time to see how at *peace* the man appeared.

Hargan swung a right, followed by a close left.

He-Dog skipped back, his lower legs every bit as drained as his arms. He countered with a jab, but Hargan smacked that away like a troublesome insect. Then Hargan lunged, smashing He-Dog's guts with one punch, lifting him clear off his feet.

He-Dog landed on his back, gasping for wind that wasn't there. He turned onto his stomach, feeling the grit of sand underneath. Reality rolled one way then the other, and he made the mistake of checking on his opponent.

A battering ram of a fist crunched into his face, slamming him to the wharf, stunning him to black stars.

"*Fight's done!*" The words sounded as if he were submerged in deep water. "*Hargan! Fight's done!*"

He-Dog crawled, unaware of what direction, until his hands touched a sack of grain. He got his elbows and knees under him and tried to stand. Too much, too soon. He collapsed, the coarse material of the sack scrubbing his face as he went down.

Hands grabbed him, hauling him to a sitting position. The sunlight was blinding. The world eventually smoothed itself out, and He-Dog sighted Chop, sitting against a chest. Then a fence of legs blocked his view. A hand clasped his shoulder.

"Well fought," Shay said gently. "Apologies. I forgot to mention that Hargan has the hardest head around these parts. Probably anywhere, truth be known. And he lives for this sort of thing. Apologies. But it's only a few coins."

A huffing He-Dog grimaced. "Don't have it."

"What's that?"

"The punce said he doesn't *have* it," Bartus repeated in disgust. "You unfit maggot. Wagering coin you don't have. That's dishonest."

He-Dog couldn't argue against that.

Bartus wasn't finished. "I say toss him over the wharf and see if he swims."

"I'll finish him," Hargan threatened from nearby, sounding hellishly fresh.

"You don't have it?" Shay asked.

"No."

"You don't have *five* cutaros?"

He-Dog shook his head, spotting the old mercenary with the wild bush of hair and beard nearby, gripping the hilt of a sword.

"What do you think, Bartus?" Shay asked.

"He's got a sword on him. We could take that."

Shay sized up He-Dog. "You know, you didn't do too badly with Hargan. The Nord, well, I wasn't so impressed. But you had some push." The prince lapsed into silence then, considering. "Can you use that blade?" he finally asked.

He-Dog coughed twice and nodded. "Aye that. When I have to."

"What about the Nord?"

"He's . . . better."

"Better, is he?" Shay inspected the masked man. "Doesn't look it."

"*Much* better."

A familiar smile spread across Shay's face. "We are . . . short a lad," he said to Bartus.

"Short a lad?" Bartus countered in dismay. "These two? One's *Nordish*, Shay, in case you've forgotten. Hargan gives our *own* boys a hard time. What do you think the he-bitch might do to a *Nord* after a day at sea?"

"What about him, then?" Shay asked He-Dog. "He's a long way from Nordun. A long way. He still with the Jackals?"

"He's . . . been with me . . . forever," He-Dog answered, his head clearing just a little. "We'll take any work. If you'll have us. If not, take my sword. It's good steel."

Though it would break his heart to lose it.

Shay scratched at his face, thinking matters over. "We've enough good steel, truth be known. Bad fortune to take another's blade, anyway. While he's still alive, I mean. Looking for work, are you? You know anything about the Sanjou?"

"No."

"Care to?"

He-Dog shook his head.

"Probably be dangerous. Plenty of killing, I wager. But if we find what we're searching for, the riches will be considerable. What say you to that?"

Plenty of killing. He-Dog's hate flared. Plenty of killing was something he could do. Something he'd discovered he was *eager* to do.

A glowering Hargan drifted into his line of sight then, watching him. The man's fists dripped blood.

"If you'll have us, we'll go." He-Dog didn't bother asking Chop. He knew what the answer would be.

Shay grunted. "*Hargan*. Can you work alongside a Nordish mercenary?"

"No," came the answer, deadly serious.

"Excellent!" Shay smiled. "Captain Stephanak! I'm going to bring aboard two more souls, with your approval." Then he turned to He-Dog. "Get him up, lads. Him and the other one. Meet the newest recruits. And no killing the Nordish maggot, Hargan. Don't you dare kill him. I forbid it. That man might save your life one day, so I want your word on it."

Hargan walked away.

And somewhere in all of that, He-Dog lost consciousness.

CHAPTER 6

The rolling sea failed to upset Shay's stomach.
    Standing upon the quarterdeck of the *Blue Conquest*, salty air blew across his face, scrubbing away the filth of Othil. Sea travel was always a roll of the dice for him. Some voyages were fine. Others damn near killed him, sickening him to where he wished for death. His sea legs never really seemed to develop, and just when he believed he *did* finally have them, it was usually time to put ashore. This time, however, all seemed well.

He wondered if it was something he ate or was eating.

The sky blazed a deep, beautiful blue, marking the morning of the third day of their journey. The *Blue Conquest* cut a straight line toward a horizon absent of any land. Blue waves parted before the ship, the dull roar comforting to hear. The wind blew from the east, and every now and again the *Conquest* would lift just a bit before dipping with a ponderous lurch. Shay's open shirt rippled in the wind. Fine spray lashed his face, forcing his eyes closed. In that darkness, he glimpsed Amber waiting for him back in Valencia. Radiant. Little smile on her face. Dark eyes as deep as the ocean he sailed upon. He asked himself once more why he'd left the woman, and the answer, once clear, wasn't so at the moment.

"Sailed all my life," Stephanak spoke at his left, the captain's scratchy voice rising above the sea. "Given me the best ride of my life, better than any of Zuthenia's honeypots. Watching the roll of *these* hips is far better than those of flesh."

Shay smiled at that, knowing Bartus would call the captain a silly nog for saying such a thing. The prince, however, found his respect for the old seahorse growing with every passing moment, witnessing firsthand how Stephanak commanded his crew and vessel. Tall and dour, with his cloak flapping in the breeze, he stood like a statue upon the deck. With a satisfied nod, he turned to the activity on the decks below.

"I started out as a mere boy," Stephanak continued, gripping the railing while the wind rustled his cloak. "Sleeping on bare planks. Learning knots. Cleaning pisspots and shite troughs. All that nonsense. But I paid attention. Watched. Learned. Every day I learned. The way of ships and the sea, so when the last captain of the *Conquest* died, crushed in a storm, I was the one who took command. The day he perished, well . . . it was the fiercest gale I'd ever encountered. We were in the south seas, west of here, and it came upon us like Saimon himself, throwing waves as tall as castles while his breath flung men overboard. Never saw the like before or since. When the captain died and I took command, no one questioned me. I knew it all, you see. The stars, the charts, the mood of the ship and the ocean. I took command in that unfit storm and I guided her through that hellish bluster, straight to the other side, saving what remained of the crew. We should've perished. We all should've. But we didn't. Many thought the Lords above had descended—maybe Seddon himself—and drove Saimon off."

The captain smirked at the memory. "The storm broke shortly after I took the helm. Ask any of my crew. As if . . . some power *wanted* a new captain. Not necessarily me, you understand. Just someone other than the one we had. Enough of that. I'll bring bad fortune to us all talking such gurry."

"How many days to the Sanjou, again?" Shay asked.

Stephanak's lips puckered as if about to receive a grape. "Three days in, so seven remaining. But it depends on the winds. If they decide to fight us, it'll take longer. If they're at our sails, faster. Are your men comfortable?"

"As comfortable as we're going to be. Your ship is full. I'm surprised it still floats. Some of the lads haven't gotten their sea legs yet, so they're miserable. Others are well enough. We'll make it. By the time we reach the Sanjou I daresay you'll be glad to be rid of us."

That amused Stephanak greatly, and he slapped the weathered wood of the railing. "So you may think, but I actually *enjoy* being heavy on the water. It comforts me, you see, as one would feel after a grand meal. A light ship is a quick one, mind you, but I sleep better when there is something holding her down. A good sign, I think. And *Conquest* is a heavy galley. She's fat in the middle but strikes a lovely cut from stem to stern." He chopped his hand at the front and rear. "She slices the water like a sword. I only hope that you and your men will add more weight to the return trip, may the Lords watch over our bloody souls. As for the sea legs, think of that as . . . a test. See who's got stomach for the life and who doesn't."

"One more test," Shay said, staring out over the water while the sails crackled overhead. "Been tested every day of my life, it seems."

"That is life itself, isn't it?" Stephanak's expression hardened. "Have you ever been in a jungle before?"

Shay shook his head.

"The reason being your armor," the captain pointed out. "Zuthenia is hot, but its heat is a dry and vengeful heat. An angry heat. The Sanjou is hotter still, but its heat is a wet one. You can . . . chew on the air, it's that thick. Even worse, it *leeches* the water from a man. I've never worn a shirt of mail in my life, but there? In the Sanjou? I'll wager it's damn near intolerable."

"What are you saying?" the prince asked.

"Perhaps it would be better without such."

Shay shook his head. "I don't think so, Captain. It's our skin. We'd be naked without it."

"The wildmen do well without it."

"Perhaps, but we'll make do. Have no worries, Captain. You've sided with the best, and I say that in all modesty."

Stephanak became quiet then, turning his attention to the rolling waves. The *Blue Conquest's* bow breached a particularly high crest before dropping sharply.

All color fled Shay's face as he clutched at the nearby railing.

The captain's laughter rang out across the water.

Sitting on the main deck with his back to the gunnel, He-Dog reached over his head and grabbed the railing as the ship dipped and then leveled.

That attracted the attention of the older man called Grage, one of Shay's Koor officers. The deep forward pitch of the vessel barely caused the man's expression to twitch. He-Dog was still only learning the names of individuals, but the one called Jers Snaffer stood next to Grage. Snaffer was the shaggy slayer who had eyed He-Dog on the docks, and was presently eyeing him again with the cold indifference of one undecided of another's worth.

The ship leveled out only to dip once again, whereupon He-Dog's guts threatened to leave him. When he looked about, both Grage and Snaffer were watching him. He-Dog ignored the scrutiny and hoped the sea smoothed out soon. With that he let his breath go and took in a new one.

"How are you faring over there, boy?" Grage asked, his brow lowered.

He-Dog exhaled and nodded, but the ship dipped again, forcing him to grab hold of the railing once more.

Grage smiled and exchanged looks with Snaffer before they both turned their attention elsewhere.

The question was somewhat meaningful, as few of the mercenaries paid much heed to the two new recruits. Not that it surprised He-Dog. Mercenary bands could be fickle about new lads, thinking them already dead until otherwise. The warriors of Shay's group eyed them from afar with dark looks and wary expressions, quietly gauging them, wondering if they would live or perish in the very first skirmish.

He-Dog ignored them.

Chop sat an arm's length away, black mask over his head, his knuckles white from clenching ropes or gunnels. At least he had the mask, which covered the worst of the bruises from Hargan. He-Dog had nothing, and his battered and swollen features slowed the stride of any sailor passing by. It only took a short prodding here and there with his finger to realize he'd taken an unfit beating.

But he was still alive. Still alive. With most of his teeth intact.

He-Dog sighed and checked on Chop. The pair had claimed this spot on an otherwise busy and crowded deck. Their armor and weapons lay in a pile between them, sometimes rattling across the wood until one stuck a leg out to hem it all in. They kept to themselves, eating and drinking when able, slowly nursing themselves back from their many hurts.

Hargan swaggered by, his own features also battered and swollen, and cast a death gaze at both of them before moving on. He-Dog watched his back until the Sunjan was gone.

Hargan continued on his way, passing a group of sailors fussing over ropes and rigging. All of them took even more interest in their work until the warrior passed. The Sunjan was clearly one ready to fight. It hung about him like sour-scented water. Even Hargan's fellows seemed to avoid him, but there was a reason for that. Two nights earlier, He-Dog overheard a pair of mercenaries discussing the angry brute in harsh whispers, and how he'd recently lost a brother. Oddly enough, that knowledge saddened He-Dog just a touch. He didn't resent the Sunjan for the beating on the docks. Saimon's hell, he'd *asked* for that. A part of He-Dog even wished Hargan had kept right on pummeling him. Because in oblivion, nothing hurt. Inside or out.

That state of no pain, of *unknowing*, very much appealed to him.

"You there."

He-Dog and Chop looked up.

A squinting Grage loomed over them, gripping a rope as the ship continued heaving. "Keeping to yourselves, I see." He glanced at the waters. "Don't mind that. As long as you can handle a blade better than you fistfight. What's his name, anyway?"

"Chop," He-Dog winced, feeling his guts lurch in time with the ship.

"He can't talk?"

He-Dog shook his head.

Grage became quiet for a bit, inspecting them both. "All right. See here. I don't know either one of you, but I'm here to tell you to follow orders. At any instant. And mind the others. Especially Hargan. That's the little topper that nearly took your head off your shoulders. Stay clear of him, for all you're worth. Especially you . . ."

He aimed that at Chop.

"Did he hear me?" Grage asked He-Dog.

He-Dog nodded.

The officer scowled and leaned in, lowering his voice. "Hargan doesn't like either one of you. A blind punce could see that. As for the rest of the lads . . . mind your feet around their pisspots and you'll be fine. Anger any one of them . . . and you'll go into the water."

He-Dog held Grage's stern gaze for a moment when his innards threatened violent mutiny again. Instead of saying anything, he took a breath and let it out slowly.

"Understand?" Grage asked.

Squeezing his eyes shut, He-Dog nodded.

"You nodding there? The way the ship's going, I can't—"

"Aye that. Aye. Understood."

That satisfied Grage. "Two other things."

Dying Seddon. He-Dog took another steadying breath.

Grage turned and gestured for a barrel-chested man wearing nothing more than a pair of old black breeches that ended at the knee. The scorching sun had cooked his skin into tough leather and colored his hair. The man hurried over once summoned, his mouth puckered into a shriveled blossom.

"This is Gusper," Grage introduced. "The company's healer. Of sorts. He'll see to your wounds."

He-Dog glanced at the healer then at Grage.

"Why only now?" the mercenary officer asked, reading his expression. "Well, we would have seen to you earlier, except . . ."

"We couldn't find the saywort," Gusper croaked, as if badly needing a drink.

"We couldn't find the saywort," Grage repeated in annoyance. "He'll see to you now. Straighten you both out."

Gusper's head bounced from one shoulder to another, indicating he would do what he could for the pair.

"And . . . when you feel like parting with it," Grage pointed, "hand over that leather vest you have. One of our lads might be able to stitch up the front. Make it somewhat whole again. Unless you want to be half-naked in the jungle."

Fighting down the sickness, He-Dog shook his head.

Grage lingered, as if thinking matters over, and leaned down close. "Just know this . . . If any of my lads die because of you, *any* of them . . . I'll gut you. With one hard cut. Across the guts or up the middle. And if I don't, *he* will."

Grage pointed at the one called Snaffer.

Seddon's crack. He-Dog huffed miserably and hung his head. As an afterthought, he reached for his vest between him and Chop, pulled it free of the little pile of belongings, and handed it over.

"Truth be known," Grage rumbled, his tone softening. "You're more valuable alive than dead. You're with us now, for a short time, anyway. Remember that."

He-Dog would remember.

Grage walked away with the leather vest, leaving the pair.

A sickened He-Dog glanced over at Chop. The black mask stared back.

He-Dog wished Balless was still about.

"You're fine enough for this?" Gusper asked.

The two men nodded.

"Apologies again in getting to you this late," the healer said. "No matter. We'll have you right by the time we get to land."

Gusper stooped before He-Dog first. The healer looked down the length of his nose to examine his patient. In doing so, the older man's shriveled mouth parted in a grimace, revealing nothing but one yellow tooth sprouting from his lower gums. Grunting at the task before him, Gusper placed the jar on the deck and got to his knees. A moment later, he scooped out two fingers worth of ointment and held it to He-Dog's face.

The smell of onions was strong.

"All right, lad," Gusper said, flexing his elbows. "Stay still now . . ."

Having delivered his message, Grage turned and caught the wave from Shay, indicating that he wanted to talk. Following the prince's lead, he threaded his way across the deck and into a chamber belonging to the first mate. A short time later, a handful of the prince's companions gathered in that cramped space. Shay sat on the only chair and regarded Grage and Bartus, while Snaffer and Talso stood guard outside the closed door.

"Lads," Shay said. "Our talk for the day and then I'll let you be. Grage, remind our lads to stay clear of the crew. See to it that they do. Bartus, see to it that all hands upkeep their armor and weapons while we're on board. Sooner or later, the winds blowing the *Conquest* along will drop out. When that happens, we'll take our turn manning the oars. And Bartus, remind the lads that no one should be taking a squat over the sides. There are shite troughs for that, near the front, and those black tarred ropes are for their cracks once done. I've also been talking more to the captain about the Sanjou. We'll have some work to do before we land."

A frowning Bartus held up a hand.

Shay gestured for him to speak.

"About those two you threw in with us . . ."

The prince waited for it.

"Tell me again why you did it?"

Shay rubbed his head. "You see Marrek standing here?"

"I do not. However . . . they aren't going to replace him, Shay."

"No, they are not. Not even if there were a dozen of them. But they swing swords, and we need fresh swords to replace our fallen . . . and they were right there."

"Hargan smashed them both," Bartus reminded him.

"True, that's true enough. But they weren't at their best. You heard them just after they boarded. Only a day ago they came in from the desert, where they had been marching for weeks. They'll be somewhat mended by the time we reach the Sanjou. Not entirely but enough to fill our ranks. Besides . . . I like their looks. They didn't do badly against Hargan. It's Hargan, after all. Just keep him and the Nord away from each other."

"I think you made a mistake, Shay," Bartus said.

"You're telling me this now?"

Bartus exhaled. "Not everyone carrying a blade can use one. They could have escaped any of Othil's dungeons for all we know."

Shay sighed, ran a hand over his head, and fixed his attention on Grage. "Your thoughts?"

The old Koor's eyes flickered from the prince to Bartus and back again. "Same concerns, more or less. They look hard enough, but so will any starved rat."

"Bit harsh."

"I'm more hopeful than him," Grage continued, nodding in Bartus's direction. "As you say, they're not going to replace Marrek. Not ever."

"We needed the swords," Shay stressed. "You know as well as I do, Othil will be under siege within a week. Maybe sooner. Much sooner than any can reinforcements arrive from the mainland. Othil will want every able soldier, mercenary, and cutthroat to help defend the city until then. Word was they were already recruiting swords. Only a matter of time 'til they pressed us into service, and we all know there's no coin in sieges. Not when you're being *sieged*."

The prince eyed his trusted men. "Look. We're fortunate to get those two, even though, yes, they're not known to us. We'll find out what they're worth soon enough."

"Unless the voyage rots out their guts first," Bartus noted.

"They have the sickness?"

Bartus nodded.

Shay sighed. "Well, perhaps they'll get their sea legs and that'll be the end of it."

"And if not?"

"Then we won't know their worth until we're in the Sanjou."

A dubious silence followed that.

"All right, look . . ." Shay stressed. "I understand your concerns. Truly, I do. Truth be known, I hope *I* haven't made a mistake by bringing them along. Any other time I'd be far more careful with taking on new lads, but we *needed* new swords. Just keep watch. Let me know how they get on. Make sure Gusper gets them on the mend. I'm sure they'll do well enough in the Sanjou when we get there. And if not . . . if I've made a mistake, well . . ."

He let that hang in the air. ". . . I'll kill them myself."

The seas finally calmed at the end of the day.

The winds died away to the barest breeze, and the ship's heaving settled into a gentle rocking. All manner of snores ripped the quiet, coming from the mercenaries stretched out and sleeping upon the decks. A black cobweb of rigging hung between the masts, and beyond that a vast field of stars shone.

Unable to sleep, He-Dog watched the heavens as he lay across scrubbed planks. The stink of saywort clung to his battered hide, which did nothing to help him rest. Twice he ran a finger over wounds coated in the shite and twice he forgot he'd done so when he rubbed his eyes, causing them to burn and blur for long moments. His guts had settled a bit, so that much was good. In between the snoring he sometimes heard the odd whisper from the sailors assigned to keep watch. Every now and then, a mercenary rose and pissed over the side.

Of course, He-Dog heard every sizzling drop.

Chop slept nearby, stripped down to his mask and loincloth, fingers laced together on his belly. His skirt of hardened leather strips lay in a heap next to him, along with his remaining sword and a replacement for the blade they had to give up back in Othil. Right after Gusper had finished applying his salve, the healer noticed the Nordish man's second empty scabbard and asked about it. He-Dog told him they were forced to sell it for lodgings and food. Gusper offered Chop a replacement if he wanted it. Chop did, so the healer took the scabbard and went off with it. A short time later, he returned with a sword the Nordish man approved of and thanked him for.

A new blade, freely given. Passage from Othil and Big Rock in exchange for some mercenary work. Food and drink. Healing. He-Dog had to admit, once he got to thinking matters over, he appreciated Shay for taking them both on board.

Despite the battering he and Chop had taken back on the docks.

Some good fortune at least. For a change.

That caused He-Dog to sigh, long and hard. As the ship drifted beneath the glowing heavens, his thoughts strayed. He thought about the Kratoe of Foust. And the man called Galt. And how he would very much like to find both of them and exact some revenge for their betrayal.

He also thought of Balless. Dare he admit it, he missed his brother. Missed Rige.

And just before sleep finally took him, it occurred to him, of all the things he *thought* he hated, he realized he hated one thing above all.

He hated being alone.

CHAPTER 7

Breakfast was a handful of dried beef strips, a hard biscuit, an apple, and two long pulls of water from a covered barrel. He-Dog and Chop ate in silence, seated in their spot against the railing. The Nordish man still wore his mask but had rolled up the ends to uncover his mouth.

While they ate, He-Dog caught sight of Hargan stopping by the water barrel. The battered man held an apple, which he only seemed half-interested in, and he was looking over at him and Chop. Studying them. After a few moments, he scowled, remembered the fruit in his hand, and took a big bite.

Hargan nodded toward Chop. "He's got no lips," the Sunjan declared mid-chew. "You see that? Unfit punce's got no lips. Like the gills off a fish. See him? Right there. That's why he wears the mask. What else is he hiding under there? Can't be much worse than that."

He-Dog and Chop stopped eating.

His beard flecked with juice, a sneering Hargan stuffed one last bite into his mouth and threw the rest into the ocean. Wiping his hands on his chest, he sauntered over to Chop and stopped before him. The Sunjan bent over, still chewing away, and inspected the mask not an arm's length away.

"What happened to you, Nord?" Hargan demanded quietly, one side of his face crinkled by the sun. "Hm? What happened to that sore crack you call a face?"

He-Dog and Chop exchanged looks before lowering their heads and continuing with their breakfast.

Hargan kicked the Nordish man's feet. "I said . . . what happened to you? Don't make me ask again."

As a reply, Chop slowly withdrew both legs.

"Go away," He-Dog said simply, not bothering to meet the Sunjan's heavy gaze.

Hargan scowled, as if he'd just swallowed something unpleasant. "Wasn't talking to you, kog."

Sighing, He-Dog peered at something farther down the ship. "He can't talk."

"What's that?"

"He can't talk."

"So you talk for him?"

He-Dog ignored that. "He was on patrol in Paw Savage lands. The patrol got butchered. Paw Savages took his scalp. He tried burning his head to stop the bleeding, cooked his face instead."

Hargan feigned horror. "He *cooked*... his face... *instead*?" He absorbed that, sizing up Chop before regarding He-Dog again. "How well you know this man?"

"Well enough."

"And that's what you got from him? His story, that is."

"Aye that."

He-Dog distantly remembered that day on mainland Zuthenia, in the city of Vukedos, when he and Balless sat in a tavern, unfit drunk, listening to the Nordish man retell his history through grunts and gesticulations. Now that He-Dog thought on it again, there might've been an old bastard in there as well, reading a bit that Chop had written down. For those parts not easily explained... which cleared up a few mysteries. That was the trouble with hard drink—gave you great happiness, but in the end, also took away one's memory.

"So you've been with him for a long time?" Hargan pressed.

"Long enough."

The Sunjan leaned into the face of the Nordish man. "*Lies*," he quietly said. "All of it. Just like a Jackal."

Chop stopped eating.

"Oh, you heard me," Hargan warned. "You unfit stream of gurry."

He-Dog glanced at his companion.

Without warning, Hargan yanked the mask off Chop's head. The Nordish swordsman didn't resist as the material came free, exposing the melted face underneath. The hateful Sunjan stood back, balling the material in his hands, and glared at the ruined features.

"Cooked, indeed," Hargan declared. "Trouble is," he pointed at the man's face, "I know what that means. I *know*, you lying Nordish topper. You might have fooled *this* punce, but not me."

Dark eyes hooded and twinkling, Chop's hands slid to his blades.

All activity upon the deck ceased as mercenaries and sailors alike took a greater interest in the conversation.

He-Dog tensed, somewhat confused. "Go away," he again warned the Sunjan.

"You don't know who's sitting beside you."

"I said go away. Or it won't be a fistfight this time."

Hargan straightened. "Pull steel on me and I'll gut you. And heave what's left over to—"

"*Hargan!*" shouted Bartus, emerging from the ship's inner chambers. "You unfit he-bitch. Get away from those men. You've heard Shay say they're with us, so they're with *us*. Get *away*, I said, you flyspecked crust of shite. There'll be no blood spilled this day. Not on this ship and not between sword brothers."

Hargan stiffened at the word *brother*, as if he'd caught a whiff of rancid meat. "He's no brother of mine," he said and threw the leather mask to the deck. "You're shite," he said with a poisonous glare at He-Dog and Chop. "You're *both* shite."

"Go on," Bartus warned the Sunjan.

Hargan stomped off and disappeared below deck, with all eyes watching until he was gone. The situation dispelled, Bartus waved away the others. The tension eased off and Shay's hired swords went back to eating. High on the captain's deck, Shay and Stephanak, unnoticed until now, resumed their conversation.

Although Shay's eyes strayed back every now and again.

He-Dog ignored them all.

"That Sunjan," he said in a low voice to Chop, "will be trouble."

Not showing any indication of having heard, the Nordish man gathered up his mask and spread it across one thigh. Some of the other mercenaries studied him from afar, some blatantly so, eyeing the destroyed face. If their attention bothered him, Chop didn't show it as he arranged his mask on his leg.

He-Dog warded off a few of the more annoying looks with a scowl of his own. After a time, he checked on his companion, not blaming him for not wearing the mask. Not under the hot sun.

He remembered what Hargan had said, however.

Lying Nordish bastard.

One of them was lying. Knowing Chop for as long as he had, He-Dog decided it was the Sunjan.

And left it at that.

After breakfast, a cool breeze blew in from the east, and an order came down to exercise the mercenaries. The ship wasn't a big one, with a crew of about forty or more and an additional thirty of Shay's hired swords. Space was a prized commodity on board, and though He-Dog had not been below deck, he'd overheard that the cargo hold was near bursting with supplies of food, fresh water, and the odd barrel of wine. Barrels and chests cluttered the main deck as well, so Shay's men cleared a small area. Once the arena was set, Grage selected a pair of mercenaries to fight each other with lengths of wood.

Under the morning sun they doffed their shirts, revealing physiques corded with muscle and scratched by scars old and new. Using improvised swords, the paired off mercenaries verbally jabbed at each other while attacking or defending. Thrusts and slashes, parries and dodges, the skillful exchanges drew the attention of Stephanak's sailors, who would pause from their work to watch. As the morning drew on, the mercenaries fought until one jabbed the other with their practice swords. Regardless of who won or lost, smiles were flashed and shoulders slapped.

Not moving from where they sat, He-Dog and Chop watched.

Grage glanced their way every now and again, and He-Dog knew what was going to happen. Hated to consider it, really.

After the seventh or eighth match concluded, Grage chopped a hand at them. "You there! Dog!"

He-Dog hung his head and sighed.

"Get over here." The officer tossed him a bare length of wood, and the stick clattered at He-Dog's feet. He exchanged looks with Chop. The Nordish man didn't look too eager to fight, either. Not with sticks. He-Dog suspected that refusal would be worse, however.

So he climbed to his feet.

Chop muttered something, but damned if He-Dog understood.

A circle of hired killers waited.

"Stand right there," Grage ordered. "You should be up for a little knockabout."

Little knockabout. He-Dog inwardly groaned. It was only a few days ago that he'd nearly had his head taken off in a *little knockabout*.

Still, Grage insisted with an unwavering glare.

"Kellic," the officer shouted.

A hairy brute of a man with no neck lumbered forward. He-Dog recognized him from the last few days aboard the ship. Kellic was one of the larger men of the company, not tall, but bulky, with a youthful but sad expression, as if he'd done far too much killing in his time. Kellic was shirtless, thick with muscle, but possessed a hairy belly that hung over his belt, almost daring someone to take a swing at it. His scalp had been shorn down to a thick shade, while a menacing point of a beard punctuated his brooding features. He swished his wooden sword back and forth, inspecting it with those sad eyes, and finally regarded his foe like a bad cut of meat.

He-Dog winced at the Koor officer. He didn't have the patience for any of this unfit foolishness.

"First hard crack wins," Grage declared, retreating to the edge of the ring. "And no fists," he warned He-Dog.

The two fighters faced each other, though He-Dog clearly wanted no part of what was about to happen.

"*Begin*," Grage yelled.

Kellic lashed out once and broke his sword across the meat of He-Dog's left shoulder, the wood spinning over ducking heads. The onlookers flinched and cried out at the blunt smack.

Kellic backed off and made ready to defend himself.

A scowling He-Dog didn't press matters, however. He took the hit. Took the pain. And dropped his stick.

"He wins," he growled, flicking an unappreciative look in Grage's direction. Flexing his shoulder, he returned to the railing and plopped down next to Chop.

"Lords above," he muttered. "I wish there was firewater to drink."

His shoulder ached as if Seddon himself had just stomped on him. Kellic was a powerful man, and He-Dog suspected he hadn't impressed anyone with that display. Most certainly he would not have impressed Balless, but he didn't rightly care.

Across the way, Grage scratched at his face, perhaps undecided if he should call the new lad back for another round.

As it turned out, the decision was made for him.

"I'll fight next, Grage, if that's fine with you." Shay's voice boomed as he walked among the mercenaries. Bare-chested and twirling a length of wood in one hand, the prince stopped at the edge of the makeshift clearing.

Grage gestured that the floor belonged to the prince.

"Who will try this day?" Shay asked with a smile, scanning the gathered brutes for a challenger.

A heartbeat later, one stepped forth and hailed the prince. He was the same size, with a muscular torso and arms.

Cheers rose from the gathered men, and the prince nodded in approval.

"Once more, Carodo?" Shay asked with a knowing half smile.

"Once more, Prince."

They met in the middle, not two strides apart. They crossed swords, and the smiles disappeared.

The fight started without a word from Grage.

Carodo swung at the prince's head, then at his arm. Shay ducked and stepped back, avoiding both attempts. The prince's smile returned, and he nodded in approval before feinting at his opponent's head, freezing his foe.

An instant later Shay slapped his wood across the man's midsection, buckling him.

Whereupon the prince tapped the back of Carodo's neck with the length of wood.

"You just lost your head, Carodo," Shay informed him.

The mercenary straightened, holding his gut, while a mix of cheers and groans erupted from the audience.

"I heard that, Talso," a beaming Shay pointed. "Hope you didn't wager your boots."

Wincing, Carodo made it clear he was done. He left the little arena to the prince, who bowed ever so slightly at the waist.

When the circle was clear, Shay spun and exhibited a flashy series of strikes and lunges. He stabbed and slashed at imaginary foes, sank low and stabbed high, whipping his wooden sword about in a flashy weave that left more than a few shaking their heads. Shay continued prancing about the circle until it looked more like a dance. His men cheered him on, encouraging the show, and Shay did exactly that.

Well past what was comfortably necessary. Or so He-Dog thought, his shoulder still aching. It dawned on him that Shay enjoyed the applause perhaps *too* much. To He-Dog, if the prince was attempting to make a point, he'd made it long ago.

He was good with a stick. Fair enough.

He-Dog rubbed his forehead, unable to watch any more, drawing the attention of Chop. Who was no doubt thinking the same thing.

Eventually, Shay ceased twirling his stick to the general approval of the watching men. He-Dog studied the grain of the planks before him, keeping quiet, because he knew one word, one *look*, would most certainly get him into trouble.

Seddon above, he hated such swagger.

Not quite ready to leave the circle, Shay took on two more of his mercenaries and defeated both, raising He-Dog's suspicions that the men weren't really trying that hard.

"Who are we?" Shay asked at the end, baring teeth.

"Lost men!" came the shout.

"Who *are* we?" he demanded again.

"*Lost men!*"

With a satisfied smile and a wink, the prince tossed his stick away. He slapped shoulders as he passed through his ranks, on his way to rejoin Stephanak on the upper deck. There, the two men conversed pleasantly enough.

Below, the fighting circle continued its sparring. Hargan was noticeably absent, however, which surprised He-Dog. He wondered if Hargan would've danced with Shay like the others had. Something told him *that* pairing rarely happened.

A long time later, after the foolishness of the bouts was over and done with, Shay's mercenaries took shifts at the oars below deck, propelling the vessel along with powerful strokes. He-Dog and Chop took their turns with the rest, hardly lasting but feeling better for the exercise.

Something felt mislaid, however, for the two men. A presence missed.

Neither man spoke of it.

Supper was more meat, bread, and halves of ripe fruit. Sailors took to humming or singing comforting tunes of the sea, in time with the dips of the bow, while the rigging creaked off-key. The ocean drank the sun, turning the sky a frightening red and purple. Captain Stephanak walked about, a shadow against the evening, gazing up at the galley's masts or peering ahead at the horizon. A wind lifted his cloak, waving it against a smear of darkening colors.

The voices died away. Men settled down for sleep. But the ship and sea continued to creak and groan.

Sometime later, under a clear night sky, He-Dog rose from where he lay, annoyed at having to empty the bull so often. He pissed over the side and, once finished, gazed over black waters as fine and smooth as silk. The moon and stars sparkled off those waters. So He-Dog stood there, staring, hearing sailors singing in his head. Balless danced a destructive shuffle and step, possessing a brutish elegance that was both comical and endearing. His ugly grin blazed.

Feeling an awful ache within, He-Dog turned away from the night.

CHAPTER 8

Just before dawn, while the others were still sleeping, He-Dog woke and stood. The railing beckoned once more and he leaned against it, scowling just a bit as he took in all that awesome ocean. He understood it was going to be a lengthy trip, but part of him, the hateful part, wanted it done today. Locating his scabbard, he pulled forth the sword he'd taken from the armories of Foust. The dog skull with bared fangs and missing lower jaw glared at him.

"Interesting design," Shay said, appearing as suddenly as a curl of sea mist. "Good quality. Anyone can see that. I was wrong not to take that blade. It's easily worth a hundred cutaros or more. Much more. Where did you get that?"

"Armory of Foust," He-Dog rumbled.

"You were in Foust?"

"Aye that."

"Never been there," Shay said, turning to the water. "Probably never will now, if what they say is true. These beastmen are on the march. Did you see one?"

He-Dog didn't want to talk about them.

"Doesn't matter," Shay said, filling the silence. "I've been watching you these past few days. Not much to do on a ship like this. You seem a thoughtful man. Deep of thought, really. If not a shade dark, if I may. Bit ragged about the edges, truth be known, but the regular feedings are agreeing with you."

"They are."

"Good, good," Shay said pleasantly. "Certainly an improvement over when we first met. Hope you'll have fully recovered by the time we reach the Sanjou. I think we're in for a hard landing there."

The sun broke the horizon, and He-Dog bared bad yellow teeth at the flash. "You sound worried."

"Me?" Shay scoffed. "I'm eternally optimistic."

He-Dog wasn't certain what optimistic meant.

"My lads and I have visited and survived many dangerous places," Shay continued. "And we've lived. Well, *I've* lived. There are always some casualties, but this group, which you are now a part of . . . is as hard as iron. As iron *should* be, with a few scratches and scars. Guard their backs and flanks, and they'll guard yours. Even Hargan. Oh, he's a right saucy knot, that one, I know. Even a nuisance at times, but he'll watch your back. Guaranteed. A good man to have on your side."

"Seems unfit to me," He-Dog said.

The prince shrugged. "We *all* are, to some degree. Except myself, or so I think, and perhaps that's unfit in itself, hm? Hargan, though, yes, he's in a difficult patch right now. Lost his brother back in Othil. A lout cut his throat from behind. As ferocious as Hargan seems, his brother Marrek was three times so. He was also a keeper for Hargan. Kept him out of trouble. Not an easy man to replace."

"So who watches him now?"

"I do," Shay said simply. "He still obeys my commands, though reluctantly. He listens, but . . . a little slow to move at times. Marrek placed the fear of the Lords above into him and Hargan wasn't one to cross his brother. I have no family ties, just rank."

He-Dog frowned, feeling an odd understanding with the Sunjan.

"Keep all that to yourself, now," Shay warned with a good-natured frown.

"He worries you?"

The prince's good-naturedness cooled then, and his smile hardened. "Nothing worries me, lad. No man. No beast. Not Seddon in his heavens above or Saimon in his hell below. And certainly not you. Which brings me to the usual speech I give new men. A few days late, but it's there and to be understood. These men about you are the most dangerous lot of brutes and hellpups you'll ever find, and they address *me* . . . as 'Prince.' This is *my* command. You follow *me*, and me alone. You obey me and my officers. Cause dissent . . . and punishment is death. Understand me, He-Dog?"

Dislike flared up at being addressed in such a manner, but He-Dog suppressed his baser instincts. Shay stood before him, unblinking and with set jaw, his smile hard and without warmth. The self-styled prince smiled far too much for the trade.

He-Dog nodded exactly once, willing to obey orders, but knowing he wasn't ever going to hail the man as "Prince."

"Excellent," Shay said, the frost disappearing. He regarded the breaking dawn and took a breath. "Get strong again. We'll all be suffering soon enough. We'll get this done, right and proper. You've heard about the emeralds?"

"I have." Overhead the story from Shay's own war dogs, in fact. And a few sailors. They talked of little else.

"Riches abound in the Sanjou," Shay said. "Or so they say. So the captain of this vessel says. I believe him. And *we* are going to find those riches. Enough to make us all kings, thrice over. More than anyone could want or make use of. These men? Watch their backs, follow my orders, and that will be your prize."

Smiling again, Shay nodded and strode for the upper deck, where Stephanak's cape-flapping bulk appeared.

"Op-ti-mizzic," He-Dog whispered, facing the sun.

He didn't rightly know the word's meaning, could perhaps guess at it, but he suspected the prince was eternally . . . something.

Shay left the newest member of his company and wandered toward the captain. He very much enjoyed Stephanak's grandfatherly warmth and his tales of the sea. Two men intercepted him, however, emerging from below deck. One was the silent yet threatening Kellic, and the other was an equally imposing warrior by the name of Sunbar. The pair reminded Shay of the black bears that inhabited the great forests of Pericia: hairy, quiet, and somewhat unwieldy, with a few layers of fat.

Animals that would kill a man with one swipe of a paw.

And they both looked exceptionally dour that morning.

"Yes?" Shay asked pleasantly with his voice lowered. "How is he?"

Despite what he'd said to He-Dog, Shay *was* concerned about Hargan. Worried enough to assign men to watch over him . . . but also relieved that the man was staying away from the Nord.

Sunbar leaned in close. "The same," he reported. "Short times on deck but when he's below, he sits with his back against the hull. He looks asleep but, truth be known, I don't know if he sleeps anymore. I wake and see him just sitting and . . . staring. Sometimes," Sunbar glanced at Kellic, "sometimes he's whispering to himself. And I don't know what it is. It *sounds* like words, like he's speaking, but damned if I can understand him. Otherwise, he barely makes a sound. He eats but you've seen that. The only other time he does anything is when he gets up to empty the bull. Or have a squat."

Shay rubbed his face.

"He barely says a damn word," Sunbar carried on. "To us or anyone. We've watched him, as you ordered, but . . ." he grimaced. "The only one that attracts his attention . . . is the Nord."

"The Jackal?"

"When he's above deck, he watches him," Kellic rumbled, showing a gap in his front teeth. "Doesn't hide it either. He watches him. Like he's thinking about taking his head."

"That outburst yesterday?" Sunbar said. "That was the most . . . life we've seen in the man since the fistfight back in Othil."

"Sunbar's right," Kellic added. "He's got the look of one ready to kill."

Shay sighed and rolled his eyes. "Well, see to it that he doesn't. If he kills the Nord, the *other* one will no doubt want satisfaction. And those two are supposed to replace Marrek."

The pair nodded but didn't look so confident.

"Damn shame," Shay muttered. "A bloody unfit shame. Who'd've thought Hargan would get on like this?"

Neither man answered but, then again, no one ever believed Marrek could die either. Men died *around* Marrek, but never the man himself.

"Carry on, then," Shay ordered. "Keep watch. Let me or Bartus or Grage know if there's a change."

"We'll be right there," Kellic said.

Shay knew both these men greatly respected Hargan. Where brute strength and sheer ferocity were concerned, Hargan was second only to Marrek. If Kellic and Sunbar were regarded as bears, they were mere cubs compared to the once-Sujin.

"Maybe even talk to him," Shay suggested as an afterthought. "Maybe that'll right him."

That stopped the two men.

"Talk about what?" Sunbar wanted to know.

"Damnation, I don't know. Whatever you butchers talk about. How many hearts you've eaten raw. Or heads you've bashed in. Arms you've broken. I don't know. Just get him talking sensibly."

Neither man appeared happy about that idea.

Shay dismissed them and they returned below deck. Shay really didn't care *what* they did as long as Hargan unlocked himself from his current state. The prince didn't know what to do to help the man, but he *did* understand Hargan was a force too valuable to be abandoned. Once again, he wished Marrek were still alive. He was the only one who could control his brother. Now, Hargan wasn't only becoming a worry, he was becoming . . . unsettling.

Even a touch frightening.

Beyond Marrek, only Kellic and Sunbar had any semblance of friendship with Hargan, and that was solely based on their common interest in splitting heads.

He hoped the old Hargan reappeared soon. Before they reached the Sanjou's coastline.

Sensing eyes upon him, Shay glanced around and saw the masked figure of the Nord, on the open deck. He nodded at the warrior.

And the man nodded back.

Sunlight crept below deck as the day began anew. It made its way down worn steps leading to a cargo hold packed with barrels of rations and arms and shone its morning rays upon the sailors sleeping among the supplies. Shafts of light seeped through the floorboards and into the lower decks where the oars powered the ship on windless days. The smell of old wood, foul breath, and sour sweat wafted through the hold as the crew awoke. Boots clattered as the men attended to their morning duties.

Hargan sat with his back against the hull, in the darkest place he could find, away from sunbeams or swaying lanterns. Darkness for a creature of darkness. He dwelled in the gloom. Kellic and Sunbar watched him, but he didn't care. At times, he didn't recognize them. At times, he forgot where he was.

Not that it mattered.

Nothing mattered anymore except for the light in Marrek's wide eyes going out, and the warmth of his brother's blood spraying across his face.

The memory tormented him. Hargan tried countering it by focusing on how he had torn Mobos apart. That helped for a bit, but with each passing day it seemed to help less and less. Now, whenever he closed his eyes, he saw his brother's throat slit, again and again. The sensible thing would have been to keep his eyes open and he tried that for a time. But as time passed, it seemed his memories of his brother only grew. Eventually, forgotten childhood memories—of happier times—leaked into his mind, creeping back like something wild once frightened away. Vivid images of him and his brother, each one scratching at him like an unfriendly cat.

Two boys fishing off a short wharf.

Play fights with sticks.

Marrek falling onto the ground and splitting his head open on a rock. Hargan stripping his shirt and applying it to the wound.

What had *happened* to them? Why had the last few years been so bitter?

Sadness welled up inside Hargan, threatening to reach his eyes. Remorse, cold and endless black, comparable only to the sea beyond the hull. *Pain.* If the loss of a limb would relieve it, he would do so. Seddon above, *he* was supposed to die before Marrek. *He* was the reckless one. Yet, here he was, alive and hurting in the dark. All his life, he had built walls around himself, armoring his flesh against the spectacles and horrors of the battlefield, but Marrek's death pushed a mighty icicle through those barriers and skewered him through the chest.

Worse still, the hole was healing but the stake was still there, fashioned from memories of good times and bad, melting into a terrible poison.

One that burned.

So very badly.

Hargan let out his breath in a hiss.

He would survive this.

He could . . . he *knew* he could. But it was so very painful.

And a growing part of him wanted to share that pain.

The days on the water dragged from one morning to the next. The winds barely breathed into the sails, forcing sailors and mercenaries alike to work the oars. Shay made certain his warriors took their turns. All those sword arms were useless if they were in poor condition.

A haunted Hargan worked the oars more than any other, pulling them with powerful conviction. He ignored the men informing him his time was up and continued hauling the wood. Some believed he was attempting to sweat out whatever poison infected him, and so they left him alone. Over time, his demeanor worsened, and the rest of the crew avoided his company altogether. Even Shay found other things to concern himself with rather than confront the moody warrior. Only Sunbar and Kellic kept in contact with the man, sometimes nearby, sometimes at the fringes, keeping an eye on the Sunjan and ensuring he stayed out of trouble. At times, when they found him with his back to the hull, they would sit and talk in low voices about one thing or another. Hoping Hargan would overhear and join in.

It didn't work, but they continued anyway, following the prince's orders.

He-Dog and Chop rowed with their new companions, learning their names and their stories. Grage and Jers Snaffer were perhaps the oldest hellpups on the ship—they were in their late forties and appeared far from done. Both commanded a great deal of respect from the others, the hard kind earned by surviving where many had died. Grage delighted in shouting out Shay's commands on a regular basis while the brooding Snaffer had no problem being the Koor's murderous shadow.

He-Dog grudgingly began to favor Grage, the graying war dog, eventually losing his urge to throttle the topper.

Talso became another familiar face, an ugly, muscular shagger whose appearance could scorch a man's eyes from his head. He lurked about the ship like hellish Saimon himself searching for the weak of stomach. Every day Talso tended to an evil selection of blades in his possession—inspecting, sharpening, and oiling the weapons with deadly intent. He nodded a lot and spoke little, as if constantly deep in thought. Ink covered his powerful arms from wrist to shoulder, and a fearsome collection of scars crossed his chest and back. When he worked his blades, everything rippled and writhed.

Whenever Talso cared for his weapons, a swarthy Sarlander named Zozz usually did the same. The Sarlander rubbed a stone along a sickle of a sword, and that constant grating lick irritated He-Dog to the bone. Zozz even drew Stephanak's unexpected wrath when he took to testing his weapon on the railing of the *Blue Conquest*. In the evening, the Sarlander put aside that nasty weapon and settled near the prow of the ship, gazing at the horizon as it darkened.

The second Koor, Bartus, usually stayed close to Shay, discussing matters not concerning other ears. When he wasn't talking to Shay he prowled the ship, scowling as if expecting trouble from every quarter.

Then there was the brooding scout, Ungla. It was said Ungla had traveled most of the known lands with the prince, surviving countless campaigns. No one knew where Ungla hailed from, but he seemed every bit as cautious as one in his profession might, and kept his own company over the others.

The blocky healer, Gusper, drifted through the ranks daily, telling stories of the Sanjou to anyone who would listen. Stories of missing ships and the crews populating them. Gusper, who hailed from Vathia, was the most unfit healer He-Dog had ever met. The man hung a menacing assortment of throwing knives on his chest and waist, which he had the unsettling habit of pulling and throwing, sinking them deep into various wooden targets about the ship. Stephanak warned him twice for gouging his vessel, and promised that a third instance would find the healer hanging from the prow by his thumbs.

Then there was the rest of Shay's company, all banter and bluster like bears at play. At times, they threatened each other with worn blades and were laughed at for doing so. Swords were commonplace and well cared for, but there were more personal weapons as well, strapped to backs, sheathed to forearms, or hanging from waists. A tall Ghedian possessed a greatsword that could have been the same length as Chop's body. A brute from Orvasia carried a spiked mace the size of a melon. Another powerful lad, wearing a helm adorned with bull horns, carried a battle-axe as if it held no weight at all.

In his time, He-Dog had seen such packs of butchers before, and decided this one appeared capable enough. Whether he could depend on them to protect his back was unknown. He rarely spoke to Chop, and when he did his gaze lingered for a bit before he turned away.

Wishing he could better understand the bastard.

CHAPTER 9

A fine string of light crested the horizon, giving way to a dark and worrying red sky that preceded the dawn.

Wearing a light sleeveless tunic that revealed his muscular arms, Shay climbed up onto the top deck and greeted Stephanak with a nod.

"Good morning," Stephanak returned. Bright blue and sea green covered his frame, and a dark cape rustled in a southern breeze. A wide hat covered his head, lending a twinkle to his shaded eyes.

He pointed to the sea, directing the prince's attention.

Far away, across mild waters, a dark landmass rose from the middle of the ocean. A jagged crown of peaks and uneven slopes, as if fashioned by a smithy with a broken hand.

The prince squinted. "That's it?"

"That . . . is the Sanjou."

Shay gripped the railing, appraising the distant island.

"Are your men ready?" Stephanak asked.

"We were ready when we stepped aboard this ship, Captain. Now? They're just eager."

Stephanak chuckled. "Excellent. Truth be known, my Prince, I have never been beyond those cliffs. I have stood *on* them, for I am as curious as the next man. An unfit jungle lurks past that mountainous coastline. An unspoiled wilderness of the deepest colors. You will see far more than I ever did. You will discover its mysteries. Its riches. Its horrors . . ."

After nearly two weeks or so, Shay had learned that the captain of the *Blue Conquest* enjoyed telling tales meant to frighten youngsters.

"I've stood here since it was still dark," Stephanak continued, "watching the dawn sear the horizon, slowly turning the sky red. The Sanjou was barely there. But as the light strengthened, so did my old eyes. And though the air grows warmer, I feel a chill. The very sight of that haunted place disturbs me. I feel as if . . . I'm delivering you to your deaths."

Out of respect for the old officer, Shay lowered his head, waiting for the rest of it. He'd listened to variations ever since they left Othil, and it was beginning to grow tiresome.

Stephanak gestured at the island. "Some final words of advice, even though I know you've heard enough. Please . . . practice caution. *Always*. This is one of those places from which people rarely return. It is a nest of legends. A den of beasts and ghosts and all manner of frightful things that would leave a man trembling."

Shay forced a smile. "We'll be careful. And we'll return. Have no doubt."

"You truly are a brave lot. But once more, please be cautious."

"Understood."

"Can you feel it?"

Shay could not, and his expression reflected that.

"The *heat*," Stephanak snarled for emphasis. "And we're still on open water. The ocean's winds will not touch you in there, beyond the rocks. I say this because I've seen your armor. How heavy it looks. It will be . . ."

The old captain's face screwed up, searching for the words.

"Difficult, aye that," Shay said. "No doubt. It's our skin, Captain. Our hides. We have padded shirts underneath, of course. To soak up the sweat, but I know. The heat will be unfit."

Stephanak stared at the Sanjou's foreboding mass.

Shay joined him. "You'll feel better when we return with the stones."

"Yes, daresay I will." Another breeze rustled the captain's cape. "Know this, Prince Shay. I am getting far too old for these waters. These travels. Truth be known, I believe this will be my last voyage to this accursed place. I wish . . . to live the last of my days on another, far more pleasant shore."

"Spending your riches on a castle on a beach, somewhere?"

"Lords above, no," Stephanak said, dismissing the thought. "I'll purchase a new ship. A bigger, much grander ship . . . but one more suited to just the docks. The more *noble* docks, you understand."

Shay did and they shared a smile for a moment while the *Conquest* pressed ahead.

"We'll make the cliff's shadows by afternoon," Stephanak said.

"Afternoon," Shay whispered, eyeing those craggy heights. When he'd had enough, he turned his attention to the deck below and spotted Bartus. "Bartus! We land just after noon."

The Valencian waved and went to the railing. There, he peered ahead, seeing the distant mass sitting upon the waters.

A moment later, he started barking orders.

Tall stone cliffs formed a small bay protected from the open sea, and therein the *Blue Conquest* dropped her anchor into calm blue-green depths. The wind had dropped out completely and Stephanak kept a respectable distance from the shores of the Sanjou. Beyond the gravel beach jutted great big towers of rock, grooved and lined, like the scraggly throat of an impossibly ancient man, with tufts of green clinging to it. Menacing clouds drifted in and hooked themselves on craggy mountain spires, suggesting a powerful rain might fall at any time. Those spearheads loomed over the bay, casting long shadows across the water.

More than a few faces lifted to study those formidable heights. The island was no longer the wellspring of frightening tales told by sailors around a sea-washed deck. The Sanjou loomed before them all.

Stephanak shouted orders, directing his men as the deck teemed with preparations to go ashore. A pair of longboats hauled behind the *Conquest* were pulled to the ship's broadside. Bartus strode among the mercenaries, inspecting the readiness of his butchers.

Amid it all, He-Dog and Chop stood at their usual perch, watching the activity with wary interest. He-Dog had already donned his leather armor, the same he'd taken from Foust's armory. Leather twine, sewed by one of Shay's men, stitched the front of the vest together. His dog skull blade hung in a scabbard at his waist. The mercenaries had provided him with a rectangular shield that rested against his legs, a helmet, and a backpack filled with provisions. Bronze greaves protected his lower shins and knees, while a skirt of hard leather strips covered his thighs. Daily applications of the saywort had partially healed the worst of his wounds, allowing him to get about. As an afterthought, he adjusted his war braid. Thoughts of cutting the damn thing off had crossed his mind, but the women seemed to enjoy twiddling with the length, and truth be known, when you looked like him, every little bit helped.

The imposing island filled He-Dog's vision as he gazed up and down the cliff walls, from the sea-rounded stones at the base to the storm clouds masking the tallest peaks. Not a sea bird flew about those heights. Not a cry could be heard. The Sanjou radiated evil, pure and hot and warming the very air surrounding it. Its spires imposed long shadows across the water and the *Conquest*, as if issuing a final warning.

"See anything?" Grage asked. Snaffer stood just behind the Koor officer.

He-Dog considered them both before shaking his head.

The Koor smirked and pointed.

There, high above them all, was a split in the cliffs, where the clouds hung the lowest.

He-Dog sighed, knowing they were going to have to climb all that nonsense.

"That's where we're going," the officer informed him.

He-Dog sighed again, hating himself for being right. "Hand over foot, I imagine?"

"I suppose, if you must. Look there. No, not there, you git. *There*. See it? That's a trail. All the way to the top."

He-Dog squinted but Chop spotted it first and pointed.

A beaten path, thin. It resembled the hide of a crushed snake. It angled up the cliff wall and disappeared near the top.

He-Dog exhaled softly. *Dying Seddon*. The sight failed to lift his miserable spirits. Damned *beastmen*. He reminded himself of what had brought him here in the first place. Fleeing from doomed Othil. Was probably overrun by now.

Still, compared to the sight of that death trail, the Zuthenian city on the brink of siege didn't seem like a bad place at all.

"Not much of it, I know," Grage said, sensing his thoughts. "But we'll be up there by nightfall, or so thinks the first mate. They've made the hike before. Says it's the safest way. The *surest* way."

He-Dog kept silent about that and chewed on the inside of his mouth. His left hand, the one once squished by catapult shot, twitched and itched.

Stephanak appeared on the top deck then, with Shay by his side. The captain raised his hand, and the activity on board gradually stopped.

"My friends," the captain said, his croaky voice carrying. "My very good friends. Just a few words before your grand adventure. My first mate will guide you up and over those cliffs and peaks. Once you climb those heights, strike inland and stay quiet. Always quiet, for the jungle and its mysteries will be listening. I can't tell you much else about where the stones are. Such details were not given to me. So search inland for as long as your supplies last. You'll find plenty of fresh water in the Sanjou's rivers. And fruit, for that matter, which will be a welcome fare from the dried meats we've packed for you. We will stay here for as long as we can, but by the first *full* moon, roughly twenty days from now, if you have not returned, we will sail *back* to mainland Zuthenia. There we will resupply and return. Here. *Right* here. For you. By the following full moon. We'll wait here then, for as long as we can. If you have not appeared by then, well . . ."

Stephanak nodded grimly as a sad smile leaked across his face. "Well, know that I will not bring another soul to this place. I am greedy, but not so much to continue ferrying good men to their deaths."

Shay patted the captain on the shoulder then. The two men clasped forearms and a solemn Stephanak held on a moment longer before releasing.

"Understood, Captain," Shay said for all to hear. "And we'll return. I promise you. If this place holds riches of any kind, we'll bring them back."

A moment of meaningful silence then, while the rigging creaked overhead.

"Over the sides, lads," Shay ordered.

Long boats bobbed at the waterline of the *Conquest*. Stephanak's men jumped feet first into the sea, disappearing with a splash before clambering into the boats. Bartus and Grage gave their orders and big men wearing tough leather cuirasses and shirts of mail climbed over the side. Sailors handed down backpacks full of provisions, where they were stored away in the smaller boats. Shields, weapons, unstrung bows, and quivers stocked with arrows went over the side to be packed away.

Having said his goodbye, Shay left the captain and joined his remaining men upon the deck. He-Dog and Chop were among the last to climb down into a longboat, and when they did, they sat next to Ungla, the stoic scout said to have been with Shay the longest. Ungla pressed the upper curve of a bow to his cheek while he sized up the Sanjou. He-Dog didn't know the man, so he urged Chop to sit next to him.

Sailors and warriors took up the oars.

"Pull!" a voice cried, and the boats left the shadow of the large galley. Oars dipped in an uneven beat, soon working in unison.

The boats inched toward the rocky shore of the Sanjou, the smell of brine thicker in the secluded bay.

Working an oar, He-Dog glanced back at the *Blue Conquest*.

His cloak hiding his figure, Stephanak had not moved from his place on the high deck.

The old captain leaned forward, clutched at the railing, and watched the two boats drive for land.

"Lords watch over them," he whispered, eyeing the impassive heights of the cliffs . . . and rapped the wood three times for good fortune.

CHAPTER 10

In short time, the mercenaries reached the shores of the Sanjou.
Sailors jumped over the sides, splashed down, and hauled the boats onto the beach. The mercenaries followed, watchful of the towering heights. Surf foamed around the men's ankles as every step fell upon a rattling, shifting mat of rounded rocks. Packs and supplies were quickly off-loaded, and once done, the mercenaries pushed one boat back into the water.

For a brief moment, He-Dog watched the sailors rowing back to the *Conquest*, then he glanced at Chop and the rest of the group, already marching in single file toward the cliffs. The cliffs leaned over them all, shading them from the worst of the midafternoon sun.

He-Dog started his hike. The trail was barely the width of a single man, and a dangerous mix of loose gravel and pebbles. Clumps of squat bushes colored the cliff wall with greens and dollops of white and yellow. The burning grew in He-Dog's legs as he ascended, placing a hand on the imposing rock face on his left. A huge wedge in the cliff face narrowed the trail a short distance, forcing the men to carefully move around it, gripping the thing with their backs to the water. When it was He-Dog's turn, he glanced down over the edge beneath his feet and let his breath out in a hiss.

Dying Seddon, he thought, blinking at the drop. Some fifty paces down, at least. The surf smoothed over the beach in a soft, wet rattle.

In the middle of the blue-green bay, the *Blue Conquest* floated, tall and hauntingly resplendent in the cliff's shadow.

He-Dog realized Chop, the last man in the line, was waiting for him. With a scowl, he got moving.

Seventy-five paces up the trail.

A hundred.

Truth be known, He-Dog figured falling at twenty would be enough to kill a man. Anything above that only bettered the chances.

The trail switched back several times, at points made even more treacherous by the path's smooth rocks. Water from unseen springs slicked a few of those slabs. Pointed outcroppings poked at him, scratched at his arms, warning him he should consider heading back to the beach. He slipped twice, despite concentrating on the trail. Men spoke in hushed tones above him, some even managing to laugh. He-Dog didn't know what was so damned funny. A few pebbles rained down on his head at times, from the mercenaries climbing the next level overhead. One rock shard came down before him, bouncing off the trail with a puff of dust and spinning into space. It clacked off the cliff wall twice before landing on the beach, or so He-Dog believed. He didn't actually hear it land.

Three times the mercenaries stopped along the trail. When they did, the men leaned against the wall and stared out over the spectacular sight of the bay and the lone galley, fine and noble on shimmering waters.

The fourth time the line stopped, He-Dog reluctantly peered down, sweat dripping from his face.

Sweet Seddon above.

Two hundred paces up? Perhaps three?

He glanced at Chop, who was pressing himself against the wall and looking up instead of down. Chop was always the smartest of their lot.

It was just unfortunate no one understood the bastard.

Overhead, the clouds thickened and stretched beyond the cliffs, smothering the sun and further darkening the land. Bartus and Grage waited at the top, standing among the rocks like stern gatekeepers of the realm. Bartus beckoned for He-Dog and Chop to hurry while glancing over his shoulder at things out of sight. The Koor grabbed He-Dog by his forearm when he was close enough and hauled him onto a rough platform of stone.

A warm breeze blew into He-Dog's face, so sweet it stopped him in his tracks—until Chop slapped him in the back, urging him to move along.

Their guide, Muggins, the first mate, stood a few paces back. The older man nodded at the last two climbers, baring all three of his remaining teeth in a lopsided smile.

A tired He-Dog smirked in return.

"Step to the rear," Bartus ordered. "Have a rest but keep quiet. StayKeep alert."

He-Dog did as told, his lower legs on fire after the strenuous hike. They shuffled off the rock and onto a flat shelf of packed earth that extended some fifteen paces back, where tall, olive-green grass grew along the inner edges. That wide rim extended right and left in a dramatic ridge of stony peaks and dips, a dazzling sight that not even the low-hanging thunderheads could darken. Those tall walls of green and earthy brown formed a natural bowl that stretched off to either side, far into the distance. Too far for He-Dog to see, but stunning to behold.

"Like a crown, isn't she?" Muggins asked.

He-Dog nodded. She was indeed that, and they were the itching mites upon her brow. He walked ahead, past mercenaries with no interest in the view, toward others who stood and stared. A massive valley waited just beyond the inner cliffs, and from where He-Dog had stopped, carved slopes flowed downward in broad wedges of earth, ending in a wide step fit for giants. It then cascaded downward a second time, disappearing into a dense jungle that concealed the base of a vast caldera.

Not a jungle, he thought. "Jungle" was too ordinary a word to fully describe the wondrous sight before them all, and a stunned He-Dog left it at that. He'd visited his share of jungles in the interior of Big Rock, but this . . .

This was much grander. Much more ancient. A place where a hundred civilizations might have risen, flourished, and fallen to yet a hundred more before being swallowed whole by all that relentless vegetation. An ocean of green lay before him, as far as the eye could see, where huge domes of foliage spread across the whole of the valley floor, broken by hills and mountains drenched in plant life. Birds flew across the sweeping expanse, black specks that sped above the tallest trees, only to disappear within a natural canopy of limbs, leaves, vines, and nests. The sheer scope of the Sanjou was such that its outer bounds disappeared in the hazy distance. Beneath He-Dog's feet, below the outcropping they stood upon, earthy ridges and channels descended at a sharp angle and disappeared under a domed patch of trees looking soft enough to dive into. Plumes and tufts of mottled color both light and dark covered the lower slopes, their pigments glistening despite the gloomy clouds overhead. Lazy birdsong drifted throughout, low melodious squawks that rose above and pierced an unmistakable chatter of life, all well-concealed below.

He-Dog stared. Stared until sweat slid into his eyes, annoying him until he wiped it away.

For a place only talked about in hushed tones of dread, the Sanjou was unbelievably lush and vibrant. Immeasurably ancient. And shockingly beautiful.

For a brief moment, He-Dog wished Balless were there. And the man called Rige. Lords above, even the one-eyed archer called Borus. Big Rock had its share of forests and jungles south of the desert belt, but *this* . . . this was . . . something otherworldly.

The armored men spoke in hushed whispers, basking in the view or fussing over backpacks and weapons.

He-Dog didn't bother with either. He just couldn't get over the sprawling jungle depression stretched out before him.

"Right," said Muggins, his sea-blasted voice jarring in the quiet. "When you're ready, Captain Prince Shay, sar. This way."

He-Dog and Chop turned to see the old sailor leading Shay and Bartus toward the far end of the ridge they stood upon.

Muggins stopped and pointed at a spot below where the hardpacked earth dropped out of sight.

"Right, trail starts here. Snakes back and forth all the way down to the valley floor." He chopped a hand. "That's the place. Strike hard but for the love of the Lords be quiet about it. Don't be raising your voices like you were up here. Seddon only knows what's listening. Now then, mind the trail. It's packed tight but can be muddy in places. Made by adventurers and explorers long gone and Seddon only knows what else. But mind yourselves. There's savages about. Savages. Dangerous and bloodthirsty wildmen. If they're near, they might pick up your trail. Smell your blood, even. And that's just the wildmen. Seddon above knows what else lives in that wretched patch down there."

He-Dog wondered that himself, stealing another glance at the awesome overgrown garden below.

"Remember," Muggins continued in a harsh whisper. "We'll be waiting. I'll wager you'll be dreaming of the *Conquest* by dawn tomorrow."

Gripping his sword and shield, Bartus placed one boot atop a rock and peered into the valley. Grage and Snaffer wandered over, taking in the sight. The little company looked quite fearsome with their assortment of blades and armor. Restrung bows were at the ready. Spears held at the high. Shields hung off arms. He-Dog grudgingly approved.

"Quite the drop," Shay commented, marveling at the heights.

"It's getting late," Bartus said. "Perhaps we should camp here for the night."

"Camp where? Too damn narrow. The lads would roll off the cliff in their sleep. And we're exposed. There's nowhere to hide up here. Anyone along those ridges would see us easily. We still have plenty of daylight left. Let's head down while it's still light. Get along as far as we can before we have to stop for the night."

Not looking too pleased with the decision but keeping quiet, Bartus once more peered down into the valley.

Grage wiped at his bare head and flicked the sweat from his hand. "Hellish heat."

Shay studied the mercenaries and beckoned Ungla to come forward, his features serious. Wearing an old vest of leather armor with forest-green breeches tucked into well-worn boots, he plodded to the front. He barely made a sound as he reached the end of the ridge and studied the path ahead. Ungla passed off his bow and pulled forth a short sword. Without a word, he descended in short hops until he dropped from sight.

The mercenaries followed in single file.

The prince turned to Muggins as his men walked by. "Right, we're off. Until the next time we meet."

He held out a fist and the first mate pressed it with his own.

With a nod and a wink, Shay stepped into line with the remainder of his company.

He-Dog watched them all take the trail down, snaking out of sight. He shared a look with Chop, and they both turned to see Hargan watching them. Armored in chainmail, the sweating Sunjan stood with the head of his battle-axe head down in the dirt. He showed no inclination of going before either man.

He-Dog gestured at Chop to get moving. The swordsman did so, and He-Dog followed, glancing back at the stern Hargan.

The Sunjan glared.

He-Dog ignored him, not in the mood for hateful looks.

After they had all gone, Muggins and the few sailors with him stood at the trailhead and watched the mercenaries descend from the cliffs. He scratched at his corded throat, fingernail picking at some unfit protrusion there, and checked on the worrisome clouds overhead. He noticed the hard looks between the last few lads, especially the one with the axe. No trust there, that much was clear. And they had the looks of something heavy on their minds.

Muggins didn't care for those looks. Trust was everything in a place like the Sanjou. If you didn't have it, someone or something would have *you*. He hoped the mercenaries would sort their matters out long before any trouble.

He watched the mercenaries descend farther, keeping to the cliff wall. The trail was an uneven one, hardpacked, with irregular drops. The other sailors lagged behind, uneasy of the heights and feeling exposed to anyone who might be watching from below.

Muggins dropped into a crouch before finally sitting on that first earthy step of the trail. He watched the mercenaries all the way down, until the jungle thickened and swallowed them up one by one.

The short one with the battle-axe was the last to disappear from sight.

Muggins again checked on the clouds. Ignoring the mutters of sailors behind him, he gauged the gathering storm as well as that infested pot of vegetation below. He waited until he decided the mercenaries were well away before giving his chin a rub.

"That's it, then, lads," the first mate said to his crew, suddenly anxious to be back out on the water. "Let's get clear of this place."

CHAPTER 11

H*eat.*
 It wasn't the dry heat of Big Rock's desert. This . . . this was a different kind of monster, but every bit as hateful. A steamy heat, dense with moisture and thick enough to drink. Perhaps even *chew*, in He-Dog's mind. As a result, sweat covered him in an unruly sheen, slick and dewy and unpleasant. Sweat coated the inner grip of his shield. More sweat ran down his back and seeped into cracks, souring his mood all the more.

One would think that the clouds above would make the heat more bearable.

It did nothing of the sort.

He-Dog wiped his eyes again and bared bad teeth.

The trail was every bit as narrow going down as it was going up, but with even more uneven steps and awkward slopes. The earth was hardpacked, well-traveled, and did not leave prints. At least as far as He-Dog could see. He hoped Ungla saw the same and had passed that information along to Shay.

Chop shuffled in line just ahead of He-Dog, with Gusper before him. It grew darker the deeper they descended, until the sky disappeared completely under an impenetrable roof of foliage. A primordial gloom enveloped them then.

"Perhaps we should light a torch," someone muttered from up ahead, somewhere through thickets of huge palm leaves splaying off from massive trunks. He-Dog glanced around. A forest of odd trees surrounded them, with pale, segmented trunks that curved upward toward the dark ceiling above. They brushed against wreaths of alien flora and dark strands of cotton hanging in multitudes, in swaths both thick and thin, where gray daylight either bled or shafted through. Black, fist-sized globules hung from above, clinging to the foliage and perhaps ready to fall.

Thick tangles of dark green vegetation with splashes of yellow, red, and white threatened the boundaries of the path, striving to hide all traces of it. Low walls of creeping vines bearing barbed hooks scratched at knees and thighs. The air grew heavier with every step into that steamy, shadowy cauldron, and every breath went down like soup. Swarms of black flies found them, drifting in like a fine but murderous drizzle, covering cheeks and necks and anything exposed.

Unseen birds cried out while the men brushed aside and pushed through the overwhelming vegetation. Leather creaked. Metal clicked and rustled while hands slapped at biting insects. Whispered curses spiced the air. The weight on He-Dog's back, distributed as evenly as possible, became a burden, squeezing more perspiration from him.

Unfit heat.

Only moments off the cliffs and already he was cooking.

He-Dog picked a black fly off his neck, crushing it dead. The amount of blood on his fingertips surprised him.

"Lords above," Bartus whispered, pressing a hand to his cheek instead of slapping, crushing several insects. "This is *unfit.*"

"Bartus," Shay cautioned, and the Koor quieted. The prince wiped his brow, squishing his own share of flies. He focused on the task ahead. *The riches of the Sanjou*. If they found them, if they found the stones, Shay and his lads would be wealthy beyond imagination. Truth be known, however, wealth held little interest to him. Riches were good and all that, but *recognition*—that was something he valued far and above coin. To be the one to survive, explore, and finally *conquer* a place like the *Sanjou*, well, that greatly appealed to him. Being known for it, being *recognized*, was power.

For Shay, recognition was everything.

He hoped this adventure, like those before it, would be the stuff of stories and songs.

All those thoughts ceased as he realized the jungle had quieted. His scout called Ungla stopped on the trail with a hand raised, gazing at the shadowy heights overhead.

Shay halted, as did everyone else. *The birds*, he realized.

Their calls had all stopped.

"You hear that?" whispered Grage from behind.

Shay did. He raised a hand while studying the surrounding thickets.

Ungla remained on the trail, hunched over as if sensing danger. Shay caught his attention and motioned for him to return.

He-Dog noticed the missing birdsong just as Chop and Gusper stopped in their tracks ahead of him. They stooped while eyeing the shadowy jungle. Dark. Nowhere near night, but all those towering trees, proud flowers, drooping petals, and outstretched leaves would provide excellent cover, even if the sun *was* shining. As it was, anything could easily hide and remain hidden.

Before him, Chop extracted both his swords.

Following his companion's lead, He-Dog eased his own weapon free. Over the shoulders and heads of crouching mercenaries, Shay waved for Ungla to return. The scout started back, rustling leaves as broad as bucklers.

Ungla halted halfway, suspicious at something near his feet.

An unmistakable hiss split the air, raising the hair on He-Dog's neck, and Ungla's head snapped back with an arrow halfway into his face. The impact knocked the scout off his feet and he disappeared into the bushes.

"*Get down!*" Shay roared and crouched, bringing up his shield.

Back on the cliff, a distant shout perked Muggins's ears. He paused before taking the first step down the other side. The few sailors around him did the same.

Muggins waited, listening for more. He wavered before hurrying back over the ridgeline, toward the interior of the island, where the mercenaries had taken the trail down to the valley floor. There he stopped, unwilling to go any farther, and peered below.

Nothing. Only that overgrown cauldron of deepest green.

The old sailor held his breath and gripped the hilt of a short sword hanging at his waist.

He waited.

Listened.

And *waited*.

More shouts from below, from civilized men giving orders. Those commands seemed to hang on the air for long, agonizing heartbeats.

Muggins shook his unbelieving head. Lords in their heavens above, he had warned them to be *quiet*.

Then the valley below erupted in the war cries of hundreds. Perhaps even thousands. A throaty explosion of hateful glee that sent a flock of birds flying hard to be clear of it. It was the sound of wildmen springing a trap well prepared, signaling the reaping about to begin.

That roar rooted Muggins to the spot, his eyes popping wide.

There was a *nest* of them down there, just waiting.

And Shay's lot had marched right into the middle of it.

One thought speared through Muggins's mind.

Tell the captain.

He hurried back to where his sailors waited.

A soft padded step caught his attention and he whirled—just as a spiked club smashed his face, salting the air with whatever teeth old Muggins had left in his head.

CHAPTER 12

Upon hearing that nerve-shivering explosion of noise, Shay's mercenaries didn't panic. Didn't run. Rather, they reacted. With practiced discipline, the mercenaries bashed through the vegetation, trampling everything underfoot as they overran the trail to form a small circle. A wall of large shields slammed into the ground, their edges clapping as they overlapped each other, creating a rounded barrier. Men crouched behind those defenses, shoulder to shoulder, as an inner rank of mercenaries lifted their shields over the heads of the outer rank. A sizeable tree became the backbone of the formation, where Shay squatted, peeking around his own upraised shield.

Then the arrows slammed into them.

A killer rain fell, striking the shield wall in a death rattle, the feathered shafts either splintering or bouncing away. No sooner had the first wave finished, when a second and third salting of the formation struck. Arrows exploded off low-hanging tree limbs. One bounced off a helmet, dropping a bulky Vathian.

"*Stand firm, lads,*" Shay bellowed over the onslaught, arrows bouncing off his own shield. "*Stand firm!*"

Cringing, He-Dog crouched on one knee, his shield braced against his shoulder. Chop stooped behind him, without any shield and dependent on nearby Gusper. The healer leaned over both men with his own barrier, providing extra protection.

Gusper caught He-Dog's worried look. "Nothing, this is *nothing*," the fearsome healer assured him. "We've lived through worse. I'll tell you sometime."

A fourth wave of arrows crashed into the mercenaries from all quarters. The explosive clatter nearly drowned out the angry sizzle of those shafts. An arrow cracked into the helmet of a Sarlander, knocking his armor askew and blinding the man. More insulted than surprised, the man held onto his shield while adjusting himself, and his sword brothers shifted to close the finger-wide gap.

Gusper winced. "These bastards do seem eager, however."

He-Dog did a double take of the man.

"Once," the healer continued, making himself heard, "back when we numbered close to a hundred, we walked into an ambush. Much like this. Up went shields, like this. Held the formation for a dozen volleys. A *dozen*."

Another round of arrows fell, punching metal and bouncing away or simply sinking into the jungle floor. Arrows clipped shoulder pauldrons, rang off helmets, and just missed boots or sandals. Arrows crashed into trees or continued on, missing the formation entirely.

Gusper shifted a bit and kept on talking. "*Those* were archers, mind you. Trained Anvar killers. Able to loose four arrows at your face in a heartbeat. From a *horse*."

A flurry of arrows stuttered into the healer's shield, forcing him to hold on.

He-Dog spared a look as the next squall crashed into the defensive ring, several shafts slamming into his own shield, shaking his arm. He tightened his grip on the piece, cringing as the volleys became a steady downpour that fell without pause.

"When the Anvar emptied their quivers," a squinting Gusper continued, "the boys went hunting. And caught their fill, I can tell you."

The healer chuckled. He-Dog didn't join him.

His own shield held over his head, an angry Grage hunkered down beside the three men. "Shaddup and concentrate on what's afoot, will you, punce?"

Gusper scowled. "You're calling me punce now, but you'll be singing my name when I'm stitching you up."

The Koor ignored that and checked on He-Dog. "Keep ranks. Wait for the order."

Amid the harsh patter of arrows, the officer lurched away to the others in the cluster.

Gusper smirked. "Wait for the order. These maggots aren't Anvar archers. No sar. No unity here. No thought for coordination. Just loose and loose again. *Pah*."

Like beastmen, He-Dog thought and squeezed his eyes shut. *Pound and pound and pound again, until they fall.* The dreaded realization then, of boarding a ship to escape Othil only to land in a place inhabited by some distant tribe of beastmen. *Lords above*, surely Shay hadn't brought them to some forgotten island inhabited by those unfit brutes. No, He-Dog knew that wasn't the case. No beastman could overcome their natural fear of the ocean.

Or so he hoped.

Arrows continued falling, panging off upraised shields and causing arms to shiver. Arrows rebounded off the tree anchoring the formation. Shafts sank into the ground inside and out of the formation, the feathered ends quivering for an instant. One glanced off He-Dog's shoulder and spun off behind him, the blow both staggering and startling but failing to penetrate. Another arrow shot through a gap and skidded along Chop's armored back, reeling the Nordish man. More arrows studded the jungle floor in such numbers it became hard not to brush a boot against them.

All the while, the shadows deepened, the jungle darkened, and no foe could be seen. He-Dog peeked out from cracks in the shield wall and saw only the dense undergrowth of the Sanjou.

"*I can see them, lads,*" Shay shouted from behind. "Darting in and out. Behind the trees. Short little toppers. Short bows. Quick release but nothing like the Anvar."

Gusper glanced at He-Dog and Chop with an expression that said, *See?*

"Keep your heads down," the prince said. "They'll be coming soon enough. Maybe even now . . ."

No sooner did he say it when the downpour of arrows tapered off to nothing, the harsh sizzles and whistling of falling shafts fading away. The panging upon the shields lessened gradually, until nothing struck at all.

Silence descended upon the wilderness, filled by the underlying drone of insect life.

"Oh my," Shay said, his voice laced with satisfaction.

A gray ray of light pierced the shield wall, big enough to allow a peek if He-Dog wanted one. He leaned in for just that and scowled.

Not twenty strides out appeared a man, stepping out from behind thick curtains of foliage. Just one man, his features shaded by the dense roof overhead and the diminishing daylight. The figure was not overly large, but his shoulders appeared rounded and poised, corded with wiry muscle. His legs, what could be seen of them, were twice as thick as those of an ordinary man, and powerful. He held a spear, crude but lethal, the pointy bit scorched by fire and aimed at the mercenary formation. A rope secured a stone knife around his waist. A filthy loincloth covered his fruits, ragged but it did the job. Not a slab of armor on the stout little bastard, nor did he carry a bow.

What he did have, apparently in abundance, was a clear hatred of the mercenaries invading his territory. Those rounded shoulders heaved with breath, as if he'd run a long distance and was ready to run much more.

As He-Dog watched, the wildman—for this was no civilized man—turned his head left and right, as if checking on something.

Lords above, He-Dog thought, realizing what was about to happen.

The lad came forward two steps, and a beam of daylight, weak and fading yet just enough, revealed the wildman's face. Thick, perhaps gray-green slashes of pigmentation covered him . . . from his bare head all the way down. A thick jutting jaw, flat nose, and round eyes, impossibly so, glared ahead, at the holding formation. Hate contorted that face, promising all manner of primitive tortures when the Sanjou hellions captured them. *Hate*. Raw and unchecked and positively *boiling*.

Hate was something He-Dog understood.

And the Sanjou native was *livid* with it.

The wildman drew himself up and lifted his spear—two-handed—over his head. He set his thick legs apart and screamed. Screamed long and hard, enough to make the earlier howling sound like annoyed whispers.

"Steady lads," Shay yelled out, making himself heard.

Then, after emptying his chest, the gray-green wildman, still the only adversary in sight, lowered his spear and charged the formation.

While screaming.

If he'd had time, He-Dog might have compared the savage's screaming to that of the beastmen. He did not have that time, however. The sprawling garden of exotic flowers, drooping vines, and towering trees festooned with broad leaves, suddenly erupted with furious life as scores of Sanjou wildmen sprang forth and charged the mercenary force.

Shay squawked orders, but all that rampant screaming drowned out the prince's voice. Rocks pelted and cracked off shields and helmets, surprising the mercenaries huddled behind their improvised wall. The arrows fell again, from everywhere, smashing the shields squarely or hissing straight down upon the mercenaries. Arrows clacked off metal rims and sliced past ears. Shafts bounced off the iron plates of armored backs. Some men grunted in pain while others straightened. One arrow pitched deep into the face of a burly Ice Kingdom brute, who fell back, dead before he hit the ground, his shield clattering.

That first kill left a frightening hole in the wall.

The mercenary on the edge of that opening clamped a hand to his neck, around an arrow that pierced him underneath his helmet. He dropped to his knees as blood spurted between fingers. The gap in the shield wall widened. Arrows shrieked through those empty spaces. One shaft embedded itself into the shoulder of a nearby mercenary, paralyzing him an instant before he cried out in pain.

"*Form up!*" Grage roared, staying low himself behind a set of shoulders. "Keep your heads—"

An arrow skewered his shoulder, bypassing his armor and knocking him off balance. Grage staggered to a knee, leaning against another. Then the one called Snaffer appeared, eyes narrowed and beard wild as he pulled the Koor back, toward the formation's backbone, which was the tree. Shay shouted orders to fill the breaches.

A spear punched through a seam in the shield wall, flashing past He-Dog's head. That scorched black length squealed along the metal rim, reached full extension, and then struggled to withdraw. The owner—the same gray-green pisser glaring hate from afar—grabbed onto the shield and pulled it down, just enough for He-Dog to see the face beyond.

What he saw stunned him.

Gray and green slashes covered the wildman's face, but in greater clarity, applied with an artist's touch. What was truly unsettling, however, were the round and entirely orange eyes, perched above a thick and jutting fish-shaped jaw—festooned with pointed teeth. Teeth . . . no, the wildman possessed ragged triangular *fangs*—some missing, some black—and spitting hate and wide-eyed fury.

Gusper staggered back, unable to strike the rabid spearman.

A Sarlander next to He-Dog turned to kill the savage, but He-Dog was faster—thrusting his dog skull blade through the wildman's neck, parting meat in a great oily gout. The wildman crumpled and He-Dog shoved the corpse off.

As he did so, he glimpsed what was coming. He got his shield up and braced it an instant before the main wave of savages crashed into the formation. The weight and fury of all those bodies bent the wall, buckled it, close to breaking.

But the mercenaries held.

Baring teeth and groaning, straining, they dug in boots and pushed back, leaning into their shields with shoulders. Mud-stained hands with filthy claws grabbed at the upper rims, attempting to pull them down, while crude spears stabbed through cracks anywhere they found them. The Sarlander on He-Dog's right grabbed his throat and collapsed. That opened an unwanted door in the wall. A multitude of hands pulled the dead man's shield away as He-Dog and the next mercenary over attempted to fill the gap. Spears shot forth, some clacking off shields. Chop and Gusper stepped in. Chop disemboweled one savage across the middle, releasing a torrent of gore. Gusper heaved his shield into the gap. Arrows continued to fall, from all directions, zipping over heads, smashing off metal and wood, or simply stabbing deep into Sanjou soil. Several gray-green pissers fell, nailed by their own archers.

Behind his shield, He-Dog shoved back against the masses smashing into the formation. The other mercenaries pushed with him while striving to close the gaps, step by aching step. The inner ranks of the company kept the savages at bay, stabbing dead any attempting to enter. Gusper leaned into his shield. Chop stood at his back, thrusting both swords into whatever was available. Savages screamed. Blood spritzed the air, showering He-Dog in a warm rain. He shoved and shifted his shield, finally linking it with that of another mercenary, shrinking the formation. Other men strove to adjust their position as the pressure against them doubled, then tripled. Wildmen swung and stabbed and chopped while another wave behind them pressed their brethren into the shield wall. The ground shook and seemingly rolled. Spears pierced the edges of He-Dog's shield, dividing his attention.

"Stand *fast*!" Shay shouted, barely heard over the unfit shrieking. "Standing men *kill whatever you can*."

Not that they needed to be told.

He-Dog stomped on a spear jutting past the lower rim, snapping the thing off. He dug in his heels and heaved back. Cracks appeared in the defensive barrier, revealing glimpses of green faces with orange eyes and protruding jaws. Those faces barked and raged. Chop stabbed at them, the resulting gush dousing He-Dog again and again, which he didn't appreciate.

Chop killed every wildman within reach, until the dead could not fall, because of the unfit press of bodies behind them. Beyond those bleeding corpses, orange eyes flared and faces howled. Those wildmen stabbed spears blackened by fire over the drooping dead. Then came stone axes and wooden clubs, hammering the shields. A frenzied wildman stampeded up and *over* the undulating backs of his brethren before *leaping*, spear-first, over the shield wall. Down he came, burying half a charred length of wood into the head of a thickset Ghedian. Both dropped near the center, where Chop turned and hacked down the killer.

Another of Shay's mercenaries fell back, clutching at his face. His shield dropped and the formation again weakened by one. Chop spun and killed the wildmen bulging into that gap. A mottled screamer jabbed a spear at He-Dog's head, but Gusper caught the blow on his shield, and split the primitive spearman's skull in two. Another burst of blood showered the line as the corpse collapsed. He-Dog closed ranks with Gusper, sealing the breach.

The battle intensified. Another savage leapt over the shield wall, hurtling himself over the crest with stone axe reared back and ready to brain someone. A blood-soaked Valencian with a broadsword sliced the flying screamer in two.

The deaths and the mounting stink only energized the wildmen of the Sanjou.

They howled with frenzied might and constantly wrestled for control over the invaders' shields, while their companions behind them stabbed spears or swung clubs and stone axes. A pair of wildmen grabbed He-Dog's barrier and he brained both, shoving them back into the heavy press. Other mercenaries hacked at hands seeking better grips, and fingers jumped into the air. Two hands latched onto Gusper's shield next to He-Dog and yanked open a gap. A spear streaked through, blunting its scorched tip against the hardened leather cuirass He-Dog wore, until the weapon slid harmlessly under his arm. Another savage grabbed He-Dog's sword arm and bore it down while the spearman released his weapon. The creature wrapped its hands around the back of He-Dog's neck and *pulled* his head toward an open maw.

One savage on his arm, another hauling him in.

If he wasn't awake before, He-Dog awoke then, as an orange-eyed wildman sought to bite his face off.

And among all that pulling and shouting and screaming and bloodletting, where every breath left blood on his face and tongue, He-Dog's own anger rose to a boil. Weeks of pain and suffering, of long starving walks and blazing suns, of hard looks and barely contained contempt, of being battered senseless upon a wharf, had led him *here*—among the mounting chaos and rotting fangs and the darting red tongue eager to taste him.

"*Kill them all, lads!*" Shay roared above the racket.

That was all He-Dog needed.

He leaned back and Chop was there, killing both attackers with hard thrusts to their faces. He-Dog retreated a step, digging bootheels into the dead underfoot as the press of bodies fell into the gap. Clearing a space, he got about the dirty business he knew so well. He stabbed and hacked. Arcs of black ink fanned from his blade. Savages fell, while others struggled to reach the warrior. He-Dog split one savage from mottled scalp to black teeth. Mashed his shield into nose and facial bone. The tall Ghedian with the greatsword strapped to his back joined him on the left. The Ghedian slashed with a lesser blade, taking a terrible toll on the enemy. Screams were gutturally cut short. Blood splashed boots and spattered faces. Though the savages were unarmored, a raging He-Dog was still faster. He hacked off an arm and hewed open a face. A savage clung to his shield, but He-Dog heaved him back into oncoming attackers, impeding the rush.

Then Chop stood next to him, his blade opening an unarmored foe in bursts of gore. One of Shay's mercenaries hacked and slashed to the right of the Nordish swordsman, and the formation opened up and started taking heads.

Wildmen died in droves, piling up before the straining circle.

The momentum began to shift, or so it seemed.

He-Dog slashed one wildman across the middle and took his bowing head off with one chop. He readied himself for his next foe and what he saw shocked him.

Wildmen.

The jungle was *alive* with them.

If they'd just killed dozens, then scores more sought to replace them, converging on the mercenaries from all sides, trampling through whatever vegetation lay before them. Dark gray-green bodies topped with hairless scalps and screaming faces—and they *howled*, as if their blossoms were afire and their fruits were smoking.

That screeching, seething mass of primitive weaponry and terrible energy *charged* the mercenaries, rushing the formation in a massive, bowel-loosening flood.

Seeing all those hateful faces and bodies, He-Dog heard Rige's voice from beyond the grave.

A rock will break a thousand waves. But in the end, the sea will break every shore.

He-Dog whipped up his shield to deflect a stone axe as that wave of fresh fighters slammed into the little formation.

Then it was all fight.

War clubs pounded metal. Spears blanched off shields or hissed around their edges. Arrows sliced through humid air, their sizzling flights unheard because of the screaming. The screaming peaked. The mercenary brute wearing the helmet with the bull horns collapsed when five savages jumped atop him. Three more piled in, their thin arms pumping, stabbing with primitive knives. Others grabbed for Chop but the swordsman killed them, ending that nonsense.

Then the shield wall crumbled in another quarter, and the wildmen surged inside, splitting the formation. He-Dog quickly lost sight of Chop and Gusper in the deluge of painted torsos, and Shay's remaining mercenaries placed their backs to each other. The momentum shifted, and the fighting descended into a new level of mayhem. Wildmen rushed He-Dog from left and right, separating him from the Ghedian. The Ghedian hacked down two screamers before he was taken down in a pile. An instant later, a savage stepped up and crushed the man's skull with a stone axe.

He-Dog was already retreating, darting back, stabbing and bashing, while mindful of the dead underfoot. A tree appeared, the trunk pitted from arrows and spears. He spun around and placed his back to that tall column. Arrows struck his chest, either exploding into splinters or bouncing off the hardened physique of his armor. Two shafts zipped along his arms, drawing bloody lines before smashing into the tree behind him. He-Dog braced himself, realizing he stood against the same tree Shay had backed against earlier.

There was no sign of the prince, however, and that was the last thing to race through He-Dog's head before *everything* got tossed into Saimon's overflowing shite trough.

Mercenaries stood their ground in twos and threes, killing the war-painted wildmen in droves. Every chop of a blade, every thrust, felled a wildman, but for every three the mercenaries slashed, stabbed, or chopped, five new attackers replaced the dead.

Worse, the savages were killing mercenaries *back*, at times overwhelming warriors in a green and gray avalanche of sinewy muscle. They stabbed and hacked with crude knives and stone axes. They smashed with heavy war clubs. A shrieking figure *dropped* from the dense foliage overhead, falling spear-first and skewering the mercenary Sunbar through his shoulder. The pair fell to the ground and an unsteady Sunbar rose first, a curved club in hand, when Kellic split the attacker apart with one chop.

A nearby Vathian fell, his helmeted head cracked by a stone axe. Then Shay was there, grimacing, stabbing, seeking to turn back the onslaught. He stopped a spear on his shield and sliced his attacker up the middle. He took the leg off another, spun and half decapitated a third. The dead sprawled upon the ground hampered his rally and when he turned to face new foes, he stumbled in the knots of limbs underfoot.

He-Dog bounded from the tree and sprinted to the prince's side, remembering the man *had* taken them on this bloody venture.

Two wildmen got in his way.

He-Dog split one head apart and bashed the other's face in with his shield.

"*Get up!*" He-Dog yelled, but his voice was drowned out by the screaming from the living and the dying.

A grimacing Shay struggled to rise, placing a knee atop a carcass and slipping.

Chop magically appeared and protected their flank, killing every attacker within the path of his blades. He slashed one savage open to the backbone. Another lightning cut removed an arm from a second screamer. A flashing backhand removed a head entirely from another's neck.

But others sought to reach them. Livid shrieks split the air. A continuous rush of hellions emerged from the dark thickets of the Sanjou. They ran and jumped, baring black fangs.

A war club smashed into a mercenary's helm, dropping him to his knees as a spear pierced his chainmail and burst through his back. Three other wildmen tackled the dying man, stabbing him as he buckled over. The sight distracted He-Dog long enough for two brutes to crash into him. He staggered under the weight as primitive daggers stabbed his waist but failed to penetrate the armor. He-Dog shoved them off, stabbing one and smashing the other upside the head.

"*Here!* They're over here!" someone shouted.

"Move *back*!"

"They're *behind* us!"

"To the cliffs!"

"They're *coming* from the cliffs!"

Hard men cried out, and the jungle raged back.

The brutish mercenary from Orvasia crushed a head with his mace, then a spear slammed into his mail shirt. The impact staggered him long enough for nearby savages to batter his head and shoulders with clubs.

The Mademian called Talso stabbed one of the Orvasian's killers through the chest, but a handful of wildmen piled onto him and forced him down. A fearsome spearman stepped in and nailed the mercenary's head to the ground.

He-Dog faced his own problems. Savages leapt and grabbed and swung at him, forcing him away from the prince. A sickly body tackled Chop around the Nordish man's waist and both disappeared through a flimsy curtain of foliage. Wildmen plunged through the gap, chasing after them.

He-Dog sought to help his companion, but a pair of screamers swung clubs at his head. He parried and slashed and went cold at the sight of all the Sanjou killers remaining. Spears punched his shield, testing it and further separating him from Chop. He spiraled that iron slab, finished off the spearman, and then the healer Gusper appeared, red-faced and no longer smiling.

Their eyes met an instant before a war club hurled through the air and smashed into the healer's face. He dropped like a heavy curtain, revealing a wall of painted bodies teeming forward.

"*Move back!*" Bartus shouted from somewhere nearby. "Mind your *backs*!"

Instead, armored men labored to turn around, some breaking into runs and crashing through the jungle. A squall of arrows and spears fell, further spicing the madness. Those evil missiles pattered off helmets and armor, and also sank into the unprotected torsos of the pursuing wildmen. A grimacing Snaffer staggered in and out of sight, swordless and pulling free the arrow that had disarmed him. He threw the bloody shaft away before getting his shield up in time to block another attacker.

A heavy weight crashed against He-Dog's shield. He stabbed back and got only air. A club smacked across his helmet, dazing him. A spear nicked his sword arm deep. Something hard slammed into his back, straightening his spine and almost toppling him. He-Dog spun, whipping both blade and shield around him, catching several faces, drizzling all with blood and crumpling them. The jungle darkened and all those screaming faces warped into something even more fearsome.

Too many. Far too many.

There was no escape.

In the middle of all that slaughter, where tethers of receding light punched through the leafy heights overhead, where the mindless screaming peaked, and where Shay's mercenaries died one after the other, an odd feeling of relief filled He-Dog.

His end was near.

That feeling eased the burn in his limbs and the sting of his new wounds.

Here, in the Sanjou, he would finally perish.

Underneath that vast rooftop of vegetation, perhaps a heartbeat away from being overrun, He-Dog faced three wildmen baring rotten fangs and brandishing clubs.

Then he heard a voice at the back of his skull, a voice that belonged to Balless. And Balless said, *Run.*

CHAPTER 13

Run, Balless had said.

Or at least it *sounded* like Balless.

Trouble was, there was nowhere to go.

One of the green-faced bastards crunched a club into his shield. He-Dog stabbed the asslicker dead before shoving him off. He killed the other two with quick cuts that sprayed gore over everything. More savages rushed forward. The jungle was alive with them. Dressed in loincloths and wiry of muscle, they stabbed with their crude spears or smashed with clubs and axes. They screeched at him and fought with a frenzied, frightening energy.

And those eyes . . .

Orange and speckled with ink.

Mad. *Livid*. And hate-filled.

Furious shrieks blasted He-Dog's senses. An ordinary man couldn't produce sounds like that, and whatever could was unquestionably *evil*. It was in the blackness of their teeth, the wildness of their eyes, and their total abandonment of self-preservation.

They were almost as bad as beastmen.

Beyond the wildmen He-Dog had just fought and killed, he glimpsed the savages of the Sanjou dancing over armored corpses like hellions enjoying an open fire, their spirits high on bloodlust. One stood over a fallen man and speared him repeatedly through the chest. Another cavorted about and shook a hacked off head by its hair, jerking the bauble about like a leaky gourd.

He-Dog put down another wildman flailing at him, earning the briefest respite.

Run, the voice had said.

For perhaps the first time ever, He-Dog listened to what Balless was saying.

No longer ready to perish, he whirled and plunged through jungle growth as screams sounded behind him. He bolted through the underbrush, pounding over the jungle floor in high-leaping strides. Figures charged him from his flanks but he outpaced them, putting trees between him and his pursuers. Trees rushed by. Foliage whipped at his face. There was no time for stealth, only the mad rush of escape. A monster of a tree towered before him, with huge black roots as high as his waist. He-Dog leapt over the first twisting length as if it were a fence and flipped over the second. When he hit the ground, he tumbled head-over-blossom, dug in, pushed off, and launched himself into the wilderness beyond. More leaves and branches lashed at him. A sticky net suddenly covered him at the same time an exceptionally hairy coconut—with *legs*—swung into and bounced off his shield.

That frightened him badly.

He'd just hit a spider the size of a wine jug. And the net clinging to him was its web.

That realization made him run harder.

The hot air of the Sanjou filled his chest, burning him from the inside. Each footfall over the uneven ground stung while sweat found his eyes. On his right, the jungle became a twisted wall of dark colors, but to his left was a shaded pathway that plunged deeper into the gloom. Someone had shouted that the savages had come from the cliffs, and that troubled He-Dog. *Had we walked right by them?* If so, he had failed miserably to detect them. Not even so much as a whiff. Painted as the wildmen were, it would've been an easy thing to walk by them, but being unable to *smell* them was something else.

He swung onto the trail, twisting off deeper into the Sanjou. No doubt it was carved out by the same hellions who had ambushed them.

He-Dog ran on.

A clump of wild bushes rustled an instant before a wildman tried to take He-Dog's head with a stone axe. He ducked, spun, and slashed, opening the topper across the midsection and buckling him in two.

Two more savages burst onto the trail.

He-Dog blocked the war club and unleashed an uppercut, opening the first one from crotch to chin and throwing the man-thing back into the bushes. The second one lunged with a spear, driving the black charred tip into the tough leather protecting He-Dog's guts. The spear skidded inward, toward the bindings, and He-Dog twisted in reflex to avoid the stabbing tip. Not fast enough, however, as the spear pierced flesh. Pain exploded as He-Dog cracked his shield across the stabber's face, sending teeth and wildman crashing to the ground. The spear fell, and the strap binding his shield to his forearm snapped. Flinging it away, he pressed a hand against his wound and searched for other attackers.

None.

He-Dog glanced at his hand, then his armor. Blood covered his palm and seeped down his legs, dark and alarmingly thick.

He got moving again.

Blood spattered the path in his wake. Tree limbs whipped and clawed at his face and shoulders. The trail curved through the jungle, and a single shaft of light stabbed through the canopy overhead, briefly illuminating the way before descending into jungle gloom. That fleeting flash of light, quick enough that he wondered if he saw it at all, confused him. Thunderclouds had masked the skies before they entered the jungle. He didn't spare it any more thought and pressed on. In time, he slowed down. His legs and arms began to dearly ache. His chest threatened to burst. Panting, he halted in the shadow of a towering tree and swung left to right, scanning the jungle. With a huff he sank his blade tip first into the soft earth, pulled his helmet off to let it drop, and placed hands to knees. Heart pounding, sweat dripping, he watched the wilderness, struggling to hear over his breathing.

Forcing himself to quiet, He-Dog gulped down humid air and held it.

Listened.

The Sanjou had become silent.

The pathway behind him appeared empty, but so had the trail Shay had followed to lead his company down from the cliffs. Just before they were all taken by surprise.

Then he heard it, and the sound narrowed his eyes.

Shouting, ghostly and eerie. Then howls. Coming from a place more terrible than any nightmare, but not getting any closer.

As bad as beastmen, He-Dog thought again, letting his breath go in a rush. He checked on his wounds and grimaced at the alarming rivulets covering his legs.

Dying Seddon, he swore, and held his breath again.

The noise in the distance held steady, but then another, more worrying sound perked his ears.

The soft crackle of undergrowth, coming from his left, stemming from a thick curtain of vegetation. Footfalls, quick and sure and none too concerned with being silent. He-Dog snatched up his helmet and slipped it back over his head. The surrounding bushes were dense and perfect for hiding, so he pulled his sword free and backed into the foliage.

No sooner did he hide than the tip of a fire-blackened spear emerged from across the path, parting the bushes. The owner emerged—a Sanjou wildman, hunched over and hunting, his fishy eyes wide and alert.

He-Dog held his breath. This hunter hadn't made the noise he was hearing.

The Sanjou hunter stopped then, fingers flexing on the spear. He inspected the ground. Appeared to listen. Even sniffed. Before looking directly at He-Dog—who stabbed the creature through his throat in a crunch of flesh and bone and a gruesome spurt of mud. The thing crumpled, and *another* screamed out a warning, just out of sight.

Perhaps a hundred voices answered the call, the closeness startling He-Dog as a stone axe whipped through the foliage, chopping down the plant life and revealing his hiding place.

Orange-eyed and jutting jaws, the wildman shrieked and sought to swing again.

He-Dog's sword flashed up, cracking the savage's head back and spraying the trail behind him with blood, brains, and black teeth.

The screaming didn't stop, however.

He-Dog ran.

Another savage burst onto the path.

He-Dog cut him down.

Two more emerged.

He-Dog slashed one's chest to the backbone, killing him instantly. As the corpse fell, he parried a hard thrust from the other, then stabbed him through the middle and shoved him aside.

Dying Seddon, He-Dog thought, staggering into a run. Leaving a trail of corpses was *not* going to help him escape these hellions. Nor was his bleeding over everything. Ominous droplets spattered the land, reminding him that the maggots had left their marks.

Worst yet, the shrieks echoing throughout the jungle sounded like a sizeable number was after his hide.

Tropical colors dulled by the oncoming night flashed by him. Hoots and screeches spiked the air in his wake. They kept up, so He-Dog ran harder, feet slamming the ground. He crashed through a small clearing, leapt over a dirt-ringed hole, and continued his straight run. *Cliffs*. He could not see any cliffs. Only more jungle. Then another open space ahead of him, and he smelled water. Glorious unfit water.

There was a rumble of a thunderhead, a great throat clearing from Seddon himself, perhaps peering down from his heavens. A new sound reached He-Dog's ears.

Rain.

The trees and bushes ended, and the rim of a cliff forced He-Dog to skid to a stop, spraying dirt and debris over the edge. The other side of the chasm was a wishful thirty strides away, where white stone held up a thick scalp of earth, all trussed together by a black lace of roots. The stone shelf seemingly stretched the length of the whole ravine, as if the very ground had split apart at one time to allow a river passage far below.

A river dotted with rocks.

The storm clouds appeared even drearier as a steamy rain showered his face. Hearing the yelps and shouts of his pursuers, He-Dog trotted along the cliff's edge, mindful of the drop. His limbs grew heavier with every step. Though the trail was a full stride wide along the edge, he knew cliffs lied at times, as solid ground might only be a thin outcropping waiting to plunge an unfortunate topper into the rocky depths below.

Nearly exhausted, he stopped midstride, swayed, and glanced back. He badly wanted a drink. His blood dotted the ground, betraying him, and the rain wasn't falling fast enough to wash it away. The seaside cliffs were nowhere in sight, and the ones next to him were sloping upward. He-Dog took a deep, chest-expanding breath and forged onward, hoping to cross the ravine at some point. Trees and brush hugged the edge, hanging over the drop like grand displays gone mad. He trudged along as close as he dared, becoming grimly aware that the land was not only rising . . . but circling back the way he'd come.

Another rumble of thunder, and his ears perked at something more.

The grass and soil of the trail led to an outcropping of pale rock glistening with moisture, where trees with broad leaves leaned over as if studying the ravine's depth. The gap widened even more, from thirty strides across to maybe fifty, where a mighty wall of jungle flourished on both sides. A great rush of water could be heard, and a haze drifted over everything.

The slightest breeze teased his face.

Waterfall, he knew, and again stopped to put fists to knees. Pain spiked through him, stemming from his many cuts and bruises, the worst from the spear wound in his midsection. He-Dog straightened, pressing a hand to his side and sucking down great gulping breaths. The shouts and yelps were farther behind him now, as if his hunters had taken a wrong turn, which was odd considering how much he was bleeding. He hobbled onward, peering over the cliff's edge at times, drawn to that great rush of water just out of sight. Rumbling. Thundering. An immense and unending crash hidden by a growing mist that filled the ravine, obscuring everything below, rendering it all a dream.

He so very badly wanted a drink and remembered his pack. He reached for one strap and realized it was gone, ripped away without him knowing.

Seddon above.

Then a lull, where the only thing he heard was the crashing waterfall.

Instinct pulled him back from the cliff and turned his attention to the wet trail ahead.

There, standing upon a white rock and against a backdrop of cliffside jungle, a single figure waited for him.

One of the wildmen.

Armed with a spear.

Like those before him, a crumbly green and gray pigment covered his muscular body, right down to its filthy loincloth. The wildman wasn't nearly as tall as He-Dog, but he was squat and corded with powerful muscle. Under a lowered brow, orange eyes watched him with alien loathing. The Sanjou native pointed his spear at him, showing off an iron head forged by a more civilized hand. No fire-scorched gut sticker there. The spear had obviously been fashioned by a craftsman.

Blocking the way, the wildman waited for the larger invader.

Near exhausted, bleeding, and disbelieving that one of the little gray-green maggots had managed to get *ahead* of him, He-Dog scowled and sized up the unfit wildman and his weapon. He also realized that *this* savage wasn't screaming his head off, which made him wary of the topper. Was the wildman angry? Aye that. One look at that painted face left no doubt.

As He-Dog studied his foe, he gradually became aware of the approaching clatter at his back. A tired groan left him. The pack on his heels was closing in. If he wanted to escape, he had to go through the asslicker before him.

And, as if understanding that very thought, the wildman stepped forward, snarling a challenge and brandishing the spear.

Scowling back and dripping fluids, He-Dog hefted his heavy arms and went to meet his foe.

They met upon that rocky outcropping, where a cool mist drifted over and enveloped them both.

The wildman greeted him with a feint—two quick jabs at the gut—before fully committing to a thrust. He-Dog parried and countered with a straight-armed stab, surprised to see the Sanjou native spryly leap back. He-Dog lashed out again, two reaching chops that split only air as the wildman darted out of harm's way.

The waterfall rumbled nearby. A mist coated them, beading upon bare flesh, as they assessed each other, searching for weakness in the other's defense. Blood from He-Dog's wounds spattered the rock. The savage crouched behind his spear, holding the weapon at guard as he crept closer, his jutting jaw flexing like some rabid thing.

They engaged again, more fiercely than before. Thrusting and parrying, spear and sword clattering off each other. After a vigorous chop that left He-Dog panting, they backed away and sized each other up, as the waterfall continued to roar. Moisture dripped from their features, and He-Dog took a moment to wipe his face clean.

Behind a low guard that bobbed and weaved, the savage muttered something, his protruding jaw working, black tongue flickering. To He-Dog, it was a jumble of nonsense syllables. When the wildman finished speaking, he stabbed for He-Dog's head.

Fast.

He-Dog barely knocked the spear away and countered with two swift, flat cuts. Both swings missed, but the effort drove his smaller foe back. Not too far, however, as the wildman stopped and adjusted his grip to overhand. He hunkered low and again stalked his foe, weaving his spear in short menacing half-moons. Orange eyes stared as he stomped his forward foot, as if testing the stone, all the while closing the distance.

Then he lunged.

He-Dog parried and didn't bother with a counter, fearing a swing would off-balance him. Feeling the last of his strength leaving, he knew he had to finish off this pisser. As an afterthought, he glanced toward the cliff edge on his right.

The savage lunged again with that startling speed, backing He-Dog up on his heels where he slipped on wet rock.

The Sanjou *warrior*—as this was clearly no savage—spun about and whipped the spear around, droplets flying from the arc. The wooden end smashed across He-Dog's jaw with all the force of a catapult shot, cracking his head back. A field of black stars filled his vision. On pure reflex alone, he lashed out drunkenly, a dazed counter that sliced only air and left him exposed.

The wildman drove that awful iron head tip into He-Dog's hardened vest, piercing armor and the flesh underneath. The spear sank in, the pain paralyzing, spinning He-Dog around and causing him to grab for his foe's head as he went.

Missed.

The wildman did not, however. He shoved his spear into He-Dog's lower bits, where the armor was thinner, piercing leather and missing the root of his topper by a fat finger. A grunt of pain burst from He-Dog as he pawed at the impaling weapon, his arms finally failing him, and his legs not far behind. The white rock underfoot became a watery red.

The Sanjou warrior yanked the spear free—before leaving the ground in a spinning leap. That awful length of wood whirled in a blur, the end smashing He-Dog's head yet again.

This time, however, connecting with his temple.

Despite wearing a helmet, a sun exploded against his head. For a beat, he didn't know where he was. Didn't know *who* he was.

A drunken stumble followed, and he didn't have the presence of mind to realize the spearman stood *right before him.*

The Sanjou warrior stabbed, driving forward with all the power of his thick legs, *driving* that iron tip squarely for the leather twine binding He-Dog's vest together. Somehow, He-Dog twisted at the last instant, and the spear struck hardened leather instead of running through guts.

There was still enough force to stagger the larger man back a step.

Where his rear foot touched only air.

And the last thing He-Dog saw, before he fell from the cliff, was the hateful gaze of his killer.

Then the spinning flash of white stone and gray sky . . . and he was gone.

CHAPTER 14

As fortune went, after being knocked senseless, He-Dog fell into the ravine and landed in the river below, just missing the rocks looking to break him open. He surfaced, more dead than alive, while an angry current rushed him away. Tossing and spinning him along, he bobbed and banged off rocks above and below the waterline, gulping down breaths of air when the river allowed him to surface. Several times his helmet *gong*ed from hard contact on unseen head-splitters. All the while, he floated toward the rumbling waterfall he'd heard but was still too unfit senseless to realize what he was hearing.

And, seeing as He-Dog was blessed with bad fortune, he went over those falls and crashed down into even deeper water.

Oh, there were a few frantic moments where he struggled to clear the current, until his chest damn near mutinied for air. He eventually clawed and kicked his way back to the surface though, at times, he touched bottom. Or submerged rocks looming up from the bottom. In any case, those fleeting contacts were brief as the current pushed him along, cracking him off *more* rocks. A series of smaller falls followed, each one a torturous crash, followed by a moment's disorientation. Somewhere along the way he lost his helmet. Twice he'd almost blacked out.

Which was around when fortune—bad fortune, that was—decided to leave He-Dog.

With even worse fortune.

The river's flow quickened again, and it seemed every rock in existence had lined up to smash his carcass. And smash they did, battering his arms and legs, though he managed to keep his head clear of it all and above water.

One last set of falls dropped him five paces down, where he barely missed being impaled upon a collection of broken tree roots. As it was, He-Dog touched the bottom, exhaled a watery burst of bubbles, and pushed off. He didn't go far before he broke the surface with a gasp.

Before sinking again.

His arms were done—exhausted, as heavy as iron. His legs weren't that much better, but he lumbered, finally touching bottom in an area where the shore was a short wade away. The river ride calmed down considerably, the surface mirroring the huge slabs of orange and white rocks jutting over it. A high embankment of muck lay after that, one laced with veiny tree roots and shaded by trees and tall grass. Shade that mercifully leaned out over the peaceful water.

Thank the Lords, a battered He-Dog thought, spitting water. The river bottom sloped upward, enough that he didn't have to bounce anymore. The waterfalls continued crashing behind him as he waded for the shore. He rose, the water lapping at his lower chest, drenched and dripping and all the heavier because of it, but still breathing. His hand strayed to his lower wounds, fingers below his belly and partially submerged. A tentative pressure caused him to hiss at the contact. Tender as a hundred boils. A thousand, even.

He was perhaps a dozen paces away from the shoreline when something other than the waterfall caught his attention.

To his left, perhaps some thirty strides downstream, the water darkened in the shade and flowed out of sight.

Except for the one patch which churned and bubbled.

He narrowed his eyes and paused, studying the spot with suspicion. At first, he thought it was another set of falls, but the rest of the river remained quite calm. The idea it might be rocks lurking just below the surface came to mind, but he dismissed that as well as the current wasn't moving near as fast as before.

The curious thing was that the violent churning was moving *toward* him.

Then his eyes popped wide and a coldness spread through him despite the warm river depths.

He-Dog broke into a run.

At least, as much of a run he could break into while half dead and partially submerged.

A safe slab of rock waited not eight paces away.

The swath of violent rippling water approaching him was a chilling *twenty* paces away.

Sweet Seddon, He-Dog thought and hauled his bleeding carcass along until he slipped. Down he went with a splash. He floundered and swallowed a mouthful, before planting his hands and knees on the bottom and pushing off.

He glanced downriver.

That frothing patch sped for him, growing to half the width of the waterway.

Energized by fear, He-Dog staggered for the rock, splashing with every step.

Four paces away from the shore and he chanced a look.

The frenzied waters were only *five* paces away, and beneath the surface only just beginning to churn, the quickest of the fish lanced forward.

He-Dog lunged for the stony perch. He cracked his knees on the lower edge, but the rest of him landed on rock. Wheezing, he clutched at the edges but failed to find a grip, when a series of gnashing bites pitched into his *boots* of all places. With a burst of frantic energy, he found a handhold and scrambled free of the churning water. Everything splashed and sloshed as he collapsed on that flat pan of rock and pressed a cheek to the warm surface.

Land, he thought, in delirious relief. *Lords above, precious—*

The water churned and sloshed in a froth below him, distracting him, as did the *pinching* sensations about his lower legs. Rolling over, He-Dog didn't have the strength to swear. A good dozen of what could only be bloodfish thrashed upon the rocks. A dozen *more* of the fiendish bastards held onto his boot leather, where they had sunk their sizeable red fangs deep and refused to let go. A few of the fish flopping about splashed back into the river. A few more relinquished the boot leather and fell wriggling and twisting upon the land.

He-Dog kicked at the little muck-colored hellions, knocking off a few before pulling the remainder off his boots, grimacing at their slick, writhing lengths. After clearing the chunk of rock he sat upon, he discovered the bloodfish had gnashed through his leggings just above the boot leather. Dazed and dismayed, he pulled back the tatters of cloth and saw, in horrified wonder, the bleeding outlines left by exactly four bloodfish.

One of the little killers remained on the rock, one red eye wide and staring, its lipless, many-fanged mouth flexing as it perished.

He pulled himself clear of the thing, until his back hit a boulder. The bloodfish in the river continued to rage, the water rippling fiercely, as if a stunning downpour of rain centered on that very spot. *No doubt wondering where the meat has gone*, He-Dog figured. Just to make sure all was well, he pawed at the rest of himself, checking this and that, starting with his fruits. Still where he left them and thankfully intact. He sighed in relief.

Bloodfish, he mentally groaned, staring at the frothing waters only just beginning to subside. The Sanjou had bloodfish in its rivers. Right. No bathing, then, and even that failed to produce a smile. Bloodfish could rip a man to shreds in mere heartbeats. The interior jungles of Big Rock had them. Then there were the legendary monsters of the Harudin. The ones belonging to this river were no more than the length of a man's hand and just a little thicker in the middle. An angry, ravenous muscle of a creature, with a protruding jaw filled with small but sharp triangular teeth.

He leaned back, head shaking in disbelief.

Savages. Bloodfish.

The Sanjou was earning its reputation. What else might be waiting for him? He didn't want to think about it.

Despite his latest escape from certain death, He-Dog slumped, his chin resting on his chest, and allowed himself a moment's rest. He woke with a lurch, reaching for a sword he no longer had, and grimaced at the tightening stab wounds. Suspecting he might have been tracked motivated him to crawl up and over the embankment and hide himself in the jungle. Several strides later, he sat and placed his back to a tree. There, he ripped off a length of cloth from his breeches, bundled it into a thick wad, and shoved it up under his armor, against the worst of his licks—the stab wounds. Given how much he was bleeding, he realized why the bloodfish had come for him.

The steamy heat and ever-present humidity left him uncomfortable. Birds squawked overhead, their voices accompanied by that familiar underlying buzz of insects. Drenched in shade as he was, a gap in the vegetation granted him a view of the river. Leaves hung in thick bunches, but he could see the calm current and the far shore. Quite the picture, really, if one didn't think about the unfit terrors lurking underneath it all.

Damn . . . damn bloodfish, He-Dog reflected, his eyelids growing heavier.

And then he lost consciousness.

It was morning when he woke. Or at least he *thought* it was morning. Sensed it. Felt the pain as well. No, not pain. *Agony*. The kind where you were beaten to within a finger of your life, only to wake and realize you weren't dead at all, and were greatly disappointed by the fact. Everything was stiff. Like any good spice working into a roast, the flavor was stronger a day later.

Then he felt things crawling up his arms.

A probing, hairlike touch, creeping along the outer curve of his left arm. Then a second crawler, up the inside of his leg, while another paused in his left ear, as if wondering what lurked inside.

*Crawler*s. If it wasn't the heat, it was crawlers. He hated them. Big Rock had a loathsome collection of insects as well, and sleeping outside invited any number of them to slink and skitter over you during the night.

He-Dog extracted the crawler from his ear, frowned at its finger-sized length and its many energetic legs. He flicked the thing away and located the other invaders, starting with the ones heading for his crotch. He pinched every one away. Then he listened.

Birdsong, bright yet indifferent. The constant buzz of insects. And other sounds he didn't recognize.

Something started crawling up his leg again, up the back of his knee.

Lords above. He reached around, located the insect, and crushed its shell with a pinch. Detecting no more of the things, he stayed still, content to watch and listen, sitting underneath broad, oar-shaped leaves. Nothing moved, nor did he hear anything like Sanjou savages searching for him.

As he suspected they would be.

Thoughts of the wildmen turned to the single savage who had defeated him upon the cliff. The creature had been strong and quick, much faster than He-Dog, and had bested him.

He sighed through his nose and even that hurt. He took a moment to check on matters, grimacing at the many pains, and discovered nothing broken. His prized sword from the armory of Foust was gone, however. Lost in the river. That annoyed him. He'd very much liked that blade. Probably the best he'd ever owned.

Mosquitoes buzzed in his ear, and he rattled his head. Grimacing, He-Dog reached under his armor and checked on the wad he stuffed under there. Watery blood saturated the bandage, dappling his fingers, but he wasn't sure if he was still bleeding.

Spears. He grumped, wanting to snap off every one. Along with the asslickers who used them.

Sparing a look around, He-Dog considered where he was, and hated his predicament. He had survived a brutal ambush where most, if not all, of Shay's mercenaries had been slaughtered. He had managed to escape, however, and by that reasoning, he expected Chop to have escaped as well. The Nordish swordsman was every bit the survivor that he was. Perhaps more. Where his Nordish companion might be, however, He-Dog had no idea. And no idea how to safely find him.

Dying Seddon, he thought. Alone. In a savage land. A land he had no knowledge of, except the stories he'd overheard from the sailors and mercenaries.

His entire frame pulsed with discomfort then, as if pressing the point.

And to add to his misery, the crawlers had returned.

Grimacing, he staggered to his feet, brushed himself off, and suffered the agony erupting from all quarters. Weaponless, he limped back to the river, step by painful step, stopping just short of the water.

There, hunched over with a hand pressed to his bandage, he listened and watched. The bloodfish he'd left on the rock was gone, and nothing except a few dark smudges—which he figured was his own blood—marked the spot where he had pulled himself from the river. The shade allowed him to gaze into the much calmer depths of the waterway, all the way to the bottom. No bloodfish, so he got down on his knees, dipped a hand to sample, and found it very good to drink. He drank deeply, filling that need, and then splashed some over his head and face.

Seddon above. That was unfit good.

Nothing lurked or prowled along the riverbanks. No sign of the wildmen who had ambushed them. He-Dog stood, grunting as he did, and kept to the shade. A nearby rock was free of crawlers, so he slowly sat down upon it, aching all the way.

His pack had been ripped away so his food was gone. The plan had been to eat and live off whatever the Sanjou offered while searching for the emerald treasure. If he could find any familiar fruit, he'd eat that but no fires for cooking unless he wanted to attract another war party.

The *Blue Conquest* entered his mind then, and He-Dog remembered the plan. The ship would remain anchored until the next full moon, whereupon it would sail back to mainland Zuthenia, and then return the following full moon.

Which meant the ship was still anchored in the bay.

Heading back up the river, however, risked encountering the same maggots who had surprised and butchered them. Taking the long walk around might avoid the wildmen, or whatever they were. *Fishmen*, he decided. With their unnerving features and round orange eyes. Like a two-legged bloodfish. He took note of the sun, barely visible through the foliage overhead, and got his bearings. It was indeed morning, and a bright one at that.

Downriver he would go, at least until he could find a safe place to cross.

If he fell into the water again, however, the bloodfish would have him.

He started walking.

If the morning had been hot, then noon was unfit boiling.

Big Rock had its own jungles and He-Dog had endured those, but the Sanjou's heat felt thrice as strong. Where a desert might cook him with sheer scorching power, the jungle sought to boil him from the inside out. Trees and layers of green ceiling provided shade from the sun, but it trapped the moist heat, making matters worse. A dewy sweat coated him from morning 'til night, and any part of his skin covered in fabric or armor felt glued down. Everything was soaked, right down to his fruits, and he dared not check on that as some things were best left alone. Every footfall landed on a soft and rotting floor, mottled with dead colors, where things chittered and fled into the underbrush. He-Dog hoped he didn't need to squat anytime soon, for fear of falling over and staying there.

He stopped to rest and wiped his face, studying the moisture coating his hand. *Seddon above.* How much water did he have in him? How much water could he lose before falling over? He'd come close with Chop when they marched to Othil, but the river was just there, and so he supposed he wouldn't die from thirst.

Chop filled his thoughts then. He hoped the Nordish man had escaped. Perhaps he was doing the same as He-Dog. Circling, taking the long way back to the cliffs, avoiding any savages while trying to get back to the *Blue Conquest*.

It was something to hope for.

Suffering with every step, He-Dog continued on, treading softly, trying not to disturb the foliage around him. A skilled tracker would spot a bent or broken flower. A heel driven hard into the ground would be like a posting sign of his location. Anything could hint at his passing . . . if one knew what to look for.

The jungle buzzed around him. Birds flittered through the air, dark shapes sped along the edge of sight. No animals crossed his path, nor did he spot recent feedings or cow kisses. Insects continued to plague him, and he crushed them under a firm hand. Spiders *infested* the wilderness, crawling away from him at an unsettling pace or becoming as still as statues until he walked by. Some were huge, as large as two hands placed together and just as hairy. They often hung in webs big enough to trap a man. Desiccated husks of birds and rats hung in those disturbing nets.

It took time, but He-Dog limped around those spectacles.

At one point he stopped and rested against a gnarled tree trunk. A flicker of movement prompted him to turn his head. Not a finger's length away from his face dangled a spider the size of a child's hand, suspended by a single glistening strand of webbing. It hung before He-Dog's face, close enough to show off its brown and green spotted body and long, elegant legs. Those legs flexed ever so slightly before freezing in place. Perhaps inspecting He-Dog in turn.

And after deciding all was well, it continued lowering itself to the ground.

He-Dog watched it all the while.

Spiders.

Surprisingly, he didn't hate spiders so much.

Probably because most people did and killed them outright. He-Dog believed spiders hated people in turn. That he could understand.

Deep thought over, he resumed his torturous hike.

The vegetation thickened around the riverbanks, hiding everything above and beyond. The mountain ridge they had climbed only yesterday remained hidden from sight, though he knew it lay someplace to his left. Getting there would be a challenge.

Distant voices from up ahead interrupted his thoughts.

He-Dog eased through bushes and tall grass, wary of the riverbank's edge. Tall thickets of wilting trees dipped their roots into the water. A parting of huge fronds provided a view downriver, where two of Shay's mercenaries stood, partially obscured by the grass growing along the edges. Their names came to him at once. The older, shaggier one called Jers Snaffer, who looked perpetually angry, and the barrel-shaped one called Kellic—the one who had fought him on the deck of the *Blue Conquest* and had broken a wooden sword across his shoulder. Both men resembled two butchered shanks of meat that refused to fall over.

Very glad to see them, He-Dog pushed free of the vegetation.

Jers Snaffer spotted him and pointed, turning Kellic around to see.

A relieved He-Dog shambled ahead. The two men stood upon a broad, white sheet of rock that sloped into the river. A thick smear of dried blood coated that rock, all the way down to the waterline.

Drawing closer, He-Dog saw where the blood came from.

The unconscious form of Prince Shay, more dead than alive, splayed upon the rock with one pale leg in bloody tatters below the knee, right down to the bone. All the leader's toes were gone, bitten off in a feeding frenzy that He-Dog had nearly experienced firsthand. A length of cloth was bound just above the afflicted limb, in an effort to stop the bleeding below. The other leg was in better shape, but there were bite-sized chunks missing, and raw holes glistened.

"Seddon above," He-Dog whispered. "He's alive?"

Kellic glanced at Snaffer. Both men looked like bloody cow kisses drenched by a passing thunderstorm. A long red gash split Kellic's left cheek, spilling meat and promising a gruesome scar, while the flesh about his right eye was blacker than any Mademian plum. A grim collection of crusted-over cuts, colorful bruises, and egg-sized welts covered Snaffer. Dirt and grime spattered their chainmail vests, but where Kellic had a helmet, Snaffer did not, and his steely gray hair flourished.

"Aye that," Snaffer replied. "Just barely."

"He went swimming in the river?" He-Dog asked.

"Fell into it." Kellic nodded at one grassy bank. "Yesterday. Over there."

"Fell into it?"

The mercenaries exchanged pensive looks.

"I fell into it," Snaffer admitted. "Lost my way. The grass too damn high. Ground disappeared underfoot as I was walking. Went down with a splash. Him with me." He nodded at the prince. "He sank. Nearly to the bottom. Almost lost him. I grabbed his arm, dragged him out. Had two feet on land when the waters around him started boiling."

Despite the heat, He-Dog's guts chilled, knowing what happened next.

"Bloodfish," Snaffer finished, glowering at the word.

He-Dog's cheeks puffed as he sighed. "Unfit."

"Unfit," Kellic agreed.

"Just you alive?" Snaffer asked.

He-Dog nodded. "And just you two?"

The older warrior nodded.

"So this is it, then?" He-Dog asked.

Another nod, as Snaffer hooked his thumbs into his belt, his gaze returning to Shay.

He-Dog stopped where the rock rose high above the river. Grimacing, he eased himself down onto the smooth surface and hobbled over to the prince, taking on the full angry might of the sun when he left the shade. He stopped at Shay's side and studied the man they called "prince."

Seddon's holy knob. Only just barely, indeed, just as Snaffer had said, and perhaps better off dead. Though the leg was ruined, everything above the knee didn't look very promising either. Bloody rivulets drooled from split flesh and ran between a bulging assortment of purple and blue welts. Something had split part of Shay's upper lip, exploded it really, swelling it to an unnatural state with oozing things best left inside. His nose was squished to the left, perhaps the worst break He-Dog had ever seen. The prince's left eye was swollen much larger than his right, but both were closed and slitted, blissfully unaware of the damage sustained to his face.

"A savage knocked him upside the head," a squinty-eyed Snaffer said. "With one of those clubs. Drove him to his knees. I killed the maggot, but the prince was gone. Alive but senseless. I carried him away. This one here got between us and any following."

"All the way?" He-Dog asked, impressed.

Snaffer ignored that, as if saying it once was enough. He nodded at Kellic, whose sad eyes studied the ravaged prince lying on his back.

"We only just got away," Snaffer said.

"Bartus is gone," Kellic revealed. "A savage skewered his leg. When he fell, a half dozen more jumped on him. Speared him dead."

"What about the other one?" He-Dog asked, meaning the other older officer.

"Grage is dead," Snaffer said bluntly.

Silence, then, for a moment.

"Your healer got killed as well," He-Dog said quietly. "I saw him fall. Nothing I could do."

"They're all dead," Snaffer growled while watching the jungle.

A gloomy Kellic nodded agreement.

"So, we're the last," He-Dog let out softly.

No one commented on that.

"What were they?" Kellic asked after a time.

Snaffer had no answer.

Neither did He-Dog.

"They looked like men," Kellic carried on. "But... their eyes. And their mouths."

"Fishmen," He-Dog rumbled.

"Monsters," Snaffer growled. "Nothing more than that. And plenty of them."

"A small army," He-Dog added, remembering too well. "Well... that's it, then. I was heading back to the ship."

"As were we," Kellic said. "We couldn't go back that way. Those he-bitches would still be about. So we headed this way, looking to cross the river... which was when he fell in."

"You weren't tracked?" He-Dog asked.

Kellic shook his head.

"Where's your lad?" Snaffer asked. "The one without the face."

He-Dog paused. "He has a face."

"Just not a good one."

That earned the old warrior a dirty look.

"I don't know," a scowling He-Dog replied. "I'm hoping he's alive. And that he's headed back to the ship."

That quieted the men.

"We stayed here for the night," Kellic said, breaking the stillness. "On this very rock. Too dangerous to do otherwise. We were just about to move when you came along."

A little good fortune for He-Dog. "We best be moving then. In case they find our tracks."

That they all agreed upon.

"We can't go back that way," He-Dog said. "And we can't cross the river. Not on foot. Not with the bloodfish about."

The mention of the unfit creatures darkened their faces.

"Downriver, then?" He-Dog asked. "Until we get to a point we can cross?"

"We could hack down one of these trees?" Kellic suggested.

"Too much noise," Snaffer said. "Might draw any nearby screamers."

That thought sank in.

"That way then?" He-Dog pointed.

The men looked downriver, which snaked around a bend and disappeared behind a wall of trees and lush vegetation.

"That way," Snaffer said, unimpressed with the choice.

A nearby pack caught He-Dog's eye, lying underneath a large shield. "You got anything to eat in that thing?"

Kellic exchanged looks with Snaffer, who nodded after a beat. The younger man waddled back to pull out the pack. A quick search, and he handed over a few strips of dried meat.

Taking what was offered, He-Dog nodded his thanks.

CHAPTER 15

Heat.

Punishing, war hammer–force *heat*.

With every exhausting step and stagger, the temperature rose to sweltering levels, bleeding the men of moisture and coating them in an unwanted sheen. Sweat oozed from their cracks and pits and seeped into their eyes. Even better, tormenting clouds of insects enveloped them all, looking for a taste. He-Dog wiped a hand across his brow and rubbed it off a thigh still soaked from the last time. He felt terrible, from the murderous heat and his punishing wounds. Everything pulled and ached or was relentlessly sore. The others didn't look any better, wearing their chainmail shirts spotted with iron slabs and suffering for it. They also bore the extra weight of the prince, who one would carry over a shoulder while the other stayed nearby, preventing Shay's broad carcass from sliding off. At least they had stripped the man's armor and left it by the river. Shay also had weapons, one being a broadsword. It wasn't a sculpted piece of art like the blade He-Dog had from Foust's armory, but he took it and strapped the belt and scabbard around his waist, discarding his own.

He-Dog didn't like leaving a trail of bits behind, but by that point, he didn't care. None of them did. All they wanted was to get away from where they'd been ambushed.

And to get back to the ship, at best speed.

So they trudged on, suffering immensely. In single file they marched, through a landscape overrun with vegetation and at times sun-freckled. He-Dog led them, watching for danger while keeping the river on their left. Enormous trees towered overhead, forcing them to march around their wide bases and push through the annoying undergrowth sprouting up between the monsters. Vines, bushes, and springy limbs sought to trip He-Dog and the others, further slowing them down. Bright flowers of all shapes and sizes dappled the foliage with swaths of color, while weeds with long needles stabbed for ankles and legs. At times, the river disappeared entirely and the jungle became an oppressive tangle that rubbed against them. The ceiling was an even denser collage of leaves and outstretched limbs. There were birds up there, somewhere, never seen but heard, their calls haunting and worrying, as if alerting some greater predator about the mercenaries. Spiders the size of one's fist abounded, hanging in fishnet-sized webs. Crawlers as long as a boot moved underfoot, strange creatures with honey-red carapaces that resembled armor plating. No other wildlife could be seen, however, and for that, He-Dog was grateful.

A few strides behind him, Kellic limped along with Shay. He said not a word about his hurts or the weight of the unconscious prince slung over one shoulder. Snaffer was nearby, equally silent, scowling at everything as they all shuffled along.

It was nearing noon when He-Dog halted, his shoulders sagging, and everything saturated. "Stop here," he huffed, keeping his voice down. "Before I drop."

A nearby tree looked to be free of insects, so he leaned against it before sliding down its base, landing in a patch of wildflowers with drooping yellow petals.

Kellic unloaded Shay nearby and then plopped down beside the unconscious leader. A red-faced Snaffer stood guard, watchful of the jungle, his fists resting on two hilts. One hilt belonged to a long-shafted hand axe, the other, a thick dagger nearly the length of a short sword.

Kellic removed his helmet and ran a hand over his soaked hair and beard.

He-Dog waved away the flies around his head and sized up Shay. The man remained mercifully ignorant to how unfit his half-eaten leg was festering. Black flies pitched for a quick taste before darting off, covering the limb in patchy sheets. Kellic fanned them away, if only for a short time.

"That can't be good for him," He-Dog said quietly.

A puzzled Kellic questioned him with a glance.

"That," He-Dog said, indicating the ruined leg.

The bearded man sized up the wound with greater scrutiny. Snaffer even leaned in for a peek. After a moment considering it, the older man lumbered off into the jungle.

"Where are you going?" He-Dog asked.

Snaffer did not answer.

Kellic shrugged, indicating he wasn't Snaffer's keeper.

Not pleased, He-Dog figured the man was emptying the bull. He gripped his new sword and waited. On impulse, he glanced down at the prince and scowled. In the short time Shay lay upon the ground, a huge slug, yellow and glistening, with black stripes across its back, had fastened itself to the ravaged leg.

Kellic saw the thing as well and extracted a dagger. Working fast, he hooked the creature—which was the length of two fingers—and flicked it away.

The slug landed with a soft thud among the flowers.

"I hate this place," Kellic muttered.

He-Dog agreed. The Sanjou was quickly becoming an unfit hole of the worst possible kind.

Snaffer returned.

"Where'd you get off to?" He-Dog asked him.

"Needed a squat," Snaffer grumbled and stood over the prince. A beat later, he hunkered down and inspected the ravaged leg. As he did, his expression became even more grim. "Lad needs a healer," he finally said. "If we don't do something for that leg, it'll go rotten. Might already be too late."

"There's a healer back on the ship," Kellic said.

"There is?" He-Dog asked.

"Aye that. One of the sailors. He and Gusper spoke often."

He-Dog didn't remember any of that, but then again, he hadn't kept track of all the men on board the *Conquest*.

Snaffer grunted and picked at the knotted cloth above Shay's knee. He untied it, releasing a trickle of blood.

The sight worried He-Dog. "Maybe you shouldn't do that."

Snaffer glanced at him. "Can you do it?"

"No."

"Then shaddup. Daresay I've seen it done enough times to know how. Best to try, at least." Snaffer took hold of the ruined leg. He bent it twice, then with dirty fingers prodded the leftover tatters of skin clinging to the limb.

He-Dog was certain the man should *not* be doing any of that, but he didn't argue the point. He wasn't a healer himself, though he had been cut up enough times to recognize Snaffer was letting off bad blood to stave off the rot. Whether or not he would be successful was unknown.

Kellic went through his pack and handed over a wad of cloth. Snaffer took it, cut off a length, and tied off the leg above the knee once again.

He-Dog wagged a couple of fingers at Kellic. "You have any more of that?"

The mercenary did and handed over a bundled clump. With a nod of thanks, He-Dog took the bandages, and unlaced the front of his vest. Everything stung as the air touched it. Everything was tender. It took some effort but he shucked off the vest. Once he had freed himself, he peeled away the saturated wad covering the worst of his wounds and inspected the slit.

Ugly. Purpled. And trickling blood.

The sight made him sigh. He jammed fresh bandages against the cut, taking the pain. When finished, He-Dog rested for a bit, inspected his work and, as an afterthought, considered his bloody hands.

Before wiping them in long swipes on some nearby bushes.

Kellic helped him pull his vest back on, and that was that. A long and sullen silence where none of the men talked. Snaffer inspected his forearm, touching the rosy bloom of what looked like a stab wound. Kellic offered him the last of his bandages, but the older warrior shook his head before releasing a wet cough and quieting.

The three of them didn't speak, while unseen wildlife called out all around.

"How far you think we're from the ship?" Kellic finally asked.

Snaffer didn't answer.

He-Dog studied the shaded heights. "Hard to say. We need to get clear of this."

"Seems like we're getting farther from the cliffs," Kellic said.

That felt true enough as the river curved this way and that, slinking deeper into the jungle, and not offering any chance to cross it.

Becoming impatient and knowing it was going to hurt, a groaning He-Dog slowly stood. "Best we get moving."

The others rose, and He-Dog held up a hand. "Wait a moment."

With that, he pushed his way down to the river where tall grass hid the shoreline. Some nine or ten strides across was the other side. The nearby trees were monsters, far too large to chop down. Eyeing the shallows, He-Dog wandered a few steps, sinking ankle-deep in muck, and dared not go any farther. He held the soiled bandage he took off his lower bits and considered it before tossing it out into the river. The cloth floated for a short time before the water frothed and jumped around the material.

Then it was gone.

Bloodfish, He-Dog grumbled to himself, and returned to the others.

Once again traveling in a single line, they followed the waterway deeper into the sweltering Sanjou. At times, the river widened to twice its width, or narrowed to perhaps seven or eight paces across. They pressed on, every suffering step unnaturally loud, but so was the unseen wildlife that chirped, sang, or rustled vegetation just out of sight. The only things not caring if they were seen or not were the spiders, freakishly large, with their long-segmented legs poised and ready. They hung in curtains of webbing tethered between trees, webbing festooned with the corpses of insects and small animals.

The spiders didn't bother the men, but the black flies did. Clouds of them buzzed in their ears and attacked their faces, mercilessly tormenting the mercenaries. Despite all that, Snaffer and Kellic endured their wounds while sharing the weight of the unconscious prince.

Until they all lumbered to a stop, on the cusp of falling over.

"Lords above," He-Dog breathed, waving at the scores of black flies before his eyes. "This is unfit."

He smacked a cheek, crushing several insects and coating his fingers in blood.

Without comment, Snaffer and Kellic lowered the prince to the ground. They plopped down, wincing as they did, and placed their backs to nearby tree trunks. He-Dog borrowed Kellic's helmet and carefully filled it with water from the river, wary of any lurking bloodfish. He filled the helm and splashed its contents over his face and back.

Warm but good, he thought, and sighed with relief.

That little effort brought on a spell of dizziness, forcing He-Dog to sit until it passed. When all was right again, he refilled the helmet, drank, and filled it again before bringing it back to Kellic, who used the water to wash off the prince's face.

Once done, the mercenary opened his pack and handed out portions of whatever he had. Hard biscuits. Strips of dried meat. A pair of apples, cut into sections. Each pack had contained enough food for one man for four days or so. With the three of them feeding from the pack, it would go fast, even faster if Shay came to his senses.

They ate in silence, though there was plenty of noise. Kellic chewed with his mouth open, sending things flying. Snaffer smacked his lips and ate with a soft, audible moan, just loud enough for He-Dog to puzzle over what he was hearing.

"Can't see any mountains," Snaffer said while eating. He swiped at black flies.

"Nor I," He-Dog said.

"Are we lost?" Kellic asked.

"Not yet," He-Dog answered.

"The river's a snake," Snaffer noted.

That much was true. A bloated snake at times, refusing them any point to cross. Not unless they wanted to swim, which wasn't going to happen.

None of the men spoke after that, using what little energy they had to slap and wave at attacking insects. A short time later they got moving again, and marched until the sky turned orange, then pink, with great swaths of purple. As the jungle grew darker, the shadows twisted into increasingly menacing shapes.

Not wishing to travel at night, they stopped at the edge of a small glade where the river gurgled, behind a hedge of tall grass.

"I'll take first watch," He-Dog said quietly, swatting the back of his neck.

"Wake me when you've had enough," Snaffer said, and that was that. He stretched out beside the senseless prince. Without a word, Kellic did the same.

Headed for a tree near the water, it struck He-Dog that the two surviving mercenaries weren't much for idle conversation. Understandable, if not appreciated. Balless could talk. Talk endlessly at times, especially when drinking, until He-Dog told him to shut up. Not that Balless always listened.

He-Dog sat against the tree, adjusting his scabbard as he landed. Sighing, he realized he longed to hear his brother's voice once again. *Damnation.* He could barely stand the topper when he was alive—now a simple thought nearly broke him. Scowling, he checked for crawlers before making himself comfortable. As comfortable as he might get with the black flies hounding him.

With an aching weariness that would not go away, He-Dog watched the darkness spread across the Sanjou.

The cries of birds woke him, just before dawn.

The night sky faded, and the air wasn't as steamy as the day before. He-Dog scratched at tender places and dug thick fingers into both ears. The black flies had eased off greatly during the night, which made him wonder what might be eating them. Wanting to stand, he shifted his legs and a bolt of agony lanced him below the waistline. Then the rest of his wounds started to screech, aching furiously.

He-Dog grunted, heeding the warnings, and checked on Shay. Before Snaffer had relieved him from guard duty, He-Dog had noticed a length of rope easing across the prince's midsection. That rope had turned out to be a crawler almost the length of his forearm, with a thickness of his thumb. He flicked the beast off the unconscious man and ground that nasty, twisting length under his heel. The earth was soft, however, and the crawler armored, its unfit strength repulsive. Killing the thing took longer than expected. Just the one insect, which he had discovered by chance. Who knew what else might have been creeping about during the night?

He-Dog glanced around, spotting Snaffer at the edge of the glade, facing the river. The old war hound had stayed up the remainder of the night. Kellic still slept, and He-Dog let him be.

The prince, however, looked worse than the previous day. Dark lines underneath his eyes gave them a sunken look, while his skin took on the pasty hue of a dying man. His leg, the bits not chewed away, festered and oozed.

While He-Dog examined the man, Snaffer wandered back while Kellic stood without a word and joined them.

"Looks like a strung-out length of shite," He-Dog remarked quietly, drawing a hard look from Snaffer.

Kellic tried waking the man with a few pats across the face. When the prince failed to respond, the mercenary slapped a little harder.

"Just *wake* him," Snaffer warned. "Don't take the face off him."

Kellic placed a hand over the prince's mouth and nose. "I can't feel a breath."

Alarmed, Snaffer slapped away Kellic's hand. He promptly did his own inspection, placing an ear close to the prince's mouth.

"It's there, though barely," he said after several heartbeats.

"You say he was cracked upside the head?" He-Dog asked.

Snaffer nodded.

He-Dog pointed at the leg. "Give that a sniff."

Kellic smelled the limb and jerked his face away. "It's festering."

He-Dog shuffled to one side, to allow what sunlight there was to strike the prince. The leg was a mess. The skin not chewed away had taken on a sickly yellow color, and a dull sheen coated the exposed meat. Blots of matter mushroomed around the raw bits, while other parts resembled a rotten plum.

Kellic prodded at the edges with dirty fingers, and in one spot the contact released a squirt of rotten-smelling juice.

"Festering," Snaffer repeated under his breath.

"Let me look," He-Dog said and dropped to his knees, hurting all the way. He crowded over the leg and sniffed. That one intake of stinging foulness shoved him back. After a fresh breath, he checked again and got the same result, the stink harsh and choking.

Damnation. He rubbed his face, as if that might dispel the smell. It didn't.

"Festering?" Kellic asked.

He-Dog nodded.

Snaffer shook the unconscious man's shoulder and failed to wake him.

"What do we do?" Kellic wanted to know.

A fair question, but He-Dog didn't have an answer. Neither did Snaffer, who stood and glared at the prince.

And damnation, the smell was only getting stronger. *Infection*, He-Dog knew. Good meat going bad. The smell guaranteed it. "He truly needs a healer now," he said. "And the only one nearby is on the *Conquest.* If we continue following the river, we may not get back in time to save him. And if we go back to the cliffs, where we *came* from . . . we know what's waiting for us there."

Their glum expressions said they knew.

He-Dog grimaced. It was far too early for such hard thinking. "We're dead if we return to the cliffs. And we can't stay here. So . . . what do we do?"

"We keep moving," Snaffer declared. "Down the river. Find a way across and make for the ship. We can't bring him anywhere if we're dead."

"We're nearly dead as it is," Kellic said in a low voice.

"And if he dies along the way?" He-Dog asked.

The scowl on Snaffer's woolly features deepened as he sighed. "Get him up."

The sun had barely risen in the hazy sky, but its heat was already scalding. The three surviving mercenaries left the glade and marched on, eventually reaching a vast, open patch of marshy grassland that stretched off into the distance. Staying with the river, they pushed on, crossing the open wetlands, gambling that they would not be spotted by any murderous wildmen. The march became a slog. Wet mud sucked their feet down past their ankles. Even worse, the black flies returned. Ravenous clouds buzzed around the men, pitching and flying before hands could crush them. The little hellions went for any exposed flesh—ears, eyes, even clogging their nostrils. Twice, Snaffer stopped and pressed a finger to each side of his nose to blow out the invaders.

Sweat streamed down He-Dog's face and into various cracks, and the Sanjou offered not a breeze. He fumbled at drawstrings on his vest and cracked that open, getting the barest relief upon doing so. The effort irritated his stab wounds, summoning long and lingering aches. The extra patch of bare skin also attracted more black flies.

Kellic and Snaffer plodded along behind him, suffering from their own hurts and melting in their heavy chainmail hides.

At a glance, He-Dog figured they were halfway across the wetland, spying a wall of trees where the jungle surged up again.

Seddon above they needed that shade.

They also needed to cross the river, which continued meandering along without any real direction. The surface of the water appeared peaceful enough, but the depths were dark, suggesting a muddy bottom. Wary of bloodfish, they avoided getting too close, where the ground became a watery muck that disappeared in the tall grass.

Halfway to noon, they crossed the wetland and plodded into the welcome shade of the trees. The many layers of foliage overhead diminished the sun to just a few lines of light. The men collapsed upon a flourishing carpet of wild grass and flowers, breathing in humid but scented air. He-Dog slapped his neck and drew away a mash of insect guts and his own blood. He was dizzy, his throat parched. Kellic had food, but no water, and no one wanted to wade back to the soft sides of the river and chance a drink.

"Unfit," He-Dog whispered, and tongued his lips.

That little bit of effort ruined him and drained all of his strength.

The others didn't speak, and He-Dog couldn't think of their names. His head ached. Black flies whined in his ears and about his head. He grimaced and covered his eyes with one hand while swatting his attackers. He quickly tired of that, dropping his arm as if chopped from his shoulder. That puzzled him greatly, considering all the hardships he'd recently been through. He'd sustained a terrible beating from a stubborn pack of beastmen—the same ones who killed Balless—and survived the scalding desert of Big Rock. A hard fistfight on a pier and a wretched crossing on the Big Water. And yet, here he was, near death. He-Dog pressed a hand below his waist, and the contact fired back, stealing his breath. The spot was dearly tender, perhaps even worse than he suspected . . . but still . . .

He couldn't finish the thought. Couldn't remember what was bothering him. The chaotic whining rose in his ears, reaching a feverish pitch. Things crawled over his face and he pawed at them, sending up an angry puff that quickly descended again.

"Snaffer," He-Dog croaked, remembering the name, spitting away the flies upon his lips.

Snaffer lay on his belly, his face buried in his arms while insects swarmed the back of his neck and crawled through his hair. He was livid with the things. Black flies. Large and mindless and voracious drinkers of blood. They covered the backs of his legs and his arms and anything exposed. In fact, the mercenary resembled a roast drizzled with spice and ready for the fire, except all that seasoning teemed with movement.

He-Dog dragged a hand across his eyes, clearing the insects again, glimpsing Kellic face down and unmoving. The man had covered his head with his pack. Shay lay nearby and his face *rippled* with the things.

Black flies.

Hordes of them.

A sense of dazed amazement overtook He-Dog. Of all the hardships He-Dog had endured, he was on the cusp . . . of being killed . . . by *insects*.

Unfit, he thought, not daring to say the word, as it would allow the hungry things to enter his mouth. They had already invaded his nose, flittering inside. His strength waning, He-Dog inhaled, tasted them at the back of his throat, and barked them out in reflex. With a grunt, he blew out both nostrils before rolling onto his stomach. No longer able to fight them off, he hid his face in his arms. His senses spun, threatening to sicken him, while the flat whine of thousands filled his ears.

Just before he lost consciousness, he lifted his head a few fingers.

There, emerging from the brown-green folds of the wilderness and creeping toward him, was a line of spear-wielding shadows.

CHAPTER 16

With the sun nearing noon, a long procession of figures emerged from the Sanjou, plodding along a bare trail long since stomped into hard earth. The trail was a wide one, perhaps five paces across, and hemmed on either side by creeping, thorny vines, low-growing spider bushes, and mottled, slug-shaped gourds. Intimidating crawlers, as long as one's arm, slunk or skittered through that undergrowth. The insects stayed clear of the well-traveled path, however, and the grim, hunched over things walking upon it. The stooped creatures called themselves Iruzu in their language, and they were returning home, victorious in their battle with a group of invading Hard Shells.

As evident by the number of heads spiked upon their spears.

Fish-jawed, orange-eyed, and squat, with powerful legs and sinewy, gray-green torsos, the Iruzu lumbered across an open field. At the center of that foul, flattened rug of troublesome vegetation rose a wall—a disturbing barricade some twenty-five strides high, constructed of ancient trees cut straight from the Sanjou's dark heart. Skulls of animals and Hard Shells garnished that wall, and the rotting juice of the land stained the grim decorations and logs alike. Each log ended in a sharpened point high overhead, creating a fearsome battlement that lay long shadows upon the ground. Figures patrolled those impressive heights, eyeing the returning warriors as they headed for a set of crude gates, open and waiting.

Beyond that imposing portal waited the Iruzu village, as old as the roughshod fortification protecting it. Hundreds of jutting wood peaks and domed thatched roofs loomed through the gates. To call it a village was perhaps a touch misleading, as it had existed in the Sanjou since forever, swelling in size over many, many generations of Iruzu.

The returning war pack lumbered into the battlement's shadows and carried on through the gates.

Shouts salted the air, alerting the populace of their warriors coming home. Young and old Iruzu stopped their work or play, dropping simple hammers and lowering stone axes. Some ceased strangling the necks of dead animals and tossed aside monkey skulls bound in old skins. A filthy tide of hunched humanoids kicked aside free roaming pigs and chickens and gathered along the main path. Old female folk elbowed their way to the forefront. Mouths of fish-jawed youngsters hung open in rabid, puzzlement, displaying yellow fangs just beginning to develop. The male folk shoved aside the youngsters and females alike, to get closer to the procession, sparking shouting matches and near fights. All the while the crowds thickened until, finally, a weird hush fell over them all.

Before a shocking, rock-splitting burst of glee erupted from the masses.

The young warriors shook fists at their returning brethren. The female folk shrieked and clawed at the air with blackened talons. The youngsters jumped and bobbed while waving monkey skull rattles and toys made from teeth. Filthy fingers pointed at the trophy heads among the war pack and the screams rose louder and louder. Male folk leaned over the path and spat thick yellow gobs before the feet of the returning warriors. The older male folk produced shards of rock and slashed at their own hands to fling black blood upon the path. Some of the younger male folk, not yet of warrior age unsheathed their pelvic roots and released hot streams onto hardpacked ground. The family and brood of those warriors missing—presumably killed in battle—cheered even louder, as it meant a prosperous existence in the Other World.

As impressive as all that was, none of those celebratory gestures moved the war party's leader. One Spear—the impassive Iruzu warrior named for the weapon he carried—ignored the cheering masses. He continued to ignore them, even when they darted into his path, delivering killing thrusts to imaginary foes before releasing wild and wicked peals of delight.

One Spear walked by them all, shoving aside any getting too close.

Although his face resembled a fierce mask seemingly cut from sun-split stone, inside he was *soaring*.

In the distance, a single hill loomed, easily visible beyond the many roofs.

Upon that hill sat a lodge, built of the biggest logs of old wood, belonging to the Iruzu elders. Vines and fungal matter festered and thrived upon the walls of the dwelling, sprouting from a thick sap coating the wood. That rancid, vile juice seeped from within the lodge itself, through crevices and cracks, staining the very rock it rested upon. A foul glaze tarnished the roof as well, but in wide, disturbing blotches, as if something had been smashed against that unsettling shell. The lodge was a dark place. An aboveground cave that should have collapsed long ago. It continued to stand, however, surviving the most violent of the stormy seasons, defying the cloudless skies and the harshest suns.

One Spear fixed his attention upon that grim structure as it came into greater clarity with every step.

A pack of squealing pigs scampered away from the procession. An old Iruzu male, near toothless and one-eyed, stood behind a fence of bones and wood. The old male stuck a dirty skull atop a sharpened post. He drew back, slow and deliberate, and brandished an equally aged war club. He waited until One Spear was a few paces closer, whereupon he bashed the skull into bits. Bits that sprayed across the path of the returning warriors.

A gesture that very much pleased One Spear.

The Iruzu greatly prized the skulls of their dead enemies. *Smashing* those same skulls before warriors returning from battle was the highest compliment. The skull shattered before One Spear no doubt belonged to an enemy from long ago. The gesture heaped praise upon the warriors, done by those who wished they could still hunt and fight with the younger packs.

As One Spear and his warriors continued on, more skulls were shattered. Some on fences. Some on bare rocks.

One Spear could not get enough of it. He carried two heads of his own, freshly taken from dead Hard Shells. As was the Iruzu way, he planned to stake the heads upon a pair of poles and let the sun dry them out, from this day onward. One day, he would be the one smashing old skulls.

In the last few days, much honor had been heaped upon One Spear's name. His warriors had killed many Hard Shells invading their land. The Hard Shells possessed thick, shiny skins not easily broken, but the Iruzu had killed them anyway, proving yet again they were the strongest of the Sanjou. The most vicious, and certainly the most feared. One Spear himself had killed four Hard Shells, and later harvested their heads and their teeth—also highly prized. He had mastered killing the Hard Shells, punching his spear through their faces or skewering bare limbs, before peeling away their shiny skin. He killed the last one by stabbing it and pushing it off the inner cliffs. That one's head he couldn't claim, so he offered the invader to the water gods. One Spear wasn't one to care what the gods thought of him, but sometimes he believed it was good to offer up something. Just to quiet them.

Shortly after killing the invaders, One Spear led his warriors to the cliffs, to the Hard Shells' Great Mother still floating upon the sea. They waited until night, and then swam to the Great Mother. There, they proceeded to climb up her slick sides and kill the sentries. The battle that followed was not really a battle, but an outright slaughter.

Which the Iruzu greatly enjoyed, staining the Great Mother's wooden bulk red with the blood of their enemy.

The Hard Shells aboard the Great Mother did not have hard shells and were easy to kill. After the battle was done, the true work began. The Iruzu scraped teeth free of their enemies' faces—some of which were still screaming—before removing the heads from their bodies. Then fire was set to the Great Mother, and she sank to the bottom, with only her tallest points showing where she lay. Not finished, One Spear ordered a handful of heads to be stuck atop spears and left along the shore. That grisly line would serve as a warning to any other Hard Shells seeking to invade Iruzuland. Such butchery pleased the Other World spirits. It had greatly pleased his warriors.

Such an act would most certainly please the elders.

Enough for them to give One Spear what he wanted.

The title of War Pig, leader of *all* Iruzu warriors.

If the elders gave him that honor, One Spear's voice would be heard and heeded within their lodge. For one so young, it would be a great accomplishment, even though he'd been walking the path ever since the day he was born. His legs were thick with muscle, while his torso was shredded and formidable. His weapon, a spear taken from a Hard Shell long ago, was sharp and unbreakable. No one had ever wounded him in battle, and death was a concern as trivial as squatting and dropping filth upon the land. Fear did not concern him. Fear was something he projected.

This recent massacre would lift his name and worth among his peers.

He would be War Pig. No one else was worthy of the title.

Those thoughts occupied his mind as he led his warriors through the maze of dwellings. Sometime later, they climbed the hillside to the elder's lodge and sat outside it. A dried sheet of skin, stitched together from many enemies, covered the entrance. In time, servants brought a feast of roasted pig and water, as well as dream weed. One Spear ate, but he didn't partake of the dream weed. He wanted his mind sharp for the elders, even though the elders' lodge reeked of the stuff.

Later that evening, as a red sun sank below the surrounding cliffs, a servant beckoned One Spear to enter the elders' lodge.

Leading a smaller group of warriors, One Spear entered the huge structure built upon a stone foundation. Such foundations were a rare thing among the Iruzu. To have one meant power. The sun had been hot, but inside the lodge it was moist and juicy and good to breathe. Dream weed smoke filled the chamber, nearly obscuring the thick cuts of wood holding up the roof. Skulls decorated those posts, some missing their bottom jaws, and all hanging from pegs. Each skull's teeth had been plucked free long before they were fixed to the wood. Smoke curled and drifted around the leering faces of bone. A many-legged worm glistened as it extracted its fearsome length from one eye socket and slunk down the post.

Unfazed, One Spear stopped at a smoldering fire pit at the center of the lodge. The elders sat around the pit, their features partially hidden in smoke and shadow. Necklaces of teeth and bones adorned their hazy silhouettes. One of the elders, old Stone Axe himself, beckoned One Spear to come closer. The old killer's orange eyes were heavy-lidded and wrinkled from where his youth had leaked away over many years.

One Spear sat just beyond the ring of figures. The dream weed threatened his senses, trying to wobble him. He gestured at the shadows and his pack of warriors came forth, bearing gifts.

Two Hard Shells, still alive, their shiny skins intact and saved for this very occasion. The two gifts hung from poles, bound by wrists and ankles, and had screamed as they were carried through the jungle. They had quieted upon entering the village, no doubt exhausted from their travels, and fearful of their fate.

As they should be.

The Hard Shells began screaming again as the warriors placed their struggling lengths over the fire pit, resting the poles atop the highest rocks. The screams reached even greater pitches as the flames slowly cooked their tough exteriors. A servant emerged from the dream smoke, a curved club in hand. Without warning, the servant struck the first gift, shivering the poles and lessening the noise. The servant then did the same with the second gift.

Having silenced the two Hard Shells, the servant considered the fire pit before prodding it to an even greater heat. Glowing embers floated about the lodge. Flames rose, licking at the two gifts, and new smells filled the air.

One Spear waved a hand, and five additional heads, hacked from the necks of invading Hard Shells, were laid out before the elders. Five trophies, their pained and terrified expressions still intact.

One Spear waved his warriors away after delivering the gifts.

And yet, while the fire crackled and the smell grew stronger, the elders did nothing for long troubling moments.

Stone Axe eventually pointed at One Spear and spoke for all to hear.

Stone Axe heaped praise upon One Spear's name, calling him the most feared, most respected, and most dangerous of all Iruzu warriors. Stone Axe called him the thunder that flattens the hills, the beast that drains the waters, and was pleased that One Spear had many years of youth left in him. The elder said One Spear would have many females, and spawn many, many young Iruzu. The elder finished with one last thought, saying how the many gifts pleased the elders.

The other elders, orange-eyed and snarling sleepily, rocked back and forth as Stone Axe spoke.

One Spear kept his features impassive as those words fell upon him. Inside, however, he was elated. He was *War Pig*. *All* Iruzu warriors were his to command. Thoughts of glory filled his head, of hunting down the Sanjou's other tribes, even going into and beyond the mountains, digging all their enemies out from their hiding places, and killing every last one.

Stone Axe cleared his throat, and a slug of yellow spit stretched from his lower lip and fell to the ground. The elder informed One Spear of a hunting pack that had discovered another hunting pack, all dead, and all killed by Hard Shell weapons.

Tension filled the lodge then, and One Spear became very aware that all eyes were on him. He realized he had not returned to a victory ceremony that would've rewarded him with the highest decoration of the Iruzu, second only to the chieftain. He had returned only to discover he *hadn't* finished the wishes of the elders—to kill *all* Hard Shells trespassing in Iruzu territory.

One Spear's spine stiffened.

All the gifts he had brought the elders, all the offerings, had perhaps persuaded the elders *not* to punish him, for only partially completing their wishes.

One Spear squirmed. His thoughts raced. He remembered the one falling off the cliff. The one he'd offered to the water gods. If the rocks below the cliff didn't kill the Hard Shell, the fish of the river would.

One Spear's eyes narrowed.

Stone Axe commanded him to go back into the jungle and find the Hard Shells killing Iruzu hunters. The elder declared that if One Spear did this, he would be War Pig.

One Spear glanced at the other figures sitting around the fire pit. Old and drooling Leech On His Face. Heavy Foot. Fat Belly. Long Chin. And Big Cut.

They all watched One Spear.

Stone Axe said that the Drinkers were nervous. He said that the Drinkers and the Spirit Hags believed the Hard Shells were not happy to be slaughtered in such a way as One Spear had done, and that the gods of the Hard Shells were angered. And vengeful.

Stone Axe's lips parted in a smile, revealing the jagged shards of his remaining fangs. He said that the elders were greatly pleased, however, and that they squat and piss rain on the gods and ghosts of the Hard Shells.

Gruesome chuckles erupted from the others. Fat Belly snorted laughter while scratching at his enormous midsection.

One Spear relaxed, sensing he was in no danger.

Stone Axe spoke again. He said that gods were still gods, and spirits were still spirits. And that they could do things from the Other World, if their hatred was strong enough. The elder said the Drinkers and Spirit Hags agreed that One Spear had offended the gods by spiking the Hard Shell heads on the beach.

That prickled One Spear's spine. No one from his pack had spoken to the elders about what they did on the beach.

Fire crackled in the elder's pause for breath. Fat sizzled. The smell of roasting meat laced the air.

Stone Axe spoke again, informing One Spear that the elders still didn't care about any of that, and that the spiking of heads greatly pleased them all.

Again, rumbles of amusement around the fire pit.

Stone Axe leaned forward and told One Spear to keep offending the Hard Shell spirits, their gods, and anything connected to them. Stone Axe said that if the gods and spirits were angered enough, they would send *more* Hard Shells to kill. More Hard Shells meant more killing, more meat and blood, and more fear heaped upon the Iruzu name.

All around the fire, the elders nodded. A spot of drool shone in a corner of Fat Belly's mouth.

Stone Axe told One Spear that if he did that, if One Spear could show that the Iruzu had no fear of gods and spirits and Hard Shells, then . . . One Spear would be War Pig.

Stone Axe lifted a wooden cup, its sides stained black. The other elders did the same. They drank, only to spit-spray their mouthfuls onto the fire as was the custom. To show any lurking spirits they did not believe their blood was worth drinking. To the Iruzu, lurking spirits were like crawlers within your bedding, troublesome and needing to be dealt with.

Ribbons of flame weakened before crackling back to life.

One Spear accepted the elders' decision. He would find the Hard Shells that had escaped him. He would find them and crush them underfoot, like the fat crawlers they were.

With nothing else to say, Stone Axe gestured for the young warrior to leave.

One Spear stood and left the lodge.

Outside, the warriors who waited for him climbed to their feet, but One Spear waved them off. Visibly puzzled, they fell into line behind their leader and followed him a short distance to another lodge below the hill. A much smaller dwelling, built on common ground, and nowhere near as imposing as the elders' structure. One Spear entered that dwelling, and his most trusted warriors followed.

They sat in a circle, around a small, unlit fire pit, where disheveled mats covered the ground.

The imposing warrior called War Club asked about what the elders had said.

One Spear didn't answer right away. He considered the faces before him.

Blood Fingers. Worm Eye. Red Bone. Gut Eater. Rock Jaw. And War Club. They were the fiercest of the fierce. The most terrifying of the Iruzu. Warriors who would make even the dead stumble and run for the Black Beyond the Dawn. With Iruzu such as these, it was no wonder One Spear was destined to be War Pig.

One Spear studied them each in turn and told them they were not yet finished hunting Hard Shells.

CHAPTER 17

Under a brilliant sky of stars, distant campfires and their smoky wisps marked the settlement nestled in the valley below. Chop surveyed the village from his cliffside perch, amid a dense thicket of weeds and foliage teeming with life. He lay on his belly, close to the dirt and vermin, where every breath tasted just a little foul. The Nordish swordsman did not move, however. Did not swipe at the many legs skittering across him.

Chop watched the village. Studied it. The place was a huge, noisy thing, located a day's travel away from where he, He-Dog, and the others had been ambushed. An imposing log wall surrounded the settlement, tall and black with shadow. Figures crept along those impressive heights, patrolling the battlements. Wildmen they might be, but the wall showed they knew something about fortifications.

Something brushed underneath Chop's chin, clipping the edge of his mask, yet he still did not move. Wide traps of sticky silk spanned the space above him, where spiders the size of fists hung and waited. Their legs flexed, sewing together threads meant to capture their next meal. Night birds called out, hidden in the trees, their cries soft and seemingly mindful of the walled village.

The thing under his chin rustled his mask yet again. Chop drew back and located the creature. It wasn't one of those large spiders but a monster of a crawler. A long, many-legged brute that tensed at being discovered. Sensing a retreat was in order, the creature scurried away, the honey-red armor of its shell undulating until it disappeared in the surrounding growth. Chop watched it go and when it was gone, he checked on the spiders above him. Venomous moss spiders existed in Nordun, ones that could paralyze a man or woman with a single bite. Or kill a child. Those creatures were barely the size of his thumb. With that thought, Chop eyed the spiders above him, warning them with a look. Satisfied, he cautiously returned to watching the village.

His mind drifted as the night wore on, back further and further, until it reached the point of the wildmen's attack and being separated from He-Dog.

After his escape from the ambush, the wildmen had hunted Chop without pause, thrashing their way through the jungle. Nordish Jackals, of whom Chop was once one, were light infantry trained to conceal themselves in the wild until it was time to strike. That it was a jungle didn't matter to Chop. It was still a wilderness, with an abundance of places to hide. After creating some distance from his pursuers, Chop hid within the lush growth and remained there, listening to his hunters' search for him. A skilled swordsman he was, but he was also a master of hiding, and his enemies passed him without knowing he was underfoot.

Until night, when all noise from the hunt had diminished, and Chop decided to go on the offensive.

What followed were a number of silent slayings, performed by a master of the craft. He would blend into the jungle and wait for the precise moment to strike. When the opportunity showed itself, strike he would, eliminating one wildman after another. He repeated this several times throughout the night, often dispatching enemies without them realizing it. When the sun rose the next morning, Chop stood over his last victim. Though these wildmen had used weapons of stone and wood, they weren't exactly precise with them, preferring to smash and stab instead. Their true strength lay in their numbers, as *hundreds* of warriors had attacked Shay and his mercenary force.

Once Chop was satisfied he'd picked off his last pursuer, he decided to return to the place of the ambush. There, among the trampled vegetation and the blood-spattered weapons and the flies covering it all, were the remnants of a huge fire pit. A heap of charred armor and blackened bones filled the pit, and ash drizzled it all.

Among those bones, however, not a skull could be seen.

Nor was there any sign of He-Dog.

So Chop decided to follow the trail back to the cliffs. There, he discovered the wildmen had attacked the *Blue Conquest,* and sunk the ship in the bay. Only the tips of her tall masts were visible above the surface. Worse still, a ghastly fence of heads had been erected on the beach below, likely as warning to anyone considering landing upon the Sanjou's shores.

Chop recalled descending the cliffs to study that dreadful collection of heads. He remembered seeing several familiar faces of the crew, including the one belonging to Stephanak, the captain. He-Dog's was not there, which strengthened Chop's hope that the big man was still alive. He knew his friend had much better fortune than he believed, and when he didn't have fortune on his side, he had the tendency to make his own. If only He-Dog could see it for himself.

Chop had believed his companion might be following the wildmen, so he left the beach. Returned to the jungle. Followed another trail, which led deep into the southern reaches of the Sanjou. Which eventually led to this place.

He eyed the set of rough-hewn gates. *Village,* he scoffed. Truth be known, it was a massive fortress, surrounded by a dark, grand palisade. Numerous skulls of animals and men hung from the walls, easily visible under the sun earlier in the day. Not only did sentries roam the gloomy heights, but several dozen guarded the main gates.

Another many-legged crawler trekked over one of his legs, but the Nordish man ignored it, and the insect didn't bite. Which was wise on the crawler's part.

For at that moment, Chop considered himself to be the most dangerous creature in the Sanjou. He'd fought free of the wild fishmen ambushing Shay's company and lived long enough to find this cursed place. And he intended to survive, to take revenge on those residing in the fortress below. Hate powered him, energized him, and for the first time since joining He-Dog, Chop believed he finally understood the man's constant loathing.

He-Dog.

Chop felt a stab of sadness. His companion had become a shell of his former self since the death of Balless. Chop hadn't known the two men were brothers, much less had beastmen blood running through their veins, but it explained much. Balless, ever the brute, was always ready with his wreck of a smile, whether Chop wore his mask or not. That was something the Nordish man warmed to, perhaps faster than he cared to admit. The days spent marching back to Othil had been marked with grief, as memories of Balless and their travels together filled Chop's mind. He-Dog had dwelled on something beyond that, though, lost deep in some prior memory. For long stretches of their journey to Othil, it felt as if the man's body was in this world but his mind lingered in another. Even after leaving Othil aboard the *Conquest*, He-Dog's spirits had barely improved.

Then the ambush separated the two men, for the first time in a long time.

Still, there had been no sign of He-Dog's corpse anywhere around the ambush site or on the beach. If he was alive, the *old* He-Dog, he would not be so easily killed.

In the meantime, Chop would become a ghost, and inflict as much death upon the wild fishmen as possible until they finally killed him.

Pipes and drums carried some unfit tune from within the city's walls, interrupting his thoughts. Shrieks spiked the air.

Chop regarded the stronghold one last time before slowly withdrawing back into the jungle.

CHAPTER 18

An explosive flutter of wings woke Chop, and he clutched at tree limbs to steady himself. There he waited, high in a tree, roosting there for half the night. Senses scrambled but alert, he was able to register the frenzied squawks of unseen birds. He adjusted his mask awkwardly and arched his back to stretch out the stiffness from the night before. He disliked sleeping in trees, but he wasn't going to sleep on the jungle floor, not with the myriad spiders and crawlers lurking below.

With a rub of his nose, he inspected the vine around his chest that fastened him in place. The air was somewhat cooler this morning, so he took a deep breath and peered out through the foliage at that unpleasant stronghold. His perch provided him with a good view. The gate itself was no more than five or six men across—small, considering the impressive size of the wall—but Chop saw it well enough.

Then he saw the reason why the birds had scattered.

The gates were opening.

Slow and ponderous, those mighty timbers creaked open, and a vile, gray-green stream of hunched fishmen issued forth. They trudged through the widening gap, hooting and hollering, their postures poor as if buckled by the heat. All manner of weapons bristled among them—bows, spears, clubs, and stone axes.

The fishmen flowed in a lengthy column from the gates. The sight of all those warriors filled Chop's mind with concerning thoughts. *Why so many? What could be happening?* Then he had it.

They were looking for him.

Hunting for him. Crowing as they marched forth, leaving the protection of their nest, shrieking and shouting in their language.

The screamers thought themselves fearless.

Chop scowled at the parade.

He would make them fear.

At the head of the column, One Spear stopped and planted the butt of his namesake weapon firmly into the ground. The Iruzu behind him halted, their shouts tapering off to throat-clearing grunts, quietly aware of their leader. One Spear peered at the jungle, eyeing its steamy depths.

One Spear pointed straight ahead and with a guttural cry summoned the Iruzu pack leader behind him.

Worm Eye, stern and frightening to gaze upon, with his one dead eye that always stared straight ahead. Beads and bones decorated the Iruzu's chest, rattling as he moved. He brandished a curved club studded with fat wooden spikes. Worm Eye led twenty warriors past One Spear, headed in the direction indicated.

When Worm Eye and his twenty were gone, One Spear pointed in another direction and shook his iron-tipped shaft.

Gut Eater strode forward, orange eyes wide and staring, his lower lip and chin studded with flecks of black stone. Gut Eater led another twenty. They too disappeared into the jungle.

One Spear summoned the next leader and his pack.

Tall and imposing Red Bone.

Short but frightening Blood Fingers.

Unkillable Rock Jaw.

Each led a group into the jungle, all with the same instructions—find any surviving Hard Shells and take their heads. The elders would want those.

One Spear did not think there were many Hard Shells left alive. Not really. And if there were, no more than a handful. This hunt did not have a feeling of danger at all. This hunt felt . . . *playful*. Dare he think it, One Spear considered this task no more than sport, and that annoyed him.

The last leader approached with his pack of Iruzu. War Club carried his namesake in a huge fist—a heavy cudgel of knobbed wood that had killed hundreds. Of all the pack leaders, he was the biggest. Vicious, possessing towering height, broad shoulders, and draped in heavy muscle, War Club's eyes shined the brightest when he was cracking open heads.

One Spear ordered him to go to the southeast.

War Club screamed, a hateful note that carried across the clearing, and the Iruzu at his back screamed with him. The imposing warrior lurched off into the brush, leading his pack away.

One Spear watched him go for moments before he summoned the final forty. They knelt at his very gesture, lowered their heads, and laid their weapons upon the ground.

Gazing over their backs, One Spear hefted his namesake and turned for the jungle, taking the same path as Worm Eye.

Just in case their prey fooled the first wave.

Behind him, his hunters rose and followed without a sound.

Pack after pack of savages bled off from the main line of hunters and entered the jungle, spreading out in a wide pattern.

Chop knew they were searching for him.

There were many. Too many, really. The notion to run entered his head, but he pushed that away, knowing there was no place *to* run. His parched throat clicked when he swallowed, and his lips were dry, longing for a drink of wine or firewater. One last group remained in the shadow of that horrific palisade dressed in skulls. A much larger group. As he watched, the leader shook his spear and the rest dropped to their knees.

Chop realized then the jungle had become quiet. Very quiet despite all the screaming from earlier. He looked at the ground below, this way and that, as a feeling of dread welled up inside him.

Then he heard it.

Snap. The softest footfalls, made by hunters trying very hard to move in silence.

They were coming straight for him.

A chill overtook Chop, despite the heat and the muck and mud he had lathered upon himself. He wondered if he was high enough in the tree to remain unseen. Wondered if the layers of branches and their foliage would be enough to hide him.

The sound of feet gently treading across the jungle floor grew closer.

Chop pressed his back against the trunk and drew up his legs so they did not dangle. He steadied himself and watched the ground some fifteen strides below him, through tattered layers of leaves. It seemed high enough yesterday, but right now he wasn't so confident.

If he could see down, *they* could see up.

Chop swallowed, suspecting he had lingered here too long. He should have retreated the instant the gates opened. He then realized that was exactly what the fishmen would want him to do—to panic and run. To flee. Then it would be an easy thing to hunt him down and take his head.

But he wasn't going anywhere.

A crunch of twigs beneath him, the foliage looking much too thin.

Chop held his breath.

Not so far below, things moved.

A soft rustle and then something else moved into view. *Heads.* Shoulders and torsos. Spears and clubs. A pair of hunters slunk toward the base of the tree, even glanced up—which tightened Chop's blossom. They eventually moved out of sight. More twigs snapped, and a flicker of movement from another angle attracted Chop's eye, but he dared not move.

The head and shoulders of another screamer appeared.

Then a fourth, just a stride away, looking this way and that.

The hunters moved toward Chop's tree, so he remained stone-still, fighting down the urge to scratch his nose or head or even breathe. Sweat slid down the inside of his mask, glazing his face, and eventually finding an eye. He closed it, but more sweat oozed from him, perhaps falling away. Chop quietly let out his breath and stayed still. Something pitched around the eyehole of his mask and crawled along its curve, until it found a bit of skin between his eye and upper cheek. Chop frowned, mentally swearing on the thing, enduring that awful sensation. He waited for a yell of discovery from below—a hate-fueled shriek of triumph and the frantic rush to the tree's base.

Nothing of the sort happened, however.

The line of hunters moved past him. The insect muttering about his face flew off.

Chop listened, waited, forced himself to remain still, until he could no longer hear their slinking through the undergrowth.

He relaxed just a little, knowing he'd come far too close to being discovered. Sensing the danger had passed, he wiped his face, scratched at the more troublesome itches, and relaxed his arms and posture. Not yet ready to move, Chop continued waiting, giving his hunters plenty of time to widen the distance between them. When he was certain of his safety, he would climb down and become a snake in the underbrush.

Ready to strike when the time presented itself.

No sooner did he have that thought than he heard *more* movement from below, approaching his tree.

Dying Seddon, Chop thought, tensing again while searching for the source. Closer they crept, gliding through the vegetation in a wave that snapped and crackled. Every hushed step and rustle caused Chop's heart to race. He took deep breaths, barely moving while sensing movement all around down there, closing in on his perch.

He glimpsed a shoulder passing underneath. As quiet as a fish through deep water, the body passed beneath him, making no sound at all. That concerned the Nordish Jackal, as he had only just been playing with his face.

Another figure drifted through his line of sight.

Then he saw the others. A creeping surf that moved past him, their footfalls barely a patter. No one stopped at the tree's base. No shouts of discovery. Chop held on, his heart pounding, when one of the hellions *stopped right underneath him* and rapped the tree trunk. The hellion looked up and Chop froze, staring back, knowing the slightest movement might reveal himself. He waited for the devious little topper to start shouting. Or climbing. Or both. But the hellion showed no signs of recognition. It continued to tap the tree a bit longer, as if it were killing a crawler or two, then the tapping ceased, and the figure moved on.

Needing a moment's peace and a good long squat, Chop closed his eyes. When he opened them, he believed the entirety of the second pack had walked right past him.

Chop realized he was behind them now. This presented several deadly possibilities, but first he would stay in his nest a little longer, in case a *third* pack lurked about. No other savages were coming from the stronghold, however. In fact, the gate to the place had closed. Once he knew for certain his hunters were ahead of him and that there were no stragglers, he would descend and follow. Follow them until nightfall.

Then . . . he would kill.

As many as he could without being discovered. Until he'd killed them all. Or perished in the attempt.

CHAPTER 19

After a day of scouring the jungle, the hunting packs did not find any sign of the hated invaders. Which was strange. The Hard Shells were noisy, smelly things with no mind for concealing their tracks or themselves and were usually easy to find. As a result, One Spear decided to head southeast in the morning, into the deeper parts of the Sanjou, which a Hard Shell might think was a better place to hide. With no objection from his pack leaders, One Spear ordered them all to camp for the night in a wide line, well within shouting distance of each other.

They possessed no fear of being attacked at night. They were Iruzu. They were as numerous as the stars scattered across the great blackness overhead. And they feared next to nothing within the Sanjou.

Still, when War Club and his pack of twenty hunters stopped for the night in a dark glade, he chose a handful of guards to keep watch. The Iruzu then gathered brush for a fire and unrolled sleeping mats among tall, wild grass. Warriors gutted the wild game they had killed during the day—flightless birds, huge rodents, and a pair of hoary jungle hogs. A sizeable anthill also provided crunchy sustenance, and several Iruzu dug out red crawlers from the soil and ate them.

After they were sufficiently fed and weary, War Club settled back on his mat, scratched at various parts, and stared at the night sky. Reaching tree limbs framed the sight. Even though they had not found a Hard Shell, War Club was content. He was in the jungle, leading a pack of warriors, with good skies to watch over them all. Tomorrow would be another day, and he had no doubt they would find whatever had been killing Iruzu. When they did, well, he hoped he would be the first. He imagined many torments to inflict upon the Hard Shells, from gutting them while they still breathed, to eating them alive. Even better if he alone found them, to impress One Spear and the elders. And if they could not find any Hard Shells, then perhaps they would find a great beast and kill that instead. Anything was better than returning home with nothing.

His eyes drooping, War Club scratched at his head, digging at something crawling over his scalp. An Iruzu guard lumbered close to the fire and stoked it with a spear. Embers fluttered in the night as the guard walked away.

Yawning, War Club rolled onto his side, folded one muscular arm, and laid his head upon it. His great club rested beside him. Soft snores rumbled nearby. As he drifted off, he thought of standing over captured Hard Shells before smashing their chests. Their arms. Their legs. He would save the heads for the elders.

Those were his thoughts when a hand clamped his mouth shut and a knife pierced his throat, stabbing upward, deep into his brain . . . before being twisted. The hand kept the Iruzu's spasming figure in place until it relaxed.

Chop waited, grimacing from the effort needed to control the powerful reflex of the dying fishman. Lords above, it took effort just to shut the thing's mouth. When the creature was well and truly dead, he released it and eyed the other sleeping bodies around him.

Not one moved.

So he lay there, covered in muck and grassy filth, more dirt than flesh, or so it would seem in the dark. The fish thing's blood seeped through his fingers, warm and sticky. It was the fourth one he'd killed that night, having already disposed of three guards posted around the clearing. As far as he could tell, only the sleeping ones remained.

The pissers had been at it all day, searching for him, and not too concerned with leaving their own trail. It was an easy thing for Chop to follow and hunt them in turn, leaving his armor in a place he hoped he could find later. He waited until night, listening to their gibbering until they settled down to sleep, perhaps a little too confident in their numbers.

Chop had learned long ago, when in an enemy's territory and facing numbers greater than your own, it was best to strike, strike *hard* . . . and then slip away.

Provided you *could* get away.

There was plenty of time before dawn.

He selected his next victim, sleeping not five strides away.

When the next snore ripped through the night, he started crawling.

The sun rose at One Spear's back, draping the ruined corpse of War Club in shadow. A dewy mess of blood covered the dead husk. One Spear's jaw shivered with building anger as he dropped to a knee to examine the gaping wound under the thing's chin. Orange eyes glaring, One Spear reached out and traced the killing blow. A clean cut, made by a weapon not of the Sanjou.

Hard Shells.

Anger gripped the Iruzu leader as he stood. His warriors filled the surrounding glade. One Spear looked past them, into the vast depths of the jungle. Hard Shells prowled the Sanjou. A handful that had escaped the trap set for them and now . . . they were killing Iruzu in turn. One Spear fumed at the thought, strangling his weapon while thinking matters through. An entire hunting pack gone. Killed in the night while asleep. The Iruzu enjoyed doing exactly that to their enemies. One Spear wondered how many Hard Shells might be out there. There would have to be many to kill an entire pack without a sound, in the night, giving the Iruzu a taste of the same poison they'd fed to so many others over the years. Only one thing angered him more, and that was the absence of enemy corpses.

Not a single carcass lay among this slaughter. Not one.

The Iruzu leader drew in a deep, murderous breath and let it out, resisting the urge to scream. Hatred boiled within him. He hated the Hard Shells. Hated their boldness. Fuming, he planted the butt of his spear in the ground and leaned into it, once more inspecting the dead scattered about the camp. They lay on their backs or sides, lifeless faces staring, their weapons nearby and untouched. Including War Club. That surprised One Spear, because he had been a dreaded killer. One who had earned his name for a reason, time and time again.

Now he was dead and gone.

One Spear pushed down his building anger, needing to think. Could something else have killed these warriors? Another enemy of the Iruzu? All manner of ghosts and monsters lurked within the Sanjou, which was the very reason the ancients built the wall surrounding the Iruzu's village. One Spear shook his head as if shaking off flies, dismissing the thought. Hard Shells had killed War Club and his hunters. The nature of the wounds proved it.

Hard Shells.

He sent off his warriors to summon the other hunting packs. In time, those groups gathered around the encampment.

Worm Eye, with his dead eye, watched One Spear. Menacing Red Bone waited for orders. Blood Fingers and Rock Jaw glowered at the dead Iruzu at their feet.

The only one not there was Gut Eater.

One Spear paced in a small circle, flattening the grass further, wondering where his warrior could be. Gut Eater. The other pack leaders noticed the same, and they glanced around for the crafty warrior. Sometime later, three warriors came running into the clearing, turning heads as they rushed to One Spear. There they dropped to their knees and reported news that shocked the gathered army.

Gut Eater was dead. His pack was dead.

That revelation shocked One Spear and left him staring, his lower jaw flexing in confusion.

Then he started running himself, and the remaining packs followed him.

By midmorning, the Iruzu leader was walking through a familiar sight. Another campsite of nothing but slaughtered remains. The same manner of cuts marked the corpses, and clouds of flies buzzed about the butchery. One Spear stopped at the fallen Gut Eater, still on his sleeping mat, his green and gray skin noticeably pale in death. The Iruzu had his throat opened to the bone by a Hard Shell knife, leaving a sticky feast for all manner of Sanjou insects.

The pack leader's club lay beside his mat, untouched, suggesting he never knew what killed him.

That angered One Spear enough to get over his shock. *Two* of his prized warriors had been butchered during the night, along with their hunting parties. War Club was a monster for anyone but Gut Eater . . .

One Spear knelt beside the corpse, and a drunken plume of insects rose from their feeding. One Spear dug two fingers into that awful gash in Gut Eater's throat, tugging one way and then the other. A single, many-legged crawler slunk up the side of the corpse's face. One Spear crushed its berry-sized head with one quick pinch, the resulting crack sharp upon the air. He then tossed the dead length away.

Hard Shells. One Spear hated them. *Hated* them.

One Spear vowed again to kill them. Every last one. Kill them over *days*, until the sounds of their dying became a haunted song all would remember.

One Spear stood and regarded the surrounding Iruzu packs and their leaders. One Spear told them the Hard Shells had again killed their companions during the night. He told them the Hard Shells thought they owned the night, but that was wrong. The Iruzu owned the night. He told his warriors to find those responsible for the killings. To find them and feast upon their living hearts while they still screamed. He told them to rip apart the very jungle in their search, to overturn every rock, to stab a spear into every bush and body of water. Until the Sanjou revealed the offenders.

One Spear vowed the dead would be avenged, and that the Hard Shells would be slowly gutted.

When he finished speaking, the gathered Iruzu thundered in agreement, and that blast caused birds in far-off treetops to take flight.

Blood Fingers stepped away from his pack and approached One Spear. Blood Fingers had been a very good friend of Gut Eater, and the hatred upon his face pleased One Spear. Many of the other Iruzu also wore angry faces. Even One Spear's own pack looked ready to tear apart the land to find the killers.

The sight of all those angry faces pleased One Spear very much.

They were Iruzu. The most feared in the Sanjou. The nightmares that walked. Ruthless slayers who would devour their enemy alive, if given the chance.

And they wanted to impart that truth upon any Hard Shell they found.

One Spear ordered Blood Fingers and his pack off into the jungle. When they were gone, One Spear sent the packs led by Worm Eye, Red Bone, and Rock Jaw in their respective directions. One Spear then turned to his own dreaded pack and split them into two groups, to cover more ground.

Within moments, over a hundred Iruzu warriors bled into the Sanjou, searching for signs of passage. Any sign at all.

As long as it led them to Hard Shells.

CHAPTER 20

A storm-wrecked fence of ancient trees sprouted from the jungle floor, their crooked limbs reaching in all directions, holding up bushels of green, dagger-shaped leaves. That dense ceiling doused the land in a soft emerald shade, and through that miasmic color and the clawing, clutching tangles of the underbrush, a masked swordsman retreated north.

Enduring the morning heat, Chop retraced his steps from two days before, back to a giant tree that dwarfed all others. It was a monster. An abomination. Its oddly segmented trunk was as tough and knotted as iron plate. Its limbs, thick as a man's torso, spread wide as if effortlessly holding back the advances of lesser trees. There was no missing the giant, the very reason why Chop chose it as a hiding spot for his items. There, tucked between two massive roots that reached his chest, the Nordish man pulled away clumps of bushes, disturbing an assortment of reddish-brown crawlers drawn to what was hidden beneath.

Two backpacks. His own and one belonging to another mercenary, taken from the ambush site. Both contained modest supplies of food and water. He brushed off the few insects skittering over the heavy cloth and untied the flaps of both to inspect the contents. Things moved inside, so Chop emptied the packs and picked out more invaders. A quick check informed him his food—mostly dried meats—was intact. As were the few fist-sized baubles of orange fruit he'd picked along the way. One water skin remained full, while the other was half-drained. Chop took a quick swig from that one, gasped, and put it away. He glanced around that vast jungle cavern and saw no signs of pursuit.

Not yet.

But there would be.

Working quickly, Chop checked on his blades and ensured they were secured tightly. Then he slung one pack across his back and the other over his front. He reached for the other weapon he'd found at the ambush site, one he was surprised to find, considering its quality. A short bow, its curved wood thick and bullish in the center, tapering off to finely wrought tips. A rigid length of sinew stretched between those tips, and a quick flick of the fingers strummed out a deep tone. Vathian characters (or Valencian, damned if he rightly knew) were etched into its length and gave the weapon an exotic look. And if Seddon above had smiled upon the Nordish man with such an impressive gift, as an afterthought he had bestowed another: a quiver, filled with iron-tipped arrows. Ones made to penetrate armor at close range.

Or punch clear through a bare chest.

Chop hung the quiver over one shoulder, grimacing at the awkward burden, and picked up the bow. Sweat found his eyes, so he removed his mask and wiped his face and brow. The warm breeze felt good, so he decided to keep the mask off. As he was stuffing the material inside his armor, he noticed the skin on his hand bleeding through the mud he'd covered himself with. A fresh layer would be needed if he wanted to mask his scent from the wildlife of the Sanjou.

With everything gathered, Chop patted the nearby root of the giant tree and thanked it for guarding his few possessions.

Then he hurried away.

Trails crossed his path. Some were well trodden and worn, maybe used by the largely unseen game of the Sanjou. Perhaps by the very creatures searching for him. Some trails looked older, reduced to subtle partings of underbrush, no more than a week away from being completely overgrown. He stayed upon a path as long as it went in the direction he wanted. When it deviated, he left it and eased back into the bushes. The ceiling of interwoven foliage spread out overhead, thick in places, thin in others. Where the greenery was tattered, light shone through in long shafts broad and thin, diffusing the shadows. A moist sheen coated the vegetation, gleaming in both light and dark. Alien flowers with petals spread wide dotted the landscape, their many colors brightening the ground, even in the places where the sun failed to reach. Chop moved around huge flowering bushes of yellow and red. He ducked and weaved through the green-infused light, until he stopped on a slope. There, daylight spilled through a wide gash in the overhead canopy.

Through that rip he saw hills, perhaps less than a day away.

High ground.

Chop started moving again, through hazy veils of sunshine, through a haunting wilderness of unchecked vegetation perhaps thousands of years old. Things crawled and slithered away as he approached. Twice he stopped for snakes. Big, brutish creatures the length of four or five men, colored in diamond-shaped patches of slick yellow and brown. Chop avoided their heads and stepped over their slow-moving lengths, watching where he put his foot down. Bushes and vines brandishing stabbing needles and evil hooks tore at him. A part of him wanted to hack through it all, but he would do no such thing, knowing the Sanjou trackers would easily spot such signs. The Nordish man also had to be careful about where he squatted, for that matter. When he stopped for a rest, he did not sit, and he frequently adjusted his packs and quiver. The extra weight caused more sweat to ooze, enticing insects to pitch and probe, drawn to his smell despite his layer of filth. When he felt them, he pawed them away, tired of their bites.

The ground dipped and rose as he descended into thick jungle. Overgrown thickets clutched and clawed at him as he pushed through. Even worse, the plant life grew waist-high or higher, hiding his own boots, until he fell and splashed into a hidden stream. Thankfully, his fall stopped short on a small embankment. The knee-deep drop rattled him, and he took a moment to size up the water before pulling himself clear. Foamy clumps floated upon the stream's surface, stopping him from chancing a quick drink. He kept trekking forward, slowing his pace, a little more mindful of his footing as the land leveled out.

Daylight eventually dimmed, and he wondered if he'd lost his way. Not the case. The jungle ceiling thickened into a many-layered mesh, blotting out the sun. Shadows deepened, replacing the diffused light. He made his way through halls of wild-growing wonder, and not until midafternoon did the leafy covering thin out. Tattered holes in the foliage ceiling appeared, spilling sunlight onto the ground.

By evening, the Nordish man was near exhaustion, and unsure of how far away he was from the hills he'd glimpsed earlier. With no desire to travel at night, he chose to rest in a tall beast of a tree with thick limbs and its height concealed by dense vegetation. Slinging his bow over his head and shoulder, he tested both his grip and footing before starting up the trunk. In short time, he reached a suitable collection of branches well-hidden from the ground, one where he could nest without fear of falling. Below him was a screen of leaves thicker than any curtain. To either side, more leaves.

Chop peeled away his bow and packs and hung them from branches. His roost wasn't comfortable, but it was safer than sleeping on the ground. Settling in, he carefully fished out some strips of dried meat and a water skin. The food was edible, the water piss warm but wonderful, and he had to stop himself from gulping it all down.

Once fed and feeling somewhat content, the Nordish man leaned back and hooked his arms over a pair of tree limbs. Birdsong and buzzing insects filled the jungle heights, assuring him that he was alone. At least for the time being. He rubbed his nose and studied the many layers below him.

Nothing would see him up here. Smell, perhaps, but not see.

Feeling somewhat safe, he closed his eyes and relaxed.

And knew no more.

A great roar woke him, and he nearly jolted out of the tree. A deep nighttime darkness surrounded him, so he perked his ears, listening for danger. Eventually he settled back and wondered if he had dreamed the noise. A second roar cut through the stillness, however, a cavernous throat rattle that shivered the very air.

Worse still, the sound was getting closer.

Vegetation crunched under heavy but hesitant footfalls, as if a creature was finding its way. Wood splintered and snapped, the sound sharp and spine-straightening. More footfalls, long ponderous things that came down slowly, followed by branches rustling against an unseen mass. Then a great chuffing, low and wild, flaring from something massive.

Despite all his experience in the wilds of Nordun and Sunja, regardless of all the sights and frights he'd seen in his travels since then, Chop had no intention of investigating whatever was below him. None at all. So he stayed where he was, locating the sound as coming from his right. He licked at what was left of his lips, held on tight, and waited. Whatever the monster was, it had no concern for being quiet. And considering the amount of noise it was making, the thing had little concern of being challenged.

A great sinewy crackling then, slow and deliberate, of perhaps a tree being broken, or its limbs. A frustrated rattle of a grunt followed, loud enough, *close* enough for Chop to hold on even tighter.

Then nothing.

As if the creature had vanished.

There, in the dark, while perspiration trickled down Chop's face, all that noise simply ceased to be, as if he hadn't heard it at all. Which was troubling. He didn't move, didn't breathe. Fearing discovery, he steadied his breathing and waited. The mud and filth coating him from the day before had nearly worn off, and he hadn't bothered reapplying any more before climbing the tree. *Lords above*, he mentally groaned, and hoped the thing did not have his scent. Chop swallowed, and the resulting click warned him not to do it again. Still no sound from below. Time passed, instilling hope the creature had moved on by some sorcerous means. He slowly looked down and saw nothing but darkness, when a great huffing erupted, followed by a hurried walk. A thunderous, many-footed march.

Coming straight at him.

The ground trembled. The tree shook. Then a great and powerful intake of air followed by a death rattle of a growl right below him. A massive force hammered the base of his hidden perch, throwing him to one side. Leaves rustled as branches snapped under incredible force. The world trembled, then shook, and Chop held on for whatever he was worth. Something clapped him upside the head and withdrew. Leaves rained down as the beast slammed into the tree again, sending a shock through the base that shivered everything to the top. That deathly growl continued as the monster slammed the tree a third time, hard enough that Chop thought he heard the trunk *crack*. He braced himself as his world began to tip. The giant presence below had dug its heels into the earth and was *pushing* the tree, seeking to topple it. Things groaned and shuddered. Sinewy fibrous notes stretched out, reaching their breaking points before snapping with dull pops. The tree lurched with alarming intention, the roots straining against being unearthed.

The monster roared again, mustering all its strength for one last shove—before conceding in a wheezy huff and giving up.

As that terrible pressure relented, the tree righted itself just a little. Footsteps mashed the ground while the unseen thing drew in great, considering breaths.

Before moving off.

Chop waited, eyes wide and darting, listening to the creature lumber away. The footsteps receded, the noise softened into a distant thumping that haunted the dark wilderness. Then it faded away entirely, unaware of how close the Nordish man had come to squirting out a cow kiss.

Chop allowed himself to breathe. He listened, fearing that whatever had tried to uproot him might return.

And at some point, he eventually drifted off into an uneasy sleep.

CHAPTER 21

At dawn, Chop gathered his belongings and returned to the ground. It was a slow and awkward descent, where he had to constantly check his footing, until the previously impenetrable foliage disappeared beneath him. Chop stared in narrowed-eye wonder. Whatever had sought to topple the tree had left its mark. Most of the thick branches had been snapped off, leaving a series of raw stumps or limbs dangling by yellow fibers. That swath of destruction stretched some ten paces to the jungle floor, where a heap of wood lay, mashed flat.

With the way cleared, Chop had an easier time climbing down the tree. Once back on solid ground, the Nordish swordsman adjusted his things. He took a moment to marvel at the barrel-sized prints sunk deep into the soil. The monster had wandered in from the northeast, did a slow turn, and scrubbed its back on his tree before continuing south.

Chop headed northeast.

Whatever the creature was, it was enormous, and it had flattened much of the vegetation, allowing Chop an easy hike in the direction he wanted to go—toward a range of green mountains resplendent in the morning sun. The trail eventually veered away to the west, but Chop continued northeast. The underbrush and bright plants thinned. The land gradually sloped downward. The mountains' lush heights grew closer, rising dramatically and towering over the jungle floor, while flocks of winged specks glided across their faces.

Those mountains offered a safe place to rest, with a clear line of sight of anything coming after him. Even better, there would be little to no chance of being shaken from a tree by some unseen monster.

Chop strode down an incline, cutting through broad swaths of wild grass that reached his thighs. By noon, he had reached the bottom of the valley, where the grass flourished among a collection of crooked trees and white boulders perhaps tossed off the mountains by giants. The trees possessed grooved trunks and weren't nearly as tall as those behind him. They also grew strangely, with their limbs fanning out near the top, holding up broad flat hats of leaves.

Chop headed for the mountains. He glanced back when the urge took him and saw no sign of pursuit. At one point the grass thinned out into a rocky shoreline of orange-speckled pebbles. A shallow stream lay beyond, perhaps a dozen paces across, the surface sun dazzled. Seeing it was not deep, he waded in, the water warm and pleasant and reaching midshin. Once on the other side, he stopped upon a flat length of river rock and sampled the stream. One cupped handful and he deemed it good. Slabs of rock lay strewn along the shore, stretching off on either side for dozens of paces. Birds chattered nearby as he refilled his water skins, and when he finished, he stopped and gazed at the landscape he'd just left behind. It struck him that, while the Sanjou might very well be a place of legendary danger, inhabited by all manner of fiend and foe, it wasn't entirely unfit to the eye.

Returning the water skins to his packs, Chop started hiking for the nearest mountain. The incline rose sharply, letting him know his casual walk was over. Low shrubs grew underfoot, prettied up in places with small clumps of orange and yellow flowers. No trees grew for hundreds of strides on either side of him. At one point he stopped and turned around to see the stream he'd just crossed, and its jagged cut along the base of the mountain.

Then he was back at it.

Upward the Nordish man climbed, putting the occasional hand to a knee and pushing for that extra bit of effort. A breeze found him, making the ascent almost pleasant. The wind blew cooler the higher he went, lifting his spirits and suggesting he take a rest. So he stopped, turned around, and studied the lowlands he'd just crossed.

And blinked at the sight.

Beyond that wide stream far below lay a vast, unspoiled painting, with broad strokes of open grassland. Rising and falling flourishes of unspoiled nature dotted the jungle floor. Fat thickets of vegetation fanned out in pleasing green tiers on the far side, looking quite lovely despite Chop knowing better, having experienced it the night before. Those thickets and tiers stretched off into the distance and disappeared beneath a band of fog. Craggy mountains rose above that. Dark clouds drifted in from the west, warning of rough weather. Now that Chop stood above it all—what he considered the worst of it—the breadth and beauty of the land caught the Nordish man off guard. He scanned the vista from left to right and back again, unexpectedly moved by the Sanjou's plentiful charms, and breathed deeply of air hinting at rain.

The dark edge of the rain clouds crept in his direction, and even though it was blue sky over his head, he wanted to get higher before anything started to fall.

A fourth of the way up the slope, the underbrush frayed away in places, into grainy soil dusting flat rock. A crooked outcropping of boulders resembling an ogre's lower jaw jutted out some twenty strides straight above him.

Bent at the hips and truly pushing himself, Chop climbed for those rocks. A path crossed his trail, zigzagging upward, and after a moment's consideration he followed it the rest of the way. Hardpacked and grainy, the path eventually ended at the base of the outcropping. Chest heaving, a snarling Chop tossed his bow up and over those rocky battlements and heard it clatter on the other side. Then both packs went over, their cloth hides plopping on firm ground. Shallow indentations and grooves marked the stone, ideal for handholds, and he used them to haul his carcass up and over that irregular wall.

With a grunt and a flick of his legs, he dropped onto a grassy floor. Tired, Chop pushed away the packs and took a moment to compose himself. He lay upon a small but sizeable mountain shelf, covered in thin grass and ringed by boulders the size of barrels. A little courtyard, really, some forty strides long and twenty strides across. A single tree, tall and skeletal, sprouted from the courtyard's center. Beyond the tree stood a pair of white boulders, shaped like columns, leaning away from each other as if forced apart.

Revealing a dark cavern mouth between them.

The rest of the mountain rose steeply around Chop, covered in stubby plants. There would be no more hiking from this point, unless the cave turned out to be a tunnel that led all the way through to the other side. Truth be known, he wasn't that fortunate. On impulse, he clutched at the scrubby soil and felt the dirt under his fingernails. Letting that little fistful fall from his hand, he glanced back and beheld the Sanjou once again. The lofty nest offered an even better view of the valley, and an excellent place to camp. The slope below offered no protection for anyone seeking to climb up, all the way to the ribbon of water he'd crossed a short time ago. From there, the odd tree dotted an otherwise empty grassland, and anyone coming over all that in full daylight would be easily seen. With his bow and full quiver, Chop could hold off a large force for a very long time if needed.

Feeling uneasy with his good fortune, he considered the cavern behind him, curious about what might lie within. He kicked aside his packs, glad to be free of the weight, and leaned his bow and full quiver against the rocks. One hard snort of mountain air and, with his hands on his swords, Chop admired the view once more.

Lords above. The sight made him feel like a king. Or something like a king, he supposed. He'd still have to squat over the edge of the drop there, and clean his own blossom. That thought left a smirk on his ruined face. Having enough of that, he turned for the cave and hoped he'd found the perfect shelter.

The smell hit him not halfway to the tree, offensive enough to stop him in his tracks. *Shite.* The unmistakable smell of fresh shite. Pure and fragrant and repulsively hot, and strong enough to halt him on its gaseous border and back him up a step.

As there was nothing but grass and rock around the swordsman, Chop eyed the cavern as the probable source. Something was having regular squats up here. Mountain bears were not uncommon in mainland Zuthenia, or his native Nordun for that matter, but Chop had no idea what manner of beast might exist in this place.

Then he heard it.

Pebbles rolled and crackled off the mountain floor, followed by a feral snorting, a guttural rooting, from a creature aware it was no longer alone. An odd scratching then, short-lived but harsh, and a dark outline appeared within the shadows of the cave. There the shape lingered, shy of the day, yet drawn to investigate.

Chop extracted both blades, wondering if he could frighten the thing away. It was tall enough to be a mountain bear, but it stayed out of the light, giving doubt it was a bear or some similar beast. The brutish snorting grew louder, interspersed with a shuffling of padded feet over pebbled ground.

Whatever it was, it had the Nordish man's scent.

Chop flexed his arms and waited, expecting the worst . . . and stared in disbelief at what emerged from the cave.

A figure lurched into the light. Hunched-over and man-shaped, it was a broad mass of forest-brown fur, well adapted to hide within the shadows of a jungle. A squat anvil of a head lay between huge shoulders, and within a dirty orange face, a pair of bulbous red eyes fixed upon the Nordish man. Weeds and dead leaves dangled from its frame, including several gray slivers resembling bones. A few of those clattered to the ground as the thing lumbered forth, muttering all the way. It halted a step outside the cave and flexed its shoulders, as if stiff from narrow confines. Impossibly long arms reached out, ending in oversized hands. Spidery fingers stretched, tipped in claws, curved and black.

Those unblinking eyes glared at the man before it.

Heart pounding, Chop clanged his blades together, hoping to ward the thing off. The creature answered with a deep-rooted growling . . . but it didn't retreat. Didn't run away.

Instead, it charged, as if launched from a siege weapon.

An eye-watering, nose-rotting stink enveloped Chop as the creature closed the distance and lashed out—and missed. Chop nimbly ducked and darted away, allowing the thing to speed by.

The wall of boulders halted the monster, where it whirled, its long fur flying. It straightened, claws at the ready, and snapped a doglike maw. Yellow teeth flashed and stringy froth stretched to its chest.

It lunged again.

Those oversized hands repeatedly swiped for Chop as he ducked and dodged, avoiding the claws. With a frustrated peal, the creature swung for Chop's head, seeking to rip it from his shoulders in one powerful blow. The swordsman bobbed, escaping the claws, but not the lethal blast of putrid wind.

Stunned by its foulness, he lurched for the tree in the center of the little arena and got behind it.

Instead of pursuing, the creature straightened its loathsome frame and stared, as if surprised its meal still lived. Then the thing's eyes narrowed. It lowered itself into a predatory crouch, extending those fearsome claws. Bent over as it was, the creature matched Chop's height, and those egg-sized red eyes glared at him, their centers speckled by ink.

The eyes fascinated the swordsman.

Huge and red and staring, Chop found himself gazing, until the creature lunged—surprisingly closer than expected.

A claw hammered the tree, drizzling the air with splinters and driving the swordsman back. Chop sprang back in stunned wonder at the bit of sorcery he'd just witnessed. *The eyes*, he realized. The eyes had charmed him, *mesmerized* him, just long enough for the thing to get close and strike. Aware of the danger, he kept the tree between himself and the monster as it stalked him. He matched its moves, swords at the ready, keeping his eyes on the thing's chest.

The creature showed no fear of his edged weapons.

Chop decided to make it fear.

He leaned right, baiting the beast, then leapt back as the red-eyed fright darted forward, crashing its bulk into the tree while grabbing for the much nimbler swordsman. Claws slashed and clutched as it snarled yellow teeth and sprayed strings of slobber.

Rearing his arm back, Chop stepped in and hacked off one of those hands in a burst of scarlet and a flash of bone.

The growl switched into an agonized hiss as the monster yanked back its arm and clutched at its spurting wrist. It retreated, all the way to the wall of boulders.

Sensing the end, Chop pursued—when the beast abruptly halted and charged him, spreading its arms wide for an embrace.

With a speed unnatural, the Nordish man ducked and cut—three blinding slashes across the thing's midsection as it streaked by him. The creature staggered away, releasing another hiss of pain . . . before it rushed the swordsman again.

Chop avoided the sweeping arms, sliced the hairy torso to the bone, and sprayed blood in broad swaths.

Off-balance and bleeding heavily, the stricken monster stumbled away, red eyes wide and glaring. Its lower chest was a seeping wreckage, and every step left a red print. It retreated behind the tree, lumbering for the mountain wall, when it lurched to a stop and faced its adversary once more.

And again attacked.

This time, however, its wounds slowed both its speed and thinking.

Swords flashing, Chop parried a handless arm and hacked upward, splitting the monster's chin and whipping back its head. The thing crashed to the ground in a splash of dust and blood. There it trembled, releasing a growl that tapered off into a miserable mewling. With a shudder it rolled onto one side, conceding defeat, and drew up its thick legs.

Not trusting the creature, Chop skirted around those legs and sank a sword deep into its torso, stabbing for its heart. Steel rasped bone as the mountain monster seized up, pawing weakly at the killing blade. Then it crumpled and moved no more. Those great red eyes stared past the swordsman.

When Chop was certain it was dead, he set his legs and yanked his blade free. Tired but relieved, he sized up the beast, wiping his swords clean on its meaty corpse. He then withdrew, wincing at the stink and the blood seeping from the carcass. Those baleful eyes held his attention for moments longer. He'd seen tapestries in Zuthenia depicting great apes, but this creature was huge and powerful, its claws short and curved like filthy daggers. Hair covered its frame but failed to conceal the muscle beneath its hide.

It stank *worse* in death.

Repelled but also curious, Chop hesitantly leaned over the dead heap, studying this and that, mentally replaying the short but meaningful battle in his head.

When a familiar growl spun him around.

A second monster shambled forth from the cavern, hunched over and much larger than the first. Earth-brown hair covered its massive frame, while even bigger claws drooped from two enormous hands. Red eyes the size of fists squinted, flickering from Chop to the corpse at his feet.

The growling hitched to a meaningful stop.

Only to resume a touch harsher as the monster turned its baleful attention back to the Nordish man. That deep rumbling grew as the beast straightened, reaching an imposing height perhaps half a torso taller than the one before it. Bones popped. The monster rolled its broad, burly shoulders and stretched arms as thick as a man's chest. The jaws flexed, revealing knobs of black teeth, its maw more than large enough to fasten around a skull.

But the eyes . . . red and bright with hate.

The thing shuffled forward, watching the swordsman. The growling turned into a disturbing *chuffing* that ended with hard rolling clicks.

Bracing himself, Chop backed away, his swords unwavering.

Then the creature's chuffing ceased . . . and it roared. A bone-shivering blast that rooted the Nordish man to the spot. That shocking burst tapered off into a throaty growl, whereupon the monster's weaponized hands clenched and relaxed.

Chop rushed the towering creature.

That startled the beast. It reared back and clumsily swiped at the attacking man. Chop ducked under one arm and slashed at a meaty leg. The sword cut, cut *deep*, but failed to strike bone. He barely evaded a backswing, the wind alone nearly rolling him over. Wanting space, he retreated past the tree, stopping halfway to the rock wall.

Before him, his new opponent clamped a hand over its wound. Blood pulsed through its fingers. With a snarl it released its leg and crept forward with barely a limp, though its blood spattered the ground.

The hot sun pressed down as Chop backed up another step.

The fright stalking him matched his moves, flexing claws, while its mouth hitched up in a leer. It halted beside the tree, eyeing the swordsman and his weapons. Then, the creature did something unexpected. It gripped one of the nearby limbs and snapped the length free in a splintering of fibers.

Club in hand, the monster faced the swordsman once again.

A chill gripped the Nordish man, realizing the beast wasn't quite so mindless after all. Knowing what was about to happen, Chop again clanged his blades together, hoping to scare the thing off.

The monster instead charged.

Unhindered by its bleeding leg, the beast rushed forward a few steps and *threw* its weapon. That heavy, crooked length glanced off a dodging Chop, twisting him off his feet. Arms splayed, he fell flat on his spine.

No sooner did he hit the ground than he sought to regain his feet.

A shadow fell across him—much faster than expected—and claws hooked into his leather armor. With a roar that blasted the mountainside, the monster jerked the squirming swordsman off the ground and swung him around—all the way around—his arms and legs whistling through the air. The sky whirled blue and gray before Chop's vision, and he lashed out with his swords, flailing in all directions.

Until he struck meat.

A piercing shriek erupted from the beast then, but instead of releasing the Nordish man, it shook him. Shook him *hard*, like a living baby rattle. Chop's swords flew from his hands. His chin bounced off his chest. His remaining teeth clapped together, nipping his tongue while his limbs flopped about wildly. The cavern flashed by twice as he was again whipped around.

Before the monster flung him away.

At the tree.

Spinning end over end, Chop glimpsed the fast-approaching mass of unyielding wood a split instant before he slammed into it. Chest-first. His face punched *past* the granite trunk—just barely missing it—while his torso took the brunt of the impact. His breath left him in an explosive puff. Black motes burst within his vision as mind-robbing agony seared him from shoulder to hip and everything in between. Chop hung there for a heartbeat, dangling really, before crashing upon rocky soil. There he lay, crumpled, buckled, his senses unfit and swimming. His ears crackled and popped as if he were three paces underwater. He tried to rise, thought he was rising, until he realized he was tasting far too much dirt and rolled onto his back.

Claws grabbed the front of his armor and jerked him from the ground.

The monster shook him again, sloshing him and his juices about like a jug of cheap wine. His head snapped back and forth until a blast of hot, putrid air enveloped Chop's face. He glimpsed that awful maw spiked with black and yellow teeth, some pointed, some snapped off, but all opening *wider*. A second gust of rancid breath blew past him, threatening to melt his face completely from his skull, and *that*, along with the fact that he was about to have his head bitten off, jerked his senses back in a frightening snap of clarity.

The monster's face was *right there*, close enough to see the foul dew glistening upon its teeth.

Dazed and desperate, Chop aimed for a nose and smashed his forehead into the thing's lower jaw. Fragments flew while wet matter spattered the swordsman's face. A tooth gouged the curve of his skull, etching a spurting line over his right eye.

The monster squawked in pain and its eyes squeezed shut.

Half blinded by blood, Chop slammed his head into the mouth a second time.

The jaws clamped shut, becoming an oozing wreckage.

Chop grabbed two fistfuls of hair covering the thing's massive head. He dug his boots into something solid beneath him and rammed his forehead into that cringing face again and again.

An eye squeezed shut.

Its brow burst apart in a spurt of red.

Its nose flattened to one side upon a *fifth* blow.

Yet the thing held onto the swordsman.

Chop released the hair. He mashed his forearm against the creature's yielding nub of a nose. He shoved that face back, drawing another peal of pain while creating distance between him and a blood-spattered face. The thing wheezed with fury, speckling Chop with color and tiny shards. It wrapped its mighty arms around the swordsman's back and squeezed, buckling him. An agonized grunt left Chop as the beast crushed him against its chest and face.

Then its hold relented just a touch, as its grip wasn't yet set.

Half-dead as he was, Chop knew the next squeeze would break him, despite his armor.

Signaling that very intention, the monster screamed.

Chop screamed back.

And in the instant *before* the beast could crush him in one mind-freezing constriction of brute force, the swordsman stabbed both thumbs deep into those glaring red eyes.

The thing's scream became an ear-splitting shriek. Its arms tightened in reflex, the force overwhelming.

Gripping the head from *inside* of its ruined eye sockets, Chop shoved that wailing face away as his lower ribs shifted and creaked under irresistible pressure, igniting a sheet of pure, breathless fire that flashed up his spine and shot down his limbs. His breath left him in a gush and his chest compressed, coming dangerously close to not simply breaking but collapsing. He ceased all thinking except for his last fleeting action—worming his thumbs *deeper* into the monster's skull.

But still the thing held on.

The crushing pressure increased. The beast shook its head, jaws snapping, missing Chop's face as his vision blackened. His chest and spine edged closer to a shattering point, while his head and throat swelled close to bursting.

Whereupon he jerked his hands free in arcing black gouts and sank his fingertips deep into its throat.

Which collapsed like a rotten plum.

His body on the cusp of shattering, Chop ripped and clutched and ripped again. Red matter flew. Blood sprayed across his face. His consciousness waned, spun, and the world shimmered and darkened . . .

When the monster dropped him.

Chop landed in a heap. Reality continued to spin, but slower, becoming a soup of sparkling blackness that sounded like a wheezing old man. His back and chest greatly pained him. Every breath rattled and hurt. His senses left, only to return an instant later, while his chest fought with his guts—one wanted air, while the other wanted to purge. Unable to move, he stayed still, slowly becoming aware of the dreamy chatter of birds. His breathing evened out. His guts simmered down. The world returned, shapes formed within daylight, and the spinning slowed to a stop.

Breathless and nearly dead, Chop rolled onto his side, one hand pressed to his ribs. His whole chest ached dearly and every breath summoned fluttering black stars. With a groan he collapsed again on his back. There he stayed, breathing, able to move things and grateful to do so. The day seemed overly bright so he closed his eyes and rested a while, listening to the buzzing of insects.

In time, he turned his head to check on his adversary, and even that caused him great stabbing pain.

The creature lay not three strides away, in a pool of its blood. One huge hand clutched at its ruined throat, while the shattered shells of its eyes were turned to the sky. Flies covered the carcass in a teeming rug.

Chop looked away.

Cringing, moving feebly, he managed to get to his knees. His lower back felt wrecked, and when he chanced climbing to his feet, pain seized him and took him back down. The world tilted and bobbed, and there he stayed until the ground stopped tipping. In time, a wetness of some sort touched his lower legs, and he realized it was the juice stemming from the nearest carcass. The widening, spreading edge of the mess had reached him.

Remembering the unfit stink of beastman blood, Chop crawled away as best he could, to escape that terrible flow. As he moved, he neared one of his blades. Still not quite right in the head, he managed to get a hand on the hilt, and hauled it in close. The weapon didn't help, but he felt better having it.

Bleeding, dazed, every breath a stabbing intake that caused his eyes to water, Chop dragged himself back to the boulders. At some point he eased his back against one, and there he slumped. Colorful bruises bloomed up and down his body. An equal number of cuts bled. Another bolt of pain paralyzed him as he eyed the cavern, looming beyond the two carcasses splayed across the ground. He watched that opening, cringing, waiting for the worst. If there was a *third* pig-bastard lurking in there, he was as good as dead.

Metal tinkled as his sword slipped from his hand. Not that it mattered. He had no strength to lift it, anyway. A terrible thirst overcame him then, one not felt since his walk through the desert with He-Dog. The thought of his old companion brought the ghost of a smile to his ruined face. A terrible burning grew within his chest then. His entire frame trembled. The world darkened once more, and Chop's chin drooped, unable to stop himself.

Then he was falling, and the storm clouds moved in.

Unfit, he thought.

And blacked out.

CHAPTER 22

Ghosts filled He-Dog's vision.
Flittering, shadowy things, outlined by sharp flashes of light. They fussed over him. Leaning in, leaning out. Prodding and picking. They wiped down his face and body with wet cloths that felt soft and wonderful. Then they left. When the ghosts departed, He-Dog lay on his back, staring at a slanted moon overhead. Or at least he thought it was the moon. It was certainly round enough to be one, but squished for some reason, like a face. One that had been slapped by a maul. And when the light went out, the moon disappeared.

Which was all unfit in He-Dog's mind.

Also unfit was the time he spent sleeping. It seemed he slept a lot. The ghosts usually woke him. Once, when He-Dog felt he was a little more lucid than usual, he looked up and beheld the ghostly face of a smiling woman. Young, dark-haired, and lovely, and when she noticed him watching her, she smiled.

He-Dog noticed movement behind her. A dark figure tossed something onto a small fire. The shape disappeared, but the ghost in front of him remained. She leaned over He-Dog, the tips of her long hair tickling his face, the contact puzzling him. Flames flickered just beyond her outline, while an odd yet pleasing smell grew upon the air. Long poles arched upward all around them, meeting in a knot at a point above. High above that knot, the moon cast its pale light down upon them.

Then she was gone, and he slept again.

Echoing voices roused him, making no sense at all. That pleasant wood smoke hung about him in a deep yet comforting haze. He reached up to scratch at his face, and even that bit of contact felt . . . odd. As if his arm were stretching and contorting to do so. Something wet covered his chin, and when he inspected his fingers, the tips shone like melted wax.

"What's this gurry?" he asked.

"What's what?" a man's voice asked him back.

He-Dog didn't pursue the matter, forgetting what it was he wanted to know. "The . . . smell . . ."

"That . . . is what the Anoka call *wan-shol*."

"*Wan* . . . whaaat?"

Another ghost leaned in and smiled, this one male. "It's meant to relax you."

"Smells like . . ."

"Like sunbaked shite," another voice said.

The ghost frowned. "Well, I don't agree with that. It's supposed to relax you. And you all need relaxing. As well as healing."

"Healing?" a confused He-Dog repeated, trying to make sense of it all.

The ghost nodded. "Lords above, yes. You were all near death."

"Near death?"

The smiling woman returned. She placed a hand upon He-Dog's head and his eyelids grew heavy.

The ghost spoke again, but used a string of words that made no sense.

"We have to go now," it said. "Else I'll be dropping beside you. Just . . . relax. You're among friends. You're on the mend, so . . . let yourselves mend."

That hooked He-Dog's consciousness but did not arrest his slide into oblivion. "Chop?"

But the ghost was gone, in one of those bright flashes and a fluttering of distant thunder. Then the woman floated over his face again, the ends of her hair brushing his chest.

She smiled.

Just before he closed his eyes, He-Dog managed a little smile back.

When he woke again, a sheen of sweat covered him. The moon was back, but he saw it wasn't a moon at all, rather an oval cut in the ceiling above him. Daylight shone through that cut, illuminating the interior of the dwelling. Long, segmented lengths of wood ringed the walls like ribs, and a patchwork of dark material enclosed everything. He lay upon a mat, the only thing keeping him off the ground, and that ever-present smell of whatever was being burnt had diminished. The fire at the center of the floor had burned itself out.

A hand rested across his forehead, and He-Dog's breath hitched in his throat at the contact.

An older woman, her face familiar, hovered over him. She said something under her breath, the words a mystery, and stood.

He-Dog grabbed her wrist and held on.

"Where am I?" he croaked.

The woman's features creased in confusion and she tried to pull away.

"Where *am* I?" he repeated, louder that time, and held on even firmer.

Too firm, and the pain showed on her face.

He tried to rise but his frame would have no part of it, which was when he noticed he had been stripped down to nothing but a cloth covering his fruits. What wasn't covered had been painted in a dull coating of what might have been honey. The heaviest amounts were concentrated around the worst of his wounds.

"Lords above," he whispered.

The woman yanked her wrist free and fled outside in a flare of sunlight. The material covering the entrance rippled as she left.

A heavy aching pulsed from He-Dog's many hurts, the worst around the points where he'd been stabbed. He glanced around and saw two others, also stripped down to their covered fruits. Also gleaming with the same honey. Honey that smelled like an odd mixture of ash and exotic spice.

He let his head drop onto the mat.

"Scare that one off, did you?" asked Jers Snaffer.

He-Dog sighed. "Not on purpose."

A groan then, from the one called Kellic.

"Hurt?" Snaffer asked the younger man.

"Aye that," came Kellic's pained reply.

"Either one of you know who she was?" He-Dog asked.

No answer.

"Either one of you know where we are?"

Again, no answer. The lack of conversation from the two men was going to annoy him greatly. He-Dog grimaced. With Balless and Borus, it was getting them to shut up, but these two were a chore just to get talking.

"No idea?" he asked again, feeling something pull in his lower bits.

"None," Snaffer grumbled. "Where's the prince?"

He-Dog still didn't rightly care for calling Shay a prince. "I don't know."

"Have you seen him?"

"I haven't seen a thing. Been . . . sleeping, mostly. And when I was awake, it seemed like I was dreaming."

"I was the same," Snaffer muttered, a note of discomfort in his voice.

"As was I," Kellic added.

"We're not dreaming now," He-Dog noted. "Though I wish otherwise."

"Where's our armor?" Snaffer said, a hint of alarm in his voice. "And our weapons?"

He-Dog didn't know. Didn't bother answering.

"Where did she go?" Kellic asked, ignoring the question.

"Outside," Snaffer answered. "Probably to get the closest wildman."

He-Dog frowned at that.

"She was taking care of me," Kellic said. "I remember that."

"I remember that as well," He-Dog added.

"She was wiping me down," Snaffer growled. "All meat gets cleaned . . . before being tossed in a pot."

That deepened He-Dog's frown, and he was about to say something about how they were all still alive, when a hand pulled back the hide hanging over the entrance. A dark-haired man walked in, bare-chested, muscular but not overly so, and quite tall, crouching to fit within the dwelling. A great black beard, perhaps trimmed by a stone knife, covered his face. Like them all, he only wore a loincloth. Glaring button eyes studied them from underneath a low brow, and on one side his mouth hitched upward in a scowl.

"Lads," he spoke in Zuthenian with a dip of his head, surprising the lot of them. "Who grabbed the woman's wrist?"

Silence, for a good three heartbeats, before a wary He-Dog raised a hand.

"Bit harsh," the man said. "You put a right and proper fright in her, and she's been looking after you. Washing. Cleaning. *Feeding.* Minding your bandages and oils. All that. So don't grab her again," he warned with a finger. "Not unless you want me cracking your head. Not unless you want the whole *village* cracking your head. You understand me?"

A harsh burn of shame overcame He-Dog. "Apologies," he said in a tired voice and meant it. "I wasn't thinking."

The man studied him, weighing the apology, and his stern expression softened. "Well . . . I'll tell her that. So, you're all awake. I can see why. The fire burned out. No wonder you're . . . in a grabbing mood. The smoke relaxes you but when it's gone, well . . . no matter. We'll get that going again."

"You're one of us," He-Dog said.

"He's not one of us," Snaffer growled.

"No," the man smirked. "I'm *not* one of you. Suppose I *look* like one of you. Been a long time since I've spoken Zuthenian. Spoken to anyone from Zuthenia. Or anywhere else for that matter. And your accent is one I haven't heard in years. What are your names?"

He-Dog stared for a moment longer before answering. "He-Dog."

"He-Dog, you said?"

"Aye that."

The man regarded the others. "What about you two, then?" He got the sullen replies of unwell men knowing they'd been captured.

"Kellic, you said?" the man asked. "Snaffer? Must say, you're both brutes. You're *all* brutes, truth be known. Hard on the eyes. *Hard.* You were harder still to look at when they first found you. Smelling of blood and unwashed blossoms. Unfit. No one wants that, I'll tell you. They said they smelled you a day before they found you. A *day.* You look like you just finished a war."

No one spoke.

"Well then," the man continued, nodding. "I'm called Broska. Of Zuthenia, which you've already guessed. Welcome to the Sanjou."

No one said anything to that either, until Kellic cleared his throat. "Where's our captain?"

"He's alive. Being cared for. Unlike yourselves, the Anoka are still burning the *wan-shol* for him."

The *wan-shol.* He-Dog remembered that, and he placed the Zuthenian's voice as the one who had been talking to him before, when he was dreaming. Or when he *thought* he was dreaming.

"What took his leg?" Broska asked.

"Bloodfish, in the river," Kellic answered.

The Zuthenian let off a distasteful sigh. "Bloodfish. Hm. Not surprising. We found you at the very edge of Iruzuland. That whole area is surrounded by a sloppy lace of rivers, and each one is infested with the damned things. Murderous little pissers. Murderous. They're not as big as those found in the Harudin, but they're every bit as vicious."

The three mercenaries absorbed that.

"You got your senses back?" Broska asked, changing the subject.

"Senses?" He-Dog asked.

"Think you can talk? Without sounding like you've downed a jug of firewater? Hm? Or taken a bootheel to the face?"

"That what you've been giving us?" Snaffer asked. "Firewater?"

"Had to give you something," the Zuthenian explained with a sniff that wiggled his beard. "Either the smoke of the *wan-shol* or a club upside the head. Don't think you wanted a clop, the hard way you all look. Lords above, you were fortunate. The *wan-shol* is what the Anoka give their warriors wounded in battle. It . . . lessens your senses, as you've found out. It pinches time, makes a week seem like a day. They say you were being devoured by the *krila* out there. You know what the *krila* are? Unfit insects. Clouds of them. They swarm a man just like bloodfish. Worse, the flying maggots carry a venom. Mild enough when it's only one, but if you're caught in a swarm? Like you lot were? Weakens you. Enough to drop you. Then the *krila* drink you dry. Until you're nothing but skin. Bones. Gurry for the crawlers. You were covered in the *krila* when they found you. Fortunate for you . . . you all decided to lie on your bellies and cover your faces. The *krila* attack the eyes first. Blind whatever it is they're feasting on. Not so mindless, I'd say. Not at all. I've seen dead men without a drop of blood in them. Not a *drop*. And their eyes? All shriveled up like, like . . . I don't know what. But shriveled up inside their faces. Horrible to see. Horrible. In any case, you were all close to dying."

That silenced the three men.

"If you have your senses back," Broska said, "I'll answer your questions. You probably have a few, right?"

He-Dog didn't hesitate. "Where are we?" he asked, not entirely certain he did have his senses back.

"In the village of the Anoka, the people that saved all three of you."

"Four," Snaffer corrected in a wary tone.

Broska's bearded face darkened. "Your captain is alive, but . . . well . . . the bloodfish took his leg. And what was left was rotting. Rotting. All yellow and red and festering. We had to take it off. Burn it. It was that or . . ." he trailed off. "The other leg isn't much better but it's there. He might be able to use it. Maybe."

"Where is he?" Snaffer demanded.

The Zuthenian pointed at the wall. "In the next lodge. You can see him anytime you wish."

Snaffer made to rise but stopped halfway, all color leaving his face. With a sickly scowl and a shiver, he lay back down and held his head.

"The smoke does that," Broska explained, teeth flashing in a little smirk. "When you've been sucking it in as long as you have. It'll wear away. But until then, don't stand up. The world will spin on you and there's a good chance you'll empty your guts on whatever's nearby. Don't do anything fast. And mind yourselves when you squat. Use both hands when you—"

"We need to return to our ship," Kellic weakly interrupted. "And leave this place."

Serious once again, Broska frowned and scratched at an ear. "Apologies. Your ship was sunk. Our scouts traveled to the coast. There's an inlet where ships usually drop anchor. It's well-known to us. I don't know why ships like to drop anchor there, but they do. Anyway, yours? Sitting on the bottom of that inlet right now. Or at least I'm guessing it was yours. They saw her masts sticking out of the water, and some debris on the beach. Along with the crew. What was left of them, anyway. Dead to a man."

The news stunned the three men.

"Dead to a man?" Kellic repeated. "What do you mean? Do you mean . . . we're—"

"Stranded here, aye that," Broska said, nodding. "Mind now, it's not so bad, so don't look like that. You'll . . . get used to it. And if not . . ."

He shrugged, as if there was little choice in the matter.

"If not *what*?" Snaffer pressed with rising, but sleepy, anger.

"You'll live or perish," came the plain answer. "By something. Someone. Or by your own hand. You're not prisoners here. At least not yet."

Again the smirk.

That bit of information silenced Jers Snaffer, perhaps still affected by the *wanshol* smoke. Kellic looked as if he'd taken a long-barbed lance through the belly and had watched it go through him.

He-Dog . . . didn't know what to think. At least not yet. "There were others," he finally asked.

"We found only you," Broska said with a hint of sympathy. "Might I ask . . . why are you here?"

"Treasure," He-Dog said, ignoring the hard look from Snaffer. "Searching for treasure."

"Ah. And you found death instead. This is the Sanjou, right? No doubt you've heard the stories. You should have heeded them. Stayed clear. Well . . . you're not the first looking for riches. Won't be the last."

"Is that how you came to be here?" He-Dog asked.

"What? No. No, I was here for a different reason. To explore this place. For Zuthenia. They had notions of claiming the Sanjou for their own. Like you, we found only death. Death, death, and more of that unfit slop. The whole expedition. Strung up, chopped down, or just right and proper butchered. Dead. I was fortunate, however. The Anoka found me. Allowed me to stay. Been here ever since."

As he finished, another man entered the lodge in a blinding flash. A gray-haired individual, with skin nearly roasted to leather by the sun, and wearing only a sliver of clothing that barely concealed his manhood. The old man squatted next to Broska, giving He-Dog a glimpse of aged fruits he did *not* need to see. The old man carried a makeshift torch, while a tanned satchel slapped against his thigh. He quickly dropped the torch into the fire pit while speaking to Broska. The Zuthenian answered. The old man then reached into his bag and pulled out a handful of what looked like ordinary shrubs, which he tossed onto the flames. Wiping his palms, the old man studied each mercenary in turn, his lips tightening into a knot of appraisal. Then he rose again, satchel swinging off his bony hip, and left the lodge.

"That was Peaceful Moon," Broska informed them. "He's the Anoka healer and spirit man. He's also been taking care of you. The woman you grabbed? She helps him."

"The lad's unfit," He-Dog muttered.

"Unfit? Why do you say that?"

"The topper's wearing less than you," Snaffer said with distaste.

The smoke wafting from the pit gave Broska's answering smile an odd glow. "Different land, lad. Different style of dress. You'll see. I must leave. That's *wanshol* burning. Peaceful Moon just threw it onto the fire. If I stay, I'll fall under its spell, which won't please my missus. Then again, I suppose I wouldn't care. Anyway, I'm off."

With that, the Zuthenian rose and turned to leave. When he moved, waves of shimmering light rippled about him.

"Rest a bit more, lads," said Broska. "And know this . . . you're among friends here."

It was the smoke, of course, but He-Dog believed every echoing word.

CHAPTER 23

Searing heat brought Chop back to consciousness.
   With a pained snarl, he cracked open his eyes and stared at a dead monster, the one clutching at its ripped-out throat. Black flies buzzed about and festered the carcass, from its gruesome eye sockets to the bottoms of its toughened feet. Worse was the smell from the thing, a putrid stink of meat spoiling in the sun, tainting the very air around it. Something was wrong with the sight, however, and it took Chop a moment to realize it was his own right eye. A careful prodding revealed that side of his face had swollen to epic proportions, narrowing his vision to a slit. Dried blood crumbled upon further poking, from an assortment of crusted over cuts and ugly rashes. Even better, he discovered a collection of raised welts and tender bruises.

Chop sighed, knowing he had suffered a right and proper thrashing.

But he still drew breath.

Groaning, holding his ribs, he rolled onto his stomach with all the grace of a half-crushed corpse, suffering, whimpering at the debilitating pain in his chest and lower back. He pushed himself, but the pain seized him every time, forcing him to stop. Every deep breath sparkled, and since his ribs hurt, all he wanted were deep breaths. His armor hid the damage underneath but considering the red and purple blooms covering his exposed bits, he suspected the worst. He swallowed thickly, wishing for water, and remembered the packs he carried. The urge to cough took him. He did so, weakly, spitting at the end, gasping from each boot kick of agony that took him. When he recovered, he examined what he'd spat onto the ground, and saw no blood. Small mercies there, he supposed. He felt his face again, hissing at the worst of it. His limbs were intact, but his lower ribs and spine felt crushed. Flies droned around his face.

The vermin scattered as Chop struggled to rise. He planted his forehead (careful of the tender spots) to the ground and drew in his knees.

That effort alone nearly dropped him.

Sunburned and stiff, every movement stabbed at him like daggers through his joints. When he made it to his knees he wavered and glanced around, sputtering for breath.

His packs leaned against the rock wall . . . a good ten paces away.

Unfit.

Groaning, Chop started crawling, moving as if he'd taken a dozen iron-tipped arrows to the front and back. Several times he stopped, blacking out twice, for unknown lengths of time. The sun was still shining when he opened his one good eye, so that was fine, and he eventually reached the packs.

It took time to crawl over to the boulders. There he rested, gathering his strength for the next two feats.

One was sitting up, getting his back to a rock. The other was opening a pack.

A water skin waited within, warm and bloated. The smell woke an urgent need that he hadn't felt since crossing the desert with He-Dog.

He-Dog.

He hoped the man was doing better than he was.

Hands shaking, Chop labored to extract the skin. He nearly dropped the hateful thing when he uncorked it. If that had happened, daresay he would have licked the water from the ground. He fastened his ruined lips around the spout and drank.

Sweet Seddon above, that was good.

Water dribbled down his chin and neck, and he let it, feeling—almost hearing—the sizzle upon his skin. The Nordish man downed two cups' worth, mindful of drinking too much too soon. He then sealed the container and dropped it in his lap. Panting, cringing, he adjusted himself against the rocks and slumped.

After a time, he lifted his head and saw he was still alone.

How long had he been on the mountain? No idea. He arched his back too fast and a spear's worth of agony ripped through his guts, snatching his breath away. Relaxing, Chop considered the backpack. There was food in there. Despite his wrecked condition and the unfit stink hanging around, he realized he was ravenous. After a feeble search, he pulled out some of the orange fruit he had picked and bit into it.

Sweet. And full of juice.

The first rotation of his jaw shifted a tooth near the back of his mouth, resulting in a spike of agony he could have done without. Chop dropped the fruit, stuck a pair of fingers in his mouth and poked around. Three back teeth were missing. Two below, one above. All on the right side. The one remaining tooth there wobbled under a fingertip.

Upon a little extra pressure, the whole thing came out.

A weary and disbelieving Chop extracted the tooth, not remembering when any of that had happened. He examined its bloody roots and sighed. Good thing he'd started with the fruit. And he supposed he would have to be even more careful with the meats. Those dried strips were tough.

Not having the strength to toss the tooth, Chop let it fall from his hand. The rest of his teeth remained, so he was thankful for that. He picked up the fruit, blew gently on it, and managed another bite. Flies landed on the raw cavities dimpling the food, but they quickly sped away as if the sample was not to their liking.

Chop ignored them.

Long shadows stretched from the mountain face, creeping toward the stricken swordsman, informing him the day was getting old. Chop felt as boiled and cured as the armored vest he wore, and he patted the thing fondly, thanking it for saving his hide.

He decided he needed to move. If he stayed in the open, he would become a strip of boot leather. A fit of coughing overtook him, dry hitches that hooked and hurt with every bark. When it passed, he spat in his hand and again saw no blood. Broken ribs, he supposed. Just enough to make his final days miserable.

He regarded the cave entrance.

His broken and battered body warned him to move slowly as he pulled himself to his feet, using the boulders at his back. With a loud groan he stood and swayed. The world spun, threatening to topple him, so he plopped down on a rock until it passed. When it did, he regarded the packs and his swords. His bow and quiver rested nearby as well.

It took time, but he managed to pick up one blade, and felt better for it.

Then he eyed that dark cavern mouth once again.

Shuffling past the two blood-matted creatures that had nearly done him in, Chop dragged himself toward the cave. The flies ignored him, their shiny numbers flickering over pools of gore dried to a black gruel. He again wondered how long he had lay there, unconscious, and thought that a day was about right. At least a day. Maybe two, but no more.

His shrunken stomach rolled and threatened to revolt, warning him he'd drunk too much water. And the fruit wasn't treating him fairly either.

Shadows of birds sped across the white rock around the cavern entrance. Chop reached the opening and leaned heavily against one side. A gut-twisting stink backed his head up on his shoulders.

Unfit, he moaned inwardly, recognizing the smell of a den. If the walk over here hadn't upended his guts, going in *there* most certainly would.

Hating the next part, he tapped the rock with his blade and waited.

When nothing showed itself, Chop proceeded inside.

Walls of smooth, bare rock were split by cracks and veins of dirt where clumps of weeds sprouted. The cave itself was not wide. With his shoulder against a wall for support, he was able to easily reach the other side with a fist. A rug of fur and debris covered the ground. Scarlet crawlers slunk underfoot and along the walls, many-legged and longer than a finger. White spiders skittered away in a hasty retreat.

Chop ignored the insects and headed deeper within the cave. At one point he stopped and rested. Listened.

No sound. And the dark cave continued deeper into the mountain.

Unwilling to go any farther without light, he returned to his packs, learning his limitations with every agonizing step. Once outside, he fished out a flintstone and steel from a pack. Groaning, flustered with his lack of motion, he gathered up a small pile of grass, twigs, and branches. It took time. A lot of time, really, but he cobbled together a makeshift torch. Took even more time to light it, with frequent rests, and he didn't care about the smoke.

Chop returned to the cave, torch held waist-high and practically dragged his sword behind him.

The light repelled the crawlers, sending them scurrying into cracks. What stayed behind he gave a taste of fire as he crept deeper into the dark. The air cooled, and some thirty paces later, or his staggering equivalent, he reached a grand inner chamber. Firelight flickered over an oval-shaped room, stretching away from the corridor he'd just come through. A startling collection of animal bones, big and small, covered the floor. Human skulls peeked out as well, colored orange by the torchlight, the jaws clamped shut or missing entirely.

Those bony remains held Chop's interest for a short but meaningful moment, before the sound of trickling water reached his ears.

A ledge the length of three men ran along the northeast wall. At one end, water spilled down the side. It pooled in a natural basin of stone, before overrunning and emptying in yet a larger one below it. From there, the overflow emptied into a split in the rock floor. Even more interesting was a fat vein of white rock that sparkled in the torchlight. It wasn't gold. Nor was it related to a gemstone, but its bulging streak reached from floor to ceiling.

The rest of the rock shelf was dry, resembling a hard bed big enough to keep two Sanjou ogres off the floor. Chop stumbled through the bones and, with a sigh, sat on the edge of that stone bed. He slid over to the water basin and brought a handful to his nose. Sniffed and tasted. Clean and good. A pure natural spring. He now understood why the creatures had chosen this place as their home. It was located on high ground, offered a perfect shelter with its own clean water source, and was hidden away by boulders encircling it all (although part of him wondered if the beasts had placed those there themselves).

And the stupid things had turned it all into an unfit pisspot.

The stink of unwashed fur and dried offal threatened to overcome him, so Chop decided to leave. His torch died within a few strides of daylight, so he tossed the thing aside and staggered to a stop upon the cavern's threshold. Though the sun had passed overhead, granting shade to this side of the mountain, it was still insufferably hot.

Letting out a breath, Chop leaned his sword against a wall. He then winced as he removed his bracers and greaves. After that, he unfastened the buckles along the sides of his leather vest and slid carefully out of his armor, mewling all the way, before letting the hateful shell drop. The saturated cloth shirt underneath stank from sweat both old and fresh. Peeling himself free from that was harder to do than the armor, and his skin gasped at being separated from the filthy layer.

He got it off and dropped it on the armor.

At the end of his strength, Chop lowered himself to the ground, the rock clawing at his sides and back. Not satisfied with sitting, he studied the cloth over his leather and decided it would do. It took energy he didn't have, but he lay down, placing his head on the hard, stinking pillow of cloth and leather.

In no time, he was asleep.

The next day Chop decided he'd get his matters organized.

Moving at a slug's pace, Chop went about cleaning his little mountain fortress.

With another crooked branch taken from the tree, he swept what he could from the cave, starting from the very rear, back into the light. What he couldn't sweep, he carried, suffering all the way, heeding his body when it warned him to stop. The two carcasses continued to stink, and even attracted the evil attention of large birds circling overhead. Fearing further damage to himself if he attempted to lift the corpses, Chop decided to carve them up. He tied his fragrant shirt around his nose and mouth, pulled out his sword, and proceeded to cut the creatures apart, right down to the grisly bones.

Eventually, Chop was able to heave the chunks over the boulder wall. It was bloody, nasty work. Filthy and rotten, staining his hands and arms to the elbows, and spattering his lower bits to his knees.

He did it, however, over the course of two days.

He ate what he had in the backpacks, rationing as much as he could, knowing he'd have to replenish his supplies soon somehow. Water wasn't an issue, as the cave provided plenty. He drank from the high basin and washed himself and his few bits of clothing in the lower one. He used fire sparingly, burning the part of the cave the monsters had used for squatting. During that one cleansing burn, the resulting smoke forced him outside, and every barking cough threatened to split his ribs.

While he recovered, he looked out over the Sanjou valley, searching for any signs of the fishmen. The gray curls billowing from his cave worried him—the longer the smoke lasted, the more time he spent scanning the valley, listening, watching. Before he knew it, the sky had faded from blue to gold, to a deepening band of purple.

He fell asleep against the rocky battlements just as the first stars appeared in the night sky.

A few days later, Chop couldn't decide if his cleaning efforts had improved the smell of the cave, or he'd simply become used to it. His ribs and assortment of bruises had not improved, nor did he expect they would for a while. Worse, his food supplies were down to nothing. He had one piece of orange fruit remaining, squished and soft, and a handful of meat strips. Enough for one more day, and that would be that.

Not ready to perish from hunger, Chop considered the stream far below and thought of fish. Or some other wild game, either drinking from the water or hiding in the surrounding grassland. A little flock of those evil carrion birds with mottled feathers and hooked beaks feasted on the remains of the mountain beasts he'd thrown below. The creatures had steadily devoured the decaying mess over the last few days. The birds stayed clear of him, however. One of them would make a meal, but Chop wasn't steady enough to take one down with an arrow.

The stream might be his best chance, but that meant going down there.

And though it was a long walk down, it would be a longer, harder walk back up to his mountain lair.

Not going down there meant he would have to start eating crawlers.

He got to work.

Using a blade, he stripped down the same branch he'd used to sweep the cave and made a walking stick. Then he pulled on his boots, fastened his belt around his narrow hips, and picked up a single sword. He left his shirt and armor, as pulling them on would have been agony. He did manage to get a pack across his back, and hoped he wouldn't perish on the way down.

The boulders ringing his nest caused him to wince. They were unfit to get up and over before. They would be torture now.

And he was right. Getting over that wall proved to be an excruciating experience, but he got down without killing himself, though at times he wondered where the ground was as his feet kicked at empty space. Once below the rocks, he sized them up and hoped he would be able to haul himself back over them when he returned.

From there he hobbled down the slope, every shuddering step feeling like he was lowering himself into a boiling pot. The sun cooked him. His chest and knees ached from the exertion. Perspiration coated him in a shiny, annoying sheen. His stomach rumbled constantly, joining in on his unhappy mood. He shook his stick at the carrion birds when he neared them, failing to drive the bone pickers from the last of their feast. Chop eyed the grisly remains of the two dead monsters, surprised at how little was left of the creatures.

The birds eyed him back. They were large, ruthless creatures, a dozen of them, as tall as his waist. Killing one of the evil things might not drive the rest away, and he wasn't sure if they would fight back.

Wary of the feathered bastards, Chop moved on.

In time, he reached the bottom of the slope and soon located the same orange-speckled rock he'd stopped at when he first crossed the stream. There, he searched for signs of danger before deciding to go fishing.

Nothing. Not a dart nor a flicker.

Grumbling, he trudged along the shore, minding his step while weirdly shaped insects buzzed past his face.

Still nothing, and the exertion of his search was more taxing than he expected. He hobbled along another hundred strides or so (each step really half a stride) to a cluster of trees leaning over the stream. The shaded water looked deeper, perhaps thigh- or even waist-deep. Fish breached the surface, stirring up fat flies that dotted the water. Fish streaked underneath as well, flittering over a pebbled bottom.

Chop edged closer to the bank when one rock rolled out from underfoot and he was launched into the water with a splash. His back slammed against the shore, leaving him breathless from the impact. There he lay, grunting at the fiery aches along his ribs. In time the sensation receded, and he flopped onto his belly. Suffering, angry with himself, he pulled himself out and stood.

Damnation. The very last thing he needed right now.

Dripping, aching, he shambled away, his interest in fishing gone.

He picked his way back up the slope, looking this way and that, stopping several times to rest. By late afternoon, he struggled over that ogre's jaw of rocks surrounding his mountain nest, collapsing on top from the effort. There, he took long moments to recover, watching the small valley, bright and certainly charming under sunny skies, right up to where the jungle began.

Hard rock pressed against his cheek as he stared at the sight. There was food out there somewhere. All he needed to do was find it.

Until then, he ate half of what little of his supplies remained.

When he finished, he retrieved his bow from beside one of the boulders. He tested the drawstring, pulling only halfway before his back and chest warned him to stop. Ignoring both, he took a quick breath, assumed an archer's stance, and pulled the string all the way back to his ear.

His ribs protested but he held the pose, long enough to loose an arrow. Pleased that he could handle at least one shot, he relaxed the bowstring and inhaled sharply without thinking. Pain clutched him throughout, causing him to bare teeth. Chop dropped the bow and pressed a hand to his tender spots.

Lords above. He was in a troublesome knot.

That night, after a scorching day, Chop lay on the stony bed at the rear of the cave. Water trickled in the dark, the sound oddly comforting, until he heard and felt the deep rumble of his stomach. Felt the nagging pangs of hunger, soft at the moment, but promising to worsen. He placed a hand over his belly, hoping it might quiet until morning.

And that's how he fell asleep.

CHAPTER 24

Two days later, his pack long empty, Chop feebly descended to the stream once again.

This time, he carried his bow and quiver.

The fish proved to be far too fast for him, however. He released two arrows at his targets, missing both times. Not willing to retrieve the shafts in the watery depths, he let them be. He drank a few handfuls to ease the grumblings of his stomach, which helped matters for only a short time.

Giving up on the fish, Chop trudged back up the slope, searching the grasslands for berries or edible greens along the way. He picked a few thistles and weeds that looked favorable but spat them out quickly upon tasting them.

The carrion birds were gone, and no bird of any size flew near him, as if knowing full well he was dangerous. There were no signs of rats or mice or similar vermin—but there was one creature that thrived all around him. Some the length of his fingers.

Crawlers.

The very thought slouched his shoulders.

It wasn't the first time he'd had to resort to eating such fare, but he'd loathed it enough to not want to do it ever again. Still, he needed something in his belly.

From that point on, Chop started prying rocks free from the earth. The smaller ones he flipped over and examined the pockets beneath. Some had spiders too fast to catch, but others held the familiar, many-legged frights that he was looking for. Those he killed, crushing their heads with a quick pinch, ignoring the brief resistance of their shells before the unpleasant crunch.

By midafternoon, he returned to his roost and laid out his catch on top of a waist-high boulder. Nearly two dozen of the monsters, their orange-brown carapaces intact and edged by a multitude of nasty little legs. And the crown jewels of the hunt—a pair of beetles, green-shelled and horned, each roughly the size of a fat plum. These were the juicy ones, the ones he could pick up and behead with his fingers, leaving the white contents of their fat shells intact.

He gathered what wood he could scavenge off his home's single tree, then piled his bundle into a little fire pit he'd dug out near the cavern entrance.

Dropping to his knees, he filled the pit with twigs and grass. He figured his sword blade was just wide enough to lay half his catch upon, so that he could at least warm his meal to a point. The thought of eating something solid actually made his mouth water . . . until the flapping of wings whipped his head around.

A mottled carrion bird, poised over Chop's catch on the boulder, gulped down one crawler and helped itself to another.

Chop yelled at the thing, an inarticulate bark of rage.

Not enough, however, as the beast plucked up another beakful and gobbled it down.

The Nordish man limped to his feet, grabbed a handful of dirt, and flung it at the bird.

The animal took wing, hopped off the rock, and disappeared from sight.

With an angry squawk, Chop hobbled over to where he'd laid out his meal. Three crawlers were missing—robbed and devoured by the winged hellion. Fuming, he gathered up the remainder and returned to his fire pit. There he kept his food close while he started the fire. Once he had it going, he placed what was left on the flat of his blade and laid the weapon across the pit.

Not long after, he popped the first crawler into his mouth.

Crunchy. Gummy. With a taste close to a tree nut. A *warm* tree nut, with some burnt bits that couldn't be helped. He then rushed the beetles onto the fire, mostly because he was impatient with hunger. The thickness of their shells prevented him from biting into the things, so he cracked and picked off the scorched bits, enough to suck the contents out.

Soup. Just like warm soup . . . from the filthiest pot. The taste wasn't unpleasant, but the texture was a touch . . . runny.

He ate everything.

That night he lay on his back, on a cool bed of stone, staring up at the dark sky. Every now and again he shifted, releasing a little grunt of discomfort for his trouble. When he lay still, trickling water filled the silence. The day's events filled his head, followed by thoughts of tomorrow. He'd have to scour the slope again for food, but he had a feeling he would not collect nearly enough. Crawlers lived in the cave, but those would be harder to catch as they lived within the cracks in the rock. And he would need to light another torch to see what he was hunting.

Crawlers.

That hitched up a corner of his ruined face. The unfit thing was . . . they didn't taste that bad. He'd heard tales of Nordish soldiers running out of food for one reason or another and having to consume awful things in order to survive. He'd done the same once, which was enough for him. Until now. His father would have been amused to know what his son had done to survive the day.

That unlocked a memory. Chop had never really known his father, except that he was a Nordish soldier, a Jackal, like himself. The Jackals were the twisted dagger within the Nordish army, excelling at stealth and silence rather than the slow procession of infantry or booming charge of lancers. His mother had perished when he was young, as had his two sisters and older brother. Chop had been a boy of merely five or six. His family had lived on a farm, at the very edges of a small forest. Chop . . . well . . . that wasn't his name back then, but he remembered his mother, sisters, and brother, had gone into that forest one day in the summertime. Looking for wild herbs or shrubs or something to put into a pot of soup. Chop was with his father when it happened. His father had been showing him how to fashion a wooden pipe.

Chop hadn't heard the screams, but his father had—or so he overheard him say later. At the time, however, his father threw down his knife and length of wood and told Chop to stay in the house. His father then grabbed his scabbard hanging from a peg near the front door and rushed outside.

Chop could not remember what happened next. Didn't need to. His father had returned home, but the rest of his family had not. Chop believed they were later buried on the farm somewhere, but he couldn't be sure. He remembered being very sad at that time. Remembered missing his mother, sisters, and brother dearly. He also remembered his father and some other men going back into the forest, but not all of them returned. His father had and would never speak of what had happened in those woods. Chop assumed something had killed his family, whereupon his father and a hunting party went out and killed the creature back.

Or so he liked to think.

A few years later, his father went off to war—the Nordish-Sunjan War—and left Chop with an elderly couple. His father never returned, and word was he'd perished somewhere in that foreign land, his body never found. He had been a brave man. A kind and good man. Or so the elderly couple told Chop, and he believed them. His father had been all those things and Chop, like most young boys, wanted to be like him. So he stayed in that little home until he was in his midteens, and every now and then his departed mother would visit him. In his dreams. Sometimes his sisters visited him. Sometimes his brother.

His father never did.

Chop left that little home just after entering adulthood and joined the Nordish Jackals, as his father had done. The Jackals trained him in a very specialized aspect of war, and over time, fashioned and sharpened him into a weapon. And it was after that, fighting alongside other Jackals on the Nordish-Sunjan front, that he'd lost his old name. Along with his face.

And became nameless.

For refusing to carry out an order from his commander. An order Chop did not want to remember.

He had lost his face, and perhaps a little bit of his mind, as punishment but Chop had survived. He abandoned the Nordish army and fled from Nordun entirely. Since then, he had taken part in some particularly vicious campaigns, all of his choosing, surviving them all. Until he'd reached this place. Alone once again, broken but not quite dead, reduced to picking up insects from under rocks on the side of a mountain.

And very far away from civilized lands.

He had survived to this point, however, and he would continue to survive tomorrow. And the day after that. For as long as he could. Like all those times before, for his father, whose face he could no longer remember. And for the memory of his mother, sisters, and brother, all of whom no longer visited him in his dreams.

Until he finally discovered the greatest mystery besides death itself . . . how *he* would finally perish.

At this point, it looked like starvation.

No one would know how he died. Or where. Or . . . if he'd even perished at all.

Starvation.

After all the things he'd done, he supposed he'd earned it.

CHAPTER 25

Shadowy underbrush rustled as a wave of green and gray torsos crept through it, brandishing bows, spears, stone axes, and spiked clubs. Through the lowlands the Iruzu combed, spread out in a lethal line, sending the wildlife into hiding. It had been days since the killing of War Club and Gut Eater. Not one Hard Shell had been found, forcing the hunting parties to widen their search. Wildlife abounded in the jungle, so most tracks were ignored . . . until this hunting pack, led by Worm Eye, stumbled upon a partial print left in the soil. Just a hard wedge, really, but it wasn't barefoot, as most denizens of the Sanjou were prone to be.

It was enough to continue following.

So the Iruzu pack spread out, searching for other signs, and finding them. Another mark in the soil. A broken strand of grass. Prints along the edge of a stream. It took time, the signs spotty at best. They eventually found the devastation left by a thunder beast, which immediately placed the hunters on guard. One side of a tree had been shredded, which prompted the Iruzu to search the area. They eventually followed the trail of the thunder beast, and glimpsed green mountains in the distance. The sight of those mountains stopped Worm Eye. Monsters lurked there—terrible creatures with no fear of the Iruzu. Those same creatures possessed a strength and cunning not to be taken lightly, and they would feed upon the Iruzu if given the opportunity. A few of Worm Eye's warriors wondered if the trail they followed was, in fact, a lure, made by one of those monsters.

No one said anything of going back, however.

Not with Worm Eye leading them.

And not with One Spear somewhere behind.

Wearing a grim assortment of beads and bones, Worm Eye studied those peaks, green and bright under the morning sun. His dead eye fixed straight ahead while the other flickered here and there. Sweat trickled down his profile and seeped into that unseeing orb, not bothering the Iruzu leader in the least.

Worm Eye believed the mountains would provide a good hiding place for Hard Shells . . . a place just beyond the edge of Iruzuland. A place where the Iruzu did not go.

Worm Eye would go there, however, and he would make certain there were no Hard Shells hiding there. He did not want to return to One Spear empty-handed. One Spear was a different kind of monster.

Motioning his warriors to follow, Worm Eye led them through the jungle, down a slope, and into a small valley. The sun brightened, and the wild knots of the unforgiving wilderness thinned away. The Iruzu reached the bottom and waded through wild grass growing between a smattering of warped trees and white boulders.

A shallow stream halted their search.

There the hunting pack gathered, twenty strong, and gazed across the water. The broad back of a mountain waited, covered in dark shrubs and freckled with flowers of orange and yellow. Trees grew on the far sides of the slope, but the middle was clear of vegetation, as if a giant had scraped it all off. The mountain rose sharply, rising in uneven lines and terraces, and was the foremost of a glaring range.

Worm Eye motioned for his warriors to search the shoreline, as all manner of creatures must drink sooner or later. Sometime later, in the shade of a nearby tree, a hunter discovered a pair of discarded arrows at the very bottom of the stream. He dove in, retrieved them, and presented them to Worm Eye. There was no doubt in Worm Eye's mind. The arrows, with their heavy heads, were the kind used by Hard Shells.

Worm Eye gave the arrows back to the hunter who had discovered them. He then ordered the hunter and another to return to One Spear, to tell him where Worm Eye and the others were going.

The pair of Iruzu hurried off, back across the grassland.

Worm Eye turned his attention to the mountain. He held a curved club bristling with wooded spikes.

Then a sight hooked his attention.

A red-black cluster of bones stained the ground in a big splotch of rotten color. A pair of scavenger birds with crooked necks hopped about the bones. Only two, but when the scavengers gathered in any number, it meant a recent kill, at most a few days old.

Sensing something close, Worm Eye waded into the stream.

His hunters followed.

Peering out from his rocky nest, Chop watched the enemy as they moved along the shoreline. He'd spotted them earlier while he was emptying the bull over the rock wall, and immediately pinched off his piss stream while ducking out of sight. Ignoring the sting in his fruits, Chop scuffled to a craggy parting in the boulders, where he could see below without lifting his head.

His stomach sickened when the fishmen found his arrows. He cursed when two of their number sprinted back the way they'd traveled. Then he cursed himself for being so careless. At the time, however, if he had gone into the water, he might not have crawled back out. Still, he should not have left them behind.

Now the fishmen had his scent.

Moments later, they bled across the water. They were dark things in the sun, hunched over and focused, wielding all manner of primitive weapons. Close to twenty, at least. Chop sighed at the battle that lay ahead.

Onward they crept, searching for a sign, each one leaving a path in the grass as they neared the slope. A pair of scavenger birds flew off as they approached, which Chop thought wise. The fishmen paused again at the base of the mountain, interested in the ground.

Chop gently thumped his forehead against a boulder, realizing what they had found.

The overturned rocks, from when he was foraging for crawlers.

He would have smiled if it didn't hurt to do so. In his search for food, he'd unwittingly left a trail to follow.

And now the enemy had found him.

Below, the group started up the slope.

Chop rubbed his forehead. He had the high ground and was well protected by the boulders. The shelf and cavern would be easy to defend. His aggressors below him, however, had nowhere to hide.

He was only one man, though, and a broken one at that.

They were many.

Knowing a good bit of butchery was approaching, he withdrew, careful to stay out of sight. It hurt to stand, but stand he did, swaying as he stumbled into the cave, one hand pressed to his ribs. Perspiration beaded his face and torso. Some of that was from the hellish heat, but most was not. His stomach rolled and threatened mutiny, and Chop growled in annoyance at its timing. He pawed at his leather vest and winced as he pulled it on. Fastening the buckles was easier, and he drew them as tight as he could stand, as the armor was the only thing keeping him together. He reached for his swords then, hefting the belt and scabbards and lashing them around his waist. The leather about the grips felt fine in his hands, and he hoped he could pull the steel cleanly when needed. Another short rest, only a few breaths, before he adjusted his belt so that everything hung just right.

Chop listened and heard nothing.

He returned to daylight and went back to the rock wall. With the full power of the sun unfairly pressing down on him, he picked up his bow and quiver and readied both. *Lords above*, it seemed everything wanted him dead. His swollen eye had opened a bit, so he could aim without issue. Pulling the drawstring, however, tested his ribs to the point of a grimace. Not that he had a choice.

Nothing could be heard, nor did anything show itself. That would change soon enough.

If they capture you, a voice in his head warned.

He would just have to make sure they would not capture him.

That didn't relieve his swelling unease.

A fly buzzed close to his ear, so he rattled his head to avoid it. He didn't black out, which was good. Only a few days ago he would have had to lie down and wait for his senses to stop spinning. Chop took a short, calming moment. Then he eased out until he spied the fishmen below—a teeming gray-green mass picking their way up the slope. There appeared to be more, which caused the Nordish man to draw back for a moment, to reset his eyes.

Didn't matter how many were coming up the mountain. There was nowhere for him to go. No place to hide. He would make his stand here. The thought of cutting his own throat came to him, but that wouldn't do. His father wouldn't have it, nor would the Jackals. No. Whatever was coming, whatever his fate, he would meet it.

With his bow. And swords.

He would make certain they regretted finding him in the first place.

Chop adjusted the quiver, standing it upright between the rocks, just at his knees. He withdrew an arrow and gently nocked it. He sighed through his nose and tested the hard draw of the string. Not quite as smooth as he would have liked, but it would work. It would hurt, but he couldn't think about that. Not now.

At least he could see enough to aim.

Again, he checked on his hunters. With the sun overhead, he remained practically invisible to them. That would change soon enough. The fishmen advanced, spread out in ones and twos, well within range of his bow. Chop sniffed, and a flare of pain scorched his sinuses, hard enough for his left eye to water. When the moment passed, he warned himself not to do that again. He then leaned over the rocks as far as he dared and sighted a target. He ducked and nodded, knowing the next part would hurt. Would hurt right and proper.

The sound of their approach reached his ears. Panting. Breathing. Short, guttural bursts. The clicking of rocks skidding down the incline.

Chop took one last breath, filling his lungs to the point of pain.

Then he went to work.

In one not-so-subtle movement, he leaned out over those rocky battlements while pulling his arrow back to his ear. The bowstring croaked. The resulting hot ache was a sword slash across his ribs.

Chop sighted his target.

A fishman carrying a spear.

He released, the bow bucking with power. The arrow punched through the warrior's chest with a misty spurt, pitching him back down the slope.

The fishman next to the fallen creature spun about, watching the corpse skid to a stop.

In that beat of time, Chop already had another arrow in hand. A harsh bluster of voices as the Nordish man sighted his next target and released.

The fishman ducked as soon as the arrow left the bow.

In fact, the whole pack scattered, ducking and weaving in an attempt to avoid the archer.

Leaning back, Chop grabbed another arrow, slowed by the burn in his chest. He readied the bow, took several shallow breaths, and leaned out once again.

There.

Iron-tipped and merciless, his arrow sped out of the eye of the sun and slammed into another fishman, flipping the thing over a low rock, ankles flying over gray-green ass.

Shrieks and yowls of anger spiced the air. Chop knew then he'd been spotted.

No matter.

Broken as he was, he was still a Jackal.

A quick peek told him that the fishmen had scattered like tossed pebbles. Worse, they were climbing up the slope faster.

Chop readied another arrow.

Loosed.

Missed, the shot sped past screaming heads and crashed into the rocks below.

He readied another arrow.

Loosed and nailed a screamer through the chest, halting the creature as if he had been bashed with a heavy plank.

The arrow after that sank deep into a fishman's face with a grisly spurt, shoving the head back on his shoulders before the body crumpled.

Chop dropped from sight, his heart hammering. His chest demanded more air yet threatened to tear him apart upon getting it. He readied another shaft and paused, the discomfort forcing him to a knee. He squeezed his eyes shut while drawing shallow breaths, ignoring the yammering howls and shrieks from below.

Getting closer.

They liked screaming? He would give them something to scream about.

Chop rose and leaned over the rocks, quickly aimed and loosed—but the target ducked, and the feathered shaft clattered off the incline.

That missed shot elicited a round of evil taunts.

Suffering dearly, Chop reached for the quiver. He leaned out and released three arrows, one after the other, as fast as he could manage, aiming at whatever unfortunate bastard caught his eye.

He killed one through the chest.

Snapped back the head of a second, shutting him up with a startled *yurk!*

His third arrow missed its target entirely.

A shaft zipped by Chop's head, forcing him back. He crouched behind the boulders and saw he only had a handful of arrows left. Worse, after his sustained barrage, his arms pulsed with numbness from his elbows down. Hot slivers squeezed his chest with every intake of air, threatening to kill him there.

The fishmen whooped and hollered, their cries much, much louder.

Then their arrows fell about him.

The returning volley bounced off the rocks in explosions of dirt and dust. One arrow buried its tip in the ground, the shaft thrumming a finger away from Chop's right knee. Others barely missed his shoulders, while one zipped past his ear, hissing all the way. Chop pressed himself into the rocks and clutched his bow. More shafts fell about him, their flights ending in blunt explosions upon dirt and stone.

The entrance to his cave beckoned, in what seemed like a very long sprint away.

Not yet, he thought and popped up, sighting one attacker not fifteen paces below. He released. His arrow sped through the screamer's gullet in a burst of scarlet, twisting the thing off its feet.

Spears were hurtled as a reply, thrown with such power that Chop was forced to drop from sight. He grabbed the quiver and hobbled a retreat to the cave. The land seemed lopsided, and the entrance swayed. He wheezed, every breath feeling like a flourish of needles in his chest, the agony hot and bright. Angry voices shrieked and barked behind him as he charged for that black maw.

A spear whistled past him in a slant, missing him by a full stride.

Another bounced off the rock shelf, much closer, sending a dusty wave of pebbles down the mountain's face.

Then a squall of arrows salted the earth, each one looking to bite him. They fell all around, crashing off the rock in shattered, ruined arcs.

The cave mouth loomed closer.

Despite his best intentions, Chop's breath quickened, his chest killing him with every filling. He forced himself to move faster. Blood thundered in his ears and temples. The hateful shouting became a nightmarish chattering. Any moment, he expected a terrible punch to the back, ending him right and proper quick.

But then he was inside the cave, alive and untouched and gasping with relief.

A hard corner clipped him as he entered, as if the very earth wanted to wake him up. He got inside and around that meager bend in the cave, granting him some protection. Out of sight, he collapsed against the wall, managing to keep upright while sweat raced down his face. He did good, he told himself. Did very good, even though his chest felt like he'd downed a bottle of burning pitch. That put a terrible smile on his face, one that didn't stay long. He puffed out a breath and chanced a peek at the rock barrier where he'd stood only moments before. The shouting drew closer while arrows continued to break upon the ground.

Chop readied his bow and aimed at the rocks marking his fortress. Sweat dribbled into his eyes, forcing him to lower his bow and scrub the drops away. Once done, he took aim once again.

The shouting was closer. *Louder.*

Then nothing, as if the entire rabble had fish-hooked themselves all at once. Chop didn't think he was so fortunate. He waited. Blinked. Licked his upper lip and drew back the bowstring, waiting for a target.

He didn't wait long.

Harsh war cries shattered the silence, a horrid screeching that hurt the ears. A long and undulating drone grew in strength, rising into a much greater, meatier roar. The noise possessed a bloody melody. A hungry braying of dogs, knowing they had chased their rabbit into a corner. Voices faltered then rose again in a long and maddening pitch.

Snarling, Chop watched the rocks, his arms *burning* from the prolonged draw, the feathers coarse against his cheek.

The shouting stopped.

And a deluge of bodies spilled over the rock barrier and onto the ground.

Chop released his arrow, blowing one screamer back, hurtling the thing into the emptiness beyond.

The others surged forward, a wave of insanity that charged the cave mouth from both sides.

Chop reached for another arrow and knocked over the quiver instead. No time to retrieve it, he threw the bow aside and pulled steel. He stepped back, just around the bend, and waited for the mass rushing toward him. The natural corridor was only so wide, allowing no more than one or two at a time. Grimacing, *hurting*, Chop struggled to breathe as he raised his guard.

The screaming died away as the wildmen reached the cave, their footfalls hammering to a stop. There they gathered, just out of sight, close enough that Chop could hear their breathing—harsh, recovering from their run, but far from exhausted.

A mass of figures stormed into the cave, daylight fluttering across their heads and backs. Hunched low and faceless in the shadows, they piled into the narrow confines of the tunnel, which constricted the charge into a single line. Snarling, yelling, the lead warrior rushed forward with several behind him in a ragged tail.

Chop stepped out to greet his visitor.

The fishman reared back a stone axe and hacked for the Nordish man's head.

In an almost casual *one-two* combination, he took the wildman's hand off at the wrist before slashing him across the face. The next warrior hopped over his crumpling companion, thrusting a spear at the swordsman. The weapon's tip grazed one bracer until it nicked flesh near the elbow. That sting energized Chop. He stabbed back, punching a sword through the wildman's neck and slowing the charge with two corpses littering the cavern floor.

But there were more.

Shrieking, the third attacker leapt over the dead and swung an axe. Chop parried, the connection nearly tearing his blade free of his hand. The fish-thing bashed the cave wall, spraying rock and dirt across Chop's face. The swordsman stabbed and slashed, working the familiar combination that had killed so many in the past. The fishman slammed himself against the wall, avoiding the blades, and hooked one weapon from Chop's hand. The right blade left him, but he opened the wildman to his backbone with the left, the burst of blood heavy and shocking. That one fell as the press of bodies lurched over him, further crippling the rush.

Every breath bringing him agony, Chop faced the oncoming figures. He retreated two paces and swore not to give any more ground.

He killed the lead screamer as quick as a thought, his short sword flashing up and down the fish-thing's face.

The next one died clutching at his throat, dropping a club to stop that dreadful flow.

Another fishman shoved the falling corpse aside and thrust a spear into Chop's lower ribs. His hardened leather vest deflected the blow, but the impact staggered him, forcing him to retreat another two paces.

Shrieking, the fish-jawed spearman sought to stab Chop a second time.

The Jackal parried and jabbed, driving the thing back into the fishman behind him. The light dimmed further, and black and purple motes exploded in Chop's eyes. He retreated, leaning heavily against the walls, taking his remaining blade in both hands. He barely had time to tighten his grip when they were on him, a rabid rush of torsos and weapons that filled the passage.

And out of that darkness, visible briefly against distant daylight, a shape flew straight for his head. An *axe*-head shaved the side of his face in a sparkling *whoomf* that was more surprising than painful. Chop twisted, pushed away a club before stabbing the owner. He retreated again, deeper into the cave, his chest blazing while the sounds of battle became oddly muffled.

A broad-shouldered fishman closed in far too quickly and thrust a spear. Chop barely deflected it, spiraling the weapon into the wall. Another fish-thing pushed past the spearman and swung a curved club. Chop parried it to the ground before smashing an elbow into the screamer's face, taking the creature off its feet. Another warrior piled in, grabbing for the Nordish man's sword arm. Chop crushed his attacker's nose with one straight arm punch, freeing his weapon. Others advanced, their orange eyes gleaming despite the dark, their protruding jaws gnashing, flashing crooked black teeth.

A spear shot forward and connected with Chop's chest, hard enough to stun him.

Another glanced off his armored stomach, twisting him aside.

Still on his feet, though, Chop stabbed and slashed back, his blade connecting with the cavern walls. Dirt and sparks sprayed. He avoided a spear thrust to the guts and ducked under a spear for his head. That near miss forced the Nordish swordsman to stagger against the wall.

Then they had him.

A wildman tackled him and they crashed to the ground. Chop twisted, but the precious air in his chest left him in a gush. He squirmed weakly, gasping, but couldn't push his attacker off. Couldn't bring his sword about. Got a hand underneath a fanged jaw and pushed the face back. More fishmen crowded in. A heavy foot pinned Chop's sword arm to the ground. Hands clutched his face and throat. The yells and shouts became a distant dreamy thing, and a hideous face leaned in close to Chop's own. One with a terrifying assortment of beads and bones hanging from his neck. Above all that, one orange eye narrowed to a slit, while the other, glazed and ruined, stared ahead.

The one-eyed fishman raised a stone dagger, poised to stab.

The hands held Chop's head firmly in place. He struggled for breath, mewling really, close to mercifully blacking out but also aware of that pointed rock descending for his face. A loud clattering rose above the yelling. Then the fishman with the dead eye and dagger was looking back to the entrance. The hands holding the swordsman released him, and their cries took on a different note.

One of angry surprise.

Then the impossible.

Chop's attackers fell one after the other, seemingly all at once. The one death that surprised Chop the most, however, was the fishman with the dead eye . . . and the flash of steel that swiped his entire head from his shoulders.

What felt like a pot's worth of hot soup splashed across Chop's stunned face.

Sputtering, still on his back, he pawed at the slop blinding him, while daylight flickered from beyond. The screaming ended, replaced by the grim smack of steel sinking into meat.

In time, even that ended, and all grew quiet.

A rattle of pebbles broke the silence, followed by a heavy thud of something hitting the floor. Someone grunted, breathing heavily, and shuffled through the dusty light. A broad figure, and for a moment, Chop thought another ogre had returned to the cave, drawn to the bloodletting.

He rubbed weakly at his eyes and stopped, his mouth hanging open.

There, standing against the light, was not an ogre, but a knot of a man, knee-deep in the dead. The battle-axe he held blazed.

Narrow-eyed recognition then, and Chop's head thumped as it hit the ground.

Death had found him after all.

"Dying Seddon," Hargan dragged out in mutual disbelief, breathless from his exertion. "That you, you Nordish prick? Under all that shite?"

Which was the last thing Chop heard before he lost all consciousness.

CHAPTER 26

Bits of dust settled in the hazy gloom of the cave. The battlefield stink of death and hot fluids already going rancid in the heat filled the cramped passage. Hargan stepped over corpses and slogged through the dirt-spattered muck stemming from the carved-up dead. One of the dying maggots stopped him, however, as it clearly did not resemble the fishman gurry littering the floor. Squinting, Hargan leaned against a wall and sized up what looked to be the Nordish bastard at his feet.

"Dying Seddon," he whispered. It *was* the Nordish bastard, entangled with two of the fishmen toppers and coated in a steaming gravy of carnage.

Chop. That was his name. Not that Hargan cared. The man was still Nordish, despite the melted face.

"Of all of them to live," Hargan said in dawning, *poisoned* resignation. "Had to be you. Seddon above."

Hargan examined the mess from head to boots. A little smirk bled across his face. The bastard wasn't looking so smart now. In fact, he looked like flattened shite.

With a feeble ray of daylight reaching past him, Hargan considered the row of dead savages strung out in the cave. Then he regarded the Nordish punce. Overheated and weary from all the killing, Hargan was of a mind to leave the unfit kog in his own juices, until death took him.

Then something occurred to the Sunjan.

"You still there?" he asked, and kicked a leg. "Hm? Alive?"

And to his disdain, the Nordish maggot moved his head. Just a little, to the right, as if it was his last gesture before dying. Hargan sighed mightily and set his axe down among the slaughtered, leaning on it like a fearsome cane. He cocked his head and smirked. Watching a Nord slowly perish was entertainment on *any* day.

The pig bastard's face was a mess, resembling raw meat mashed into the mud and pounded by many hooves. Then he noticed the grisly mark where an ear should have been, still dribbling blood.

"Oh-ho," Hargan chuckled softly and got in close. The light truly was unfit. Could barely see anything. He stooped, trying for a better look, and inspected the still oozing wound.

A soft exhale left the Nordish man, and a wet bubble exploded from one of his nostrils.

Hargan scowled at that.

The Nordish man didn't look good. In fact, he looked as bad as any dying man gasping out his last few breaths. Hargan straightened and hefted his axe, one palm slapping the wood eagerly. He squared up and touched the scratched edge to the Nord's forehead, right where he meant to split the melon down the middle. Hargan was not particularly bothered by how he killed his enemies. Especially an enemy to his homeland, whose guts he'd despised from the moment he saw him.

Axe held with both hands, he brought it up, knowing from experience it wouldn't take much effort on his part . . .

Birdsong from beyond the cave. Just a few calls, then nothing. A black fly, or what passed as a black fly, buzzed around his face. Sweat ran down cracks of flesh and soaked into cloth underneath his chainmail. Things grew quieter still in that upturned offal barrel of a mountain cave, where the smell was only just starting to flower, and the gore would eventually seep through his boots.

If he stood in it long enough.

Hargan lowered the axe.

Memories of his days as a Sujin filled his head, along with thoughts of Marrek. And the battles fought against Nordun's Jackals. Nothing noble about those matches. Nothing glorious. Just a lot of tension, some right and proper frightful moments, and plenty of flying blood.

Hargan scoffed and lifted the axe. "Right," he let out, and lined it up with the melon once again.

Except, again, he hesitated, and the axe didn't fall, not for long moments, until his arms ached from the weight.

Features twisting from his deep thoughts, Hargan lowered the weapon, puzzled at his dithering to execute the rancid dog at his feet. The Nordish prick deserved a hard chopping, truth be known, but for some damn reason Hargan couldn't bring himself to finish the unsightly prick.

A few paces behind him, one of the unsightly fishmen moaned with life. The sound surprised Hargan, as he thought he had finished them all. So he located the maggot and brained him without a thought. No reservations there, so that was all very well and good.

The Nord was another matter entirely.

In the following silence, Hargan became aware of trickling water from the back of the cave. Curious, he proceeded a little deeper until the walls fell away into a much larger chamber. A short search found two stone basins, both filled with fresh water. A broad, crooked vein of white rock stemmed from ceiling to floor, and a slab of stone stuck out of the wall like an oversized bed.

S'all right, he thought with approval, sizing up the place. Better than sleeping in trees. He drank from the lowest basin of water and deemed it good. Then he returned to the Nordish blossom still on his back. There Hargan stood, pondering, vacillating, until he mentally shrugged with a sigh. He untangled the nearly dead man from the surrounding mess, kicking aside the head of the last maggot he'd killed. Not willing to carry the Nordish topper, he grabbed his ankles and dragged the lifeless weight across that rocky floor to the lowest pool of water. There, the Sunjan dropped him with a thud and then took a moment to drink his fill. Even splashed a few handfuls over himself. Lords above, it had been trying days. Damn trying days. Eating and living off a foreign land. Wondering if the fruit he ate would outright kill him or merely leave him sickly with the squats. Then it was avoiding the hunting parties and killing stragglers where he could, all while moving about, leaving false trails, and making his way to higher ground. The mountains. Along the way, he'd stumbled onto a fresh trail leading out of the jungle. There he met two eager, mottled shite-pigs on the edge of a swath of grassland. After quickly gutting them, he noticed they carried, of all things, a pair of iron-tipped arrows.

Hargan thought, *hoped*, the arrows belonged to one of his sword brothers, so he pretty much tore across the grassland, thundering along like a red and rosy topper after a honeypot. Then it was across a stream and up the side of the mountain, hurrying all the more after hearing the screams and grunts from above.

Those last few paces had been the hardest. The worst. He had almost spent himself scaling that slope. Fortunately for him, the toppers that had gathered at the jutting rocks above were more concerned with *screaming* than checking who was coming up behind them. Still, if any of the pissy hellions had waited for him at the top, behind that stony outcropping, they might've killed him. Easily, too. All they would've had to do was spear him as he tried to climb over the battlements. Or bash in his head.

As it was, they hadn't waited. And they didn't kill him. Hargan had climbed over the rocks, and the reaping he witnessed at that moment—as every one of the noisy punces was in the cave and *still* facing *away* from him—was right and proper butchery.

The way Hargan liked it.

He sliced through the backs of the wildmen. Only to find . . . *him*.

Of all the mercenaries to survive the ambush of so many days ago, it just had to be the Nordish topper.

Unfit madness. Right and proper insanity.

Equally poisoned and mystified, Hargan sat down on the stone bed and stared blankly into the cavern spring, puzzling over why he'd decided to spare the man. Topper was a Nord. Reason enough to gut him and not think twice on the matter.

Much to his dismay, he realized he couldn't execute the kog.

Couldn't figure out why. The Jackal certainly deserved it. Jackals would murder soldiers in their sleep if they found them. Truth be known, *Hargan* had murdered plenty that way. Killing an enemy in their sleep was perhaps the best way to end one. They went to sleep thinking all was fine . . . and then they were dead. Just dead. The very thought hitched an evil smirk on Hargan's face.

He looked in the direction of the fishman he'd only just axed, and that got him puzzling some more. One fish-jawed savage was no better than the other, and yet . . .

Chop stirred nearby. "*Aaagaa*," the ruined face barely got out.

That was right and proper unpleasant. "Aye that," a scowling Hargan replied. "It's me, if that's what you're trying to say. You undying crust of pig shite, you."

Sighing, Hargan smoothed out his wet beard and regarded the way he'd come. Something buzzed past him in a bumbling flight.

The Nord did not speak again.

Hargan nudged him with a foot and got a groan of pain. It sounded like the man was attempting to talk.

Having had his fill of that nonsense, Hargan stepped over and studied the man. Hearing the beginning of another miserable moan, the Sunjan punched the Nord, snapping his head to the side and shutting him off.

"Best you sleep, anyway," Hargan muttered, flexing his hand. "You'll heal faster."

In truth, Hargan didn't know if the topper would live to see the evening, let alone the next morning. Didn't really care if he did.

But . . . being stranded at what felt like the boiling pisspot of the world, left with a sworn enemy of his homeland, got Hargan thinking some more.

Figuring the Nordish pisser would be unconscious for some time, Hargan sat and rested his head against the wall. He studied the cavern again. Decent enough place. Easily defendable, with the right person doing the defending. The little basins of water were a gift as well.

"You found a fine enough place," Hargan said to the unconscious man. "I'll give you that."

It would serve as a shelter for a time. At least until the next hunting party came through. Hargan rubbed a hand across his nose. The bodies couldn't stay, and he knew what his next bit of work would be. He sighed and felt the tired ache in his limbs.

"I know," Hargan said. "Give me a moment, and I'll start dragging them out."

He eventually straightened and wandered back into daylight, leaving the Nord behind. Once outside, he noticed that the sun, that hateful, flesh-cooking sun, had dropped below the mountains.

He drifted over to the boulders and took in the sprawling bowl that was the Sanjou.

"Lords above," he whispered. "I ran across all that?"

The race had been a blur at the time, but he took a moment to appreciate it all the same, attributing the feat to good Sunjan blood. More important, no fishmen in sight. He sat down heavily, placing his back to the rock. His axe he lay across his lap. A short sleep was needed. He thought better with one.

And in one breath, he was gone.

In the morning, he woke and discovered he'd stretched out on the mountain floor. He sat up with a groan and a throbbing in his shoulders. Odd that, as it wasn't the first time he'd slept on hard ground. Feeling around his lower arms and legs, he discovered a number of troubling bites. Then he noticed the red and black insects scurrying all over him, each as big as a thumbnail.

With a snarl he jumped to his feet and swept the little blood drinkers off himself. Then he took a few moments to claw through his head and beard as well. Another odd thing. He could slice up a man into the bloodiest pieces and not think twice about it, but being bitten by insects? While *sleeping*?

A shiver passed through him.

Satisfied he was clean of the little monsters, he stretched and peered at the valley below. It was a magnificent view, and he watched the misty layers of cloud hang over the treetops of the opposite mountain. Waking up to that sight in the morning wasn't a bad thing at all.

The smell of dead creatures rankled his nose, however, ending the moment.

Hargan checked the slope below, all the way to the stream, and saw no signs of fishmen. Or wildmen. Fish-jawed toppers shaped like a man. Whatever they were, they were nothing. Gurry, even, and not even that. He gripped his axe and thought about breakfast.

Then his head whipped about.

There, just inside the cavern entrance, lying on his back with his hands in his lap, was Chop.

The Nordish man watched Hargan with a pair of badly swollen eyes. The night had done him no favors, as he appeared even worse in the morning light. The spot of his missing ear was a grisly mess. Bruises covered his face. Crusted-over cuts covered both his arms. In fact, his armor was probably the only thing keeping him together.

The next thing Hargan noticed were the swords lying near the Nord's legs, well within reach.

"Nordish," he said. "You truly look like . . . a freshly flattened cow kiss split up the middle. By a wagon wheel."

Chop slowly nodded, just the once, and that seemed to take the good out of him.

"You have anything to eat?"

Perhaps close to passing, Chop gave a little shake of his head.

"Nothing?"

The dying man didn't repeat himself.

"You best answer when I ask a question," Hargan warned. "Shake, shiver, or roll over for a squat. I don't care what you do, but you give me an answer."

Taking his time, or perhaps half-deaf from his missing ear, Chop eventually nodded.

"You have something?"

A shake of the head.

"Damnation, man," Hargan swore softly, unimpressed. "Can't you talk at all?"

Another shake of the head.

"This is going to be damned annoying."

Chop grimaced, and it wasn't lost on the Sunjan. "Hurts? You're hurting?"

Another nod, more dead than alive, barely noticeable.

Hargan's face hardened. "Good."

Without warning, he approached the battered Nordish warrior.

Chop groped for a short sword but clearly didn't have the strength to lift the weapon.

Hargan ignored the effort and placed his axe against the rocks. Then he grabbed the ankles of the corpse near Chop and dragged the body over to the cliff, leaving a black streak in its wake. Once at the rocks, Hargan hefted the creature up and heaved the body over the side.

That was one.

"This won't take long, Nordish," Hargan grumbled as he walked back for the next body, trudging over the smear from the first. "You'd probably devour these maggots raw if I let you. But I'm a *civilized* he-bitch. Not like you Nordish kogs. Devour your own youngsters, you would. Right before their mothers. I've seen it."

He grabbed the second corpse by the feet, thought better of it and, loathing the next part, hoisted the body up and over his shoulder.

"Lords above," he muttered, repelled by the mottled ass next to his face. He glanced at Chop. "This smells like you."

Not waiting for a reaction, Hargan continued his work. Place had to be cleared of corpses if he meant to roost here, else it would become unfit. And it *was* a good place for a nest. Just needed to be cleaned of all the blood and bits and whatever else was lying about. There was no one else to do it. The Nord looked ready to perish at any moment. So Hargan had to do it, and had to do it fast, before the bodies started to swell and truly stink. Else there would be no more pleasant mornings to enjoy.

When he plopped the second carcass over the edge, Hargan stopped and studied the dead scattered below, killed by arrows. Some of those had been well placed. *Nordish*, he mulled darkly. They might be unfit pissers who would cut your throat in the middle of the night, but they knew how to place an arrow.

"Where's your bow?" Hargan asked.

Chop was slow to move, but he pointed inside the cave.

"In there?" He tossed his head back in exasperation. "I didn't see it. Probably stinks of shite now. This was a nice nest you hid yourself in. Now? It's a full pisspot. Hm? An overflowing *shite trough*. One that badly needs emptying."

Chop slumped and moved no more.

"Not a bad idea," Hargan noted. "Just remember, if you feel like *dying* . . . just do it today. Hear me, Nordish? Die *today*. So I can heave you over like the rest of them."

He turned to leave and then turned back. "What were those things you hacked up and left on the slope? Those heaps of bones?"

Chop barely shook his head.

"You eat any of that?"

The Nordish man's swollen eyes actually widened at that. He locked eyes with Hargan for a few beats. A hard look delivered quite well considering the man resembled a half-dead maggot. Ignoring him, Hargan grabbed the next corpse and carried it over to the rock wall. There, he dumped it.

The brazen smack of flesh on stone brought a satisfied smile to his face.

"I get this done first," Hargan said, returning to the cave entrance. "And I'll have a look about. You're fortunate I found you. I came across a pair of these unfit honeypots out there in the jungle. Going that way."

He pointed.

"Killed them both, and realized they had a pair of arrows. Proper arrows, I mean. Not the gurry they use. Saw that and I hurried all the way here, pissing on the run. Figured one or two of the lads was fighting them off. Imagine my surprise . . ."

He grabbed the next corpse, thinking that they stank even more when dead. "Dog balls. If I'd known it was *you* they were after, I'd have . . . stood back . . . and *watched*. Saimon's hell, I probably would've *helped*."

Having cleared the bodies outside the cave, he stopped for a breath and leaned against the mountain wall. As an afterthought, Hargan checked on the near-dead Jackal. "Still alive?" he asked, wiping his forehead and flicking the sweat away. "Not that I care, mind you. I don't. No more than those few drops I just wiped from my face. Or the few taps off my pisser."

Having not moved from where he lay, Chop watched him, his breathing slow and steady.

Hargan watched him back. "Listen, now. You fish that water down there? Hm? Drop a hook or what have you? Eh?"

Chop squeezed his eyes shut and shook his head.

Hargan sighed in annoyance. "Lazy tit. Stuns me at times. When I think how the war's gone on for so *long*. *Stuns* me. Supper will be a little later, Nordish. When I'm through here I'll take a stroll through the market. Perhaps I can buy a nice, seasoned roast. For me. The likes of you might choke on it." He looked toward the valley. "Looked like a decent river, though. Or a stream. Whatever you want to call it. Fresh water. Should be something in it, right? Right? I fished when I was a boy. Was good at it. Maybe I'll take that bow of yours. And a few of your arrows. See what I can see."

Hargan checked on the sun. "You die anytime you like. Save me from killing you. Out of mercy, you see. Damned if any of you lot deserve a single drop of that."

Scowling, he went inside the cave and hauled out the next body. On his way out, he again kicked Chop's outstretched legs.

For the rest of the morning, Hargan heaved bodies over the side. After each dumping, he would return to the cave and drink his fill from the spring. A little past noon he finished clearing the cave of the dead, took a moment to empty the bull, and gathered up the fishmen's weapons. They were crude, well-used things, and he heaped them in a pile outside the entrance. Hargan inspected them all before discarding them, less than impressed.

"Unfit," he muttered, brandishing a club. "Seddon's rosy ass. To think this lot killed us all. Killed *any* of us. Turns my guts to think of it. Turns my guts."

He tossed the club away and picked up a crude stone axe. "Look at this. Hm? Who made this shite? It works, I suppose, but damn certain they don't cut down trees with one. Might crack open your head well enough, but fall apart doing so. Well, let's see what we can do."

Axe in hand, he walked by Chop—once again kicking aside his feet—and went back into the cave.

Hargan hacked at the cavern wall, focusing his effort on the softer patches where he could see dirt. He spread the debris that fell onto the floor with his foot. Every swing came with a grunt of effort and a short stream of curses. Dust filled the interior, and he coughed when it became too much. It was dirty work. Loud work. But he doubted anyone below the cliff could hear it. Still, whenever he needed a rest, he headed back to the rocks for a long, considering look across the valley.

Sometime after midafternoon, Hargan leaned against the mountain wall, a few paces from Chop.

"Feeling better, Nordish?" he asked, not interested in the least. "Wish I could sit back and enjoy the day. No chance of that. Our little war here needs to be cleaned up, before someone notices."

Chop grunted in agreement.

Then the Nord's chin touched his chest, and he fell asleep as quick as that.

A kick to the leg woke him with a jolt.

"Dead yet?" Hargan asked, standing over him, stripped to the waist. Clear blue skies at his back.

Chop lifted a hand and even that hurt. He noticed the rising sun. *Morning*, he realized.

"Damnation," the Sunjan swore with a murderous scowl. "That's a disappointment. Hm. Well. Day's only starting. Here."

He dropped a fat, brown fish on Chop's belly, the contact wet and wonderfully cool.

"That's your breakfast," Hargan grumped. "Probably your last meal as well. That river's got fish in it, but damned if I know how they taste."

The Sunjan dropped Chop's pack and sat down heavily, his back to the mountain wall. He exhaled mightily, sniffed at himself, his face screwing up at the stink. He then produced a large knife, much larger than the fish. Ignoring the difference, Hargan slapped the thing down on a slab of rock. He split open the belly, rooted out the guts, and ate the meat raw.

Juice beaded to his beard.

Chop watched the man.

"Rather have it cooked, would you?" Hargan asked while chewing. "Figured this is how you Nordish dog blossoms like to eat. Seeing as you eat youngsters and all. Aye that, I've seen it."

With that, he took another bite, making a show of it.

Chop's ruined features crunched in suspicion. He'd never heard tell of such foolishness, but twice now the Sunjan spoke of such gurry. He studied the fish. After a time, he picked it up and managed to brush it off. Once cleaned—or, at least, cleaner than before—he brought it in close.

Without hesitation Chop bit off the head. Spat it out. From there, he chewed through the upper bit, down the length of the fish, eating whatever would go down. He weakly rooted out the guts, picked needle-sized bones from his mouth, and discarded the tail.

Everything else went down his gullet.

Hargan had ceased eating and, instead, watched him.

This time, Chop ignored him. Eating a raw fish wasn't pleasant, but it was better than picking at insects, and much better than starving.

As if realizing he was staring, Hargan shook his head and stood. He pulled out one of Chop's water skins and drank from it. Sloshed around a mouthful and spat it out. Then he tossed a few handfuls over his back, front, and washed his face.

"Thirsty, Nordish?" he asked plainly.

Chop reluctantly nodded.

Hargan went into the cave. Moments later, he returned with the second water skin, and dropped that into the Nordish man's lap, right on his fruits, jolting him. Not appreciating the surprise, but grateful for the water, Chop lifted the thing and drank. Drank until the effort left him weak and weary.

"Got your fill, Nordish?" Hargan asked after a time.

Chop nodded.

"Those two things at the bottom of the slope? Their bones, anyway. You kill them?"

He nodded again.

"What were they?"

He shook his head.

Hargan frowned. "You must have killed them earlier, then? Before I got here."

Feeling dizzy, Chop closed his eyes.

Hargan kicked a leg. "Don't pretend to sleep around me, Nordish. Don't. Else I hook out both your eyes and thread my topper through the holes. Understood?"

Chop nodded.

Hargan simmered down, put a hand to his belly, and looked around. "Tell you one thing. That fish tasted like shite. The next one I eat will be over a fire. Lords above. I'll be squatting not long after. Must be other animals running about this place. I'll see what I can hunt down."

Squinting from the daylight, Chop cocked his head in a question.

And Hargan saw it. "'Course it'll be *me* doing the hunting, you unfit kog. *You* can't. You can't do much of anything except bleed, and you look about done with that as well. Truth be known, I'm surprised you're still alive. Truly. I know I said that *before* but you don't see what I see. Or maybe you do. Well, you're a *mess. Worse* than a mess. You look like you clawed your way out of a rock-filled grave. You understand? You look like, like, a butchered pig that wormed its way off the spit, right near the end of the cooking. Hm? You hear me? That you're hearing *any* of this stuns me. Listen . . . if you think about perishing during the night," Hargan swept his hand before him as if clearing a table, "you go right on and perish."

Chop gurgled a reply, forgetting his limitations.

Hargan held up a hand. "Just nod. Or shake your head. Squat even. Just don't make them noises at me. Makes you sound unfit in the head."

Chop didn't respond.

"Smart lad. Smashed like a slab of flattened shite, but smart."

Picking at his teeth, Hargan looked away. He rooted away at something for a bit, spitting with vigor at times, before settling back.

"Have you know . . . Thought I was the only one left alive here. In this place. This hell. Make no mistake, this is hell. To be stranded here with the likes of you? *Hell*. Dying Seddon above." Hargan contorted his face and let out his best impression of the Nord. *"Arrg uuug arrrrum."*

Though Chop had experienced worse from the Sunjan, he didn't need to receive more while in his current condition.

"Don't like that, eh?" Hargan said in a low voice. "Well, why don't you do something about it then? Your swords are just over there. Right there. Get them—if you can. You heard me go on and on about you looking dead. Did I say dead? You look like you've been squashed. Under a boot the size of a boulder. Truth be known? Truly? I don't want to kill you, Nordish. Not really. To kill you now would put an end to your suffering, see."

Hargan leaned in close. "And I find . . . I like to see you suffer."

Chop stared back.

Message delivered, the Sunjan straightened. He glanced around and gathered up the bow and quiver, which contained a handful of blackened arrows. Slinging that around his shoulder, he picked up his axe and walked over to the rim of the mountain shelf. He took his time easing over the wall and soon disappeared. Chop heard a rattle of rocks and a squawk of anger, followed by a blue string of curses. Then nothing.

Chop waited, as there really wasn't much else he could do. When Hargan didn't return, he took another drink from the water skin. Even splashed its warm contents across his face. Then he stared at the blue sky and wondered.

In the company of the Sunjan, he wasn't sure if his fortune had improved . . . or had become much, much worse.

CHAPTER 27

Smoke.
Just a whiff, laced with the smell of cooking meat.

Enough to wake Chop, who opened his eyes to see Hargan hunched over a small fire just inside the cave entrance. A pair of good-sized rocks supported a spit and the charred and drooping carcass of what looked like a sizeable snake. The smell alone got Chop's stomach rumbling.

Unaware he was being watched, Hargan sniffed and idly scratched at one ass cheek. Grunting, he shuffled in close to the cooking snake and, with a dagger, sliced free a small strip. Holding it aloft, he blew mightily on the portion. After a few stalwart puffs, he popped the whole thing into his mouth. Hargan huffed hard, sucking in air while chewing, occasionally licking at filthy fingers. He then took a quick drink from a water skin and let out a growl of relief. After that, he continued to feed himself with those fingers.

Feeling the stare, Hargan glanced over at the broken man and kept right on chewing. "Still alive?" he asked. "A true wonder. You've been lying there for two days, maggot. Two *days*. Asleep or dying or both. I'm disappointed now. Thought I was going to enjoy this all by myself."

He tapped the remaining roast with his blade. Then he swallowed, choking it down with some effort, and rapped his chest with a fist.

Before slicing off another piece.

Which he again ate.

Not that Chop cared. The news of being unconscious for two days stunned him. *Two days?* he thought, mesmerized by the little fire.

"Found this in the jungle," Hargan muttered as he helped himself to another bite. "Snake. Unfit thing. Thick as my arm and three times as long."

Flames crackled in between bites.

Chop's stomach rumbled again. His mouth was as dry as the rock he lay upon. He spied the plump water skin.

"Something's been puzzling me," Hargan said, popping another piece into his mouth. He took his time chewing before speaking again. "You see . . . I know you,

Nordish. Fought you and your likes for years. Became *like* you, in fact, to better kill you. Right? So, here and there . . . you learn things . . . about your enemy. About their customs. Their laws. Mostly within the Nordish Ikull, but that's it. Enough really, truth be known."

Chop didn't like where the conversation was going, so he pulled over the water skin. Uncorked the thing and tipped back a mouthful, until his strength failed and he dropped it onto his chest. Water spilled over him until he pushed the container aside with a huff of frustration. It took whatever strength he had left to replace the cork, and that one action seemed to take forever. When it was secured, he wet his hand with what he spilled and dabbed his brow.

Chewing away, Hargan watched him. "I know you lot are butchers. To the last man. Butchers. Strike at night and cut down everyone you find. Seen enough of that to know. Butchered soldiers. Butchered men. Women. Whole families, young and old. Cows. Horses. Dogs. What do you call it? A campaign of terror? Or some such foolishness? I'm saying all this . . . because I hate you, Nordish. Hate your likes like . . . like no other. Took an oath, in fact, to kill off every last one of you maggots with my dying breath. So you understand my hatred for you. For all your unfit kind. But I'm . . . divided here, Nordish. Because . . . as I've said, over the years I've learned a thing or two about your country. And I've known . . . I've *seen*, one or two Nordish Jackals with their faces cooked off. Just like yours. Melted right down to the skull, in fact, much worse than yours. The puzzling thing is . . . they were dead at the time."

That got Chop's attention, and a chill that had nothing to do with the heat gripped him. He turned his head to face Hargan, who continued to watch him.

"For crimes, I was told," the Sunjan went on. "Usually striking down their own. Maybe an officer. Maybe a fellow crust of pig shite like yourself. Not so horrible to me, you understand. I took an oath to kill you all anyway. But the Nords . . . cook . . . your *head* . . . to mark you as a traitor. As they've clearly done with you. And yet . . . when I smashed you about, on the wharf back in Othil, you wore your mask. Right? That executioner's gurry all you dogs wear."

Hargan exhaled then. "So, you get right down to it . . . I'm no longer sure what to do with you. Kill you where you are and end your miserable, unfit life . . . or just watch you and see what happens. Do what I swore to do with every last Nordish knob I encounter . . . or not. Be a lot easier if you could talk, to tell me why they burned you, but I don't think that's going to happen. Just letting you know, is all. In case you go to sleep and don't wake up."

Chop didn't move or make a sound.

Hargan gazed into the fire for a long, silent moment. He stood and walked over to his side.

"You did *something* to earn that," he declared softly. "I know it. I'd even wager you did plenty of killing before you turned traitor. Should just kill you and finish it. But as bad as I *am* . . . I'm not like you, Nordish. At least . . . you should *hope* I'm not like you."

With that, he regarded the broken man at his feet and kicked his head. The swordsman went limp.

Chop didn't wake up, but he was still breathing.

Inspecting the unconscious figure at his feet, Hargan turned back to the fire. Lifted what was left of his meal off the flames and left it on the rock. He took a sliver and ate it as he strolled over to the wall of boulders.

Evening, with the sun somewhere behind the mountains and a sheet of pink sky beneath thickening dark clouds. A single star hung low in the sky, weak but making itself known. It would be night shortly, and that summoned a memory, of waking up in his warm bedroll. Hargan remembered getting up and stepping outside the tent he'd shared with Marrek and others. He could still recall the spicy breeze coming off the greater Hrand Forest . . . only to see the outer ring of firelights all gone out. He remembered seeing shadows flittering between the outlines of other tents . . . followed by the flash of metal and the cries of alarm. Then full, bloody mayhem. Marrek's hand on his shoulder, and his brother leading him away from the mass butchery of the Sujin camp.

Hargan remembered he wanted to fight.

He also remembered Marrek saying the fight was already lost.

More memories, then, of a long, terrifying night where they escaped the killing and the hunters that pursued them.

"Seddon above," Hargan whispered, gazing out over the Sanjou. It was every bit as forbidding and deadly as the Hrand Forest was on that night.

He considered the sleeping Jackal back in the cave.

One hard thrust of his knife and he'd be rid of the bastard. The same bastard that belonged to the group that damn near killed him and his brother so long ago, that turned him into a deserter and a traitor to his own country. One hard thrust and the legs would kick, the body would spasm, but then all would be just fine. Hargan thought it over. Thought and thought, while chewing on his lower lip, feeling the scraggly hair of his beard there.

The Field of Skulls.

He and Marrek fled that slaughter out of self-preservation, or so they told themselves, but to the Sujins it did not matter. Death was the penalty for desertion, no exceptions. So the brothers thought. Either way, they didn't dare return to their homeland to find out.

Since that day at the Field of Skulls, and every day afterward, Hargan and Marrek tried to cleanse their guilt and shame by taking on any fight that came along. Any conflict. Any time. They were there. Especially Hargan. As if spilling more blood might drown the memory of their escape, by proving that he was *anything* but a deserter. Or a coward.

And Hargan had spilled plenty.

Yet the memory haunted him still.

"Damnation," he whispered, mouth twisting into a snarl.

He faced the cave, the interior lit up ever so slightly by the little fire just within. And thought on matters some more.

In the end, he surprised even himself.

At some time during the night, Chop woke with the urge to piss. He eased onto his side and hauled himself up against the wall. Hargan sat with his back against the rock, his head lowered. Ignoring him, Chop considered the little fire pit from earlier while his hand found his crotch.

"Not there, you motherless punce," a sleepy voice warned.

Chop stopped moving.

"You thought about it. I saw. If you're going to empty the bull, do it away from the cave. Unfit kog. S'all I need, is to be smelling more piss."

With a mighty breath, the Nordish man stood and leaned heavily against a wall. Alive but shaky, he limped toward the entrance, every step rattling his innards.

He stopped at a set of legs attached to the faceless Sunjan, who sat with his axe at the ready.

The Sunjan did not move his legs.

"Fall on me and I'll smash you," came the warning.

Chop stepped over him, which took more effort than he realized, while the urge to relieve himself grew. He reached the outside, where a hint of daylight glowed just beyond the horizon. A short shamble later, he reached the boulders ringing the area. With one hand planted on a rock, he freed his pisser and arched a stream over the drop. Dizziness threatened him and his knees trembled, but he kept on pissing. It was a near thing, but he did not pass out. Upon finishing, he tucked himself away, catching a whiff of soiled cloth and realizing he had pissed himself while unconscious. Chop grimaced. Not since being burned had he been in such a dire situation, at the mercy of such a land. And a brute like the one called Hargan.

All because a beast had thrown a *tree* at him.

Now he had the Sunjan to worry about, and whether or not the man would try to kill him. As of now, it would be an easy thing to do. Chop considered killing the Sunjan first, while he slept, but the notion made his head hurt. Here he was, swaying, barely able to hold onto his topper, considering using a blade. Unfit.

It also occurred to him that Hargan was the only one who could deal with the fishmen if they came back.

Chop wondered which was worse—death by Hargan or death by fishmen.

Feeling unwell once again, he lowered himself to the ground. There, he leaned against a boulder and realized the place had been cleared of the dead. The Sunjan had done it all himself. Chop remembered, just before his senses whirled and mottled specks bled into his vision. His stomach churned and he felt himself slipping.

Then he was gone once more.

CHAPTER 28

Time drifted and carried He-Dog with it.

Most of the time he slept but when he woke, he found himself staring at a moon at the center of a starless night. At times, the moon was blue. Sometimes gray. Sometimes there was smoke. And sometimes he couldn't see it at all. But then the stars came out, twinkling down upon him.

Figures moved around him now and again, speaking a language he had no knowledge of. Sometimes they leaned in close to check on him, and their eyes were huge. One face belonged to a man, older and wise, who would linger until He-Dog blinked, whereupon the man would leave. Other times, a woman would lean in and check on him. These people wore not a stitch, except for strips over their lower bits.

The woman was a strange one as her face appeared youthful at times, and much older at others. He-Dog liked her as she smiled a lot. And she washed him, or so he thought. He could smell the water and feel a wet cloth against his skin. Heard it dripping, even, and every drop smashed down like the beat of a huge drum, but not unpleasantly so.

In the state he was in, it never occurred to He-Dog to move. If he did, he had no memory of it. So he stayed. Rested. And ate . . . mostly fish, he thought, seasoned with sweet greens. Every now and again the faces fed him a little meat, roasted and garnished in herbs that made everything taste good.

The faces provided pisspots, large and deep oval pans carved from wood, and periodically emptied them.

In time, He-Dog learned the old man's name was Peaceful Moon—and it was he who usually relit the dream leaves. Once in the morning. Once in the evening. Which was apparently enough to leave the three men pleasantly stunned and senseless for both day and night.

He-Dog would wake, at peace and without pain, his mind distorted by the burning leaves. Reality oddly elongated, yet shortened.

Time went on drifting, carrying him along with it.

He-Dog opened his eyes.

Rough lengths of wooden ribs held up a dark material, converging at a circle of daylight at the very top. That glowing hole of sky held his attention for long moments. Strange but not entirely unpleasant smells spiced the air. He lay on his back and realized he was still within the lodge. His hand strayed to the worse of his two stab wounds. A mysterious crust covered them, and He-Dog frowned in puzzlement at the touch. With a grunt, he inspected himself. A thin blanket covered him from his neck to toes. He lifted the blanket, revealing a patchwork of greenish-brown streaks and tied-off bandages of rough cloth. Wasn't so bad, he supposed, until he raised the blanket further, and scowled at how he was bare-assed underneath. A heavy dab of that foul-looking substance coated him right below his belt line, where the spear had taken him. The sight reminded him of a day-old cow kiss, wet after a rain, and still fragrant.

"Unfit," He-Dog whispered and dropped his head with a soft thud. Sighing, he glanced around and caught sight of his leather vest and other pieces of armor jammed into the base of the wall. Another mound lay nearby, covered by several blankets. A tuft of gray chin whiskers peeked out from one end, revealing the mass as Jers Snaffer. Kellic lay on the other side of Snaffer, similarly buried, with his face uncovered and his mouth wide open. Piles of weapons and armor lay at their feet, shoved against the walls, as He-Dog's possessions were. As such, with an unlit fire pit at the center, there wasn't much floor space remaining.

The fire pit captivated He-Dog for moments. He remembered an earlier conversation with a man. A Zuthenian calling himself . . . no, the name would not come to him. That annoyed him, so he focused on Snaffer. A boot to the head would wake him, and He-Dog considered delivering it when someone yanked back the entrance curtain. Blinding daylight flooded the interior, forcing him to shield his eyes with a hand.

A dark shape entered carrying things that rattled softly. The shade considered the three men and shuffled to He-Dog's side. It was a woman, older than he but not overly so, and nimble. Considering he'd been laid out like a corpse dead for days, anything appeared right and proper nimble to him. What was truly disconcerting for He-Dog was the female visitor's bare chest. A long triangle of cloth covered her lower bits, but the sight of all that swinging matter alarmed him greatly and he quickly averted his eyes.

Not that it helped as she crouched beside him and dropped what she was carrying. Much to his shock, she leaned over him, studying him, until she lifted a hand to his face. Not daring to move, He-Dog endured the woman pulling at his eyelids up and down, stretching the skin one way and then the other. She then pinched his lips, repeating the pulling and ending each inspection with a curt nod. Once finished with his face, she gripped the blanket covering him.

Well aware he wore nothing, He-Dog fumbled for her hand and held on, preventing her from doing whatever she was about to do.

That bit of action swung her scowling attention back to his face,

"Mind yourself, now," a voice rumbled from the entrance. "Who do you think stripped you bare in the first place? I can tell you it wasn't me."

He-Dog switched his attention to the Zuthenian whose name he still couldn't remember. "Tell her to stop."

"She has to see to your wounds. See how they're coming along."

"See them another time," He-Dog said.

Not pleased, the Zuthenian spoke to her.

She protested softly, or it *sounded* like that, and that started a conversation between the two. In the end, she regarded He-Dog for a lingering moment before patting his broad chest. She then stood and turned her attention to Kellic, who remained asleep.

The Zuthenian sat just inside the entrance. "You were much more ... *willing* ... when you were breathing in the *wan-shol*."

He-Dog scowled. "The what again?"

"The dream leaves. Or at least that's the closest I can name it."

"The gurry we've been breathing ever since we came here," Snaffer grumped from underneath his covers, no longer asleep.

"It was the best way to get at you," the Zuthenian explained. "Your wounds, I mean. While you're senseless. Big lads like you. You might not have let her tend to your wounds. And make no mistake, that woman has tended to countless people. Men. Women. Girls and boys. She's seen all ages. All shapes. All sizes."

"Where's the other one?" Snaffer asked.

"Peaceful Moon? Has other matters to look into. She helps Peaceful Moon when he's busy."

The woman spoke then, leaning over an uncovered and equally bare-arsed Kellic.

The Zuthenian smirked. "She said it might be best to burn more leaves in here."

Silence to that, except for the woman, who continued inspecting an unaware Kellic.

Someone spoke outside the lodge, and the Zuthenian moved aside to allow another woman to enter. Younger. Slender. Dressed as the older nurse, which was to say, in barely anything at all. More pleasing to the eye, without question. Long hair, dark eyes, and a slim figure, she moved to the fire pit and dumped a pile of mysterious leaves into it. Showing her bare back, she knelt at the pit and threw the few stragglers in. She paused once to gather up her hair and flip its length over her shoulder.

He-Dog noticed Kellic—suddenly very much aware—watching the younger woman closely. Until the mercenary realized *he* was being watched in turn and averted his eyes.

"The first time you take in the leaves," the Zuthenian continued, "is usually the harshest. By which I mean the strongest. You get used to it in time, but ... ." He rattled his head, dismissing the thought. "In any case, they have instructions to keep you under its sedation."

"Sedation?" Kellic asked.

"Senseless," Jers Snaffer grumped softly. "What's your name, again?"

"Broska. From Zuthenia."

"We've been breathing that shite since last week?" Snaffer asked.

"Well . . . longer than that. It's been . . ." he trailed off. "Over a month now, truth be known. As I said, the first time is usually the strongest. And we might have used a little too much of the more seasoned stuff."

Pain seized He-Dog when he turned his head, although not nearly as bad as before.

"Have no worries," the Zuthenian assured him. "Dream leaves are . . . much better than any ale or beer. Or firewater. You don't feel a thing upon waking. And your sleep is deep and dream-free. Oddly enough. I mean, with a name like dream leaves one would think—"

"I've been lying here for a month?" He-Dog blurted, gnashing his bad yellow teeth.

"Oh, at least. Maybe more. Here? Days go by like water in a brook. And while your care is of importance to the Anoka, well, we do have other things to tend to. And the *wan-shol* doesn't really let you talk. Not about anything you can remember. It's best this way. Let you heal to a point where . . . what we have to say will be remembered. You were all barely alive, truth be known. And getting your armor off? In your state? Easier for all involved that you were senseless."

The younger woman left the lodge, leaving a flickering of flames in the fire pit. And even though the fire had only just started, He-Dog got a whiff of what was to come.

"Zuthenian," Snaffer slowly asked. "The women. They're not wearing clothes."

"They cover up their lower bits. Same as the lads. It's the heat. Too hot for much else. Much hotter than Zuthenia. It never grows cold. Never. And because of that, most wear only the barest clothing. They think nothing of it. In time you'll be the same way."

He-Dog doubted that.

"In any case," the Zuthenian said, "just don't stare at the prettier ones. Shouldn't have to tell you that but there it is. Mind yourselves. Else I'll have a talk with you. Now then. It's time to leave. I cannot, ah, partake of the *wan-shol* with you. My missus wouldn't be happy if I did. But before I leave, how are you feeling?"

He-Dog and Snaffer grunted at the same time, realized their timely agreement, and traded glares.

"Where's the prince?" Kellic asked.

"He's nearby," Broska answered. "Not enough space in here for all of you. And he's in the worst condition."

That was news.

"He alive?" Jers Snaffer asked.

"Alive. And awake, as you are. But much weaker. He's missing a leg, after all. They're burning leaves for him as well. It helps him . . . understand . . . what's happened to him."

But only while the leaves are burning, He-Dog thought and blinked sleepily. *Lords above,* the smoke well and truly worked sorcery. He scratched at his face and barely felt his own touch.

The older woman spoke to Broska who then translated. "Right. Any of you hungry?"

He-Dog was that. Famished. He raised a hand. The others did the same.

Broska spoke to the old woman and she left the dwelling.

"She'll bring you something," Broska explained in a strained voice, waving a hand before his face. "Fish and sweet greens. Goes well with the smoke. You'll eat it. And daresay you'll ask for more. Apologies. I have to leave . . . before I drop."

He-Dog could understand that, as he was already on the ground. He raised his hand all the same.

"Yes?" Broska asked.

"Pisspots . . . ?"

"You need one?"

". . . Not right now."

"Then don't worry," Broska said, his expression pinched as if holding his breath. "She'll tend to you. As will Peaceful Moon. They want you healed up." Light blazed through the entrance, shadowing the Zuthenian's features. "They're eager to meet you."

Those last few words struck He-Dog as odd, but before he could ask anything more, the rising smoke worked its sorcery upon him.

And he knew no more.

He regained a little more awareness around midafternoon, when the leaves had burned away into gray ash. He lay there on his mat, covered in thin blankets, and stared with a drunkard's attention at that hole in the roof. Voices often spoke outside the lodge, but he didn't understand a lick of anything being said. Nor did he have a need to investigate matters any further. At times, Snaffer and Kellic rolled over onto their own pisspots and voided, sometimes loudly. None of that bothered He-Dog, however. He'd been cut up and left for dead plenty of times, and he wasn't always fortunate enough to have an infirmary nearby to nurse him back to health. He'd heard enough of others squatting, the worst from Balless. The lads had been with him the last time he'd been in a healer's house. In Foust, he remembered.

Morning. Noon. Night. All floated by seamlessly, with the occasional interruption of reality when the leaves had burned up and the air cleared a bit. Each time He-Dog was on the verge of having a real, lucid thought, one of the caretakers would enter the lodge and replenish the unfit sedative. Either Peaceful Moon or the older lady would bring in another fistful of those damned leaves, toss them into the pit, and light up the pile. They would scurry back out, because the smoke—all that comforting smoke—would render anyone unfit. The leaves hit hard. Harder than firewater, truth be known.

Not that it bothered He-Dog.

Then, one morning—Seddon only knew how many—He-Dog arched his hips and dragged out the wooden pisspot from underneath him, barely remembering he'd done so. What surprised him even more was his ability to do it alone. Once the receptacle had been put aside, he lowered himself onto the mat, fumbled with the blanket, and pulled it over his chest. Daylight shone through the opening overhead, and He-Dog stared at it until a hazy flash roused him.

He turned his head to see a *clean* pisspot on the ground next to him, while white smoke rose from the fire pit.

"Sorcery," He-Dog whispered.

"What?" Kellic croaked, well affected by the medicinal leaves.

"I said . . . sorcery."

"What?"

He-Dog flopped a hand. "The . . . thing. Gone. One squat. Rather, half squat . . . and it's . . . Then there's . . . a fresh one. And more . . . leaves."

"That's not sorcery, you tit," Snaffer growled like a sleepy animal. "That's . . . that one. The older one."

"I like her," Kellic said.

"I do as well." He-Dog liked them all, really. The leaves no doubt had a part in that.

"You don't?" Kellic asked, and Snaffer did not reply.

"I like them all," Kellic repeated, answering himself. "Truly. To take in three savages . . . like us? And nurse us back to health? That's . . . right and proper . . . noble."

"They have . . . reasons," Snaffer replied, struggling to make sense of it all. "We just . . . don't know them yet."

Kellic didn't answer him, maybe because his senses had departed.

Which ended the conversation.

Snaffer's words remained with He-Dog, however. He supposed the man was right about one thing. He-Dog suspected these people . . . had reasons for nursing them back to health. He-Dog also believed these people . . . weren't like them at all.

And they were better because of it.

Another day.

The older woman placed a bowl of rice and sweet greens by He-Dog's head, waking him. She sat down, gathered up his head like the ugly melon it was, and nestled it against her bare thigh. Once in place, she fed him.

He didn't resist. Didn't want to.

There was a flash of light, and suddenly another person stood in the lodge. He-Dog thought it was Broska, but when the older woman spoke, a younger voice answered her. They talked for a short time, and even shared a soft laugh, which sounded like bells ringing across an open field.

Curious, He-Dog lifted his head and saw a younger woman, her hair in long braids that flowed over her back. She tended to Kellic, fussing over his blankets as he lay there. Kellic simply stared, watching her every movement. Sensing something amiss, the woman questioned his stare with one of her own. Only for a moment, however, before the young woman lifted a bowl and started feeding him.

He-Dog thought to say something, but the older woman pressed a second bowl to his mouth, urging him to drink. So he did, tasting water.

A third woman appeared in a hazy flash of light, another long-haired beauty who took away the empty bowls as they were handed over. He-Dog stared after her, wondering if he was awake or locked in a dream.

Then all three women were gone, as if they had never been there at all.

"Unfit," He-Dog muttered.

"What's unfit?" A disembodied voice startled him.

He-Dog cranked his head, surprised to see Broska sitting on a mat.

"When did I get here?" the Zuthenian asked, plainly amused. "While they were tending to you."

"Who were they?" Kellic croaked.

Broska scratched at his beard. "The women?"

"Aye that."

"The older woman is called Little Bloom. The younger one is Bright Leaf. The third is Summer Wind."

"What were they talking about?"

Broska finished scratching his beard and went to work on his head. "Oh . . . the usual things. I really wasn't paying attention. They did mention you, however."

"Me?" Kellic asked.

"Aye that. Said you were a handsome man. Or some gurry like that. Can't say I agree, but then, you know. Said you were well-built, if not more than a little cut up. As you all are. Little Bloom said you will sire many children. Strong ones . . . according to her, anyway."

"I will?"

"So she said," Broska replied.

"And they'll all look like him," Snaffer muttered.

If the jab bothered Kellic, he didn't show it. "Children," he scoffed sleepily. "Not likely. I'll be long dead before that."

"And the world a better place for it," Snaffer remarked.

He-Dog's eyes narrowed at that one.

"Bit harsh," Broska said.

"Don't mind him," Kellic said. "That's Jers Snaffer. Old . . . two-legged war dog. When you're around him long enough, you'll . . . understand him."

Though He-Dog didn't know Kellic very well, it was the most he'd ever heard him speak at any one time.

"You don't know me," Snaffer grumbled softly. "You've only been with the prince, how long? A year? If that?"

"Two."

That clearly caught the older man off guard, whereupon he said no more. In the peace that followed, a few voices could be heard outside the lodge.

"Well," Broska resumed. "You might be surprised about the children."

"What do you mean?" Kellic asked, in a tone which suggested the man might remember the conversation.

"Just mind yourselves," Broska said. "Especially with the women minding you. They might not speak your words, but they understand well enough. Be civil around them. Well then. Enough of that foolishness. You lads feeling well?"

Grunts and feeble waves at that.

"Excellent. You're looking much better. The color has returned to your faces. And your bruises are fading. All good signs. Now then, I have to go. Just seeing how the mend is going. As you grow stronger, they'll stop burning the leaves. Too much of the smoke for too long isn't good. Or wise. You risk slipping back the other way, into sickness. One where you're unfit for anything. Where you're a different person entirely. Weakened so badly of mind and body that you can barely squat. Barely *care* to squat. You don't want that."

No, He-Dog supposed. *Don't suppose we do.*

Bright Leaf returned in that blinding flash of daylight. She dumped two handfuls of leaves into the fire pit and dropped a lit branch on top. The leaves burned, and white flowers of smoke curled upon the air.

She quickly left and Broska turned to follow.

"Broska," Snaffer said, stopping the man. "How long have we been on the mend now? Since last time . . ."

"Ah, don't worry about such things."

"*I* worry about such things, you Zuthenian asslicker. How long have we been here?"

Broska's expression darkened.

Jers Snaffer waited for his answer, and He-Dog had to admit he was curious himself.

"Perhaps two months," came the quiet reply. "Certainly no more than three."

That struck the three mercenaries as senseless as any dream leaves.

"As I said," the Zuthenian reminded them. "Don't worry about such things."

With that, he left.

A day later, no dream leaves were burned.

That night was a restless one. He-Dog spent most of the time twisting and turning. His senses were sharp, however, and his pain all but gone. He flexed one leg and then the other, then his arms. *Perhaps two months*, Broska had said. They'd been living in a dream for perhaps *two months*. At *least. Certainly no more than three.*

Sorcery, in He-Dog's mind. To him, it seemed no more than a few days. Certainly no more than a week.

"Unfit," he whispered, staring at the opening in the ceiling where the night sky shone through.

"You're awake?" Kellic asked from the shadows.

"'Course he's awake," Snaffer grumped. "He just spoke."

"Some lads talk in their sleep."

"Some lads haven't been breathing smoke shite for two months."

"I'm awake," He-Dog said.

"How do you feel, then, other than awake?" Kellic asked.

"Good enough. Though I'm nowhere near sleeping this night."

"I'm the same," Snaffer said. "The leaves."

"We've slept for two months," Kellic added.

"At least," He-Dog added.

"Like a dream."

"Shut your guts," Snaffer quietly scolded his companion. "Like a dream. Like a *nightmare*. Near dead when we got here and lying on our spines ever since. All the while, the *Conquest's* long returned to the mainland."

The Blue Conquest. He-Dog remembered. He hadn't thought of the ship or its captain until now. "The ship's sunk," he reminded them.

Silence followed as the others remembered.

"These people want something," Snaffer said after a time. "Guaranteed."

"We'd be dead if it wasn't for them," He-Dog softly countered. "They saved our unfit hides. Fed us. Cleaned us. All that time. I'd say we owe something."

Neither mercenary said anything to that.

Not long after, He-Dog heard the two snoring, that lengthy conversation too much for either to maintain. Considering how much they spoke months ago, He-Dog supposed it was an improvement.

He tried to sleep. Surprisingly he did, not too long after.

In the morning, the older woman called Little Bloom entered the lodge, along with Bright Leaf and Summer Wind. The morning meal consisted of rough bowls filled with strips of tender meat placed over warm vegetables of orange and green. Water to drink, poured from a large gourd.

Everything tasted just fine.

As they were well enough to feed themselves, the women left them to their food.

Broska entered just as they finished. "Sleep well?"

The three men shared looks.

"No," He-Dog said.

"Not in the least," Kellic added.

The Zuthenian smirked. "No smoke, that's why. Well, if you can make it through the day, you'll sleep tonight, because you'll be exhausted."

He-Dog fixed the man with a question.

"Don't worry," Broska said. "We won't have you building any castles here. Though that would be a sight. But that does come around to some business. Are you well enough to walk?"

There was a moment of reflection as the question sank in, and the men struggled to stand.

"Suppose you're anxious," Broska said, backing out of the lodge. "The Anoka elders wish to see you. And I imagine you want to see your captain. I'll take you to him first."

The men reached for their tattered underclothing and leggings. It took time as they were all slow-moving from weeks of inactivity. Once dressed, they started for their armor, heaped in piles near their sleeping mats.

"You won't need that," Broska dismissed with a frown. "It's hot out there."

Snaffer traded looks with Kellic before both hauled on belts and scabbards with their weapons. Feeling better with a blade of his own, He-Dog strapped on the broadsword taken from the prince. That bit of movement got him sweating and brought on a dizzy spell, forcing him to stop. The others experienced the same, and Kellic's cheeks puffed out, as if he were on the verge of emptying his guts.

"You lads all right?" Broska asked uncertainly.

"Feeling a bit unfit," He-Dog replied for them all. "On the legs."

"Guaranteed it's the *wan-shol*. It'll fade. You'll be a touch clumsy for a day or so. And you've been on your backs for a long time. The more you move about, the faster you'll improve."

"Anything more you want to tell us about the smoke?" Snaffer grumbled, his face glistening with sweat.

Broska absorbed that before shaking his head. "When you're ready, then," he said.

After a necessary moment to steady themselves, they stepped outside where the full might of the day struck. It wasn't so much the heat as the bright rays of the sun. A snarling He-Dog held a hand over his eyes, as did Kellic and Snaffer.

"All that time inside," Broska said from nearby. "It'll pass as well."

Squinty-eyed and scowling, the three men spotted the handful of armed warriors before them. A fierce-looking fellow, standing a full head shorter than He-Dog, leaned into his long spear planted firmly into the ground. He barely wore a stitch, showing a wiry frame devoid of fat except for a mildly protruding belly. Unlike the wildmen that had attacked them, the Anoka man was . . . actually a man. Black of hair and eyes, with a nose that might have been broken once in his life. White streaks of pigmentation decorated both cheeks and forehead, as if clawed by fingers. Beneath the near lipless slit of his mouth, shiny pebbles studded his chin.

The warrior studied the newcomers with one side of his face hitched up in obvious dislike.

"This is Half Tusk," Broska said, gesturing at the man. "He's the leader of the group that found you."

If Half Tusk understood what was being said, he showed no sign.

He-Dog nodded at the man, who didn't acknowledge it at all.

"Ah, he's a stern one, Half Tusk," Broska explained, somewhat apologetic.

"Where's the prince?" Snaffer demanded.

"That lodge over there."

The four of them stood on a low ridge, on the edge of a well-shaded hollow populated with lodges. The dwelling that had provided them shelter stood at their backs, between two others, with a thick wall of jungle some ten strides beyond. Strange blooms of orange and purple dotted the ground right up to a healthy thicket of vegetation. A heavy roof of leaves provided shade to the whole area, but the sun bled through in places, touching the land with broad beams of emerald-infused daylight.

Somewhat unsteady, Snaffer headed straight for the lodge containing the prince.

The Zuthenian got ahead of the mercenary and held up both hands. "Before you go in . . ."

Snaffer went around him and whipped aside the flap covering the entrance. Smoke puffed from the opening, a scented cloud that He-Dog recognized right away.

The *wan-shol*. Dream leaves.

Snaffer waved away the smoke and peered inside. There, on his back and bare-chested, with a thin blanket draped over him from the waist down, was Shay. And Shay reacted to the bright daylight with a pickled expression both harsh and humorous, before he slapped hands to his face and groaned.

"Shay?" Snaffer asked.

The prince didn't answer. Instead, he rolled over to face the dark. The blanket did not go with him, however, baring one hairy ass cheek.

"They've been burning more dream leaves for him," Broska explained from behind. "And for a longer time."

"Did you not say the shite makes one unfit in the head?" Snaffer asked.

"I did, but there was no choice. He was near death. The worst of you all."

"Stop burning that gurry so I can talk to him." Snaffer glared at the Zuthenian.

Broska eyed him back. "I'll tell the healer."

"You tell him *now*."

"You'll still have to wait. For the effects of the smoke to leave him."

Scowling, Snaffer shook his head.

"I'll tell the healer, I said," Broska repeated. "Now . . . may we go to the elders?"

The older mercenary barely nodded, while Half Tusk and his guards watched the exchange.

Broska stopped the mercenaries with a hand. "First a word to you all . . ." He glanced over his shoulder at the village below before facing the three men. "Now listen. Listen good. You're the first outsiders they've seen besides me. They're curious. They will look at you. They *will* stare. But that's all. So, mind yourselves. Remember where you are. Remember what they've done for you. All right? Mind your manners, especially in the presence of the elders. Understood?"

They did. Even Snaffer nodded, though impatiently.

"Good," Broska said, eyeing them all. "This way, then . . ."

CHAPTER 29

Children's laughter chimed near and far and the faint smell of smoke seasoned the air—*clean* smoke and not that from dream leaves. Broska led the slow-moving mercenaries—testing their legs after being bedridden for so long—over a well-used dirt path that cut through the center of the village, where many lodges stood in the shadow of the dense jungle's edge. In the distance, however, the Anoka had built their homes upon ridges that lifted them above the others. Paths weaved in and around the many dwellings, and He-Dog suspected Broska could have brought them another, less visible way instead of straight through the middle.

Through the middle they went, however, allowing the gathered Anoka a good look at the three mercenaries.

And look they did.

Men halted their woodwork. A group of women openly stared, their baskets full of berries forgotten. Several children who'd been laughing and chasing one another along the main road stopped all at once, bumping into each other. They all stared, slack-jawed and squinting. The notes of a flute ceased with a shrill squawk, and a deep and considering silence fell upon the village as He-Dog and his companions made their way through.

"Ah," Broska said. "Again, pay them no mind. They mean no disrespect. Merely curious. That's all. They've only heard about you until now."

And the Anoka didn't appear to blink for fear of missing a detail. There was no malice in those looks. No distrust. Just curiosity, as Broska had said . . . even though it felt unfit in He-Dog's opinion. Still, there were no hateful smiles or snarls among them all, just unchecked curiosity. Even wonder.

More people gathered, stepping out from their homes, no doubt hearing the thunderous silence and wondering what was afoot. On ahead, through the pointed tops of the lodges and leaning trees, Anoka formed a line along a ridge.

He-Dog frowned, no longer comfortable with the attention. This simple visit to the elders had become an event. He met the eyes of a few onlookers, nodded at fewer still, and then concentrated upon Broska's back. A few of the children bobbed and giggled, holding hands to their mouths as if knowing they would be scolded afterward.

On impulse, He-Dog glanced backward.

A wide-eyed Kellic met his gaze. Clearly, he did not expect such attention from the villagers, and he looked unsure of what to make of it all.

A grim Jers Snaffer glared ahead, ignoring everyone.

The three of them were big men, standing a full head over the tallest Anoka. Thick, knotted muscles covered them, marked with scars both fresh and faded. Snaffer, however, with his wild mass of silver hair and beard, garnered more attention than the other two. His recovery in the lodge had left him looking even harsher than usual, truth be known, and his fearsome demeanor warned all to stay back.

Perhaps it was his unruly bush of hair. Maybe it was his imposing frame. Or maybe it was the fiercely projected promise of pain if anyone crossed him.

For whatever reason, the children singled him out.

They pointed and whispered among themselves, smiled and gesticulated at just how much hair the man possessed. When he walked by, a few of them kept abreast of him, looking up in wide-eyed wonder. Some broke into skips while others fell into step beside the warrior, correcting their posture and walking as he did.

A full half dozen of them.

The Anoka did nothing to drive the children away.

Nor did Jers Snaffer, choosing to pay them no heed.

"Don't worry about them," Broska said at one point. "They're all very impressed with you. All of you."

None of that talk impressed Snaffer, however, whose features darkened even more.

Kellic faltered in his walk, his attention hooked upon a familiar face in the crowd. He-Dog spotted her right away. The same young woman who had been caring for them at their lodge. Only a glimpse, however, as she was quickly lost among the press of villagers. Kellic teetered into a full circle as he walked, until he noticed He-Dog watching him. That ended that.

A short hike later, Broska led them up a short slope, the path beaten down by many feet, toward the lodge of the elders. It was a large structure, much larger than the others, its roof broad and bony and covered with mottled hides. Bowed and bulky, the lodge waited behind a protective line of about two dozen Anoka warriors with spears planted into the ground. Slashes of dark pigmentation covered the eyes of each warrior as they watched the mercenaries approach.

The presence of the guards did not slow Broska, however, and they parted for him at the last moment. The Zuthenian walked straight to the entrance and pulled back the flap. Nodding, he bade the three men to enter.

A cone of daylight shone down from the central hole in the ceiling, illuminating great bowed stalks of wood crisscrossing the interior and holding up the roof. A fire pit ringed with sooty rocks marked the center of a matted floor, while the remains of wood glowed within that circle. A scattering of small, blackened bones had been discarded in the fire pit, and the faint smell of cooked meat lingered on the air.

Broska directed the mercenaries to individual mats and gestured for them to sit before the fire pit. Which was good because the walk had drained He-Dog more than expected.

Facing them from the other side sat the Anoka elders.

As the men lowered themselves, Broska greeted each elder in that quizzical language. The elders responded with subtle nods. Broska then spoke at length and finished by swinging a hand at the visitors.

"I'll introduce them to you now," Broska said, and did just that.

The first elder was Skin Like Sand, who might've once been a huge, burly man, but now looked withered and frail. The next was Smiling Dog, with a wide jaw and abnormally long teeth. Warmest Wind was the smallest of the elders, and ailed by numerous spots on his skin. Smiling Rock was just that, fat but solid, with narrowed black eyes that watched and judged. Peaceful Moon was present and greeted the three with a short bob of his head. Bite Of Night acknowledged the newcomers with a nod, and of all of them he looked the most miserable, as if plagued by a terrible disease. No Tooth possessed an incredible number of scars scratched onto his near-naked body. His crossed legs cradled a huge paunch, but stringy muscle stitched the rest of him together.

Broska then introduced the last of the elders and the chieftain—Three Cut, who waited with the barest amused look upon his round face. Three Cut's eyes missed nothing, and long snowy hair reached for his shoulders. He wasn't quite as small as Warmest Wind but he looked solid despite his old age. Broska added that Summer Wind, one of his daughters, was part of the group tending to the recovering mercenaries.

"Very notable, indeed," Broska added with a nod.

Three Cut's smile grew just a little wider as he studied the visitors. With introductions finished, Three Cut squared his shoulders and spoke in a deep and clear voice that fooled He-Dog into thinking he almost understood the man. With Broska translating, the chieftain informed the mercenaries that they—the three *Slayers*—looked strong indeed. As strong as any of the elders when they were young men and able to run around the hills. Three Cut stated he could plainly see why the Anoka had named Kellic "Sad Eyes" and Snaffer "Hateful Face."

Snaffer's scowl deepened.

"It's just a name," Broska assured him. "And they mean it in the highest regards."

That failed to lessen the look upon the mercenary's face.

Kellic's name left him thinking as well. Not in disapproval, however, but in thoughtful reflection.

He-Dog waited for his own.

Three Cut studied the third man. The chieftain asked Broska what they should call him.

With a level of politeness reserved for kings, Broska responded that the Slayer's name was He-Dog.

"He-Dog?" Three Cut repeated, his accent thick but not unpleasant to the ears. Broska said that it was so.

Though it was not polite to show favoritism, Three Cut very much liked the man called Broska, whom the Anoka had adopted as their own—and not for the strange way he sometimes spoke the Anoka's words . . . though it was amusing to hear at times. Sometimes so amusing that Three Cut could not hide his smile quickly enough. No, the man called Broska spoke and acted carefully and with proper manners—at times even more polite than some of the Anoka.

Three Cut liked that.

Broska even showed Half Tusk respect and honor, more than the war leader deserved in Three Cut's mind. At times, Half Tusk's harsh bluntness could make the spit bubble at the back of the elder's throat. Three Cut did not care where Broska came from—only that he was *here,* as one of the Anoka, and a worthy addition to their people. It had been Three Cut who cast the deciding vote to adopt the man into the Anoka, after Broska had lived among them for two years. A decision Three Cut did not regret.

Three Cut spoke then, slow and precise, inquiring if Broska had informed the Slayers of their purpose yet.

Broska answered that he had not.

When Three Cut didn't speak, No Tooth did, wanting to see the weapons belonging to the Slayers.

Bite Of Night said he also very much wanted to see the weapons of the Slayers, having heard that they were very fine. Such fine weapons should be inspected by the elders before being used in battle.

Smiling Dog also wondered aloud if their weapons were strong enough to slay the Paw, and also wished to see them. The elder's teeth flashed in the firelight as he spoke.

Warmest Wind said the weapons were no different than those belonging to Broska, and that they were very fine, having the color of water when the moon shines upon its surface. He added that they were well cared for, unlike those belonging to the Anoka.

No Tooth said that he had cared for his war club all his life. And that he would use it across the spine of the Paw if Three Cut would allow it.

All became quiet then and looked to their chieftain.

Three Cut did not answer right away, as he did not like everyone speaking at once. It slowed matters down to a snail's crawl. When a good amount of time had passed, he reminded them all of his dream. The *shared* dream—as Peaceful Moon had dreamed the same—of three Slayers with weapons that shone like moonlight on water. In the shared dream, the Slayers fought and killed the Paw. And with the Paw dead, the Anoka could leave this place, travel north, and live in peace. Free from the curse of the Paw and the threat of the Iruzu.

A deep silence followed Three Cut's words, and the elders' expressions darkened.

No Tooth said the Paw would demand its offering soon.

Smiling Rock agreed, saying the Day of Offering was drawing near, which marked the year half gone, when the jungle became just a little cooler at night.

The others also agreed. The Paw would want its sacrifice soon. And it would leave signs.

Three Cut raised a thin arm, silencing the others before they prattled long into the night. He then settled his gaze upon Broska and asked him to retell his words to their guests. Three Cut then formally welcomed the Slayers to the Anoka village, explaining that the Anoka considered them their personal guests, and that their leader, Sleeping One Leg, would be well cared for.

Broska translated everything.

He-Dog waited for the fishhook. He didn't doubt Jers Snaffer was waiting for the same thing.

Kellic, however, surprised them all. "Thank you," he said, a touch gruffly, but with a little bow directed at the elders.

A pleased Broska translated but Sad Eyes' message had already been understood, as several elders cast subtle glances at each other.

All pleasantry faded from Three Cut's face then. He spoke at length, stopping to allow the Zuthenian time to translate every word. Broska told the mercenaries that Three Cut and Peaceful Moon foresaw their arrival at their village. In dreams, they saw three Slayers without faces, brandishing weapons of the sharpest stone, standing before the one terror the Anoka were powerless against. That terror was the Paw, an unseen monster that dwelled within the Sanjou, emerging every so often to prey upon the Anoka. Three Cut and Peaceful Moon and many others grew up hearing from their mothers and fathers how no Anoka could kill the beast, and because of this, their people's existence was a cursed one.

In their most recent dreams, however, the Paw was seen dying in a gray mist, at the feet of three faceless Slayers. With their weapons of gleaming stone.

"Our weapons of stone?" Jers Snaffer grumbled. "You have a steel blade, Zuthenian. Why didn't you cut up this beast?"

"They wouldn't let me," Broska replied with a wry look at the elders, as if he'd argued that very point at one time.

"We're not the first to come here," He-Dog said. "That's clear enough. I imagine there's plenty of steel weapons lying about. Only a matter of finding them and using those."

"True enough, but . . ." Broska shrugged. "They prefer their own. And even if they did find some, none of their warriors would use them to hunt the beast. They're a superstitious lot, and their fear of the monster is a strong one. Things have changed, however, since those two shared a dream. A dream of three Slayers. *Three* is a number of power to the Anoka. Very strong. They're hoping it's enough to kill the Paw, and lift this . . . curse upon them all."

"They want us to kill this Paw?" He-Dog asked, deciding the task not so unfit after all.

"Aye that," Broska replied.

A killing He-Dog could do. "I'll do it."

That took Snaffer off guard, who scowled a question. "Do what?"

"The killing."

"You can't do the killing alone," Broska said, drawing their attention.

"Why not?" He-Dog asked.

"Their dreams have *three* Slayers, not one. It's three or nothing. One simply won't do."

He-Dog regarded Snaffer. "Not a heavy price, for all they've done for us."

Snaffer eyed him back. "Until we get sight of the monster. And see it bigger than all three of us combined."

"We have a debt. They took care of us."

"All without asking. This whole time they've meant for us to kill a monster they can't. Sly way of doing things in my mind."

"They could've left us for dead in the jungle," He-Dog countered.

"Maybe they should have," Snaffer said, his mouth barely moving underneath his massive beard. "We might be better off. Look." He leaned toward Broska, flicking a finger at He-Dog and Kellic. "You might get these two youngsters . . . but I've learned to not agree to *anything* without knowing *everything*. These old bastards—"

He aimed the same finger at the elders and the reaction was immediate.

They collectively flinched as if threatened by a blade.

That confused Snaffer long enough for Broska to reach across and lower the offending digit. "Apologies. I didn't tell you. Never point your finger at a person. Do so with an open hand if you must but never with a finger, and never at their face. They consider it bad magic here. Bad sorcery."

Snaffer frowned at the display. "Good thing I didn't use my topper," he muttered and reset himself. "Look. It's sly dealings to give shelter for nothing one day, only to ask for gold the next. I *know* they aren't asking for gold, so clean that look from your face, Zuthenian. You know my meaning."

"What about you, then?" Broska asked Kellic . . . who wasn't prepared for the question, and it showed. He looked at Snaffer.

"Speak your mind," the older warrior said. "I won't tell you what to say."

Kellic remained quiet, not ready to answer.

So Snaffer spoke again. "What can he tell us about gemstones?"

That narrowed Broska's eyes. "Gemstones?"

"We came here for a king's treasure in gemstones. They know anything about that?"

That got He-Dog's attention.

"They probably don't," Broska answered.

"Ask *him*," Snaffer pressed, nodding at Three Cut. "They want this Paw killed? I want to know about gemstones."

"Why do you want to know about these stones?"

That was met with blunt surprise. "They're *stones*, man," Snaffer insisted. "Have you forgotten? That's *coin* back in our world. A lot of men came here to *get* them and they *perished* doing so, but the stones are still *here*."

An undecided Broska glanced at the elders, who waited for an explanation.

"They want me to kill their monster?" Snaffer asked. "That's my price. A true bargain in my mind."

Clearly not comfortable, Broska asked the question.

Three Cut's stern expression melted away as he spoke at length. The other elders listened, nodding at whatever was being said. All except one. The elder called Skin Like Sand held up a hand, asking to speak. Three Cut waved permission, and Skin Like Sand spoke for a long time.

Rubbing his forehead, the Zuthenian listened, struggling with the story. When the elder finished, Broska closed his eyes. "Give me a moment," he said, holding his chin. "It's not often I have to translate so much. All right. Skin Like Sand remembers something from long ago. But things may have changed. In any case, it will do you no good."

"I'll decide that," Snaffer warned.

He-Dog glared at the older warrior—who glared right back.

The hard looks didn't bother Broska. "It'll do you no good because he says those stones might be in Iruzuland, which is the worst place they could be. It would take . . . forever to search there—*if* the Iruzu allowed you, which they won't."

"Not afraid of any wildman," Snaffer growled.

An annoyed Broska waved that away. "You can't go back there. You *came* from there. Most of your group *died* there, killed by the Iruzu. Yes, these stones *could* be in Iruzuland but they have hundreds of warriors. *Hundreds*. And every one of them is looking to prove themselves to their own elders. If you go there, gemstones or no, they'll butcher you. And after you're dead they'll search for those who've helped you. That's the Anoka. Without the Anoka to guide you and hide your tracks, the Iruzu will eventually find a trail back to this village and slaughter everyone. The Iruzu are . . . Saimon's *hellions* in the flesh. A forgotten race of man-shaped fish creatures that left the seas behind thousands of years ago. Once provoked, they kill everything in sight. They . . . *delight* in butchering. And they've taken the heads of thousands. *Thousands*. Though they would never admit it, the Anoka cannot match that kind of ferocity. If you go fumbling about Iruzuland, you'll not only perish yourselves, but you'll most likely doom these people."

That silenced them all.

The Zuthenian reset himself and nodded at Three Cut. "Understand this. My life is now with these people. I've married that one's daughter and she'll soon have our first child. I'll not risk their heads or anyone else's by rousing the Iruzu."

Three Cut spoke then, and the Zuthenian listened. "Well," Broska said. "He says that if you kill the Paw, he'll allow a handful of scouts to take you to the edge of Iruzuland."

Three Cut continued talking.

"*If* you kill the Paw," Broska went on. "For if you do, that will lift the Anoka's curse, and will allow them to leave this valley without fear of being hunted by the monster. Then they could travel to a place the Iruzu will not find them. What you do after that is entirely your business."

That narrowed He-Dog's eyes. "Why can't they leave now?"

"I think I said they're a superstitious lot. I mentioned a curse just now. This Paw was a curse bestowed upon them generations ago by some unknown sorcerer. A curse carried down through the ages. The Anoka's best warriors have never been able to kill it and they've long since given up, convinced that the Paw will not die at their hands. They also believe that if they did kill it, the whole tribe would be hunted by things *worse* than the Paw. Unfit gurry, in my mind, but there's no swaying them otherwise. Until now. Two elders shared the same dream. Three faceless killers. You arrive days later. Right and proper odd in my mind, but to them? Magic. Sorcery. Whatever you call it, it does seem . . . promising."

Broska regarded Snaffer. "They've told you what they know. Now, will you help them?"

Snaffer didn't move. "Before I kill anything I'll have to wait for Shay to wake. With his senses."

"Done," Broska said. "But truth be known, your captain won't be of much help."

That quieted the old mercenary.

Lords above, He-Dog sighed. "Look. The Anoka saved our hides. Truth be known, they're still saving us. That's a debt owed, and I don't like owing debts. I'm for killing the thing. You two do what you want."

Silence again as the two mercenaries mulled over matters. Kellic looked the most uncomfortable while Snaffer glowered at the floor.

"I'll need to talk to the prince," Snaffer decided. "But I daresay . . . he'll agree if that one there lets his scouts bring us to Iruzuland."

Broska informed the elders of the decision. The old men barely nodded, masking their thoughts about the bargain.

It wasn't the reaction He-Dog expected. "None too happy, are they?"

"Nothing is for certain," Broska replied. "They *are* hoping on a dream. A shared dream, but a dream all the same. And the Paw is a beast. A thing of the darkest might. It's terrorized these people for generations. But if you do manage to kill the thing, there'll be smiles all over the village. That I can guarantee."

He-Dog watched the elders. Only Smiling Dog looked away with a quiet muttering of words.

"What's that about?" He-Dog asked.

Broska glanced at the elder. "Well, truth be known, not all believe you can kill the Paw."

That bit of news didn't surprise He-Dog.

He'd been doubted all his life.

CHAPTER 30

After showing off the three Slayers' weapons to the elders, Broska led the men back through the village.

Twice the number of Anoka waited in the road to watch them pass. They crowded the pathway and the spaces between their homes to see the three Slayers. The children once again marched alongside Snaffer, gazing up at him with huge, blazing grins. Until Half Tusk's men surrounded the three to keep the crowd away.

"Where are they coming from?" Kellic asked in blunt surprise.

"And why don't they stay there," Snaffer muttered.

Though he didn't say it, He-Dog agreed with him.

"They just want a look at you," Broska said as he walked along with the men. "It's common knowledge now. They've all heard about the shared dream and the three Slayers. You're special. Looked upon like . . . like Sunjan Cavaliers. Or those similar from Gheda. Or Sarland. And if you kill the Paw, that removes the curse the Anoka believe they're under. It lets them travel north, through the mountains and into the valley beyond, to get farther away from the likes of the Iruzu."

"Broska," He-Dog said, changing the subject. "What manner of creature is this Paw?"

"I don't know," the Zuthenian admitted. "No one does. No one has seen the thing and lived."

"Perhaps a troll?" Kellic provided, glancing at the villagers around him. "Or an ogre?"

"Or worse . . ." Snaffer added.

"There are monsters in the jungle," Broska conceded. "Great cats and lizards that will turn your shite to water if you cross one. But I've yet to see or hear of a troll or ogre. Not to say they're not there. I just haven't seen any. Creatures like that tend to keep out of sight. The Anoka have told me about monsters that lurk deep in the jungle. Vicious things that can tear a man in two. Everyone avoids those places. And not one Anoka has seen the Paw and lived. Which should tell you something."

"The thing likes to kill Anoka?" Kellic asked.

Broska nodded, suddenly grim. "And it's very good at it."

As the group neared the men's lodge, Half Tusk and his warriors stopped at the base, preventing the curious villagers from hounding them any further.

"Don't worry about them," Broska said of the villagers. "They'll go back to whatever they were doing before. In time, they'll lose interest in you. One last thing..."

The three men waited for it.

"Are you well enough to hunt the beast? Speak the truth, now."

"I can do it," He-Dog said. "I'm a little weak in the limbs right now, but I can do it."

"As I," Kellic said.

Snaffer did not answer.

"Keep resting," Broska told them. "Move about the village if you want. Get strong again. The Paw leaves signs when it becomes active. A cow kiss here or there. A tree with its limbs snapped off. It's been... quiet for some time. But everyone believes it will soon leave a trail of activity. Until then... get strong. And prepare yourselves for what's to come. There may be little warning."

"What did these people do in the past?" He-Dog asked. "To try and escape this thing?"

Broska faced him. "The Paw is... a thinking creature. The Anoka have been able to survive by offering one sacrifice every year or so. The elders make the decision, carefully considering among the grown men and women of the village, so that the rest might live another year. As you can guess... they can't keep doing that. But they remember what happened the one time they didn't offer a sacrifice."

He-Dog and the others waited.

"The Paw came to the village," Broska said. "Destroyed it. Killed dozens. Mostly warriors, but really, anyone it found. Happened when Three Cut's father's grandfather was alive. After that, the Anoka didn't hesitate with offering sacrifices."

"This is all gurry," Snaffer grumped. "How can they know it wants a sacrifice? They spoke to this thing?"

"From what I understand, elders from generations ago somehow scratched out the agreement, and it's been upheld ever since. I think it's gurry myself, but what I think doesn't matter. *They* believe it. Truth be known, they *live* it. And it's kept the village safe—or at least somewhat safe. As long as you're not chosen as the Paw's next meal."

"A yearly sacrifice," He-Dog said dourly. "How many Anoka are there again?"

"Almost four hundred," Broska said. "Seventy-three of whom are warriors."

"That's all?"

"Here that's a respectable army... but as for the total number of Anoka. Aye that. That's it. Though they do make the effort to increase their numbers."

Broska cocked an eyebrow and let that sink in.

"Unfit," Snaffer muttered, regarding the crowds gathered beyond Half Tusk and his warriors.

"I'll be ready," He-Dog said. "When you give the word."

Kellic didn't answer, thinking matters through.

Snaffer went inside the lodge and returned with a mat. He threw the thing down upon the ridge and sat on it. There he stayed, letting his legs swing over the earthy embankment.

"Angry one, isn't he?" Broska said to the others.

He-Dog agreed.

"Well," the Zuthenian said, "you're free to do as you will. That area behind your lodge there? Use that to swing your steel if you like. Half Tusk and his lads will keep the villagers away. Not that you've anything to fear from them, you understand. Even walk about the place if you wish. Might be best anyway. Get the looking over with."

"Where will you be?" He-Dog asked.

"About. If you need me, just shout. I won't be far away. My own lodge is just over there. Otherwise, get strong."

The villagers standing beyond Half Tusk and his warriors evidently had their fill of studying the three newcomers, and in ones and twos they returned to whatever they were doing. Three young boys and a girl stayed, however, watching the three mercenaries but mostly focused on Jers Snaffer. They waved at him with smiles on their faces, trying to get his attention. They rubbed their chins and tugged on the ends of their hair, pointing at the impressive mane belonging to the mercenary. When Snaffer looked away, they followed his line of vision.

Snaffer shook his head in disbelief.

"Don't mind them," Broska said. "As I've said . . ."

Snaffer dismissed that with a wave and an exasperated look.

Broska said a few words to Half Tusk. The Anoka warrior barked at the children, scattering them, the smiles gone from their faces.

". . . You'll be doing these people a great service," Broska said after a moment.

"You *hope*," Snaffer growled back. "Just bring the prince back to his senses, and I'll decide from there."

Broska glanced at He-Dog. "Angry, indeed."

With that, he left them.

He-Dog watched him leave. "We owe these people something."

"Maybe *you*," Snaffer said. "I know differently. All I see is a pack of dogs trying to use me to do something they should have done long ago. Three Slayers. Gurry. Weapons of stone." He shook his head. "As you said . . . there's been enough treasure hunters coming here and dying over the years for them to get proper weapons. Just take the blades from the corpses."

"Perhaps they like using their own," He-Dog said. "Perhaps they wouldn't know how to use a proper blade if they had one."

"Lords above," Snaffer winced.

Annoyed with the old mercenary's perpetual misery, He-Dog turned to Kellic. "You think the same?"

"I don't know what to think," the man replied. "I'll . . . wait to see what the prince says."

That seemed to lighten Snaffer's mood, but only by a touch. "Don't be too surprised at that, lad," he warned He-Dog. "That's loyalty. That's the one thing we all have for the prince. He's saved us all one time or other. Or have you forgotten that?"

"I don't forget much," He-Dog muttered.

"Then we're split. You're for this killing. The lad's of a mind to wait for the prince's word. And you know what I think."

"I know."

"Then let's do the one thing we can," the old mercenary said. "Get strong again. Paw or no Paw. I have a feeling there'll be plenty of killing to do soon enough."

They agreed on that much, at least.

Taking his leave, He-Dog didn't want to return to the confines of the lodge right away, so he wandered behind the dwellings, to that open space behind them. Ten paces or so wide, and a little longer in length. He-Dog inspected the green-tinted shade, with orange and purple blooms around his ankles. He glanced around. The only way for someone to see him back here was if they intentionally entered the field themselves, as the lodges hid him from sight. He couldn't even see Kellic or Snaffer where he sat.

So he pulled free the prince's broadsword and hefted it. Held it. Then whipped it about his head. He cut through the air in front of him, then chopped this and that.

Until his arms grumbled with fatigue.

Surprised at the burn, he lowered the weapon, feeling a chill overcome his face. Then the rest of him. It took him three tries to sink the sword back into the scabbard, whereupon he staggered a step and needed to sit. So he did, taking in deep, settling breaths. After a while the coldness went away, replaced by that heavy, clinging humidity of jungle air. A spider crawled across the back of his hand. Sighing, He-Dog flicked it into the mass of flowers growing nearby.

"Lords above," he muttered, wondering if there was any peace at all in the Sanjou.

The rest of the day was a lazy one. The only event of note was the men moving their mats outside the lodge. The shade within shielded them from the sun, true, but the walls kept the heat heavy and moist. They sat strides apart, each man as silent as ever, giving each other the space their lodge couldn't provide. They sat and stewed and watched the Anoka village until sleep took them, one by one, dropping them on their backs. Their sleep wasn't deep, however, or peaceful, as the relentless humidity left them restless. Little Bloom and Summer Wind roused them in the evening, bringing wooden bowls covered with broad leaves. The meal consisted of little roasted birds' legs, served over lumps of rice, and flavored with strange but pleasing herbs.

They ate, watching the village over the heads of the Anoka guards, who stood with their backs to them as if Broska had advised them to do so.

The activity in the village waned with the fading of the day, and He-Dog was the first to retire inside the lodge. Finding his spot, he plopped down and spread himself out, feeling the heat thicken around him. He wondered how he had ever survived during his time in the settlement. *Dream leaves*, he realized, and remembered being wiped down.

Kellic wandered in a short time later, pulling back the hide covering the entrance and hesitant on entering.

"What?" He-Dog asked.

Kellic grunted, studying the portal. He eventually hooked the hide to allow a weak breath of air to enter, stepped inside, and found his own spot.

The man rested his head not far from He-Dog's, which wasn't so bad until the man got into a fit of sniffing and blowing his nose.

"What?" He-Dog asked again.

"Nothing."

"Why all the sniffing then?"

"Ah . . . something flew up my nose."

"You drew back the hide over the doorway."

"It was hot in here. And it smells."

Which was true, and the last Kellic had to say for the day.

Snaffer wandered in as the first rumbling snore erupted from Kellic. He lingered on the threshold, deciding on whether to sleep inside or out. Then he crossed over the fire pit and settled down at the back, his feet a step away from He-Dog's.

Snaffer didn't speak, nor did He-Dog bother to start a conversation. He stared out the entrance, where faint lines of smoke drifted up from the quieting village.

The night's sleep was little improved upon, as the heat kept He-Dog awake and suffering. Not a lick of a breeze blew into the lodge, leaving him to lie in a clingy gruel of his own juices.

The next morning, food waited by their sides. Mostly greens this time, but sweet and chewy and good to eat.

Broska entered while the men ate. "Sleep well?"

Unhappy grunts answered him.

"Feeling better?"

Indifferent looks that time.

"You'll get used to it," Broska assured them. "Now then. Ready to visit your prince?"

Snaffer and Kellic rose, but He-Dog took his time following them to the prince's lodge.

"They stopped burning leaves for him yesterday," Broska explained at the entrance. "He might be a touch unfit. It will pass."

With that, he pulled back the flap and waved them inside.

"Lads," Shay greeted sleepily from within.

Light shone down from the hole in the ceiling, exposing motes of dust floating about. Flies buzzed as well. Shay lay on his back with a rolled-up lump of hide under his head and a disheveled blanket covering him from the waist down. Stripped as he was, he looked smaller, leaner, as if his months of inactivity had sucked away all the fat. An assortment of healed scars and sweat covered his torso while a beard flourished on his face, aging the man ten years. His missing leg silenced them all, as the blanket failed to hide the empty space below the knee.

"Prince," Snaffer greeted.

"You're alive . . ." Shay quietly marveled. "I mean . . . he *said* you were here, but I didn't believe them." He spied He-Dog. "You. Last I saw of you, you were running. Wasn't impressed, truth be known."

He-Dog frowned, feeling the looks from the others. "I *stayed* . . . until it was clear that to stay any longer meant to perish."

"You *ran*," the prince accused.

He-Dog didn't care for that. He was about to say as much when Kellic spoke. "It was a bad time for us all, Prince. Once the formation broke, you either stood and perished or . . . you ran."

The prince studied Kellic. "You're defending this unfit bastard?"

"All respect, my Prince. Truth be known, I ran as well."

That visibly stunned Shay, and the interior of the lodge became noticeably cooler. "You what?"

Kellic glanced at Snaffer, who became gloomy. "Aye that. I ran as well, my Prince."

That admission visibly horrified Shay.

"When the formation broke," Snaffer rumbled. "There were too many bodies piling onto us. It was either run or perish. So we ran. And we carried you off when we did."

"So the others . . . ?" Shay asked.

"Dead. Every last one of them."

Shay stared at his men before settling on He-Dog. "Leave us," the prince ordered. "Wait outside."

Not caring in the least, He-Dog left.

"You go with him," Shay ordered Kellic. "See that the maggot doesn't listen at the door."

Kellic nodded and left as well.

Once they were gone, Shay regarded Snaffer. "Sit down. The place dips and rolls when I look up."

The older warrior did just that, placing himself across from the prince.

Shay's features twisted in annoyance. "Closer," he said.

Snaffer did as told.

Shay grabbed the man's beard. The prince was surprisingly strong, despite the dream leaves, and he pulled Snaffer close. "The lads have perished, but make no mistake . . ." he whispered into Snaffer's face, his breath hot and terrible. "We'll honor them when we get back to the mainland. Who are these people, Jers? Why have they spared us? Why have they kept us alive for so long? What *reason* do they have?"

Held fast by his chin whiskers, Snaffer shook his head as much as allowed.

"Look at what they've *done* to me."

Snaffer couldn't look. "Prince . . . there was no other way."

A horrified Shay stared at him as if he were unfit in the head.

Snaffer pressed on. "Your leg was taken by *bloodfish*, in a river. I fell in while carrying you. They got you before I could get you back to shore. What was left began to rot and had to be cut away."

Shay released him and fell back to stare at the ceiling. "It couldn't have been you," he muttered. "It was *him*, wasn't it? The new lad. He cut it off."

"Apologies, my Prince," Snaffer said. "He did not. The Anoka have a healer. He cut off the leg. To save the rest of you, you understand."

"You let them take my leg?"

Snaffer blinked. "It was already—"

"You've killed me," Shay whispered. "You . . . unfit kog. You *killed* me."

The charge stunned the old mercenary.

"Butchered by my own," Shay trailed off in disbelief.

Snaffer found his voice. "It was that or—"

Shay waved that off like foul gas. His mouth thinned to a poisoned line as he glanced around the lodge. "Who are these people?" he asked in a low voice. "What have you learned?"

Snaffer steadied himself. "They call themselves the Anoka."

"Number of warriors?"

". . . About seventy."

"That all?"

Here that's a respectable army, Snaffer almost said, but wisely did not.

"They're nothing," Shay continued in a whisper, not waiting for an answer. "You're worth a *hundred* of them, Jers. A *hundred*. Sunbar's another fifty."

Sunbar, the mention of the long-dead warrior brought a frown to Snaffer's face.

Shay nodded at the entrance. "We easily outmatch them. *Easily*. What else is there? Tell me everything . . ."

So Snaffer did everything he could remember, including the conversation with the elders.

"They spoke to you?" Shay asked, his eyes narrowed in disbelief. "Why didn't they speak to *me*? *I* should be the one speaking to them. *I'm* the captain."

He grabbed for Snaffer's beard again but missed, his hand flopping to the mat. "I'm unfit," he moaned. "Not quite ready. Not yet. I will be. One day soon. I will be. Then I'll speak to them. I'll speak to them. When I'm ready, I'll walk to them. *Walk*." Shay squirmed before settling back. "That one out there. The Zuthenian. Lords above. He said I've been here almost two *months*. Is that true?"

Snaffer nodded. "He said the same to us."

"You know what that means?"

Snaffer did, but he let the prince say it.

"That means," Shay went on in a rabid whisper, sweat glistening on his face, "that Stephanak has left. *Gone*. Gone back to the mainland."

"My Prince . . . The Zuthenian said Stephanak and his crew were killed. The ship sunk. By the same wild fishmen that attacked us."

"That's what *he* said . . ." Shay countered. "I don't believe it. Did you see any of them dead?"

". . . I did not."

"See? They'll tell you *anything* to keep you here, to do their bidding. Stephanak isn't *dead*, but he might very well think *us* perished. He'll return. He'll return by the next full moon. The next one. We have to be on the coast by then. We have to be there and *ready* by then. If we're not, we'll *rot* in this forsaken place. Learn all you can about these people, Snaffer. All that you can. Until then, wait for my word. Wait for it."

Snaffer stared. "My Prince, what about . . . the Paw?"

"The what?"

"The creature these people want us to kill."

"What about it?"

Snaffer hesitated, remembering what Broska said about anyone breathing in too much of the dream smoke. "Do we kill it?"

"Kill what? Speak sense, man!"

"The Paw. The monster—"

"That? You're asking me about a killing? Aye that, kill it. By all means. *Butcher* the thing. Just don't lose sight of leaving here. We must reach the coast and Stephanak's ship."

"And the gemstones?"

Shay's eyes flashed. "We'll take them, too. We can't go back without them. We've lost too much. Where are they? Have you found them?"

Snaffer shook his head.

"We'll find them," the prince vowed. "We'll find them and return to Stephanak. The riches, Snaffer. The *riches*. Enough to buy castles back in Valencia." Shay slammed his stump upon the mat. "Go on then. Do what they ask. Whatever they want. If they want you to kill their monster then do it, but find out everything you can. Watch everything. Miss nothing. *Nothing*. We'll talk again. When the time is right, I'll let you know. Off with you then."

With that, Shay relaxed and closed his eyes.

Obeying his leader's orders, Snaffer turned to leave.

Outside the lodge, He-Dog and Kellic waited, barely able to hear the conversation inside the dwelling. Broska was nowhere to be seen, but Half Tusk and his warriors stood guard below the slope where a few villagers watched the mercenaries.

"He said they would stare," Kellic said under his breath.

"He did," He-Dog agreed. He glanced at his companion. "How did you get in the trade?"

"How?" Kellic thought about it. "Was always good at cutting down things. Mostly trees when I was younger. When I was old enough, I saved my coin and bought an old sword. Left my home. Mother and father had died two years earlier, so . . . it was easy to leave. Did some guard work. Learned how to use a blade. And . . . one day joined the prince's lot when he was passing through a town. He was looking for sword arms to fill his ranks."

"To replace the ones who perished."

"Aye that." Kellic shrugged, gazing at the village. "Wasn't a hard choice."

"And you've been doing this ever since."

"Truth be known, I'd rather be at something else. Not much good at anything else, though. Figure I'll carry on with it. Until I have enough coin to leave. Or get too old for it. Or perish."

Or perish, He-Dog thought. "How long have you been with Shay?"

"Long enough."

"He's good, is he?"

Kellic thought for a moment. "He's good. Fair. About as much as anyone can ask for in this business."

"And Snaffer?"

That brought on a frown. "He's a hard one. Been with the prince a long time. Him and Grage. Long before I joined the company. Grage was more even-tempered of the two. Snaffer listened to him. And the prince. Not that Snaffer is . . . unfit, or anything. He just let Grage and the prince think for him."

He-Dog could believe that. He ceased his questioning, not wanting to offend the other man. He sensed Kellic was an even-tempered sort, despite his choice of trade.

Snaffer came out of the lodge, and Broska wandered back into sight.

"All done talking with your man, there?" Broska asked.

A grim Snaffer nodded.

"Well?" the Zuthenian asked. "What did he say, then? About the Paw, I mean."

Snaffer nodded again. "We kill it."

CHAPTER 31

Birdsong flittered from the valley below, breaking the morning stillness while a groggy Hargan handled his pisser. Half-naked and swaying, he generously doused the slope below the rock wall. At times, he peered at the other side of the valley, taking in the lush greenness that thickened higher up in the hills. A dark rug of clouds obscured the day far to his left, releasing rain and drenching the land in a gray mist. Far to the right, however, were blue skies.

Hargan sniffed, snorted, and hoarked. He finished his business and tucked himself away, inside tattered breeches that had become pure rags midthigh. He shivered and spat again, sending a gob out over the cliff—which he watched fall until he lost sight of the thing. The valley got his attention again. Some might call the view lovely. Or majestic. Some might even sit and watch the moving storm. Hargan dismissed it all with a pick of his nose and a flick. He then scratched at his kog and bells, truly rooting around down there while walking to the other end of the mountain shelf he'd declared home. There, he stopped and peered down into the valley again.

Unfit, he thought, scratching his chest. He checked his fingertips for lice. Something was feasting on him during the night. The cave he and the Nordish slept in was either plagued with some Saimon-born mites or something had crawled off the Nord and onto him. Hargan couldn't see anything on his fingers or under his nails, so he proceeded to chew on one tip, spitting fragments as he went.

Yesterday's heat had damn near split the very rocks around them. The humidity had lessened during the night, but only a touch. This day would be cooler, bringing some much-needed relief. The rain clouds appeared to be creeping toward the mountain, or so Hargan thought, and figured he thought wrong. So he stretched, making fists in the air, and returned to the cave.

There, outside the entrance and sprawled on the ground, lay the Nordish crust of shite whom Hargan had dragged outside by the ankles. The man had snored terribly until the Sunjan could take no more.

With a disdainful glance at Chop, Hargan retrieved his axe from the cave. He returned outside, stopping a stride away from the sleeping punce. He strummed the weapon's edge with his thumb before holding it at arm's length.

"You alive, topper?" Hargan asked.

A sound leaked from that mess of a face, perhaps a week into healing.

"You look sickly," he said, and meant it, studying him with greater scrutiny.

"Here's the problem I have . . . with you," the Sunjan said. "I want to split you down the middle. One cut. Right now, in fact. Put you to sleep and be done with it. End the misery. Yours and mine. Save the bit of food you'd be eating for myself. But killing you now? As you are? Would make me no better than a Jackal. Understand? Which is also . . . unfit. Since I despise your guts."

The Nord didn't answer, so Hargan held his axe just under the man's ruined face. He tapped a sunken chin. "You hear me, maggot? Better be listening when I'm talking to you."

Squinting, Chop grunted.

"That's better," Hargan said. "Nordish kog." With that, he marched to the far edge of the shelf. There, he picked up the bow and a quiver partially filled with arrows—good ones collected from the fishmen corpses.

"I don't have the best aim," he muttered and sighed. "Never did. Was much better with the axe. Half these shafts probably won't even fly true. They look straight enough, however."

As he spoke he slung the quiver over one shoulder. Then he considered his axe in one hand and the bow in the other, wondering how he would manage it all.

"All right," he said, pointing the axe at Chop. "Your task this day . . . mind the fortress. You manage that?"

As a reply, Chop squinted back.

"If not," Hargan peered at the valley, "daresay you'll be killed by something while I'm away. Not that I care, mind you."

With that, the once-Sujin climbed over the rock wall and eased his way down the slope. Pebbles rattled underfoot as he descended. In short time he reached the bottom and waded through tall grass toward the stream. Flies and other buzzing insects found him as he passed the fresh holes he'd dug and dumped the corpses into. Took him two days to do all that, but he'd done it, and was glad of it. The mass graves would be easily spotted if someone walked by them, but the jungle eventually would hide them. Or something would dig it all up and eat what lay beneath. He didn't care. Hargan didn't care about much these days. Certainly not being discovered by more hunting parties. He'd deal with them like the rest. As it was, he'd kept vigil up on his mountain roost—what he considered his, anyway—and saw no one approaching.

He stopped at the little river and looked for fish in the shallows. Finding none, he moved on along the shore. There were few signs of animals moving about the mountain, so he figured the jungle would have the best chance of game. He crossed the river and hiked the width of the valley, keeping in the shade when possible.

In time, the grassy plain ended and the jungle began.

Hargan found the first marker he'd left behind, studied it, and sighed, wondering if he should really have done such a thing. At the time he was angry. These days, it wasn't so hard to be angry and to *stay* angry. It powered him, truth be known. He wondered if he was becoming a bit unfit in the head, or simply outright mad. He didn't think so. And yet, even after all the effort to find a safe place to hide, here he was, practically announcing himself to the enemy.

He simply didn't care.

Not at all.

Hargan frowned at the rotting head of a fishman he'd killed. Its flesh had paled considerably and its jaw hung low, revealing a black slug of a tongue. One eye was clamped shut while the other was open just a slit, revealing a peek at the sickly orange beneath. Hargan inspected the grisly thing and the mess of crawlers and flies feasting upon it. He waved them away, stirring up a loathsome cloud that made him back off a step.

When he'd had enough, he turned and inspected the other heads.

Each one he'd hacked off a corpse and spiked on narrow posts of cut wood. He'd spaced them apart some five or six paces, creating a line across the face of the Sanjou. It was the kind of work he didn't mind doing.

It was a warning to any fish maggot coming this way.

One that Hargan hoped would anger the enemy.

Chop awoke, smelling rain in the air.

His shoulder ached from how he slept, so he lay on his back, and that little bit of motion made his stomach roll. Dark clouds filled the sky, low and ready to piss upon everything below. Not wanting to be in the rain, Chop struggled to sit up, his hand straying to the crusty place where his ear had once been, leaving it when he made tender contact.

Sacred Curlord, he almost hated the Sunjan for saving him.

He should be dead, truth be known. Not suffering like this. A few grunts left him as he slowly stood. The land dipped and tilted, forcing him to grab for nearby rocks. A sour grumbling from his guts reminded him he was hungry. There had been food. He remembered a fish, eaten raw, and that nearly caused him to retch. Then he remembered a snake.

And Hargan eating all of it.

Fearing a need to squat, Chop eased himself into the cave, shuffling to the little fire pit Hargan had made just inside the entrance. There he leaned against the wall and slid to the base, drained of what little strength he had. He remembered the spring water, which prompted him to crawl deeper into the cave until he reached the basin. It seemed to take years to fill his near empty water skin. Once done, he drank a little before the effort overcame him and he settled down on the rocky floor.

Then he knew no more.

The smell of smoke brought him back.

Dark, from the dying of the day, and not quite night.

Hargan was across from him, his back against the wall. He was staring at a new fire pit near the middle of the cavern. Dark lumps of meat hung on a spit over weakening flames. Hargan poked a stick into the pit, stirring up little embers. Sensing he was being watched, he glanced back.

"Still not dead?" the Sunjan asked. Then his expression hardened. "Truth be known, I don't expect you to last much longer. You should have perished long ago. I'll offer you a mercy. All right? When you've had enough, truly had enough, and you want to be on your way, you tell me. And I'll end you. One crack. Right here." He tapped his forehead. "Quick and without pain. All right?"

Truth be known, it wasn't a bad offer.

In the silence that followed, wood crackled softly, and the smell of cooked meat caused Chop's stomach to rumble. It was a pitiful, begging noise, startling in its volume.

And it crinkled the Sunjan's hard expression. "Damnation," he muttered. "That you, Nordish? It wasn't me. You starving over there?"

Chop supposed he was.

"Want some of this?" Hargan nodded at the lumps on the spit. Dark and scorched and looking cooked of every drop of juice.

Chop hadn't seen anything better in a very long time. He swallowed at the sight, the sound loud in the cave. He slowly nodded, sensing a trap and expecting the worst.

"Feed a dead man, or one who wants to live." Hargan mulled. "You want to live, then, Nordish? Hm? Because I'll not waste food on a dead man."

Chop agreed that would be a waste.

Hargan became quiet, thinking matters over, long enough for Chop's guts to beg once again.

What happened next was unexpected.

Whether the Sunjan was tired, didn't want to listen to that sad stomach, or some other unknown reason, Chop didn't know. Hargan, however, lifted the spit off the fire and without pause leaned forward to offer one end.

Clearly it was a trap. If he reached for it the Sunjan would strike him. No doubt.

Hargan rattled the spit, warning the offer was for a limited time only.

So Chop reached out and took one portion. To his surprise, the Sunjan gestured to take two. So he did, and Hargan didn't strike him once. Chop placed one chunk on his thigh and held up the other. The morsel was black, cooked to a crisp, and devoid of any juice as suspected. Crunchy to the bite, it tasted wonderful. Dry and chewy, he gnawed every bit and strip off the bone.

"That . . . was a monkey I killed," Hargan revealed while watching him eat. "Small one. Some thirty paces up a tree. Saucy, red-arsed little bastard. Actually swore at me. At length. A stream of little monkey chirps. Little monkey screeches. Brazen little monkey *punce*. He thought I couldn't reach him up there. Thought he was safe. Little kog was wrong."

Chewing on the last bite, Chop weakly tossed the bone into the fire pit. His hand found his stomach, feeling full. It hadn't taken much to fill it.

The Sunjan leaned across and offered a fat gourd. Water sloshed within.

Here it was, *now* would be the time for a smack upside the head. Followed by a fist or three to the face. Chop knew it. And he had his own water skin nearby.

Still, Hargan was offering.

Warily, Chop looked from the gourd to the Sunjan, who frowned and shook the container again. So Chop took the gourd. Drank a few mouthfuls before stopping to gasp.

"Drink it slow," Hargan cautioned softly, eyeing the fire pit. "You empty your guts in here and I'll toss you outside. You should know better. And keep that thing over there. With you. I don't need it. I have another. Found them in the jungle. All over the place. Most were rotten . . . but a handful weren't. I cleaned them in the river. Let them dry for a bit. Brought them back here. Better than tipping back that skin all the time. Or drinking with your hand."

Chop agreed. He finished the second piece of meat, his belly becoming dangerously bloated.

"No more," Hargan said. "We'll eat what's left in the morning."

That was fine by Chop, who relaxed with a hand upon his full stomach.

Hargan scratched his beard, then his thigh. He stoked the little fire then rested his head against the wall, looking darkly thoughtful as he gazed out at the night.

"Did you fight at the front?" he finally asked. "The Sunjan front?"

That prompted the Nordish man to study Hargan's stern features. Wary, he nodded that he did.

"You ever kill anyone in their sleep?"

No, Chop shook his head. Not at the Sunjan front, anyway.

"You at the Field of Skulls?"

No.

"The truth now . . . Did you take heads and put them on spears?"

No.

"No, eh? You better not be lying. Not to me. My whole Klaw got butchered by Jackals. Nearly butchered me and my brother. We were the only ones who escaped. The only ones. The Jackals took the heads of everyone they killed. Filled a whole field. That's Sunjan history now."

Chop knew, but had not been a part of it.

Hargan studied him, searching for a hint of a lie. He must not have found one, as he made no move to strike.

"Why did they burn you?" the Sunjan finally asked.

The question was as sharp as a spear to the guts. For moments, Chop couldn't answer. It would have all come out in nonsense anyway. So he met Hargan's questioning gaze with one of his own.

"You did something wrong. I know they burn traitors. You a traitor?"

A short pause and he shook his head.

"Not a traitor. Well. Damnation. This would be more interesting if you could talk," Hargan rubbed his face. "You get on someone's dark side?"

Yes, he nodded.

"And you ran?"

Chop bobbled his head on his shoulders, *yes and no.*

Hargan thought for a moment. "You kill another Jackal?"

No.

"Steal another's woman?"

No.

"An officer's woman?"

No.

"An officer's *man*?"

No.

"Alright, alright. No lover's vengeance then." Hargan thought about it. "You disobeyed an order, perhaps?"

An energetic *Yes.*

"Disobeyed an order?" Hargan smiled coldly. "You crooked kog, you. What could that be? Something you couldn't do?"

Yes.

"Someone you wouldn't cut up?"

Yes.

That wiped the humor off Hargan's face. "Seddon above, you wouldn't kill someone? A *Jackal* wouldn't kill someone?"

Chop nodded, suddenly oblivious to his many hurts and his full stomach. On impulse, he cradled an imaginary baby in his arms.

"A baby?"

Chop waved that off and measured the air before him, the height of a child.

"A child then."

Yes.

"You refused . . . to kill a child?"

Chop held up two fingers.

"Two children," Hargan said in dawning horror.

A third finger, then, followed by a hand placed much higher than before.

"And a bigger child?"

No.

Hargan took a breath. "Their mother?"

Yes.

"Were they Sunjan?"

Yes.

"You refused to kill a mother . . . and her two children . . . and they burned you for it?"

They burned me for it, Chop remembered and nodded. It was the slowest, most wretched gesture of the entire conversation.

Silence then, for long considering moments. "Damnation," Hargan said softly and studied him for a few moments more before looking away.

The Sunjan did not ask any more questions that evening.

A mewling of stiff limbs and sore wounds woke Chop the next day, reminding him he was still on the mend. Of the Sunjan, there was no sign. Chop rose on unsteady feet and staggered into daylight. The rain had passed, and the sun had cooked off all of the clouds, leaving only a deep blue. He wandered over to the rocks and voided, and while he emptied the bull he looked into the valley.

Again, no sight or sign of the Sunjan.

A cool breeze staggered Chop. He finished up and made it back to the cave. There he sat just inside, out of the sun, feeling hungry but nothing compared to the day before. The "conversation" he'd had with Hargan coursed through his mind. He hadn't even told He-Dog any of his history, in all the years he'd traveled and fought with him. There were times when they'd all been drinking, and stories had come out, in a sense, where Chop let them think what they wanted. Chop didn't want to remember that decisive moment in his life, when his homeland cast him out. But if his homeland wanted him to kill innocents just for terror's sake, for cruelty's sake, then he had no use for his homeland.

More important, Chop knew his father would have approved of his decision to leave.

That was one thing he liked about He-Dog and Balless. They had simply accepted him as one of their own, and that was that. A rare thing.

Hargan, however, his once-sworn enemy, knew more of the truth than they ever had.

The sun hung low on the horizon, blazing into the cave and slowly baking it. There Chop sat, oozing perspiration from head to toe and front and back. When thirst scratched at his throat, he drank from the gourd, taking the odd handful to splash over his face. At times he drifted, unable to do anything more than pinch dead the few crawlers that came too close. He held onto those little bodies, wondering if he should save them for later, in case Hargan didn't return.

He hoped the Sunjan would return, however . . . with something to eat. And willing to share it.

At one point Chop woke with a lurch. He listened, sensing something nearby. His swords lay deeper inside the cave, but he stayed where he was, with his bare back pressed against stone. He leaned forward, spying part of the rocky battlements beyond and nothing else. It looked late in the afternoon, with long shadows stretching across the ground. He strained to hear, fearing another of those ape beasts might have found the cave, when a hard clopping froze him.

The noise grew louder, closer.

Just beyond the cave, Chop caught sight of what looked like a tail whipping about.

Chop tensed, ready to make the lurch for his swords.

A white tip of something flickered along the edge of the entrance, up and down before swinging out of sight. Then a long, brown horn lumbered into view, followed by a nose, attached to what looked like the head of a goat. Except this goat had three curved horns above its face. The animal wandered into full view, its hooves clicking as it climbed on top of the boulders enclosing the mountain shelf.

It was a goat, clear as the sun in the sky, but all Chop saw was a roast with legs.

The animal tensed, realizing it was being watched, and bolted from sight in three long strides. Rocks clattered as the animal made its escape, the noise receding.

In time Chop managed a little smile.

If he saw himself, he would run as well.

Much later, he opened his eyes and listened. A dull, unbreaking chirping filled the night, one not unpleasant to the ear. Chop turned his head, realizing he lay on his side. Outside, stars blazed upon a black canvass framed in the stone arch of the entrance. All was quiet, except for that soft pulsing of distant wildlife.

Hargan still hadn't returned.

Chop wondered if something had killed the man.

Somehow, he doubted it.

Sensing nothing amiss other than the nagging of his empty belly, Chop went back to sleep.

Hargan returned the next afternoon.

Chop heard him swearing as he climbed over the rocks, so he leaned out of the cave to better see.

"Still alive, Nordish?" the Sunjan asked upon nearing the entrance.

Chop lifted a hand to show he was still indeed alive.

Indifferent to the fact, Hargan carried his backpack over to where the man rested. "Still alive. You're like a half-crushed crawler clinging to every breath, you are. I expected you dead. Fully expected it. Well then. Look here . . ."

He opened up the pack and pulled out a gourd filled with bright red berries. As Chop watched, Hargan took a handful and jammed the lot of them into his bearded face.

"Sweet things," he said, chewing. "And see this."

The Sunjan extracted four dead birds that resembled tropical hens. Each one roughly the size of water skins with deep brown feathers.

"They couldn't fly for some reason or another," Hargan said while chewing, sending bits scattering. "I wonder what they'll taste like. Here." He handed over the gourd. "Eat those. A handful or two at least. I'll pluck these birds. Daresay we'll eat like kings this night, Nordish." He paused. "Any fish maggots about?"

Chop shook his head and tried a handful of the red fruit. The Sunjan was right. They were sweet.

"Don't eat too many of those," Hargan warned. "They bring on the squats. They did for me, anyway. All right. Here. I've changed my mind. Help me pluck the feathers from these. Don't give me that look, you Nordish dog blossom. You'll pluck if I say pluck, especially if you want to *eat* . . ."

So Chop finished his berries and helped with the plucking. Hargan collected a bit of wood and got a small fire going. By evening, they roasted all four birds.

When the food was ready, the two men sat across each other and ate a quiet yet civil supper. In time they finished and settled back while the sky grew dark.

"I'll be leaving again in the morning," Hargan rumbled, watching the night. "You'll have to mind yourself as best as you can. Don't expect me back . . . until I come back. And if I don't . . . I'm dead."

Chop regarded the man, waiting for more.

But Hargan only lowered his head and went to sleep.

CHAPTER 32

*H**unting.*
Hunting was on Hargan's mind that morning as he strode across the valley floor, back to his fence of skulls. *A fence.* He wondered what the Nordish asslicker would think about that. Not nearly on the scale of a *field* of skulls, but that was fine with Hargan. He would do what he could, to create his own little bit of history in this Seddon-forsaken pit of misery.

He wore no armor, having decided stealth would be better. He wore only his ragged breeches and boots, carried his axe and his pack, and nothing else. Thus, near naked, he went into the thickening jungle. An immense ceiling of interwoven foliage blocked the sun from reaching the ground, thick in places, thin in others. Where the greenery was thin and tattered, long shafts of light shone through. Alien flowers with their petals spread wide dotted the scene, their colors brightening the ground—even the darker places, where the sun failed to reach.

It wasn't long before Hargan caught a whiff of the smell, grimacing at the ripe tang up ahead. There, bathed in shadow, the heads of the dead waited in a neat row, their awful skulls picked clean by the denizens of the Sanjou. Nothing of sustenance clung to the faces, at least nothing that Hargan could see. When he came closer to inspect them, he found he was wrong. He stopped beside a pair of mottled skulls, not picked as clean as he first thought. The crawlers and flies had only moved inside the facial cavities, to dine on whatever festering gurry lay within.

He gazed upon the dead faces.
Lords above.
Hargan arched his head, studying the foliage above him. He'd once had the idea of hanging a few bodies off the branches to frighten any fishmen coming this way. Or enrage them enough to come charging forward. He wondered if that was why he was butchering these creatures. To enrage them . . .

He glared at the decaying faces and decided it was much worse.
He was going mad here. Unfit mad.
Which was one reason he had to leave his mountain roost. To burn off the hateful energy growing inside him. To search for the dog blossoms that left him sharing a cave with a near-dead Nordish topper. That scratched a smile across his

dirty face. Oh, how far he'd fallen to end up here. And if he allowed these thoughts, if he let these feelings of self-loathing burn . . . well . . . it was just best he bled them off.

By hunting the ones responsible for his situation.

The fishmen.

Hargan looked around him and decided it was time to venture deeper into the jungle. He concealed his tracks most of the time but also intentionally left blatant signs of his presence to confuse them, to trap them, and, ultimately, to slaughter them. To spike their heads across the whole forsaken Sanjou. To tighten their blossoms with a little fear, if such creatures could be frightened. He didn't think so.

Regardless, he believed he had a plan. A good one, even.

To that end, he slipped into the underbrush and allowed the jungle to swallow him right up.

Over the broad backs of hills he traveled, into shallow valleys and shadowy recesses, looking for the fishmen. He wanted them to know he was out here somewhere, everywhere. The Nordish Jackals terrorized Sujin patrols back in the day, leaving trails that led nowhere or into ambushes. The Sujins didn't know which until much later, one way or the other.

Hargan hoped to do the same in the Sanjou.

His strength finally failed him by the evening, so he stopped near a small stream bordered by tall reeds and a fallen log stretching off into the jungle. The surrounding woodland was a jumble of high grass, coarse brush, and clinging branches. Tall trees with gilded trunks dipped their roots into the stream. Insects looking for a bite ignored him, thanks to a layer of filth he'd slapped on his skin earlier in the day.

He rummaged through his pack and finished off some of the bird meat he'd cooked the day before. After eating, he sat upon the soft bank with his back against a tree. He ignored the colorful insects clambering over the surface of the water. He'd kill them dead if they bothered him, and he mentally projected that threat to the little creepers.

In the morning he'd make his way southwest, toward the fishmen's fortress. He'd stumbled upon it just days after the ambush had torn the mercenaries apart. He hoped he would meet some of the sickly maggots along the way.

With a hand on his axe, he tipped his head and went to sleep.

And opened his eyes, blinking.

It was daylight, and Hargan realized he'd slept like a dead man. His back was a little stiff, but it wasn't exactly the first time he'd slept in discomfort. He scratched, cranked his neck, and inspected his filthy chest.

And saw the bites.

Huge, brazen red marks the size of a thumb pad spotted his chest, each peaked with a ripe, yellow bulb. Enough of them to turn his skin into a gruesome pattern. He frowned and studied himself further, noting that the majority of the bites appeared on his chest, but there were also a few on his arms. His legs felt untouched.

Something had feasted on him during his sleep, and he hoped the little maggots had choked during their meal.

The marks were swollen, a little elevated, and itched upon touch. Scowling, he scratched one of the rounded mounds dotting his forearm.

One rake of his fingernail and the pustule broke open.

And a black worm oozed out.

Hargan's jaw dropped in horrified dismay. He brought his arm closer, inspecting the maggot-sized larva wriggling about in that yellow dollop. For a single shocked moment, he could only stare at the creature.

Then panic seized him.

With a moan he swiped the worm off his arm and smeared his fingers across the bare trunk of the tree. Gasping, he went for the next raised welt upon his arm. He dug out a second grubby occupant—this one a bit more active.

"Oh, sweet Seddon," he swore, gawking at the remaining marks covering him.

The next few moments were spent in a rabid urgency to pop open all the welts. He clawed *deep*, rooting out his unwanted guests and ignoring the blood. Sickened by the infestation, he lurched to the nearby stream and waded up to his knees. There he frantically splashed water on himself, washing the dead things off.

An itch told him to check his shoulder then. A whimper squeaked past his lips as he spotted a rosy boil on his right shoulder, a milky, sightless eye rising from the skin. Hargan ripped at the thing. He got the worm out, splashed it off his back, and immediately probed his other shoulder. Finding nothing, he began clawing at his lower back, raking fingernails deep into his own skin.

A dawning sense of dread stopped him.

He hadn't checked his breeches yet. Although his legs *felt* fine.

Fear gripped him again.

His kog and bells.

Oh, Lords above, he thought, the fear stabbing through his heart.

Have to be sure. Hargan thrashed back to shore. He stripped off his clothing and, panting with fright, lifted this and shifted that. He pawed at his fruits, examining them before finally releasing everything with a sigh of relief. No worms infested his bits or his legs, and he figured the rough cloth of his breeches might have protected him. Still appalled, Hargan studied the blood seeping from his self-inflicted ruptures. Anyone else would have dropped senseless long ago, but not him. Scowling, regaining control with every heartbeat, he waded back into the water and washed himself.

In between splashes, however, he realized how quiet the jungle had become. Alerted by the lack of sound, he straightened and listened. A snap of dead brush whipped his head around.

A flicker of movement beyond the trees.

Crouching, Hargan got out of the water and grabbed his axe. Held it across his waist and waited, watching the bushes. He edged forward, staying low, moving for the fallen log along the shore and kneeling behind it.

A peek over the top revealed things moving just beyond where he'd slept. Hunched things creeping through the wilderness. The underbrush parted, and low shapes, their faces painted in shadow, crept toward him in a wide line. *Fishmen*. At least a dozen of the maggots.

They'd found him.

He checked his flank. Sunlight sparkled off the stream's surface, but no enemy tried to encircle him. Ahead, however, a pair of fishmen emerged on either side of the log, not ten strides away. Their oddly aquatic faces turned, searching, listening. Jutting jaws hung open, revealing racks of fangs. Orange eyes narrowed into slits.

One of them climbed onto the log.

Hargan lowered his head. He remembered the last conversation he'd had with Marrek, before his throat was cut. Perhaps his brother was right after all. Maybe there *was* something wrong with him.

As soon as the thought left his head, Hargan sprang from his hiding space, catching the pair off guard.

Hargan hacked a leg off the one standing upon the log, just above the ankle. The fishman collapsed, mashing his groin into old wood. Hargan stopped the spear thrust of the other, and his answering cut split apart a throat, slashing the Sanjou with a black mist. The Sunjan turned and brought his axe down, taking the head off the twitching fishman sprawled over the log, freeing that grisly bauble with a little jump. Hargan shoved the body off as he climbed onto the wood. He ranted. Raved. Shook his axe at the rest of the fishman patrol emerging from the jungle. They hesitated before realizing there was only one foe.

Then they rushed him, howling as they charged.

Hargan screamed at the nearest fish-jawed creature as the thing raised its club. The mercenary moved faster, swinging his axe, splitting the hellion's skull to the jaw.

Then they were coming at him from everywhere.

Hargan lopped off a hand and lashed the axe across a livid face. He kicked a head, bashed another to the side, and killed a third with a ruthless downward chop. Then he was running, bare feet slapping wood, leaping over clubs and axes, pushing fishmen off the log as they strove to climb on. Spears flashed by him. Hargan ducked and bobbed, smashing heads and shoulders while punching those too close for the axe. He caved in a face, hacked apart a shoulder while the owner shrieked, and left fishmen clutching at killing wounds in his wake.

Then he ran.

Naked and wailing, he bounded through the tall reeds, knowing the fishmen clamored after him.

He turned right for a few bounding strides.

Then left. Then straight on.

A howling fishman appeared before him, stabbing a black-tipped spear at his face. Hargan knocked the thrust aside and slammed his forehead into the other's. The fishman fell. Hargan charged another foe, parrying a spear before upper-cutting with his axe, swinging from the hips. Steel blade connected with a jutting jaw, destroying it in a crack of bone, lifting the lout off the ground.

On instinct, Hargan ducked and a stone axe hummed overhead. A scream followed it. The pissers attacked from all sides now. Hargan rushed through the jungle but rounded his way back to the log by the stream, his pursuers yammering wildly in confusion. The log appeared and Hargan leapt onto its girth. There, he skirted to the middle, bellowing all the while. The fishmen closed in. Yowling nonsense, they scrambled onto the wood, sticky with gore.

The mercenary met them one after the other.

He took a head off at the shoulders.

Severed a leg at the knee.

Hacked into an arm, which fell to the jungle floor with a burst of ink. He split a jaw in half and the face above it, and when the fishman dropped, his back broke across the log.

Hargan jumped off the wood, landed running, and nearly fell. He stumbled, righted himself, and thumped into the same tree he'd slept against the night before.

He placed his back against the trunk.

The last of the fish maggots crowded in, and then . . . nothing mattered.

Hargan slew half of them before burying his battle-axe too deeply into one of their shoulders to pull it back out. Whereupon the Sunjan grabbed a club from one of the dead and bashed whatever stood before him until it broke in two over a skull. Then he grabbed a stone axe and continued killing . . . until nothing stood at all. He swung about on giddy legs, stumbling, bruised and bleeding from a few stinging licks. Panting, he leaned against the tree and glared, smeared with a foul blend of perspiration and oily blood. Wiping his face, he regarded the battlefield.

A mess of carnage lay across the back of the Sanjou.

With no one else to fight, Hargan stumbled to the water's edge. As he moved, the noises of the forest shyly crept back into existence. The danger had passed.

Almost.

A fishman twisted onto his back, orange eyes glazed and dying. The thing pressed both hands across his slashed midsection. Upon spying the Sunjan, the creature gnashed charred fangs and grumbled gibberish.

Hargan watched the thing for a short time before dropping the stone axe in favor of his own. He wrenched his battle-axe out of the fishman corpse's shoulder and lumbered over to the dying creature. The fishman squirmed a little more. The orange eyes opened just a little wider.

The thing screamed just before a bloody wedge of steel split his face, right between the eyes.

When it was done, Hargan left his axe in the dead creature's face and rested his bones on the log. Unmoving bodies crushed weeds and bushes, while the ground soaked up fluids splashed about. Wrecked and bleeding carcasses hung across the log, soaking it. More corpses lay strewn around the trees, underneath a shimmering haze of heat.

Knowing there was no time to waste, Hargan remembered what he wanted to do, so he went about doing it.

The next morning, a group of Iruzu wandered through the area, following the trail left by another hunting pack. The first of the hunters stopped and stared, drawing the attention of the leader. Then they all saw and looked upon the bodies of their missing hunters.

The heads gone from each of the corpses.

All except one, spiked on a spear, his dead eyes festering with the crawling filth of the Sanjou.

CHAPTER 33

Two ships raced along the Inner Sea.

The first vessel powered through the rough waters, her full sails harnessing the winds, her bow cutting through waves in explosive white mists.

Standing on the high deck of the second ship, peering intently at the fleeing quarry, was a well-dressed individual, dark of hair and beard. A white shirt lay open at his sternum and fluttered violently, revealing a muscular chest. This individual leaned into the breeze, war braid trailing, squinting at the distant ship to gauge its distance and speed. He stroked a pointed beard and smiled a toothy yellow grin, being one of the few men on board to still possess a full set. That made him handsome. Or so he believed.

His name was Black Korraz, one he'd chosen for himself, mostly because of his full head of hair. In some circles, however—mainly the nautical ones—if you heard his name, it was best to hear *of* him and not *from* him.

"She looks to be breaking away from us," an intimidating character yelled, making his voice heard over the winds. He was a big man, broad of shoulder and powerful, barely fitting into the leather armor he wore. His long hair had been tied back, letting a tail perhaps half an arm long snake in the wind. Scars decorated his face. A number of blades hung off his figure, the most notable being a broadsword at his waist.

"She's not breaking away," Korraz replied, his voice crisp, cultured, and utterly chilling. "Keep watching, Sobaba. You'll see."

Determined to do just that, Sobaba's face screwed up a touch more.

Korraz checked on the helmsman behind him. Then he glanced at the rigging, the sails full and powering his ship—the *Bloody Thorn*—along at a brisk pace. With nothing amiss there, he looked down upon the main deck. A collection of leering killers talked among themselves while slapping on armor and checking their weapons. Shiny bracers and greaves flashed under the sun. Edged steel rasped and clicked as swords were pulled free of scabbards and inspected. Sixty-five cutthroats assembled, with another thirty maintaining the ship as she sped across the Inner Sea.

Korraz smiled and nodded. "This rabbit's a quick one."

Sobaba said nothing to that. Sobaba didn't say much of anything, truth be known.

Korraz leaned over the railing, watching his men prepare for battle below. An unshaven Timmer strode through the works of them, cursing at some, slapping the shoulders of others. The once-gladiator wore a black skull rag, pulled tight over his head and tied off at the base of his neck, with two tails dangling. Shirtless, the man displayed a lean torso wiry with muscle. A scabbard housing a short sword hung at his waist, his hand never straying far from the pommel. While Sobaba had been with Korraz for years and served as his chief enforcer, Timmer was a welcome addition. Hailing from Sunja, the lad had developed his fighting skills by competing in the yearly gladiatorial games. Eventually tiring of that, he decided to apply his murderous expertise to other trades.

Piracy being the one he preferred.

Much to Korraz's delight.

Oh, Sobaba was a monster, make no mistake, but Timmer was . . . an artist with a blade. Where Sobaba would kill a man out of bloodletting necessity, Timmer could and would duel, gauging an adversary—playing with him—until delivering the final chop.

As Korraz watched the boarding party, he noticed Horlo the Cruel smiling that unfit smile of his. Tall, bulky, and cursed with an ogre's grace, Horlo stood near the starboard railing. His huge belly spilled over his waist, despite a wide leather belt attempting to hold it back. A matching pair of bands crisscrossed his front and back. That huge jiggling gut, coated in a dew of hair and sweat, seemed like a tempting target for one so ponderous on his feet. All an illusion, however, as Horlo had proven himself time and time again to be skilled with a blade, and exceptionally useful when assigned to watch prisoners.

Sobaba. Timmer. Horlo the Cruel. Three notable names among the collection of killers that made up a most vicious crew.

Korraz included.

His attention returned to the fleeing ship. Something was not right there. She was too far away for him to see exactly what was off, but something was amiss.

Sobaba saw it too, clutching the railing and leaning forward.

Then the two masts of the ship lurched and Korraz smiled. "Grounded," he whispered in dark delight and turned to his helmsman. "Where are we exactly?"

"Not far off of Zuthenia, Captain."

"How far?"

"We'd see land soon enough if we struck that way, sar," the helmsman reported, nodding in one direction.

Korraz knew himself, but he liked to double-check. He wasn't about to be set upon by vengeful galleons. He eyed the surrounding ocean. "We're out of reach of old Narijo's navies? *Far* from reach?"

"Aye that, sar, that's correct."

"And that way," Korraz indicated west. "Roughly four- or five-days' sail is what the beastmen call Big Rock?"

"Aye that, sar."

Korraz studied the helmsman. His name was Nillot or some such gurry. "So then, we're well clear of the Serpent's Teeth?"

They were the fabled rows of reefs and shoals guarding the Zuthenian southern coast.

"Oh, aye that sar," Nillot answered immediately, well-aware his life *depended* on knowing that very crumb of knowledge.

"Carry on, then," Korraz warned with a cold smile. "On this course. Bring us alongside that stricken sea hen. Mind her feathers. And the hidden shoals. She's run aground something out there. Something not on her charts. Or ours, apparently." He shot a warning glance at the helmsman, who suddenly looked fearful for his throat. "Have whatshisface mark these waters on his charts. For future reference."

"Aye that, sar," answered the helmsman.

Korraz turned back to his crew. "*Fish!*"

A stick of a man appeared, at the edge of the activity on the main deck.

"Get up front and start dropping stones," Korraz ordered. "Watch for the backs of dragons."

"Sar!" Fish scrambled off with his orders.

Sobaba's eyes widened at the mention of dragons.

"Our rabbit has hooked its furry fruit on something," Korraz said and sized up the boarding party below. "Ready for some bloodletting, lads?"

A shout went up.

"Kill what you want. Take prisoners if they throw down arms, but make no mistake, we'll kill them later. Bring me the captain of that vessel alive, if possible. Or the first mate. That is all . . ."

Another shout went up.

"Timmer!" Korraz shouted.

The black-capped head popped up. "Sar?"

"Have the lads ready their bows. We'll drift by her side. Salt her tender bits. Then . . ." Korraz clawed at the air, hauling in a fistful.

Timmer relayed the orders.

Korraz regarded Sobaba. "Help me with my armor, would you?"

A short time later, the *Bloody Thorn* leisurely passed alongside the stricken two-mast galleon, and arrows drizzled the air as both ships exchanged greetings. Shafts hammered the *Thorn*'s deck, the impacts shockingly loud, drowning out the few grunts of surprise from lads not nearly as protected as they'd thought. Korraz's men released thicker waves of arrows, however, and by the time they had passed, they had inflicted their own share of damage to the other ship and crew.

The order came to circle back.

And make ready the hooks and boarding planks.

The *Bloody Thorn* made its turn, further wetting a rack of iron barbs lining the underside of the bow. Water frothed as the pirate vessel bore down. Word came back from Fish, leaning over the spar. He believed the crippled ship ran afoul of the absolute edge of a hidden shoal.

Which was all Black Korraz needed.

The *Thorn* drifted alongside its quarry while the leering faces of pirates waited for the opportunity to board. Nillot, the helmsman, brought the ship in as close as he dared, the hull raking submerged sand and moaning as it did so. A tremble went through the vessel, widening more than a few sets of eyes. Korraz grabbed for the railing and held on, waiting, dreading, for that abrupt halt which would make things even more interesting. Arrows flittered from both sides, keeping heads down. Then the hooks went over the side, flying across a space of a dozen strides. Several found purchase and were immediately hacked away. More sailors died, struck down by arrows.

Korraz stayed below the raised walls of the deck. He cocked his head at the sounds of the dead and nearly dead.

This dying rabbit was being saucy.

The gap between the two ships narrowed more. Planks were shoved across. Korraz's pirates, the foremost carrying large shields, lumbered over those shivering bridges. Some fell into the gap, disappearing with a yell and a splash below. The rest breached the rabbit's side and jumped aboard, swinging steel as they went.

Where the true reaving began.

The unmoving galleon held a crew of perhaps eighty, with maybe a score of those shaved off by the volleys of arrows. Given their situation, and the reputation of their attackers, anyone who could fight . . . did so.

Not that it made any difference.

Timmer crossed in the first wave. Korraz glimpsed him going over with sword and shield, and a stream of cutthroats at his back. Other waves followed, amid the tempered clanging and yelling from the stricken ship. Horlo the Cruel lumbered over, leading a wave. Then Sobaba. Cries and screams stabbed the sea air, and Korraz glimpsed both armored and unarmored men perishing on the other ship. One lad of the other crew was descending a ladder when a spear nailed him to the wall. An instant later his whole body fell back. Sailors fell into the waters between the two ships, trailing blood and dead before they hit. A few pockets of resistance appeared upon the deck as the battle dragged on, but Timmer and Sobaba found them and put a bloody end to them all.

In time, the fighting died away.

When it did, Korraz adjusted his sword hanging from his waist and carefully crossed the plank himself.

There was something glorious about one's boots landing upon the deck of a conquered ship, but Korraz didn't rightly know what it was. Perhaps it was the cheers and blood-streaked smiles from his killers as they greeted him. Maybe it was the wood beneath his boots, littered with the dead and awash in crimson. Certainly wasn't the smell, which for some reason no one mentioned in their songs of pitched battles at sea.

Korraz nodded at his surviving crewmembers, judging they'd lost no more than a score, which would be later weighed against whatever valuables they found.

Of the enemy, only a score and three remained, which would also be weighed against the loot they came away with. Timmer and Horlo the Cruel had the prisoners on their knees and their heads lowered.

"Excellent," a pleased Korraz told them all, nodding and winking at the bleeding faces. "Simply . . . excellent. Well done, all. Very well done."

A leering Horlo stood before the row of prisoners. He held a shortened gaff hook, presumably one found on board.

"Did you find the captain?" Korraz asked Timmer.

The once-gladiator nodded and gestured at an open door, one spattered in blood and hair. "In his cabin."

"Thank you, Timmer. Sobaba? With me, please? And bring a few lads."

"A few lads are waiting inside with the captain, sar," Timmer said.

Korraz approved. He studied the defeated remnants of the ship's crew and didn't give them another thought. Inside he went, cautious of where he stepped, thankful for the much larger room. Officers' quarters, complete with rope hammocks that gently swayed over nailed-down chests. Nothing of any great value. He walked by it all, toward a second door. There, inside a white-painted room, were three men on their knees. A handful of Korraz's men stood guard, bloodied weapons bared and ready.

The lads nodded at their captain as he entered.

Korraz stopped just over the threshold and placed his hands on his hips. Most of the furniture had been overturned, as if the prisoners had braced for a siege. The three men waited, heads lowered. One heavy-set individual wore a white shirt speckled red, half of it upended over a fine belt of leather. Of the three, he was the oldest, with thinning hair and a couple of fleshy barnacles sticking off his face. The other two were much younger. In their twenties, if Korraz guessed correctly.

"Which one is the captain here?" he asked, already knowing the answer.

As expected, the lads pointed to the older dog blossom, who slowly lifted his head.

He sported one blackened eye and a bleeding gash above it, as long and wide as one's little finger. A thin stream dribbled from his left ear as well, down to that white collar where the material had stained a deep maroon. His jaw twitched in a blend of fear and rage, which was understandable, at least to Korraz.

"Your ship is mine now," he informed the defeated captain on his knees.

The older gentleman blinked and made no reply.

"Your . . . crew . . . or what's left of them are at my mercy."

The defeated captain prodded his inner lip with a tongue.

"Do you know who we are?"

A deep sigh through the man's nose, and an equally deep nod.

One that Korraz matched, but with a much different sentiment behind it. His fingers rested on the fancy pommel of his sword. "What do you have in your hold?"

"Food and water mostly," the older man croaked, sounding in need of a drink.

"Don't you all?" Korraz smiled knowingly. "Is that it?"

"That's it."

"What's your name?"

The older man puckered his lips into an angry knot and fumed, not believing his predicament. "Tycuro."

"Captain Tycuro?"

He nodded.

"Hailing from?"

". . . Zuthenia."

Korraz smiled. "This will all end the same way for you and your men. There's no changing that. What I want you to consider, however . . . is how you *want* it to end. Quickly. Or slowly. Hm?"

Tycuro tongued his lips again and glanced around, as if remembering much better times. Perhaps even that morning.

"Where are you sailing?" Korraz put to him.

"The Sanjou."

"What's that?"

Tycuro met his eyes. "The. Sanjou."

"The cursed Sanjou? The haunted land? The land of all manner of monster?"

Tycuro nodded as an afterthought.

"People still sail there?" an amused Korraz asked Sobaba without expecting a reply. And he was right. "For what purpose?"

"Exploration."

"Exploration? With this rabble?"

Tycuro nodded wearily.

"You have a royal command from good King Narijo or something?"

Tycuro answered that with a spiteful glare, which Korraz met with a puzzled one of his own. Without warning, he walked over to one of his lads and held out a hand.

The man slapped a broad knife into his captain's palm.

Korraz approached one of the younger men beside Tycuro. He smiled, briefly, at the old captain, and then grabbed the chin of the young prisoner.

Before plunging the knife into the man's eye.

To the hilt.

Where Korraz left it, as the prisoner fell twitching upon the floor.

Raw shock flashed across Tycuro's bruised features and the other remaining prisoner. Shock that quickly transformed into rage. "You—"

Sobaba slapped the old captain hard across the face, knocking him over.

The other pirates lugged the battered Tycuro back to his knees, where he saw Korraz holding the face of his other companion.

Korraz waited until Tycuro saw him . . . and what he was about to do.

The captain was about to talk when Korraz opened the second man's throat with another blade, producing a horrific gargle that quickly bled away.

Korraz let that one drop as well, mindful of the spreading mess.

"Now then," he said to the outraged captain. "Those were two examples of how it will end quickly. And let me remind you, I have twenty more of your crew outside these walls."

"You unfit hellion."

". . . You're not wrong there, I suppose."

"You . . ." Tycuro sputtered, red-faced and still bleeding, unable to finish.

"I see you're one of those stubborn types."

"I hope they hunt down every last one of you Ossaki asslickers. And put each and every one of you to the hooks. Where you'll swing. By your ankles. While crows pick your eyes from your screaming faces."

Korraz let him have his say before locking gazes with him. "You've made your choice, I see."

"There was no *choice*. You Ossaki *shite*. Unfit pirate *bastards*. I know what will happen either way, and yes, I've made my choice, damn you."

Weathering all that, Korraz's face became a stern thing. "So be it."

He glanced at his men. "Lads . . ."

"Wait . . ." Tycuro spat, just as the grips tightened around his neck and shoulders.

Korraz took a dagger from Sobaba, a straight one with a wicked serrated edge.

"I'll tell you," the old man said.

Korraz stepped up to the captain and grabbed a fistful of thinning hair. He yanked up the head and stared down at his face.

The serrated blade touched a shaved jawline.

"We're looking for riches in the Sanjou," Tycuro said, clearly hating himself for breaking, but very much mindful of the sharp edge upon his face.

"Riches?" Korraz paused. "What kind of riches?"

"A mountain of gold."

"A *mountain* of gold?"

"We have a map."

Korraz squinted. "Where is it? And for your sake you better not have second thoughts."

"In the corner. There's a floorboard underneath the pisspot. Strike one end and pop it up. Slide it out. It's in there."

Sobaba went to the indicated corner. The big man started stomping, breaking wood. Moments later, he returned with a scroll in his hand.

"What is it?" Korraz asked.

"It was given to me by an official of King Narijo," Tycuro explained as Sobaba inspected the map. "I wasn't told how he got the map, only that there *was* a map."

Korraz leaned over to better see the thing. There, in a series of rough drawings indicating trails and landmarks, were two lines resembling a mountain. And a number of shorter lines coming from it, as if shining like the sun.

"That's a mountain of gold?" Korraz asked.

"Aye that."

"You're sure of it?"

Tycuro squeezed his eyes shut. "Nothing's for certain. Which is why we're only one ship and not a handful. The king wanted us to find it first."

"And the provisions you speak of? To keep you alive for the duration of this . . . treasure hunt?"

"Aye that."

"All supplied by the king's man?"

". . . And financed. Aye that."

Korraz's sinister features brightened. "A mountain of gold, you say."

Tycuro shook his head. "Truth be known, I don't know if it's there or not. I was sent to find out for certain."

"I see." Korraz nodded and stabbed the captain through the throat. The older man collapsed, gargling blood, clutching at the blade driven deep into his kinkhorn and left there. He twitched and twisted for only a few heartbeats, kicking once before the life left him.

"Let me have that," Korraz said and took the map from his henchman. "Mountain of gold," he mulled, studying the details. He thought for moments before regarding Sobaba. "What do you think?"

The big man shrugged.

"Not this time," Korraz warned him. "Say what you think."

Sobaba frowned. "Maybe."

"It is the Sanjou."

"It is cursed," Sobaba plainly pointed out. "More tales of men going to their deaths there than treasures coming out."

"But those that do come out . . ." Korraz held up a finger, "have riches."

Sobaba nodded, supposing that was true enough.

Timmer appeared in the doorway, catching Korraz's eye. "Have you checked the hold?"

"Aye that," the once-gladiator reported. "Filled to capacity. Dried fish. Cured meats. Biscuits. Water and a dozen kegs of beer. Three filled with wine."

"Anything else?"

Timmer shook his head. "No room for anything else. They filled the hold with everything they could. Even weapons. Bows. Spears. Arrows. Extra swords. Armor."

"Enough for how long?"

Timmer thought about it. "Long enough, I figure. Several weeks at least."

"Long enough to explore a large island?"

"Aye that. Easily."

Sobaba met Korraz's sly gaze. "Timmer . . ." the captain said, still staring at his henchman. "Feel like looking for a bit of treasure?"

CHAPTER 34

He-Dog and Kellic sat behind the lodges in a sweat, wearing only their leggings. They faced the jungle, reflecting on the past few days, since they'd woken from the last of the dream leaves. Not sociable at any time, He-Dog sat and stewed in his own juices, at times pawing at his face and other parts to rid himself of the annoying moisture. Kellic didn't say much either, staring into space for long periods that He-Dog thought strange at first, then annoying, then right and proper unfit. Upon having enough of that nonsense, He-Dog stood and ignored the mildly questioning look from the other man.

It was brighter out on the little ridge in front of the lodge, but not enough to brighten He-Dog's spirits. Half Tusk and his lads noticed the mercenary and turned about with inquisitive looks. He-Dog stared at the guards. The guards stared back. Ordinarily, he would be up to a contest to see who would blink first, but not that day. Growing increasingly contrary, He-Dog rumbled his disdain and plopped down on the embankment. He let his legs dangle, swinging them a few times just to get the blood moving, and planted his hands into the grassy dirt.

Apparently having seen enough, Half Tusk turned away, slowly, clearly unimpressed with the big man. He-Dog didn't blame the topper. He'd be unimpressed as well. With that thought lingering, he kicked his legs, realizing he was drawing the attention of a few villagers.

Lords above, He-Dog mentally groaned. At least it wasn't scornful attention—but it was uncomfortable. To that end, he leaned forward and let his head hang, sneaking peeks here and there every so often.

The Anoka watched him, their tools forgotten and hanging at their sides. Some held cups just below their chins or watched him over rims. Children pointed and laughed. A few even waved. One woman held a dead jungle bird by its neck, with half its feathers plucked.

Well, He-Dog reminded himself. *Broska* said *they would be watching. He did indeed.*

With that, he alternated between studying his knees and the ground below.

Not long after, Kellic joined him. Without a word, the mercenary thumped his arse down on the grassy dirt and slouched forward. Just a little too close to He-Dog, however, and he let the man know with a questioning glare.

Except Kellic ignored him.

Sighing, He-Dog slid a half stride away from his companion. If Kellic noticed, he didn't show it. Not a grunt or glance. In silence, the two mercenaries faced the village and the Anoka watching them from afar. A few of them even wandered in closer for a better look. Half Tusk and his warriors prevented the villagers from getting too close, saying a few words in that odd language of theirs and sending them on their way. Two little ones walked up to Half Tusk and spoke to him, but the leader shooed them away as well.

He-Dog appreciated that little courtesy.

Realizing they were not allowed anywhere near the two Slayers, the children and villagers returned to whatever they were doing . . . but continued to steal peeks from afar.

"They like to watch," He-Dog muttered.

Kellic grunted in agreement.

Scratching at his chin, which was rough with stubble, He-Dog studied the village as daily life resumed. A lot of things were happening. Wild birds, perhaps freshly killed from a morning hunt, had their feathers plucked. Women fussed over stitched blankets or cleaned hides. Men stretched more hides over bare wooden stages. A handful of young men sat in a circle and made arrows. All the while, children scampered throughout the dwellings, squealing with delight at being chased.

He-Dog rubbed his throat while watching it all. "I'm bored," he muttered after a bit.

Kellic didn't say anything to that.

He-Dog glanced over. "Are you bored?"

Kellic answered with the barest of frowns, indicating he was. A little.

"You don't talk much, do you?"

Sighing through his nose, Kellic shook his head.

Clearly, He-Dog thought and glanced around. He uprooted himself, dusted off his legs, and again wandered behind the lodges. Green daylight soaked the little glade. Needing to do something and wondering what he *could* do, He-Dog started trudging around in a circle. In short time, he'd created a path through the colorful flowers dotting the ground. The prince's scabbard hung off one hip, the sword within slapping against his leg. Sweat shone upon his muscular frame, the heat and humidity slowly steaming him despite the shade.

Heat.

He-Dog couldn't decide if he hated the jungle's heat more than the desert's. One meant to boil every drop of juice in you while the other simply wanted to scorch you down to nothing. But he was walking. And after all that time breathing in the dream smoke—not that it seemed like a long time—it was good to be up and walking about. Good to be moving for more than a few paces. That nagging sense of being just a touch off-balance still plagued him, but not nearly as bad as before. Broska said it would pass. All he needed was a little more time to recover. So he walked, mindful of the surrounding jungle when he came close to it, glimpsing the village beyond the lodges when he made his turns. The Anoka knew he was pacing back there and they watched him as if wondering what he was doing. He didn't mind that.

After some time, he stopped and pulled out the sword. He gripped it with both hands and held it over his head before swinging it down in a chop. That felt all right. Heavier than he remembered, but his accuracy was still intact. So he weaved a figure eight in the air. Easy enough. Then two more straight chops from overhead, with a little more power, as if he were splitting an imaginary skull.

A wave of dizziness came on strong after that, warning him not to get unfit with things.

"All right," He-Dog muttered, putting the sword away. He would try again when the feeling passed.

"Feeling unsteady?" Kellic asked, watching from between the lodges.

He-Dog squinted back, wondering if the bastard realized he was following him around. "Aye that," he admitted. "When I swung the sword."

"Broska said we would get over the sickness in two days."

"He said we'd get over it soon."

"He said that?"

He-Dog nodded.

Appearing to think that over, Kellic followed the path He-Dog had already stomped out. The man hitched up his leggings before scratching at his considerably hairy torso. He also wore his sword, and after a while, he pulled it free.

He-Dog got out of his way, thinking the man truly did have sad eyes.

Kellic took a few practice swings before stopping to gulp down some air. He bent over, propped up by his sword and a hand to a knee, and looked to sit down.

"Watch for the crawlers," He-Dog advised. "Unfit things grow big around here."

While Kellic recovered, the sound of children laughing nearby hooked their attention. A frowning Snaffer skulked behind the lodge, clearly looking for a spot to hide from watchful eyes. He sat with a thump and crossed his legs before him.

"How's your prince?" He-Dog asked, knowing the man had left them earlier to check on Shay.

Snaffer regarded him for a moment before answering. "The man's unfit in the head," he grumbled. "One moment he thinks we've been here days, the next it's months. He should be better than this. That Zuthenian asslicker said he would get better."

He-Dog remembered Broska saying that. He also remembered his warning about the dream leaves changing a person for the worse if they breathed in too much for too long. Not that Shay had had much of a choice, given the extent of his wounds.

"He told me he wants to walk," Snaffer said.

". . . But that's good," Kellic said with an uncertain look.

"The man only has one leg," Snaffer muttered while staring at the jungle. "And the bloodfish had a good chew off that one as well." The old mercenary winced. "He wants *walking* sticks. Already asked Broska, he said. Said he'll be up and walking in no time. Also said he wants to talk to the elders."

". . . Will he?" He-Dog asked.

"I don't know," Snaffer admitted in a tired tone. "All I know is . . . the lad's not right. Not in the head. You lads better this day?" he asked as an afterthought.

"A touch better," Kellic said quietly.

"As I," added He-Dog.

Snaffer met that with a scowl. Then, as if he was sick of sitting, he stood and pulled his hand axe from his belt. He straightened his arm and sighted a tree. Without warning he threw the axe, *hard*, and placed it dead center in the trunk, the impact loud and blunt.

Snaffer ignored the looks and sat down again, message sent.

For moments, no one said anything, and He-Dog didn't think much of it. In fact, he was getting sick of the bouts of silence from the pair. So he decided to take a walk. At least that didn't seem to sicken him.

"You're off?" Kellic asked.

"I'm off."

"Where?"

"About the village," He-Dog said. With that, he adjusted his belt and left the pair.

The sun bore down as he stepped out from between the lodges and skidded down the embankment, kicking up dirt as he went. Half Tusk and his handful of warriors watched him with sunny scowls.

"Lads," He-Dog greeted stoically and walked by them all.

To his surprise, no one stopped him. He knew Half Tusk and his boys had orders to keep everyone away from the three lodges, but they didn't have any orders to stop the Slayers from wandering about. And Broska had recommended the men take a walk around the area if they so desired.

He-Dog suddenly desired, so he followed a path through the village, keeping to the shade. Lazy trails of smoke drifted by, as did the sounds of wood hammering wood, and the soft clucking of the odd wild birds that Kellic had once called jungle hens, which strutted freely throughout the settlement.

The first Anoka he encountered were three older women, weaving material into long strips while sitting before a lodge. When they noticed him, their eyes opened wide and their conversation ceased. Another group of women sat before the next home, sifting through baskets of berries and greens. They also stopped what they were doing and stared in unchecked wonder at the Slayer as he passed. Children appeared in twos and threes, girls and boys no older than ten. They spotted him and lost all interest in their sticks and balls of crumpled hides. One little boy waved energetically.

He-Dog awkwardly nodded and increased his pace.

He passed raised platforms with piles of skinned animals, where the men fussing over them paused in their work and watched him go by. Far ahead, the lodge of the elders loomed on the little hill, through the trees. Guards stood at the trailhead leading to that lodge.

With a familiar nagging feeling, He-Dog stopped and glanced back, halting two of Half Tusk's warriors a dozen paces behind him. He frowned, but neither man reacted, waiting for his next move.

So He-Dog cut between a pair of homes, turning heads as he went. Children squealed and pointed. Older folks glimpsed him as he hurried by, stopping all conversation. The Anoka tongue was a maddening language, sounding familiar yet incoherent. Then the village abruptly ended at a wide river, some two dozen strides across, with the jungle raging on the far side. Several children swam in the current, while a pair of families lounged on the shore not a few paces away from him.

They gawked the moment they noticed him.

He-Dog rolled his eyes and looked about. Scowling, he moved down the shore, darting around a knot of trees that shaded the water's surface. Things got right and proper tropical then, as dense greenery grew and spilled over the river's edge. A narrow path led along the riverbank, so He-Dog followed that, shielding his eyes from the bladelike leaves whipping at his face. At times, he glimpsed the river through the tangles, and at others, it disappeared completely. He eventually passed a large orange rock extending into the water, where the surface resembled a dark mirror. Jungle crowded both sides of the stone, offering a sense of seclusion. Enough to gather one's thoughts.

He-Dog glanced around.

The two warriors remained not ten paces behind him.

"I'm not gone far," he told them. "Just here. Just for a bit . . ." He shut up, wanting a moment of solitude to sort through matters. Needing to figure out if matters had improved or become much, much worse. For that amount of figuring, he needed to be alone.

The two lads didn't understand what he was saying, anyway.

Solitude. Here he was as close to being alone as he was going to get, he supposed, without venturing any farther into the lush tangles of the Sanjou. Memories then, of all the countless times he'd wanted to be clear of Balless. *Wished* he could be clear of the man. And here He-Dog was . . . clear of him . . . and wishing the punce was back. That was the way of things, he supposed, and he hated himself for thinking it.

So he adjusted his sword and sat upon that rock. The thing was big enough that, if he wanted, he could easily stretch out for a nap. Perhaps he would. So there he sat, propped up on his hands, legs splayed, taking in the great green wall rising from the opposing waterline.

He glanced over his shoulder.

The two lads were still there, crouched on the trail and nearly out of sight.

At least they were making an effort to hide themselves. To a point. He-Dog wiped the sweat from his face and stared across the river. *The Sanjou*. Even if he did try to escape the place, he didn't know where to go, how long it would take to get there, or what might lurk out there in the wilds—besides an unseen monster that demanded a yearly sacrifice from the very people who had saved and sheltered him. Some manner of beast that, if it didn't get its meal, would tear through the village in bloody retribution.

The thought deepened He-Dog's usual scowl.

The conversation had not improved since He-Dog left the glade, and Kellic didn't feel much like swinging a sword around in such sweltering heat. The kind of heat where simply scratching one's head would thicken a sweat.

So he stood and brushed himself off.

"Where are you going?" Snaffer grumped.

"Off. About. Somewhere."

"Don't mind them watching you?"

Kellic shook his head.

"Or talking about you?"

"Talking about me?"

"Talking about you, guaranteed," Snaffer said.

Kellic thought about that. "Talk never hurt anyone."

"Lad." Snaffer's perpetual scowl darkened. "*Wars* have been started over talk. Remember that."

Kellic was inclined to remember a lot of things. With that, he wandered out of the glade. Not too far, for as soon as he passed the home of Peaceful Moon, a pair of Half Tusk's warriors started following the mercenary. Kellic didn't mind that, however, and though he wore his belt and sword, he kept his hands clear of them. So he moved along until the little ridge sloped downward, where he encountered another Anoka home. A family of four—a mother, father, and two daughters—sat around a large basket filled with yellow berries, picking small leaves from the fruit. The family stopped working upon seeing Kellic, who lifted his hand in greeting before moving on.

In his mind, Kellic wasn't a cruel man, and what he'd said to He-Dog about his past was true enough. Fighting was merely a trade he was good at, *very* good at, and he earned a fair amount of coin when there was fighting to be done. Oh, he knew it was only a matter of time before someone better with a blade took his life or limb. Knew he faced a messy death every time he strapped on steel, truth be known. Even if he did leave the business, the challenge then would be figuring out what to do *next*. One thing he knew he *didn't* want, was to reach Snaffer's age and still be in the trade.

He did not want that at all.

Fighting for coin. *Killing* for coin, really, when you chewed through the meat of it and bit into bone. Mercenaries, bandits, or like-minded maggots deserving to die. Steady, bloody work, but nothing that prevented him from sleeping at night. By traveling to the Sanjou, he had been prepared to kill for even *more* coin. More than he could imagine, if, in fact, it was there. Now, however, with Shay crippled, and his group of hired soldiers reduced to three, Kellic sensed his time with the prince was nearing an end, if it had not already.

The Anoka had saved his life. He knew that. They wanted him to do a killing in return, and the killing was a monster. While under Shay's command he'd killed more than a few beasts disguised as men. Killing an unseen monster and freeing these people from its curse appealed to him. Felt good. *Noble*, even.

Maybe he would even survive the encounter. If he did, he'd figure out what to do from there.

A group of old women waved at him as he strolled by. He waved back and their smiles widened. Some children ran between him and the two warriors following him. The children sounded like any others enjoying the day, and it put him a little more at ease.

Then he saw what he was looking for.

Broska's lodge stood on the edge of the village, with a wide clearing behind it and a little brook that flowed to the west. Broska sat outside his home, concentrating on weaving together a basket. A young boy sat next to him, clothed in only a strip of hide around the waist. The boy saw Kellic first, and he patted the man's leg.

"Broska," Kellic greeted, and nodded at the child.

"Kellic," the Zuthenian returned, putting the basket aside. "Doing a bit of wandering, I see."

"Aye that."

The boy spoke, getting Broska's attention. "He says he saw you when you were visiting the elders."

Kellic again nodded at the boy, which very much pleased the youngster. "You're in need of a basket?" he asked, pointing.

"The missus wanted me to make them. I'm her servant. Though she lets me pretend otherwise when I'm around other menfolk."

At that moment, a woman pulled back the hide covering the entrance and stuck out her head. She spoke to Broska before regarding their visitor. "Hel-lo," she said with a disarming little smile, robbing Kellic of a reply. She was lovely, dark of hair and eyes.

Kellic nodded a greeting in return.

"Drink?" she asked.

"Good manners to accept," Broska informed the mercenary. "Even if it's warm shite. Not that she would do that, mind you. Or anyone else in the village. Just bad manners to say no."

"Then, yes. Please."

She withdrew into the lodge.

"That's it, then," Broska said with a sigh. "She'll be talking about you later on. Daresay she won't shut up, either."

"You're a fortunate man. She's lovely."

"She's unfit wonderful, truth be known. Her name's Sunny Smiles. Makes me wonder how she ever came to be with me." He winced and scratched his head. "I figure it's my hair. Certainly not the face below it. In any case, I'm hers. Until she decides to let me loose."

Kellic wasn't sure how to react to that.

"Ah, have no worries," Broska assured him. "I think I'm safe. For a while, at least. As long as I can put together one of these."

He held up the half-finished basket.

"And she can speak?"

"Zuthenian? Not really. A few words, but we usually speak Anoka. I make her smile. I think that's why she really keeps me, because of the way I butcher the language. I'll tell you this for nothing . . . there are many here who wish they could speak with *you*."

That interested Kellic.

"Oh, aye that," Broska said, seeing the other's expression. "They're a shy people. Too shy, really. Except for the children, perhaps."

"You speak the language well enough."

"Ha! To your ear, perhaps. I'm still learning . . . But, better than when I first started, I tell you. A lot of mistakes were made. But I learned, while keeping a smile on my face."

Kellic was about to ask something else when Sunny Smiles returned. She offered a wooden cup filled with water. Kellic took it with a nod of thanks, and she disappeared back inside.

He studied his drink. "I'd like to learn a few words. Just enough to get by."

That interested Broska. "Truly?"

"If you're willing to teach me. I'm . . . not the quickest learner. But if you're able. And willing. I'll try to learn. Just a few words. Enough to be understood. You understand?"

"I do," Broska said. "I'm surprised. Harsh-looking topper like yourself? Wanting to learn the language? Well, then, when do you want to begin?"

That took Kellic off guard, as if he wasn't expecting Broska to agree.

"What about now?" the Zuthenian asked.

"Now?"

"You'll get me away from weaving this unfit basket. Truth be known, I'm utter shite at making them. But my wife hates making them as well. She gets me to do it. I can weave while teaching, I suppose. Just a few words, right?"

"Aye that."

"All right then. Let's begin . . ."

Later that afternoon, He-Dog wandered back through the village. The two warriors trailed him, though he paid them little mind. A few hunters—or warriors, he couldn't be sure which—sat around a small fire pit, working on arrows. One cut away a length of wood. The second had what looked like a stone spike and wooden mallet, poised to tap a hole into the cut shafts. The third lad fixed feather flights into the ends. All three stopped working when He-Dog walked by, eyeing him with more reserved curiosity. More people noticed the big man walking by, and the children stopped and stared.

Trudging through the maze of homes, He-Dog noticed how some lodges stood closer to the jungle than others. He wondered just how large an area the village was, and with that thought, he altered course and kept on walking... until he came to a large dwelling at the very edge of the wilderness. There he stopped, deciding which way to go next, when a woman stepped out around the lodge. She stood with her back to him, carrying a basket filled with leaves. A long strip of hair tied in a neat knot at the base of her neck flowed down to her waist. Unlike the other Anoka, she ignored him. She placed her basket on the ground, next to a deep shell taken from some sizeable creature long dead. Water filled the shell. She knelt gingerly and felt for the two containers. Measuring the distance from one to the other, she took a handful of greens before cleaning them in the water.

Blind, He-Dog realized. She was blind.

She worked quietly, her face deeply sun-browned and heart-shaped, with high cheeks. A few loose strands hung over her forehead, reaching her eyes, and she puffed at them. That little action alone rooted him to the spot, until he realized *he* was the one staring. On impulse he glanced around.

The two lads following him had stopped a ways back, watching him *watch her*. Worse still, other villagers had noticed him. Some had little smiles. Others did not.

One of them was the spirit man, Peaceful Moon, and his catty eyes twinkled.

Feeling his cheeks flush hot, He-Dog marched away.

CHAPTER 35

The next morning, He-Dog and the others woke up to another cooked meal. Roasted strips of meat, garnished with seasoned tubular greens and cloves of soft, sweet orange fruit. The three men ate in silence, in their lodge, peering out at the day through the open portal. Once finished, they set aside their bowls and stepped outside.

He-Dog and Kellic tried swinging their swords again that morning. They cut and stabbed at imaginary foes, with only marginal strength behind their swings, all under Snaffer's scornful eyes.

"You don't feel unfit?" He-Dog asked the older mercenary at one point.

"Only when I watch you."

That prompted the two men to practice their sword work a little longer. To their surprise, the dizziness took a lot longer to take hold of them. When it did, they stopped swinging and sat down.

After a short settling rest, He-Dog stood and fiddled with his scabbard. "Off for a walk," he said and left.

Snaffer and Kellic watched him leave. They also saw Half Tusk notice him leave, when the big man dropped below the embankment. With a curt nod, the leader dispatched two of his warriors to follow the mercenary.

"Look at that," Snaffer said, annoyed by the display.

"They did the same yesterday," Kellic said.

"They did?"

"You didn't see them?"

"I saw three of them sitting down there."

"Two of them followed me. The others, well . . ." Kellic gestured at He-Dog's departing back.

"Lords above," Snaffer swore softly.

Kellic started walking away.

"Where are you off to?" Snaffer demanded.

"Just walking. Looking about."

"The prince will be awake soon."

"The prince doesn't need me," he said and kept on going.

Suppose not, Snaffer thought, noticing how two more Anoka warriors left their group to follow Kellic.

That left three, one being the brazen punce called Half Tusk.

Who locked gazes with the older mercenary. Snaffer glowered back, letting it be known he wasn't one to be making eye contact with. A stoic Half Tusk didn't blink, however, sending a message of his own.

Two months Snaffer had been in this place, in a dreamy daze he barely remembered. A few heartbeats into this stare with Half Tusk and Snaffer realized he didn't have the patience to continue. Realized that if he *did* continue, he would eventually walk over there and chop down the little blossom. If that happened, he might not stop at just one.

Snaffer didn't consider himself a smart man, but he knew he couldn't kill Half Tusk. Wouldn't be right. Or proper. The man had saved their hides after all, and the thought poisoned him.

So Snaffer fumed in frustration and marched for Shay's lodge.

"Prince?" he asked, stopping at the entrance.

No answer.

"Shay?"

"What?" came a groggy reply.

Snaffer paused. "It's Snaffer."

"I know."

"May I enter?"

No answer, and time passed until Snaffer's brow creased in question. "Shay?"

"*What?*"

Snaffer rubbed his forehead. At least the man was awake. "May I enter?"

"Do what you like."

Which wasn't the reply Snaffer expected, but he entered all the same.

A cloud of bad air engulfed him, smelling of rancid breath, unclean sweat, and piss. A beam of daylight shone down from the hole in the ceiling. The interior resembled the lodge where Snaffer stayed, except Shay had the whole of the floor to himself. Which the prince used. Splayed out, a blanket covering him from the waist down, where one end had been pulled up to expose the rounded stump of his missing leg. He looked sickly, as a feverish sheen coated him.

The smells didn't bother Snaffer, but he took a fistful of the hide flap, intent on hooking it back, to let some fresh air inside.

"Leave that," Shay groaned, squirming like an old snake close to perishing.

Snaffer left it and sat down. A bowl of food waited next to the prince. The same meal they had all eaten, as well as a wooden cup filled with water.

Shay turned his head just a touch, his jaw and eyes sunken. "What do you want?" he croaked, badly in need of a drink.

Snaffer shook his head.

That narrowed Shay's eyes. "Then why are you here?"

". . . Just seeing how you are, my Prince."

"Seeing?" Shay repeated in annoyance. "By all means, have a good look. See here." He lifted his stump. "Nothing's grown back yet. Same meat and bone left to rot. And I'm rotting with it, lying on my back and never to recover."

Snaffer decided to remain quiet.

"Where are we?" Shay asked miserably.

"At the Anoka village."

"Still?"

"Aye that. Still."

"When do we leave? We have to get back to the coast. Stephanak will be waiting. Next moon he said."

Snaffer didn't hesitate. "Stephanak and his lads are all dead, my Prince."

"What?" Shay asked in horrified wonder.

"They're all dead."

"Who told you that?"

"The Zuthenian."

"And you believed him?"

Snaffer took a breath and with it, the prince's rancid smell.

"Where are the gemstones?" Shay demanded. "Have you found them?"

"No."

"Well, get *looking*. We'll start today. As soon as you bring me my walking sticks."

"I thought the Zuthenian was going to bring you those."

"You can't trust that one. You do it. Once I'm well enough to walk we'll gather the lads and get moving."

"The lads are all dead, Shay."

That earned him a sour look. "What are you rambling about? Who's dead?"

"The lads."

"The lads?" Shay repeated, clearly confused. "Where's Grage?"

"Dead."

"Nonsense. Get him. Bring him to me."

Snaffer scratched his chin and considered the food. "You should eat."

But Shay wasn't listening. Instead, he lifted his head and inspected his lower self. He moved his stump, studied it, and dropped it with a thud. "Where's my leg, Snaffer?"

"Bloodfish took it, my Prince."

"Bloodfish? In Othil?"

"We're not in Othil, my Prince."

"Not in Othil?" Shay screwed up his face. "What gurry is that?"

"We're in the Sanjou, Prince Shay."

"The where now?"

"The Sanjou."

"Bartus."

That silenced Snaffer, and he ruefully shook his head.

"Where's Bartus?" Shay asked.

"Dead, my Prince."

"Bartus . . . Where's my leg?"

Snaffer glanced about the interior, as if seeking an answer.

"Bring me walking sticks, Bartus," Shay grimaced, as if being stabbed by a sword. "The kind that hold a man up. Do that and I'll walk out of here. I'll walk about the whole village. I'll show them all."

Snaffer nodded at the food. "You should eat something."

"What's that?"

"Eat." Snaffer pointed. "They brought that for you. And drink. So you can get strong again."

Shay turned his head and what he saw didn't impress him. He screwed up his face and returned to staring at the ceiling. "Have you found the gemstones?"

"Not yet, my Prince."

"Well, find Grage. Enough of this foolishness. We didn't come here to be laggards. There are riches to be found."

Snaffer lumbered to his feet.

"Where are you going?" Shay asked.

"To look for those gemstones."

"Don't be long then . . . and don't forget my walking sticks."

Snaffer stepped outside.

Not a dozen paces away a pack of youngsters had gathered to watch him. The same three boys and two girls from before, standing just below the ridge with huge, expectant smiles on their faces. The presence of Half Tusk and his two men prevented the youngsters from getting any closer, but that didn't bother the children. One little girl waved, which got the rest of them going. Then they started waving both hands, until it looked like they were fending off a swarm. The group started jumping not long after.

Snaffer ignored the excited display. He marched around the dwelling, into the cleared patch of land where the wildflowers grew. There he held his forehead and stared at the near impassable jungle.

"Walking sticks," he whispered.

The prince wanted walking sticks.

Truth be known, it wasn't a bad idea. Getting up for a walk might clear the man's head. He inspected some of the nearby trees. A moment later, he pulled the hand axe from his belt and took a reassuring grip.

Not difficult work at all, he supposed, and he discovered he was eager to hit something.

He-Dog returned to that spot along the river, sitting on the orange-colored rock, in the shade. Sunlight twinkled off the water while insects pitched and played on the surface. At times he laid back and took in the sky above . . . or at least the bits he could see through the leaves and branches overhead. His two guards were somewhere nearby. The lads seemed to realize his desire to be alone, so they hid themselves. Very well, in fact, as he couldn't see or hear them at all back there.

At one point, as he idly listened to birdsong, a rustling along the path lifted his head. He sat up to see seven Anoka warriors carrying spears and bows creeping past him. The warriors noticed him but continued on, disappearing one by one into the bushes.

Thinking nothing more of the matter, He-Dog lay back once again and closed his eyes.

He woke sometime later, the air hot and humid and thick enough to drink. His back stuck to the rock and he unfastened himself with a grimace. Sunbeams no longer freckled the water, and the sky glowed from the oncoming evening. His stomach rumbled, reminding him not to miss the last meal of the day. The food was always good—the greens sweet, the meat tender, and everything seasoned with mysterious spices.

That thought got him to his feet.

His two protectors were nowhere in sight, but He-Dog figured they were nearby. The smell of cooking food led him back to the village, where people gathered around fire pits that burned surprisingly little smoke. Faces lifted as he walked by, some of them smiling, but he paid little attention to them.

Until he spotted a familiar one walking through the village.

"Broska," He-Dog greeted, startling the man and halting him in his tracks.

"He-Dog. Exploring this fair city?"

"Aye that."

"You have your friends, I see."

That prompted He-Dog to glance over his shoulder. His two shadows were strides behind him. "Never too far away, it seems."

"Don't think of them at all. Now then. The alehouses are over there," Broska winked and pointed. "The palace, as you already know, is up that way. And the town square is just over there. But if you need a smithy or armorer, you're in for a walk."

"Many thanks. What do you have there?"

Broska hefted a wooden cup. "Tree sap. Very sticky. They use it for their roofs. Whatever they can't tie down they rub this over it. Rub it on, under, and in between. Seals very well and prevents leaks."

"You're repairing your roof?"

"Aye that, but not mine. Another's. Anoka custom. No one repairs their own home here. They wait until someone else sees the problem, who usually will let them know what's wrong and then go about fixing it."

He-Dog scowled in puzzlement.

"Unfit, isn't it?" Broska said brightly. "Oh, I know. In the beginning I would let them work on my home all day long and just watch them go at it. Now, however,

I, ah, am one of them. So I'm obligated to do the same. It's not a bad thing. You're thought well of when you do work for others."

"And you take no coin?"

"Coin? *Pah.* You see any coin here? Have you ever seen any coin? That's right. None. You do get paid, however. In a different currency. Maybe one even better. You'll get offered new tools. Weapons. Choice cuts of the hunt. Cleaned hides or cooked food. You're paid in some manner or other, and the place is better because of it."

He-Dog didn't believe that. "I saw a group of hunters outside the village."

Broska nodded. "Groups go out every day. They usually bring something back. Something they'll clean and cook. Or preserve for when the hunters don't bring something back. The ones you saw might be out searching for signs of the Paw. That time is close."

"How close?"

"When they find its sign. Which could be any day now."

He-Dog glanced around.

About a half dozen of the Anoka were listening to their conversation, their brows furrowed as if attempting to understand what was being said.

"They're a quiet lot," He-Dog noted.

"The quietest," Broska said. "How are you lads doing with your recovery? Can you fight if needed?"

He-Dog felt as if he had barely lifted his blade at all. "Aye that, if needed."

"Excellent. Not that there's any danger nearby. We're well away from Iruzuland. Well hidden. They don't come this far north. Don't like it up here for some reason or other. The people say they prefer to hunt in the south. One thing about the jungle . . . plenty of game running about. And it's always growing. Any signs of a trail are hidden by new growth in only a few days."

He-Dog glanced around.

"These lodges," Broska went on, "are not built to last forever. They are . . . quick homes. Easy to replace. To repair. And just as easy to abandon, if needed. Well. Enough of that. I must get back home. As you can see it's not far from yours. Just a few turns." He pointed. "Your man Kellic found me. Anyway, get on back. I expect they'll be bringing you food shortly."

That lifted He-Dog's mood.

"It's good, isn't it?" Broska said, noticing the reaction. "Damnation they can serve up a right and proper feed. Try it all, I say. Whatever they give you. Have the crawlers or biters been bothering you?"

He-Dog thought about it and shook his head.

"Because of the seasonings they douse the food with," Broska explained. "Some wild shrubbery they tear up and throw on everything. The smell clings to your skin days later. Some scent we can't smell but it keeps away the insects. They don't care for it at all. Another reason to eat what they give you. Well, apologies. I must go. If you need me . . ."

With that, the Zuthenian nodded and walked away, saying something to the curious faces around them. The Anoka chuckled at his words and reluctantly left He-Dog alone.

On his way back to his lodge, He-Dog sniffed at one arm and frowned. He couldn't smell anything beyond his own sweat.

All three of them returned to their shared home. Kellic hooked back the flap covering the entrance, to allow fresh air inside. It also allowed a view of the pitched roofs and jungle beyond. Sitting inside their lodge, the three men settled down for supper, soon brought along by Little Bloom. Wooden plates with white vegetables of some unknown variety, garnished with, once again, strips of stringy yet well-seasoned meat and curved chunks of soft and sweet orange fruit. The mercenaries ate without conversation, but not in silence.

In He-Dog's opinion, his companions chewed their food like sick cows.

It wasn't long before they finished everything before them.

"That was well done," He-Dog said and wiped his mouth.

"Some of the best I've ever eaten," Kellic agreed. "What is that meat? I think we've had three different kinds now."

"Probably the jungle hens strutting around," He-Dog said. "And some manner of pig. No idea what that was."

"It was good."

"It was good."

"It's the seasonings," Kellic decided, examining his empty bowl. "Puts a fine taste to it all. A fine taste."

Keeping his thoughts to himself, Snaffer spat a stream into the unlit fire pit and wiped his beard.

"How are you recovering?" He-Dog asked after a moment.

"Fine enough," Kellic reported and glanced at Snaffer, who inspected his hands.

"I talked to Broska not too long ago," He-Dog said. "The Anoka are sending hunters out into the jungle. Perhaps searching for signs of the Paw. Broska says we could be called upon at any time."

"That Zuthenian asslicker is happy he doesn't have to hunt down the beast," Snaffer fumed.

That earned him a hard look. "He's explained why he hasn't," He-Dog said.

"Gurry."

"But you do believe there's a monster out there?" He-Dog asked. "One that's killing off these people, one by one?"

"They're *offering* themselves to it, one by one," Snaffer countered. "Instead of killing the beast."

"And we've heard their reasons for that. I'm just telling you they have men out there now, searching for signs. If they find any, we'll be called upon. Now you know."

"I'm ready," Kellic said.

Snaffer lifted one arse cheek off his mat before scratching at his neck.

At that time, Little Bloom returned and gathered the empty bowls, clearly pleased they had eaten everything put before them. As she took Kellic's bowl, he spoke a few halting words which stopped her. She spoke back, and Kellic shook his head and muttered a short stream of syllables, correcting himself as he went.

Whatever he said pleased her, bringing about a little smile, which stayed with her as she left.

"What was that?" Snaffer asked gruffly.

"What?" Kellic asked back.

"What you just said to the savage."

Kellic frowned. "She's not a savage."

"What did you say to her?"

"'Thank you.'"

"You said what?"

Kellic's eyes narrowed in confusion.

"You thanked *that*?" Snaffer demanded.

"Snaffer . . ." He-Dog warned in a low voice. "Shaddup."

Snaffer didn't spare him a look. "How do you know how to say *anything* in their gurry tongue?"

"I learned," Kellic replied simply.

"*Learned*? You're *learning* it?"

"From Broska."

"That Zuthenian *kog* is teaching you how to speak that foolishness?"

"Snaffer . . . I said shaddup," He-Dog warned, a touch stronger that time.

That earned him an evil look. "You don't warn me, topper. Not when it comes to this place. This place killed off my whole lot. Killed off your lad as well, and you'd best remember it."

Heat flared in He-Dog's face. "These *people* didn't kill anyone I knew. But they saved my hide. Looked over me and fed me for weeks and they're still feeding me. That's what I'll remember."

A fuming Snaffer waved that away.

"He's right, Snaffer," Kellic quietly said.

"You go on then," the older mercenary growled and stood. "Learn that gurry tongue." He adjusted the weapons hanging from his belt and walked out of the lodge.

He-Dog exchanged looks with Kellic.

Suppressing the urge to strike something dead, Snaffer lowered his head and walked to Shay's dwelling. There, he yanked back the hide covering the entrance, nearly ripping it off the support beam. Fuming, he looked in on the prince. Shay lay on his side facing the wall, showing only his back.

"Prince?" Snaffer asked.

Shay didn't stir. His food from earlier in the day had been taken away, and the man did seem a touch cleaner.

"Prince?"

No response. Snaffer lurched to enter when Shay let off a snore, shifted ever so slightly, and thumped his remaining leg.

Snaffer left him.

The mercenary snuck behind the dwelling and followed the jungle wall, to avoid Half Tusk and his lads. When the clearing narrowed into tall standing tufts of vegetation, he continued on, checking to see if anyone saw him. No one had. Not yet, anyway. And Snaffer was of a mind to continue slipping away. The day had the look and feel of evening about it, but he wasn't relaxed, as one might be. As one *should* be.

No, Jers Snaffer wasn't remotely relaxed.

In fact, he was right and proper *boiling*. Perhaps even murderously so.

And it showed. He bunched his hands into fists. Lowered his head and scowled hard enough to leave permanent lines. As he threaded his way through the village, curious villagers eventually spotted his furious march. The Anoka said nothing and wisely left him alone.

Which was a good thing.

Snaffer might have beaten them into the ground if he heard a word of that shite tongue.

The villagers stayed away from him. A few even quickly backed away from the approaching mercenary. The children that once walked beside him did not follow or even appear. One of the old Anoka men, squatting and holding a handful of filthy rock, chuckled as the shaggy warrior from the Ice Kingdoms strode by. That wheezy outburst stopped Snaffer in his tracks. He whirled on the old villager, who stared back without fear.

Sensing trouble, other villagers drifted into sight, their faces drawn and concerned about the next few moments. Men, women, and children. All watching him. They were *everywhere* Snaffer turned. Broska might enjoy their attention, but Snaffer saw the Zuthenian as little more than a pet—smart enough to be taught how to talk and squat in the right places.

Dismissing them all with a hand, he stomped away. They watched him leave. They *all* watched him. He felt it like how a dog would feel lice. Every moment he was in sight they watched, studying his every feature, his every movement. Daresay they'd watch him have a *squat* if they could, and that spiked his anger even more.

It was maddening.

Worse still . . . it made him want to hurt people.

Snaffer didn't like this place. And it didn't like him. He very much wanted to leave. Ever since all his lads had been butchered in the ambush, including his constant companion, Grage. The last friend he'd had. If Grage were still alive, Snaffer would tell him a secret . . . that he believed his mind was fraying at the edges. A little at a time. Like some great length of ancient rope. He could feel it. With every passing moment, another strand snapped, putting that much more stress on the rest. The ambush had been the start of it all. Being unable to save any of the lads greatly bothered Snaffer. Falling into the river with the prince and not being able to save him bothered him even more. If he closed his eyes, he could still see the thrashing waters about Shay's leg, and the rising bloody foam. Then there were the Anoka, and their gawking and their gibberish that was somehow a language. And the *heat*. The wretched torturous *heat*, that trapped him in a boiling cauldron, one that barely cooled at night.

All of it.

Face drawn and darkly pensive, Snaffer snorted.

Only a matter of time before he broke. He recognized that, at least. It happened to other warriors, where countless campaigns turned their minds to muck and left them unfit. Snaffer never thought it would happen to him. Now with Grage gone, the lads gone, and only *him* still alive . . . it was happening to him. He could feel it—a terrible, terrible energy welling up inside, demanding release.

He had to get clear of the village. Before something wicked happened.

With that, Snaffer stomped through bushes as tall as himself. That energy continued to build, creeping up his legs and reaching for his chest. He doubled his pace, shoving his way through the jungle. Leaves whipped at his face and shoulders, angering him even more. A huge web loomed before him and he smashed through it. A spider the size of his fist dropped to the ground and he squashed it with a foot. A heavy spurt of green and yellow shite burst from the thing, staining his boot, which fouled his mood even more. Branches clawed at him as he pushed through, until a river stopped him. There he adjusted course and stomped alongside the water, kicking up waves with his dirty boot. The shadows deepened. The sounds of the village diminished. The colors sharpened as did the cries of unseen wildlife. Snaffer had always preferred the wild, *any* wild, to a settlement. A forest had its secrets, and if one were quiet enough, *respectful* enough, it might reveal one or two. Snaffer had spent a lot of time in the Black Forest of Kold Keep, and in that time, he'd seen many secrets. Sights and sounds that had calmed him, pleased him, and even allowed him to forget his problems, for a little while at least.

He needed that now. That solitude. That time to forget where he was. What he was doing. And especially to douse the dire thoughts gathering in his head.

The jungle pressed in, crowding him, as he swept aside large leaves. Sweat coated him. He wiped at his features before cleaning his hands on his breeches. Black flies buzzed about but, surprisingly, didn't bother him. Jers Snaffer turned one way and then another, feeling lost and in need of deep steadying breaths. The need to scream swelled within his chest, the pressure building behind his eyes. *Lords above.* Snaffer looked at the darkening sky and spotted a faint scattering of stars. Kold Keep was under those same stars, he supposed, but his homeland was an ocean away. A *world* away.

That dreadful energy spiked again. A crackling, desperate surge very close to madness, needing to be bled off. His lower legs ached and trembled. His heart hammered against his ribs. He needed to move, move fast, or split down the middle.

So he ran.

He sprinted, crashing through heavy vegetation, guided by slivers of evening light. He tripped and fell, stood, and ran again, smashing through walls of leaves and barely seeing where he was going. He ran through another gigantic web and kept on running, not seeing what had built the thing.

And in time, it wasn't evening anymore.

It was the ambush once again.

Wildmen killed his sword brothers, and Snaffer pulled steel. He slashed and chopped, hacking out great gushing cuts of anything nearby. Dark matter flew and fell. Tatters of material drizzled the air. Vines swung and spewed fluids. Then the Anoka were there, laughing and pointing, gibbering in their hateful language. The sound clogged his ears and wormed around, maddening him further.

Someone stood behind him and Snaffer whirled, his weapons ready.

And there stood Grage, not a dozen paces away, spectral and shimmering, the jungle growth reaching his waist. At least it *looked* like Grage. Snaffer couldn't see the man's face, but the shape resembled that of his dead friend. Snaffer scrambled toward him, but the shape fled. He wasn't worried. Grage was back. The mercenary ran faster. Through the Sanjou he stormed, following his friend. Several times he fell, only to look up to see Grage leaving him behind. That forced Snaffer to his feet.

He followed that ghost all through the night.

Followed it until there was no longer a jungle. No longer the Sanjou. Only a long black tunnel that ended in gloomy silver.

Snaffer ran . . . until he collapsed.

Dawn's light bled into the jungle and Snaffer stirred.

Then he sat up with a lurch.

Something crawled through his beard and over his head. Little invaders realizing their choice of safe refuge wasn't so safe after all. With a growl, Snaffer scratched at himself and stood. His weapons lay about his feet, so he gathered them up as an afterthought and put them away. With that done, he took a few steps, pushed through a fence of green, and felt the land vanish underfoot.

Arms splayed, he fell, splashing face down in a river. His hands sank into a muddy bottom, the texture repulsive yet cool to the touch. After a moment's thrashing followed by another moment of realization, he sputtered a few dribbles. Then sampled some. The water tasted fine, so he took in a few more mouthfuls, until he remembered the bloodfish. Frantic, Snaffer rose with a bark and sputter. He splashed back to shore, expecting those flesh-ripping bites to tear into him at any moment.

He crashed through the bushes in a panic, heedless of where he was going. Just before he realized he was perfectly fine, an unseen root hooked a foot and sent him flying.

Thorns and branches stabbed at his face as he landed hard. Things snapped, and more things went up his nose. He flared out the bits of leaves and twigs, then pawed at his face. Rubbed his eyes. His mind cleared, as if everything had been knocked free. After a time, he sat up and had a moment of reflection.

A bed of pink and white flowers surrounded him. Dripping, soaked to his skin, Snaffer glared at a narrow body of water through a ragged parting in the greenery. A quick check revealed his weapons were still at his waist. He relaxed, his shoulders slumping. Memories of the night before put a scowl on his face, and he sighed in sour disappointment.

There had been no Grage. He'd been chasing a ghost.

Worse still, he didn't recognize this part of the jungle at all, which meant he was probably lost.

Lords above, he fumed, when he heard the sound of rustling leaves to his right.

A woman emerged—an old woman, brown-eyed and gray-haired, with a satchel hanging off her hip. Her back was badly warped, hunching her over to the point of toppling, if not for a walking stick she used to keep herself upright. Despite her curved back and that length of cut wood, she slipped through the bushes with surprising nimbleness.

She halted two strides away and squinted at him, her mouth puckered in a question, as if trying to make sense of what she was seeing.

Snaffer could only imagine, since he was dripping water and partially covered in mud. "Oh, go away, would you," he groaned, and looked back at the river.

The woman did not, however.

After a time, she ambled toward him and sized him up with even more scrutiny, perhaps searching for injuries. Snaffer shook his head at the intrusion. Even frowned when she tapped his arm.

That was enough for him.

"Look, you hag—" he started, and faltered.

The woman held out a piece of orange fruit. She peeled away one section, ate it, and offered the rest. Snaffer considered it. He had been ready to drive the spidery hag away but his stomach grumbled in disagreement.

She offered again.

"You won't give up, will you?" Snaffer rumbled at her.

The Spider Hag whispered back, her voice pleasant but her words a mystery. Until she stuck the food in front of Snaffer's dripping face.

Sighing, he took it, sensing she wasn't going to go away until he did. The fruit was sweet, juicy, and went down well. While he ate, the Spider Hag opened her satchel. She pulled out strips of that odd but unquestionably tasty meat, cured and seasoned, and offered a handful to him.

The display brought about another lengthy stare from the mercenary.

She didn't flinch under his gaze. She shook the handful, insisting he take it.

Stubborn, Snaffer thought, but he *was* hungry.

She nudged his arm again.

"You . . ." he started quietly, thinking about barking—*roaring* about how he wished to be alone . . . but he didn't finish the thought.

Instead, with a defeated nod, he took the food.

CHAPTER 36

A day later, just after breakfast, He-Dog and Kellic idly paced behind their lodge. Their heads were clear, the dizziness once plaguing them gone. It was early, but the village was wide-awake and bustling. Snaffer had already left them—left directly after eating, in fact—without a word. No doubt to check on Shay, or so He-Dog figured.

Which left him to puzzle over what to do with the day. He wasn't looking forward to swinging steel about. That thought stopped the man in his tracks with a heavy sigh. "I'm bored."

Kellic nodded but said nothing more.

Among the three of them, He-Dog still believed he was the best to start a conversation. This wasn't one of those times, however, and He-Dog was about to say something to that effect when Shay limped into sight.

Walking upon sticks.

A hopeful smile stretched across the prince's face as he swung himself forward, placing his full weight upon the supports tucked under his arms.

"Lads," Shay greeted as he came to a halt. He swayed, just a bit but enough to worry Snaffer, who followed him.

"Get away from me, man," the prince snapped. "I can do this. Walking is the least of my concerns."

With a cranky gait, he hobbled around the clearing, testing his new makeshift legs. Shay swung himself a few strides in one direction, turned with the care of a person still learning to do so, and returned to where he started.

"Easy," he remarked, sweat beading down his face. "See that? Hm? A bit off-balance, but I expect that'll pass. My thanks, Snaffer. For making the legs. See this, lads? See what he has done for me? Made me legs. An extra set of legs. Being able to get up and move around is . . . well . . . it's good. Better than good. It's *wonderful*. Wonderful, I say."

He adjusted the sticks under his arms, offering a peek of the padding wrapped around the ends.

He-Dog glared at Snaffer, who ignored him. Message sent, He-Dog watched the prince as he continued to swing himself about.

"What are you looking at?" Shay eventually asked him.

"A dog walking on wooden legs."

The prince let that jab go, but it got Snaffer glaring.

Which He-Dog ignored.

Shay stopped. "What? You don't think I can walk? Well, clearly, I can."

"Clearly," He-Dog muttered.

"You're moving well enough," Kellic said.

"I am," Shay said, adjusting his sticks again. "One leg won't stop me, Sunbar. Snaffer has given me a true gift here. A true gift."

Kellic's features frosted over. "It's Kellic, my Prince."

"What?"

"Kellic."

Appearing confused, Shay walked to the edge of the clearing. There, he teetered before lurching back, taking much faster strides.

He-Dog frowned.

"Watch yourself, my Prince," Snaffer warned.

Shay stopped with a wobble. "Watch yourself? I'm doing damn fine considering. Look! I'm walking!"

"A step away from dancing," Snaffer said.

That deepened He-Dog's frown as he rubbed at an ear.

"Why not?" Shay remarked. "If I wanted. Perhaps after we find our way back to the mainland. A shame about Stephanak. I'll miss that one. He had character. Well. We'll find a way. Until then, I'll practice walking. And learn how to hold my sword again."

Those last few words narrowed He-Dog's eyes. "Learn how to what?"

"Hold a sword."

He-Dog glanced at Snaffer before returning to the prince. "What do you mean, hold a sword?"

Shay faced him. "I think I said it well enough."

"You can't fight, Shay."

"What do you mean?"

He-Dog looked at the others for agreement and saw very little. "You can't manage a blade with one leg."

"You'll see."

"I'll see what?"

"Me handling a blade. That blade, in fact." He nodded at the weapon hanging from He-Dog's waist. "That's mine. And I'll want it back."

He-Dog exchanged looks with a suddenly equally concerned Kellic. "You can't *fight*, Shay. You . . ." Words failed him. "All a butcher needs to do is kick out one of those sticks. One kick. One *push,* and you're done. And I mean gutted."

"I'll practice for that very thing. Already been thinking about it. Having you guarding my flanks will work."

"I'm not *guarding* your *flanks*, Shay, because you can't *fight* anymore. You're *done*. Your days of pulling steel are over."

"You're wrong," a sweating Shay said and smiled. "I can do this. Then we'll go hunting for this Paw."

That left He-Dog scowling in confusion. Again he glanced at the others, but they kept quiet. "Unfit," he muttered and walked over to Shay.

The prince's smile wilted upon the larger man's approach.

He-Dog shoved him, slamming a single palm into his chest. Shay toppled, crashing onto his back, his crutches splayed at his sides.

Sensing movement, He-Dog spun about to face Snaffer closing in, his long dagger and hand axe out and ready. The shaggy warrior cut for a head and a belly, two swipes thrown hard, but He-Dog jumped back and circled. Snaffer pursued and He-Dog pulled steel, broadsword flashing in the green-soaked daylight. Snaffer stomped to a halt, and there they faced each other behind raised guards.

"No one strikes me, you brazen blossom," Shay seethed while struggling to sit up. "Lads, punish that unfit bastard. I'll tell you when to stop."

Snaffer didn't move, but nor did he lower his weapons.

Kellic remained where he stood, visibly struggling with the command.

A breeze pushed through the clearing, rustling leaves overhead but failing to break the hard tension that followed.

"You both saw that, "He-Dog said and pointed at Shay. "It'll take even less effort if some maggot truly wants him dead. Saimon's rosy bells, why am I even saying this? *Look* at him."

A stern Snaffer did nothing. He huffed and fidgeted as sweat dribbled down his bearded face. Then his eyes flicked to and from the prince.

"Snaffer, Sunbar," Shay ordered. "Gut that topper where he stands."

Orders heard, Snaffer flexed his arms . . . but made no move to attack.

He-Dog watched him. "If you think . . . he can fight, on three *legs* . . . then you're as unfit as him."

"Shut your *mouth*," Shay blurted, grabbing his walking sticks and trying to stand. "Kill him, Snaffer. *Kill him*. Sunbar, pull your damn steel and—Dying *Seddon*!"

Halfway to his feet, the prince leaned on one stick not firmly set and all of him toppled over. He lay there, staring at the heavens, before struggling to rise once again.

"What are you waiting for?" Shay croaked. "*Sunbar!* Listen to me!"

An unimpressed Kellic folded his arms and looked at Snaffer. The older warrior glared back, then considered He-Dog. He still made no move to strike.

A red-faced Shay toppled a second time. "*Damnation*," he blurted. "Don't kill him yet, Snaffer. One of you help me up. *Kellic!*"

Surprised at hearing his name, Kellic hesitated before moving to help the fallen prince.

He-Dog watched Snaffer. "One shove and he's in the mud, yelling for you. You truly need to think about that? If anyone wants to bash his head in, and I mean really crack it, it would be an easy thing."

Snaffer remained silent.

"Shut your guts," Shay snapped as Kellic helped him to his feet. "You're *finished*. You miserable—after all I've done for you and that masked he-bitch that came with you. After saving your unfit hide back at Othil. You treacherous shite-stained punce. You unfit bastard. Get out of my sight. Get out of it! You're no longer part of this company."

"What company?" He-Dog said. "It was killed off. Only what you see here is left. Him and *him* and *me*. And I don't keep company with . . . *fools*."

That nearly popped Shay's eyes from his face. "You unfit *kog*. Kill him, lads. Cut him down!"

But neither man obeyed the order.

Still, He-Dog watched them all as he backed away, and when he was far enough, he turned and left.

They let him go.

A steaming, fuming Shay was only getting started. "That treacherous pisser *pushed* me! Without warning. Pushed *me*. While I was trying to walk! No need of that gurry. No need at all. Without provocation. I'll kill him right and proper dead if he does that again. If he comes within arm's length. I'll slice him right up the middle and let everything fall. Lords above." Shay regarded his two companions. "Get after him and butcher that pig-bastard. I mean it. He's not one of us. Never was. He's the—the ruination of all of us. Of *everything*. Everything was *fine* until I brought him into the fold. One act of kindness I should never have done. Never have done. The lads warned me about him. Bartus and Grage. Said that one looked as trustful as a Marnite pisspot. And they were *right*. Saimon drag me down by the bells for it all. Get after him and bring me back his *head*."

Without a word, Snaffer sheathed his weapons and retreated.

That took the rage out of the prince. "Snaffer?" he called out. "Where are you going? He went *that* way. Snaffer? *Snaffer?*"

But the older warrior didn't answer. Didn't stop walking either, disappearing from sight around one lodge.

A confused Shay stared until Kellic also wandered off without a word.

"What?" Shay sputtered, on the verge of falling once again. He steadied himself and watched the last of his remaining men leave him.

"Wait," he said. "Wait . . . you . . . you—"

The prince shut up. *Damnation.* He fumed. Once again, he couldn't recall the lad's name.

The morning's confrontation had rattled Kellic, so he decided a walk would help him think matters over.

As before, a pair of Anoka warriors followed him.

Growing concern troubled Kellic. His instincts had guided him through some harsh times in the past, and they were warning him about the prince right now. Something had unhinged itself in the man's mind, and Kellic wondered if the loss of the leg was the root of it. Or was it too much of the dream leaves? In the time he had served with Shay, he knew the man could have a lofty air about him. The men addressing him as "prince" no doubt encouraged such behavior. Shay could be generous as well, and had been in the past. Kellic sighed. He had to respect the man for not sinking into a mire of despair over losing a leg, but he wasn't about to cut into He-Dog for proving a point. The prince's notion of wanting to take up a blade *was* unfit. Perhaps the man could use a bow, but not a sword.

Kellic also wished Shay could remember his name and not call him Sunbar.

Sunbar. His friend and sword brother might have a word or two about the prince. A part of Kellic believed Sunbar was still alive somewhere, perhaps searching for survivors belonging to the company. At times, he imagined his old friend walking right into the village. Nothing of the sort had happened, of course. Nor would it. Sunbar was dead and gone and that was the end of that.

Kellic meandered through the village, past women sitting outside their homes, weaving baskets, stitching hides, or working on other mysterious handcrafts. He passed the menfolk as well, sturdy men working with stone tools or shaving the hides off carcasses. Despite his troubled thoughts, Kellic greeted them all, in their language, leaving little smiles on their faces.

Until a group of children stopped directly in his path, pointing fingers and giggling.

Kellic told them to stop pointing.

Which stunned them for a moment, before they squealed with laughter and ran off.

Scratching his neck, Kellic thought about what he'd just said. He was certain he'd said the words right. He'd have to ask Broska. Which didn't seem like a bad thing to do. He'd meant to see the man later in the day anyway, to keep on with his lessons, but he didn't think the Zuthenian would mind starting earlier. Learning the language of the Anoka was far better than seeing the prince again.

A short time later, Kellic found himself at Broska's home.

The Zuthenian's wife, Sunny Smiles, greeted him at the entrance. She spoke slowly and Kellic was grateful for it, though he understood not a word beyond her initial greeting. She motioned for him to wait as she disappeared inside. Kellic glanced around, watching the villagers casually go about their morning. He wished he could learn the language faster, but his head could only remember so much, and speaking it—speaking it *well*—was more challenging than expected. His entire life had been spent honing the natural strength in his arms, legs, and back. Not in his head. Thinking was something his officers did.

A smiling Broska stepped outside. "Managed to get away from the others, did you?"

"Aye that."

"We heard you yelling over there."

A frowning Kellic said nothing.

"All is well?"

"Well as expected. Though it's best I don't return there for a bit. For the morning, anyway. Could I speak with you for a time?"

Broska shook his head. "Sadly, I cannot teach you this morning. The missus has work for me, and it involves her family. Hunting. Filling the larder. That sort of thing."

"I could help," Kellic offered.

The Zuthenian waved that off. "I can't help you today . . . but I have a friend who can."

The flap covering the entrance rustled again and the woman called Bright Leaf emerged, the same one who had cared for him while he was on the mend. The Anoka woman wore rough breeches and a vest. She glanced at Broska before settling her gaze upon Kellic, pleased she could surprise him.

"You don't mind, do you?" Broska asked with a smirk.

The mercenary blinked. "No," he said, clearing his throat.

Broska spoke to the young woman, far too fast for Kellic to understand. Bright Leaf answered, nodding at times, all the while sparing looks at the red-faced mercenary.

"Here . . ." she finally said and took Kellic by the hand.

That soft yet firm contact disarmed him completely, and when she led him away, he didn't resist in the least.

He-Dog marched out of the village.

Pushing thoughts of Shay from his mind, he wandered down to the river, needing a moment's peace to right himself. Just far enough to get away for a little while. He went to his little hiding place on the shore, nestled in the jungle. There he sat and took in a deep, calming breath. Sunlight twinkled off the water, offering a much-needed distraction.

Shay.

That was a right unfit bit of business there.

He held his head, attempting to quiet his buzzing thoughts about how much trouble Shay might become.

Until the brazen slap of something wet and heavy startled him. The surrounding trees with broad leafy overhangs prevented him from seeing any farther than a few strides.

Then another wet slap, the noise rousing He-Dog's curiosity. He figured one of the villagers was washing clothing—*the scant bit of clothing they wore*, he reminded himself. Not that he blamed them. The days were unfit hot despite the shade, tempting even him to run around with only a rag over his fruits.

He stood, dusted himself off, and wandered toward the noise just around the nearest tree.

Not ten strides away, he located the source of the disturbance.

There she was . . . the blind woman from before, washing garments downstream from the village. She knelt at the water's edge, absorbed in her work, slapping rags against bare rocks. Some children waded into the water, just farther up from her, splashing about and shrieking laughter. He-Dog paid no mind to the children. He crouched, tore a few blades of grass from the soil, and his mind wandered. Chop would have liked this place, if he were still alive.

The man was dead, He-Dog was all but sure of it. He figured even if the Nordish swordsman had somehow survived the ambush, the Sanjou's many dangers would have eventually claimed him. He wondered what Balless or Rige would have thought of the Sanjou. It was different from Big Rock. Sometimes he dreamed of his childhood and burly old Rige. In those dreams, Rige did very little except smile every now and then or place a warm hand on He-Dog's shoulder. Sometimes the old man tried to speak, but He-Dog always woke before he heard any words at all.

A feeling of sadness welled up inside him then, and He-Dog didn't need that either.

He ripped out another handful of grass and continued watching the woman at the river. Her hair occasionally fell into her eyes. When it did, she stopped and tucked the offending strands behind her ears. Not that it helped. When she stooped, her hair fell over her shoulder, eventually dipping into the water. At one point the children called out and she answered with a wave before returning to her work. At times she straightened and stretched, arching her back and holding her hips, rolling her head from side to side.

Feeling awkward, He-Dog tossed the grass away and intended to leave. He stood, turned, and flinched, startled by Peaceful Moon standing there as if conjured from the very air.

"You again?" He-Dog asked of the spirit man.

This time, however, Peaceful Moon said a few words, practically a whisper, really, and nodded at the blind woman downstream.

He-Dog shook his head, not understanding.

The spirit man continued speaking, ending each sentence with a flex of his jaw, as if he were chewing on the next thought.

He-Dog listened, for respect's sake, but the meaning was lost. He wondered how long the spirit man had stood behind him, watching him watch *her*. That soured his mood just a little. Then he had a thought.

"He-Dog," he said, tapping his chest.

Peaceful Moon smiled back.

"He-Dog," he said once more, and pointed at the spirit man's chest with an open hand.

Peaceful Moon's face softened with understanding. "*Ee-ah-Lun,*" he said.

"He a Loon?"

The spirit man shook his head. "*Ee-ah*-Lun."

"*Ee-ah-Lun,*" He-Dog repeated, this time earning a nod from the other. He-Dog pointed again with his open hand. "What's her name?"

Peaceful Moon gestured at the woman in the river.

He-Dog cringed and gently pushed the hand down. "Aye that, she's the one," he said, glancing around to see if anyone else was nearby.

"*Huu-hun-on-ni,*" Peaceful Moon said.

He-Dog tried to say it, but failed. Peaceful Moon repeated the sounds until he got them right.

Huu-hun-on-ni.

He-Dog had to admit. It wasn't bad on the ears at all.

CHAPTER 37

Displeasure hung over the Iruzu council.
Their hunters had discovered more Iruzu corpses . . . hunting packs sent out to find whatever was killing off Iruzu, only to die themselves. Even worse, not one body of the enemy had been taken, yet the Sanjou reeked with the blood of their own. Heads, either skewered on spears or kicked underfoot, littered the jungle floor. Trails led off to nowhere, further puzzling their hunters, or ended in more heads and their corpses.

It was no longer a hunt, but a slow and steady slaughter of entire packs.

The Iruzu elders yammered angrily, cutting each other off as one shouted over the next. They wondered if a monster from the mountains had wandered into their territory and was feasting on the packs. They then wondered if they faced a regrouped invader . . . or perhaps if a second Wooden Mother had appeared on the Great Water. One that had released yet another pack of Hard Shells upon their shores. Maybe the ghosts of angry Hard Shells were responsible? Could ghosts even be killed? They agreed that a ghost could not. But if the ghosts became flesh to kill Iruzu, could they be killed again?

Possibly.

Sitting on the other side of the council's fire pit and the bearer of such terrible news, One Spear remained silent for much of the discussion. His mind began to drift, revisiting memories of when he was a young hunter of the Sanjou. His first hunt, in fact. One Spear had a spear even then—a wooden one—sharpened to a point as fine as a stone's edge would allow. He remembered branches brushing past his head as he struggled to keep pace with the other hunters. They ran through an unknown part of the jungle, charging over hardpacked ground, screaming, enjoying the hunt.

Then the air filled with arrows and everyone started falling. An Iruzu fell with several shafts in his chest. Another had his head slapped to one side by an arrow sunk deep into his ear. An arrow struck One Spear's shoulder, twisting him off his feet and launching him into the underbrush. The ground buckled his back when he hit, while the stiff barbs of the underbrush scratched and stabbed at his limbs.

Broad leaves shivered above him, and when he turned his head the Hard Shells came into sight. A line of them, shoulder to shoulder, emerging from the jungle. They trampled over the wounded Iruzu, stabbing them dead as they passed. Sounds of fighting then, as the few remaining Iruzu who hadn't been struck down fought back . . . but quickly died.

Hard Shells talked as they killed. Even laughed.

Somehow, they missed One Spear, lying in a thicket of leaves and barbs.

When the sounds of killing died away, when all became quiet, One Spear contorted himself until he got his legs under him. He remembered wanting to run, and run he did, springing from his hiding place and crashing into a Hard Shell warrior. One Spear remembered peering into a face of bright stone, where only the eyes moved and narrowed. The Hard Shell also had a spear, and he backed up to use it. One Spear had been faster, however, stabbing his own weapon into the Hard Shell's throat, feeling it strike bone.

The Hard Shell collapsed, and One Spear grabbed the creature's weapon.

Then One Spear ran . . . not stopping once . . . until . . .

One Spear blinked, his attention back with the elders—old Iruzu who had killed one or two Hard Shells in the past. None of them had been with the hunt on that fateful day, where only One Spear had survived. In the years that followed, One Spear had killed more Hard Shells than any of them.

The elders spoke to him, asking what he intended to do next.

One Spear didn't answer right away, and the silence swelled like a painful boil.

When the elders again appeared on the edge of shouting, he spoke.

One Spear said that whatever was killing Iruzu was mighty indeed. For such a mighty enemy, they would need the best hunters to kill the thing, as anything lesser would fail. Had already failed. He said he would choose twenty warriors. The best killers of the Iruzu. The strongest. The fastest. And, certainly, the most vicious. He then asked for a ceremony, in case they *did* encounter ghosts, to bestow sorcerous charms upon himself and his chosen twenty to help dispel such creatures. When all that was done, One Spear would lead the pack out into the Sanjou, day after day if needed . . . until they finally found this hidden killer.

Or died trying.

That pleased the elders, and they sat and waited for more.

One Spear then explained their enemy was only killing them in the thickest patches of the Sanjou, where the creature could blend into the shadows and surprise its prey. He said they should bring all the hunting packs back into the stronghold. That might lure the creature out of the thick jungle, from which it enjoyed killing Iruzu so much. The wilderness surrounding the Iruzu stronghold was not so dense, so the thing would have a much harder time hiding.

One Spear believed if they could lure it closer to their walls, he and his chosen pack would find it. He vowed to find it. And kill it. Slowly.

All that greatly satisfied the elders.

They agreed to let One Spear choose his twenty, and then they sent him away.

Later that evening, One Spear returned to his lodge where Red Bone and Rock Jaw waited for him. All the others, War Club, Gut Eater, Worm Eye, and Blood Fingers, had either been killed or disappeared. That angered him even further. He considered Red Bone and Rock Jaw, and after a time, he informed them of his plans. One Spear told them to choose their best warriors, until they numbered twenty, as twenty was a number of power to the Iruzu. He told them to choose their quietest warriors, ones who could tickle the hairs of monsters and let them think it was the wind. He told them to choose the fastest ones who would make the great cats lie upon their backs in defeat. And he wanted the strongest and most vicious, as they could be grappling with legends softened by flesh.

Red Bone and Rock Jaw exchanged looks. Twenty warriors of the Iruzu. Their best, all in one pack . . .

One Spear continued. He said that on the next full moon, the spirit hags would perform rituals and anoint the twenty in the blood of fiends, to protect the pack against the very things they hunted. He said the drinkers would also bestow powerful charms upon their weapons so that nothing would miss or break. All these sorcerous enhancements would thwart any magic used against the Iruzu.

One Spear told them he believed there was no need for such magic. That he didn't care for the planned ceremonies at all, and that it was merely being done to satisfy the elders.

Such talk shocked the two other Iruzu, resulting in even more uncomfortable silence. Such ceremonies could evoke powerful magic and it was wise not to speak badly of them. Even if the one speaking was as dangerous and determined as One Spear.

One Spear noticed their unease. He told them not to fear. Told them they were going to gather a hunting pack of their strongest and fastest, the quietest and most fearsome. He told them their combined might would be enough to find and kill anything within the Sanjou. Hard Shell or any other monster.

One Spear then boasted the spirit hags and drinkers would do better *not* to work their magic in the Twenty's favor . . .

But rather, for whatever the Twenty found.

Three days later, One Spear and his chosen pack of Twenty waited among a ring of torches, lit by the spirit hags. These were warriors that One Spear, Red Bone, and Rock Jaw had chosen from among hundreds. Twenty Iruzu, strong and fast, fearless in battles, and possessing exceptionally violent temperaments. Iruzu warriors that would eat each other *raw*, if given the chance. All qualities which One Spear very much prized.

A full moon blazed above, and a multitude of stars prickled the night sky. Under that combined glow, the spirit hags and the drinkers stalked, hunched over and wearing the skulls of their victims. They circled the gathered group of the best hunters and warriors, their voices scratching out incantations in unison. The spirit hags and the drinkers represented two ancient groups within the Iruzu, possessing a deep connection to the dark arts. For such a sacred hunt, nothing was spared on the group of Twenty. The hags broke old bones of their enemies so that the hunted would not escape. They tore apart rotten animal flesh so that the strength of the hunted would fail. The drinkers took in mouthfuls of spiced blood and spat out plumes upon the Iruzu's Twenty, so the pack would find their prey all the faster. The spirit hags then danced about the pack and heaped chants, ointments, and even more blood upon them. The drinkers approached the warriors next. They placed bony necklaces upon each warrior and hung jawless skull masks over their faces. Masks painted in blood.

The Twenty focused on the distant gates as all this happened—listening, trembling, their collective strength building with each successive ritual. Some of the warriors thought only of the honor they would receive upon return. Red Bone thought of ghosts and wondered if ghosts could die. Rock Jaw believed it was only Hard Shells beyond the night, and was eager to crack their skulls open.

One Spear just wanted to find the enemy and drink from their opened throats. Just drink. And *drink*.

Smoke spiced with intoxicating herbs rolled over the Twenty, and they breathed in deeply of its magic.

Then the spirit hags stopped their chants. The drinkers stepped away. The elder called Big Cut spoke, his fangs red and gnashing. Big Cut spoke loud and long about bringing back the night to the Iruzu. He talked about punishing those who would take it from the Iruzu. He talked of killing. He talked of faces. Of Death.

When Big Cut finished, the spirit hags resumed their chanting, strengthened by a thousand more voices of Iruzu young and old gathered beyond the mystical smoke. The rising voices ignited fires inside One Spear and his warriors. One Spear knew they were ready. If there was an enemy waiting outside of the gates, he alone could tear them apart. He *wished* something waited outside. The anticipation grew, threatening to burst his chest. The chanting grew louder, rising to a peak, while Big Cut shook a huge skull rattle at them all.

Then everything stopped, and all became quiet.

A spirit hag pointed.

The gates to the outside opened with ponderous grace.

With the power of the ceremony bursting within him, One Spear was aware of everything. His limbs burned with strength. His mind buzzed with spiced blood.

The spirit hags screamed, and he broke into a slow run for the gates.

His hunters—his *Faces of Death*—followed.

Iruzu not partaking in the hunt trotted beside them, screaming bloody encouragement.

One Spear and his Twenty charged the gates and poured through, into the night.

CHAPTER 38

Wood burned in the fire pit, its light, smoky scent flavoring the air within the lodge. Three Cut, chieftain of the Anoka people, breathed deep and let it out slowly, his frame sagging as he did so. The fire brought back memories of when he was a young man, quick as a snake. Strong as a boar. Not the skin and bones he'd become. Memories of friends and council members no longer present, their lives taken by time or one of its many snares. If only Three Cut could stare into the flames forever, its comfortable heat warming his face, remembering happier times and the people living them. Those thoughts lifted his spirits, but just for a short time, as there were matters to be decided upon as chieftain of his people.

That made him even more miserable, and he struggled to hide his feelings.

The decision he had to make was a monstrous one, one which he'd been delaying for as long as possible.

Smiling Rock grunted, breaking the chieftain's trance, and asked the other elders when Half Tusk would arrive.

Warmest Wind said the warrior would arrive soon.

Flames crackled in the silence that followed.

The elders shared the responsibility of ensuring the best for their people. Especially in matters concerning the Paw. Only days ago, the elders had sent a group of hunters to the land of the accursed monster, in search of its sign—footprints, droppings, or broken trees. All indicators that the fearsome creature wanted its offering, and wanted it soon. When the monster's sign was upon the land, the Anoka had to appease it or suffer its considerable wrath. It had done so before. It would not hesitate to do so again.

The Paw would not allow the Anoka to leave this part of the Sanjou, keeping the people trapped between the mountains to the north and Iruzuland to the south. To spare the village from the constant threat of attack, a bargain had been struck between the Paw and the long-dead forefathers of the Anoka. A bargain that had been upheld through generations until it was Three Cut's time to continue upholding the agreement.

The Paw would not bother the Anoka if they gave it a fully grown man or woman, no older than thirty, once a year, on the Day of Offering. Choosing the sacrifice was always difficult. Warriors were especially valuable, considering the constant threat of the Iruzu. But giving up women brought other problems to the Anoka, that of creating and raising *more* Anoka. After so long, it was clear that the yearly offerings were slowly destroying the Anoka people.

There were times when Three Cut wondered just what kind of bargain the other tribes had made with the beast, for there were five in the Sanjou, separated by several days' worth of rough travel. At one time there had been fourteen tribes, or so Three Cut's father's father had told him. It was said the Paw had destroyed one tribe completely. The other tribes had locked spears with the Iruzu and had been killed to the last.

Three Cut often wondered what the monster ate *between* offerings. Probably hunters or warriors gone astray. Or women or children lost in the jungle, snatched off the path and never seen again. Three Cut also wondered if the Iruzu had ever paid such painful tribute to the monster. He doubted it. The headhunters feared little and perhaps the Paw realized it, sensing that which the five tribes already knew. To make war upon the Iruzu was to make war upon death itself. It was also known that the Iruzu prayed to dark spirits. Maybe those same spirits were in league with the Paw.

In any case, the Anoka had honored their horrific agreement with the Paw for years.

But Three Cut no longer had the stomach for it.

The time for this year's offering drew near, and with it the decision none of them wanted to make. The last few offerings had been men. This year, it would be a woman.

Smiling Rock cleared his throat and said they should gather up every warrior the Anoka had and challenge the Paw. He said they should show the creature they were as strong as the Iruzu and would no longer honor the bargain.

Three Cut forbade it. The chieftain reminded the elder of the shared dream he and Peaceful Moon had about the three Slayers. Three powerful warriors from across the Great Water, bearing weapons that none of the tribes could make or wield. Warriors who wore hard shells and who were not easily killed. One shared dream of three Slayers—who were already in the village.

Only the Slayers could free the Anoka of the Paw. Only their weapons could kill it.

The elder called Warmest Wind spoke then. He worried about what might happen if the Slayers *didn't* kill the Paw. He worried that the monster might discover the Anoka had sent the Slayers against it and would punish the entire village for the act.

That started a long talk, spoken with an intensity that hurt Three Cut's head. Each one spoke of their hopes and fears, causing them to forget their manners. They wondered aloud if the Slayers could do it. Could they kill the Paw with their weapons that shone like moonlight on water? They spoke of warriors from other tribes attempting to kill the Paw, using similar weapons scavenged from the depths of the Sanjou. The same warriors had been torn apart by the monster, and their pieces hung about the jungle as warning to everyone else.

Three Cut silenced any more of that talk with a raised hand.

He reminded them that having the weapons alone would not kill the Paw. The Slayer's weapons were not only different, but required a different skill and knowledge, gained from years of experience. Which was no doubt why so many had fallen to the Paw in the past. Three Cut then said the very fact that the Slayers had arrived meant the time was near. He said the Paw would leave its sign upon the land, and when it did they would send the Slayers after it. He believed the Anoka would soon be forever free of the Paw. When *all* the remaining tribes would be free of the monster.

That quieted the other elders, and for that Three Cut was relieved. He'd said the same many times before, but he did so again, knowing the elders were nervous. They'd been nervous the day the Slayers had arrived, because the three warriors were all so battered and bleeding. Nor could Three Cut or Peaceful Moon explain the presence of the *fourth* Slayer, the one near death, whose leg had been taken by the bloodfish. The dreams had shown only three warriors, and not the near-dead group discovered in the jungle. This caused the old men to worry.

In any case, the Anoka had brought all the Slayers back to health, even Sleeping One Leg, even though they knew he would not—*could* not—hunt the Paw.

A clattering of wood outside the lodge silenced the elders.

The animal hide over the entrance fluttered and Half Tusk entered, covered in a sheen of sweat. The stoic warrior greeted the elders with a solemn bow and knelt before them all.

Three Cut asked if any sign of the Paw had been found.

Half Tusk informed him his hunters had seen no new signs from the creature. The fire crackled as the warrior leader took a moment to settle himself, and then proceeded to explain the depth of the search. He revealed his hunters had traveled to the land of the Paw and found nothing. They went farther north, toward the herds of thunder walkers, and found nothing. Then they went east, toward the hips of the mountains and the pastures of the long necks. Nothing. No sign of the Paw.

Half Tusk let that settle in, and the elders didn't doubt him. The warrior could be brutally direct with his words, and he had little patience for laziness or stupidity. He was also their best fighter, a skilled hunter and tracker, and without question loyal to the Anoka.

If Half Tusk said there was no sign, then there was no sign.

Skin Like Sand asked if the hunters had visited the offering place near the mountains.

Half Tusk said they had, and again they found no sign. He then suggested the creature might have wandered out of its territory.

The elders disagreed, saying the offering place had remained unchanged for generations. After so many years of *giving* an offering, it was puzzling that the Paw had not shown its sign yet. The elders wondered if it might be prowling the jungle, lurking, watching the Anoka. There were whispers that the monster did such things, but no one knew for certain. No one had ever seen the creature and lived to speak of it. Some even believed the Paw possessed powers beyond understanding, which seemed probable, since it lived well beyond whole generations of Anoka.

Three Cut spoke then, telling Half Tusk to choose a fresh group of hunters and to lead them back to the mountains, first thing in the morning. He told his best warrior to return to the offering place and search for signs of the monster. Search it from one end to the other.

Half Tusk nodded that he would.

Orders given, Three Cut motioned for Half Tusk to leave. The warrior bowed, stood, and left the lodge. Silence again from the elders. No Tooth looked to speak but Three Cut stopped him with a hand. He and Peaceful Moon then exchanged pensive looks.

Three Cut had one more decision to make . . . and that was who would be this year's offering.

But the old chieftain faltered, his shoulders slumping. It was so hard choosing one to die, even though this time they would be protected by the Slayers. What if they were wrong about the dream? Three Cut stared into the flames and saw no answer there.

In the end, he asked his elders if he might choose the sacrifice tomorrow . . . and allow the person at least another day of peace.

The next morning, six Anoka hunters rose before dawn and painted themselves in green pigments to match the shades of the jungle. They packed their food into their pouches and hung them off their backs. Upon leaving the village they proceeded north, ghosts trickling through the dense underbrush leaving no discernable trail. They made little sound, gave off no scent, and kept to the safety of the shadows where they could.

All while looking for signs of the Paw.

Any odd sound caused the Anoka hunters to stop and crouch, until Half Tusk deemed it safe to continue. Any broken twig or snapped leaf was inspected. Trails were examined before being followed to their ends. Half Tusk spread out his hunters behind him, warning them to stay quiet, to stay alert, and above all, to stay within sight of each other. They did so, not wanting to incur their leader's anger, and fearful of being taken by the Paw.

With this heightened state of caution, their progress was painfully slow, but that didn't bother Half Tusk. He and his hunters had done this before, and he was glad to be doing something other than standing guard over the three Slayers. That task aggravated him to no end. He often wondered what he'd done to annoy the elders so much to give him such a boring undertaking. He wasn't a mother to three children, tasked with keeping them within the village. He was the strongest warrior and hunter for the Anoka, and while he was wise enough not to openly declare himself as such, he certainly conducted himself in that manner. In his mind, when he became too old to hunt or fight, if he lived that long, he would be an elder himself.

With that, Half Tusk returned to the task at hand, grateful to be away from the village. Even if it was to search for signs of a monster.

A day later, they reached the valley of the offering place. From that point on, they crept from one end of the valley to the other, searching for any signs of the Paw and finding none.

The day was sweltering. Sunlight bled through the dense vegetation overhead and not a breeze made it through. At times, mountains peeked out of tattered holes in the vegetation, their peaks hidden by low clouds. Realizing they were close to the offering place, Half Tusk signaled his hunters to be extra careful. Birds flittered overhead, screaming harsh greetings, which the hunters took as a good sign. They smelled water and soon heard a gentle rushing of a river.

Not just any river. But *the* river.

The place where the Anoka left their offerings.

Half Tusk was well-known among his people. None could best him with spear or arrow or club, and some called him fearless.

Well, Half Fear felt a tingle of unease upon coming to this haunted place.

Creeping through the jungle, he gestured at his men to stay hidden. A tall barrier of reeds rose before him, and he slunk through them all, staying low and careful not to break any. Eventually he parted the reeds and gazed upon the river.

It was a wide serpent of a waterway, perhaps forty paces across at its fattest, and twenty in the narrows. Sunlight dappled the water as it flowed with a low and lazy current. In the stormy season, however, the river could swell to monstrous proportions. The lower levels revealed barren rocks lining its sides, below craggy embankments of soil and exposed roots. The roots were huge, twisted things that slunk into the edges of the water, while the trees leaning over it provided gloomy shade. In the center of the river lay a stark strip of land consisting of white rocks barely above the waterline. In the middle of that little island, a single tree towered. Blight covered its white trunk, while a few shreds of gray fluff hung from dead and crooked limbs. Those same limbs clawed upward, reaching for the sky, spread wide above the considerable girth of its trunk.

Nothing moved on the far embankment. No signs of life at all. Still, Half Tusk waited, listened, and watched, up one side the river and down the other. Insects slid in graceful lines over the slow-moving waters, their bodies glittering in the scant sunlight.

Half Tusk studied the tree.

It resembled a skeleton licked clean, a haunting presence in the middle of the river. Not a leaf covered the thing. Not a bird nested in its heights. Many an offering had been tied to that tree. Chills trickled through Half Tusk as he gazed upon the thing, followed by a flood of unpleasant memories. It was a cursed place, where terrified individuals were brought to die by their own people. Sometimes they slipped into unconsciousness as they were tied to the tree. Sometimes they went mad even before then or became violently ill. Half Tusk knew these things because he was usually the one leaving them. Their pitiful cries forever haunted his memories, but still, he always came back to this place, as only he had the fortitude of mind and body to do so. When he did come back it was usually with different groups of warriors, to spare them the same awful memories as much as possible.

And because of all that, Half Tusk hated this place. Hated it with all his being. It made him feel weak. Even guilty, since he was unable to kill the Paw. Forbidden even to try. And he hated that as well. Struggled with it. For the Anoka did what they did to ensure the lives of the rest of their people.

For a little longer, at least.

That's what he told himself, but it was becoming harder to believe.

He thought about the three Slayers, wondering if the shared dream was indeed true. As much as he doubted it, he found himself secretly hoping they would kill it, and that his people would be forever free of the monster.

Gurgling waters invited him for a swim, but Half Tusk scowled at that. Not even eating the fish from those foul shallows tempted him, believing them to be every bit as cursed as the dead tree that marked the river's terrible heart. With every passing moment the urge to leave grew stronger. Half Tusk didn't want to linger, but he forced himself, loathing it, looking for signs.

There weren't any. Not a track nor a single scratch.

Even then he stayed, ever watchful, at times checking on the light of the sky. The low hush of the river remained constant, and nothing disturbed the scene before him.

After a long and tense period of waiting, Half Tusk decided it was time to go. Wasting no more daylight, he moved back from the riverbank to where his hunters waited. There, he signaled they would continue along the shore and eventually cross over to the other side. Get a little closer to the mountains.

If his hunters disliked his plan, they did not voice it.

No one spoke as they moved downstream. They reached a narrow point and waded across, one by one, the warm water lapping at their knees. Half Tusk tightened his grip on his spear as he crossed, disliking the exposure. Once they reached the other side, they climbed the embankment and slipped back into the undergrowth, safely concealed once again. The relief was a welcome thing. With one last look at the tree on the island, Half Tusk led his hunters back into the jungle. There they continued their search, not speaking unless Half Tusk broke the silence first.

By early evening, in the deepening shadows of the mountains, Half Tusk led his men to a well-hidden patch bordered by giant bushes with huge drooping leaves. The bare earth would be their beds for the night, without worry of crawlers since they all wore scents that repelled them. Half Tusk chose one man as a sentry, with orders to rouse another when he could no longer stay awake.

With that done, they crawled underneath their selected bushes like worms burrowing into fruit and settled down for the night. Curled up in his own hiding spot, Half Tusk dared to wonder what it might mean if they *didn't* find any sign of the

Paw. He wondered if they would be spared a sacrifice. He even dared to consider the creature might have died or been killed at long last by some unknown force. Perhaps it knew the Slayers were near . . . and feared them.

Such thoughts were dangerous for the hope they brought and Half Tusk dismissed them with a scowl.

A thing like the Paw would not forget about the Anoka.

Nor did Half Tusk believe the monster was dead. The monster was merely late, or worse, torturing his people with its patience. Nothing more. It was foolish and dangerous to think otherwise.

They would find its sign soon enough.

Half Tusk woke the next morning, not daring to move anything except his eyelids. All was quiet, and when he believed it was safe, he eased himself up onto his feet. Narrow beams of sunlight lit up patches of jungle and all remained still as he stood. A much-needed stretch then, and Half Tusk thought about Iruzuland for some reason, even though they were nowhere near that awful place. Thoughts of what to eat crossed his mind, before he became even more aware of the deep, reckoning silence of the morning.

Half Tusk gripped his spear and hunched over, eyeing the surrounding wilderness.

Something was not right.

The other hunters emerged from their hiding places and converged on their leader. Seeing his wary stance, they readied their weapons and gathered around their leader. On guard, they listened and watched as that menacing silence pressed down on the land. Nothing moved. Not a branch. Not a twig.

Half Tusk thought he smelled blood, then realized only three of his hunters stood with him.

Motioning for silence, Half Tusk led them through the underbrush, following the trace scent toward the spot one of the missing hunters had chosen for his night's rest. Along the way, the last sentry to take watch for the night joined them.

The one chosen for the first watch was missing.

Near noiseless, they slipped through brush bearing prickly leaves, leaves that clawed at them with every step. Eyes narrowed, Half Tusk crouched below the tall vegetation and quietly searched the missing hunter's sleeping spot.

Then he heard it.

An unmistakable buzzing, low and disturbing enough to stop Half Tusk in his tracks. Taking a firmer grip of his spear, he signaled his hunters to be on guard and pushed forward. He parted the dense greenery and entered the imposing shade of a huge tree.

The buzzing grew louder.

Using his spear, Half Tusk lifted a branch covered in broad leaves. The leaves dripped water, and the air became charged with the smell of spent carnage. Underneath, a spattered ring of gore and rubbish covered both the ground and the segmented trunk of the tree. There was no corpse in the revealed space, just an enormous amount of blood. An oily, teeming mat of flies and crawlers gorged themselves on the slaughter, full to the point where they did not fear the Anoka hunters.

Ready to fight, Half Tusk scanned the surrounding area.

The grim discovery caused the others to break their silence.

It took him! they whispered in horror. *During the night, while we slept like youngsters. The Paw took* him.

Half Tusk hushed them all with an angry hiss and a wave of his hand. The men quieted, clearly nervous, eyeing the depths of the jungle.

Still, they were Anoka hunters. Anoka *warriors*. And this was not the first time they'd seen blood. Half Tusk reminded them of that with an angry whisper—reminded himself as well, as his stomach tightened into a knot and his legs pleaded for him to run.

A cold realization gripped him then. The thing had walked *among* them last night and plucked one man from his nest without even a rustle of leaves.

That prompted an even greater urge to flee, yet Half Tusk did no such thing, his heart hammering to the evil buzzing of flies. Feeling vulnerable, he organized his warriors into a tighter circle, vigilant of the surrounding wild, its lush greens and splashes of color no longer welcoming. Now it was a dangerous place. Worse, it was the lair of a monster, perhaps still nearby, watching them.

Half Tusk hefted his spear.

The Paw was . . . is here.

All the old tales flooded his mind then, of the monster creeping about the Sanjou's dark, twisting paths, lurking within its hidden reaches. Tales of unwary men, women, and children being snatched from trails and devoured. Horrible slayings without warning, without sound, leaving nothing more than a few tatters of ruined flesh upon the land.

Sweat beaded down Half Tusk's face until he wiped it away. He signaled to his hunters his intention to leave. Taking care to remain quiet, he led them back in a painfully slow procession, fighting down the swelling urgency to run. Half Tusk chose stealth over speed, at least until stealth failed them.

The jungle seemed darker, providing more places to hide, to aid their retreat. Drooping vines brushed their arms and shoulders. Old wood sought to trip them. Insects whined in their ears. Otherwise, the Sanjou seemed empty of life as if it had witnessed yet another killing within its borders and was already hungry for the next.

Half Tusk watched everything as he crept through the jungle. Every thicket of vegetation, every leaf, every shadow. His growing fear sharpened his senses, and he doubted a snake would get by without him knowing it. Several times he stopped his hunters and listened, continuing only when he deemed it safe. He finally pushed through a wall of bushes spotted with purple blooms as big as a person's head . . . and stopped.

The river lay before them. The same one they'd crossed the day before. Senses thrumming, Half Tusk edged forward, gently parting the flowers and their reeds, until he saw the offering place.

The sight stopped him.

His eyes widened as he gazed upon that haunted tree in the middle of the river, where so many had lost their lives to a monster. Shadows darkened the water and the little island at its center.

Except for the tree.

Stark and white and wicked, its limbs reached for the sky.

Half Tusk's breath hitched and his guts went cold.

On the bare white bark of the tree lay a partial, yet gruesome print of a hand. A *huge* hand, the blood splayed across the whole trunk.

The Paw had returned.

And, as expected, it had left its sign.

Half Tusk blinked, realizing they had to get word to the village. He faced the four hunters, about to convey his thoughts, when a massive, oversized hand with rust-speckled claws reached out from the bushes *behind* the last Anoka man and clutched his entire head. The hunter released a short scream smothered by mottled flesh, followed by the awful crackle of a shattering skull. Bloody matter spurted from between those huge, crooked fingers, just before the claws yanked the corpse back into the jungle, gone in a flutter of reeds.

The remaining hunters shrieked and scattered.

The instant that giant fist had pulled the unfortunate hunter away, Half Tusk had turned and bolted, hurling himself over the embankment and landing with a violent splash. He fell to his knees, hobbled with pain, and sprang up soaked and sputtering. More screams twisted him around, in time to see two other hunters leap and land in the shallows.

A third hunter burst from the vegetation, jumping for the river. A monstrous arm shot out after him, seizing the man around the waist. Huge claws sank deep, spraying blood and other horrible matter, and yanked the hunter out of sight.

In that shocking moment, Half Tusk glimpsed a scaly shoulder, brown as sun-baked dirt and impossibly huge, along with a flicker of an oily black mane . . .

And the flash of what might have been an eye.

Run, he screamed at the others, and they ran *hard*, stomping across the shallows with enough energy to skim across the surface. Twice Half Tusk nearly tripped, righting himself with his spear—a spear that would not do anything to the monster behind him.

He didn't look to see if the others followed.

The Paw had returned.

And he wasn't going to stop running until he reached the village.

CHAPTER 39

His legs dangling over the edge, Hargan sat on the rocks fencing in the mountain shelf. The sky boiled with storm clouds that slowly tumbled their way. Winter was coming, or what passed as winter here, and that made him wonder if it got cold here at all. It remained scorching hot during the day, but recently he felt it was a touch cooler in the morning and evenings. Just a touch. Which got him thinking of Sunja and wondering how long it had been since he'd been home.

He then thought of heading back out, to see if he could hunt down and kill off more of the hated fishmen. Something felt different these past few weeks, however. He'd left heads and carcasses all over the land as markers to frighten and confuse the maggots . . . and it might have worked. He had not been able to find another pack of the dogs. It was strange. Almost as if . . . they knew he was out there and were planning something.

As a result, he didn't go anywhere beyond the valley, wary of walking into a trap.

Hargan mentally shrugged it off. Whatever they were planning didn't bother him. First, they would have to find him, and up here he could see almost everything. His only concern was the fish maggots attempting to creep up on him during the night. He looked down over the mountain slope. A few simple traps would alert him to any of that gurry.

Birds darted over the rolling roof of treetops on the far side of the valley. Some would fling themselves up high over those soft plumes of green before diving hard and disappearing from sight.

Hargan wondered if he might be able to kill a few of those and eat them.

Chop stepped beside him, startling the Sunjan.

"Noisy topper," Hargan muttered after a bit.

Chop didn't react to that, content to gaze at the valley. Over the last few days, the Nord had seemed increasingly spry. He'd been walking more and his cuts and bruises had long disappeared.

"Must be the meals I keep feeding you," Hargan grumbled.

The ruined face turned to him.

"Oh, you heard me," the Sunjan said. "Don't think I don't see what you're doing."

Hargan cocked an eyebrow when the Nordish man stiffened. He must have struck a tender spot.

"Didn't like that, did you?"

Chop slowly shook his head.

"Well, there's plenty I don't like," Hargan complained and rubbed at a poorly trimmed beard. "*Plenty*. I don't like the notion of spending the rest of my life on this mountain with *you* as company. Truth be known, topper, you aren't that pretty. I'm also feeling we should do more about those fish maggots out there. Bloody their noses. Smash them square. Take more heads. They're planning something. I can smell it. And I'm getting tired of waiting for them here. I figure with you, we might well and truly break some spirits. Crack some faces. When you're ready, that is. *If* you'll ever be ready. Oh, that's right. I've noticed. You aren't moving so slow these days. Or grabbing about your ribs. Makes me wonder what you're waiting for."

Silence to that.

"Then again," Hargan continued, nodding toward the valley. "All this is probably fine for you, you no-faced bastard. To think we're losing the war to you sour blossoms. Not like *you*, you understand, but the *other* Jackals. If we'd had to fight the likes of *you*, the likes . . . *like* you, the war would've been finished *years* ago. Been done . . . what's the word? Ah, *decisively*."

Chop weathered that storm with slitted eyes. Then, without warning the Nordish man walked back toward the cavern.

Annoyed, Hargan watched him go. "Aye that. Start a fire back there or something. Clean the cave. You woman. You *punce* of a woman. Might get you to wash the rags covering my arse crack. You think all I'm about is sharpening my blades here and prowling about the jungle? Hm? Like some vengeful he-bitch? Saimon's crusty knob."

Having had his say and meaning every damned word, a simmering Hargan turned back to the valley. "Decisively," he repeated, pleased with himself. He knew a few big words. Just never got much chance to use them.

There was a grind of metal on metal, jerking Hargan's attention away from the view.

Chop returned . . . with both short swords unsheathed and held low at his sides, the blades dull with menace.

The very sight turned Hargan completely around, swinging his legs back over the rocks. "What's this?"

Chop positioned himself in a guarded stance, one sword flashing high, while the other pointed at Hargan's chest. A cool mountain wind blew around them, whistling high overhead.

The Sunjan sat there with a crooked look of disgust. "What? You offended or something? Because I called you a *woman*? Don't mind *that*. Truth be known, a woman would be much angrier with me for calling you that. Go on, now. Put those things away. Before . . ." he smirked. "Before you cut those soft hands of yours."

The Nord didn't move.

Hargan sighed. "Go on, I said. Else I take those bread knives and use them to cut the hairs on my nogs."

As an answer, Chop whipped the swords around him, the metal flashing. He continued weaving both blades in the air, flexing his steel before his adversary, until he returned to the same guarded position as before.

"That was very pretty," a nodding Hargan sneered. "You've been secretly practicing. Do it again."

Chop did not. Instead, the Nordish man bared teeth. Or at least Hargan *thought* he bared teeth. The maggot had no lips, so it was difficult to say, but he suspected he'd been snarled at all the same.

Hargan reached for his nearby axe. "You're annoying me now, topper."

Chop clanged his blades off each other.

"You're unfit . . ." Hargan concluded, lifting his weapon. "Mad, even. All this time up here, I suppose. Stupid, stupid topper. Come on then. Let's have some exercise. See how much you've recovered."

Chop circled to his right, and Hargan matched him. "Oh no, you're not going that way, topper. Come straight on if you want it, you miserable—"

The Nordish swordsman streaked forward, swords whirling.

Hargan barely deflected the first thrust. He narrowly turned aside the second, then the third and fourth before deciding he needed more space. He broke away, glimpsing Chop leaping high, just as the Nordish man brought one sword down at Hargan's head.

The Sunjan stopped it on the shaft of his axe.

Somehow, Chop snaked his sword *past* Hargan's block. Edged steel licked the Sunjan's forearm a good finger's length before he turned the blade aside and retreated.

But the Nordish man pursued him and was deadly fast about it.

Two flicks of the wrists later and a pair of stinging red cuts marked the Sunjan's chest. Dark rivulets ran down Hargan's belly, reaching the waistline of his tattered leggings. A few drops dappled the earth.

Hargan retreated again and the Nordish man didn't pursue. Hargan stopped with his back against a boulder and inspected himself. His chest bloomed with heat. *Angry* heat.

No more than a few heartbeats into the fight and he'd been scratched thrice.

Resetting to his guard position once again, Chop waited.

"You ripe—" Hargan said and charged with a bullish roar, splitting the air with his axe.

Chop ducked with a speed damn near sorcerous, and countered with a spinning slash so rapid that Hargan felt the breeze along the back of his neck . . . It was so close that he stopped with a squeal of outrage. He slapped a hand to feel for a wound. Nothing. Not even a nick. But it had been a near thing.

Too near a thing.

He sized Chop up. The swordsman was perhaps seven paces away and practically bouncing on his feet.

And motioning Hargan to come at him.

"All right, then, you no-faced stain of shite . . . you want a fight?" Hargan charged, crossing the distance in no time. He swung his axe with all his might, the weapon near weightless in his hands. He cut and slashed, reared back and chopped, unleashing blows meant to sever arms or legs or even free a head from its neck.

The Nordish swordsman, the fully *mended* Nordish swordsman, ducked, dodged, and deflected every attempted assault. Then, as if he'd had enough, he broke away well out of reach. His speed was frightening. His strength was formidable, for it took a strong arm indeed to parry the killer sweep of a battle-axe. Chop bobbed and weaved, nimbly stepping one way before darting back the other, all while shadowing Hargan.

Who still bled, still, and stalked his adversary with hateful eyes.

"You going to fancy dance all day long, maggot? Or—" Hargan charged again and doubled down on his efforts to take the Nordish punce's head.

Chop charged from the other side.

They met in the middle, steel clanging, echoing across the slope.

And again, what Chop didn't evade, he deflected. Twice Hargan tried hooking swords, and twice his opponent twisted free, meeting brute strength with effortless skill. With a dangerous mindset that the fight had become quite real, Hargan lashed out with short, vengeful slashes, looking to split the man up the middle. Chop dodged everything, content to forgo parrying to better avoid his foe. Hargan tried to get in close, but Chop twisted away from looping fists and elbows, danced with stomping feet, and did not allow either limb or sword to be grabbed or locked up.

All done with a speed almost twice that of the Sunjan's.

It made Hargan *furious*.

He slashed at the Nord's legs. Chop leapt *over* the axe and slapped the Sunjan's shoulder with the flat of a blade. A bellow of rage from Hargan as the swordsman landed in a crouch . . .

And swept the Sunjan's legs out from under him.

Arms flailing, Hargan crashed to the ground.

Chop backpedaled, rolling his shoulders and flexing his joints, placing the whole of the valley at his back.

Spitting dust, Hargan looked up from where'd he landed flat on his bleeding chest. The Nordish bastard was *flowing* through a series of thrusts, parries, and strikes aimed at imaginary enemies. His speed was shocking. And when Hargan thought the man could not get any faster . . . he *did*. Punching the air, punctuating each set of moves with an unexpected pause and click of crossed steel. There, Chop held his blades at arm's length for a single beat before starting up again, whipping up a truly dazzling storm of gleaming metal and whistling wind.

Where Chop stood at the center.

Seddon above, Hargan thought in dismay.

The Nordish he-bitch had healed, well and truly.

Chop stopped hacking up ghosts and met Hargan's hateful stare, a heartbeat before motioning for him to stand up.

Pah!

A furious Hargan jumped to his feet. Seething, he charged two steps and *threw* his axe—with the might of both arms behind it—straight at the Nord's head.

Except the Nord's head was no longer there.

The man ducked and the axe split only air, spinning end over end, over the rock wall, until it disappeared from sight.

Horrified, Hargan roared, balled up both fists, and plodded forward.

Chop threw down his swords.

Hargan swung first—missed—and Chop countered in a thunderous barrage of hooking rights, lefts, and a final jaw-breaking uppercut that streaked through Hargan's crumbling guard. The punch connected like a hammer smashing an anvil and crossed the Sunjan's eyes.

Hargan hit the ground with a teeth-rattling thud. The wind jumped from his lungs and left him gasping. He grunted and groaned like he was in a painful squat and unable to move a thing. In time his eyes cleared and he lay there, taking in much needed air. With an effort, he struggled onto his side, wavered, and landed flat on his back.

There he stayed, unfit to continue.

Chop placed the tip of his blade to Hargan's throat.

Very much aware of the sword at his kinkhorn, Hargan's breathing evened out. He squeezed his eyes shut as if clearing his head, and his anger bled away. He peeked right to left before finally fixing on the Nordish man's face.

Without warning, Chop warily withdrew the weapon and retreated a few steps.

Not quite ready to rise, Hargan begrudgingly waited a few moments before he pushed himself to his feet. There, he swayed, steadied his stance, and ignored Chop entirely, taking the time to look for any open wounds. He dusted himself off, grumbling under his breath, and dabbed at his chest. Frowning, sighing, he inspected the blood covering his fingers, ignoring the Nordish bastard as well as he could, for as long as he could. With a scowl, Hargan placed hands to hips, nodding at the swordsman standing across from him.

Chop was untouched.

The mountain wind died away. Clouds drifted overhead. After a time, the Sunjan cleared his throat.

"All right then," He muttered. "You going to help me look for my axe or what?"

They found Hargan's battle-axe not far down the mountain slope, which pleased the Sunjan very much. Chop didn't understand why, however. Their fight had proven the weapon to be a clumsy thing.

"It's the mind, you see," Hargan said, as if sensing the swordsman's very thoughts. "When most people see a proper battle-axe, especially coming at their *head*? . . . Scares them piss dry."

Chop didn't react. The axe certainly didn't scare *him* piss dry.

"Well, you're different," Hargan grumbled, detecting his thoughts. The Sunjan spared him a glance then, one that, dare Chop think it, almost looked approving. Which wasn't completely odd. While they had searched for the battle-axe, Chop felt Hargan's attitude toward him change, somehow. The Sunjan seemed almost affable, truth be known, and Chop wasn't certain why that was. He doubted it had anything to do with helping him find the axe. A little part of him suspected that it was more about him besting the Sunjan in their fight.

Just perhaps.

Rain clouds held off as they made their way back up the slope.

"You damn near snapped my leg when you tripped me," Hargan muttered, halfway back to their shared home. "You hear me?"

Chop did not reply.

"Shaddup," Hargan warned, but the once-Sujin was smiling when he said it.

And the Jackal, as much as he was able, smiled back.

CHAPTER 40

Under a bright morning sky, a ragged Half Tusk staggered into the Anoka village.

No one else followed him.

Half Tusk cried out, a harsh, half-dead sound that startled the children. Women and men paused in their work and emerged from behind their lodges, their faces filled with concern.

Whereupon Half Tusk collapsed in a heap.

A throng of villagers engulfed him. Worried faces crowded in, gathering up the fallen warrior. A near-delirious Half Tusk did not resist, and with his last bit of strength he gasped out the last thing they wanted to hear.

The Paw was somewhere behind him.

The reaction was swift. Parents swept their youngsters into their homes. Warriors snatched up weapons and rushed to their guard posts. Fire pits were lit and maintained.

Half Tusk was carried by a handful of Anoka men to the elders, where his unconscious body was placed upon a soft mat. When he came to, the tired warrior sat up and bathed in the friendly glow of the lodge's burning fire pit. His features drawn and haggard, his voice a wasted croak, Half Tusk told the elders of how he and his hunters had run for the village, stopping only when their legs could carry them no farther. And when they stopped, when they thought they had finally escaped, when they couldn't believe that the Paw had kept up with them, a set of claws would reach out from the undergrowth and snatch away whoever was closest. By the head or by the arms, the Paw yanked them back into the shadows, prompting those remaining to flee again.

The Paw killed off all his hunters, Half Tusk told the elders. And each time, only the *hands* of the beast were ever seen, huge, far-reaching things of meat and bones and talons. As Half Tusk spoke, his head sank between his shoulders. He admitted to fear. *Terror*, even, whispering he had never felt the like before. Never had he felt so helpless in the wild. Or closer to death.

With haunted eyes, Half Tusk said he could still hear the breaking of his men's bones, the cracking of their skulls. So fast were the attacks, so surprising, the victims barely had a chance to scream.

After a moment to compose himself, Half Tusk stressed that there be warriors watching the edges of the jungle, in case the Paw showed itself. He didn't know if the monster had tired of the chase or if it had followed him all the way to the village.

He also said the three Slayers should be made ready to fight, as the monster might not want to wait for an offering. The thing had killed five hunters. It might be looking to kill *all* the Anoka this time.

At the end of the telling, Three Cut gestured for Half Tusk to be removed and allowed to rest. Anoka warriors helped the man away, leaving the elders alone. No one said anything, and the only sounds they could hear were coming from beyond the lodge, where the village readied itself for the worst.

No Tooth broke the silence first, saying that it was careless to lead the monster back to the village. His words brought a grim agreement from Smiling Rock.

Peaceful Moon spoke then, and the spirit man believed that if Half Tusk had led the monster back, then the three Slayers would kill it. Just as they had in his dream.

No Tooth warned that they should prepare for war in case the Slayers failed. He also said the Paw might lurk in the jungle surrounding the village, feeding when it needed to, until the Anoka gave it what it wanted.

Bite Of Night spoke then, agreeing it was time to call upon the three Slayers, but also to bring the latest sacrifice to the offering place. If the Paw was near, it would see the Anoka bring out the offering and would follow . . . drawing the monster away from the village.

Three Cut spoke then with a very sad heart. He informed the elders that he had decided the name of the sacrifice for this year. Unable to choose any of his people for the danger that was to come, he decided—though it pained him to do so—to offer his youngest daughter of twenty years—the unseeing Gentle Rain—to the Paw.

Silence greeted his words.

Bite Of Night eventually spoke up. Using his words carefully, he acknowledged that it was good of Three Cut to offer his youngest daughter. She was a good offering . . . but perhaps she was not the best. The Paw would want the best, would demand it, and would sense anything . . . less. If the Slayers failed, it would be wise to have a worthy sacrifice in place . . . just in case. To avoid the Paw's wrath and the destruction of the Anoka village, Bite Of Night suggested a healthy offering would be best. An offering with . . . no troubles.

So he suggested another.

Three Cut's second-born daughter, Summer Wind, who was twenty-two years old.

Peaceful Moon spoke then, saying that while it pained him to offer anyone to the Paw, Summer Wind was a good choice. She was strong of will and limb and could endure hardship if needed. They would need someone like that to survive the days ahead.

Three Cut held up a hand, silencing any further discussion. He agreed to offering Summer Wind. He forced hope into his voice and reminded them all that this offering would be the last, and that the Slayers would kill the monster . . . as shown in the shared dream.

Bite Of Night looked at the ground and his voice became low. He said he hoped the Slayers killed the Paw; otherwise, the monster's vengeance would be a terrible thing.

Three Cut barely heard him. He was again hoping the shared dream would come to pass. None of that, however, eased the sadness pressing down upon him for his beloved daughter. He'd carried such high hopes for Summer Wind, his second daughter and, secretly, his favorite. Many would have sought her heart for marriage.

Three Cut caught himself. Many would *still* seek her heart for marriage. The Slayers would kill the Paw.

Steadying himself, he informed the others he would tell his daughter that she'd been chosen.

"That . . . is . . . a . . . tree," Bright Leaf said carefully.

Kellic repeated the words in Anoka.

She clapped at his efforts and they shared a smile.

They sat beside the river, away from the village, on a secluded embankment.

"That . . . is . . . a river," she said, nodding.

"A stream?" he asked.

"Stream?"

"It's a small river."

She looked confused at that, and Kellic knew it was because of him. "That is a river," he said, and then tried the same sentence in her language. He mispronounced the final word, which earned him a playful slap about the shoulder. During his time spent with Bright Leaf, it had occurred to him that Anoka women—or at least the one teaching him—enjoyed slapping their men around the head and shoulders.

"Un-fit dog blossom," Bright Leaf laughed. She covered her mouth as her brown eyes opened wide.

Kellic matched her expression with one of feigned shock.

It was interesting what the ear picked up at times, and that particular phrase was no doubt her overhearing a few too many conversations between Kellic and the others. The Lords above would frown on him teaching her such gurry, to ensure she said it correctly, but he figured if she was going to swear, she might as well say it right. Still, he knew he was tempting Saimon's hell because of it.

Kellic tried to hide his growing smile and failed miserably.

Whereupon she swatted him across the shoulder yet again.

What was unfair, at least in his mind, was that she would not teach him the equivalent swear words in *her* language. Broska had further explained that, surprisingly, the Anoka did not swear like people on the mainland. When the Anoka were truly angry, they simply screamed and waved their hands about as if throwing away a handful of gurry. Then they stomped off somewhere to let off steam, like gathering wild vegetables and herbs, or marching around the village to mend fences and roofs. In their minds, anger was a poison that had to be bled off with some kind of activity that benefited others.

The notion made sense to Kellic.

"You are very . . . smart," he told her, tapping his temple.

Bright Leaf smiled. "*You* are . . . very smart . . ." she repeated, shoving him back with a light push, rocking him in place.

"Me?" Kellic asked in Anoka and waved the notion away. "No . . ." he replied, wanting to say *not at all*, but could not. *No* was the best he could do with his current vocabulary.

She squinted at him—which was something else Bright Leaf enjoyed doing for some reason. "Sad Eyes," she said, using his Anoka-given name.

Sad Eyes. Kellic didn't think he had sad eyes. Certainly he might look *glum* from time to time, but not enough to be called that. He checked on who might be listening nearby as he prepared himself to deliver his next thought. A few words he'd learned from Broska for this very moment: telling Bright Leaf how so very lovely she looked. Fidgeting a bit, he faced her, took a breath, and caught sight of an Anoka warrior emerging from the bushes. Not just one, but several, and Peaceful Moon.

None of the menfolk looked very happy to see Kellic with the young woman. Sensing trouble, he stood and made certain he was a respectable distance from Bright Leaf. She stood as well, brushing off her backside as she did so and no longer smiling.

Peaceful Moon spoke then. Too fast and far too many words for Kellic to understand. However, he could understand faces well enough.

As the spirit man spoke, Bright Leaf's expression withered into deep worry, before becoming one of unchecked horror. All color fled her cheeks. She covered her mouth while Peaceful Moon continued.

Broska appeared from behind the elder.

"What's happening?" Kellic asked, bracing for the worst.

"Everything," the Zuthenian replied. "You best come with me."

Within the lodge of the mercenaries, a dour Broska informed the men of Half Tusk's return and the Paw. Shay was even present, having hobbled his way over. The elder called No Tooth sat beside Broska as he spoke. The old man had his eyes closed, as if enduring the harshest nightmare.

Once Broska finished, the mercenaries exchanged pensive looks.

"So that's why everyone got out of sight," He-Dog remarked.

"And why the warriors were surrounding the village," Kellic said.

"And that pisser led it right to us," Snaffer grumbled, more grim than usual.

"Half Tusk had no choice," Broska said. "His task was to find the Paw's sign and return as soon as possible. Which he did."

"They think the thing is watching the village?" He-Dog asked.

"We think so, but we're not certain. If it is, the elders hope it won't attack as long as the offering is made. Within reasonable time."

"Five men isn't enough of an offering?" Shay asked.

"Maybe it's just a start," suggested He-Dog.

"More of a warning, I suppose," Broska said.

"A hard warning. Killing those men."

"I'm not . . ." Broska sighed heavily. "I don't know *why* the thing does what it does. Or what it thinks. Or wants. All I know is what the Anoka are doing *now*. Preparations are being made. You will take the offering to the place where . . . this will happen."

"She has a name," Kellic said in a low voice, watching the Zuthenian.

"You're right, she does. Apologies. You will take Summer Wind to the offering place. And there you will kill the Paw."

Kellic lowered his eyes.

"What's your problem, then?" Shay asked.

Kellic sighed. "She's Bright Leaf's best friend."

"Bright who?"

"She's also Three Cut's daughter," Broska added, exchanging looks with No Tooth.

"How many daughters does that one have?" Snaffer asked with blunt curiosity.

"Three. Summer Wind, who tended to you lads. Gentle Rain, and my missus. She's the oldest. Gentle Rain is the youngest and was born without sight. You've seen her. About the village."

That got He-Dog's attention.

Shay scratched his head, clearly not interested. "Well, then. When do we leave?" he asked.

That drew a hard look from He-Dog.

"You'll leave in the morning," Broska answered. "Half Tusk will take you there. And then leave you."

"Not the first time to be left somewhere," Shay said. "Except we won't fail. Tell your man there not to worry. We'll kill the monster."

"You're not going, Shay," He-Dog rumbled.

"Of course I'm going," the prince scoffed, suggesting the very thought was the most unfit thing he'd ever heard.

The elder called No Tooth spoke then, for a long time.

Broska listened, nodding, and took a deep breath when the old man finished. "He says that Sleeping One Leg—that's you"—Shay's jaw twitched—"will remain in the village. He says you'll be cared for while the three Slayers kill the Paw."

"But—" the prince started.

"He *says*," Broska insisted, "that the Slayers in the dreams were *whole* . . . and not . . . so wounded as Sleeping One Leg has been."

"Stop calling me that."

"They call you that."

"Well then, tell *them* to stop calling me that," Shay stressed. "And I'm going."

He-Dog was about to say otherwise when Broska spoke. Sternly. "You were not in their dreams, Shay. And because of that the Anoka won't let you go. Three Slayers. Not four. Whole men with all their limbs. To go or do otherwise would draw bad spirits to the Anoka. Or so they believe. They won't allow that to happen, not when there's a chance they can be free of the monster once and for all. And certainly not when it's Three Cut's middle daughter. I've said this before, they're very superstitious. You will remain here."

Shay squirmed on his mat and sighed. "He said all that?"

". . . Most of it," Broska admitted.

An uncomfortable heat swelled within the confines of the lodge. A fuming Shay gazed upon his missing leg as if it were a length of chain, none too pleased with the decision. He then cleared his throat and quietly stated, "These are *my* lads. I *have* to go. They only follow *me*."

"I'm not your lad," He-Dog said.

"I don't mean *you*."

"I'm not your lad, either," Kellic said. "Not now. Not ever more."

That struck the prince hard, and he struggled with a reply.

"Best you stay here, my Prince," Jers Snaffer rumbled. "Truth be known, you would only slow us down."

That visibly mortified Shay. "Snaffer . . ."

"There'll be no more talk of this," Broska said.

"Look . . . I can . . . I can be *useful*."

"No, you cannot. Not for this."

"And not when it's her," Kellic said quietly.

"Sunbar . . ."

"Shaddup," Kellic said and Shay flinched. A moment later the prince looked away, unable to match the other's harsh eyes.

"You'd only be bait," He-Dog muttered, uncaring of how it sounded. "And we have plenty of that already."

Shay absorbed that, his jaw clenching, but he kept his peace. Without a word he pulled his crutches underneath himself and struggled to his feet. It took him a bit of work, but he did it, and no one offered to help. He righted himself and regarded them all. "Do what you will, then. Best of fortunes and all that. If you do need me . . . I'll be about. Somewhere."

With that, Shay swung himself toward the opening. He fumbled with the entrance flap just enough to prompt Broska to help.

"I can open an unfit door," the prince snapped and shoved his way through.

In the quiet moment that followed, Broska regarded the others. "I didn't mean to offend him."

"Pay no mind," He-Dog said, eyeing Kellic with newfound respect.

The mercenary frowned. "I can't remember when he's called me by name . . . if ever."

"He's called you by name," Snaffer rumbled.

He-Dog studied Jers Snaffer with a lot less hate.

"Don't say a word," the grizzled war dog warned him. "Not a word."

"Do you need time to talk matters over?" Broska asked carefully, not wanting to start an argument with these men.

"No," He-Dog replied flatly and nodded at No Tooth. "They want this thing dead? I'll kill it for them."

"As will I," Kellic said, straightening his back.

They waited for Snaffer then, who looked darkly thoughtful. "As will I," he finally released.

A smile spread across Kellic's bearded face.

"Shaddup," Snaffer warned with a slow, disdainful shake of his hairy head. He noticed He-Dog a heartbeat later. "And *you* shaddup. I know what's owed and what's not owed."

He-Dog kept his mouth shut on the matter. Dare he admit it, however, he liked the nobility of it all. It was the same feeling when he, Chop, and Balless had helped the last few handfuls of survivors escape the doomed city of Foust. Except better. There was no coin involved here. Balless would have approved.

"Why can't we thrash the jungle about the village?" Snaffer asked. He looked at Broska with accusing eyes. "Because the Anoka are a superstitious lot and we do what they want."

Broska said nothing.

"I know why," He-Dog said. "Because if we fight it here and fail, the Paw will tear through this place, killing everyone within reach. If we're at the offering place and we fail, then it's just the four of us and no one else dies. That right?"

A sad smile crossed the Zuthenian's face. "Something like that. But we're hopeful that you will not fail."

"Lords above," Snaffer muttered.

"Alright then," He-Dog said. "When do we take the girl?"

Broska asked the elder No Tooth.

And the Slayers listened.

CHAPTER 41

The next morning, a group of women led Summer Wind to the river. There, in clean, slow-moving waters, they washed her until her skin was almost raw. When they finished that, they clothed her in the best hides from the most recent hunt and walked her back to a lodge where Peaceful Moon waited. Within the dwelling redolent of calming smoke, the women rubbed scented oils squeezed from wildflowers onto Summer Wind's shoulders, arms, and legs. They combed out her long hair and placed red petals within it. While the women worked, Summer Wind closed her eyes and breathed deeply of the smoky curls floating about her head. She thought of her family for a moment. She thought of her wonderful mother, her father, and her cherished sisters. She didn't blame her father for choosing her for the offering. She was especially thankful that Gentle Rain had been spared. To be born without sight and finally given to the Paw would have been a terrible ending to her life and memory. Summer Wind thought of her own life then, and what she had done up to that point. She did not think about what was to come, for fear of being overwhelmed with terror.

The women covered her cheeks in pigments of green, shaped in Anoka characters of blessings. Once all preparations had been completed, they told her she was very brave. They told her that if the elders' shared dream was true, the three Slayers would save her. The three Slayers would save them all, and they would never *ever* have to offer another life to the monster in the jungle.

Summer Wind listened, but her thoughts were elsewhere. The elders were not the only ones who could dream, though she never spoke of hers. A dream she'd had well before the Slayers arrived at the village, well before she'd even heard of the shared dream. Her dream, one she'd had three times already, had her in great peril. She was never sure why she was in danger, or where, only that a faceless figure with shining skin appeared by her side to lead her away from that danger.

Only one.

And yet, there were three Slayers.

Still, it was just a dream. Oddly comforting in the end. She wasn't sure if any of the Slayers would save her, but knowing they would be with her, well, that made her less afraid.

Enough that a little smile touched the corners of her mouth.

One of the Anoka women saw that smile and felt a pang of sorrow. *She was so beautiful, this one . . .*

In another part of the village, preparations of a different kind took place.

He-Dog and the others sharpened blades and inspected chainmail links. Thumbs flicked across edges and leather bindings were tightened. Hands slapped toughened leather slabs meant to protect one's guts, front and back. Mail shirts were donned and fitted into place. As they fussed over their weapons and armor, performed with the air of deadly experience, Broska translated No Tooth's words. He told the three mercenaries what to expect. They and a group of warriors would escort the offering to the offering place.

Kellic stopped sharpening his sword. "You keep doing that," he said, fixing the Zuthenian and the elder with a dark look. "Call her by her name."

Mindful of the warrior, Broska translated and No Tooth's eyes narrowed.

"He didn't like that," Snaffer muttered, his smile nearly hidden by his beard.

"Neither did I," Kellic said.

They returned their focus to their preparations. With Broska's help, No Tooth explained that Summer Wind would be tied to a tree at the offering place. Half Tusk and his warriors would then leave but the Slayers would remain to protect the girl. When the Paw appeared, they would kill the beast. No Tooth's expression brightened when he conveyed those last words.

"Glad someone believes this will work," He-Dog grumped as he strapped on his scabbard and adjusted his leather vest. "What about Half Tusk? Isn't that one near dead or something? From exhaustion?"

"He's recovered," Broska answered. "And very much wants to help. Feels ashamed to be the only one of his group who survived. Wants to show he's still worthy of being the lead warrior and hunter."

"How many warriors then?"

"About half. Perhaps thirty or forty."

"What's the reason for that?" He-Dog asked bluntly. "Might that frighten off the beast?"

"It's how it's always been done. And nothing will frighten off the Paw. Also, remember, the elders hope this will be the last time."

No Tooth spoke again and gestured at the three Slayers.

Broska translated. "He says that he hopes you kill the monster and that you all live to be a good old age."

The mercenaries glanced at one another.

"Tell him . . ." He-Dog said and took a moment to think, "If he wants it . . . we'll bring back its head."

Broska translated for No Tooth.

The elder smiled broadly, displaying his namesake.

From within his own lodge, Shay sat in sullen silence and watched a group of Anoka warriors gather at the base of the embankment. Both elders and villagers stood nearby in crowds, and the prince suspected they weren't there to admire him. Things were certainly afoot. He remembered the commotion the day before. Saw the warriors scamper throughout the village and the villagers run for their dwellings. Things were much more subdued now, however, and he detected a note of hope and purpose in the air. He could see it in their postures.

The expedition was about to get underway, and he wasn't going to be a part of it.

That thought burned his guts and left him miserable. He glanced down at his missing leg, shook his head, and looked back at the gathered villagers.

A few moments later, the Zuthenian and an old man emerged from the other mercenaries' lodge. Following them were Snaffer, He-Dog, and the one whose name Shay had once again forgotten. They faced the villagers as a murmur of excitement rippled through all present. Shay recognized it right away. Had experienced it firsthand, in fact, usually moments before first contact in a battle, when spirits were at their highest.

Their armor shone, at least Snaffer's and the other one whose name he still couldn't recall. Shay placed a hand to his head, wondering if he would ever regain his mind. Perhaps he would. Perhaps not.

He considered his three lads, or what he still thought of as his three lads. Even the asslicker called He-Dog. He-Dog wore a damaged vest of hardened leather but at least it looked decent enough. The bastard had Shay's sword as well, which the prince meant to take back when all this gurry was over and done.

His lads descended the embankment amid the cheering crowds. Shay had to admit, even though it damn near killed him, they looked *fine*. Bitterness welled up within his chest and he let the hate flow unchecked. He hated them for going, for going without him. He hated himself for having only the one leg. He glanced down at the vacant spot where his missing limb should be. It was not right. How could he . . . how could he *exist* like this? How could he get back to the mainland, and what would he do there if he could? Beg in the streets? His doubts doubled and nearly took control of him, but he shoved it all down and away, taking back control. Then he firmed up again and nodded at the truth. The hard truth. But he could accept it. He *would* accept it. With a sigh, he told himself he would only hamper the lads' efforts. He knew that. Aye that, he did.

The lads knew that.

Shay chewed on the inside of his cheek while watching them.

But damnation . . . it was a hard thing to know.

This adventure would be told to generations thereafter, around dying fires, to children who would remember it as a favorite and retell it to their own children. Of the men who came to this place looking for riches, but instead saved an entire village by felling a monster straight from Saimon's hell. A fine story indeed. Except

Shay figured he would not be mentioned at all. If so, he'd be the one left behind . . . with the one leg.

Right about then, one of the women tending to him appeared in the frame of the entrance. She was the older one, and as their eyes met, she released a comforting little smile.

Shay very much needed to see a friendly face.

She held up a bowl filled with his usual meal, which he was becoming well-adjusted to, he had to say.

"At least you haven't forsaken me," the mercenary captain said quietly.

Broska spoke loudly to the gathered crowds, yammering away in that nonsense tongue they spoke, of which Shay could pick no sense. The prince wondered if he'd ever achieve such a mastery over the Anoka's spoken word. The Zuthenian had, the ignorant brute, so it must not be too difficult.

"Easily," Shay whispered, knowing he could.

Nearby, the older woman—*what was her name?*—turned to watch the departing Slayers.

"Damnation," Shay swore softly and met the hard eyes of He-Dog, who was sending a message with one look. *Stay there*, He-Dog warned. *Stay* right *there*.

Setting his jaw, a none-too-pleased Shay stared back.

He-Dog hadn't missed the prince's stern expression, and he wondered if he had time for a few parting words.

A figure stepped before him.

He-Dog faced the blind woman he'd been watching from afar. All anger bled from him in an instant.

She stepped in very close to He-Dog. She touched the hardened leather of his vest and her hand lingered there, causing his heart to race. It nearly stopped when she reached up and cupped his unshaven chin. Strong hands felt his face, explored it, while the smell of her hair—fresh and clean and scented like, of all things, berries—left him speechless.

She spoke then, her breath warming his face. When she finished, her hands dropped, leaving him blinking.

"That's Gentle Rain," Broska explained from nearby. "She asked you to bring her sister back to her. She says she has only two, and they are so very dear to her."

He-Dog studied Gentle Rain's face. Saw the earnest pleading there. Then he noticed all the expectant faces of the Anoka listening nearby.

"You should say something," Broska prompted him.

He-Dog chose his next few words very carefully. ". . . I'll bring her back. Or perish doing so."

Broska translated, and Gentle Rain smiled with unchecked relief. She was so unfit lovely that He-Dog struggled to take his eyes off her.

"We'll bring her back," he repeated, meaning every word.

If he'd said he would protect Summer Wind before, he was determined to do so now.

Behind Gentle Rain, her father, Three Cut, stiffened with ill-concealed discomfort. He'd seen the way He-Dog stared at his daughter.

He-Dog didn't blame him.

A group of elderly women appeared, accompanying the disoriented Summer Wind. A blanket of grave-like silence swept over the crowd as the Anoka woman stopped in her tracks. Her father, Three Cut, appeared close to faltering, perhaps no longer so confident in the shared dream. At his side, Summer Wind's mother, Warm Cloud, wept, her breath trembling in small hitches. The family embraced Summer Wind. Perhaps for the last time.

He-Dog looked away, to allow them a moment.

And he noticed Kellic staring at the young woman called Bright Leaf, who was staring right back.

CHAPTER 42

They left the village at noon.

Broska accompanied the Slayers. The Zuthenian wore no armor, but he had strapped on a belt and scabbard containing a serviceable short sword. The Slayers walked just ahead of Three Cut, Warm Cloud, and Summer Wind, along with Peaceful Moon and three dozen Anoka guards protecting the lot. Half Tusk, recovered from his ordeal with the Paw, led them all. His task had originally been to escort the Slayers and Summer Wind to the offering place. Now, however, he had the added responsibility of protecting Three Cut and Warm Cloud, as well as the Anoka's spirit man. The parents would not let their daughter walk to the offering place without them.

Half Tusk led them north, into what Broska explained were the highlands of the Sanjou. They traveled through verdant halls of dense, sweltering jungle, along a trail well-known to the Anoka. As they pressed forward, Three Cut and Warm Cloud stayed close to their daughter. Kellic followed a few paces behind them, helmet lowered and carrying a shield. His usual somber expression was a few shades darker, and much more serious.

No one talked except for Summer Wind and Warm Cloud, and those whispered exchanges were lost upon He-Dog. Kellic, Snaffer, and Broska were well within earshot if he desired to speak with them, but conversation was kept low. Clouds of black flies buzzed around them but never came close to touching them. He-Dog noted that whatever they'd been eating in the village did indeed repel the little maggots.

The group trudged along until nightfall, whereupon they camped upon a small hill. A dozen guards were posted to keep watch.

The three Slayers stayed close to Summer Wind and her parents during that time, ready to be called upon if needed.

In the morning they rose with the plan of journeying until nightfall again. When the sun began to sink below the trees once more, Broska explained to the Slayers that they would reach the offering place the following day, perhaps before noon.

Despite the long and hard journey of the day, sleep did not come easy.

They arrived at the river by midmorning.

Trees crowded the shoreline as if afflicted with a terrible thirst, slipping thick roots into the shallows. Pebbles freckled the riverbed. A small island of rock and gravel split the river up the middle, and a single tree, oddly pale from either death or disease, rose from the center like a blighted crown. Compared to the other trees of the Sanjou, this towering trunk of twisted wood radiated evil, as if it had been rejected from the very jungle itself because of unknown impurities. Its bare, creeping roots plunged into that scant stain of land like sick snakes, whitened and petrified by the sun. While its base was barren of any limbs at all, the top frayed and fanned out like the ends of a wretched length of rope.

He-Dog scowled at that horrendous growth, half-inclined to burn it until nothing remained.

The Anoka warriors waded into the river up to their knees while keeping a keen eye on the thickets along the shores. The Slayers followed, escorting Summer Wind and her parents to the tree. Rocks shifted and rattled underfoot as they gathered upon that narrow lick of land. He-Dog and Snaffer stopped along the shore of the little island and stared at the loathsome tree, where so many had been taken before.

"Biggest unfit shrub I ever saw," Snaffer grumbled.

He-Dog agreed. "I'm of a mind to burn the thing."

That got a hard, considering look from the silver-haired warrior, who didn't say no to the idea.

A short outburst of grief split the gloomy quiet, as Warm Cloud clutched at her child. Three Cut pulled his wife away. A dour Peaceful Moon stepped in and motioned a pair of warriors to tie Summer Wind to the tree. They bound her upright with her back against the trunk, her wrists tied behind it. Her arms didn't reach all the way around the trunk, so the Anoka added enough length to keep her in place. They wrapped a second length of rope around her waist. An impassive Three Cut watched all of this and held onto his grieving wife.

"Bit much, isn't it?" He-Dog muttered to a nearby Broska. "All that rope?"

"Aye that," the Zuthenian whispered back.

Peaceful Moon then placed a hand upon Summer Wind's forehead. He spoke in a low voice easily heard over the river.

"Placing a blessing upon her," Broska whispered. "Wishing her existence will be a fine one in the other place. That her death will mean another year or so of life for her people. That all will be remembered and her name will live on . . ."

His eyes red and weeping, Peaceful Moon stopped and pinched the bridge of his nose. He took a deep steadying breath before backing up and nodding to Three Cut. The old chieftain spoke in that calming voice of his, pausing when his emotions threatened to overwhelm him.

"He says," Broska translated quietly, "that he hopes that he will see his daughter soon. And that she will be alive and well."

"No mention of us?" He-Dog asked.

"None."

"In case the Paw is nearby?"

"Suppose so," Broska said, sniffing mightily while wiping at his own weeping eyes.

Anoka warriors stood guard up and down the water's edge, watching the jungle. A fidgeting Half Tusk leaned on his spear and glanced around. Peaceful Moon spoke one last time before nodding and turning away.

Not before looking at He-Dog, sending a message that needed no interpretation.

Half Tusk said a few words to Broska, nodding at the three Slayers as he did. When he finished, he spat out two short hisses and his warriors surrounded Three Cut and Warm Cloud.

Three Cut then spoke to Broska before leading Warm Cloud away from their daughter, back the way they'd come.

Broska rubbed at his head as if in mortal pain.

"Well, I have two messages for you," he said to the three Slayers. "The first is from Half Tusk. He said . . ." Broska winced, "to tell the savages to kill the monster."

He-Dog almost smiled at that.

"The other one is from Three Cut." Broska cleared his throat. "He said . . . if the Slayers can save his daughter from the Paw . . . he will forever welcome them with the Anoka. And he will help them find the gemstones they are searching for, if that is what you wish. Anything you want, really. Just . . . save his daughter."

Her cheeks wet with tears, Summer Wind watched her parents leave.

Kellic moved closer to her, leaning his shield against the base of the tree.

The Anoka waded back across the river.

"You staying?" Snaffer asked.

Broska wiped at his eyes again and chuckled darkly. "Lords above, no. I'm leaving as well. You're on your own. Stay with Summer Wind. Guard her. Wait for the Paw. When it shows itself, you kill it. We'll move back to last night's encampment and wait there. If we interfere and you fail to kill it, only the Lords above know what will happen next."

"You truly believe the gurry stories about the thing, Zuthenian?" Snaffer asked.

Broska shook his head. "After hearing about it for so long and living with it . . . I suppose their beliefs have become my own." He checked on the departing warriors before regarding the Slayers. "But you *will* kill the thing," he insisted. "You *must*. Just remember . . . whatever you've done in the past, whatever you might've been, or whatever reason you came here for . . . all that means *nothing* now. Now you're that woman's protectors. And you carry the hopes of the Anoka people who wish to be free of this nightmare. Remember," he held up a pair of fingers. "*Two* men have seen you save them all in their dreams. Remember that."

Sighing, Broska studied the frightening tree and the woman lashed to it. "Just save her," he finally said. "Save us all. If you don't, one day it might very well be my child left here."

Fixing them all with a darkly pleading look, Broska nodded goodbye and left.

Water sloshed around shins and rocks rattled as the Zuthenian and the others made their way back across the river. Upon the embankment, the Anoka looked back one last time before disappearing into the jungle. Broska raised his hand, waved once, and slipped out of sight along with the rest. Then, all grew quiet again. The three Slayers stood their ground on that little island of rock. In time, He-Dog became aware of the sound of the river flowing gently by.

"Savages," Snaffer said, considering the word like a bad piece of meat.

"He called *us* savages," Kellic clarified.

"I *know* the topper called us savages. I'm saying *they're* . . ." but he frowned instead and didn't finish.

He-Dog knew why—because Half Tusk spoke the truth. "Right," he said under his breath. He faced Snaffer. "We have a little arena right here. We guard the girl. When the thing comes . . . we kill it."

"He-Dog," Snaffer said, actually saying his name for the first time. "Did anyone say *when* the thing would come here?"

That was a good question, to which he shook his head.

"So we just wait?"

"We wait."

"It won't be long," Kellic added, standing next to Summer Wind.

No, He-Dog didn't think it would be long at all. "I'm on that point," he said, nodding to one side of the tree, rattling rocks as he walked away.

"I'll be over here," Snaffer reported, and moved to the opposite end.

Kellic stayed with Summer Wind.

With the tree at their backs, the Slayers took a grim appraisal of their situation. He-Dog pulled out his broadsword. He hefted it, brandishing the weapon at arm's length, and studied the embankments flowering with trees and reeds. A longing filled him to be back in the sprawling deserts of Big Rock. There, at least, it was impossible to hide.

Behind him, Kellic turned to a tired and grief-stricken Summer Wind. "You're very brave," he told her.

With a miserable grimace, she leaned forward and rested her head against his armored chest.

After a moment, he lowered his head onto hers.

And their surroundings seemed to dissolve around them.

CHAPTER 43

On the first day of travel, well after the Anoka and the three Slayers had left the village and headed north, they'd passed through a landscape not unfamiliar to them. With the burden of the Paw on their minds, no one suspected they were being watched from afar.

Perched high in a tree and surveying the land for a direction to take, the Ossaki pirate Timmer rubbed a near odorless ointment on himself. They had discovered the shite in a pair of small tankards within the hold of the captured vessel, much to the disappointment of the lads hoping they could drink it. Timmer, however, was one of the few who could read, and he informed his companions of the true nature of the contents. The shite seemed to repel most of the insects of the jungle, for which the crew was—mostly—thankful.

And by Saimon's swinging dew sack, Timmer believed there were some accursed mites that didn't mind the lotion at all. He slapped at a sudden nip at the back of his neck. Checking his hand, Timmer wondered if the earthy brown slop made them all taste better.

Snarling, he used the last of the lotion on his neck and put the rest away.

Which was right about when he spotted one wildman emerge from the foliage, and then others. At first, the once-gladiator supposed they were a hunting party of sorts. Then he spied the woman. And what looked to be an unhappy mother and father walking alongside her—perhaps on their way to some kind of primitive marriage nonsense. That thought scratched a smirk across his face. Such gurry didn't interest him much, but the presence of so many near-naked men carrying clubs and spears caught his eye . . . until he spied the *other* warriors. Armored hellpups looking for a battle. Seeing those prompted him to double-check his hiding spot, to ensure he was indeed out of sight. Timmer cocked an eyebrow, sizing up the three butchers plodding among the savages. And butchers they clearly were.

In all his years cutting up men in Sunja's Pit, in all the bloody ventures since, Timmer never thought he'd see civilized men walking alongside Sanjou wildmen as if they were all the best of friends. The wildmen were of no concern to him. The warriors, however, the *real* warriors—they would be trouble. Timmer had faced enough brutes in his time to recognize an experienced killer when he spotted one, and here were *three*. Three tried and bled hellions, bearing steel, bad intentions, and full armor that flashed in the sun.

Timmer's thoughts raced. Perhaps some gurry mating ritual wasn't afoot after all. Perhaps the savages were going to some tribal war ground with those three he-bitches, who walked with the burly swagger of trained gladiators. It was no secret the Sanjou had long been a fabled destination for many treasure seekers over the years, and Timmer suspected only a fraction of the stories were true. Those that *were* true, however, attracted those like himself. With those thoughts, three civilized warriors seemed a paltry number, and this confused him all the more. He wondered if there were others. He wondered why they were so friendly with the wildmen. Then he wondered where they were going, if they were headed for some treasure trove hidden deep in the jungle . . . Perhaps even the mountain of gold Black Korraz sought to discover.

All that presented something of a question to Timmer, one he had to carefully consider.

Black Korraz and his crew had made landing several days earlier, and, as they all feared, the mountain of gold shown on their map was *not* in the place marked. Unwilling to abandon the search so easily, Korraz chose a handful of men and informed them they were now scouts. Every morning since, he sent them out, scouring the jungle for clues as to the location of the mountain.

Timmer had been one of those selected.

He stuck a finger under his vest of hardened leather and scratched at his private bits. He then adjusted himself in the tree, taking the stress off his legs for just a moment. When he did so, a bead of sweat ran down his profile. The rag he had tied around his head was once again soaked. *Sweat*. He'd never done so much sweating in all his days. It was no wonder the wildmen had to reapply scented oils upon their hides every morning, oils that repelled the murderous clouds of insects plaguing the wilderness.

Timmer shifted again, the wood hard against his backside. In short time, the three mysterious butchers and their pack of savages vanished into the jungle and were gone from sight. Only then did he climb down and head for where he'd spotted the group. Easing through the underbrush, he eventually crossed the trail upon which the party traveled. A sly smile spread across his unshaven features as he inspected the flattened earth between his boots. Like a widening cut, Timmer's mouth opened even further, revealing uneven yellow teeth. He looked in the direction the group had come from and started walking.

Not much later, he found a village nestled in the wilderness, with light smoke drifting from hidden fires.

Taking care to remain unseen, Timmer settled down and studied the place.

Warriors carrying spears and clubs patrolled the village. Timmer didn't mind them, considering himself equal to ten wildmen. They were alert, however, vigilant of the tree line, and Timmer had to be wary of that. The wildmen could *smell* civilization, from what he understood. Smelled it like a queen's scented water. Or a king's, he supposed. In addition to the warriors, men and women of all ages strolled through the village, as well as children. No riches to be seen, though, and certainly no mountain of gold. All he had to be wary of was stepping into some wildman's cow kiss.

Even more interesting . . . he saw no other civilized warriors.

A thoughtful Timmer rubbed his chin then his skull rag, once again soaked and dripping.

He'd found a village. *Dying Seddon above.* He'd found a *village.*

One ripe for the taking.

He needed to report back to Black Korraz, gather their forces, and march to this place. Who knew what might be down there, but if civilized men walked among them, well, they were there for a reason.

And the only reason *anyone* came to the Sanjou was to search for treasure.

Timmer slunk back into the foliage.

"It was very good," Shay said loudly, as if raising his voice would instill understanding. He wasn't lying, however. The evening meal had been good. Say what he might about the Anoka . . . they knew how to prepare food.

Smiling—which was the extent of her speaking ability—Little Bloom set aside the empty bowls and brought forth a pan of water. She dipped a rough cloth and wrung it out, right about Shay's bare chest. Warm water dripped, providing little respite from the unrelenting heat. *Heat.* Day after day. No wonder he was constantly miserable. It felt like he was trapped in a Valencian bathhouse forever filled with steam.

Little Bloom wiped down his chest. His belly. Her fist guided the cloth over his skin. She stopped at his waistline and gradually retraced her work back up his frame, to his shoulders, arms, and finally face. Shay closed his eyes all the while, and when he opened them, Little Bloom smiled at him. Just a hint of one, fading like pleasant smoke, but there all the same. She was an older woman, with wisps of gray streaking her long hair, but certainly not hard on the eyes. Or so Shay had decided.

She went over him again, concentrating on her work. Shay lay there in sullen silence, letting her clean him up.

No gemstones, he thought.

No company of fighting men.

No leg.

And perhaps worst of all, no way back to the mainland—with the very real prospect of spending the rest of his days in the Sanjou. With the Anoka. Given the Sanjou's deadly reputation, it would be a good many weeks, or even *years*, before anyone ventured so far south upon such troubled waters.

Lords above. He'd fallen into a right and proper shite pit with this venture. Stephanak had been right. The Sanjou was a cursed place. An evil place. With the betrayal of Snaffer and the one whose name he still couldn't place, no doubt influenced by that treacherous He-Dog bastard, Shay again decided he was next to finished. And by finished he meant dead and as good as forgotten. After all he'd done and everywhere he'd been, it was difficult to accept that everything had come to an end . . . *here*.

He let out a huff and stared at the open doorway. The Anoka homes lay beyond, and the rustling of activity had died down to mere whispers.

"Dying Seddon," Shay murmured, bitter to the core.

Little Bloom pulled back, wet cloth dripping, a question on her face.

"What?" he asked before sighing in frustration. "No, it's . . . it's not you. It's . . ." His eyes rolled while his arms flopped to the ground. She couldn't understand him anyway, and he didn't have the mind or patience to try.

Lords above. He was in a special place of Saimon's hell.

Little Bloom leaned in and placed a hand on his forehead. She kept it there.

"Aye that," Shay grumbled softly. "Check for a fever. Maybe I am still unfit. Lords above."

She kept her hand there for a time. A very long time, in fact, much longer than Shay thought necessary. Not that it was unpleasant. The touch of her hand . . . well, a bit of contact was never a bad thing. He peered at her, sending a question. As an answer, her hand slid down his profile, past his ear, gently rubbing the thickening beard along his chin. In the shade of the lodge, she looked much younger.

Little Bloom noticed his scrutiny and didn't say a word. Her fingers fluttered in his beard, gauging it, while her eyes met his, in that way that needed no words at all. With a little smile, she pulled her hand away and patted his chest. Slowly, at times, making a circle, the contact warm and tingling. On the final tap, her palm lingered, as if pondering what to do next.

Shay blinked, needing no translation for what was happening, and yet not believing *any* of it.

Then, without warning, she rose to leave.

"Wait," he said, stopping her. "Ah . . . please. Wait. Apologies. Look. I'm not . . . usually this unfit. Please understand that. My leg is only part of it, and truth be known, I can overcome that. It's simply . . . all my plans . . . my lads. Dare I say my *friends* . . . Everything. Is lost. Everything is lost. And I doubt I'll ever leave this . . ."

Shay faltered, not knowing how to get his meaning across, and Little Bloom watched him all the while. He finally gave up, his mouth a tight button. With a defeated wave he dismissed Little Bloom, who left without a word. The last thing she did was unhook the hide flap, letting it fall into place over the entrance.

Shay watched her go, knowing full well he'd done something to ruin the moment . . . *Lords above*, he sighed and stared. Leave it to him to drop a fresh cow kiss on the table. It was a good thing Grage wasn't around, to see him wave off pretty women washing him down and feeling his goods. *Unfit*, he decided, hearing the Anoka outside talk their talk.

She'll come back, he told himself. *In time.* She always did . . . which got him thinking again. Clearly she saw he was crippled, and yet he remembered her hand on his chest. He clasped his hands over his belly, his full belly, and he remembered how good the food was. And after the meal, Little Bloom cleaned him up from the day's sweltering heat. Not as good as the bathhouses of his homeland, but clean enough. As good as one might get, given the circumstances. And it didn't cost him any coin at all. Not that he had any, but he knew what he was getting at.

There, in the dying light, he found himself staring at his walking sticks—studying them.

He remembered Little Bloom washing him again. Touching him.

A child laughed somewhere in the village, the sound pure and ringing, and far too short.

It took a while, but it happened. In perhaps the clearest thought he'd had since being taken off the smoke. Shay admitted, begrudgingly, despite all the bad fortune on this venture, that maybe, just *maybe* . . . things weren't nearly as unfit as he believed them to be. As long as his lads came back with the head of the Paw. Of that, however he had no doubt.

At some point in the evening, as the light of day faded into night, and the pleasing smell of wood fires drifted into his lodge, he fell asleep.

He woke up only an instant later, it seemed.

Someone was screaming. Outside his lodge. A *lot* of screaming.

He propped himself up on an elbow. *Saimon's hot blossom*, it sounded like a small *war* had begun . . . right outside his lodge.

And did he smell *smoke*? He did, and much more than the curls of a dying fire pit.

Scrambling for his walking sticks, Shay quickly pulled himself to his feet. He reached for his sword and realized the pig bastard He-Dog had taken it. Fuming, he swung himself forward and yanked aside the flap over the entrance.

The sight before him stopped him cold.

The Anoka village was in flames.

Multiple fires ravaged several lodges, turning the dwellings into raging bonfires that belched smoke and glowing embers into the night. Shay inhaled a harsh whiff of it all and drew back a step. In the distance, through the haze, he glimpsed the lodge belonging to the elders. The lodge appeared untouched but the fires colored its shell a ghastly orange. Beneath it all, villagers sprinted and screamed, seeking safety in a blazing labyrinth.

Over the screams, Shay heard shouts.

In a language he understood.

Being among the Anoka for so long, he'd grown accustomed to shutting out their babbling, but he could *swear* . . .

A pair of spear-wielding Anoka warriors stopped before the embankment and hollered at him. One motioned for him to leave his lodge. Shay checked the roof and saw nothing amiss. When he looked back, a hand axe flashed in the firelight and stuck deeply into one warrior's head.

The man dropped while his companion whirled and brandished his spear.

A lean executioner of a man swinging a short sword emerged from the smoke and flames.

Shay stared at what was obviously an armored individual . . . but *not* one of his.

The Anoka spearman screamed at Shay again before turning to face the advancing swordsman.

It took Shay a heartbeat to realize these Anoka warriors, the same ones he despised, cursed out, and even at times looked down upon, were about to *defend* him.

"*Wait!*" Shay yelled, but neither the spearman nor the swordsman paid him any heed.

The swordsman closed with the Anoka warrior, who jabbed the spear at a cruelly smiling face. The swordsman parried and countered, a powerful sweep meant to cut his foe in two—but the Anoka man bobbed away. The swordsman rushed forward, parried a spear thrust, and smashed a fist into the warrior's face.

The Anoka man fell, and the swordsman wasted no time stabbing his fallen opponent through the chest, the crackle of bone sharp to the ears.

The blatant killing unlocked Shay. "*I said* wait *you unworthy punce!*"

The swordsman glanced up, his face marred by flickering shadows.

Frantic, Shay waved at him. "*These are good—*"

People he was about to say, when he glimpsed a fist coming at his head.

An instant before it hammered his chin.

Then he was falling, and the screams died away to nothing.

CHAPTER 44

The raid on the Anoka village began in earnest when the pirates closed in from both sides and slew anyone holding a weapon. Young warriors and old men fell in droves, cut down by sword or axe while the fires raged all around. Timmer and his group stormed through the sleepy settlement, killing and yelling as though they were herding frightened cattle. The confusion wrought a terrible toll upon the villagers roused in the middle of the night, caught between combating the fires and fighting off their attackers.

Surprisingly—to Timmer, at least—not many ran.

The once-gladiator, brandishing a short sword and dagger, strode through the flames as if he were impervious to them. A spearman rushed him. Timmer parried the primitive weapon before slashing the savage's throat. A stone axe whistled out of the smoky night, crashing against his back and bouncing off his hardened leather armor. The impact straightened him, however, and he barely managed to deflect the thrust of a stone knife. Timmer's answering cut opened his attacker from pisser to chin and left him cradling his last moments on his knees. Another screamer rushed him, and the once-gladiator split the skull apart with one hard chop.

He had to admit, these near-naked punces had push, but ultimately, they were poorly matched. All the pirates wore armor. Some carried shields. None of them possessed a lick of mercy. In the smoky firelight his fellow killers butchered anyone opposing them. Spears bounced off shields and armor plates. Clubs splintered against iron-forged battle-axes. Timmer struck down an old man holding a club and smashed his head with two heavy-handed blows.

Men shrieked. Women and children wailed. The night became a frenzied panic. Fiery ribbons consumed the village with a hateful fury, spewing smoke that Timmer breathed in and savored. He spied a pair of pirates opening up a keg of lamp oil, while another stood nearby with a ready torch. Other pirates herded the survivors, pulling them along by the hair or shoving them to their knees. Timmer stalked through it all, and eventually met Sobaba amid that roaring destruction.

Then Black Korraz appeared, tall and menacing, materializing in the smoke and striding toward him. Horlo the Cruel and a half dozen other pirates followed. The captain raised his hand and Timmer waved back.

In what seemed like a very short time—certainly shorter than creeping around the jungle surrounding the settlement—the pirates had mercilessly completed their assault. All done with relative ease.

The village ceased to be. The inhabitants were captured. Victory was theirs, as expected.

Timmer allowed himself a smile.

Someone slapped Shay's face.

Hard.

He shuddered and cracked open an eye, inhaling smoke as he did. For some reason it was difficult to breathe through his nose. When he tried to move, he discovered his hands were bound behind him, his palms flat against what felt like a plank wedged between them. He also discovered, with a lick, a thick crust of blood around his mouth.

Wasn't the first time he'd been struck. He tried sniffing again, drawing air through clogged passages, when a man loomed over him. A *large* man. The large man grabbed Shay's chin and shoved it back, bouncing it off the wooden post to which he was tied. That fresh clap of agony distracted the prince from his other hurts. Shay's head rolled and when he looked up, what he saw horrified him.

The Anoka village had been scorched to the ground.

Smoke obscured the morning sky while angry shouts of men peppered the air. Children wailed while women cried out. Screams spiked the scene, but Shay couldn't see anything more, because the lad before him had reared back and slapped him again. A hard mallet of a palm that cracked the prince's head crooked, rattling him against the post.

Spitting blood and wincing, Shay tongued his remaining teeth and found he'd lost not one. He almost smiled at that. He flexed his jaw before focusing on his torturer. The lad looked quite civilized with his leggings, high boots, and leather armor. Blades of assorted sizes hung from the man's waist, including the hilt of a broadsword. A slash of soot smeared his stubbled face. Narrowed eyes inspected Shay.

"You *punce*," the prince slurred in dreamy agony, surprising himself. One of those blows had been harder than he thought.

The torturer stared, his bare, muscular arms slick with filth and perspiration.

"Well, who are you then?" Shay demanded weakly.

No reply. Instead, a man screamed horribly before what sounded like a head being crushed. Shay had the misfortune of knowing the unpleasant noise.

"What about it?" he asked, getting his senses back. "Where are you from? You can at least tell me that."

Smoke drifted across the torturer's face when he spoke. "You will answer his every question," he said plainly. "Tell him everything you know. Do you understand?"

Shay frowned. "Tell who? What about introductions? Where's the harm in that?"

No response. The torturer merely stepped around Shay, grabbed the prince's wrists, and pulled them up. That, in itself, wasn't pleasant. Shay gasped. His shoulders screamed as his arms nearly popped from their sockets from the upended pressure.

But then the torturer grabbed the smallest finger on Shay's right hand. Without warning, he snapped it all the way back, mashing knuckle to skin, breaking it like a string on a stubborn harp.

Shay yelped.

The torturer twisted the finger.

Despite his best intentions, the prince shrieked, a cry that quickly lost power. When he sucked in a breath, the torturer again twisted the broken digit, causing Shay to buck and wail against the post, his entire hand singing and, worse still, holding the note.

The torturer released the finger.

And broke the *next* one on the prince's suffering hand, just like the first, before twisting it one way and then the other.

Every yank summoned a wounded squawk that, truth be known, Shay didn't think he had in him. But he felt every snap and crackle, explosive and bright and taking a year to ebb away.

When it was over, a sweating and spent Shay lifted his head.

The torturer crouched before him. "You will answer his every question," he repeated, black eyes intense. "Do you understand?"

Shay believed he did. Aye that, he most certainly did. When he didn't answer, however, the torturer went behind his back once again. Shay's breath quickened and he tried to make a fist, which seared like a ball of fire. Strong fingers scrabbled at the next unfortunate digit.

"*I do! I do!*" Shay blurted as his third finger broke as easily as the previous two. Again he shrieked and sputtered and thrashed against the post, eventually collapsing in exhausted agony. After a time, he weakly beheld the torturer crouching before him again.

Black eyes studied the prince. "You will tell him everything. Do you understand?"

"Yes," Shay moaned. "Yes, I do. I do."

Message delivered, the torturer stood but remained by the prince's side.

Before Shay knew anything else, the world tilted and reality bent and stretched before leaving him. He later woke to thin spires of smoke lingering about the burnt village. The worst of the screaming was over, but a few voices lingered, crying out in misery. The torturer remained close by, turning this way and that, perhaps wondering if the day's work was done. Shay peeked around, saw the broken beams and smoking wreckage of the village. Charred tatters of hides fluttered off blackened posts. Bodies lay heaped before some of those ruins, and armored men prodded spears through debris.

Shay's first impulse was to say something, something right and proper saucy, but the torturer stood right *there* . . . and he liked his remaining fingers.

"I'll speak with him now . . ." a voice said, and the torturer moved behind Shay once again.

A second man stopped before the prince. The newcomer resembled one of Saimon's hellions. Black, short-cropped hair and pointed beard. Thoughtful eyes underneath a furrowed brow. Smeared soot streaked his face, as if he'd wiped at it not too long ago. An expensive vest of leather armor protected his body, complete with bracers and greaves, and leggings of fine cloth. The hellion looked down upon the prince. He fiddled with the scabbard of his sword so that it hung just so off his hip. Fancy stones glittered in the pommel.

"I imagine," the man began, "that after speaking with Sobaba . . . you will be very glad to speak with me."

Shay smiled weakly. "I do have a few fingers left," he said, unable to help himself. "Could've waited a little longer, I suppose."

"Even longer then, if you count your toes. And for the exceptionally stubborn, Sobaba has been known to break wrists. Ankles. Arms. Truth be known, most are very willing to answer my questions long before then. Sobaba does it as often as he feels it's needed. To make one a little more willing to talk."

". . . Nice lad."

A cut of a yellow smile appeared upon the newcomer's face. "I am Black Korraz. These are my men. You have already met Sobaba. He *is* a nice lad. While others have come and gone, he still remains by my side. Been with me for all of ten years now."

Shay could appreciate that kind of loyalty.

"He is very serious about his work," Korraz continued. "And I am very fortunate to have him in my crew."

"Your crew?"

"Aye that."

The prince squinted at the fellow before him. "You're not a *pirate*, are you?"

The yellow smile widened. "Belonging to the Ossaki."

Shay released a defeated sigh.

"I see you know of us."

A miserable Shay nodded as if barely alive.

"The power of reputation. Excellent. It is better that way. Saves us both so much time. And yourself?" Korraz pointed with an open palm, and Shay remembered Snaffer mentioning the Anoka's custom.

Shay told him his name, rank, and title.

The title interested Korraz. "You're a prince?"

"They only call me that."

"Mercenaries. Killed off to a man, you say?"

"Aye that."

Korraz smoothed his beard. "So how is it, one of my scouts saw *three* armored men walking through the jungle with a group of warriors *leaving* this village?"

Shay struggled to hide being caught in a lie. "Oh . . . them . . ."

The pirate leader waited.

"Wasn't thinking properly," Shay muttered, scratching at his upper lip with his bottom teeth. "Something about having my fingers broken. And my head banged about."

"I suppose so," Korraz granted. "Please, think very hard on your next answer. Are there any more of you about?"

Shay shook his head.

"These three soldiers of yours, walking with the savages. Where were they going?"

Oddly enough, Shay didn't like the pirate calling the Anoka savages. He answered him, however, which arched Korraz's eyebrows.

"An offering, you say? To a monster called the Paw?"

"Aye that."

"When will they return?"

Shay shook his head. "I don't know. Eventually. If they live, I suppose."

"What brought you here? To the Sanjou?"

"Treasure."

"Tell me everything."

So Shay did, leaving out not a single detail, and Korraz listened without interrupting. When the prince finished, the pirate captain's eyes had narrowed to slits.

"You've had a poor go of it . . . Shay, that's your name?"

Shay agreed with a weary nod.

Korraz smiled without a drop of sympathy. "Ambushed by savages. One leg taken by bloodfish. The other crippled. Your force cut down to three men. You've had a poor go of it, indeed. But, as we all know, this *is* the Sanjou."

Shay nodded again. *Indeed, it is.*

"Well," Korraz concluded. "Seems we have the same purpose. We're here for the same."

"You're looking for gemstones?"

"No, not that," Korraz dismissed. "*Other* riches. We're here to search for the legendary gold mountain of the Sanjou."

". . . Legendary . . ."

"You've not heard of it?"

"Truth be known, first time I've heard tell of it."

"We have good information that it exists." Korraz studied him for a few moments. "Did you find these gemstones?"

"No."

"A shame. Well . . ." the pirate captain crossed his arms. "You've been very cooperative. I appreciate you talking to me in such a civil tone, despite your condition. And . . . misfortune. We have a problem, however. We have no intention of waiting here for your warriors to come back. They will see this smoke. We must move away from here in case your men decide to follow us. We cannot take you, for obvious reasons." Korraz gestured at Shay's lower half. "Thus . . . it's best to kill you now and be done with it."

Sobaba pulled steel.

"You can't kill me," Shay blurted.

"No?" asked a bored Korraz.

"I know where the gemstones are."

"You do?" Korraz said, folding his arms. "Then tell me."

"What are you going to do with these people?"

"Kill them, of course."

Of course, Shay realized, his thoughts racing. These were Ossaki pirates. "You can't kill them."

Korraz's smile became a cold thing, and his eyes flickered to the killer called Sobaba.

"The gemstones are to the south of here," Shay said, remembering what Snaffer had learned. "Maybe three or four days. I think I know the way."

"You think?"

"I'll take you there."

Korraz smirked knowingly. "In exchange for your life . . . ?"

"And theirs, these people. You'll need them."

"I do?" The pirate's brow cracked with amused puzzlement. "Please, tell me why?"

At that moment, the last of a fog lifted from Shay's mind, as easily as a shirt being pulled over one's head. His head cleared and he was suddenly aware of his situation, and thinking better and faster than he had over the past few weeks. A breeze lifted the lingering smoke, revealing the smoldering village. The last of the Anoka had been rounded up, not nearly as many as Shay remembered, and the sight shocked him. Then he saw her, the older woman who had touched his chest. Her name came to him in a flash. *Little Bloom*. Her eyes wide and fearful, her face dirtied by soot, she stared at him from across the way. Around her, a clutch of crying children, clinging to the remaining adults like rocks in a fast-moving river.

Mercenary he might be, but Shay still knew what was right and wrong . . . and he wasn't about to let the Ossaki massacre any more innocents. He needed time, however. The *Anoka* needed time, if they were to survive the pirates.

So Shay would *get* them that time.

"The gemstones . . . are in a village," he said. "Like this one. But it's full of savages. The same blackhearted kogs that cut us down. They're the worst of the land. And there's an army of them. The gemstones are in their land to the south."

Korraz listened, but the one called Sobaba was close, readying his blade to lop off Shay's head.

"Iruzuland," the prince blurted. "That's what it's called. To the south. Gemstones. They don't even realize their worth because they're savages. There may be other riches as well, perhaps even your hill of gold. You need *these* people, however, to get any of it. The Anoka hate the Iruzu. And the Iruzu hate them. If you bring them into Iruzuland, *all* of them, you can perhaps trade your Anoka prisoners for the gemstones. Or this hill of gold you're searching for."

"Mountain," Korraz corrected.

"Whatever. Just keep as many alive as you can. Each one of these people is worth *something* to the Iruzu, and whatever riches they might have. To them, the gemstones are *nothing*. Gold is *nothing*. The Iruzu get something they want for giving away *nothing*, you understand. You get what you want. You give them what *they* want . . . and you don't risk the life of a single man."

Korraz thought about it. "And why shouldn't I kill you again?"

"You need me to bargain with the Iruzu."

"Can you speak with these Iruzu?"

"No," Shay admitted, very much aware of Sobaba behind him. "But I can bargain."

"I think I can bargain just as well, *Prince* Shay."

"You're forgetting something."

"I don't think I am."

"The Iruzu slaughtered my company. They hate *us* as well. You present me to them, in addition to the Anoka, and that will sweeten the pot all the more." Shay swallowed. "If you decide to do it, that is."

"I'm deciding now."

The prince waited, not daring to turn his head, until Korraz waved off his henchman as an afterthought. "How do you know all this again?"

"One of these people could speak our language."

"And where is he?"

"Dead. One of your lads killed him. The spearman who guarded my lodge."

Korraz frowned at Sobaba before turning back to him. "You say this village is to the south?"

"Aye that."

"Only a few days?"

"About that. I think."

Korraz appeared thoughtful again.

"The Iruzu have never been able to find this place." Shay lied, not knowing one way or the other. That was the way with lying. Once you started pouring the gurry, it was difficult to stop. "You found it. And you captured their enemy. They'll trade, because they have nothing to lose. Everything to gain. As do you."

A blanket of smoke drifted past, but Shay could still see Korraz thinking, and he didn't miss another exchange of looks with the one called Sobaba.

"Well done, Shay," Korraz said with a smile. "Very well done."

With that, the pirate captain walked away, into the lingering smoke.

Shay watched him go, still very much aware of Sobaba standing behind him.

A short time later, Korraz returned, inspecting the contents of a small leather sack. He stopped before the prince and cocked an eyebrow.

"Gemstones, you say?"

Shay sensed something wrong, and it showed.

Korraz pulled out a black rock. He brought the thing in close to Shay's face. The pirate scratched the surface with a fingernail, then revealed what was underneath.

Creamy green.

Shay's mouth dropped open.

"One of my lads discovered this," Korraz said. "Covered in soot. Part of a fire pit, you see. From the big hut on the hill there."

"They have them?" Shay asked in breathless disbelief.

"They *had* them," Korraz corrected. "They were part of a fire pit. As you said, they're only rocks to the savages. And these stones are damaged. Paled and split by the heat. Perhaps worth only a pinch of their original value. Are these what you're searching for?"

The rock the pirate held was the size of one fist. What was it that Stephanak had said, a lifetime ago?

Shay couldn't remember, but something about there being more. Much more.

"Shay," Korraz said with feigned endearment. "I think you should come along with us . . . until I decide to kill you myself."

CHAPTER 45

Sunlight streamed into the mountain cave, brightening the interior. Hargan woke, lying near the entrance, taking in the craggy gray of the ceiling. After a moment's reflection, he rubbed his face and sniffed.

Something smelled good.

Two skewers of meat roasted over a small fire farther in the cave. Chop tended to them, turning the sticks this way and that. A flat rock rested nearby the fire pit, where a handful of wild onions waited to be sliced and added to the food. Certainly didn't look like onions. Not to Hargan. But they were. Worse, he had walked right by them the day before, believing their stalks to be nothing more than weeds. The Nord had seen them, recognized them right away, and dug them up. They had eaten the purple vegetables last night, along with the first of two wild birds the Nord brought down with his bow.

Hargan begrudgingly had to admit, the man was much better with a bow than he ever was.

The Sunjan sat up and stared at the day.

When the food was ready, Chop cut up one onion and draped the slivers over both skewers. One of which he held out to Hargan, who dragged himself over to accept it.

They ate in silence, their backs to the wall, while the fire died away. When they finished, they laid the sticks over the fire pit rocks.

Hargan dug out trapped gristle in his teeth. "Damned thing," he said and flicked the piece away. "It smells good, but it goes down like knobby shite."

Chop agreed with a nod.

"Think you can find more of these onions out there?"

Another nod, but with a touch of *maybe*.

"Maybe there's some corn out there," Hargan said. "Hm? Wouldn't that be grand? Lords above, if you're looking, maybe you can find a beer keg hanging off a tree? We'll have a little alehouse if you can do that. Right here."

More nodding, perhaps even the glimmer of a smile, if that wrecked face could smile.

"Right here," Hargan said, remembering better times. He picked at his nose, twisted vigorously at the insides, and sniffed. Sniffed again and glanced at the fire pit, which burned low. Curious, he stood, wiped his hands together, and stepped outside.

"Chop."

The Nordish man looked up to see the Sunjan gesturing to join him, so he did.

Hargan didn't bother to point.

Smoke. Great black clouds of it.

To the north, beyond a series of tree-topped hills.

"Thought I smelled smoke," Hargan said. "Someone is having one lovely cook-up by the looks of that."

The clouds coiled and thickened, ruining an otherwise lovely morning. The smoke stemmed from a patch of jungle at least a day or two away, in territory beyond what they knew.

"I'm going to see what that's about," Hargan said. "That's a big fire someone took time to light. Might be our friends. The same ones that killed off the rest of our pack."

Chop stared at the smoke.

"Need to know where your enemy is, right?"

Again, no response from the Nordish man.

"You stay here with your onions if you like. Maybe find that corn. Or something like corn. I'll be back in a day or two. Or three."

Having no more to say on the matter, he returned to the cave and retrieved his axe. His armor as well, though the jungle air had soured it. Rust bloomed in patches over the chainmail links. A stink of rot hung about the thing as well, giving him second thoughts about wearing it at all. Still, he pulled on the rags that served as clothing, despising the grubby feel of it all. Then he squirmed into his chainmail.

Heavy. Smelling of sour sweat and other foulness. As he adjusted the armor, Chop headed silently back into the cave.

Hargan strapped on a belt of daggers and slapped on his helmet. Hot. And damp.

His axe was the last thing he picked up.

When he turned, Chop stood there, waiting, ready for war. The Nord wore his leather vest and carried his bow, with both swords sheathed and hanging off his hips.

A smile crept across Hargan's face.

Chop matched it as best he could.

After a moment, Hargan looked around the little cave that had served them both very well in the time they'd taken shelter there. Thinking back, he supposed they could not have found a better place. He wondered if he'd see it again. Supposed he'd find out.

He regarded Chop. "Ready, then? You unfit Nordish bastard."

As an answer, the Jackal exited the cave.

The once-Sujin followed.

CHAPTER 46

The soft gurgling of the river failed to lull the three Slayers to sleep.

Enduring the heat of the day, they patrolled the shore of the little island, waiting for the Paw to appear. Rocks rattled underfoot as He-Dog paced. He waded into the water to let it soak his feet and eyed the thickets along the embankments—tall shoots resembling green spines. He knelt and guardedly splashed water over his back and face. Spitting into the river, He-Dog saw nothing lurking in the jungle.

He checked on the others.

Snaffer guarded the other end of the island, his great mop of hair turning this way and that. He held both weapons at the ready while he scanned the wilderness, tapping the axe-head against his lower leg.

Kellic remained next to Summer Wind, and they both leaned against the tree. The woman had regained her composure, getting over her initial fear—or at least had learned how to better control it. She scanned the riverbanks, just as watchful as any of them.

He-Dog supposed he would be doing the same. But he didn't like seeing her tied up like that. Didn't see the need.

"Cut her loose, Kellic," he finally said.

That got confused looks from the other mercenaries.

"Isn't she supposed to be tied to the tree?" Snaffer asked.

"That was before, when they left their people here to perish. *We're* here now. And I don't like her tied to that tree."

Kellic was already cutting the ropes.

"See to it she doesn't run," Snaffer warned.

"Run?" He-Dog asked, his mouth half-hitched as if fish-hooked. "Where's she going to run? The safest place is right here with us."

Snaffer ignored him, which was answer enough.

The ropes fell to the ground. Summer Wind held her wrists as she sank to the base of the tree. Kellic handed her a gourd of water but she didn't drink.

He-Dog didn't blame her.

They all resumed their watch, lingering in the shade where they could, until the sun began its evening descent.

"I hope the damn thing doesn't come at night," He-Dog grumbled, more to himself, but his words carried. No one commented, however. The river continued its whispering as the three men meandered around the banks of the island.

He-Dog rubbed his eyes and released a lengthy sigh. "I hate this."

Snaffer approached, threading the shoreline while gazing downstream. "The thing could be waiting for darkness," he said.

"Is it supposed to come here at night?" Kellic asked. "It didn't wait for night when it killed off Half Tusk's hunters."

That caused He-Dog and Snaffer to trade looks, realizing Kellic was right on that point.

"It might've gotten a sniff of us," Snaffer said. "And decided to wait until dark."

"If you keep saying so, it just might do that," Kellic warned.

He-Dog glanced at Summer Wind. "How is she?"

Using the little bit of Anoka language he'd learned, Kellic asked her, and she whispered an answer.

"She's as good as can be," Kellic reported.

"You sounded good, then, lad," Snaffer said. "Like a real wildman."

"Stop with your jabs," Kellic warned.

That turned Snaffer around. "No jab. I meant it."

Oddly enough, He-Dog thought that was the truth.

They watched the river.

"What do you think about going after it?" Snaffer asked after a while.

"Out there?" He-Dog asked back. "And get snatched away by a thing no one's even seen? Except the hands?"

"And claws," Kellic corrected. "*Giant* claws."

Frowning, Snaffer didn't pursue the idea any further.

Rocks rattled as Summer Wind curled up upon the ground. Kellic sat beside her, and without warning she moved closer and rested her head on the mercenary's thigh so that she faced the water.

"She all right?" Snaffer asked.

"Just tired," Kellic said. "She's worn down to nothing. A long march to get here. Then tied to the tree. No sleep. Wondering if we'll kill the beast or not." He placed a hand on her shoulder. A small comfort as Summer Wind did not close her eyes and kept on watching the river.

The jungle darkened a touch more.

"We'll keep watch through the night," He-Dog said. "One man guarding. The others can try to rest. We should hear the thing coming at us unless it can float across water."

Rocks rattling underfoot, Snaffer approached the tree and gathered up deadwood littered around the base. He dumped it in a pile and hacked off a few more limbs from the trunk.

"You think that's wise?" Kellic asked.

"I want a fire," Snaffer said as he continued chopping. "Maybe it'll bring the monster along."

"A fire might keep it away."

That stopped the older mercenary. "I'm not standing guard without a fire. And I want to burn this wretched tree. Piece by piece."

He-Dog understood that. The thing was unfit.

Not long after, under a purpling sky flecked with gold, Snaffer finished heaping wood onto the beach. When he was done, he sat opposite Kellic and Summer Wind, groaning as he did so, and watched the shadows deepen along the river.

"You can light that," Snaffer said to He-Dog. "Whenever it gets too dark for you."

He-Dog smirked and eyed the darkening wilderness.

I hate this, he thought.

He-Dog woke at dawn and arched his back. He rested near the tree, where he fell asleep after his watch. Summer Wind curled up nearby on the rocks, her head resting upon a backpack filled with some of their remaining provisions.

"You awake?" Snaffer asked from the other side of the trunk.

"Aye that," He-Dog said, mindful of the calm river.

"We're still alive."

"So we are."

Last night's fire left a charred stain upon the rocks. They didn't burn all the wood they had, but He-Dog was of a mind to burn the whole damn tree, he disliked it so. Kellic stood near the water's edge, his figure dark against the scant morning light. He lifted a hand at the waking warriors before continuing his watch.

Snaffer stood and lumbered off to relieve himself at the lower end of the island. Stirred by all the movement around her, Summer Wind pushed herself up on two hands. He-Dog greeted her with a nod and received one in return. The Anoka woman's mood looked to be a touch better. A little more inclined to fight, if needed.

A weary Kellic wandered in from the shore.

"Anything to eat?" Snaffer asked, returning as well.

He-Dog opened one pack. They ate a breakfast of fruit and dried meats and washed it down with water taken from upstream.

As he was eating, Jers Snaffer checked on how much food they had remaining. "Enough for the day," he judged. "For all of us."

"What then?" Kellic asked.

"Then . . . if this thing doesn't show itself . . . we'll have to get more."

"Where? Here?"

"Where else?"

An uneasy Kellic glanced around.

He-Dog finished his bite. "The thing might be waiting for us to do that. Get us off the island and into the jungle where it can surprise us. Lords above, I hope not."

"Because that means it can think?" Kellic asked.

"I know it can think . . . I just hope the unfit thing's not *smart*."

"At least not smarter than us," Snaffer added.

He-Dog agreed when he noticed a part of the bushes and reeds along the embankment shiver. The others saw it as well and they all climbed to their feet, weapons at the ready.

An instant later the familiar voice of Broska called out. "It's *me*! Me, I say! Don't kill me!"

The relieved group of Slayers lowered their blades.

The Zuthenian emerged with a handful of warriors behind him. They splashed into the river and plodded across, making no attempt to be quiet. In short order, they stood dripping and breathing heavily before them. Concern filled the Zuthenian's face and when his words came, He-Dog had trouble understanding him.

"I have news. Before dawn, this morning. One of the lads. Spotted smoke. Coming from the south. From what might be the village. Three Cut fears something has happened. He thinks the village was sacked and burned."

"By who?" Snaffer demanded.

"They don't know. They don't want to think Iruzu. It would be the first time . . . they've ventured so far north. Well beyond Iruzuland. In any case, if it *is* Iruzu, Three Cut has half his warriors guarding the village. That might not be enough. He's decided to return and see what's happened. I came here to tell you we're going back."

"We'll go with you," Snaffer said.

Broska shook his head. "You can't. You have to stay here. Kill the Paw."

"There's been no sight of the thing since you left us," He-Dog said.

"Listen to me," Broska insisted. "You *must* stay here with her. That's always been the plan. If you leave now and the Paw finds its plate empty, it'll come for the Anoka. And it won't stop until they are all dead. We'll go back as quickly as we can, and if there's no great trouble we'll return. Understood?"

"We'll stay," He-Dog said. "But we'll need food . . ."

Broska spoke to the warriors with him. In a flurry, the men dug out whatever provisions they carried and dropped it all into the packs of the Slayers. While they did so, Broska informed Summer Wind about what had happened and Three Cut's plans.

"That'll keep you for a few days," Broska said to the mercenaries. "Let's hope all this will be done before then."

The Zuthenian held out a fist. He-Dog studied it before pressing his own against the offered hand.

"Don't let your guard down," Broska warned. "That's when the thing strikes. When you think you're free of it. That's when it kills."

"You're going to run the whole way back?" He-Dog asked.

"As much as I can. My wife is back there. And my unborn child."

"Get going."

Nodding, Broska met each of their gazes before saying something to the warriors behind him. They wasted no more time and retreated across the river. In moments, they climbed the riverbank and disappeared into the jungle.

"Get ready," He-Dog said under his breath.

"For what?" Snaffer asked.

"The Paw . . . if it's out there. It might go after them."

"And if it does?"

"We go after it."

No noise erupted from the wilderness, however. No screams of terror or the clash of battle.

"They're gone," Snaffer said.

"Long gone," He-Dog added. "The beast wasn't there after all. Or it's not interested in them."

Once more he studied the riverbanks. If the Paw was going to come at all, now was the time. He sighed. He was tired, and the day was only going to get hotter. He gripped his sword and watched the wilderness.

And waited . . .

CHAPTER 47

Just outside of the smoking, smoldering ruins of the village, people bound in ropes stood in long lines. Children, women, and men of all ages battered, bruised, and defeated. Dirt and grime covered the lot of them, their coughs and soft sobbing breaking the stillness.

Timmer strode along the prisoners, eyeing the Anoka, or so the one-legged Valencian topper had called them. Some of the women were quite pretty. Horlo the Cruel had noticed the same. The pirate eyed one in particular, a sweet young berry without sight. Horlo had taken a special interest in that one, and his typical lewd, yellow smirk seemed wider than usual. Timmer could not begrudge the fat killer. A few of the captured women had caught his own eye, causing him to stop and admire them for several lecherous beats.

A pair of hunched young men, badly beaten, glared at the once-gladiator as he strolled by them.

Timmer halted and glared back. "Look away, maggots," he warned.

They did not. In fact, the glares only became harder.

Timmer pulled steel—a short, curved length of a blade—and stabbed the first one through the middle. He shoved the blade deep, twisted, and extracted the weapon in a heavy gout of scarlet.

That got the lot of them screaming.

They screamed even more when Timmer cut down the second wide-eyed maggot, cleaving apart the savage in a shallow V. The blade chopped through several bones before stopping on his ribs. The dead villager collapsed, nearly pulling the weapon out of Timmer's hand.

Snarling, the once-gladiator put a boot to the corpse to free his blade.

"*Timmer!*" shouted Black Korraz.

Spattered in red, Timmer turned with a harsh expression of *What*?

Korraz approached and stopped a few paces away. "Look, lad. I appreciate what you do. Truly, I do. In this business, you need lads willing to take a few heads upon a word or a glance. But think for a moment. You are cutting up our *trade* goods. All right? All of this? Trade goods. They are worth *nothing* to us dead. They are worth much, much more *alive*."

"If that one-legged blossom isn't lying to us," Timmer pointed out.

"Don't worry about that. Lying or not, he *will* sweeten the pot when we finally do meet with these Iruzu." With that, the pirate captain shifted his gaze to Shay near the end of the line. A handful of pirates stood around the hobbled man, one of whom was Sobaba.

"We should kill him," Timmer advised. "He'll slow us down."

"And all these savages won't? No. I . . . agree with his thinking. Trading this lot for these gemstones. Their *weight* in gemstones?"

"If the stones are there."

"They're somewhere," Korraz countered, slapping at some troublesome biter digging into his arm. "You saw that topper's face when I showed him those sooty rocks. You saw. That's all the truth I need. Even if he only has an idea of where the stones are, that will be enough. In any case, I'll enjoy watching him sicken with worry the closer we get to these Iruzu. If I don't cut him up myself and leave him for the crawlers."

"And if we don't find the stones?"

"Then we go back to looking for a mountain of gold."

Timmer mulled that over. "Kragland would pay handsomely for some of these honeypots."

Korraz frowned. "I'd sooner bathe in your rancid pisswater than become like the Ojuka, so heave that thought away."

Timmer's expression darkened. "What about these old ones then? Are we going to march them south?"

"*Especially* them. Shay says there are elders among them. If these Iruzu can be bargained with, offering them the *leaders* of their enemy might be far too enticing to refuse. One of them could be worth a score of ordinary savages."

"I think he's lying. To save as many of them as he can."

"There's that. His three dogs are out there. Just keep watch for them. Now then, did you find our lad that's missing . . ."

"*Two* of our lads are missing."

"No sign of them? No one's found them yet?"

Timmer shook his head.

"Then they're dead," Korraz said. "The savages that escaped must have killed them. Or these biters feasting on us."

"Are you using the lotion from the tankards?"

"I am. It doesn't turn these hellions away."

"Odd we didn't find the corpses." Timmer frowned, getting back to the matter at hand.

"Perhaps they took them."

"For what?"

"No doubt to eat them," Korraz said simply.

"They didn't eat that one," Timmer pointed out, indicating Shay.

"No, they did not. In any case, if the missing lads aren't here, then they're out there somewhere, and they're long since perished."

"We could search for them."

Korraz waved at something buzzing around his head. "We have no time."

Timmer adjusted his dripping skull rag. "Give me a handful of lads and I'll hunt them down. Them and the savages that got away from us. I'll find them and do whatever you want done."

"Let them come to us."

The once-gladiator's eyes narrowed. "They *could* bring back more savages. Or worse. Those three sword arms that headed north with the others. They might try and reach them. To free this lot."

Korraz smiled. "I'm hoping they will. *Especially* those three hellions. More trade goods, my good Timmer." The captain breathed deeply of the smoky air and stifled a cough. "Get them ready to move. We head south."

Timmer considered that before nodding at the Anoka. "Do we feed them?"

"Only what you find on the trail. Nothing more. Any other concerns, then?"

The once-gladiator shook his head, ending the conversation.

Around midmorning, the pirates marched their prisoners into the jungle. The Anoka moved quickly, encouraged by hard slaps to the heads or threatened outright with death. There were many of them, but Korraz was unconcerned with leaving a trail. He did assign a rear guard, however, comprising of handpicked cutthroats and led by Timmer. Any savage attempting to free their companions would be either killed or captured.

Five pirates marched ahead of Korraz, and the pirate captain gradually slowed to allow the others to walk on by. His men nodded as they moved past, herding along prisoners who stole peeks at the captain's sweat-soaked finery. One savage inspected him up and down before a pirate slapped the curiosity out of him and yanked him away.

Smiling with grim approval, Korraz waited for one prisoner in particular.

Four Anoka men approached, their faces swollen, bloodied, and crusted over. Deciding on saving time, Korraz had his boys lash together a roughshod stretcher, made from a pair of poles and animal hides. Four beaten villagers were then tied to the ends to carry the thing. To further ensure cooperation from the prisoners, a stern Sobaba walked beside them, brandishing his broadsword.

Shay laid upon the makeshift bed and held on with his good hand.

Korraz walked alongside his civilized prisoner. "This place is hellish," the pirate captain declared, dabbing his face with a rag. "Takes no great imagination to see how your lot was killed off. The insects alone . . ."

Wincing from the constant dip and rattle, Shay didn't bother commenting.

Korraz squeezed perspiration from his hand cloth. "All but three, that is."

Shay stared at the jungle roof high above and regarded the man who had tortured him. "What's this one called again?" he asked the pirate captain.

"Sobaba?"

"Aye that. The one who broke my fingers."

"He could have done far worse," Korraz assured him. "That one has killed more than you and I together. He's killed dozens with just his bare hands. Snapping necks. Ripping out throats. Or just . . . smashing in faces. Until they no longer draw breath. That sort of thing."

Shay didn't say anything to that.

"Where are these Iruzu, again?" Korraz asked.

The prince thought about it. "Somewhere to the south. Two or three days away. In a land bordered by rivers of bloodfish. That's where I lost my leg."

"Excellent," Korraz said. "And you're certain these gemstones are there?"

"That's what I believe. Even more now, after seeing the fire-pit stones."

"Hard to believe they exist at all."

"Hard to believe your mountain of gold exists. That one is new, I'll tell you that for nothing. Between the stones you found and what Stephanak told me—"

"Stephanak?"

"The captain of the *Blue Conquest*. He was our partner in this expedition. In any case, I'm certain that the stones are somewhere in the south. In Iruzuland."

"Daresay we'll see," the pirate captain said. "Truth be known, Shay, my lads believe you're lying. *I* believe you're lying. We all think you're lying merely to stay alive a few days more. Just long enough for your three killers to try and take you back. I don't care, really. I suppose I just didn't want to leave a civilized man in the jungle with this rabble, where any number of things could devour you." Korraz studied the passing wilderness. "Truth be known, I'll match my killers against yours any time. Sobaba alone is worth three of yours. My second? The fierce one with the skull rag? He used to be a gladiator in Sunja's *Pit*. Killed the best for a *living*. Until he realized he could earn more coin with us, doing what the Ossaki does best."

Shay absorbed all that with a stoic expression.

"Do you understand me?" Korraz asked.

Shay blinked as if roused from deep thought. "Can we stop? So I can empty the bull."

"No. Apologies. We're on the march. If you have to use your pisser, do it over the side."

With that, the pirate captain turned and strode away.

Shay watched the pirate as he walked up the line.

He replayed the conversation in his mind, which was becoming sharper with every passing moment. He remembered most of what Snaffer had told him about the Iruzu, whose land lay to the south, southwest . . . but finding it? Like he was? Shay sighed. Troubles upon troubles. Taking a breath, he convinced himself he could find the place. He suspected it might be near where they had been ambushed months ago. His memory with landmarks was superior, and he was confident of recognizing that place if they crossed it.

In any case, he had Korraz fish-hooked. That much was clear. Finding those burnt gemstones had certainly helped with the convincing. Shay figured he could lead these maggots around by their noses for perhaps two days at the most. Doubtful no more than that, since Korraz already knew Snaffer and the others were out there.

Two days. It was Shay's hope that would be enough for Snaffer, He-Dog, and the other one to return, find a scorched village, and then track him and the surviving Anoka down.

If the lads were still alive. Nothing was ever certain.

Life was short. Shay knew that. Especially in the bloody trade he'd chosen as a profession. He'd made a life off the lives of others, he knew. Probably treated them more like commodities than he should have, but that was that. Still, he told himself he valued loyalty. Valued good intentions, and better people. The fog and confusion caused by the dream leaves had finally lifted, enough for him to think long and clearly. His missing leg, his dead companions, but also . . . the people who had taken care of him. Certainly, they had their reasons to do so, but Shay was still grateful all the same.

Grateful and feeling more than a little indebted.

He thought of Little Bloom then, somewhere behind him, and dearly hoped she was all right. He'd gotten a glimpse of her, and she of him, and in that fleeting moment volumes had been spoken without a word. The thought almost brought a smile to his face, one he quickly forced down for fear of the pirates noticing.

Gemstones.

He'd come here for riches and perhaps found something better.

The only hope remaining for them all rested on Snaffer, He-Dog, and the other one, whose name Shay still couldn't remember. Those three had to kill the Paw first. Then maybe, just *maybe*, they would return in time to see the destroyed Anoka village. The trail the pirates left would be an easy one to follow. Korraz had said he would match his killers against his own at any time. Shay welcomed that match. He knew Snaffer's skill with a blade. Even knew what the other one was capable of. Both were two very dangerous individuals. Even He-Dog, Shay supposed, since he'd been the only other person to survive this long.

At the very least, Shay hoped they would be able to save the Anoka prisoners . . .

And if Snaffer and the others *didn't* find them . . .

Shay had no doubt that he and the remaining villagers were dead. Probably slaughtered in the most horrific fashion imaginable.

There was one thing that offered Shay a glimmer of hope—the fact that he was leading this pack of Ossaki shite to the monsters who had butchered his company in the Sanjou.

CHAPTER 48

Time took on an even slower pace after Broska and the others departed for the Anoka village.

Or so it seemed to He-Dog.

Smoke drifted overhead, just a little. Perhaps from the Anoka village, perhaps something else, but it did nothing to improve He-Dog's mood. Two things nagged him. One was Shay. As much as He-Dog had grown to dislike the man, he still felt a meddlesome sense of owing something to him, ever since Othil.

Of greater concern was Summer Wind.

Since arriving here, she'd slowly regained her composure, drawing strength from the confidence of the Slayers around her. Since learning of the potential trouble at the Anoka village, however, the woman looked more worried every time He-Dog glanced her way. Kellic remained by her side, but the looming confrontation with the Paw and the unknown fate of the village clearly weighed upon Summer Wind's resolve. Twice He-Dog saw her wipe tears away from red eyes before hiding her face behind her knees. When Kellic spoke to her, she barely responded.

So, with growing worry, they watched the jungle along the river and the smoke in the sky.

The Paw did not appear that day.

Nor that night.

He-Dog took the last watch of the night, and just as dawn cracked through the dark sky someone stirred behind him, near the tree.

Snaffer, rising and stretching. Stones shifted as the mercenary walked over to He-Dog's side. Snaffer stopped a few paces away and stared at the morning calm of the river. "Nothing?" he asked.

"Nothing."

The mercenary's eyes narrowed. "Where *is* this thing?"

He-Dog shook his head.

"Do you suppose . . . it might have attacked the village?"

"I don't know."

"That bastard Half Tusk said it followed him back."

"He did."

Snaffer chewed on that thought. "I find it hard to believe the creature reached the village, looked it over, then decided to come all the way back *here*, for *her* tender hide." He hooked his chin at Summer Wind.

The gesture caught Kellic's attention.

He-Dog sighed. "I think ... I *fear* ... this Paw ... is much smarter than we think."

Rocks crunched as Kellic wandered over.

"Have you seen any fish in this river?" He-Dog asked.

Snaffer shook his head.

"Nor I. And the food we have won't last long."

"What are you thinking?"

"I think you're right, Jers Snaffer," He-Dog said. "I think that while we were here, the Paw attacked the village. And it's feasting on every last person in that place. I think we should leave here and go back. If something's happened there, and it's because of the Paw ... then I see no reason to stay here."

Snaffer and Kellic absorbed those thoughts.

"So we go," He-Dog finished. "Now."

"You know the way?" Kellic asked.

"She knows the way. We're all going back."

CHAPTER 49

A day and a half after leaving the offering place, Broska, Half Tusk, and the remainder of the Anoka party who traveled north reached their homes.

They were greeted by a horrifying sight.

The smoke had cleared, revealing stark devastation. Fires had indeed consumed the village, as well as the trees and foliage growing in and around the lodges. The charred bones of some dwellings still stood, while others had collapsed into blackened heaps. A handful of homes had been untouched by flames, but the hides stretched over their wooden frameworks had been shredded into dangling tatters. Wooden bowls, hollowed gourds, stone tools, and other personal items lay strewn across the sooty ground. Bodies lay among the ruins, some killed by edged weapons, others burned at the center of their own smoldering lodges. A harsh and heavy stink drifted from decomposing bodies, seasoned by smoke and ash and left to rot in a place roasted to its very roots.

Above it all, only the lodge of the elders was untouched.

Sparing the hill just a glance, Broska ran for his home. In short time he saw it—at least what was left of it. The lodge belonging to him and his wife, Sunny Smiles, was a scorched heap. A horrified Broska dropped upon what had been the threshold of his home and clawed through the remains. Anoka survivors yelled behind him, calling for missing loved ones, but he barely heard any of that. Some of the beams of his home crumbled in his hands as he pulled on them, uncovering a little more of what lay beneath.

Until he slumped amid the ashes.

Sunny Smiles was not there. She was nowhere to be seen. Broska straightened and looked around, hoping to see her.

His spirits spiked with a fragile hope.

Survivors stumbled into the razed clearing, emerging from hiding places in the jungle, crying, reaching for their returning warriors. Perhaps forty or so villagers, wretched and dirty from their ordeal, and clearly relieved to have their chieftain back. Wives and children, mothers and fathers, brothers and sisters, all broken and hopeless. The sight tightened Broska's throat as he hurried to the sad reunion. The villagers clutched at Three Cut and Peaceful Moon, talking over one another, desperate to relay what had happened.

The survivors said they were attacked at night. The killers wore hard shells like the Slayers, had weapons like the Slayers, but hunted only the Anoka. The attackers killed nearly all of their warriors and set many of their homes on fire. They took what they wanted, and what they didn't want they destroyed. The survivors said that all the elders had been killed, with the exception of Smiling Rock who had been taken prisoner. They said that many of their loved ones had been taken prisoner and led away into the jungle.

Then even more terrible news for Three Cut and Warm Cloud: their youngest daughter, Gentle Rain, had been captured as well.

Broska stood at the edge of the mob and asked about his wife. No one could answer him, until one woman said she saw Sunny Smiles being taken away with the rest of the captured villagers. The news chilled his guts. His first thought was that these brutes were slavers from Kragland, the only place he knew of that still plied that unfit trade.

The villagers also mentioned the attackers had taken Sleeping One Leg as well.

That turned Broska around. The three lodges on the ridge had been untouched by fire, but obviously ravaged and searched for loot.

Half Tusk returned from the elders' lodge and reported it empty, with much of the belongings smashed or thrown about the interior.

Three Cut asked the survivors which way the attackers had gone, and the answer chilled Broska even more.

South, they said, and that the trail was an easy one to follow.

Half Tusk traded looks with Three Cut, and the chieftain ordered his best warrior to go after their people. Three Cut said that if these survivors were lost, the Anoka may never recover. Three Cut then asked Broska to go with Half Tusk and his warriors to make sure they brought back his daughters, Gentle Rain and Sunny Smiles.

The Zuthenian replied that he most certainly would.

Half Tusk vowed to find the savages and kill every last one.

The violent attack had taken a heavy toll on the Anoka, but if the slavers managed to return to the coast with those people . . . Broska didn't want to think about that. He didn't want to think about losing Sunny Smiles or his unborn child.

Saying their goodbyes and vowing to return, the Anoka war party left the destroyed village and followed the trail into the jungle. Half Tusk led them with Broska on his heels. They traveled hard, eager to close the distance between themselves and the stealers of their people.

The face of his missing wife before him, Broska pushed himself to keep up with the others. Over the trail they pounded, moving at a brisk pace until their strength eventually left them all. Forced to stop for the night, they set up camp just off the trail, with Half Tusk posting sentries.

The leader then told his warriors to rest while they could, as they would be moving again before dawn.

Broska fell asleep almost immediately.

CHAPTER 50

A hard day's march later, He-Dog and his companions came upon the charred ruins of the Anoka village.

The scale of the destruction didn't surprise He-Dog. Not really. He expected the worst. Knowing how the place looked before the fire, however, it struck him hard. The village and surrounding area had been a pretty one, with its green-infused shade and colorful flowers. A setting fit for a fine painting, truth be known. What struck even harder was the missing Anoka. Dare he admit it, he'd gotten used to all those smiling faces staring at him every day. All gone, reduced to scorched wood, charred personal belongings, and mounds of ash.

Summer Wind covered her mouth at the sight. A stunned Kellic stopped and stared, his usual gloomy expression even more stricken. The place even affected Jers Snaffer, who wandered through the area with half his face hitched up in horror.

"It's gone. Everything . . . burned," Kellic said.

Movement on the high ridge caught their attention. Three Anoka warriors emerged from the entrance of the elders' lodge. Recognizing the group below, they waved and called out, gesturing for the Slayers to join them.

Which He-Dog and the others did.

Unlike the rest of the village, the lodge was relatively intact, except for one shredded wall at the back, the resulting streamers fluttering in a faint breeze. The Slayers entered and regarded the solemn expressions of the Anoka people taking refuge in the dwelling. Summer Wind rushed to her parents, Three Cut and Warm Cloud, and embraced them.

A hopeful Peaceful Moon stepped before He-Dog. "Paw?" he asked.

He-Dog shook his head, disappointing the spirit man.

"Where's the Zuthenian?" Snaffer asked, looking over the survivors within the structure. No more than five dozen, which was considerably less than the hundreds from before.

"Ask him what happened here," He-Dog said to Kellic.

Kellic and Peaceful Moon went back and forth, with both men trying hard to make themselves understood.

"Anoka died," Kellic reported. ". . . But he's also saying Anoka go."

"Go?" He-Dog repeated.

Kellic and Peaceful Moon spoke again. The spirit man pointed south, before taking Kellic by the arm and leading him outside, talking all the while. He-Dog and Snaffer followed. Peaceful Moon motioned toward a noticeable trail carved into the jungle leading south. A trail made by a great number of people, crushing the vegetation beneath their feet.

The spirit man then gestured at the Slayers.

Confusion distorted Kellic's face. "I think he's saying the Anoka went that way."

A young warrior approached and held out a bloodstained arrow to Kellic. He took the shaft and inspected it. "Not one of ours."

"Let me see that," Snaffer said and took the arrow. He studied the thing up and down. "Well made. Not one of ours, as you said. Not belonging to Zuthenia, either. They dig grooves in the heads."

Three Cut appeared with his wife and daughter, and he spoke at length with the people gathered around. An assortment of young and old, and very few warriors.

Kellic winced, straining to understand. "He says . . . slayers—*not* Slayers—came here. Anoka die . . . Anoka go . . ."

"Aye that," He-Dog interrupted. "Someone like us came here, flattened the place, and took everyone they could *that* way."

"Seddon above," Kellic whispered.

Snaffer studied the gathered people. "Ask him where the old woman is."

"Old woman?" Kellic asked.

"The old one. Bent over with a crooked back. You've seen her about. And the pack of children that followed me."

Kellic asked, struggling again to make himself understood.

But Peaceful Moon understood who he was asking about and answered while shaking his head.

"She's dead," Kellic informed Snaffer. "They killed her."

That straightened Snaffer's spine.

"They took the children as well," Kellic continued. "Along with the rest."

The mercenary's expression darkened upon hearing that.

"We'll get them back," He-Dog vowed, meeting the solemn gazes of Peaceful Moon and Three Cut. "Aye that. Every last one of them. Tell them."

Kellic did what he could, struggling with the language. Perhaps sensing their intention rather than understanding Kellic's words, Three Cut spoke to his people. The Anoka did not have much food, but what they did have they gave to the three Slayers. As He-Dog and Snaffer filled their packs, Kellic listened to Summer Wind. She grew noticeably more worried as she spoke.

She eventually finished, getting her meaning through to a stern Kellic as he took an offered pack from Snaffer.

"What was that about?" the older mercenary asked.

"They took Bright Leaf," Kellic mumbled.

Snaffer frowned at the name.

"She cared for us. While we were on the mend. She's teaching me the language."

Much to He-Dog's surprise, if Snaffer looked grim before, he appeared right and proper *murderous* upon hearing that last bit of news.

"You both ready?" He-Dog asked and got nods. "Then let's get moving."

With departing waves, the three Slayers started down the hill. When they reached the fresh trail, He-Dog stopped and studied the crushed vegetation. The width of the path suggested the attackers had taken a good many of the Anoka away, and the thought rotted his guts.

"Who would do this?" he asked.

"Slavers," Snaffer answered, as if tasting poison.

"Slavers," He-Dog agreed.

"Kragland slavers."

"Zuthenia takes slaves as well," Kellic pointed out.

"That's beastman slaves," He-Dog said.

"Kragland will take anyone," Snaffer added.

"They might have a ship nearby."

"They might," He-Dog agreed.

Not wasting any more time, a determined Kellic started along the new trail, and the others followed.

Sunlight flashed as the three Slayers hurried through the wilderness. The trail was wide and flat, trampled by men who had little fear of being tracked. The Slayers spoke very little as they pounded over green hills, through halls of hazy shadows, and across shallow streams. Birds called out, their cries sharp and urgent as the men bounded across the landscape. At times, odd little monkeys scampered up and into the treetops, shrieking, as if telling them to move faster.

By midafternoon the three men slowed to a measured march. Even at that pace, their legs burned. They rested when they absolutely had to, only as long as it took to regain their breath, before they were on the move again.

By evening, they were reduced to a stubborn trudge, walking along a southern corridor hacked out of the underbrush. The land arched ever upward until it flattened into a plateau, where a large group had made camp among the trees and bushes. The undergrowth had been trampled over a large area, and several charred fire pits had been left behind. Rotten scraps of fruit lay strewn about, and crawlers feasted upon the gurry.

"They camped here for a night," He-Dog huffed, enduring the ache in his limbs.

"Not far ahead now," panted Snaffer, eyeing the trail.

"We may catch them tomorrow."

"We should keep moving," Kellic said.

"We stop here," He-Dog told him, and got a cold glare as an answer.

"He's right," Snaffer said. "We rest here. If we keep on, we won't have anything left when it's needed. And I'm close to dropping."

Looking just as haggard as his companions, Kellic reluctantly nodded, his frame sagging from the exertion of the day. He trudged over to a collection of fallen trees drizzled with vegetation. There he sat, his back against a trunk, and lowered his head. In moments he was asleep.

He-Dog did the same, all the while hiding his surprise at Snaffer. He believed it was the first time the man had agreed with him.

"We move before first light," He-Dog said, glancing about the jungle.

"I'll take first watch," Snaffer said.

He-Dog adjusted his scabbard and got as comfortable as his armor would allow. He folded his arms and sighed. His time recovering in a lodge and breathing in the dream leaves had healed him, but that time had also limited his strength, much to his dismay.

He feared he would need every bit of it and more in the days to come.

The day darkened. Insects darted before his face, buzzing about, but keeping a wide berth of him and his two companions.

In short time, he fell asleep.

Just before dawn, the three men rose. They stretched briefly, ate a quick handful of provisions, and started marching again. When the sun cracked the horizon, a figure waited for them in the middle of the trail. A man carrying a curved club, wearing the white stripes of an Anoka warrior. Relief showed upon the man's face as he recognized the Slayers, and he said as much, as five other warriors emerged from the edges of the path.

One of them was Half Tusk.

Another was Broska, bare-chested and more battered than usual, with his face and forehead purpled and plastered in a bandage of earthy paste.

"What happened to you?" He-Dog asked.

Broska waved that off. "Did you kill the Paw?"

"The thing didn't appear," He-Dog said. "So we left."

"You left?" Broska asked in pained wonder. "Why?"

He-Dog explained his reasoning for returning to the village, and how they had brought back Summer Wind back before setting out to track down the Anoka war party. When he finished, Broska translated for the others, which brought even more pained looks. Even the usually stoic Half Tusk took in a mighty breath and muttered something in unchecked disgust.

"Where are your people?" Snaffer asked.

Broska grimaced. "We followed the slavers south, running at a good pace, when a group of them ambushed us. They cut us down with arrows first, then their brutes waded into the fray. I'm afraid I haven't been training as often as I used to. I struck down two before one tried to take my head off. He missed, but left his mark. Left me stunned and staggering about. The lads here pulled me away while the fighting kept on. Only Half Tusk and two others returned to us, and the slavers didn't pursue. We're following them at a slower pace, but their numbers are too great."

"So they are slavers?" He-Dog asked.

A suffering Broska nodded. "They are, and they have well over a hundred Anoka women, children, and men. They killed off many of the older villagers. And those able to fight. Your man Shay is with them. The truly disturbing thing is . . . they're heading south. Always south."

He-Dog scowled at that.

"Iruzuland," the Zuthenian said. "They're walking straight into Iruzuland. And we're the only ones who can stop them."

CHAPTER 51

Suffering from the sweltering heat of the midafternoon, the Ossaki pirates halted on the trail. Half a dozen pirates went ahead, hacking their way through harsh country damn near impenetrable with all manner of strange and troublesome plant life. Patches of thorny bushes as tall as a man; gigantic blooms of unknown flowers; gardens of huge, gray mushrooms the size of helmets; and vines, unforgiving tangles and knots of vines. All growing rampant beneath a blanket of interconnected limbs stemming from towering trees, thick enough to block out the very sun. Several times the pirates shouted to halt, and Shay once saw what they were yelling about. A huge web barred their way, one of which was occupied by a spider the size of a man's head. The pirates marveled at such a monster before Sobaba marched up, brandishing his broadsword, and split the fearsome thing apart with one cut.

The pirates cursed and slapped the weary prisoners to get them moving again. The march resumed but halted soon after when, surprisingly enough, the scouts ahead discovered a well-used trail bearing south. A winding, twisting thing, where the edges of the underbrush reached out to graze Shay. Seeing no reason not to take the trail, the pirates turned their prisoners upon it. The Anoka people, beaten and miserable, looked even more uneasy as they walked along the path, if not outright frightened. The prisoners marched in two separate lines, their hands tied to two great lengths of rope. They whispered among themselves as they walked, glancing around with increasing worry. The Ossaki pirates lumbering beside them noticed their looks and went about slapping the unease from an unfortunate few, to straighten out the rest.

Shay suspected he knew why the Anoka were nervous.

Not long after, the pirates halted their prisoners once again and forced them to sit. The Anoka men carrying Shay lowered him to the ground. With all the prisoners now seated, it was easy to catch sight of Korraz walking back down the line. The captain stopped halfway, motioning to the pirate guards in charge of watching Shay. Without warning, they grabbed Without warning, they grabbed Shay's carriers by the hair and pulled them to their feet. Shay came up with them, nearly spilling from the stretcher. The pirates led Shay and his Anoka bearers past dozens of prisoners until they reached Korraz and the one called Sobaba.

"What's all this?" Korraz demanded as he pointed at the trail ahead.

Shay lifted himself up to better see . . . and stared in dawning horror.

The jungle floor sloped upward, the vegetation even thicker along the trail. There was still no mistaking what lay ahead. Hanging from trees, in grisly tiers, were a number of headless skeletons. Dozens of them, either impaled upon the blackened stumps of hacked branches, or dangling from rotting vines. Skeletons sagged some three lengths up the trunks before the leaves became too dense, hiding all but the lower legs. A grayish moss clung to yellowed bones while creepers laced themselves through shattered rib cages. Hands and arms lifted in arranged displays, as if greeting—or warning—future victims.

Seeing so many bones creased Shay's forehead with dark thoughts, and raised the hair on his dewy neck.

The sight did nothing to calm the Anoka men carrying him, who fidgeted with fear.

Korraz cleared his throat, breaking the spell. He waited for an explanation.

"We're getting close," Shay said, not knowing if they truly were one way or the other. "All this? It's . . . it's a warning. To any coming into their territory."

"A warning, you say . . . ?" Korraz asked.

"Aye that." Shay struggled to remember what Snaffer had told him, knowing he was half-delirious at the time, from that unfit smoke he'd been breathing in. He decided all the details weren't necessary, as they had killed off practically all his men. "The . . . *Iruzu* . . . are not to be taken lightly. As you can see."

Korraz chuckled and considered the sight. "*We* are not to be taken lightly. Sobaba!"

The big man stepped forward.

"We go that way," Korraz said. "Timmer!"

"Captain?" came the answering call, farther back in the line.

"Be on guard. See to it no one creeps up on us. And watch these savages. Every one of them. It's plain to see they don't like this. If anyone tries to escape, kill them. Make an example to the others."

"Aye that," the once-gladiator called back.

Korraz smiled at Shay. "Shall we?"

The prince did not answer.

With that, the pirate captain and his men marched on, eyeing the headless skeletons.

The Anoka lads who carried Shay, however, did not follow, and that stopped the pirates flanking them.

"What's the matter?" one greasy-looking killer snarled, brandishing a spear and flashing a mouth full of decaying teeth. "Get on before I slap your face."

The Anoka twitched and fiddled and looked among themselves, but would move no farther.

"Captain sar," the pirate called out.

"What is it?" Korraz said, turning.

"They won't move."

"They won't what?"

"They won't *move*."

One side of Korraz's face hitched in annoyed confusion. "Well, *make* them."

Orders received, the pirate gestured to a companion farther down the line. That cutthroat yanked a young girl—no more than ten—away from her mother. The mother screamed before another pirate silenced her with a slap across the face.

The cutthroat with the little girl dragged her back to the four Anoka carrying Shay. There the killer held the girl up, his fist knotted in her hair, and put a dagger to her throat. An exceptionally old but well-sharpened blade as thick as a sword. The weapon widened the child's eyes and made Shay very nervous for her life.

"Move, you unfit savages," the pirate hissed, displaying his own spotty set of teeth. "Before I turn the ground red. *Move*."

Fearful and miserable, the Anoka carrying Shay lurched into a halting walk. Those behind them followed, reluctantly, clearly unhappy about where they were going.

The procession of pirates and prisoners trudged through that frightening pass, eyeing the skeletons along the way. More sets of bones waited for them, all headless, decorating trees every so many paces. They hung from pegs nailed into the trunks, half-hidden in flourishing vegetation. The trees grew taller, their far-reaching limbs festooned with white wool and long slivers of leaves. The base of each of these jungle monsters plunged straight down into the ground. Their trunks were solid, formidable walls at least an arm's-length wide. Things moved in their towering heights, obscured by that cottony gurry clinging to the branches. Things that eased themselves out of sight before anyone could get a good look.

Mindful of the creatures, Korraz reminded his crew to be watchful but to keep the line moving.

The Anoka carrying Shay were now shaking with fear. Every step they took was a hesitant shuffle, as if they expected it to be their last.

Onward they marched.

Just before evening, the pirates halted the prisoners. The Anoka's relief was palpable. Shay regarded the trees and jungle growth and felt that they had thinned somewhat, when he heard a shout from the front of the column. Korraz appeared up the line and gestured in Shay's direction before turning away. Shay leaned on an elbow, trying to see around the men carrying him, when a stern Sobaba appeared. The torturer waved at the prisoners carrying Shay, and his guards shoved them all ahead.

Again, the Anoka men hesitated.

Which was when Sobaba approached one bearer and slapped the unfortunate fellow across the face, forcing Shay to grab for the edges of the stretcher. The Anoka man did not fall over, however, but stared in red-faced shock at the torturer.

Sobaba threatened again, but this time with his sword. That prompted the foursome to lurch ahead, carrying Shay along.

"I'm sorry, lads," he said under his breath and very much meant it.

Looking pleased, Korraz waited at the base of a short incline. Black, crooked rays of the sun rose around him. With a word, the pirate captain stepped aside, sweeping an arm at what lay beyond.

The sight rendered Shay speechless.

The trees and brush ended abruptly, teetering on the edge of a mighty gorge that cut the land in two. It was as if one of the Lords or Seddon himself had descended and carved a jagged line from east to west. Heaps of vegetation draped the opposing cliffs, spilling over a long face of pitted bedrock that went all the way down. Birds flew overhead, disappearing into hazy white clouds that clung to the distant treetops. The barest of breezes wafted by but failed to dispel the steamy ambiance of the Sanjou.

The scene wasn't entirely frightening.

What *was* unsettling, however, was the only way *across* the gorge.

A monster of a log spanned the chasm, huge and ancient and covered in the rich, mossy green of the jungle. The near side was jagged and scorched, however, as if it had been blasted from its mooring by a single thunderbolt before toppling across that imposing abyss. Long black roots, uprooted when the tree fell, spread up and curled inward, resembling the stiff legs of a dead spider. Shay realized those roots were the crooked rays rising behind Korraz. The makeshift bridge appeared to be several dozen strides long, and rabid vines brimming with leafy foliage crept along the entire length. Whoever had discovered the tree had realized its worth, and as such, had heaped gravel and stones into a long ramp leading right from the trail to the top of the bridge.

Where only the bravest would cross.

Korraz strolled up that ramp and onto the fallen tree. With dignified disdain, he examined the drop from one side and then the other. Satisfied with something or other, he gestured for Shay to be brought to him. Using swords, the pirates urged the four Anoka men up the slope, carrying the prince along. Shay gripped the edges of his stretcher while nervously eyeing the bridge. The tree looked to have the depth and overall width of a grown man. And while two men could cross shoulder to shoulder, it left very little room for mistakes—especially for the four lads lashed to his stretcher. One stumble, one misplaced foot, and it would be a desperate claw and scrabble to find a handhold before the long drop below.

The pirates stopped the four lads at the top of the ramp, the very threshold of the bridge. There, Shay leaned out as much as he dared, horrified at the fall. The chasm was easily two hundred strides down, and a dark river flowed at the very bottom. Long rows of wet pointed rocks comprised the narrow shores, resembling the open maw of some terrible beast. Jungle growth rotted on both sides of the gorge but appeared thinner on the opposite side. High grass sprouted along the cliffs, growing around numerous trees that jutted from the scalp of the land.

As Shay watched, a handful of pirates warily made their way across the bridge.

Korraz placed a hand on Shay's shoulder.

"Don't look down," the pirate captain advised with a smirk.

With that, he walked across with a sure step, leading the way. The pirates guarding Shay and his four lads followed. The Anoka plainly feared for their lives, and it took everything Shay had to *not* roll onto his side and sputter out a cow kiss.

He clenched one side of his stretcher and braced for the worst.

The men carried Shay across.

Behind him, pirates grabbed Anoka children and held knives to their throats, forcing the others to move. Their terrified moans laced the air as the prisoners shuffled along.

In time, the full procession reached the other side, surprisingly without a death.

Shay was already farther ahead, traveling just behind Korraz and his guards. Once past the first few rows of trees, the underbrush grew much lower and not nearly as dense. Where one could see only ten or so strides ahead from before, here the distance seemed tripled.

Korraz and his crew led their prisoners another two hundred paces or so when the captain halted the line. The pirates herded the Anoka into a small clearing off the beaten path. There, they separated the children from the adults, forced their prisoners to sit, and placed them all under the baleful watch of several menacing individuals armed with spears. By nightfall, the camp had been properly established and watches assigned. No fires burned that night. Fresh water and food proved to be scarce in the area, and the Ossaki did not share what they carried.

Encircled as they were, Shay counted perhaps three dozen pirates spread out over the area. Though their numbers were limited, they stood with the air of killers well experienced in handling large numbers of captives. With their armor and weapons, it would be a bloody and costly affair indeed if anyone attempted to escape.

Korraz eventually made his way over to where Shay was resting among his four carriers. The pirate captain stifled a yawn, having the sense not to make a sound. He beckoned for a fat pirate, the one with the perpetual evil smile on his stubbly face.

"Watch this one," Korraz ordered his henchman, who then turned his unpleasant sneer upon Shay. The prince stared back for a few beats before looking elsewhere.

"I hope we find your Iruzu soon," Korraz said in a thoughtful tone, smoothing over his beard. "I sent scouts ahead when we were crossing that hellish chasm back there. They've returned with news. We're on flat land here, but some four hundred paces that way," he pointed west, "the land slopes *downward*. They didn't see much farther than that."

"We must be close," Shay said.

"I imagine we are," Korraz agreed. "One only needs to look at these unhappy toppers."

Shay agreed. The four men around him clearly did not want to be there. The adults and children alike, moaning and whining while crossing the bridge, had all quieted once on the other side. They sat still, watchful of the jungle, as if sensing monsters lurking nearby. Even the four lads carrying Shay's one-legged carcass sat stone-still, eyeing the wilderness with an intensity that was unnerving. *They* knew where they were, even if their captors did not.

"Why don't you give them something to eat?" Shay said. "You can manage that at least."

"Something to eat?" Korraz repeated as if the idea was utterly unfit. "*Feed* them? These Iruzu asslickers can feed them once they have them. Though I believe they'll do nothing of the sort. Feed them." The pirate spotted someone he wanted to speak to. "Timmer."

The once-gladiator turned his head.

"Send a few lads back to that bridge over the chasm. Have them keep watch there for the night. In case the savages attempt to attack us again or *this* one's lads," he cocked his head at Shay, "find the bridge and decide to cross it."

Orders received, Timmer strode away.

"Did I tell you about that one?" Korraz leaned in. "I think I did."

"Aye that, you did."

"Well, I'll tell you again. He used to be a gladiator. Fought in Sunja's games for years. Until he gave it up and struck south with us. Usually, he's worth five men. Here, against these savages? He's worth *twenty*. At *least*." He straightened. "Sleep well, Shay. Tomorrow will be a hard day. Perhaps the hardest."

Shay mustered his courage. "Why might that be?"

Korraz studied him for a moment. "We finally meet these Iruzu. And see if they have a mind to strike a bargain. Either way, you'll most likely perish. And in ways I don't want to think of."

With that, the pirate captain smiled and walked away.

Shay watched him leave, dreading the morning.

And as the night deepened, he thought, could *swear* . . . he smelled smoke.

At dawn, Korraz sent men out to scout the trail. He also sent Timmer to retrieve the handful of guards placed at the bridge.

Flanked by a pair of hard-looking individuals, Timmer crept through the thin wilderness, his eyes flickering about for trouble. He did not know where the guards were hiding themselves, but he figured they would be lurking on this side of the fallen tree. When they arrived at the chasm, Timmer stood at the head of the crossing, hefted his sword, and looked around.

Of the men sent to watch the bridge, not one was in sight.

Puzzled, Timmer called their names and waited . . . and waited.

And waited still.

Nothing.

Worried, and mindful that savages *and* right and proper warriors might be about, Timmer slowly knelt and peered at the jungle on the other side. Those monstrous trees towered over there, hiding everything. He couldn't see a thing, but if his men were there, they would have heard or seen him.

No one appeared, however. No one made themselves known.

Scratching his head, Timmer leaned over as much as he dared and peered down at the river itself. No bodies hung upon those racks of stony teeth far below. Taking his time, he scanned up one rocky shoreline and then back the other way. Seeing nothing amiss, Timmer stood and glanced back at the two pirates below the slope.

"See anyone?" he asked.

They shook their heads.

A little uneasy, the once-gladiator backed off the bridge and took a firmer grip on his sword. Once below the slope, he scanned the wilderness to find hints as to what happened to his sentries. This wasn't the first time men had disappeared in the Sanjou. Timmer was very much aware of the few hands that had gone missing back around the village. Simply up and vanished in the night. Timmer wondered if those three hellpups he'd spotted days ago were much closer than he first suspected. It was either that, or there were savages about. Days before, the survivors of the village had sent a little hunting party to pursue them. Anticipating such a move, Timmer and his men had set up an ambush of their own and struck down most of them, sending the survivors scampering like beaten dogs.

Still, it was possible the handful that lived had regrouped and were now quietly killing off his men when they saw an opportunity.

"You think they're dead?" one of the pirates asked.

Timmer didn't answer right away. "Aye that," he finally grumbled. "They're dead. Be mindful, now. Something's on the prowl out there. Let's get back. Korraz will want to know."

He took three strides before he stopped and stared.

Not far back from the cliff trail, an ample swath of foliage had been swiped clear of the rest, revealing a tree with a snapped-off limb, the sinews raw and bright in the day. Timmer stared at that broken length, knowing full well it hadn't been like that the day before. He would have noticed it. His mind worked quickly. Missing guards. Disturbed woodland. Someone was nearby, or some*thing*. Timmer motioned for silence and listened, eyeing the Sanjou, all the way back to the cliffside. He stood that way for long moments before turning to leave.

If it was some monster, hopefully the thing had gotten its fill with the missing pirates and that was the end of it.

If it was the armored men from earlier, however, well, that was all fine with him.

Let the hellpups come to them.

Timmer would kill them all.

CHAPTER 52

With Half Tusk leading them, He-Dog and the others ran. Over a landscape that rose and fell, through bright shafts of daylight, and through long leafy hallways of shade. When they were too tired to run, they slowed to a walk. When they could no longer walk, they rested. Near a stream if they were fortunate, for a drink and a few handfuls thrown over their faces and backs. If there was no stream, they did without and pressed on when they had recovered.

Each day, they pushed themselves until nightfall, when they were too exhausted to continue. They rested just off the trail, taking turns guarding the others, until light split the edges of the dark. The group would then quickly eat and run, continuing south. Always south.

Broska desperately wanted to rescue his wife and unborn child from the slavers. But the thought of her falling into the clutches of the Iruzu was far, far worse.

Kellic was equally driven, thinking of the woman named Bright Leaf.

He-Dog wanted to get the missing Anoka back, knowing how cruel slavers could be.

By noon, the path they followed merged into another, one not hacked out of the jungle landscape.

Half Tusk readied the bow he carried, motioning for his warriors to spread out. The four Anoka behind him crouched along the trail. Broska dropped to one knee and gestured for silence from the others. Half Tusk crept ahead until a voice spoke, paralyzing them all.

"That you, Jers Snaffer? Squatting back there?"

Snaffer's eyes widened, while the rest of their group looked back at him.

"Never was one for much talk, were you?" the voice asked again.

"H-Hargan?"

"Aye that. Those bare-naked toppers with you?"

"Aye that," Snaffer replied. Broska waved off Half Tusk and his men.

"They're not going to sling those spears at us? Or loose those arrows?"

"Show yourself, asslicker," a relieved Snaffer ordered. He-Dog and the others straightened.

The Sunjan emerged from the bushes not ten strides from where Half Tusk stood. Wearing a filthy vest of chainmail and a helmet, Hargan carried his battle-axe in one fist, his smile nearly hidden beneath a heavy beard.

Chuckling, Snaffer strolled over to the man and held out his fist, which Hargan met with one of his own. A happy growl left them both as they pressed knuckles to knuckles. Snaffer even reached out and gripped the other's shoulder, giving it a welcoming shake.

"Thought you were dead, you unfit pisser," Snaffer said.

"Thought *you* were dead, you rosy dog blossom."

A smiling Kellic approached and held out his fist.

"Kellic," Hargan growled fondly. "You sad-looking nog, you. How'd you ever survive all this gurry?"

Kellic only shrugged.

"Only you?" Snaffer asked.

Hargan pointed behind him. "Found this one as well."

There, standing in the trail, was Chop, holding onto a bow.

He-Dog wasn't usually one for smiling. It caused his cheeks to ache if he did it too long. But when he saw Chop, all the hate and loathing simmering inside him dissipated like a foul wind, and a smile spread across his hard face.

They met halfway, marveling at finding each other alive, and pressed fists together.

"Thought you had perished," He-Dog said quietly.

Chop bobbed his melted head, indicating he thought he'd perished as well.

"Hey, Zuthenian," Snaffer said to Broska. "Now there are *five* Slayers. Did your dreaming elders say anything about that?"

Half Tusk said something then, taking the smile off Broska's face. "He wants to know if they'll fight with us," the Zuthenian asked.

"Fight?" Hargan asked, glancing around. "You got heads needing to be split, topper?"

"Getting him to *stop* will be the problem," Snaffer said.

Broska translated for Half Tusk, and the Anoka warrior responded. Broska nodded and told the men, "We should be moving, then."

"We're going to save their people," Snaffer said, about to point at the Anoka before frowning at his own finger. "You tell him."

"As we're moving," Broska said.

He-Dog studied his old companion, giving Chop's shoulder a fond shake. Then they lumbered after the rest.

Hargan related his jungle adventures, culminating in a mountainside fight where several fish-jawed hellions had the Nord under siege. He described with rancid mirth how he'd rescued Chop from near death and nursed the topper back to health. Together, they managed to not kill each other while the Nord mended, and only struck north when they saw smoke in the sky. Hargan freely admitted to getting lost in the Sanjou, to a point where they had to seek higher ground to get a sense of where they were. Which was right around when they stumbled across this very fresh trail. Since there was no smoke in the air anymore, Hargan and Chop followed the trail, hoping to find whoever—or whatever—had created it.

He-Dog and Kellic recalled their own harrowing escapes from the ambush and subsequent mending back at the Anoka village. Broska then told them of the Anoka elders' shared dream, the three Slayers, and the Paw.

"You're a *slayer*?" Hargan blurted, holding up a hand for pardon when the Anoka quieted him with looks. "The three of you?" he whispered. "Slayers? That's what they call you? Because a pair of unfit bastards dreamed of you killing this monster?"

No one said anything to that.

"And Shay was with you?"

Nods to that.

Hargan lapsed into thought as they hiked along. "Shame about his leg. That's unfit. Lords above." The Sunjan sized up the armored men. "Must say, it's good to see you toppers alive. Even you, He-Bitch."

He-Dog's glare softened at that, not offended in the least.

When daylight waned, the party prepared for camp, their spirits somewhat lifted because their numbers had increased by two. At dawn, they rose and again took to the trail. Just before midmorning, they arrived at a gruesome fence of skeletons, strung along both sides of the path. The horrifying spectacle stopped them, and they took a moment to study the hanging bones.

In the silence that followed, Half Tusk spoke.

"This is a warning," Broska translated. "Letting all know this is the edge of Iruzuland."

"Why are the heads missing?" Hargan asked quietly.

"They are hunters of heads," Broska replied with a shrug. "They kill you, eat you, and use your bones for any number of things. The skulls are trophies. Greatly valued among the Iruzu."

Half Tusk spoke again.

"He says to follow him," Broska said. "Stay in a line and stay low. Do not strut about so that the Iruzu can see your heads. And he says no talking from here, as the Iruzu always travel in large groups."

"Aye that, they do," Hargan whispered.

Warning given, Half Tusk led them down the path, past the skeletons. The trees towered over them, the trunks thickened. Several times Half Tusk's hand came up, halting the rest. The Anoka leader would then watch and listen for as long as it took before creeping forward a few steps and gesturing for the others to follow.

Just after noon, Half Tusk stopped the group again and pointed.

A slope of gravel and stones led to a massive fallen tree lying across a gorge.

Warning the others to stay hidden, Half Tusk crept up the incline before kneeling near the top. From there he peered at the far side. After a short reckoning, he returned to the others and spoke to Broska.

"He says he'll go first," the Zuthenian said. "His lads will wait here. With their bows, in case someone is waiting on the other side."

"I'll go first," Kellic said. "I have the shield."

Broska translated for Half Tusk, who added another thought.

"He says you go," the Zuthenian said, "and he'll follow you."

While they made their plans, He-Dog made his way to the uprooted tree, mindful of the bushes and high grass hiding the cliffs. He leaned out just a bit and peered down. "Lords above," he whispered, feeling his own blossom tighten. As he leaned back, Kellic crept across that fat length of timber spanning the chasm, sword at the ready, peeking over his raised shield. Half Tusk followed and the pair shuffled across. They made it without incident, descended, and disappeared from sight.

He-Dog and the others waited. Broska pressed a hand against his bandaged head, waiting for a signal. More time passed, and He-Dog's blossom tightened all the more. Just when he thought something was most certainly wrong, Half Tusk popped his head up over the edge of the fallen tree on the far side. He waved twice and vanished again.

Broska sent over the four Anoka warriors, one at a time, before turning to the others. "Don't look down."

He-Dog strode onto the fallen tree just wide enough for two. Although he had plenty of room, his stomach clenched with every step. It was one thing to gaze down into the chasm from the cliffs, but looking down from the tree gave him an even greater appreciation of the drop. Near the halfway point, two large birds streaked underneath the bridge and sped away. Then he was across and trudging down another slope.

The relief was a palpable thing.

In short time the others had crossed, and soon they were all gathered at the base of the slope. The trees stood farther apart on this side, and the underbrush wasn't nearly as dense. When they were ready, Half Tusk led them deeper into Iruzuland.

A swath of flattened foliage stopped the Anoka leader, however, and halted the rest.

"What is it?" He-Dog wanted to know.

Broska asked the Anoka leader as he stared at a tree with its limb ripped off. "He says it's nothing."

Which He-Dog didn't believe. "Is that a sign from the Paw?"

That widened Broska's eyes. He asked, heard the answer, and translated. "He says it cannot be. The Paw lives in the north. In the valley of the offering place."

"Except when he led it to the village," Snaffer pointed out. "Tell him."

A wary Broska did so, and the Anoka leader glared at Snaffer before giving a lengthy reply.

"He says it doesn't matter if it's the Paw or not," Broska translated. "If it *is* here, we'll know soon enough. There's nothing we can do but be careful. So he says be on guard. And be quiet. Because we are in the enemy's land . . . and death is everywhere."

Death is everywhere, He-Dog repeated in his head.

That, he believed.

CHAPTER 53

The sweat flowed. And flowed and flowed. Timmer dragged a forearm yet again across his brow as he marched through the encampment. On instinct he sought shade wherever he could get it, but the truth was there was no refuge here to escape the blistering heat. The rag around his head did little to stop the perspiration, so he took a moment to wring the thing out until the fibers creaked. Fuming, Timmer pulled on his skull cap and whispered a curse as he adjusted it. It took a moment, but he finally got it right, glaring at pirates and prisoners alike. The adult prisoners looked anywhere else but at him.

Horlo the Cruel, with his perpetual, yellow-toothed smirk in place, stood with his hands resting on the pommels of his short swords. A filthy sheen of grease and moisture coated his exposed skin, and his clothing was soaked through. He leered at a group of women bound together around one tree, their backs to the trunk.

When he heard Timmer approach, he turned to greet him.

"Unfit heat," the once-gladiator said.

"Unfit," Horlo the Cruel agreed, evil eyes twinkling.

"Where's your prisoner?"

Horlo pointed.

Two trees over sat a glaring Shay, hands bound behind a trunk, and a thin cord lashed across his neck.

Timmer's eyes flickered from him back to Horlo. "Shouldn't you be over there, then?"

"Why? He's not running off anywhere. Besides. These berries are much better to look at. Look there. Look at that one. Wouldn't you like to squeeze those fruits?"

Timmer ignored the question. "You have any water left?"

Horlo nodded. "Over there, Tim Tim. In my pack. Drink what you like."

That remark narrowed Timmer's eyes. He then noticed the women tied before him. The one Horlo watched certainly *wasn't* hard on the eyes at all, but she was clearly with child. Not that that bothered Timmer. Or Horlo, judging by his lecherous interest.

The woman avoided Timmer's gaze.

"Oh-ho, she *likes* you Tim Tim," Horlo whispered, his face blackened with dewy stubble. He stepped in close and grabbed the woman's chin, forcing her to look at them both. "She's a sweet one, eh? Easy to see that. Good teeth. Fine hair and skin. Look at her. Just look. Even here, in all this unfit madness, it's clear to see she's a dish. Why don't you take her? Hm? Here. Over there. Wherever you want. I won't say anything to Korraz."

"Take her . . . ?" Timmer asked. "I thought she held your eye?"

"We can share, Tim Tim."

"Call me 'Tim Tim' once more and I'll open you from your fat chin to your pisser."

Horlo's yellow smile faded.

"Leave her be," Timmer ordered.

A sullen Horlo took his hand off the woman and faced him. A moment later, the smirk returned. "I do what I like when Black Korraz is not here, Pit fighter. Remember that. This is not Sunja. There are no games here. No rules."

"You think there are rules in the Pit?" Timmer asked quietly. "Would you like to see . . . those rules? *My* rules?"

All the unpleasant mirth bled from Horlo's face.

"Take a breath, Horlo," Timmer told him. "And do as I say. Leave the woman alone. Your prisoner is over there."

Horlo glanced over and clearly didn't like what he saw. "What about the other women, then?"

Lords above, Timmer thought, picking up the pirate's pack. He'd spied more than a few of the crew sizing up the womenfolk. "You know what Korraz is planning," he said, finding a water skin. "They're all trade goods. And trade goods are best left untouched to keep their value. Wait until the bargain is struck and we're out of this place. If what Korraz believes is true . . . we'll all be rich as kings. Keep that in mind."

That brightened Horlo's grimy features.

Timmer held the water skin halfway to his mouth and grimaced, realizing Horlo had drunk from the same container. He tossed it back onto the pack and looked about.

A flicker of movement in the jungle caught his eye, rooting him to the spot. Suspecting the worst, his hand slid for the short sword at his waist.

"Horlo," he said in a low voice.

The big pirate turned, a question on his face.

"Prepare yourself. Lads . . ."

A sharp, slurping hiss pierced the afternoon quiet, ending in a man's grunt. A gaunt individual wearing leather armor dropped to his knees. An arrow jutted from the Ossaki pirate's neck, and blood spurted in time with his beating heart.

More hateful arrows sliced through the humid air then, their hisses driving Timmer for cover. Two more pirates dropped, clutching at the feathered shafts killing them. One lad fell hard, an arrow straight through the gullet, while grabbing at his fountaining throat.

Then . . . mayhem.

Five armored men bearing edged steel swept into the encampment. They tore through the pirates, dispatching them with slashes, stabs, or combinations of the two—some ending with explosive decapitations.

The quick deaths momentarily stunned Timmer.

But only for a moment.

"*Have at them lads,*" he roared, brandishing his short sword and dagger.

Two pirates converged on a much smaller foe wielding a pair of swords. Timmer sought to engage a hairy old bastard with a dagger and hand axe hacking up one of his men, but then his attention went back to the swordsman—who was already charging straight *at* him, leaving two Ossaki writhing on the ground in his wake.

"You—" bastard was the word Timmer didn't get a chance to say.

The once-gladiator and the swordsman met in the middle of the camp, falling sweat and blades flashing in the afternoon sun. Steel clattered off steel as both men stabbed and slashed, parrying what they could and dodging the rest. Twice the swordsman nearly had Timmer, raising the man's estimation of his foe, when a *third* slash and stab backed him up on his heels. Weren't many who could do that, and when one did it got Timmer to wondering. He held his blades straight out in front of him in a defensive pose and gauged his opponent.

His foe evaluated him in return.

The swordsman was good, *very* good, as Timmer considered himself no slouch with a blade. Truth be known, he should have killed this one already, but the swordsman eluded his traps and combinations and sought to ensnare *him*.

Not that it mattered. Timmer had a *score* of old arena tricks, and every one of them—

The swordsman feinted so fast that Timmer's reactive counterattack split only air. Leaving him woefully open to attack.

The swordsman darted low and sliced a bloody gash behind the gladiator's unprotected knee, cutting the leg to the bone. A voice-stealing bolt of agony stiffened Timmer a split instant before he collapsed, swinging as he went. The ground knocked all the breath from him, but the moment he hit, his training took control. He twisted and lashed out—slashing wide, seeking to lop off a foot or two—and to give himself a precious moment to recover.

Except his wide harrowing cut struck nothing.

Which was the last thing he glimpsed, before a hand's length of steel plunged through his eye, nailing his black skull-capped head to the ground.

He-Dog parried a slaver's blade and smashed the man's nose. A flashing sword forced He-Dog to duck, where he hacked at an unprotected knee, shearing a red length of meat off the bone. The owner shrieked and toppled as He-Dog chopped out the guts of his third victim—a bare-chested ogre of a man. That slaver slowly knelt, clutching at the spraying wreckage of his torso. Before the dead man hit the ground, He-Dog dispatched the one he'd punched a heartbeat earlier, twisting at the hips for power and taking off another head in a burst of red soup.

Brandishing his broadsword, He-Dog sought impatiently for his next opponent.

Except there was no one else.

Standing over a corpse with a red slab hanging off its leg, Chop straightened and yanked his sword from the dead man's head. A grim Snaffer and Kellic stood over unmoving heaps, looking for their next victims and finding none. A heavily breathing Hargan appeared on the far side of the encampment, bloody weapons in hand and not a scratch on him.

He-Dog turned again, completing a circle. Not one slaver stood to face him. Almost made him proud. Almost.

But then he saw Shay near the edge of the clearing.

And the unfit executioner that had a hold of him.

He-Dog fixed his attention on the exceptionally large slaver. He had backed up to the bark of a tree in a panic. Pulled against his knee was Sleeping One Leg himself. The slaver, desperately holding a curved blade to the knob of Shay's throat, was attempting to see everywhere at once. He realized the fight was over. His side had lost.

But he had one throw of the dice left.

"Throw down your steel," the slaver barked. "Let me be and I'll let this one live."

"Surrender, Horlo," Shay said from below.

Horlo rattled the prince for such insolence before plying him back, reapplying the dagger to his captive's throat. Feeling the blade at his kinkhorn—Shay grimaced and met He-Dog's gaze.

"Now!" Horlo shouted.

"There's a dozen more . . ." Shay strained, baring teeth. "*Pirates.* Took the villagers *west*."

Horrified, the pirate pressed the blade to Shay's throat. "Shut your *guts*!"

Blood beaded across the length of steel, slipping down skin to the prince's neckline. And though he felt the dreadful edge, Shay did not shut his guts.

"To a village there," Shay blurted in pain, his eyes flickering to Kellic and Snaffer as they edged closer. "There's a village."

"*Shut* your *guts*," Horlo yelled, leaning over the prince. The pirate snarled, threatening to saw through his captive's neck if the warriors came closer. "Stay back! Stay *back*, I said. And throw down your steel!"

Snaffer and Kellic halted.

He-Dog and Chop didn't move, didn't flinch, for fear of provoking the pirate any further.

Shay, however, kept right on talking. "They left . . . not long ago. You can *catch* them."

That stunned Horlo. "Saimon's black hanging fruit. Shut *up*, I said!"

Blood trickled down Shay's throat as he blurted. "*Save those people, lads!*"

Not quite ready to kill his prisoner, Horlo shook him again, a savage rattling that caused more blood to flow. The edges of the prince's tunic turned red.

Horlo stopped shaking him.

"And *kill these maggots*," Shay shouted. "*Especially this—*"

Which was about when Hargan threw his axe with one mighty grunt. The blade flashed through the air, end over end, a killer star if there ever was one, straight at Horlo.

Who looked up and saw the axe flying at his sneering face and made no attempt to defend himself. Not that he had any time to do so. Instead, he cut Shay's throat with a reflexive jerk an instant before Hargan's heavy axe crunched into the pirate's head.

Horlo fell backward, dead and gone, while the prince slumped in place.

Snaffer reached Shay's side first, to find the man lashed to the tree. He-Dog was there a beat later and cut the ropes holding him. Snaffer caught the falling prince, cradling his drooping head while pressing down on the wound. Blood leaked through his fingers, turning them red, spilling onto Shay's chest.

"Stay still," Snaffer growled softly, covering the grisly cut to the prince's neck. The dark and heavy flow, however, assured the worst.

"They took the trail," Shay slurred, his eyes glazed. "Went west. I tried to . . . delay. Not long enough. Find them, Jers. Get them . . . home. Lost my head. No more. Pirates. All pirates. Kill them all. You . . ." the prince directed at He-Dog. "You help him."

He-Dog nodded that he would.

Nearby, Hargan rooted his axe out of the pirate's face and joined the others at the prince's side.

Shay's eyes shifted to Hargan. "You kill him?"

Hargan nodded he did indeed.

"Well done," Shay breathed as more blood leaked from him. "That one . . . was a *kog*."

"Lie still, Shay," Snaffer advised.

"You're pressing . . . too hard."

"I'm trying to slow the *bleeding*, lad."

"I'm good," whispered the man they called the prince. "I'm good." He smiled, weakly, showing red teeth. A bloody bubble popped upon his lips. Then he closed his eyes, as if so very weary, and spoke no more, while the wilderness buzzed with life.

"He's done?" Hargan asked after a time.

"He's done." Snaffer slowly removed his dripping hand from the lifeless prince. Sighing, he regarded his palm before wiping it clean on the prince's tunic. Then, as an afterthought, he softly patted Shay's forehead.

He-Dog studied the dead man, remembering how he'd taken him and Chop away from Othil. They'd had their fair share of odds over the previous couple of weeks, and He-Dog certainly had his doubts, but in the end the prince spoke the truth. He was indeed good.

The growing cries of relief turned the men around.

Dozens of Anoka prisoners twisted and pulled at their bonds, attempting to free themselves. Their voices rose, growing louder and more insistent, until Half Tusk appeared and barked at them all.

The villagers shut up at once.

Half Tusk's men pulled out stone knives and started freeing the captives. Whispers and choked gasps of relief, along with thankful smiles, and more than a few wet eyes. Old folks clutched at their warriors for only as long as to say words of gratitude, then the rescuers moved on to the next knot of prisoners. A gaggle of high-pitched cries turned Jers Snaffer's head. He left the prince's side and hurried to a tree. There, he cut loose the familiar pack of three little boys and two girls—the same children that had hounded him from the moment they saw him. Snaffer freed them and as he did, they threw their arms around his hairy person and held on, one after the other, teary-eyed and weeping . . . until they nearly toppled the grizzled mercenary.

Whereupon a curious thing happened.

Well, curious to He-Dog anyway.

Instead of driving them away, the man who could ward death away with a glare did something entirely unexpected. Snaffer wrapped his big arms around as many children as he could and hugged them back. He hugged them all, holding on for long reassuring moments, letting them know he was there for them, and that they were safe.

Broska found his wife, Sunny Smiles, amid a cluster of survivors. He held her tight while she buried her face in his neck.

All around, the villagers profusely thanked the warriors freeing them before rejoining their families and friends. Kellic strode through the encampment, cutting loose anyone still tied up, embracing the many hands patting him across the back and shoulders.

The woman called Little Bloom approached He-Dog. He remembered her nursing them all back to health when they were first taken in by the Anoka. He also remembered her being much happier in those days. At that moment, however, she looked terribly sad as she walked right by him and stopped at Shay's side. There she knelt, held onto the dead man's shoulder, and lowered her head.

The display of emotion puzzled He-Dog, but he supposed she had tended to the prince the longest.

"All of you come here," Broska called out, holding onto his dear wife.

In short order, He-Dog and the others gathered around the couple.

"Sunny Smiles says the pirates sent men out in the morning," Broska informed them. "And they returned not long after. When they did, the leader, with a dozen men, took a group of Anoka and marched off farther down the trail. Smiling Rock was with them."

"Is Bright Leaf with them?" Kellic blurted.

Broska asked his wife, who nodded and spoke.

"And Gentle Rain," he translated.

"I'm going," Kellic declared.

"Wait," He-Dog said and glared at Broska.

"We're in Iruzuland," the Zuthenian said. "We could be close to their village."

Broska then spoke to an impatient Half Tusk, who gave his thoughts. Once finished, Broska turned to the mercenaries. "He says he's heard of that place but has never seen it. He says it's very dangerous. It's the rotten core—the *heart*—of the Sanjou."

He-Dog looked at him. "Numbers?"

"Possibly hundreds."

Chop, swords sheathed and holding onto a newly acquired bow, nodded agreement.

He-Dog noticed. "You've seen this place as well?" he asked.

Another nod.

"How far from here?"

Chop shook his head.

"Hundreds," a scowling He-Dog repeated, letting that hang upon the air while regarding each man in turn.

"I'm going," an anxious Kellic repeated.

"As will I," said Snaffer.

Chop nodded his intentions while Hargan simply looked eager.

"We best get moving then," He-Dog said and looked at Broska. "You and Half Tusk get this lot back over that bridge. We'll free those people and meet you there before nightfall. If we're not back by then, we're dead."

Broska regarded them all in turn. "You're doing a very great thing," he said.

He-Dog wore a doubtful expression of *We'll see*. "Get moving and don't look back."

Broska informed Half Tusk of the Slayers' intention. The Anoka leader scowled before he barked orders. Moans and pleading erupted from the five children latched onto Snaffer, and they held onto him even harder. Half Tusk said something, which silenced them, but they refused to let the old mercenary go. Half Tusk then directed a few of the able-bodied survivors to pick up bows and quivers of arrows belonging to the pirates. Once finished giving orders, he saw the children still holding onto Snaffer. He marched over to shoo them away, but the old mercenary stopped him with an upraised hand. One by one, he gently peeled the children away from himself. Though his beard hid most of his features, there was no mistaking the stern smile he presented to each little one. He patted their faces, one after the other, and pushed them toward Half Tusk.

The Anoka leader herded the youngsters off toward the other villagers. Little Bloom stood there, and she wiped her wet eyes before taking the hands of two of the children. The distressed little ones continued to speak to Snaffer, looking back with long faces while waving at him.

A squinty Jers Snaffer waved back.

Until he sensed He-Dog's eyes on him and glared back, ending the moment.

"I hope to see you again," a red-eyed Broska said while the Anoka warriors led the freed villagers away. "I hope to see *all* of you again."

Nodding, holding his wife, he followed the others. In short time, the surviving Anoka left the shredded ring of the dead. Back toward the bridge.

He-Dog and the others were already moving in the other direction.

Toward the Iruzu stronghold.

CHAPTER 54

The jungle ceiling thinned out, and sunlight shone through in broad swaths. Despite the light, the trees became increasingly crooked things, white of bark and noticeably thinner, as if the very ground sickened them. Creeping vines armed with little leafy daggers hemmed the trail. *Pretty*, Korraz thought, *to anyone else's eye*. He scuffed his boot across them every now and again, wherever the undergrowth bled onto the path. Such was his role in life, he believed. To kick the pretty things back into the shadows, especially those with a little bit of color.

"Unfit country," Korraz grumbled, slogging on despite the heat. Ahead, a few of his lads plodded along, hacking at branches leaning into the path. Anything chopped down would no doubt grow back in days, so the captain figured. He stopped and peered up at the hateful sun, visible through the jagged gaps in the Sanjou's roof. His thoughts wandered, dithering on his decision to leave one-legged Shay. *No*, it was best this way. Faster. The sight of Shay might lead the Iruzu to think of him as a less-than-worthy gift and incite them to attack. He preferred this idea. Find the Iruzu, attempt to communicate with them, and offer the handful of prisoners he had in exchange for more of the gemstones he carried with him.

Preferably stones *not* used to make a fire pit more pleasing to the eyes.

Korraz noticed Sobaba standing beside him.

"Yes, yes," the captain grated and began walking again. "How far is this place now?"

Sobaba shook his head.

"Dying Seddon above," Korraz grumbled, picking at his leggings. His soaked clothing clung to him in the most uncomfortable places. He kicked at those stringy vines with a little more fury. A short time later, the land sloped downward, allowing him a partial view of the way ahead. A rug of treetops, rolling away for perhaps three or four hundred paces, where everything appeared to drop away entirely.

Three or four hundred paces.

Saimon below. Korraz wiped his brow and glanced over his shoulder. He'd gotten ahead of Sobaba, the prisoners, and the remainder of his force. Korraz kept to the shade as the Anoka walked by, smiling at a pretty one with long hair. He also nodded at the blind one who followed her, holding onto her shoulder. *Lovely things*, he decided. Perhaps he'd made a mistake in bringing them. He didn't dwell on that, knowing he'd need to entice these Iruzu with the finer stock. If the Iruzu did indeed have the gemstones, or had knowledge of them, he would buy his share of women back in Kragland.

One of his scouts returned and waved, then pointed to the trail ahead.

"Excellent," Korraz said and started walking again.

He-Dog and the others hurried over the land while the sun blazed through the sparse shade, cooking them relentlessly. A sense of urgency filled He-Dog as he looked ahead, able to see much farther here than in other parts of the jungle. At any moment he expected to see the pirates. Boot prints marred the red dirt of the trail, scuffing the flowery vines growing along the edges.

They crossed a stream, and the land quickly descended into rugged terrain. It took them the afternoon to traverse the harsh, see-sawing grade of irregular ledges and drops, dappled in meager shade. A nightmarish staircase. The mercenaries paused at the top, gauging the steep descent. Exposed roots and loose rocks became dangerous pitfalls, seeking to pitch them forward over the next drop. He-Dog slid down one embankment and hooked a boot toe in one iron-wrought root. He flew forward, ramming his shoulder, the impact rattling his whole frame. The tree missed his face by a finger, saving him from a painful scrubbing. The trunk stopped him from going over the next jagged outcropping and crashing down onto a bed of green-scabbed rocks.

He-Dog pushed off and scrambled down the next drop, minding his footing even more, glancing at the fleeting backs of the others already strides ahead. They didn't slow for him in the least.

Down they went, drop after crooked drop, where every jarring footfall felt like a hot length of steel through their heels. Some drops were a stride down, while others were nearly two. In those cases, the slope was angled so they could slide, spraying earth, as the ground raked their armored hides. He-Dog slid down the last few earthy embankments, dust and debris clawing at him as he hit bottom. There, he rejoined the other mercenaries, their shoulders and chests heaving as they took a hateful moment to curse the hillside with the roughly hewn staircase.

They knew damn well they would have to come back this way.

Then they were running again.

"There you are," Korraz whispered with a slick smile.

A valley lay before them, unusually dire and dreadful despite having the full attention of the sun.

The pirates halted their prisoners a few strides back from a cliff, where a spotty barrier of trees and bushes provided some measure of concealment. The trail they followed dropped off at the cliff's edge before continuing after a short hop below. From there it snaked its way down, back and forth, through clumps of bushes and tall grasses, all the way to the bottom. After that, a straight walk across an open field of motley green, the color resembling the insides of a cauldron left unwashed for months.

At the center of the valley, rising like a charred crown upon an unwell scalp, was the Iruzu village.

Village? Korraz scoffed. Wasn't a village at all. Truth be known, the place resembled a fortress.

"You're going to be difficult, aren't you?" the Ossaki captain remarked, not taking his eyes off the prize.

Aye that, the stronghold seemed to project.

Sobaba cautioned his men to stay out of sight. The burly henchman joined Korraz and peered at the primitive fortress.

"They have sentries," Sobaba noted. "Patrolling the battlements."

"I see them," Korraz said. "Not so savage after all, are they?"

Sobaba shook his head while studying the defenses.

"Well . . ." the pirate captain trailed off, gauging the distance to the ground below. "A steep descent. Perhaps a hundred strides or so. It looks flat enough at the bottom, however."

Sobaba didn't comment.

"You don't like it?"

His henchman shook his head.

"No, I don't either," Korraz admitted with a sigh, and slapped at something nipping his ear. "You stay here on the cliff. Have the lads grease up this footpath here. Have a fire ready in case things turn foul. Line the ridge with archers and watch us. I'll take four lads down there with a pair of prisoners. Something to make the unfit nogs hungry." He glanced back at the captives. "Hungry enough to trade for a few stones they use to ring fire pits with."

"If you can get that idea across," Sobaba said.

Korraz smiled at that. "Doubting me, good Sobaba?"

His henchman looked away.

"I'll get the idea across. And when I do, we can bring down the others. For a little more. Then . . . the rest of them."

That turned Sobaba's head.

"Fear not," Korraz assured him. "I'm sure they have *something* of worth down there. If there's treasure to be had, we'll have it." He considered those imposing walls. "And if they don't have any stones or, worse, they're unwilling to trade, we'll leave them this lot anyway. We'll need to, to ensure our own escape. If I scream or wave, unleash hell until we get back. *If* we can get back."

Sobaba nodded.

Feeling positively predatory, Korraz strolled back to the Anoka prisoners. "It's time to be free of you, you lovely he-bitches and ladies," he said, bowing toward the blind woman and her companion. The one who could see watched him. She tried to look defiant, but her eyes kept darting toward the Iruzu fortress.

"Yes . . ." Korraz said, taking a step closer. "You know this place, don't you?"

She met his gaze, struggling to control her quivering jaw, and again, she glanced toward the stronghold.

"Aye that," he whispered. "You do know this place."

A half dozen pirates took up positions behind trees and rocks overlooking the cliff. Men leaned quivers against trunks well within reach. Two cutthroats lugged a small keg to the cliffside, just above the pathway leading down. One man broke open the container, allowing a thick flow of lamp oil to wash down the trail. The other pirate gathered up brush and tossed it onto the same path. When the keg was emptied, the man holding it chopped it apart. Once done, he began lighting a fire a few strides back.

The noisy preparations distracted Korraz from the women. He wandered back to Sobaba and the cliff.

"It's out of range of our arrows, isn't it?" he asked, as the fire took its first smoky breaths.

Turning, Sobaba nodded. "Well out of range."

That didn't please Korraz. "Savages, indeed," he said, glancing about the cliffs. "Someone knew what they were doing when they built that place." He pointed at the nearest man. "Take those two pretty ones over there. Just them. They'll be warmly received, wouldn't you say, Sobaba?"

His features screwed up, as if tasting something unpleasant, Sobaba nodded.

"Just the two of them," Korraz continued. "Easy enough to manage. Line them up here, behind me. It'll be slippery going down but—"

A frightening hiss cut him off as an arrow sank into the ear of the listening pirate. The dead man's eyes widened as he fell, toppling like a tree.

Korraz whirled, pulling steel, as a handful of warriors charged into their midst. His sword barely cleared the scabbard when one brute—wearing a vest of leather split up the middle—planted his foot squarely in the pirate captain's chest, knocking him back. Korraz tumbled backward, arms flailing until he landed flat, the impact stunning him.

That jarring fall signaled the fighting had begun in earnest. The pitched clatter of steel and grunts of men attempting very hard to kill each other broke the stillness upon the ridge.

Sobaba engaged the brute in the split leather vest, driving him back from the fallen Korraz with a series of heavy hacks. Again and again, Sobaba chopped, looking to split the attacker's head with one devastating cut. Hard, powerful blows rang out across the cliffs.

That constant ringing roused Korraz. He rolled onto his belly and crawled, crawled *hard*, powered with frantic energy while Sobaba and the others fought. Once clear, the pirate captain scrambled to his feet, swayed, and sized up the situation.

One pirate fell, clutching his throat as a gout of blood spattered the underbrush. The killer, bright-eyed and swinging a battle-axe, moved onto another. He slammed that executioner's blade into the guts of another crewmember, buckling him in two.

Nearby, another pirate managed to parry the first of two swords flashing at him, but the other blade sliced him across the face, spraying scarlet across the jungle.

One attacker wearing chainmail bashed the edge of a shield into the face of a pirate archer. When the pirate hit the ground, the chainmail killer stepped up with a broadsword and chopped into the fallen man's throat, opening it with a grisly burst. The same killer whirled, whipping his shield up to stop an arrow loosed not ten strides away. The hard clap echoed. The pirate archer cast aside his bow and yanked out a curved sword, ready to engage his moving foe.

No one attacked Korraz as he locked gazes with the one elderly Anoka man they'd taken along, huddled near a tree with two others tied to him. The old bastard's eyes widened, fearing the worst.

As you should, Korraz thought and sprinted to the tree. He grabbed the elderly man by his hair and pulled him away from the others, his skinny arms still bound to one length of rope. Snarling, Korraz stepped behind him, driving his knee into the wildman's spine.

"Stop this at once," the pirate captain roared, his blade pointed at the old man's bare belly. "*Or I'll gut him.*"

Whoever these armored killers were, they valued the lives of the Anoka. They ceased fighting within a heartbeat of the command.

One pirate, holding onto his gushing side, staggered away from the swordsman wielding two blades. The pirate crashed into the tree, stumbled, and kept on staggering, until he went over the cliff. He fell without a sound and was gone from sight.

Korraz took quick stock of his remaining forces, and the sight shocked him. Only three stood, including Sobaba, who warily eyed the ugly asslicker who had given Korraz the boot. That same asslicker backed off a step and held up a hand, signaling he wanted a word.

A word indeed, Korraz thought, and steadied himself for the next part.

The angry clash upon the ridge did not go unnoticed.

All along the west wall, Iruzu warriors perked up when they heard the fighting not far-off. Gripping spears and bows, they pounded over shivering planks, reaching the battlement heights and joining other sentries. Heads popped up between pointed ends of the palisade wall, searching for the source of the noise.

One Iruzu shouted and pointed at a thin line of smoke, just as a lifeless figure fell from the cliffs. Sunlight flashed off the shape as it bounced off two craggy points before crashing at the bottom in plain view. It did not rise again.

Only a glimpse, but the Iruzu knew what the falling figure was.

A *Hard Shell*.

The crumpled carcass at the cliff's base silenced the dozens of Iruzu watching from the battlements. Silenced them for all of two slow, comprehending heartbeats. Then a frightening blast erupted from them all. A collective explosion of sound so loud it snapped around heads and stopped work in the village behind the bulky walls. Old and young alike lifted their faces in puzzlement at the noise.

Then the Iruzu on the wall heard the yells from across the cliff. They *all* heard. Spoken in an unknown tongue, yet one familiar to them.

Hard Shells.

Hard Shells were fighting on the ridge, just beyond the walls.

After all their days of searching, *scouring* the land for these hated enemies, there they were . . . right *there.*

One Iruzu sprinted to the midpoint of the wall. Ignoring roughshod ladders, he jumped down two log platforms and landed hard on a lower shelf. Upon that stage rested seven very old, very well-*used*, instruments.

Four of them were horns, long and curved at the end, fashioned from the bones of monsters. They hung suspended above the platforms, in leather slings tied to great wooden frames. The other three instruments were massive drums, squat and fat. Scruffy mallets with heads the size of fists leaned nearby.

The one Iruzu grabbed a horn, placed the mouthpiece to his lips, and began to blow.

CHAPTER 55

The pirate shoved Smiling Rock against a tree and placed the edge of his sword at the older man's exposed belly. One hard thrust and Smiling Rock would not be smiling anymore.

He-Dog backed away from his opponent, a glaring monster who had swung his blade as hard as any beastman. He-Dog's hands and arms ached from the short but powerful exchange of strikes and counters. All along the cliff, standing amid scattered corpses, Kellic, Snaffer, Hargan, and Chop lowered their weapons.

"Excellent," the pirate said, a smile spreading across his face. "Step away, Sobaba. We're going to have a talk first."

Sobaba backed off, warily eyeing He-Dog.

"Excellent," the pirate repeated, looking pleased. "I am Black Korraz," he introduced himself with the gall of a dramatic flourish. Which ended abruptly when an earth-splitting roar exploded from the Iruzu stronghold, startling the pirate—who straightened as if he'd just sat on a pike.

The sound surprised them all, truth be known, and distracted them.

He-Dog glanced over at Sobaba, whose attention was divided between watching him and what was happening in the Iruzu stronghold. He-Dog craned his own neck to see better.

When the horn sounded.

A vast and dreadfully mournful note, blaring, *echoing* across the valley floor, sending up a dark cloud of birds that spotted the horizon. First there was only one horn but then more joined in, merging into a deep, chest-aching resonance that reached everyone on the cliffs.

The horns further distracted Korraz's attention. He stood there, mouth agape, in awe of the powerful overture coming from the fortress across the chasm. His sword faltered.

He-Dog glanced at Chop, then Hargan. The men nodded back.

Hargan dropped his battle-axe and, in one fluid motion, pulled and flung a dagger. The whistling blade sank deep into the unprotected bicep of Korraz's sword arm.

Korraz shrieked, a short squeal of pain, and jerked away, releasing Smiling Rock.

Chop rushed in to protect the elder.

He-Dog did not, however, because the heavily muscled monster called Sobaba had swung a sword at his head. They clashed, hooking their blades together, seeking to upend the other while the fighting resumed around them. Growling, Sobaba pushed He-Dog back, step by step, and He-Dog could not stop him. He relented, giving up ground to break away, and stopped a flurry of cuts punctuated by forceful grunts. He-Dog countered, slashing for a head, an arm, and finally a leg. Sobaba parried everything and answered with a straight arm thrust, looking to skewer his foe through the middle. He-Dog deflected the blade to the outside and whirled into a backhand cut—

And took Sobaba's head off at the shoulders.

The pirate crumpled, his neck fountaining red while his head bounced toward a tree.

He-Dog steadied himself and glanced around, searching for other foes.

Hargan delivered an over-the-head chop to a twitching corpse at his feet.

Snaffer yanked his hand axe out of a dead pirate's skull.

Chop stood over Korraz, both swords at the man's throat.

Kellic guarded the woman called Bright Leaf, while Gentle Rain stared on.

Of the pirates, none were standing. The dozen Anoka appeared unhurt.

Their fights finished, Snaffer and Hargan moved to the cliff, gazing at the Iruzu fortress.

He-Dog hurried to Korraz. "Free the others," he ordered Chop, and the Nordish man left to do just that.

"You killed him," a stunned Korraz whispered, a hand clamped over his bleeding arm. "You killed them *all*."

He-Dog put the point of his broadsword underneath the pirate's chin, silencing him. His face glistening with moisture, a sickly Korraz smiled.

"Aye that," He-Dog quietly agreed . . . and drove the blade home.

Korraz's eyes bulged. He released a curt yet startled gurgle, clearly expecting more of a conversation. Trouble was, He-Dog *hated* conversing with pirates.

Twisting free his blade with a dismissive yank, He-Dog left the carcass and joined Snaffer and Hargan at the cliff. Neither man said anything as they watched the Iruzu fortress. More horns blared to life, releasing long, haunting notes promising danger.

"Maybe they don't know we're here," Hargan said in a low voice, drawing dark looks from the others. "Right here, I mean."

He-Dog ignored him. "Kellic, can they walk?"

"Aye that," the mercenary said. Bright Leaf and Gentle Rain stood next to him, freed from their bonds.

Relief flared through He-Dog upon seeing Gentle Rain alive and unharmed.

"We best leave," he said, and on impulse snatched up a brass helmet with an open face. He inspected the thing before pulling it on. Snug, but good. A dead pirate's shield caught his attention then, its edge bound in iron. He fit the thing to his arm.

The nearby fire caught his attention, burning in the jagged palm of what appeared to be a shattered keg.

Snaffer pointed to the trail below. "Oil," he said.

"Oil?"

"On the trail."

He-Dog realized what the fire was for.

"Shame to waste it," Snaffer said, locking gazes with him.

He-Dog agreed. It would be a shame.

Needing no further discussion, Snaffer went to the fire. He picked up a burning slab of wood and returned to the oil-slick trail.

Where he dropped it.

Fire flashed outward and along the cliff, consuming not only the oil, but the grass and weeds along the edges. Smoke rose in lazy puffs.

He-Dog and Snaffer backed away, but Snaffer kicked the burning keg toward the nearest tree as well, spreading the flames.

"Kellic," He-Dog called out and pointed as he strode toward the trail they'd taken to reach this place. He stopped and studied the long, twisting path with irregular steps. Pebbly in places, it gradually rose, with exposed roots and rocks looking to trip the unwary. A dark, contemplative sigh left him as he beheld that hateful course, feeling tired. It had been a long run over uneven ground to find the pirates and their prisoners. It would take even longer to retreat.

Hargan walked past him, a quiver of arrows slung over one shoulder and hefting a bow once used by a pirate. Just behind him, Smiling Rock and Kellic led the rest of the freed villagers toward the trail.

Chop stopped beside He-Dog, swords sheathed and brandishing his own bow. "We don't have much time," He-Dog said to his Nordish companion.

Chop managed a mangled smile.

"Aye that," He-Dog agreed. "When do we ever . . ."

The dreary, near constant wail of the horns roused the entire Iruzu village.

Even the elders from their lodge.

The old Iruzu flinched and squinted as if the daylight had dealt them physical blows. The guards only sounded the horns at the most extreme times, and sounding *all* of them meant dire tidings indeed. All horns at once meant an impending attack, but since nothing in the Sanjou ever dared attack the Iruzu, Stone Axe suspected something else.

Hard Shells.

Only they would be brazen enough to venture so close to the Iruzu's dark nest. Leech On His Face stood by Stone Axe's side. Big Cut and Fat Belly were nearby. Heavy Foot was nowhere in sight but Long Chin caught his eye. He, too, knew what was afoot. They all did.

The elders waited for the word.

Warriors gathered at the base of the elders' hill, also roused by the horns. Hunched over and ready, they stood, brandishing weapons of stone and scorched wood—spears, clubs, and axes. Long, keen knives and rugged bows. While Stone Axe waited for the word from the outer walls, *more* warriors gathered, pouring into sight. Their thickening numbers resembled a great water, gray-green and teeming, deep and all mighty.

Relayed shouts from the wall, and the elders heard the message.

Hard Shells. Along the nearby cliffs.

Hard Shells.

Angered, Stone Axe faced the army before him. The elder raised a withered hand and spoke in a booming voice. His harsh words carried over all present, even over the blaring horns. He said this place was as sacred and mysterious as the great darkness beyond. He spoke of being unable to remember the last time when someone *not* Iruzu had gazed upon their nest.

Without fear, that was.

Without *any* fear.

Such a thought angered Stone Axe. Angered all the elders. And, he pressed upon the warriors present, it should anger *all* Iruzu. Stone Axe told them that someone had forgotten. Someone had forgotten who owned not only this part of the Sanjou, but *all* of the Sanjou. That someone would remember. Would be forced to remember. And a few unfortunates would live for torturous days *regretting* ever forgetting *at all*.

Stone Axe's voice rose, becoming a phlegmy gargle. He said if those on the cliff came to watch the Iruzu, then they should be given something to watch.

They should be given a *war*.

Hundreds screamed in agreement.

Stone Axe drew himself up and his namesake was handed to him. The Iruzu elder held the weapon over his head. He told his warriors to find those who would watch them. He told his warriors to find those who would tell others of the sights seen in Iruzuland. He told them to make the offenders disappear, as if the land had swallowed them whole, and spat out only bones. And he told them to scrub all trace of them from the land, to ensure no one else would come this way.

Then he told his army, seething at the base of the hill, that they were the strongest, the fiercest, and certainly the most *vicious* of *all* within the Sanjou.

And the visitors upon the cliffs had *forgotten* that.

Stone Axe nodded at the elder called Big Cut.

Big Cut called for the music of war.

That call was relayed back to the wall, and within moments, the harsh and ominous beating of drums began to accompany the horns.

Stone Axe faced his warriors and saw every face tighten with growing rage. Saw every set of slavering, grinding jaws. He told them to let none escape, and to collect their heads. Hunt them down, from this place to the other and beyond if they had to . . . but find them. And kill them.

The drums grew louder, as dark and powerful as approaching thunder.

And the eager voices of a thousand split the very day.

In another part of the jungle, well within Iruzuland, One Spear led his Faces of Death along a trail, not far from one of the many rivers surrounding Iruzuland. Ever since the night of their anointments and charms, they had been venturing out into the jungle, searching, only to return to the stronghold without any kills.

The spirit hags cast spells upon them each time the Faces of Death left the stronghold's walls. The drinkers worked their charms as well. Each time, One Spear could sense poisonous doubt growing. The elders didn't say anything, but their silent looks were growing increasingly impatient. No longer did the Iruzu run with them through the village when the pack ventured into the Sanjou.

One Spear knew what was coming. If he and his Faces of Death could not bring back a head soon, it was only a matter of time before the Iruzu elders chose other warriors for the task. The only thing that had delayed that decision thus far was that the killing of Iruzu had mysteriously stopped. Stopped since One Spear and his Faces of Death had begun venturing into the jungle. So that was good, at least for now.

Sensing his time growing short, One Spear knew they had to find the thing that had killed so many Iruzu, be it monster or Hard Shell. The only place they had not looked was the very place they secretly dreaded to go . . . the mountains . . . where all manner of fiend resided. Red Bone and Rock Jaw agreed—the best place for a foe to hide from the Iruzu was the very place the Iruzu despised to go.

That knowledge occupied One Spear's thoughts as he led his Faces away from the Iruzu stronghold late that morning, intending to finally travel to the mountains.

They were taking their time upon the trail when Red Bone stopped and listened. Rock Jaw did the same, meeting the questioning glare of One Spear.

The future War Pig held up a hand, demanding silence, and receiving it.

Heads turned and orange eyes widened. Drums. *Horns.* Coming from the heart of Iruzuland. Though they had not heard the horns sing in a very long time, they knew what it meant.

One Spear started running back toward the Iruzu fortress, and his Faces of Death followed.

CHAPTER 56

The deep, angry booming of drums and long, blaring notes of horns carried over the cliffs and chased the ragged, stumbling line of climbers up a rugged slope. The distant screaming bled away, overpowered by the menacing music rolling over the land, which urged the fleeing Anoka to climb faster. The troubling thing was the last couple of days had drained the villagers of their strength. And while they clearly understood what the rumbling music meant, their weakened frames could only muster half the speed needed. All too soon, a telling burn started in the back of their legs and extended to their thighs.

Smiling Rock stumbled on an exposed root and went down. Two Anoka men stopped and pulled him to his feet. With one on either side of him, they started walking again. He-Dog followed close behind, glancing back while mentally pleading for the men to hurry. On ahead, Kellic had paused after seeing the elder fall. He-Dog waved at him to keep going. Kellic did, guiding Bright Leaf and Gentle Rain along and offering a spare hand to those behind him.

Chop stopped on the other side of Smiling Rock and the two villagers. The Nordish man also watched the trail behind them. Despite the fewer trees and vegetation, the jungle gradually blotted out the cliffs, already some fifty strides behind them.

A red-faced Jers Snaffer huffed past He-Dog, as did Hargan. Carrying a bow in one hand and battle-axe in the other, the Sunjan also carried a noticeable stink of sour sweat and moldy armor.

Hargan got two strides away when one of the Anoka men helping Smiling Rock staggered and fell, tripped by another root. Taking care with his sword, He-Dog helped the man to his feet, who slumped against him. Alarmed by the lack of strength in the villager, He-Dog held on and steadied him. Together they managed a few steps until a younger woman took him.

"There you are," He-Dog said, knowing neither one understood a word. "That's it. One step after the other. Go on . . ."

He fumed at the unfit trail. Coming down this way—coming down *quietly*—had been a challenge. Awkward descents and uneven steps marred the twisting path, while roots and rocks threatened to bring them down at every step. At the time, He-Dog thought of the footpath as unfit. Now, he realized the thing would *torture* the weakened villagers. They realized it as well, muttering and shaking their heads at the difficult path ahead.

The exhausted fellow clinging to the woman staggered again. He-Dog sheathed his sword and lent an arm, hefting the man from the other side. Together, they helped the villager over the crooked knuckles of the slope.

A hundred strides away from the cliff.

A hundred and twenty.

A hundred and fifty.

The path ended in a ridge as high as one's waist, where fences of thorny bushes and trees extended on either side. Kellic and Chop hefted themselves up over that meddlesome edge and then turned to help others. Snaffer and Hargan lifted villagers up and over, into the waiting hands of the two mercenaries. Grunts of desperate, strained effort spiced the air as the survivors hauled themselves over the ridge, while hard music continued to boom from the valley behind them.

He-Dog helped the pair with him up and over the edge. Snaffer and Hargan heaved themselves up after that, slapping their weapons down before climbing. He-Dog turned from their kicking legs and glanced back at the wilderness they had just passed through. He squinted, squinted hard, looking for signs of pursuit.

Nothing. Except for the rumbling music and smoke rising above treetops.

Chop slapped his shoulder, startling him. The Nordish man beckoned with a hand and He-Dog took it. In short time, the little cliff lay behind them and the path snaked over level ground. Light flittered across the jungle floor as they hurried, a noticeable jump in their steps energized by the knowledge of being free. The flat floor helped them, and villagers and mercenaries alike encouraged and helped each other as they hurried along.

Until they sighted the next obstacle.

A punishing series of crooked and lopsided terraces, formed from dirt, rock, and cagey roots. Trees leaned in from the edges of these terraces, casting a dreary, steamy shade over it all. An ogre's staircase if ever there was one. The faces of the Anoka slackened in disbelief at the pain that lay ahead. They all did. He-Dog gawked as well, remembering coming *down* that punishing incline, remembering every stinging footfall.

At the front of the line, Kellic looked back with an expression of horrified concern.

"Keep moving," He-Dog urged. "Get them up and over."

"This will break them," Hargan said from nearby.

"What do you think the Iruzu will do?"

Scowling, Hargan slung his bow over one shoulder before helping a struggling villager.

"It *was* unfit coming down," Snaffer huffed nearby, wiping his face with a forearm. His dirty chainmail vest gleamed dully in the afternoon shade.

"I know," He-Dog said and again glanced back at the trail.

Snaffer sized up the climb. "What's worse, falling down or falling up?"

"Falling *behind*."

They shared a look of weary understanding, while the horns and war drums thundered in the distance.

"You think they'd stop with that gurry," Snaffer grumbled.

He-Dog didn't think they would. He started climbing, quickly catching up with the man and woman from earlier. Snaffer guarded the retreating column. Grabbing whatever handholds the ground offered, the group pulled themselves up that see-sawing grade. The land rose and flattened and rose again, at times ending in sinewy outcroppings as high as one's chest. In no time, fatigue gripped them. Their breathing grew deeper and harsher. The rough, uneven nature of the land bent the villagers, bleeding them of water and strength while they clutched and clawed at roots and rocks. They slowed to a determined trudge. Then a weary shuffle. Bare feet scuffed dirt. They swayed. Staggered. Grunts of straining effort rose over exhausted groans. Some of the Anoka lowered their heads and put their backs against the next earthy ridge, unable to haul themselves up. When that happened, He-Dog or one of the other mercenaries would help, gathering them up and heaving them onto the next ledge. Snaffer remained in the rear, ever vigilant, struggling to ascend, but always ensuring that the person ahead of him *stayed* ahead of him.

It was a slog. Punishing. He-Dog lowered his head and sweat dribbled off his chin. He pushed himself, carrying those who needed it, until the villagers ahead gasped and called out, alerting the others they had reached a much gentler incline. That little victory provided them all a little more life. Even better, another familiar landmark came into sight. Partially draped in shade and sunlight, a stream appeared, the same one they had splashed through earlier. With Kellic standing guard, the villagers dropped at the water's edge. There, they cupped water to their faces or dipped their heads entirely.

The smell of fresh water hooked He-Dog as well, and he knelt to drink. Next to him, the man and woman he'd been helping glanced over and offered wet and weary smiles.

"Don't drink too much," Kellic advised, standing over them all.

"I'll drink what I want," Hargan countered, rising and wiping his face. "Daresay we'll all be dead before the day is done."

Or worse, He-Dog thought, splashing his face and back. The contact brought back fleeting memories, of him and Chop in the roaring surf of Big Rock months before.

He labored to his feet and spied Hargan watching the trail behind them. "Anything?" he asked.

Hargan shook his head.

The villagers continued to drink, some lying on their bellies along the stream. The younger folk were in better shape, but the older ones, including Smiling Rock, looked ready to perish. Especially the elder. The old man hung his head, staring at his legs splayed before him, while his chest and belly rose and fell. Kellic stood over Bright Leaf and Gentle Rain, with Chop waiting behind them all.

Moments passed, every one fleeting. The anxious need to move caused He-Dog to glance around. He met Snaffer's gaze and the older man nodded sternly.

That was all he needed.

"Get them up," He-Dog said. "We have to go."

Kellic repeated that very thought in his broken Anoka, urging everyone to stand. Some rose on steadier legs than others, but no one lingered or complained. Smiling Rock even whispered a few words with a reassuring smile when Hargan helped him to his feet. With Kellic and Chop at the front, the group started trudging again. The short rest and level land helped, as the villagers were able to move a little faster, their strides a little longer.

They could not move fast enough for He-Dog, nor his rising sense that if they didn't flee this place soon, they were going to perish here.

Two hundred and fifty paces from the cliffs, one of the older men tripped and fell. Two women pulled him to his feet, but the earlier spurt of vigor was gone. The pace became a crawl. He-Dog walked alongside an exhausted man, his arms around the shoulders of two women. They were doing most of the walking for him and appeared close to dropping themselves. Perspiration coated the older man's wincing face. If one fell, they would pull the others down, and none would get back up.

Lords above, He-Dog swore inwardly. "You have to hurry," he urged them.

"They all have to hurry," Hargan muttered a few strides ahead, one arm supporting Smiling Rock.

"Tell them to hurry, Kellic," He-Dog repeated, edging on shouting. He glanced back again at Snaffer, who was walking backward and guarding their escape. Beyond him, however, nothing but jungle.

The sight offered little comfort. He-Dog's guts rolled and twisted, warning him matters were going to change very soon. Perhaps at any moment. The climb had been too much for the villagers. They had rested for too long, and yet, not long enough.

Kellic spoke again and Bright Leaf rebuked him, ending with a "No, no, Kellic no."

No, no, indeed. *Lords Above.*

"They can't walk any faster," Kellic translated. "They're falling over as it is."

"They know what's behind us?" He-Dog grated.

"They know."

He-Dog rubbed at one cheek, realizing his own pace had *halved* while walking alongside the group. "It's not good enough."

"They can't do any better, He-Dog."

"The Iruzu are *coming*, Kellic."

"They *know* the Iruzu are coming. I hear them say 'Iruzu' every now and again."

That knotted He-Dog's brow, worrying him all the more. If *fear* couldn't move them any faster, then they truly had nothing left. He twisted this way and that, eyeing their progress, and suddenly knew. Knew what had to be done. Snaffer caught his eye and slowly shook his sweat-soaked head of hair.

He-Dog made his decision. "Kellic," he said, "Get them to the bridge. I'll wait here for whatever's coming."

Orders received, Kellic spared him a fleeting look before turning away.

The words slowed the other mercenaries to a stop. Lines of perspiration covered their faces as they realized what was happening, understanding what He-Dog was going to do.

"I'll stand with you," Snaffer said, his mouth a grim line in his wet beard.

A heartbeat later Hargan unhooked himself from Smiling Rock. The hardened mercenary patted the old man on the shoulder and left him in the care of another. The elder said something before the villager led him away.

Chop split from the group, making his intentions known, but He-Dog waved him off. "You stay with them," he ordered.

Chop didn't move.

"Get them back to the bridge," He-Dog charged his Nordish friend. "They'll need more than just Kellic."

Clearly having his own thoughts on the matter, Chop reluctantly turned back to the Anoka.

"You trained that one well enough," Hargan observed.

He-Dog frowned at that as the little group hobbled away much too slowly. Sunlight and shadow played across their retreating backs, but they didn't look back once. Which was good, he thought, as he heard the deep notes of Iruzu music echoing through the wilderness. When the last person in the column had disappeared around a tree, He-Dog regarded his two companions. Snaffer met his narrowed eyes and, on some unspoken word, all three checked on the path behind them.

A drooping natural corridor of wood and foliage. Empty of life.

"How long do we have?" Hargan asked.

"Not long," He-Dog said, craning his neck. "If they truly want us."

"Oh, they want us," Snaffer said.

"Then they would have to get around the fire. Scale the cliffs by other ways. All of that takes time. But they're fresh."

"And without armor," Snaffer said.

"And not guarding people near death," Hargan scowled.

That quieted them all, and for a moment, they stood there and simply watched the trail.

After a deep sigh, Hargan leaned against a nearby tree, intending to rest while he could. He sniffed and pulled out a water skin. He fumbled with the cork and puzzled over what to do with it before tossing it away. He drank a few swallows and finished with a grimace. "Too warm," the Sunjan complained as he offered the skin to Snaffer. "Like drinking from Saimon's pisspot."

Snaffer scowled at that.

"It *is*, I tell you," Hargan insisted.

Snaffer drank, his scowl deepening as it went down.

"See?"

"Better warm than none at all," Snaffer said.

He-Dog took the skin next and downed a few mouthfuls. Truth be known, it *was* warm. The stream had been better. When he finished, he handed it back to Hargan. They shared the remaining water between them, resting, ever watchful, as the moments bled away.

"Warm water," Snaffer scoffed. "How'd you live this long, anyway?"

"Wasn't easy," Hargan admitted.

"You probably feasted on your own shite."

"Bit harsh."

"What did you eat, then?"

Hargan half shrugged. "Birds. Crawlers. Monkeys."

Snaffer blurted a chuckle. "Monkeys?"

"Aye that."

"You ate monkeys?"

"Red-arsed ones. Snakes as well. When we could find them."

"Unfit," Snaffer remarked, but not unkindly. Hargan didn't seem to mind.

"What did *you* eat then?" the Sunjan asked back.

Snaffer smirked and glanced at He-Dog. "What didn't we eat?"

"Unfit, was it?" Hargan asked.

Snaffer didn't answer at once, remembering. "Unfit *good*," he rumbled with a nod.

"Unfit good," He-Dog agreed. "Kings wouldn't have eaten so good."

"Aye that," Snaffer said thoughtfully.

He-Dog glanced in the direction taken by Kellic, Chop, and the villagers. How long had they been gone? Not long enough, he feared, and not moving near fast enough. Not for him.

Hargan downed the last mouthful from his skin. "That's done," he said, making a face. He looked around, wondering where to throw the thing. In the end he stuffed it inside his chainmail.

"Foul-smelling topper," Snaffer told him.

Hargan was about to speak when He-Dog crouched and pointed.

There.

Fluttering movement through the light and leaves, growing in numbers. A serpentine line of flickering shapes, bent low and bobbing, rustling bushes as they charged along the trail. The sound of their approach failed to reach the waiting mercenaries, but that would change. Not nearly as many as He-Dog expected, however. The fire on the trail must have deterred them, he reasoned, and forced them to use other ways up the cliff.

He-Dog slipped behind a tree and freed his broadsword.

Snaffer got out of sight on the other side and hunched behind a tree. Hargan ducked behind tall bushes.

He-Dog pressed a shoulder against the white bark and waited, meeting Snaffer's calm but deadly gaze across the way. Drums and horns pounded out their heavy tune, matching the thumping in the chests of the three men. Another sound soon perked their ears.

That of bare feet slapping dirt.

Then the grunts and ragged breathing of creatures in a foot race, and the harsh whispers of bushes as they crashed through them. The Iruzu hurried along, heedless of their noise, perhaps sensing their quarry was close. The creatures' low, foul mutterings soon reached the mercenaries—hateful, frightening gibberish, suggesting a keen eagerness to get to killing. Closer they came, their angry voices even more distinct while their footfalls seemed to thunder, drowning out the far-off music that continued to rattle the heavens. He-Dog eased back a step and noticed the now-murderous expression on Jers Snaffer's face as he hefted his dagger and hand axe.

And somewhere in that growing rush of approaching enemies, in that hateful murmur . . . He-Dog heard a voice. At the back of his head. A mere whisper, but one he knew well enough.

Come on then, Balless said.

That almost got He-Dog smiling. Almost.

The noise of the nearing charge swelled. Branches snapped. The footfalls grew louder.

He-Dog leaned back as the first Iruzu ran past them, its mouth open and black fangs glistening. Two more ran by, then a stream of hunched figures with livid, gray-green expressions and carrying all manner of weapons.

At least ten sprinted past He-Dog before he whipped around the tree and took the head off the first victim in a starburst of gore. The headless body stumbled knees-first to the ground before toppling while He-Dog lashed out at the next fishman. He severed a weapon arm in an explosion of rancid blood. Bashed his shield into a screaming face, shattering teeth and flattening features. He ducked low before slashing up, getting the whole strength of his arm behind the cut, and opened a torso from pisser to chin in a black spray. Iruzu fell as spears flashed by, missing He-Dog's ducking head. He pressed forward, slashing one fishman from hip to shoulder and nearly chopping off another head entirely, before shattering a knee with a heavy kick. A stone axe beat against He-Dog's shield before he braced it with his shoulder, then rammed it forward. A head snapped back. Teeth drizzled the air. He-Dog slashed and chopped, inflicting gruesome cuts in his foes, leaving them falling to their knees or gasping on their sides.

As quickly as he struck, He-Dog retreated around a tree. He glimpsed Snaffer and Hargan wearing sleeves of blood from plying their trade, hewing into the Iruzu and releasing great inky clouds of carnage. They carved a hard toll in that vanguard force, bashing aside primitive weapons before smashing faces, splitting skulls, and slicing open guts with grim efficiency.

A pair of Iruzu pursued He-Dog.

He dropped under a swinging club and sheared a leg off the first attacker, then parried a spear before cutting the second from chest to chin. A spin later, he stabbed the one-legged screamer through the chest and yanked his blade free.

Screaming. So much screaming.

He-Dog rushed to Snaffer, who faced three to Hargan's one. As He-Dog closed in, Snaffer parried and parried again before sinking his axe between the eyes of one Iruzu an instant before the *second* fishman tackled the old mercenary around the waist. Both went down. The third moved in, jaws snapping and orange eyes wide, rearing back a spiked club and none too concerned about whose skull he bashed in.

He-Dog stabbed that one through the middle, taking the ferocious little maggot off his feet. The Iruzu sagged, dragging the broadsword with him. He-Dog put a boot to the corpse and yanked the weapon free.

Snaffer rose, staggered, and kicked the head of his dead tackler.

Breathing hard, they turned this way and that, in search of other threats. Seeing none, they regarded each other's gore-spattered forms before listening to the growing noise.

Iruzu.

Scores of them, closing in from the sides, *pouring* through the wilderness in a great gush. A monstrous wave of bodies crashed through the Sanjou while screaming their throats raw.

"*Run maggots,*" Hargan shouted, already doing exactly that.

He-Dog ran, with a huffing Snaffer a pace behind him.

Daylight rippled as the three mercenaries fled along the trail, every stride a hard connection with the earth. Sweat left their faces in sparkling drops. The ground rose and dropped as the path twisted and turned. The screaming followed them, a near constant thing, a livid wall of rage growing steadily louder. He-Dog didn't look back. Didn't *want* to look back. He'd heard all he needed to know.

A steep yet familiar embankment of dirt and jungle growth appeared before them some three or four strides high. A well-trodden ridge of hardpacked earth lay heaped against it in a diagonal slant, all the way to the top. Knots of thick roots bulged through that wall, extending over the ramp. Tall trees leaned over it all, dappling everything in light and shadow. He-Dog remembered ramming his shoulder into one of those trees. He wondered how far ahead Kellic and Chop were with the villagers.

The three mercenaries scrambled up the embankment.

Hargan gained the high ground first, his legs flashing by He-Dog's head as he thundered up the natural ramp. He joined Hargan in time to see Snaffer chug up that hardpacked incline, his silver head bobbing. A wide front of Iruzu pursued no more than forty strides behind the He-Dog, and they were closing in fast. They were fresher, wore no armor, and were powered by a potent mixture of hate and rage and orange-eyed insanity.

Snaffer lumbered to the top of the embankment, gasping all the way. He-Dog moved past him, shield up, and blocked the ramp. If they wanted to breach the ridge, they would have to kill He-Dog first.

Hargan had already dumped his quiver and axe. He lifted his bow and nocked an arrow as he did so.

The Iruzu crashed toward them.

"You good with one of those?" He-Dog shouted.

"Good enough to send one up your pisser, maggot."

"Aim that way," Snaffer puffed while bent over.

"Mind your own steel, topper," Hargan told him. *"And watch my sorcery."*

Energized by seeing their enemies, the Iruzu started to truly holler, trampling the underbrush as they charged the ridge.

He-Dog licked his lips, glancing from the charging mass to Hargan.

Who worked sorcery indeed.

The first fishman died with an arrow jutting from his chest. The thing fell and tripped the three Iruzu behind him.

The second arrow ripped through a fishman's throat, snapping the head back in a spurt of ink.

A third arrow punched through a sickly chest, blasting the creature off his feet as if fish-hooked from behind.

The fourth and fifth shafts dropped their victims, further upending the charge.

By that time, the bulk of the Iruzu forces had reached the ramp.

Hargan released his final arrow not two strides away into a shrieking face, silencing the creature with a gooselike *urk*!

Whereupon the Sunjan threw down his bow and snatched up his battle-axe.

"Kill them, lads," Hargan roared over the rabid screaming.

Iruzu stormed up the ramp, char-tipped spears lowered—toward the heavy, sludge-stained door that was He-Dog. The rest of the attacking fishmen launched themselves at the dirt wall and the mercenaries waiting for them there.

And the butchery began in earnest.

He-Dog killed three in rapid succession, blocking spears and countering, stabbing, and chopping down anything coming up the ramp. The dead toppled. A severed arm fell. An Iruzu spun away with his face cleaved apart and the contents spilling. Another dropped with his chest split apart to the grisly bone. One fishman stabbed a spear at He-Dog's feet, but he stomped on the weapon and broke it in two. He adjusted his footing before slashing out a midsection and shield-bashing a fanged mouth. More bodies fell from the ramp, clutching at horrific wounds and screaming a different song. Oily blood misted the steamy air. Arrows sped by, hitting He-Dog's shield or hissing past to clatter off rocks or trees. A few spears bounced off his shield, jarring him, twisting him one way, but failing to pierce the barrier. Someone threw a stone axe at him, which he barely ducked.

Nearby, Hargan danced and dodged spears and axes lashing at him from below, seeking his lower bits. He shattered skulls, split faces, and hewed off hands reaching for holds. If a head was close enough, he greeted it with a hard boot, pitching the thing back as if it were yanked from behind.

Snaffer worked beside him, smashing skulls aside with heavy chops of his axe or bone-splitting slashes from his dagger.

Unable to breach He-Dog at the ramp or bypass the rising mounds of corpses, the Iruzu sought to flank the defenders by climbing up the ends of the embankment. Two fishmen fell backward, clutching at frayed roots that had snapped free from the ground. Others leapt to the top, heaved upward by the Iruzu below. When they landed, Snaffer raced to meet them—cutting and stabbing and striking down whatever Hargan could not. The creatures struck back with their spears and swiped at the men's legs with clubs and axes but failed to take down any of the mercenaries.

At the top of the ramp, He-Dog continued to battle.

One at a time, the Iruzu tried to reach the Slayer over an ever-growing pile of dead. He evaded a spear's thrust for his legs and countered by lopping off the wielder's hand. That screamer fell, only to be replaced by another swinging an axe. He-Dog blocked the blow with his shield and sliced a deep line across the attacker's midsection. A hunched fishman with glaring orange eyes chopped for He-Dog's head and missed. The Slayer's answering slash sent the creature sprawling from the ramp. Ribbons of carnage spewed and spattered with every exchange, but the Iruzu did not relent. Did not retreat. And certainly did not surrender. In ones and twos, they continued to attack, and He-Dog killed them all in great arcs of blood. He stopped a club on his shield, hacked into the owner's neck, and shoved the dead thing off his sword. Staggering back a step, he planted his feet and straightened for the next attacker.

Except there were no more to face him.

Amid the far-off din of drums and horns, underneath dusty sunbeams and wide cloaks of shadow, a storm's wreckage of the freshly dead lay at their feet, strewn about the ramp and the jungle floor below. Smashed and chopped corpses lay in piles at the base of the embankment, and, for a time, the three mercenaries stood and glared at the stunning massacre they'd wrought.

An annoyed Hargan pawed at his face, wiping off the bloody filth coating it.

Equally covered in spent mayhem, a spattered Jers Snaffer shook his axe and dagger, sending speckles flying. Hargan stooped and picked up his quiver and bow.

More screaming jerked their heads up, coming from farther down the trail.

Breathing heavily, sweat stinging his eyes, He-Dog dragged a dripping forearm across his nose and looked about.

"*Move*, toppers," Hargan said, skipping into a full retreat.

A winded Snaffer lumbered after him.

He-Dog backed away, lingering, before turning into a full run.

They bounded up over the land, rushing along the trampled path, leaving the long, punishing slope behind them. The ground evened out, and their speed increased because of it, much to He-Dog's relief.

A hissing arrow sped through the space between him and Snaffer.

Another one struck a tree with a loud *pak* and bounced away.

A spear plunged into the ground, its long shaft quivering from the impact.

He-Dog spied movement at the very edge of his sight. Coming in on both sides, drawn to the killing.

More Iruzu.

An unwanted chill gripped He-Dog. The savages had seen them on the ridge overlooking the stronghold. A sizeable force had left that place to pursue them, spilling forth like the rotten gruel from a tipped cauldron. Not all the Iruzu could climb so narrow a trail leading to the cliffs, however, especially one on fire, as the mercenaries had left it. Such an undertaking would take time. So the Iruzu had found other ways to the top of the ridge. From there they spread out, searching, covering as much ground as possible.

Or so He-Dog figured.

He realized all that screaming from the Iruzu they'd just killed had alerted *other* Iruzu spread throughout the wilderness. And now those packs were closing in, like a huge fist around a pebble.

He lowered his head and ran.

CHAPTER 57

Chop, Kellic, and the little group of Anoka hurried through the unforgiving wilderness of Iruzuland. Kellic stayed at Bright Leaf's side as she guided Gentle Rain along the trail. Chop paced alongside the sightless woman, watching not only her but the rest of the fleeing villagers. Treated poorly, barely fed, and weak from the long journey, they hobbled along at their best speed, which wasn't nearly fast enough. At one point, Gentle Rain stumbled, and Chop immediately arrested her fall. Bright Leaf stepped in and together they righted the woman and got her moving again.

Smiling Rock grunted a few words, and his people lowered their heads and redoubled their efforts to outpace the horrors behind them. The drums and horns played on, adding more weight to the already heavy sense of urgency. No one spoke, and the sounds of their ragged breathing interspersed with that of their feet marching over hard ground.

It seemed they'd only been walking for a very short time when the sounds of battle erupted behind them.

Kellic exchanged looks with Chop.

They had so much farther to go.

The haunting sounds of drums and horns stopped Half Tusk upon reaching the fallen tree spanning the chasm. He turned, bow in hand, and studied the jungle for long, lingering moments. Long enough for his warriors—who were helping the rest of the Anoka over the bridge—to notice.

Broska also noticed, and once he had his wife safely across, he went back to where the roots of the fallen tree stabbed into the air like the rays of an evil sun. There he waited for Half Tusk to turn around. The Anoka warrior eventually did and strode with purpose across the mighty length of fallen wood.

When he got close enough, Broska asked him what was wrong.

Half Tusk told him to listen.

Broska did just that and the Zuthenian's mouth hung open in puzzlement. The distant noise caught the attention of the warriors nearby, who peered back at Iruzuland with expressions of dawning horror.

His bow swinging at his side, Half Tusk marched down the slope to where the exhausted Anoka had stopped to rest. Broska followed him. Half Tusk spoke to his people, his words lifting their tired heads. He told them to gather up whatever dry brush they could find, whatever could burn. *Anything* that could burn. He called upon whoever was able, whoever was strong enough, to bring that brush to the bridge. Half Tusk then ordered his warriors to watch the far side. He told them to have their bows ready.

In the flurry of activity that followed, the four Anoka warriors took up positions along the cliff, while the rest of the survivors gathered dead brush and branches.

Whatever they could find. Whatever would burn.

Understanding they could not outrun the unarmored and, thus, much faster Iruzu, He-Dog, Snaffer, and Hargan stopped in a shaded area for a few settling breaths before it was time to greet their pursuers.

Then . . . war.

One swing of the battle-axe took an Iruzu's head off in a gout of watery sludge. Hargan backed up, inviting the next attackers—wide-eyed and shrieking loud enough to tighten one's blossom. The Sunjan parried a spiked club, booted one Iruzu square in the chest to knock him back, and swept an arm off in a burst of blood. One hard cut to the chin silenced another screamer and sent a fanged jawbone spiraling, end over end, trailing streamers.

The Sunjan then whirled and chopped into the guts of one unfit bastard looking to take his head.

Which was a mistake.

The Iruzu, frenzied to a point of madness, grabbed the axe-head buried deep in him—while more Iruzu charged the mercenary.

But then Jers Snaffer was there, his wild mass of silver hair soaked to his scalp. Hand axe and dagger gleamed as he ripped through mottled warriors and left them dead. One Iruzu stabbed a spear into Snaffer's lower back. The wooden shaft snapped off from the powerful blow as Snaffer straightened in pain. His armor saved him, but the strength behind the impact stiffened him to his heels.

Whereupon He-Dog slashed the Iruzu down the length of its spine, cleaving meat and bone. No sooner did the fishman drop than the next onslaught of attackers rushed in. He-Dog freed his blade and met the monsters, leaving Snaffer a chance to recover—except there was *no* time to recover, as several Iruzu charged for him.

A grimacing Snaffer staggered, slowed by the spear thrust and shaking off the effects. His arms and legs burned, and every breath left him wanting more. This day had certainly been a test, from the long run to the valley's cliffs and now the fighting retreat to the bridge. Snaffer was being right and proper challenged, perhaps more than any other time in his long, miserable life in the trade.

To make matters worse, the Iruzu had the battle-madness like none other he'd ever encountered.

But he wouldn't let them take the last of the Anoka people. Not one. And certainly not the handful of youngsters he once considered a nuisance. Youngsters he still felt in his arms. And for the memory of the Spider Hag, who fed him by the river when he was at his weakest.

The Iruzu rushed in.

The three mercenaries chopped and slashed, thrust and punched. Standing in a rough triangle, their formation stretched and shook and wavered . . . but never broke. They met mad Iruzu ferocity and numbers with a vicious mastery of weapons. The men cut down fishmen *hard*, delivering one death blow after another, transitioning from one strike into the next. Black blood spattered. Iruzu dropped like rainfall.

And yet the Iruzu continued to hurl themselves at the three mercenaries.

Then a stone axe crashed into Hargan's helmet, the connection frightful and flaring sparks. He wobbled for a heartbeat before a heap of brutes piled onto him, taking him down—where he disappeared from sight.

Two fishmen slammed Snaffer against a tree while a third crunched a heavy club into the older warrior's armored stomach.

A stone axe rattled off He-Dog's shield, the blow numbing his arm to the shoulder. He ducked and removed the fishman's leg at the knee in a burst of oily juice. The moment the creature hit the ground He-Dog stomped on its throat. A club slammed into his spine with all the force of a rolling boulder, driving him to his knees. He half turned when a spear buckled against his chest, unable to pierce the tough leather vest taken from the armory of Foust ages ago. The charred tip lanced underneath his shield arm, drawing a bright line along the tender flesh of his inner bicep. That blow twisted He-Dog the *other* way, where he cut a leg out from the attacking spearman. He twisted, whipping up his shield in time to stop a stone axe descending for his head. The weapon clacked off the barrier, and the fishman went with it, tripping in the dead meat littering the ground. The axe struck hard earth, and the owner stumbled, struggling for balance.

He-Dog shoved a length of steel through its face.

Both toppled, but He-Dog pushed clear of the mess and regained his feet. Things rolled underfoot, and he lurched until getting both his boots on firm ground. He leaned to his left, still shaken, but ready to face another rush.

When he realized very little was moving.

Hargan, resembling an oil-slicked hellion, pushed and kicked corpses off him. He eventually rose, wavering, but didn't fall. His helmet was missing, as was his left ear, where blood stemmed from the meaty nub left dangling. A welt the size of an egg blossomed over his left eye, disfiguring his head, while his cheek underneath his right eye had been split open to the red and drooling bone.

Not far from him, a battered and bleeding Jers Snaffer stooped and wearily extracted his axe from a pile of butchered carcasses. Like Hargan, it was a wonder the man was still alive. A grisly sheen of blood and teeth fragments covered him from neck to waist, drenching his armor. Gore soaked and colored Snaffer's once silver hair, as if he'd been dipped in a river of carnage. Both eyes were swollen and blackened. Cuts slashed his cheeks. Even his beard was dripping. The mercenary, however, took in great settling breaths, spat a gob of scarlet, and gamely retrieved his dagger. He straightened with a groan, wobbled but didn't fall over, and nodded at his companions.

"They're shite," Hargan muttered with a spotty smile.

"Flecks of shite," Snaffer growled.

"Blown-off cow kisses," He-Dog finished.

They shared tired smiles at that.

"You have any of that pisswater left?" Snaffer asked.

"Drank it all."

Snaffer nodded in disappointment, looking very much like he needed a drink.

He-Dog wished for a sip himself.

Then they heard it.

No Iruzu were visible in the nearby jungle, but they were crashing through the wilderness, their yells growing in strength.

"Can you run?" He-Dog asked of Snaffer.

"Aye that."

Hargan nodded as well.

So the three lumbered away, leaving another steaming massacre behind them. Their staggering gait smoothed into a stiff march. The trail blurred by, and every footfall was a jolt that raced up He-Dog's legs. Blood seeped from his inner arm, the wound stinging fiercely. Blood fell from them all, dappling the land. Snaffer labored along, clearly straining. Every so often he would slow and put fists to knees, spit a meaty gob at the ground, and resume walking. Hargan resembled a freshly animated corpse, pounded upon and dripping. And He-Dog, well, he moved, stiffly, and bled, but these were minor compared to his back, which dearly ached. The club to his spine had left its pulsating mark despite his armor, flaring with every step from his waist to his shoulders.

The wilderness thinned out and the three plodded to a stop in the encampment littered with dead pirates.

Ahead of them was a sight that startled them all.

For there, just disappearing into the foliage, were two Anoka villagers and a leather-armored swordsman guarding their retreat. Chop had both blades out while backing away.

Then they were gone.

"Saimon's black hanging fruit," Hargan swore before glancing behind him. "Only *this* far?"

"They'll be butchered," Snaffer panted, "long before they reach the bridge."

"They will *not*," He-Dog swore. "This way. And leave a trail."

With a startling yell, he ran into the brush, hacking at bushes so that the Iruzu would have no trouble finding them. Hargan and Snaffer trudged after him, cutting up the wilderness as they went. They trampled the undergrowth, moving away from the bridge. Around trees and through walls of leafy green they went, leaving a clear path. At one point, Hargan got ahead to do the brunt of the work, and He-Dog followed.

He-Dog dropped back, resting his arms a bit when, on impulse, he looked over his shoulder.

Red-faced and wincing, Snaffer had slowed to a shuffle.

"Hargan," He-Dog panted, halting the other mercenary. They doubled back and regrouped around the faltering warrior, who halted with his fists on his knees.

"No?" He-Dog asked.

Unable to speak, Snaffer shook his head and spat a grape-sized gob of blood.

"Well, then we walk," Hargan said, patting the other's back.

"You go on," Snaffer said.

"Without you, old man? I don't think so."

"Remember the youngsters," He-Dog said, remembering them himself.

That got a pained glare. A few heartbeats later, Snaffer nodded, straightened, and they started walking once again.

Excited shouts then, farther away in the jungle behind them. Someone had just discovered the last bunch of fishman carcasses.

"You lads go," Snaffer puffed out. "I'm nearly done."

"Shaddup, Jers Snaffer," He-Dog warned in a tired voice.

"You perished long ago," Hargan added, eyeing the jungle. "Lords know what you are now."

"He's a *Slayer*," He-Dog growled, glancing this way and that.

"Aye that, he is," the Sunjan agreed. "A right and proper one. Grage would say the very same."

"A Slayer," Snaffer rumbled with a note of fondness, and released a rare, if very tired, smile.

"Slayers don't die," He-Dog said.

"They just butcher everything else," Hargan added, still looking around.

Thriving thickets brushed their legs as they continued walking. "Slow, now," He-Dog whispered, leading them along.

"Slow is just his speed," Hargan said.

"Mind yourself, kog," Snaffer warned, causing the others to share knowing looks.

So they marched, treading lightly, slowly regaining their strength.

He-Dog noticed it first.

All the screaming and yelling had stopped. The distant music continued, heavy harmonies rolling over the land, but the pursuing Iruzu had ceased their yammering. The feral things had discovered the pirate camp. If so, it would distract them for a few moments.

He-Dog placed a shoulder to a tree and motioned for the others to get out of sight. They did, nearly submerging themselves in the surrounding thickets.

He-Dog pointed his sword.

There, at the absolute edge of sight, some thirty strides ahead, was an Iruzu warrior. Spear in hand and hunched over, the creature actively hunted for signs.

He-Dog squinted in disapproval as four more of the fishmen came into view, spread out in a line, partially obscured by foliage.

Then easily a dozen, blocking the way to the south.

Not that He-Dog wanted to really go that way, it was simply *away* from the villagers. He adjusted his helmet and pointed northeast. A hunched Hargan took the lead, and He-Dog and Snaffer followed. Things snapped and crunched underfoot as they crept along, all but hidden in the underbrush. Hargan eventually placed his back against a tree, bringing the others to a stop. The Sunjan, filthy and cringing, pointed ahead before holding up a hand.

Iruzu. Just out of sight.

Then the whispery crinkle of things moving through the vegetation perked He-Dog's ears—many things charging toward them.

Hargan pressed his back to the tree while He-Dog and Snaffer hid behind others.

The rush grew louder.

Hargan lifted his axe and briefly met the eyes of He-Dog across the way.

When the first Iruzu rounded the tree, the three mercenaries struck.

And struck without mercy.

He-Dog decapitated one and slashed open a second before the headless corpse hit the ground. He bashed a face and took an arm off, changed foes and stabbed another through the guts. A gray-green attacker brought a stone axe down, the blunt edges whistling in its descent—and it exploded against He-Dog's shield. His arm flaring numbness, He-Dog drove forward, smashing shield and shoulder into his foe and knocking the thing flat. Legs tripped him, however, and he fell to his knees. A shadow loomed over him. He looked up and glimpsed a blur of stone as its slab edge slammed into the side of his head. There was an explosion of force and sound, a deafening gong that ripped through his skull, tearing the helmet off him. Daylight flashed as He-Dog crumpled, the jungle suddenly lopsided. Figures cried out and struggled, darts of shadows and flickers of movement.

He lay flat on his spine and blinked.

Above him, one Iruzu, orange eyes blazing, poised to skewer him through the middle. The creature hefted a spear when a hand axe crunched into the thing's profile, freezing the hate on his face as he toppled.

Snaffer retrieved his axe and stood over He-Dog. "Are you dead?" the man demanded.

"No," he replied weakly.

He-Dog wasn't right, however. One side of his face felt branded, as if hammered by hot iron. His helmet had saved his skull, but blood coated his palm where he felt the spot. And the sound of a great surf crashed in his ear.

Snaffer held out his hand. He-Dog took it, hauling himself to his feet. Together, they stumbled into a run where the land seemed to pitch and roll. They followed

Hargan, and the sound of the great surf sharpened in He-Dog's ears, becoming the collective screams of hundreds, much closer than expected.

No longer concerned with stealth of any kind, the three men ran.

With every step, He-Dog's senses returned. His head cleared and his balance steadied. They plowed through patches and thickets, eventually swinging to their left. They charged over a landscape clear of enemies, arcing north, and finally crossing the trail they'd followed earlier. From there the three lumbered along, pushing themselves, their limbs and chests burning, calling on reserves of strength they didn't know they had. At times they glanced back, expecting to see their hunters upon the trail.

Amid the horns and drums and the constant screaming of their pursuers, as sweat fell with every step, and as that terrible weariness grew in their arms and legs . . . He-Dog and his companions plodded forward.

CHAPTER 58

A glaring Half Tusk stood at the head of the bridge on the Iruzuland side, gripping his bow. He watched the jungle while, behind him, his people heaped brush along the massive length of wood spanning the chasm. Half Tusk urged them to work faster as he kept a wary eye on the trail leading into the depths of Iruzuland.

Two concerns occupied his mind.

The first was the tree beneath his bare feet. Some trees, like the one he stood upon, did not burn so quickly despite being dead for so long. A stubborn few would not burn at all. Twice he stomped on the old wood, feeling no give beneath his feet. Not even a tremble, which told him the years had not weakened it. That worried him, and he tried hard to hide his worry from his people. He thought the tree would burn, *hoped* it would, at least long enough to destroy it, so that none of the Iruzu would ever be able to use it again.

That was his first worry.

Knowing when to *start* the fire was his second.

They needed a big one, a fire which would burn long and bright, but not so soon as to prevent the Slayers and the last of the Anoka from crossing the bridge.

If they were still alive.

Half Tusk's scowl deepened. They were alive. They had to be alive. And he would not be responsible for leaving them—for *trapping* them—in Iruzuland, where their deaths would be slow and agonizing. If they were trapped, he suspected their only choice would be to take their own lives rather than be captured—perhaps by flinging themselves off the cliffs. Anything was better than being taken by the Iruzu.

Far-off screams interrupted Half Tusk's thoughts, followed by the sound of smashing weapons. He listened, listened hard. The villagers piling brush behind him paused in their work, their faces lifting as they also heard them.

Half Tusk's lips tightened into a frustrated button. They had run out of time.

He ordered his people off the bridge, back to the far side. Men and women strong enough to fight took cover behind trees. Bows were readied. Half Tusk then signaled for his remaining four warriors to the base of the slope on the Iruzu side. There, they crouched, fitting arrows to bows, ever vigilant of Iruzuland.

Half Tusk once again studied the jungle around them. While the vegetation around them was not as overgrown as other parts of the Sanjou, an arrow would only go so far before hitting a tree.

So they waited as the noise grew louder.

Half Tusk glanced back and met the pensive gaze of Broska, who stood on the far side of the bridge. Sighing, the Anoka leader made his decision. He waved at the adopted Anoka man, and Broska got to work. All along the cliffs, the few villagers strong enough to handle a bow peeked out from behind trees. Those bows once belonged to their captors, along with several quivers of well-made arrows. Half Tusk didn't like using weapons taken from dead men. Had more faith in his own. Now, however, he reluctantly decided that all would help.

The growing commotion within Iruzuland hooked his attention. Growing anxious, Half Tusk checked on Broska, who knelt upon the broad back of the fallen tree. The man lowered his head to the worn surface and blew at something cupped in his hand.

Half Tusk rolled his eyes.

Broska might be one of the Anoka, but a sick youngster could light a fire faster.

He returned to watching the jungle. Not long after, the smell of smoke turned him around. The Zuthenian walked across, carrying a torch with a blazing head, lighting clumps of brush on both sides of the bridge.

Half Tusk faced the jungle, adjusting the quiver resting against his thigh. He extracted one shaft and nocked it, pulling it to a half draw. There he waited, staring ahead, the tension in his drawstring feeling good against his fingers.

There. Figures appeared in the distance, their arms and legs swinging like pendulums, hurrying for the bridge.

Half Tusk aimed but hesitated. A beat later he recognized his missing people and lowered his weapon.

Behind them, however, the sounds of pursuit grew into a worrisome racket.

Half Tusk urged his people to run faster.

Twenty strides, and he could clearly see them.

Ten strides and he could see the perspiration upon their exhausted faces.

The one called Sad Eyes led them, along with the warrior with the melted face. The Slayer stopped at the base of the slope and urged the weary people up the ramp. The nearby Anoka warriors lowered their bows to help the weaker ones across the bridge. Smiling Rock came into view, along with the unseeing Gentle Rain. The warrior with the melted face helped to the slope and urged them to continue. Smiling Rock obeyed, but Gentle Rain did not want to leave the faceless warrior. Only when another villager pulled her away did she leave for the bridge.

Bright Leaf also did not want to leave Sad Eyes, and the two stood together at the base, facing each other.

The villagers staggered up the slope, nearly done on their feet. Half Tusk stepped aside to allow them to pass, telling them to hurry even though he knew they had nothing left.

Then Broska stood beside him, holding the torch.

Breathing hard, Kellic stood before the gravelly incline and told Bright Leaf to go.

She shook her head.

Half Tusk shouted at them to hurry.

Kellic faced a wide-eyed Bright Leaf. A fierce urgency of needing her to be safe filled him, and he drew breath to say that, or at least attempt to say it—when she placed both hands to the metal cheeks of his helmet. That silenced him. Then, in the midst of the shouting and the hurrying and the growing smoke, she hugged him. Hard. The embrace shocked him. Robbed him of all thought and words, truth be known. And though Kellic wore thick armor, he believed he *still* felt the falling hammer that was Bright Leaf's heart.

Or maybe it was just his.

A frustrated Half Tusk shouted at them again and started down the slope.

Kellic didn't understand the words, but he understood the message. Bright Leaf did as well and she released him, her face drawn and fearful as Half Tusk pulled her away. He led her back up the slope, where people filed across the burning bridge, the thickening smoke hiding their feet and ankles.

The growing sounds of battle forced Kellic to turn back to the jungle, and he saw He-Dog, Jers Snaffer, and Hargan hobbling into sight.

Without warning, Chop took off to help them.

Kellic was only a stride behind.

CHAPTER 59

The faraway cries of Iruzu altered One Spear's course. Instead of heading back to the Iruzu stronghold, the future War Pig led his twenty Faces of Death along a river, where the land steadily sloped upward. They pawed and clutched at the ground, huffing, their muscular frames working, forcing themselves to move faster.

And in the distance, through a screen of jungle, One Spear saw fire . . .

A gasping Hargan squawked and pointed.

He-Dog saw it as well.

The bridge, shrouded in smoke and populated by ghosts. Not ghosts, but a handful of Anoka trying to cross.

And just beneath that—two figures sprinting toward them.

Chop and Kellic.

The sight nearly put a smile on He-Dog's exhausted face—when a squall of arrows screamed past his head and shoulders. Two struck him squarely in the back, driving him to the ground. Realizing the arrows failed to pierce his armor, he limped behind a tree. An angry rain of shafts fell then, bouncing off trunks or sinking into the dirt. Several barely missed Hargan and Snaffer, who also took cover behind trees.

He-Dog waited for the last of the arrows to drop and glimpsed Chop and Kellic off the trail, clearing the short but deadly pathway to the bridge. Curls of smoke rose and hung in the air perhaps two dozen strides away,

"Burning!" Hargan barked. "They're burning th—"

The collected voices of hundreds cut him off. A frightening explosion of noise as the pursuing Iruzu saw the burning bridge as well.

The very ground trembled as the fishmen redoubled their efforts to reach them.

He-Dog looked back at the bridge. Half Tusk crouched there while Broska hurried across its smoking length, on the heels of the escaping villagers. Half Tusk waved before he lifted his bow and readied an arrow. He aimed and released, and several arrows flashed overhead in a dark sleet, arching from the far side of the chasm. Most of those arrows disappeared in the foliage overhead.

Then the answering volley crashed down, splitting leaves and branches before stuttering the ground ahead of the charging Iruzu.

He-Dog's spirits soared at the sight.

They were close now. So very close.

But they were also half-dead from their retreating battles with the Iruzu. And they were so very tired. Their legs sorely ached and throbbed as if they had been running forever. If they made a sprint for the bridge now, the Iruzu archers would cut them down.

The distant war music played on as He-Dog had an even more frightening thought.

The screamers would soon see the Anoka fleeing across the bridge and strive to cut *them* down.

Lords above, He-Dog groaned, and took one last great breath . . .

. . . before stepping out into the open, broadsword and shield at the ready.

A wide line of monsters charged through the jungle, a wave of orange-eyed insanity that *howled* upon spotting him. The lead screamers ran at him, twisted faces peering over spears or waving clubs and axes, close enough for He-Dog to see the deep-rooted evil sparkling in their eyes.

Then Kellic and Chop appeared on his right flank.

Hargan and Snaffer stood on his left.

Kellic joined shields with He-Dog, and suddenly there was a determined wall of five, blocking the trail from one tree to another.

The Iruzu slammed into that wall with the heavy clap of flesh on metal.

He-Dog and Kellic braced their shields as the mass crashed into them. Digging in bootheels and bearing the weight, they stabbed their swords underneath the barriers, into soft flesh pressed against them. The twin blades of the Nordish swordsman blurred with a speed and power that devastated the headlong rush, and Iruzu dropped dead at what appeared to be the gentlest touch. Hargan matched the shrieking faces with a roar of his own, killing any attempting to flank on the left, while Snaffer straightened and ducked, cutting up foes and leaving them dying in the dirt.

Iruzu died by the dozens in that initial contact, and their corpses piled up in a mangled line.

Whereupon the Iruzu behind them leapt off the backs of the fallen.

Some crashed into lifted shields, seeking to drag the barriers down, but the five mercenaries reacted as one—chopping off arms and splitting faces. Jets of oily blood spurted from cleft heads and shoulders. Gouts of gore sprayed from opened chests. Heads and hands flew through the air or flopped about upon half-severed stumps. One screamer latched onto a shield and sought to pull it down when Kellic shoved a length of steel through his face. Edged blades licked throats in explosive lines of black, and high-pitched shrieks ended in bestial grunts. All the while, Iruzu arrows lanced overhead, no longer aimed at the mercenaries but at the far side of the chasm. The Anoka returned greetings with a steady pulse of feathered shafts.

Those arrows, loosed from well-crafted bows, killed and wounded Iruzu well before they reached the main battle, the impact punching them off their feet and hindering the advance of those behind.

For all the death and dying, however, for all the mystifying might and sheer stubbornness of the five standing their ground, drizzled in a dripping coat of carnage while killing even *more* . . .

. . . the Iruzu kept charging, throwing, *grinding* themselves against that wall of flashing steel.

Fishmen fastened claws over the rim of He-Dog's shield and pulled it down, revealing a row of livid faces ready to fling spears. He stabbed one dead through the eye while Kellic hacked a head in two. He-Dog shook off the corpse and circled his shield high. A stone axe crashed against it, splitting the barrier down the middle to within three fingers of his veined forearm. He-Dog lifted the shield and stabbed underneath, buckling his attacker. He then shook off the ruined shield and flung it aside.

"*Three steps back!*" Snaffer shouted over the shrieking and hissing of arrows.

They did, breaking contact as one.

Half the front rank of Iruzu stumbled over the dead left behind.

The five mercenaries formed another line and waited for the next rush.

They didn't wait long.

The next attack wasn't a wave like before, but thrusts of twos and threes, as the Iruzu struggled over the corpses of their own. There was no coordinated attack. No order. Reach the enemy and swing for their heads. Some flanked the five and swept in from the sides, and armored warriors shifted to meet their attackers.

He-Dog and Kellic parted. He-Dog parried a club, slashed low, and cut the legs out from his foe. He sliced open two more when they came within reach. A fourth clacked a war club against his broadsword, and the steel bit deep. For an instant, fishman and Slayer stood facing each other. Then He-Dog stomped on the Iruzu's knee, shattering it. The creature fell, and He-Dog yanked his blade back.

He then looked up.

To see a clutch of Iruzu archers unleash a pointed squall straight at him. With no shield and no time to dodge, a flurry of arrows stuttered into his torso—but the hardened leather, taken from Foust's armory and perhaps fashioned by one of the Lords, blocked every primitive shaft.

Except one. Which shoved its flame-blackened tip through the seam of the parted armor, deep enough to pull a winded grunt from He-Dog.

When a second wave struck him.

Arrows flashed by his face and shoulders. At least two rebounded off his protected chest, while one opened his bicep with a sting. Another sank into his *other* arm, robbing him of breath he no longer had. He bent over, clutching at the hateful shaft in his chest, and glimpsed an axe-wielding Iruzu about to take his offered head. Instead, a bloodied and bruised Jers Snaffer lifted the eager brute off his feet, punching his blade through the torso.

"*Back three steps*," Snaffer shouted again while extracting his dagger.

He-Dog yanked the agonizing arrow from his chest. Blood spurted as he flung it away.

The ordered withdrawal wasn't so easy.

An Iruzu fell flat while attempting to stab a spear into He-Dog. He stomped on its head, killing the thing. With no time to spare, he backed up while jerking the arrow from his arm. The Iruzu surged over the conceded ground, wailing and baring fangs. They reared back spiked clubs and stone axes and charged with leveled spears. Iruzu arrows struck the five mercenaries, hitting their armor and staggering them but failing to take them down. The Anoka answered with a drizzle of their own, giving a brief respite to the five. Arrows misted the air, nailing heads, shoulders, and arms, dropping their victims and further hindering the Iruzu charge.

And thus an archers' battle had begun.

Underneath skies showering death, filthy with dark matter and dripping long lines, He-Dog grimly eyed the next gathering wave of attackers. These Iruzu didn't scream. Hunched over and partially clouded by wafting smoke, they crept over their fallen and watched the mercenaries over ready weapons.

Jers Snaffer, glowering and soaked in a coat of blood, swayed beside He-Dog. A nearby Hargan appeared even worse as someone had flattened the egg-sized welt above his left eye, leaving a mass of pinkish meat and dripping fluid. He bared red teeth and held his axe with two trembling hands. Chop and Kellic wavered at the ends, also coated in a foul sludge, despite looking the freshest of the five.

Then, at the back of his mind, He-Dog heard a familiar chuffing. A deep-throated chuckling, that could belong only to Balless. Amid the noise and the chaos and the thickening smoke, feeling the weight of his wounds, the rotten slickness upon his skin, and the growing exhaustion in his limbs . . . well . . . that little bit of mirth sounded right and proper fine.

So he loaded up another breath. Set his feet. Gripped his broadsword two-handed and hoisted that slab of edged steel to the high guard. His arms hurt dearly, his back near breaking, and the puncture wound in his chest kept on stabbing. Despite all that, he faced the quiet ones advancing on him. He-Dog hated them. Perhaps even more than beastmen. Far too long had he listened to their feral yammering. Far too long had he been running. And for a man who drew strength from his hatred, he realized—for the Iruzu—he had enough hate to boil an ocean.

The Iruzu came through the wafting smoke.

The first fishman had his chest split apart in an explosion of black blood, while the two behind it perished a beat later. He-Dog slashed and chopped, reaving great shimmering arcs with his broadsword, carving up the Iruzu lines. Two more died. Then a third. A fourth and fifth. Then the killing became unfit as two unyielding forces didn't meet but *mashed* their points and edges against each other, grinding out the conflict in short stabs, brutal chops, and horrifying splashes of blood. Arrows showered the Sanjou while the Iruzu shoved themselves into that unbreaking wall of warriors. Axes and clubs came down hard. Spears lanced forward seeking guts. Arrows dove for heads and faces.

But the mercenaries—the *Slayers*, as they so clearly were—refused to break. They shifted in and out of reach, tapping into their final ferocious reservoir of strength before cutting down every attacker. Powerful counters splintered clubs, wrecked axes, and turned aside spears. Downward chops and upward slashes split flesh and bone. Iruzu sank to their knees clutching at life-stealing wounds or dropped dead on the spot. Heads flew. Faces split and teeth sprayed. Limbs severed in great black bursts while the owners shrieked and were silenced. The ground became ruddy with gore.

The Iruzu had no fear.

And the Slayers had no pity.

The dead piled up, flopping over other corpses already splayed upon the ground, and He-Dog continued killing any within reach. Jers Snaffer and Hargan worked on either side of him, bleeding and near exhaustion, but slicing up the enemy in great, scarlet spewing chunks. Chop appeared at times, head lowered and swords blurring, while Kellic stabbed around his shield, his chainmail no longer shimmering.

Then an Iruzu leapt over the back of another and smashed his axe down upon Jers Snaffer's left shoulder, mashing it two fingers down from his neckline. Snaffer collapsed. He-Dog rushed to his aid, killing the fishman before butchering a second. Grimacing, panting, Snaffer rose once again, brandishing his axe only, his left arm a swinging length of meat. An Iruzu sought to bash his head with a club, but He-Dog hammered the figure aside. He-Dog stood before Snaffer, guarding him while taking life after life, his arms and legs blazing but no longer from exhaustion. What he didn't kill, his companions did, denying the Iruzu another step. The line shifted and warped but did not break. Chop's shining swords lashed in and out, spattering blood and slinging back corpses. Hargan appeared, swinging his battle-axe in wide decapitating arcs. Kellic stood beside him, shield-bashing and cleaving heads before confronting the next fishman.

But the Iruzu didn't retreat. Didn't surrender. They kept coming forward in unending streams, crashing into that murderous line and seeking to break it.

Redoubling their efforts to kill those before them.

Running hard, One Spear led his anointed Twenty up a slope, climbing the rising landscape where the clamor of battle was at its shrillest. On his left the cliffs rose higher and higher, promising a long drop to the rocks below. As the future War Pig climbed, however, clawing at the land and pulling himself forward, a surprising sight hooked his attention.

It was the long-fallen tree that spanned the chasm, used for generations as the only crossing into Iruzuland among the steep hills.

That bridge *burned*.

One Spear barked at his followers to run faster. Red Bone and Rock Jaw and the rest of the Twenty followed.

As he approached the battle, One Spear heard words unquestionably alien to his ears.

Hard Shells!

Powered by hate, he ran faster.

Only Half Tusk and Broska remained on the bridge, guarding the villagers crossing it. The tree beneath their feet burned faster than expected, challenging one of Half Tusk's earlier concerns. The Anoka had prepared too well, it seemed. The streamers of vines, heaps of dry brushwood, and clumps of vegetation smoldered and smoked on both sides of the bridge, narrowing the path to a thin lane. Great hazy plumes thickened and drifted, reducing visibility and hindering aim.

Half Tusk shouted at his people on the other side, ordering them to loose arrows at will.

Broska stopped and yelled to the men still fighting the Iruzu. "*Cross, you unfit blossoms. Cross over before—*"

An arrow split the smoke and pierced a hole through Broska's shoulder as fine as a needle, twisting him around. He stumbled, his foot touched flames, and he fell with a yelp. Down he went, reaching out in one desperate act—and latched onto a vine, one of the few yet to be ignited by the spreading fire.

That vine, its length not clearly anchored, stretched out a pace before holding, jerking Broska to a halt. There he dangled by his good arm, pressed hard against old wood, his face scrubbed by chips as tough as dragon scale. Moaning through clenched teeth, Broska could not pull himself up. Worse, his shoulder blazed because of the shaft embedded there, rooting this way and that, torturing him with every rub.

His grip weakened, and he couldn't see anything above him except for smoke.

Just before Broska let go, Half Tusk dropped flat on his chest and grabbed the man by his wrist. The Anoka warrior pulled—pulled *hard*—but could not haul the larger man back up.

So he held on, and while he did, flames crept toward him . . . but he did not release Broska.

So there they stayed, grimacing, straining, concealed by the haze, with arrows hissing around them.

Breathing acrid smoke, He-Dog heard Broska's shout and how it was cut off.

But the Iruzu were pressing even harder, backing the five mercenaries within five paces of the earthen ramp to the bridge.

An Iruzu warrior with a spear lunged and had his chest slashed to bleeding ribbons. Another warrior fell with both knees nearly sheared away. Another had his fingers sliced off an instant before a sword snapped his face back. Chop waded into He-Dog's side vision, butchering foes and holding his ground. Then one arrow exploded off Chop's leather vest, staggering him, and another shaft pierced his right arm.

Hargan rushed to the wounded man and shielded him from any more arrows. The once-Sujin blocked an incoming spear and punched the owner. He dispatched two others in a series of tree-felling cuts.

Then there were none.

Exhausted, hurting, and dripping with gore, a heaving He-Dog glanced around. Smoke billowed, trying its best to hide the slaughter—Iruzu bodies piled high and stretched out across the jungle floor. Arrows protruded from some of the carcasses, but steel had killed the majority. The five Slayers, drenched in things best kept inside a body, stood no more than two strides from the slope to the bridge. In that fleeting moment of peace, Chop yanked the arrow from his forearm, staggered, and tossed the shaft away. Snaffer still drew breath, though a strip of mail hung off his stained armor, and his head resembled something dipped deep into a cauldron of boiling filth. Kellic righted his helmet, his eyes hard and alert, while bits of matter stained his beard, and several arrows studded his shield. Looking as if he'd splashed his head in a vat of wine, Hargan swayed and winced and sneered a smile.

"They're nothing," he croaked at the others.

All still standing, still alive, though they all looked as if they'd crawled through a shite trough of a war. He-Dog supposed they had. Swallowing and feeling the click of his parched throat, he motioned for the battle-weary lads to go.

Until figures materialized from the smoke, stopping them all. Coming in from the edge of the cliff. More Iruzu. Except the smoke whitened their gray-green flesh . . . and they wore skull masks. *Red* skull masks. To make matters worse, they could hear *more* screamers coming up the trail. Late arrivals to the butchery and quite vocal about the many corpses marking the way.

"Where are they all coming from?" Kellic gasped.

He-Dog didn't know.

Didn't answer.

Didn't care.

Only a handful of the hateful things stopped him and his lads from getting across that bridge. A pack of pig-bastards creeping toward them. One more pack He-Dog would send to Saimon's hell.

The skull-faced Iruzu charged, but one detached himself from the rest. One carrying a spear, who slowed to a stop and ripped the bony mask from his face. The thing's low brow and eyes furrowed with dawning recognition.

He-Dog scowled back, recognizing the creature and his iron-tipped weapon. The same spear belonged to the Iruzu killer who had bested him and hurtled him over a cliff a lifetime ago.

The Iruzu with the one spear directed his minions at the four guarding the base of the bridge. One Spear then further separated himself, choosing a little clearing among a heap of corpses, partially hidden by smoke. One Spear shook his weapon at He-Dog, spewing gibberish all the while.

The other skull-masked fishmen rushed the others, allowing He-Dog an unchallenged path to the Iruzu leader.

Which was fine by him.

"*Get across!*" Broska shouted again from the other side of the chasm.

The five men did not cross the bridge, however. Didn't even consider it. Instead, they fought on.

As He-Dog faced the Iruzu with the one spear, Chop met the new group of attackers. He struggled for a fresh breath, taking in more smoke than air it seemed, and his wounded arm pained him greatly. Still, when the first Iruzu closed in, the Nordish swordsman parried a club before cutting a throat and stabbing the skull mask of another. Too tired to dodge, he barely parried a spear before taking out a set of legs in a spray of blood.

Iruzu sped by him like a sour river split by a rock, engaging the other mercenaries. Mayhem erupted again, but with a much greater sense of urgency.

The bridge was burning, perhaps even greater than before.

Clang and grunts then, as Iruzu clashed with the mercenaries, and blood once again drizzled the air in hot sheets.

Chop challenged the last skull-faced Iruzu in the line. The thing jabbed a spear at the Nordish man's face but he turned it aside. Chop darted in close and slammed an elbow into the skull mask. Old bone shattered. The Iruzu went down and Chop plunged a sword into its heart, ending the creature.

When his senses buzzed.

On instinct alone, the Jackal whirled as an Iruzu leapt, stone axe coming down. Chop lashed out, too slow to kill, blocking the axe but not the body. The Iruzu tackled Chop, too fast for the Nordish man to react. Both crashed to the ground, the impact stunning the swordsman. A knee dropped onto Chop's armored midsection while clawed hands clutched at his throat. The Iruzu leaned forward, its skull mask leering. The hands clamped around Chop's throat tightened with shocking, eye-bulging power. Chop couldn't breathe. Couldn't draw a sliver of breath. Black stars exploded before his eyes while the skull mask bobbed and grinned—

Before a flash of steel swept the creature's head from its shoulders.

Hargan kicked the dead thing off the Nordish man. With a frantic glance around, the Sunjan reached down, grabbed one of Chop's hands, and pulled him to his feet.

Sheets of smoke drifted between One Spear and He-Dog as the old mercenary approached, broadsword at the ready. Behind him, the others fought on. Within five strides of his adversary, a hazy cloud came between them, and He-Dog lost sight of the Iruzu—until One Spear stabbed for his guts.

He-Dog barely sidestepped the thrust, and his countering slash missed his foe's head. The Iruzu ducked and spun, whipping the spear around in a familiar move— one that He-Dog remembered. He jerked his head back, the knob of wood grazing his jaw by an unfit hair. That knocked him back a step and One Spear charged in, stabbing for a leg. Then his face. He-Dog parried both, but a corpse tripped him, and he fell atop a wet cushion of bodies. A telling shriek of triumph spurred him to move. He rolled over the carcasses as One Spear stabbed for his heart repeatedly, trying to skewer him to dead meat.

The third jab and He-Dog lashed out with a foot, kicking out a leg.

One Spear crashed down as the smoke smothered them both, transforming them into thrashing ghosts. Both rose in a huff, amid the fading clatter and the grunts of the dying, and squared off again.

As the Hard Shell rose, One Spear jabbed at his foe's face. The bigger warrior knocked it away and countered, missing the Iruzu's head by a finger. One Spear stabbed twice more, but his thrusts were turned aside.

Then a second Hard Shell stepped in and swung for One Spear's head.

The Iruzu leader ducked and backtracked, skipping over the dead and placing distance between himself and his enemies.

Whereupon he realized he was the *last* of his chosen pack.

His entire pack, including Red Bone and Rock Jaw, had been cut down by the Hard Shells. Worse still, the Hard Shells—clearly on the edge of dying but simply refusing—sought to trap the still-standing leader. They stalked him, attempting to encircle him, while the bridge burned behind them. They climbed over the dead, swinging as they came.

One Spear dodged and jabbed, escaping their weapons, until he stopped with his back to the jungle. There, he leveled his spear and stared down the pursuing Hard Shells.

For a moment, he glared at his hated enemies, daring them to come closer. He wondered if he could kill all five before Iruzu reinforcements reached the bridge.

Then he realized he didn't have to.

Very much aware that his warriors—and his archers—were close by, the Iruzu War Pig—for in that instant he *was* the War Pig—shrieked gibberish.

To the Hard Shells it was just another scream.

To the Iruzu that heard it, however, it was a command.

The order surprised the Iruzu archers along the southern cliff and farther back in the jungle.

They dared not disobey One Spear, however, whose hateful bellow they recognized at once. As one, they ceased exchanging volleys with the Anoka across the chasm and instead aimed for the bridge, where they heard One Spear's shout.

An instant later, they released a killer rain high into the air.

The Iruzu with the iron-tipped spear eluded all attempts to kill him, until the little gray-green bastard stood across a mound of bodies and dared the mercenaries to attack. He screamed at them, longer than he should have, and got an answering cry from farther back in the jungle.

More Iruzu were on the way.

Not that it mattered to He-Dog, who glared at One Spear. "You're the last," he said as Hargan and Kellic circled in from opposite sides.

Then the arrows fell from everywhere.

Those surprising shafts hissed and sliced down through the overhead foliage. They hammered tree trunks. They smashed hard ground and bounced off rocks with frightening, ear-popping whacks.

A flurry of arrows struck Chop.

Three sank into Snaffer, knocking him flat.

One found Hargan's shoulder, driving him to a knee. A split instant later another shaft razored down his scalp, dropping him like a stone.

One arrow pierced He-Dog's left forearm, punching through the edge of his bracer. Another shaft punctured the leather protecting his left shoulder, while three more hit his upper torso, the impacts ringing out one after the other. One of those stabbed through his vest and sank deep, stealing his breath in one shocking seizure.

Several arrows hit Kellic, exploding against his shield. One shaft skewered his foot to the ground, the pain straightening him with a curt intake of air. Another nailed the knee of the same leg while two more sank into his shoulders. He lurched sideways, where a final arrow pierced his back—just before he toppled upon the dead.

Not one arrow hit One Spear.

The shock and awe of such good fortune clearly stunned the Iruzu leader, but only for a moment. Hefting his spear, he went for the nearest figure writhing upon the ground, intent on stabbing its head . . .

Which happened to be Kellic.

"No," He-Dog croaked.

Arrows jutting from him and holding his blade two-handed so that it wouldn't slip from his grip, he lunged at the poised Iruzu, swinging his broadsword with everything he had left. One Spear turned to parry, and the heavy blade lopped off the weapon's iron head. Livid, One Spear flung the ruined thing away and leapt at his foe. He-Dog couldn't react fast enough and the Iruzu tackled him around the waist. Staggering, He-Dog dropped his sword and locked an arm around the Iruzu's neck. The two warriors wrestled, attempting to upend the other. He-Dog shifted and stomped on a bare foot, breaking toes. With a peal of agony, One Spear straightened in reflex, jerking He-Dog off-balance and backward.

Both fell toward the cliff.

Where they landed, flat on their spines, all breath leaving them.

He-Dog recovered first, glimpsing a dewy arrowhead protruding from his forearm. He scrambled onto the Iruzu, groping for his neck. One Spear's fist shot up, smashing He-Dog's jaw and driving back his head. Stars exploded before He-Dog's eyes as he gnashed his tongue and spat blood. He clutched a slick forehead and drove a knee into One Spear's stomach. The Iruzu gasped and clawed for He-Dog's eyes and the arrow jutting from his arm. He-Dog twisted his head but freezing fire shot up his arm, crippling him. One Spear grabbed He-Dog's chin, then cheeks, digging in claws and raking bloody lines down a clenched jawline, pulling a groan from the bigger man.

Feeling his foe weaken, the Iruzu bucked, lifting his powerful hips and legs. He-Dog fell on his back among the dead, one arm splayed wide.

Where his fingers touched metal.

He-Dog's eyes widened at the contact.

The spearhead, lying atop a corpse. The same lethal sliver of pointed iron he'd lopped off only a heartbeat earlier.

One Spear scrambled onto him, trapping him. Hands clamped around He-Dog's throat in a face-purpling vice. One Spear leaned in, fanged maw open, seeking to chomp into a grimacing mouth—when He-Dog grabbed the decapitated weapon and punched the iron tip into the Iruzu's head.

Half a length of metal disappeared into the creature's ear. One Spear's mouth snapped shut and his frame went rigid. His orange eyes bulged with shock, nearly bursting from their sockets . . . before relaxing.

With a dismissive twist, He-Dog left the spear in its owner's skull and shoved the corpse off him.

In the thickening smoke, screams reached him, sounding fearful, warning him there was no time remaining. He-Dog glanced around and saw flames feasting upon the bridge.

The other mercenaries stirred and tried to rise.

Though he barely had the strength, He-Dog staggered for Kellic first.

An arrow pierced the meat of He-Dog's thigh, and he crumpled to his knees and elbows. Another arrow hit his back, exploding against the vest and flattening him. The world tilted and burned. Smoke sought to choke him. He-Dog lifted his head and stared into Kellic's sad, glazed eyes. Blood splashed the mercenary's face.

He-Dog tried to rise but couldn't—realized he had nothing left.

Nothing at all.

He was done.

When hands grabbed him.

CHAPTER 60

Snaffer's eyes fluttered open. He took in a deep breath of smoke—thick and harsh and choking—and gawked at the burning bridge. Then he wondered why three arrows were sticking out of him. Two were just below his guts, penetrating his mail, the other was halfway through his hand. Wincing, he yanked them free, the pain vicious and bright. Nearby, the bloody mess of Hargan pushed himself to his knees, while an unfit howling came from the jungle.

Then Half Tusk loomed over them, materializing from the thickening smoke with his four warriors behind him. The Anoka men pulled Snaffer to his feet. Half Tusk took the big man's weight while the others hauled up He-Dog and Kellic. Heads sagged as arms were draped across shoulders. Somehow, they carried them up the slope, into the choking coils of smoke. Across the bridge they labored, flames lighting the edges, illuminating every nightmarish step.

Hargan watched them go, cringing at the howling emanating from the jungle. Something flew over him, a heavy mangled mass that trailed ghastly ribbons, before it plummeted from sight over the cliff. That woke the Sunjan as he glimpsed figures vanishing into the smoke. Hargan rattled his head. He wiped his face and dragged his bloody palm across his armor. He spat red and found his axe, fallen not far away. It took effort, but he closed fists around the weapon and thumped the steely head into the ground.

"Not dead yet," Hargan muttered, and forced himself to stand. There, he swayed and staggered two steps before dropping beside the unmoving form of Chop. Two arrows had breached his armor, stabbing into his chest. At the sound of the Sunjan's approach, the Nordish man turned his head ever so weakly.

"Not dead yet," Hargan repeated.

Chop merely stared.

Hargan grabbed him. Grabbed him tight, his knuckles whitening. And *pulled*, getting Chop to sit up.

"Next part will hurt, Nordish," the Sunjan groaned and spat blood. "For you. And me."

Mewling, Hargan hooked one of the limp man's arms around his neck. Then, positively squealing in agony, he bent over and picked up his battle-axe, refusing to leave it.

"Next part will hurt *more*," Hargan muttered, steadying himself, drooling blood. "We walk, you lazy blossom. *Walk*. Or we both perish. But we aren't going to perish. Not me. Not you. Not *here*."

So they walked. Shuffled along, really. To the slope. Up the incline. Arrows flitted overhead, the exchanges continuing. Smoke enveloped the two men. Bright flames waved along the bridge, close enough to scorch boot leather. Chop started coughing—hard, chest-splitting barks that rattled him. He kept moving, however. And Hargan, leaning on his axe like a walking stick, helped him along.

With every step, Hargan expected a spear in his back. A stone axe to whirl out of the sky and split his skull. Or an arrow through an eye.

Nothing of the sort happened.

"*We're not dead yet, maggots*," Hargan shouted into the smoke, the wicked flames high and waving and reaching for their knees. "*Not dead yet.*"

The bridge burned mightily, cracking like whips in places. Black smoke obscured the surface, and every other step was near flames or on them. Searing heat crisped their legs. Hargan choked and coughed, sputtering dark strings, and noticed something odd.

The screaming behind him had stopped.

The horns had ceased their wailing as well, but the drums rumbled on like a departing storm. The absence of all that constant screaming, however, well, that was strange indeed. It puzzled him. Hargan knew they'd killed a good many of the maggots, a *damn* good many, but they hadn't killed them *all*.

So where were they?

A moaning Chop started to stumble.

"Don't you fall," Hargan warned, hefting him while eyeing the fires. "Don't you fall. You fall and you take me with you. You hear me? Ungrateful Nordish—"

Amid smoke and flames, a figure materialized on the bridge, coming toward him.

One of the Anoka wildmen. Then another.

Hargan's surprise at seeing them was undone by a great shuddering crunch, and the bridge trembled from a substantial weight . . . on the Iruzu side.

Heavy enough to nearly turn Hargan around.

There, perhaps twenty strides away and looming through the smoke, stood an ogre. The height of two men at least, and perhaps thrice that in weight, with mottled skin the color of sun-drenched leather, perfect for hiding in the jungle. But what really got Hargan's attention was its oversized mouth, and the knife-sized teeth filling it.

And the eyes above that. Red and hateful and glaring.

The sight of the monster stunned Hargan, until the creature lifted a hand. Dangling from its enormous clutches was the broken form of an Iruzu.

Which the Paw cast aside as if bored, flinging it into oblivion.

Then it started for the men on the bridge.

Hargan blinked at the thing. Then at the Anoka men, both poised and ready to run.

Hargan leaned Chop toward the wildmen. "*Take him, maggots,*" he yelled, unloading the swordsman into their care.

Then he faced the monster on the bridge.

The thing stopped not a dozen strides away, teetering upon a path much narrower for one so big. There it stood and wavered, considering the meaty obstacle before it while flexing rusty claws. Full-grown daggers, really, ready to snatch the life from the unwary.

Or the lone axe man standing in its way.

"Not this day, maggot *shite*," Hargan warned, his voice rising as he reared back his axe. "*Not this day!*"

As an answer, and perhaps feeling the fire even more, the Paw roared its own thoughts on the matter. An impossibly deep, ear-splitting bellow that shivered the very air and turned heads on both sides of the chasm.

Hargan charged into that gas cloud of foulness.

The Sunjan pounded across the burning bridge, his battle-axe gleaming in smoky firelight.

And before he reached the monster, Hargan roared.

The Paw swiped at the oncoming Sunjan—who ducked—and brought his axe down on one very large foot.

Splitting the extremity up the middle.

The Paw straightened, bellowed a sound bursting in agony, and jerked back its mutilated foot. It shrieked and hopped, performing a violent little jig upon the bridge holding its considerable weight.

A bridge already weakened by fire.

The great tree broke in two at the very center, having enough of that gurry. With a heart-splitting crackle, the two sections shuddered and sank into the chasm.

Taking the Paw . . . and a swinging Hargan . . . with it.

The ends yanked upward, rising swiftly in a creaking, terrifying yawn, and flinging up a storm of dirt and debris upon Anoka villager and warrior alike. Its wide roots whipped up and shivered like great malignant hooks, swiping at and barely missing the two leaping men carrying a senseless Chop. With a rocky, echoing rattle and a sinewy snapping of ancient fibers, the tree slid into the chasm's throat, its roots clawing the sides all the way down. Billowing clouds of smoke coiled and twisted over the chasm, turning a sickly shade of sepia, and obscuring the mighty tree as it plunged into the very void it once spanned.

The crash at the bottom echoed for long moments before dying away into nothing.

After being pelted by a squall of dirt and jungle matter, He-Dog unhooked himself from arms and shoulders and staggered to the cliff. He glimpsed the two Anoka warriors carrying Chop from the crumbling ramp, landing a very short distance from the disintegrating edge. Which was right about when a cloud of dirt enveloped them all. Someone was shouting in Anoka, but damned if He-Dog could understand what was being said.

Dropping to his knees, and then flat on his chest, He-Dog peered into the smoky chasm. He cringed, tasting grit with every breath, and waved against the dust clouds, trying to see. He turned his head and glimpsed ghosts peering over the cliff.

A hideous, lone howl shot up the chasm walls, frightening enough to widen eyes and quicken hearts.

He-Dog froze in place.

There. Just visible through the ailing haze, was the Paw.

Already striding for the rocky shore, and nowhere near dead.

Truth be known, the beast looked unfit *angry* as it waded across the river, whipping up frothy waves as it moved away from two floating lengths of wood. The monster swiped at the water, splashing even more, slapping the surface with bone-flattening blows. The Paw straightened on the riverbed, blasted another roar, and lashed out again. It turned, as if considering one section of the fallen tree floating away. Then it whirled about in a white froth and pushed for dry ground. Waves rolled as the monster moved through the water, determined to free itself of the river. With every step, however, it seemed to slow. A howl left the beast, a furious yet frustrated explosion of sound, and it thrashed about once more . . . before staggering to a standstill. The monster took another step, stumbling as it did, and sank to its waist.

Then its chest.

All the while, the rabid waters rippled and raged around its figure.

With an unnatural shudder, the Paw sagged and sank face down in the water, and slowly turned with the current. The water thrashed around it as if boiling.

In time, the monster disappeared below the surface . . . and did not rise again.

Of Hargan, there was no sign.

High above, somewhere nearby on the cliff, Half Tusk spoke, his voice carrying in the grim silence that followed.

Broska translated a heartbeat later.

"Bloodfish," he said.

CHAPTER 61

Smoke lingered over the chasm, thwarting falling arrows and allowing the Anoka to retreat farther into the jungle. Moans and mutters of desperation came from the survivors as they hobbled away. A half-senseless He-Dog listened to it all, realizing a pair of villagers were half walking, half carrying him away from the cliffs. He shuffled along, every step agonizing, from parts he didn't remember being struck. The fading daylight sparkled, and the air tasted of smoke. Then, his chest flared up—singing, really—his wounds letting him know he wasn't going to make it much further. His knees were in agreement, faltering, lowering him to the ground. Hands pressed against his chest, but he couldn't see the faces.

Then he was falling.

Someone patted his face, bringing him around enough that he frowned.

Broska leaned over him. "You alive?"

"Aye that," He-Dog answered softly, his eyes opened just a crack.

"Thought you were dead."

He thought that himself. "Was that . . . the Paw?"

"In the river?"

"Aye that."

Broska nodded. "We think so."

It was He-Dog's turn to look confused.

"No one's ever *seen* the thing and lived to speak of it," the Zuthenian explained. "Except Half Tusk. And he only saw its hands. But, yes, we think it's dead. As is your man, I'm sorry to say."

He-Dog frowned, his heart sinking. "Chop?"

"Not him. The other one on the bridge. With the axe. That one. He perished."

Hargan.

"He's . . ." He-Dog faltered. In the short time he'd known him, the Sunjan had been a hateful punce. A kog, even. But that was before. In the end, he had stood with them all. Even saved them.

"Perished," Broska went on. "On the rocks. Or so Half Tusk told me. The fall killed him. At least he was spared being devoured by the bloodfish. Small mercy,

I suppose. The river will take the body, eventually. The rains tend to lift the waters, but there's no way to get him. Apologies for all that."

He-Dog nodded weakly. "Chop?"

"He's alive. You're all alive. Chop. Snaffer. Kellic. Except that one lad."

Relief flooded He-Dog, but not enough to ease the many hurts his body started screaming about.

Broska saw his suffering. "Mind your strength," he said. "Here. Eat this."

Something was stuffed into He-Dog's mouth. It tasted oddly spicy, like something plucked from a tree. He chewed on it, fat edges stabbing his bleeding tongue. The flavor intensified to an unpleasant point, and he nearly spit it out.

Broska jammed a hand underneath his chin, however, preventing him from doing that very thing. "No, you chew that. *Chew* it. It'll help with your pain. There you are. Here."

Something touched his lips. Water, warm yet wonderful, dribbled to the back of his mouth, and his throat clicked to get it down.

"Not too much," Broska said, pulling it back. "Apologies. My arm was nearly pulled free of my shoulder. I fell from the bridge. Would've fallen into the river but Half Tusk saved me. Then his lads saved us. It's a short story. I'll tell you later."

"Later?"

"Aye that. Now chew. There you are. Yes, I know. I know. It tastes terrible."

"Iruzu?" He-Dog asked, on the verge of spitting again, but Broska once more pressed his mouth shut.

"Swallow. Get that down. There you go." A tired smile spread across the Zuthenian's face. "I don't think we'll have to worry about the Iruzu anytime soon. Perhaps not ever again. Not from what the lads told me." Broska marveled, shaking his head in unchecked disbelief. "You and your lads *butchered* them, from what I'm told. Bled them dry. *Dry*. In such unfit numbers . . . well . . . no. We don't have to worry about them. And if we do? We'll just have to finish what we started here today. With your help, of course."

He-Dog didn't say anything to that.

"We have to get clear of here, first," Broska said and grew serious once again. "Chew."

"*Pah*," He-Dog muttered weakly. The shite tasted *horrible*.

"Chew and swallow, I said," Broska ordered before chuckling. "Now you know why they usually *burn* it."

He-Dog questioned him with a poisoned look.

"Aye that. Those are dream leaves you're chewing on. One of the ladies found them growing along the trail. Growing all along here, truth be known. Just a matter of picking it. There you are . . . already taking hold, as fast as that . . ."

It was. He-Dog's head became a heavy thing, moving it seemed to take a day. His barking pain receded, fading into a distant, muted whisper, as if smothered under many thick blankets.

"You've done well, Slayer," Broska smiled, his voice oddly deep and serene, the words slightly drawn out. "Lie still now. Lie still. It's easier this way."

A hand patted He-Dog's chest, matching the slow booming within.

"We have a long walk home . . ."

Time passed, and He-Dog floated with it.

The *wan-shol* was far easier to breathe in than to eat, but as far as He-Dog could gather, they were on the move. He was floating most of that time, on his back, staring at the sky. Or what he could see of the sky, through that ever-thickening mat of leaves and limbs spread overhead. Before, when he was merely breathing in the dream leaf smoke, he'd been on his back in the lodge and had nothing to look at. Out here, he saw . . . so much more. Here, outside, when he had the sense to grasp what was happening, He-Dog saw the full wondrous power of the medicine.

In the *colors* of the Sanjou.

What was it, the sailors and Shay's mercenaries had said of this place? He-Dog had overheard many stories during the voyage aboard the *Blue Conquest*. That the land was a haunted place? A wretched, hostile place, full of all manner of monsters. A cursed place, even, and the few that ventured past its rocky cliffs were never seen nor heard tell of ever again.

Something like that, anyway.

He-Dog supposed all that might indeed be true, at least a little, but while choking down regular doses of *wan-shol*, all he saw were the colors of the land. Or rather, the colors revealed themselves to him, in all their glowing beauty. Vibrant. Scintillating. Dazzling, even, in the rays of the sun, and so stunningly beautiful in the shade. Bright, lavish yellows and eye-popping pinks, pretty enough to make one's eyes weep to behold them. Rosy reds that gushed into his mind, and dignified purples that demanded his attention. At times, he seemed to float in one spot, long enough to focus on parts of the surrounding wilderness, captivated by the minute details he saw. The intricate designs of the jungle canopy. The fine, arcing lines of curtsying petals. The diamond drops of water that hung suspended from their tips, perfectly crafted and sparkling. And everything shrouded in the softest glow of green, by far the most common of all the Sanjou's colors.

And perhaps the prettiest.

It was a kingly display. A queen's immaculate garden. And certainly nothing to fear. Nothing at all. The very thought seemed unfit.

And once, just once . . . while he was staring at all of those wondrous colors . . . a face looked back at him.

Balless, with a smile and a wink.

A piercing shaft of sunlight blinded He-Dog as he realized what he was looking at, and when he recovered, the face—as expected—was gone.

Time continued to pass.

And He-Dog floated with it.

"You awake?" someone asked.

"Muh," He-Dog answered, his voice scratchy and parched.

"He's not awake."

"He's awake. Just doesn't know it yet."

"Do you hear yourself?" Kellic grumbled, talking to someone else. "If he doesn't know he's awake . . . then how . . . can he be . . . awake?"

"You awake?" asked the other voice, clearly not paying any attention to the other man.

Snaffer.

"I'm awake," He-Dog whispered. Silence answered him. Not surprising, considering the company. "Where are we?" he asked.

"Good to see you alive, asslicker," Snaffer said.

He-Dog frowned and turned his head. "Good to see you alive. Jers Snaffer. And you. Kellic. And . . ."

That prompted him to look around. Just the three of them. Inside a lodge. Much like the first one they had days ago. *Days ago? Weeks? No, months*, He-Dog decided, remembering they didn't have the senses to realize where they were or how much time had passed.

"Dream leaves?" he asked weakly.

"Aye that," Snaffer said. "Dream leaves. If I ever get back to the mainland, I mean to grow and sell the shite."

"How long . . ." He-Dog started to ask.

"Months," Snaffer answered him.

He-Dog let his breath out in a hiss. *Months.* It didn't surprise him. He shifted on his mat and took a moment to inspect himself. As before, they had stripped him down to nothing, with a mangy blanket draped over his fruits, and his many, many wounds coated in a greenish paste. In fact, his whole torso resembled a mess of shite troughs and perky little cow kisses.

"Lords above," he whispered, taking it all in.

Snaffer chuckled, a hoarse sound that wasn't hard on the ears at all. "Like before. Just worse."

The old warrior had had his beard cut away, shorn to the chin. A large crust lined his jaw, from the middle all the way to his right ear. More of the greenish muck covered his face, applied heavily to his right cheek, below his eye. They had taken a knife to his hair as well, chopping it down to the scalp, but no such muck touched anything there.

Snaffer smiled at the stare. "One cut me along here," he said, tracing the wound with a shaky finger. "Thought it was some savage's blood." He shook his head before tapping his chest, indicating it was all his. "They thought the same thing with my *hair*, except it *was* some savage's blood. Not mine. They didn't know until they'd finished skinning me."

"I didn't recognize him," Kellic muttered from where he lay upon the floor.

"It'll grow back," Snaffer said and sniffed.

He-Dog squinted. "You look . . . younger."

"So I hear."

"Where's Chop?"

"In another lodge," Kellic answered. "They could only fit the three of us in here. Since we've done this before, they put your lad someplace else."

"So he's alive?"

"Alive," Snaffer confirmed. "But with a lot more scars. Like us all."

Like us all, indeed, He-Dog thought.

"You'll be able to see him soon enough," Snaffer continued. "Like before. They're already burning fewer leaves for us."

Burning fewer leaves. That made He-Dog think of Shay. "He . . . seemed fine, at the end. Shay, I mean."

Snaffer grunted. "He had a hard time of it. I knew he was having a hard time. We all were. Perhaps the leaves were to blame. I'm thinking they were. I asked if what happened to Shay might happen to us. Broska doesn't think so. Nor does Peaceful Moon, since we were all fine after . . . But Shay? That's the Shay I remember. The one who would . . . do what he could to help others. Even if it meant perishing. You best remember him that way as well. Both of you . . ."

"I will," Kellic said in a low voice.

"As will I," He-Dog said.

They grew quiet then, until He-Dog became aware of a hammering from outside. As well as voices.

"Where are we?" he asked, his strength ebbing away.

"I don't know," Snaffer said. "Somewhere. But they've been busy. Building. I've heard as much."

"As have I," Kellic said.

The hide covering the entrance opened in a flash of daylight, and two familiar faces entered. One was Bright Leaf, who knelt at Kellic's side and placed a hand against his cheek. The mercenary placed his hand over hers, and they shared a smile. The man once called Sad Eyes did not look so sad anymore.

Peaceful Moon threw leaves upon the fire pit. He then waved his hand over the mess, urging the flames back to life. Flames which He-Dog didn't see being lit. *Sorcery.*

Then there was a warm hand on his forehead, and the spirit man looked down upon him.

"Sleep," Peaceful Moon said, saying the word as well as any other.

He-Dog didn't want to sleep. There were still many questions he wanted to ask, and he wondered where Broska was so that the Zuthenian could translate.

Instead, he closed his eyes, and he knew no more.

*

Over the next few days, they burned fewer and fewer dream leaves.

As He-Dog slowly regained his senses, he discovered, that once again, he had healed and possessed a new assortment of scars. The most interesting and noticeable ones were the two on his chest, where the Iruzu arrows had taken him. He seemed to remember something about that.

As before, Peaceful Moon tended to their healing, while Bright Leaf, Little Bloom, and Summer Wind fed and cleaned them. Bright Leaf took care of only Kellic, however.

He-Dog thought they looked good together. Even said so, and, surprisingly enough, Snaffer agreed.

Which pleased Kellic, or so it seemed. It was hard to tell with . . . *no-longer* Sad Eyes.

He-Dog slept for lengthy periods of time in those days. Slept deeply. And one afternoon, he woke to find Chop sitting next to him with a hollowed gourd in his hand. He wasn't wearing his mask, and the sun had deepened the color of the Nordish man's melted face. The sight of his last remaining friend narrowed He-Dog's eyes, and for moments he didn't say anything, as if waiting for his companion to vanish.

When it became clear that the Nordish man wasn't going anywhere, He-Dog cleared his throat. "That you, Chop?"

Chop nodded.

"Not dead?"

A shake of the head.

"Damnation," He-Dog said in dawning realization. "It's good to see you . . . up and about."

Chop nodded again.

He-Dog's smile faded. "The Sunjan perished back there. At the cliffs. You know that?"

Perhaps it was a residual effect of breathing in so much of the *wan-shol*. Certainly, Chop had been treated by the same medicine. Maybe even more. In any case, Chop didn't respond right away. Instead—and He-Dog wasn't sure if he saw this right or not—the Nordish man's eyes became a little red around the edges, and his posture slumped.

Chop finally answered with a weary nod.

And for once, He-Dog faltered, unaccustomed to seeing such emotion from his companion.

"Good to see you alive." he whispered, and meant it.

The swordsman gripped his shoulder, not too hard, and held on.

Weeks later, all three men were well enough to sit outside their lodge.

Several villagers helped them stand, one at a time, and as they didn't get sick, they were led outside. Kellic went first, with Bright Leaf supporting him. Then was Snaffer, who, when he left the lodge, was greeted by a rousing cheer from the little lads and maidens—his youngsters—who recognized him, even without his hair and beard.

When the others were outside, Broska came back for He-Dog, who gnashed his remaining teeth at the brightness of the day.

"Ready?" the Zuthenian asked.

As an answer, He-Dog held out his hand. His legs were shaky, trembling from so little use, but that would be the way for the next little while.

Then *daylight* so bright it hurt. He-Dog shielded his eyes with a hand, and in doing so nearly crumpled. Broska held on to him, however, lending support, until they reached the little ridge where the others sat. When he was in place, the Zuthenian sat down beside him.

"Many thanks," He-Dog told him, who dismissed it with a wave.

Breathing clean air with only the faintest taste of smoke from wood fires and not dream leaves, He-Dog, Snaffer, and Kellic sat on a ridge overlooking a much smaller settlement. The new village the Anoka had built for themselves. In another part of the Sanjou.

Towering trees loomed around them, their tops exploding in suspended starbursts of heavy palm leaves. They grew tall enough and dense enough to douse the whole area in an emerald hue. Waterfalls splashed over high rocks in a gentle shower, visible through a break in the jungle heights, and the tranquil rush of an unseen river could be heard, pouring an aura of peace onto the new village. As before, the lodges were built in the shade, with the usual assortment of ropes and stages in between. The people, the last of the Anoka, worked and toiled outside of their homes, as on any day. Some of them noticed the Slayers right away and paused to take a look at them. Some even waved.

He-Dog waved back. As did Snaffer, and the little group of girls and boys sitting around him. As did Kellic, with Bright Leaf leaning into his shoulder.

He-Dog waved again when he noticed something that struck him cold.

Chop was down there, sitting outside a lodge, and next to him was the blind woman called Gentle Rain. They sat shoulder to shoulder, thigh to thigh, and looked like they were weaving rope together.

Much to He-Dog's surprise.

The Nordish man saw him and raised a hand in greeting, holding it high until seen. There was no mistaking the happiness upon that melted face. Chop's gesture caused Gentle Rain to regard the swordsman, a question forming on her lovely features.

"Quite the couple," Broska said nearby. "Your friend recovered faster, and Gentle Rain took a liking to him. It was explained to me that Chop helped her when he and Kellic were leading them all back to the bridge. She asked about who was helping her. Wanted to meet him. And . . . well, there you have it. She looked after him while he was on the mend. Damn near inseparable ever since."

He-Dog nodded.

"They make a fine couple, I think," Broska went on. "And the people approve."

Chop waved again, and on some unspoken word, Gentle Rain looked in the same direction.

He-Dog slowly waved back, a little smile easing across his hard features. "A fine couple, indeed."

"How long have we been breathing the *wan-shol* this time, Broska?" Snaffer asked, changing the subject.

"Don't worry about such things."

And much to He-Dog's surprise, Snaffer didn't repeat the question. The once-mercenary sat and checked on the upraised faces of the youngsters sitting around him, not a one missing from before. That pleased an old face and scratched a satisfied smile across features stubbled with silver.

"Well, this is it, lads," Broska declared. "The village. As it stands right now. The people have suffered. Suffered long and hard. Much has been lost but . . . the Anoka have remembered those they lost by rebuilding. They built all this and there are plans for more. We're on the other side of the mountains, here. Well in the shadows during the heat of the day. Plenty of good, fresh water from the falls over there. Good fish to eat in the river. My missus wanted our home near those waters. You can see it from here. Visit when you like. I'll put you to work. Always something to do. This place . . . the lads found this place shortly after we returned to the old village. There was a time the Anoka would not dare come here, for fear of the Paw. And what it would do. Well, we've been here for weeks now. Maybe months. And we're still here. No Paw has come looking for us, looking for offerings or revenge. And the Iruzu? They'll never follow us here. What's left of them, that is."

"So it's dead?" Kellic asked, sitting next to Bright Leaf. "The Paw, I mean?"

"Aye that. Long dead."

The sound of rushing water filled the silence as they all reflected on that.

"Something's been bothering me, Broska," Kellic asked.

"What is it, then?"

"Well, it's about this shared dream."

He-Dog had thoughts about that himself.

"The Paw was seen dying in a gray mist," Kellic reminded him. "At the feet of *three* faceless slayers . . . when there was really only one. Hargan."

"Also that one," Snaffer rumbled. "The Nord. He was there as well. That makes five of us."

"And the mist wasn't really mist, but smoke. From the bridge," Kellic added.

"Dreams," the Zuthenian said, watching the village. "The Paw perished beneath your feet. All your feet, as you were on the cliffs. Hargan certainly played a part in the Paw's death, but the bloodfish devoured the beast. Down to nothing. The shared dream wasn't . . . entirely wrong . . . it simply left out some details."

"Some important details."

Broska shrugged. "You'll have to sit down with the last of the elders. From what I hear, it was their favorite topic for a while. They seem to agree on one thing . . ."

He had their attention.

"The dream was mostly right," Broska said. "Three Slayers appeared in the village, and their arrival meant the death of the Paw."

". . . but," Kellic started.

"Kellic," Snaffer rumbled, gazing over the new land. "See to your missus there. Save your talk for the elders."

That cocked He-Dog's brow. Any other time, he believed Snaffer would have told the man to shut his guts.

"I have a thought . . ." He-Dog said, scratching at an ear. "Are we still to go looking for gemstones?"

"Not I," Kellic said right away, which was understandable. The man had found his treasure, and he was holding her close.

Snaffer sighed through his nose and didn't answer right away. "Nor I," he finally said, looking over his adopted children.

"All right, then," He-Dog said, noticing the pleased look on Broska's face. "We agree on that. Next thought then . . . anyone know how we're to get back to the mainland?"

Silence on that one as well.

Kellic spoke first. "Don't care if I ever get back. I'm content to stay here."

Snaffer took his time again. "Aye that. I'm . . . of the same mind."

If Broska looked pleased before, he was badly hiding a smile now. "He-Dog?" the Zuthenian asked.

He-Dog looked over at him.

"There are ships that . . . skirt the coastline," Broska said. "I would be a poor friend indeed to *not* tell you that. If you really wanted to, if you had no desire to stay here, the Anoka would bring you to the coast. Half Tusk might even bring you there himself," he said with a chuckle. "Some of those ships could be pirates. Like the Ossaki. Some, maybe worse. But *some* . . . you could perhaps signal them. Secure passage on one. If they were headed to some nearby coast of your liking. It's a slim chance . . . but it's there."

It's there, He-Dog thought, and looked over the village again. Saw Chop and Gentle Rain and felt glad they'd found each other. Glad that the people of the Anoka were well on their way to rebuilding their lives, in a place that looked prettier than the one before, if that was possible.

Then he remembered Balless . . . and the Kratoe and his killers, who had left Foust and its populace to the beastmen while they escaped to the coast. And then to the open seas.

That darkened He-Dog's demeanor.

There were things yet to be done.

And yet . . . remembering the smiling face of Balless, He-Dog didn't think his brother would mind if he stayed here. Not at all. *If* he decided to stay, that was, and make a life with the Anoka. For a little while, at least.

"He-Dog?" Broska prodded, wanting an answer.

"Ask me that another day," He-Dog rumbled, baring bad teeth, content to look upon the village and the people living there.

Broska accepted that. "Another day, then."

He-Dog nodded, and in time . . . he smiled.

ABOUT THE AUTHOR

Keith C. Blackmore is the author of the Mountain Man, 131 Days, and Breeds series, among other horror, heroic fantasy, and crime novels. He lives on the island of Newfoundland in Canada. Visit his website at www.keithcblackmore.com.

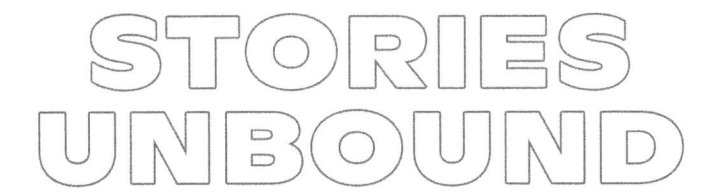